Wolf Pack

More by Brooke Shaffer

The Timekeeper Chronicles

The Chivalrous Welshman
Time to Kill
Tick Tock
Windup
Stopwatch
Free Time
Leap Second (Summer 2021)

The Hands of Time
In the Hands of the Enemy
The Hands Pulling the Strings (Winter 2021)

The Lone Wolf
Wolf Pack
Alpha Wolf (Spring 2022)

Singles
Of Saints and Sinners

Wolf Pack
Book One of The Lone Wolf
The Timekeeper Chronicles

Brooke Shaffer

Black Bear Publishing

Published in Michigan by Black Bear Publishing.

ISBN:
Hardcover: 978-1-953113-06-1
Softcover: 978-1-953113-07-8
eBook: 978-1-953113-08-5
Audiobook: 978-1-953113-09-2

For Ruby and her children and her grandchildren and her great-grandchildren and all the children of the world she loved as her own

A note on pronunciation:

"H" when coming before another consonant is not a distinct sound but a breathy huff
"Ts" may be pronounced as either "ts" as in "cats," "ch" as in chair, or "j" as in "judge"
"V" is pronounced as a short "u" as in "cut"

Allegiances

Aniyvwiya

The Cherokee

ᎣᎩᏴᎠᎬᎣᎠᏫ | Skiagvsta

Red chief, a chief or chiefs who rules in times of war

Atagulkalu | Wolf Clan, nephew of Gvnagadoga, uncle to Nanyehi, cousin of Aganstata, husband to Nayanali, Chief of Itsa'ti and later Taskigi and Mialoquo, called "Little Carpenter" by the British

Chola | Chief of Si'tiku

Ganedisgi | Chief of Itse'yi

Tawodi | Chief of Nagutsi'

Tisto | Chief of Kuwayi'hi

Ustanaqua | Wolf Clan, called "Mankiller" by the British, Chief of Tama'li

Wilinawa | Wild Potato Clan, Chief of Daqua'i

Yachtino | Chief of Talasi

ᎣᏗ | Uku

White chief, a chief or chiefs who rules in times of peace (could also be priests)

Gvnagadoga | Beloved Man of Itsa'ti, called "Old Hop" by the British

Usga'hi | Bird Clan, priest of Si'tiku

ᏴᏏᎣ | Ghigau

Beloved Woman, women who had voting rights on the Women's Council and the general council, adviser to the chiefs, could execute or spare war prisoners

Diwedalohi | Wolf Clan, grandmother to Kiyuga and Anagalisgi

Nanyehi | Wolf Clan, niece of Atagulkalu

ᎪᏢᏐᏗ | Adawehi

Priests, prophets, and medicine men who invoked the spirits for healing and guidance in matters of war, peace, and everyday life

Agodehi | Paint Clan, priest of Itsa'ti

Anagalisgi | Wolf Clan, younger brother to Kiyuga, dreamer and

prophet, priest of Itsa'ti
Nage'i | Long Hair Clan, priest of Itsa'ti
Nakatiha | Blue Clan, priest of Nagutsi'
Tsgili | Bird Clan, priest of Kuwayi'hi

DhGꝏ | Anihwaya

Wolf Clan, the largest clan, tasked with providing warriors and protecting the people, their color is red

Adahi | A warrior
Aganstata | Senior warrior, scarred from smallpox, father of Nayanali, cousin of Atagulkalu
Amadoya | First Warrior of Si'tiku
Digvnige | Uncle to Kiyuga and Anagalisgi
Gvnagadoga | A warrior, nephew of Gvnagadoga (uku)
Inga | British woman captured by Nanyehi and adopted as her sister
Kiyuga | Older brother to Anagalisgi, called Yvgidahi "Young Spear"
Selowa | A senior warrior
Uhtalugi'a | A senior warrior
Watiyel | Aunt of Kiyuga and Anagalisgi, nursemaid to Anagalisgi

DhꞭꞳꞳ | Aniwodi

Paint Clan, the smallest clan, tasked with providing priests and medicine men, their color is white

Ahtsehd | A warrior
Duwisgali | A senior warrior
Nayanali | Daughter of Aganstata, wife to Atagulkalu
Nvyohi | A warrior
Sotsena | Wife of Digvnige
Tsiyu Gansini | A warrior, son of Atagulkalu

DhUꞮh | Anisahoni

Blue Clan, tasked with keeping children well and mixing a special blue-colored medicine, their color is blue

Ani | A boy
Ganvgi | Wife to Ganulahsa'a
Kvhe | A warrior
Saloli | First Warrior of Taliqua
Uki'la | A senior warrior

DhꙨꙀ | Anikawi

Deer Clan, tasked with hunting and considered fast runners, their color is brown

Dodidoya | A warrior

Galegi | A warrior

Geluhni | A warrior

Totsuwa | A warrior

Ugidahli | An elder

Uhyesadv | A warrior

DhYGꙅ | Anigilohi

Long Hair Clan, tasked with bringing peace and considered very vain in their dress, their color is yellow

Golisdayv'i | A warrior

Kansgawi | A warrior, son of Ulvsati

Kanunu | A boy

Ulvsati | Cousin of Diwedalohi

Unisgwali | A warrior, son of Ulvsati

Yvgi | A warrior

DhALꙠꙨ | Anigodagewi

Wild Potato Clan, tasked with foraging and cooking, their color is green

Advtowa | Wife of Kiyuga

Ayohli Tsiyo | Son of Advtowa and Kiyuga

Gatsvnula | Older brother to Advtowa

Nage'i | A warrior

Totsuwa | A warrior

Ulogilv | Mother of Advtowa

DhhꙜꙄ | Anitsisgwa

Bird Clan, tasked with carrying messages and skilled in use of blowguns and snares, their color is purple

Tolatsi | A warrior

Ganulahsa'a | A warrior, cousin of Kiyuga and Anagalisgi

Saliksgwo | A warrior

Anigilisi

The British

Military Officers

General Forbes | Leader of the Forbes Expedition to take Fort Duquense, often ill and unable to keep up

Colonel Montgomery | Led an invasion of Aniyvwiya Lower towns

Colonel Washington | In charge of the colonial provincials on the Forbes Expedition

Lieutenant Colonel Bouquet | In charge of the Forbes Expedition

Major Grant | Planned an ambush on Fort Duquense, captured, later released, led massive attacks on Aniyvwiya Middle and Lower towns

Major Lewis | Part of a reconnaissance mission on Fort Duquense

Captain Demeré | Captain of Fort Loudoun

Captain Gadsden | Led an artillery force through the Lower Towns, escorting hostages from Charleston to Fort Prince George

Captain McDonald | Highland soldier who led a decoy force against Fort Duquense

Lieutenant Cotymore | Commander of Fort Prince George

Lieutenant Kettle | Led an expedition to negotiate terms to build Fort Loudoun

Lieutenant Stuart | Officer at Fort Loudoun, good friend of Atagulkalu

Politicians

Governor Fauquier | Governor of Virginia

Governor Lyttelton | Governor of South Carolina

Lieutenant Governor Bull | Lieutenant Governor of South Carolina

Lieutenant Governor Dinwiddie | Lieutenant Governor of Virginia

Other

Andrew O'Dell | Provincial soldier

Nathan Wilde | Provincial soldier

William Moore | Chaplain at Fort Loudoun

Other Peoples

Anakwanki | The Lenape
Anigalvhtsi | The French
Anigvnage'i | Black People
Anikawita | The Creek (lower)
Anikusi | The Creek (upper), Muskogee
Aninotsi | The Natchez
Aninvdawegi | The Iroquois
Anisawanugi | The Shawano
Anisenika | The Seneca
Anitagwi | The Catawba

Words and Phrases

Words expressing relation (mother, father, etc.) require certain prefixes in order to be grammatically correct, and indicate the relationship between the speaker and the object. Therefore, you would not say simply "Yes, Grandma," but "Yes, my grandma," or not "Father isn't well," but "Our father isn't well," etc.

Adahnesagi'a | He/she is conjuring/witching.
Agatena | Lace
Agi'a | He/she/it is picking it up.
Akatiha | He/she/it is peeking.
Aktiya | He/she/it is watching over him/her/it.
Ale | And
Amayi | River
Anejodi | A ball game, the precursor to lacrosse
Anvyi | Windy Moon, "March"
Asganola | Slow
Atsvstdi | Light
Digadayosdi | A ball game similar to bocceball and golf
Diga'galvnvdiha | Weeping willow
Digohwelisgi | Author
-Do | Brother to a woman (or sister to a man)
-Etsi | Child
Ge'gwogv | Pileated woodpecker
Galohisdi | Doorway
Galo'ohndiha | He/she/it is making him/her/it fall.
Gayalvnga | It is sticking to it; it is attached to it.
Guyequoni | Ripe Corn Moon, "July"
-Hnvhli | Brother to a man
Iyuwahnilvhi | Time
Kagali | Bony Moon, "February"
-Lisi | Grandmother or Granddaughter
Skala Galogwehi | Pistol or small firearm

Tsinagi'e'a | I took it from him.
-Tuta | Grandfather or Grandson
Udilegv'i | Hot
Uhlisda | Fast, quick
Uhnoyvgi | Noise, sound
Uhnoyv'nohyvhlga | It is making a noise.
Uhyvtsa | Cold
Unolvtan | Cold Moon, "January"
Vsgiyi | Snow Moon, "December"
Vv | Yes
Wado | Thank you
Watsini | Virginia
Waya | Wolf

Prefixes:

Agi- | My
Tsa- | Your (singular)
U- | His/her
Igi- | Our
Ogi- | Our (not yours)
Itsi- | Your (plural)
Uni- | Their

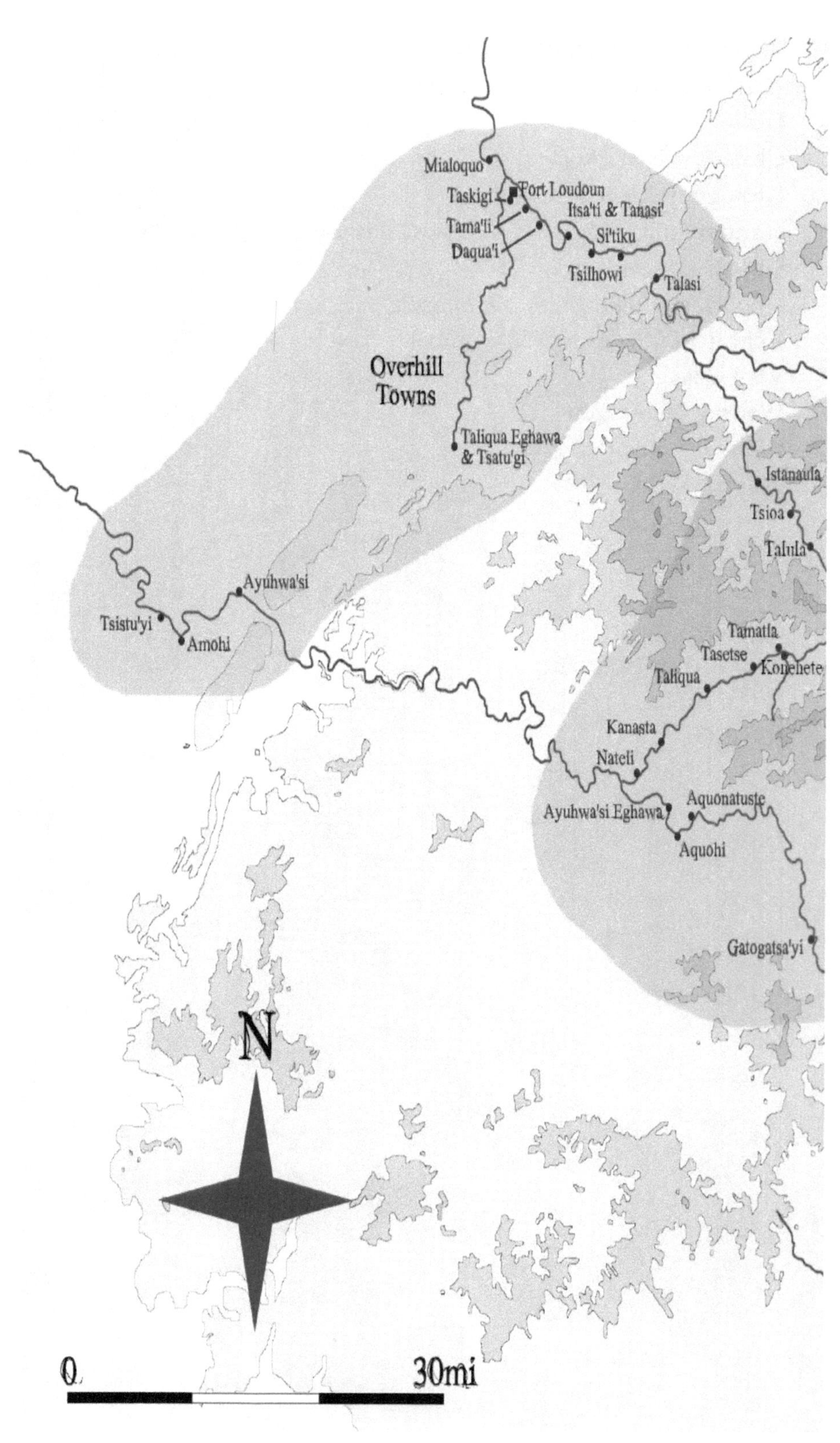

Mialoquo
Taskigi
Fort Loudoun
Itsa'ti & Tanasi'
Tama'li
Si'tiku
Daqua'i
Tsilhowi
Talasi
Overhill
Towns
Taliqua Eghawa
& Tsatu'gi
Istanaula
Tsioa
Talula
Ayuhwa'si
Tamatla
Tasetse
Tsistu'yi
Taliqua
Konehete
Amohi
Kanasta
Nateli
Ayuhwa'si Eghawa
Aquonatuste
Aquohi
Gatogatsa'yi
N
0
30mi

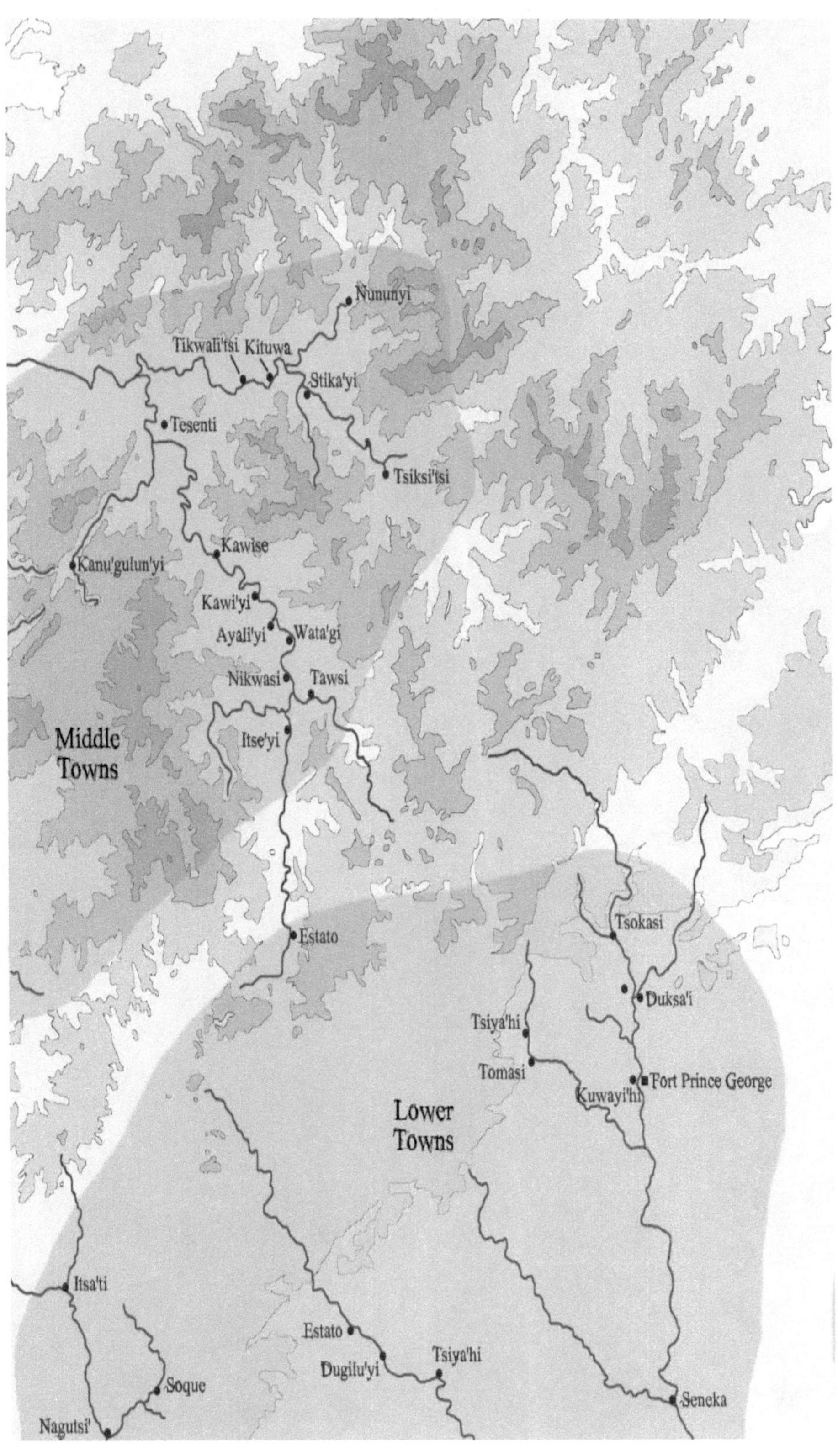

Nununyi
Tikwali'tsi
Kituwa
Stika'yi
Tesenti
Tsiksi'tsi
Kawise
Kanu'gulun'yi
Kawi'yi
Ayali'yi
Wata'gi
Nikwasi
Tawsi
Itse'yi
Middle Towns
Estato
Tsokasi
Duksa'i
Tsiya'hi
Tomasi
Fort Prince George
Kuwayi'hi
Lower Towns
Itsa'ti
Estato
Tsiya'hi
Dugilu'yi
Soque
Nagutsi'
Seneka

ᎠᏓᎳᏗ ᏚᎳ

Ayadohlv'i Sogwu

Kiyuga

Kiyuga would always remember the day his mother died, though he was only three at the time. He remembered huddling next to her, feeling the fire burn within her body. He remembered hearing her wheezing breaths, her slow heart. He'd drifted off to sleep, praying for her to get better even as he heard the wails of both the priests and others who were losing loved ones.

When he woke, his mother's body no longer burned with fire. Initially he'd been happy, and he jumped up for joy, pleased that his prayers had been answered. But when he looked, he found his mother unmoving and pale. When he touched her, she did not respond. He called her name, screamed it in fact, his voice drowned out by the cries of those also waking to find family members had walked on in the night.

He remembered sitting down and wailing like the child he was, still blubbering her name, calling for her to return to him. When the worst of his sobbing was over, he lay down beside her again and buried his face in her chest, silently willing her to wake up.

His father had walked on only a moon before, and the small child didn't know how much more he could take. Perhaps he would follow them. He wanted to follow them into the western lands. Why had they abandoned him? Why had the spirits taken them from him? He didn't understand.

At some point, someone came to take his mother's body away. He'd screamed and protested, but what could a child do? He cried again and someone held him. But he didn't want to be held, not by anyone but his mother. And now she was gone. Already he missed her touch, her embrace, even if it had been weak and feverish. It was all he had left of her, just a dim memory fading fast.

He left the townhouse. Once brimming with life, it was now a sanctuary of death, made to care for those who had contracted the disease that was ravaging all the villages. It was said to be at its peak and had to subside now. Kiyuga no longer cared. His mother and father had both been stolen from him by this disease and the evil spirits who brought it upon them. What did it matter whether it subsided or grew even worse? It wasn't going to bring them back.

All around him in the village, families were torn in half between the living and the dying. There was no merriment, no joy. Music was scarcely heard except for the now-routine beating of the funeral drums. Laughter was a luxury many could not indulge in.

Before he could stop it, someone took his hand and led him along. He didn't want to go with this person. He didn't know where he wanted to go, but it wasn't wherever they wanted him to go. He protested, but once again, he was but a child and could put up no real resistance.

Immediately upon seeing his grandmother, Kiyuga burst into tears and ran to her. She welcomed him with open arms and took him up, holding him close and letting him cry.

He wept until he slept. He wished only to see his mother, to know her spirit was well, to know that she had crossed safely. He did not see her, and when he woke, he cried some more.

"You will see her again one day," his grandmother told him. "One day, you will join her on the path beyond this world."

"I didn't want her to go on the path without me," Kiyuga said. Or that was what he intended to say. With his face still buried in his grandmother's chest, it all sounded like a mumble.

She did not reply.

Kiyuga never forgot the day his mother died. He never forgot what she looked and felt like as she lay dying, pale and feverish. He never forgot the last time she put her hand on his head and called him *akwetsi*, my son. He felt ashamed for it, for he did forget how she looked in life. Later on, he would look at all the other women in the village and wonder if his mother had ever looked as such when she was happy, or when she cooked, or when she tanned animal hides. He did forget how she said his name, and he would watch other mothers call to their children, and his heart would ache that he did not remember his mother calling to him in such a way.

As a little boy, Kiyuga remembered only the tragedy, for it was impressed upon his mind, but he was not mature enough to understand that he had to commit these other things to memory, else they would slip from him. If he did not carry his mother's memories and her spirit, how would he know it if he found her in the spirit world? Or his father, for that matter? Perhaps he would just know, something instinctive inside him, the life force that bound families together.

He wailed for his mother and father, but only Ulisi, his grandmother, was there to comfort him. His grandfather had walked on before he'd been born. What did he think of this now? What did he think of so many kin coming to walk with him at once?

Kiyuga wanted to walk with them. He wanted to walk the spirit trail and find his mother and father. He wanted to bring them back from the western lands, where spirits walked in misery.

But such were the notions of a child who did not understand death, even if it was all he'd consciously known in his life thus far. The sickness, the death, the wailing and uncertainty of tomorrow, people in his life for only an instant before they were gone, taken by forces he did not understand to a place he was not permitted to go. It was all so unfair. He didn't understand.

Eventually, he pulled away from Ulisi and meandered inside her home. They had all lived here together, but now it looked so empty. His father's things had gone, and his mother's things were now gone as well, destroyed for being unclean. All that remained was *uhnvhli*, his brother, who was named Anagalisgi.

Anagalisgi was an infant still on the breast, though he slept now in the arms of the woman who had cared for him since their mother had fallen ill. There had been fear that illness had passed from mother to son, but other than a slight fever that went away quickly, he'd shown no signs of the illness.

Watiyel, the woman, held out her hand as she prepared to exit the house. Kiyuga did not want to take it.

"I think he knows she's gone," Watiyel said. "He started crying before you did."

Kiyuga did not say anything to that, just stared at the doorway where clouds passing over the sun dappled the light streaming in. In some small part of his heart, he feared. He feared that his brother would also walk on. Such a small thing, bundled tightly and sleeping soundly. Kiyuga felt as though he had no one left in the world but him.

It was a foolish notion, of course, as everyone in the clan, in the whole nation, was family. He called his mother's sisters as mother, with no reproach or inkling that it was unusual. But there was a part of him that wanted to keep something or someone as his. Ulisi was becoming elderly, and though she would be taking care of him now, she took care of everyone, as was her duty and honor as an elder. His mother's sisters had families and children of their own. His mother's one remaining brother was courting a girl and would soon leave to join her, once the sickness had passed.

"Come, Kiyuga," Ulisi said, beckoning him forward. "We must go to the river now and let the priest do his work."

Kiyuga hesitated and turned to look at his baby brother. Tiny bubbles dotted the infant's lips as he breathed, but Kiyuga thought he looked concerned, troubled. Could one so small understand what had happened? Did he have dreams of his mother and father now gone? Did he walk with them still in some way?

When he looked up at Watiyel, the woman drew a sharp breath, as though stunned by his appearance, as if he'd suddenly grown fur or wings or a tail. Her lips parted and she took an even breath, but she said nothing of it, not what she saw or thought she saw, not what she was thinking. She turned her attention to Anagalisgi, and Kiyuga noticed that she held her breath, as though she'd had some similar revelation about the months-old infant in her arms but kept herself still to avoid rousing the babe.

Finally she closed her eyes for a moment, then reached out with her free hand to touch Kiyuga and guide him out of the home. The four of them left the village and went south, to the river. One priest would cleanse their home, dispose of his mother's belongings, then another priest would come to bathe them in the river.

They were not the only ones waiting on the banks of the river. Two other families were gathered in solemn regard. It was late in the evening before a priest came. One by one, they went into the river and immersed themselves in the waters, each time facing a new direction while the priest blessed them and declared them clean again. For Anagalisgi, the priest held the infant in strong hands and immersed him as well. The child did not fuss, but accepted it with unusually calm regard.

When they returned to their home, Kiyuga thought it was just a little emptier. It was bad enough that his mother should be gone, but now all trace of her had been erased. The only indication of her existence now was the burial mound outside their home, where she lay beside his father. Kiyuga sat in a heap. Watiyel knelt beside him and handed Anagalisgi to him.

"Watch over him a moment," Watiyel said wistfully, and departed.

Kiyuga looked down at his baby brother. Anagalisgi had roused awake in all the shuffling and looked up at him with large, dark eyes.

"I will protect you, Tsotsatanvhli," Kiyuga promised. "I will keep you safe."

Anagalisgi did not say anything, but he smiled and more bubbles foamed at his mouth as he stuck his tongue out and wiggled in his bundling furs.

They would play with the other children and call them brother and sister, but the two of them would have no more brothers or sisters of their own. They had only each other, until the day they married, and even then, the bond of brotherhood was not easily broken. Kiyuga resolved it would be so, in the innocent and yet powerful way that only a child of three years can.

"You will not walk on, Tsotsatanvhli," Kiyuga went on. "Even if I have to go before you and clear the way, you will not walk on."

Ulisi appeared then. Smiling warmly, she took Anagalisgi in one arm and Kiyuga in the other and quietly sat down. Loneliness washed over Kiyuga then, and tears blurred his vision as he found himself begging for his mother. Ulisi stroked his hair.

"I know, dear one," she sighed. "I know. But they have walked on to be with the spirits, as we all must in our own time."

Kiyuga did not speak, and when Ulisi gave him a bowl of food, he did not eat. He was starving but he felt sick. It was not the sickness that had taken his mother, but the sickness that made him long for her. He continued to refuse food, saying he was in mourning. At last, Ulisi stopped pushing. Watiyel came to feed Anagalisgi, then departed once more.

Night came, but the darkness was staved off by the sacred fire, kept going continuously since the first people fell ill, a time since before Kiyuga's clear recollection. All of the death and the funerals had run together. He'd never seen a proper ceremony before, and he would later resent the fact that he could not properly honor his mother. The best he could do was stand there at the fire and watch the priests— those who were not exhausted from over a year of death—as they sent the dead to be with the spirits, and implore the spirits to spare the rest of the living.

Kiyuga forced himself to stay awake as long as he could, but the next thing he knew, Ulisi was taking him back to bed. He rubbed his eyes and protested, wanting to stay for the whole thing. Ulisi said something kind, he knew, but he could not remember just what she said. He didn't even remember laying down and falling asleep.

Kiyuga never forgot the day his mother died. He never forgot the promise he made to his brother Anagalisgi to protect him and not let him walk on. Even when the sickness finally passed and half-deserted villages returned to normal, Kiyuga never forgot. Even as Anagalisgi began to walk and talk, Kiyuga never forgot. In fact, he worked all the harder to remember, and he frequently repeated his promise to his brother, to the point where that promise was one of the first prolonged pieces of dialogue that the boy could recite.

"I will protect you, little brother," Kiyuga told him. "I will watch over you. Even if I have to go before you to clear the way, I will not let you walk on."

Sometimes Anagalisgi repeated it back as best he could, other times he just smiled at Kiyuga and doddled after him, as little brothers tended to do.

Kiyuga took his brother everywhere and did everything with him. Everything he learned, he told or showed his brother. He repeated every story the elders told, recited every remedy the healer prescribed. He showed his brother the animals—the beasts, the birds, the insects that crawled and flitted from here to there. He showed Anagalisgi his first blowgun, his first real weapon. He showed Anagalisgi his first bow, the one that would help to strengthen his arm and improve his aim before he became a real hunter.

He showed Anagalisgi his first small club, demonstrated the various strikes he could use to disable man or animal. He took his brother with him when he practiced with his little knife upon bad furs sewn together to resemble an animal. It was a metal blade acquired through trade with the Europeans just over the eastern hills.

The only weapon he was not allowed to use yet was the firearm, *skala galogwehi*, a pistol. Such weapons had been seen as sorcery when the white men first brought them to use and trade, and many had been injured or killed. Now that the people had acquired them, they understood how the skala galogwehi worked, and they frequently traded for more, or the ammunition, but it was not something Kiyuga could well learn on his own, and Anagalisgi was much too young.

Kiyuga did not remember when he first saw a white man, a European, but when his scattered toddler images began to form into more coherent memories, he knew that it was not uncommon for them to be here. The Aniyvwiya were allied with the British, at least for trading purposes, though they had allied with the French for both trading and to bolster their offensive against the Six Nations to the north. At least, that was how Kiyuga understood it, as a six year old.

The British and French traders came by regularly, and as such, both Kiyuga and Anagalisgi began to understand them. First they parroted words they heard often or thought unique. Then they started to engage in simple dialogue. Few objected to this, as it was crucial to avoid catastrophes such as that which had befallen other peoples who negotiated in bad faith with the Europeans who used their lack of understanding against them. Being able to speak and read at the enemy's table was an excellent defense for themselves, and an offense when they turned the Europeans against each other.

When the traders left and everyone had gone to sleep at night, Kiyuga and Anagalisgi would stay up and whisper to each other, playing with their new words as much as their new traded goods. Sometimes they pretended to be the traders. Kiyuga would be a British trader and Anagalisgi an Ayvwiya man, and they would trade rocks or leaves or whatever they had to hand. Or Anagalisgi would be a French trader and Kiyuga the Ayvwiya man.

Sometimes they would both pretend to be Europeans, Kiyuga British and Anagalisgi French, and they would pretend to fight and have mini-wars. Kiyuga heard a lot of the adults laughing that the white men were so easily fooled and turned against one another at the slightest inkling. Meanwhile, they just kept trading and storing up the European weapons and goods, ready for just about anything.

Loyalty was always about family and the people first, the men said. The Europeans put their faith in pieces of paper, scribbles and ink, promises of a future not yet realized. They had no tangible loyalty to bind them to today. Their hopes were always on the horizon, always within sight but always out of reach. But not the Aniyvwiya. For the Aniyvwiya, family and the people, the things one could always see and touch. Even when distant, the spirits always guided one back to the people.

Kiyuga had no trouble absorbing this belief, for he had thrown himself into it for his brother's sake. He did not repeat his promise to

Anagalisgi every night like he used to, but he knew. They both knew.

The two of them played with the other boys in the village, whom they also called brother or cousin. They played, they ran, they practiced their hunting and fishing and tried to always outdo each other. But everyone could see that they two, Kiyuga and Anagalisgi, had a special bond.

"They will be great one day," Kiyuga once heard an elder say. "The two of them will together make our people great and save us from great tragedy."

At the time, Kiyuga paid little mind to the deeper meaning of the elder's words; he was simply thrilled to be given such high praise. But later, as he got older, Kiyuga would think back to the old man's words and wonder what he meant. What was it that the elder had foreseen? What were they supposed to do in order to avoid it? And even later, Kiyuga would wish that he had never the elder's words, had never known that everything had been apparently foretold. In his later years, Kiyuga would wonder whether ignorance would have made the loss of his brother more bearable.

DꭺᏗᎢ ᏫᏢ

Ayadohlv'i Tali
Anagalisgi

Anagalisgi did not remember his mother in any tangible sense of the word, though he would say he knew her quite well, even as a child. He knew her smell from the drifts on the wind. He knew her touch from the earth under his feet and the grass on his skin. He knew her voice and her laughter from the bubbling of the brook. He knew her spirit by the birds in the trees. Sometimes he dreamed of her, and he always felt safe, reassured that he was exactly where he needed to be. He did not know why he needed to be there, but it was a comfort all the same.

In the waking hours and when he was not listening to the world around him, Anagalisgi looked to his older brother for protection and companionship. He followed Kiyuga around, always eager to learn and proud to call him his brother. Certainly he was much bigger and faster. He was quick and deadly with the blowgun, like a serpent. He was an expert with the bow and arrow—well, he usually missed, but not by much, and he always picked up another arrow to try again. He was a deft hand with the knife and a strong arm with the club. While he could not use skala galogwehi just yet, sometimes he made pretend motions as though he were handling one.

At night, Kiyuga would sometimes recite the Promise to him.

"I will protect you, little brother," Kiyuga would say. "I will watch over you. Even if I have to go before you to clear the way, I will not let you walk on."

Anagalisgi loved and admired his brother, and he cherished the Promise as deeply as any child is capable of. But part of it also confused and saddened him, though he could not say exactly why. Later he would consider that his sadness came from the thought of losing Kiyuga, that his brother must be the one to go first, but deep down, a tiny pinprick of light said that wasn't precisely it.

These things were only conceptual to Anagalisgi at the time, as a small child, manifesting more as emotions and vague feelings rather than coherent thought and reason. But this did not bother the child right away, and he was soon going after his idol once more.

When Kiyuga became old enough to start learning how to use skala galogwehi, Anagalisgi was left to fend for himself for a time. When he was with his brother, Anagalisgi was happy to play with the other children or listen to the stories of the elders. More often than not, if it was a Sunday, a priest or a pastor would come by their village to administer religious rites to those who observed Christianity. Sometimes Anagalisgi would tag along and listen to the songs and the sermon, quickly picking up on both the French and English languages.

One time, he went to the front of the little church that they gathered in and took a chunk of the bread sitting there. When he realized that it was holy bread, he expected rebuke, but the pastor just smiled and made a comment about even a child understanding the Bread of Life.

Anagalisgi didn't understand anything, but he was permitted to eat the bread, which he did hurriedly, and just as quickly left the church. He did not return for several weeks. In that time, he pondered what the pastor had said. Bread of Life? Bread gave sustenance, but life? When he did finally return to the church, he approached the pastor after the sermon and asked about it.

"Christ Jesus is the Bread of Life, son," the pastor told him gently. "His body, broken for you, for me, for all of us, that we may live forever."

"Will you live forever?" Anagalisgi wondered. To him, the man appeared quite old, an elder of elders. Was he exceptionally old, then? Was he already living past common old age?

The old man nodded. "One day, when I have shed this mortal coil and ascended to be with Jesus in Heaven."

"Oh." The child pointed to the table where the remaining bread sat next to a cup. "What's that?"

"That is the Blood of Life. Jesus shed his blood and died on a cross for all our sins, that we might be forgiven and enter into Heaven with him."

"It's blood?!" Anagalisgi recoiled. Human blood?! Was he possessed?!

But the pastor just chuckled. "It's a metaphor, son." He retrieved the goblet and showed him. "See? Only wine."

Anagalisgi wasn't so sure, and he turned and ran out of the little church. He looked back only once but could not make out the old man's expression as he stood. The child kept running.

It was all a bit much for him, and he found he did not want to play with the other children, nor did he want to sit and listen to the elders. The pastor's words made no sense to him, and they swirled about confusingly in his mind. He needed to find a place to sit and think about things, work through this on his own.

He turned south of the village and continued running, feeling the wind push him into the bushes and up a hill into the trees. Pushing through the brambles to a path only he knew about, he snaked his way down the other side of the hill to a bluff, and from there picked his way down to the lively brook that bubbled happily along. From there, he went downstream just a hop, skip, and a jump to a small cave that formed a kind of grotto. It was here that he did his best thinking, for he was surrounded by earth and comforted by the spirits dancing around him in the cool air and speaking in the river.

He sat in the cave for a minute or two, not thinking, only breathing. Finally he got up and went to peer into the sparkling water of the brook, shining in the sunlight.

Bread of Life. Blood of Life. He was fairly certain that he'd heard Water of Life talked about in a sermon in the past. He'd seen the Baptist pastor perform a similar cleansing ritual in the river, over those who had converted, as they, the Aniyvwiya, performed over families of the dead. What did it all mean? To live forever, but only after death? And going to Heaven, ascending into the sky. The pastor had to be talking about the star trail, though Anagalisgi understood it to lead to the Darkening World.

The Darkening World was a place of unhappy souls far from home before they vanished. Yet he still sensed his mother near. The Heaven that the pastor spoke of sounded like a very nice place. If the Baptist water ritual was like the Aniyvwiya water ritual, and the river was like the Water of Life, that meant his mother and father, neither of whom he'd ever met, would be in Heaven.

Satisfied that he'd reconciled everything and solved the mystery, Anagalisgi turned his attention back to the stream. It fed into the river farther downstream, but here in the grotto there were no fish. He found plenty of frogs, though, and tracks of a multitude of animals, perhaps seeking shelter from weather or an easy meal.

He splashed around in the water a bit, wondering what made the water sacred. Was it a certain depth, a certain quality? Was it the way the sunlight hit it, that the spirits were pleased? Why did they always go to the same spot for cleansing? Was it something only the priest knew? Did the spirits tell him where the sacred spot was? And if the river was used for cleansing and purification, did that mean that all the water downstream of the sacred spot was now unclean and unfit for use?

Anagalisgi often wondered these things aloud when in the village, curious and yet hopeful that someone knew the answer. Ulisi and the elders all said that though he was only a boy of six winters, he had a spirit that already walked in the stars, and perhaps he walked in the stars at night when his waking body rested. Kiyuga and some of the hunters and warriors said that was well and good, but while he was awake and walking the land, he ought to keep his eyes on the land.

He did not understand what they spoke of, or why the men were suddenly mistrustful of the British. He did not understand the significance of the death of the man named Priber. And, really, none of that mattered when he was in the grotto, alone with the spirits. It was here that he could simply be, one with nature, pondering the mystery of existence itself.

As he played in a puddle that had become cut off from the little stream, he thought he heard someone speak, a stranger with a voice he did not recognize. He stood still and listened.

"Come here."

Anagalisgi turned, but saw no one in the entrance to the cave. He heard the tittering of a woodpecker burrowing into an exposed tree root that snaked down the slope to the river, but there was not a soul to be found.

The tittering stopped. He saw a flash of movement near the mouth of the cave, and the voice came again.

"Come here."

Curious, Anagalisgi obeyed, going to the mouth of the cave and looking over the stream. Downstream he saw nothing. When he looked upstream, he was distracted by the woodpecker, clinging to the exposed tree root. It was not only the unafraid demeanor of the pileated woodpecker, but its coloring, as it was entirely white, and its eyes and crest were silvery gray, not red. The woodpecker appeared to be studying him. Then it opened its beak and began to speak.

"Greetings, small one."

Anagalisgi just blinked. Was he dreaming? Was this a vision? He knew of grown men who fasted and sweat for days in hopes of seeing the spirits and receiving a vision, looking for confirmation of a decision. Why was this woodpecker speaking to him?

"Do not be afraid," the white woodpecker went on. "Come with me."

With that, it spread its wings and hopped off the root, swooping low over the water and gliding up the slope to a tree.

Anagalisgi broke into a run, scrambling up the gravely bluff and pulling himself onto solid ground. Before he reached the tree, the woodpecker was off again, gliding over and under several branches to rest upon another tree. The child dutifully followed, wondering what this spirit—because it could be nothing other than a spirit—wanted with him.

It went on like this until Anagalisgi was doing little more than walking hurriedly after the woodpecker, having expended all his energy. Only his curiosity fueled him now, and even that was beginning to wane. He was happy when the chase finally ended, and at another stream no less. He took a drink, then looked around for the woodpecker.

He caught only a glimpse of it on one tree before it let go and swooped to another, toward the direction they had just come. There it stopped.

Rather than speak to the woodpecker, Anagalisgi's attention was drawn to the sight before him.

Everything as he knew it was gone. The village had disappeared. All the villages had. What lay before him was pure, untouched forest over vast, sprawling mountains. The sky was no longer blue and sunny, but clouds had rolled in overhead, and a brisk wind buffeted his face. In the distance, black clouds rolled over the mountain peaks, and thunder rumbled. He saw lightning touch down multiple times. Mountains and forest disappeared in heavy rain.

Anagalisgi wanted to speak, but could find no words. He didn't know what to think. He always liked to ask questions, but he never imagined that the spirits would speak directly to him and possibly give him the answers themselves. He was simultaneously delighted and awestruck and fearful.

"Remember the storm," the woodpecker said. "Remember your place in it."

Anagalisgi stared at the distant lightning, mesmerized. He almost didn't feel the wind anymore, though he felt it in the air around him, rustling the trees.

He startled and cried out as something grabbed his arm, but it was only Geluhni, one of the men of the village. With him were several other hunters and Kiyuga.

Without a word, they ushered Anagalisgi away. The small child looked back, but the spirit woodpecker had gone, and the boy allowed himself to be led home. There, with the rain now coming down in sheets, Ulisi fussed over him to get him warm and dry, as he'd begun to shiver.

"What were you doing on that hill?" Ulisi demanded, though she sounded exhausted.

"Following a spirit," Anagalisgi told her. "A white woodpecker came to me and said to follow."

He could see his grandmother was conflicted. She loved her grandsons and didn't want to lose them like she'd lost so many others. At the same time, it was unthinkable to reproach anyone for seeking or following a spirit, and she didn't dare ask what it had told him. If he chose to tell, that was his business, but one did not ask.

Once she was satisfied that he wasn't likely to freeze to death, she released him to play with his brother. Except Kiyuga didn't want to play. He was in one of those moods where he was trying to be the adult big brother.

"I was following a woodpecker spirit," Anagalisgi said when he saw the look on Kiyuga's face.

"Why didn't you tell me?" Kiyuga asked.

"Because the spirit just said to follow it. I couldn't run away to come get you. Besides, it was my spirit."

As soon as the words came out of his mouth, Anagalisgi knew it to be true. The woodpecker was his. It would speak to him and guide him in times of need.

"All children want to find their spirit, little brother," Kiyuga told him gently. "I want to know my spirit. And I will, when I become a man."

"But it's true!" Anagalisgi protested. "It's mine!"

Kiyuga looked ready to speak, but Ulisi chuckled from her place at the fire. She motioned for the boys to approach, which they did meekly. She took them on either side of her and hummed a moment, still smiling. The rain droned overhead on the roof, like a swarm of angry wasps.

"Oh, my boys," Ulisi sighed. "The spirits are not ours to command or keep. They speak to us in times of need, when we need help or guidance, when they have a message or warning to impart."

"But why would they speak to him and not me?" Kiyuga pouted.

"Because it was clearly not meant for you. We do not tell the spirits when to speak, or to whom. Perhaps a day will come with they speak to you and not to him. It is not a cause for jealousy, simply patience and obedience. Why should we choose one hunting dog over another, except that one is talented in birds and the other in game? Why should we choose one horse over another, except that one is faster or stronger or has better temperament? Why must there be choice at all, except to bring about the most desirable outcome? Why should Unehlanvhi send a spirit to Anagalisgi except that it was His will that should be carried out?"

Kiyuga looked chastened, but Anagalisgi was mesmerized by Ulisi's wisdom and now even more curious about why any spirit should speak to him. He was a child playing in the grotto. He had fancies. He knew some of the adults feared that he would never be as great a warrior or hunter as Kiyuga was already proving himself to be. Ulisi and the elders chastised them that he was yet a boy, but in the same way they encouraged Kiyuga's skill in combat and weapons, so they encouraged him to dream.

They did not expect him to take the same path as his brother. But they were Wolf Clan. Their job was to be warriors, to protect and defend the people. Anagalisgi went to peek out the window, just barely able to see the white flag raised over the seat of the chiefs. A time of peace, when the uku ruled, when harmony with the spirits and the land was paramount, when dreaming was encouraged and indulged.

Anagalisgi could be allowed to dream for a while, but what if that changed? What happened if the white flag came down, if the skiagvsta came to power? What happened when they demanded both of the brothers? Ulisi was a Beloved Woman, but could she really only offer up one son to fight? It would reflect poorly on her and the clan if her other son had no abilities to offer, and no excuse other than his daydreams.

The rain came down harder, obscuring the white flag, and a sudden flash of lightning momentarily blinded Anagalisgi. As he was rubbing his eyes, Ulisi picked him up and brought him back to where she and Kiyuga were sitting.

"Just because you are called Anagalisgi does not mean you can stare at it," she chided lightly, "any more than Kiyuga can dig a burrow or stuff his cheeks."

"Why am I called Anagalisgi?" the younger brother wondered, still seeing spots.

"Because your mother said that she saw lightning from the spirits strike you when you were born, and she knew you would be special."

"What about me?" Kiyuga butted in.

"You..." Ulisi said teasingly, "you would not come out. You wanted to stay burrowed in your mother. And when you were born, you had big, puffy cheeks, just like kiyuga when he gathers nuts and seeds."

"Am I special, too, then?"

Ulisi gathered them to her and held them close. "Oh, my children, you are special in your own way. Who can say why we have been made except that we will know it when the time comes? We must simply let the spirits guide us and take care not to offend."

Her words were meant to be comforting, but Anagalisgi found himself even more confounded. Why had the spirit spoken to him? What was he expected to do? Remember the storm and remember his place in it? What did that mean? If the spirits had chosen him for some reason, he really didn't want to offend them, but could they maybe speak a little clearer?

The following morning, he went to the elders and the adawehi to inquire about his vision. He already knew that birds were messengers from the spirits to the earth, but what message were they trying to convey?

The head adawehi attempted to communicate with the spirits, and the woodpecker directly. He ate herbs and plants in order to do this, and he said that he saw the world from the wings of the woodpecker.

He saw visions of distant lands, of mountains, and of worlds overlaid upon other worlds, spirits walking among men. These were the things that the woodpecker saw, his vision piercing through earth and sky, through time itself.

"But why did he tell me?" Anagalisgi wondered. "What part am I to play?"

"Young child," the adawehi said, still only half-lucid coming out of his spirit trance. "You are the woodpecker. A messenger between spirits and men, destined for distant lands where ordinary men cannot go, yet remaining humble, your soul remaining tethered to the heartbeat of the earth and your people."

The six year old child had no idea what to make of this, and his mind was filled with awe and wonder and horror. He thanked the adawehi appropriately, not wishing to disrespect him or the spirits he communed with, then ran, terrified. He had no desire to return to the grotto at this time, and he found himself heading for the little church.

It was not Sunday, but the pastor was about, seeming to spend more and more of his time with the Overhill people. He smiled when Anagalisgi approached, but it faded when he perceived the boy's distress.

Again the child explained what had happened, his vision and the storm and the woodpecker. He also explained what the adawehi had told him.

"I don't understand," Anagalisgi finished, looking at the preacher forlornly.

The old man smiled and nodded. "Well, I think I might have an idea. I think God is calling you to prophecy, to prophesy before men. He will give you the words to speak, and you will go before many men, many nations, where no one else may go. Perhaps it will be that you will be the one to take the Word of God to the savage peoples of the West, bring them into civilization, into the Light."

"What about the storm?"

"Not all change is welcomed. You're very fortunate, Anagalisgi. You were born into civilization, into one of the Civilized Tribes, which is why we get along so well. It is merely second nature to you. Not all people are this way. Some people are the woodpeckers. Some people are the trees. It will take work to get through to them. But if God is speaking to you about this already, at such a young age, it means He must have great plans for you."

Anagalisgi was still unsure and his terror had dulled to a lingering fog of fear. He thanked the preacher and returned home. Kiyuga was practicing his weapons and combat with the other older boys. Anagalisgi knew he should be practicing with boys his own age, taking up the blowgun and the bow and arrow, but his heart and mind wasn't in it right now. The vision did not trouble him so much anymore as the adawehi's and the pastor's interpretations of it. He didn't know what to make of it.

Traveling to distant lands, going where no other man could go. It put him in mind of the Darkening World, the souls of the dead going west toward the setting sun and becoming ever more distressed and mournful that they left their homelands, their families, their people. Should he be expected to go to these places willingly? Well, he had no choice. If it was the will of the spirits or Unehlanvhi, he could not disrespect them or refuse their orders.

But why him? Surely Kiyuga was the better choice, if for no other reason than he was the eldest son of their parents and even now a promising hunter and warrior. His brother made a Promise to him. He would be the one to clear the way. Now it was sounding as if it would be the other way around. Anagalisgi was troubled by this as well. Did that mean that Kiyuga's Promise was in vain? Should Anagalisgi tell him? What would he say? How would his brother react?

In the end, Anagalisgi did not say anything more of his vision. He did not tell anyone what the adawehi or the pastor had said. He did not return to either of them seeking further guidance for it. In his heart, he knew it was wrong to keep such a weight, such a message and prophecy to himself, and he found himself going to the shaman more often for absolutions because of it—though he said it was always for other things which he may or may not have done. He hoped the woodpecker would return to explain more of this to him so as to ease the guilt and give him a clearer idea of what to do.

Most especially, he did not speak of it to Kiyuga, and he would not for a long time. But by then, it would be too late, and it would eventually leave Anagalisgi wondering—for decades and even centuries—whether things might have turned out differently if he had confided in Kiyuga. Maybe it would have saved him. At the very least, maybe it would have made the loss of his brother easier to bear, knowing that he had done all he could to clear the way to save him.

ᎠꮻᏞꙅᎢ ᎨᎢ

Ayadohlv'i Tso'i

A Child's Ears

The nuances of politics often escape children, and their understanding of why things were happening was limited only to what they could see and what the adults told them. But even a child could see and sense the change on the wind, Kiyuga thought.

It had started with the death of Moytoy. It was said to have been a grand affair, but Kiyuga had been too young to remember much of it, and besides, he'd still been too aggrieved of his parents' deaths at the time to take notice. He was buried beneath the townhouse, as was his right, that much Kiyuga knew.

After that, growing up, Kiyuga had expected his son, Amoskosit, to become skiagsvta. It had been proclaimed so, after all, and it was not for the child to question such decisions, though it was highly irregular as it was supposed to be a man's sister's son who assumed the mantle of leadership.

Then he started to notice something. Traders continued to stop in the village, but it was no longer a destination, as they always packed up quickly and moved north. English and French diplomats continued on the road north, rather than sit and speak to Amoskosit or any of his warriors. Even the missionaries did not linger long, preferring to move north, though the Baptist preacher had become something of a full-time resident, an elder, even.

Families started to move, cleaning their homes and moving north. There were fewer warriors in the village now. Kiyuga was quickly becoming a senior warrior, if only because there were so few left. He was spoken highly of and encouraged to go with the rest.

He returned from a hunt one day, a couple rabbits in hand, just as Ulisi was returning from the fields. But what he expected to be an ordinary evening quickly turned into anything but. He entered the house to find many things packed up. Fear pulsed through him when he saw his things set aside, and he wondered if he was being kicked out. Then he saw that everything was being packed up. Anagalisgi, now eleven years old, was busy packing and wrapping things, while Ulisi made up provisions for what she evidently expected to be a long journey.

"What's going on?" Kiyuga wondered, unsure just what to say.

"We're moving north, to Itsa'ti," Ulisi answered, mashing some berries to mix into some jerky she'd begun preparing. "Word of our family has reached Gvnagadoga and the skiagvsta."

Kiyuga blinked. "But you are a Beloved Woman of Taliqua Eghawa. This is your home, your history, your clan."

She stopped fussing with the food and looked at him. Kiyuga hadn't moved from his place at the door, and he still gripped the two rabbits. She motioned him forward and took the rabbits to begin skinning. As her hand moved deftly with the knife, she continued speaking.

"I know. If it were only me, I would not hesitate to stay behind. But he wants both of you as well. Between your strength and your brother's dreams, Gvnagadoga believes it more beneficial to have you in Itsa'ti. And myself as a Beloved Woman as well. We have a strong family line, always have. You and your brother are no exception. And furthermore, there are many families in Itsa'ti, lots of pretty girls. Maybe one will catch your eye."

Kiyuga did not tell her that one already had, here in Taliqua, but he was hardly in a position to ask for marriage just yet.

"When do you expect to leave?" he asked sullenly.

"First thing in the morning." She gave him a look. "Now don't look at me like that. We're not going far, and this is a good thing. What good is a strong warrior if he has no one to defend? What good is a dreamer if no one is around to heed his warnings?"

"But there are people here. Every village needs a warrior to defend it. And the elders and the adawehi know Anagalisgi and his dreams very well. Gvnagadoga and the adawehi of Itsa'ti don't."

"They will learn," Ulisi told him predictably. "And a warrior of great repute ought to use his talent where it is needed. You are not yet a full warrior, and to balk at this invitation is terribly disrespectful." Her gaze was mildly accusing and pricked him with guilt. Her tone became very firm. "Furthermore, a man goes where his woman tells him. Seeing how you are not yet married, I am your woman. We are going to Itsa'ti."

Kiyuga let out a breath. "Yes, Agilisi."

"Good boy. Help your brother."

He did so, not speaking until Ulisi had left the house again on some errand.

"Did you know about this?" he asked his younger brother.

Anagalisgi looked at him. "No. I knew she was worried about all the people going north, concerned about Gvnagadoga quietly consolidating power, but I didn't know until this morning. After you left, she told me to start packing. I thought she was kicking us both out, and then she told me the plan."

Kiyuga raised a brow. "But did you know?"

He knew his brother was a dreamer, and the elders and the adawehi were helping him to refine his powers of perception and discrimination so that he could better understand his dreams and help the people. He was getting better at it, but some of the child's dreams baffled even the most seasoned interpreters.

"I don't know," Anagalisgi replied shyly. "I think I might have. Some parts of a dream from a moon ago fall into place concerning this, but not all. It's very confusing sometimes." He did sound distressed, Kiyuga thought.

"But it is a good thing," he went on, sounding more cheerful. "I know that. I know you will become a great warrior."

"Everyone tells me that. I don't need a dream from my little brother to tell me something I already know."

"No," Anagalisgi insisted. "I mean, you will be a great warrior."

The way he said it, the authority in his cracked voice, made Kiyuga uneasy and he turned his attention back to the packing.

The following morning, the three of them joined a small group of other families heading north along the Great Road. It made Kiyuga feel a little more at ease, seeing how he was related to most of them in some way. His closest relative was an uncle, his mother's brother. They walked on the right side of the group, keeping an eye out for attacking animals or bandits.

"I remember I told you that we were leaving, but I didn't know you were coming with us!" Digvnige laughed.

"I didn't know either," Kiyuga replied, trying not to sound sullen.

"Ah, I'm not surprised. You are a great warrior, even at your age. You can only get better from here."

"Then why are you going?"

"Sotsena's father was from Tanasi, and all his sisters are still there. She says she wishes to be with family."

Kiyuga raised a brow. "You don't believe those are her true intentions?"

His uncle laughed again. "It is not for us to understand the minds of women, but no, I don't think so. I believe she wants to be with her family, but I don't think her intentions stop there."

"She doesn't like Gvnagadoga consolidating power, then?"

"On the contrary, she is highly supportive. They are of the same clan, and are related in some way, I think. I think she hopes to have some say in matters. She doesn't like your grandmother going, I can tell you that."

Kiyuga stole a sideways glance at Ulisi who was chatting with a couple other women. "I don't know what she thinks about Gvnagadoga."

"Of course not, you've been a child for this whole thing. Diwedalohi does not think highly of his actions. She had no problems with him, but when he began doing things quietly, behind the backs of the other uku, well, she thinks it suspect, very much like the British and French. If the white men bring their brewing war here, she's afraid Gvnagadoga will declare us for the British."

Kiyuga nodded. "She's always favored the French."

"Favored the French and opposed war," Digvnige added. "Your grandmother has never been afraid of a scrap, but she's no fool either. The French are here to trade. The British wish to conquer."

"And by accepting Gvnagadoga's invitation to bring us and serve as a Beloved Woman, she hopes to sway him away from the British."

"Something like that, I imagine."

Kiyuga didn't know what to think. Just in the last few years, his eyes and his world had opened up to see beyond himself, beyond his village, to a wider world that existed as more than stories and concepts. He no longer blindly accepted the world as a child does, but he was interacting with it, thinking about it. He was finally beginning to grasp the concept of everything being connected in some way, from the birds that touched both sky and earth, to the politics threading through their lives and connecting them to each other and the Europeans, for good or ill.

Apparently his awe and distress showed on his face, for his uncle smiled and said, "Life is easier when you do not try to assume control. The spirits will make flowers bloom or wither, so they will also direct the warriors to take up or lay down arms. I know Anagalisgi is the dreamer, but you must also allow the spirits to speak to you and guide you, and take care not to offend."

"I try. I really do. Everyone tells me how great I am, or I'm going to be, and I don't want to let them down."

"You won't," his uncle assured him. "Let the spirits guide you, and defend our people. That is the simple duty of a warrior."

Kiyuga stuck to this axiom as they continued along the road. His job now was to defend the people as they traveled. Watch out for wild animals and other unfriendly visitors. Politics didn't matter out here because they were all they had if something happened. Out here, it didn't matter who was uku or who was skiagvsta if a mountain lion suddenly sprang from the bushes. All that would matter was whether he could do his duty and keep the people safe.

He glanced at Anagalisgi. His little brother was as proficient in blowgun and bow and knife as one might expect of a boy his age, but he was no warrior. Kiyuga fully expected that he would be the one to defend and save him.

He found himself thinking about the girl he liked. Her name was Meli. She was from Deer Clan and resembled a young doe herself with her soft eyes and delicate skin. She was around his age, and he liked to think that she saw him looking and wanted him to consider courting her. He would have to bring her a deer. Sometimes it was considered bad form to accept the first deer that was offered, and he would have to continue bringing her deer until she either accepted it and prepared it for a wedding feast or until she drove him off and told him to stop calling or until he gave up. But he wasn't one to give up.

It was also bad form for a child not yet a full hunter or warrior to call on a girl. Very young children might do so simply as an imitation or at play, but he could not do so. He was too old for it to be play, and too young for it to be taken seriously. He would have to wait.

Well, he supposed it would give him time to become a warrior and find a girl in Itsa'ti. If everyone was moving to Itsa'ti or Tanasi, there had to be a few pretty girls there, right? If he proved to be as great a warrior as everyone seemed to think he would be, it probably wouldn't be difficult to court a girl. Still his thoughts wandered back to Meli.

Their trip was uneventful and they arrived in Itsa'ti no worse for wear.

To hear Ulisi tell it, Itsa'ti hadn't even really existed when she was a child; it had simply been part of Tanasi across the river. Now the whole stretch of land was full of homes and surrounded by crop fields, with horse pasture beyond that. Kiyuga took it all in as they descended the steep slopes of the southern hills. It was certainly larger than Taliqua, and except for the river splitting the two, he never would have known Itsa'ti and Tanasi were supposed to be two different towns.

Their journeying group began to say their farewells and disperse when they reached the town. Everyone had relatives here, it seemed.

Kiyuga bid farewell to his uncle as he and his wife steered clear of Itsa'ti and made for Tanasi.

Itsa'ti was a lot to take in all at once. Hundreds, maybe even thousands, of people lived here, plus there were more who were likely just passing through or staying temporarily. Cooking, talking, buying and selling, playing, carrying on with everyday life. Kiyuga saw a few dozen Europeans as well. Some were trading furs and firearms, others animals or fabrics or spices. Kiyuga identified a troupe of missionaries, preaching to a group of interested bystanders, their Bible evidently well-worn from use. Then there were other Europeans simply milling about, seeming entirely at ease in their surroundings, talking and laughing with their Aniyvwiya friends.

"It's grown up since the last time I was here," Ulisi observed.

"What are we doing here?" Kiyuga wondered.

"We have relatives in Tanasi, but I want to find Gvnagadoga first. I want to know what's about, and let him know we've arrived."

Kiyuga did not argue, indeed could not argue. He followed Ulisi through Itsa'ti. She seemed to know her way around, despite the town "growing up" since her last visit. Since he could not recall her ever leaving him and Anagalisgi while they were growing up, it had to have been fifteen years. Nevertheless, she navigated the town like a woman who had lived there all her life, or at least visited frequently.

As one might expect, she found Gvnagadoga in the townhouse where he and other warriors were meeting with European diplomats. Kiyuga might have suggested finding their relatives and returning later, but Ulisi remained where she was, hovering outside the townhouse for the entirety of the meeting. It must have just started, for it seemed to last an awful long time, long enough to bore both Kiyuga and his brother.

When at last the meeting ended, Ulisi wasted no time in entering the building and making herself known. The Europeans seemed a bit unsettled by their sudden appearance, Kiyuga thought. He took stock of the white men.

French, he judged. Armed well enough to show themselves as

formidable and prepared, not so much to be a threat. Gvnagadoga was no pushover, and he and his warriors met the gesture in kind.

Ulisi paid no mind to the Frenchman and greeted Gvnagadoga respectfully. Then she smiled and said, "Agituta."

"Diwedalohi. Agilisi," Gvnagadoga said, grinning. "How long have you been in Itsa'ti?"

"We've just arrived," Ulisi told him.

"Ah, you should have come sooner, you could have advised me in this meeting. You've always been partial to the French, haven't you?"

"Between the coyote and the crow, I'll take the crow."

The Itsa'ti uku barked a laugh. "Of course. Ah, you've not changed a bit, Diwedalohi."

Now she smiled faintly. "But you have. Consolidating all the power of the Overhill villages. I expect you'll be going after the Middle and Lower Town peoples, too?"

Gvnagadoga's smile faded. He dipped his head. "I see we have much to discuss." He looked past her to where Kiyuga and Anagalisgi waited, trying to be patient. "And these are your sons?"

"My daughter's sons, though she and her husband are long dead now."

"Of course. The warrior and the dreamer. I've heard of them."

Ulisi nodded once and made a motion. "Kiyuga. Anagalisgi."

Both boys stepped forward. Gvnagadoga regarded them with an admiration that a father might have for his son. "Fine boys. I can already see that this one—"

"Kiyuga."

"—Kiyuga is going to make a fine warrior." He looked at Anagalisgi. "And his brother will be there to guide him every step of the way with wisdom from the spirits." He looked back at Ulisi. "Wonderful boys you have." He took a step back. "Now then, if you've just arrived, I expect you have relatives to visit, and these meetings are no place for boys. Our French friends here have their own matters to attend to for the time being and will return this evening. You may join myself, my warriors, and the other Beloved Women here."

Ulisi dipped her head. "Wado, Gvnagadoga. I will return this evening."

She turned and left the building, Kiyuga and Anagalisgi following close behind. Once they were out of range, Kiyuga spoke up, asking, "Did that go well?"

"We will see," Ulisi replied evasively. She glanced at Anagalisgi. "Keep a sharp eye on the spirits and learn well from your dreams, Anagalisgi. I feel that the spirits may be speaking to you more often now."

Kiyuga saw his brother's expression turn from mild curiosity to something resembling dread. Before Kiyuga could say anything, Ulisi addressed him.

"Train well, Kiyuga, and do become the best warrior you can be. The Europeans are trying to sway us to one side or another, and rarely does anything good come from such competition. I fear we may be fighting in their wars soon enough, and their wars are different from anything our ancestors have ever done."

Dread unfurled itself within Kiyuga now as well, and he and his brother exchanged uncertain glances. Suddenly, the common life going on around them felt distant, hollow, almost like a dream itself.

Then the moment passed and Ulisi started speaking of other things, their relatives and other history. It took a serious effort of will for Kiyuga to pay attention to it, and he found himself jumping at shadows the whole way through Itsa'ti to Tanasi.

There was no real difference between Itsa'ti and Tanasi, save for which side of the river it sat on. The biggest change that had come about in the last ten years was the Tanasi Warrior, who once ruled a sovereign Tanasi, now sat on Gvnagadoga's council and answered to him. They were all related anyway, so it wasn't a big deal.

Kiyuga and Anagalisgi dutifully followed Ulisi through the town, unsure of their destination until their destination apparently found them.

"Diwedalohi! Is it really you?"

Kiyuga looked around until he spotted a woman perhaps a few

years older than Ulisi, threading her way through a group of playing children to reach them. She and Ulisi embraced and exchanged excited greetings for a long time.

"Ah, and who is this with you?" the woman inquired, finally taking notice of the boys.

"Ulvsati, my sons, Kiyuga and Anagalisgi," Ulisi introduced. "Kiyuga, Anagalisgi, this is Ulvsati. She is the daughter of my father's sister."

"Such exciting things are happening lately," Ulvsati commented.

Ulisi folded her arms. "Exciting is one word, I suppose."

"What brings you into it?"

"Gvnagadoga."

"Ah." Ulvsati nodded slowly. "Yes, igituta has been rather busy lately. I think he sees something coming. Something more with these Europeans. He wants to be ready."

"He wants to carry on Moytoy's legacy."

"He wants peace and security for our people. The settlers are not just coming. They are here. And they bring their problems with them. You see Tanasi and Itsa'ti. You have known them. Many refugees come here. We accept them, but we cannot ignore the problems that drove them to flight. Eventually, they will come for us as well."

Kiyuga looked around and noticed that, indeed, the makeup of the people around him was not homogeneous. They were not all Aniyvwiya, not wholly. Some looked Aninvdawegi, others Anakwanki, a few he could not readily identify. Still some appeared to have European parentage somewhere. He heard the English language in bits here and there, intermixed with his own language and half a dozen others.

"I imagine that is why Gvnagadoga asked me to come and serve as Ghigau, to ensure that our interests are upheld."

Ulvsati smiled gently. "You are a strong, intelligent woman, Diwedalohi. You will steer us right."

"How can I, when my own town is practically abandoned?"

"They come here for protection and guidance. With you as Ghigau and your sons as warriors, all will be well."

"Kiyuga is the warrior," Ulisi said. "Anagalisgi is a dreamer and communes with the spirits."

"They will be spending much time with Gvnagadoga regardless, I imagine." Ulvsati huffed. "This is well and good and all, but I imagine you need a place to stay." She grabbed Ulisi's hand. "Come, you will stay with me and my family, and my boys will be uncles to your sons for as long as you are here."

Then they were moving again, only a short distance to a dwelling where two girls a few years older than Kiyuga were busy preparing supper.

"Unisgwali, Kansgawi, Diwedalohi and her sons are going to stay with us."

So followed a flurry of activity to ready extra accommodations and provisions. Kiyuga and Anagalisgi were set to the task of unpacking and incorporating their goods with those of Ulvsati and her family. She had two unmarried daughters at home as well as one married daughter and her daughter's husband who had yet to move out, though it was not rushed. With the influx of migrants to Itsa'ti and Tanasi, homes could not be built fast enough.

Ulvsati also had one son who was moved out and lived five houses down, and three more sons still at home. They were all in the process of courting women, but in the meantime, they were more than happy to assume the role of uncle for Kiyuga and Anagalisgi.

Dinner was a crowded affair, and conversation was loud as distant relatives became close. Ulisi and Ulvsati quickly had the family tree mapped out and it seemed everyone had a story or ten to tell about each person. On top of all of that, Kiyuga's newfound uncles were questioning him about the skills he already possessed and bragging about which of them could teach him which new skills the best. They bragged about it to Anagalisgi, too, though he remained more passive.

When it came time to sleep, Kiyuga no longer felt out of place in Tanasi, and distant relatives felt like family. He chastised himself for wishing for home, for Taliqua, telling himself to man up and be a warrior. One day he would marry a woman and join her, and he would follow her and go where she wanted to go and live where she wanted to live. Then he would not have the luxury of homesickness.

He rolled over on his mat to face Anagalisgi, just able to make out his little brother in the darkness.

"You're awake," Anagalisgi stated quietly.

"Yeah," Kiyuga said. "What are you thinking about? Shouldn't you be dreaming?"

"I'm afraid to dream tonight."

"Why?"

"I don't think the spirits will have good things to say."

"You think it was a mistake to come here?"

Anagalisgi sighed and shifted so he was resting on his elbow. "No. I think it's exactly what we needed to do. But that doesn't mean that bad things aren't going to happen. I think we're just avoiding something worse by leaving Taliqua."

A cool breeze swept through the warm, crowded dwelling, and Kiyuga felt the hair on his arms rise and the back of his neck prickled with unease.

His brother lay back down and shifted position. "I don't know. I don't have exact answers to tell you how much corn will be harvested this year or which tree will fall in the next storm. But I do know that our best position is here. The last island amid a rising river."

Kiyuga pretended to be asleep, if only to make his brother stop. It wasn't that he was angry with Anagalisgi or thought him a liar; it was that he completely believed him.

ᎠᏣᏗᎵᎯᏗ ᎤᏥ

Ayadohlv'i Nvki

A Child's Imagination

The sun rose over the misty valley, and Anagalisgi was there to see it as he swept over the sparkling fog. He could vaguely make out the rubble of toppled walls, charred remains of wooden roofs. He could not see the ground, but he knew what was down there. Death. Only death.

He continued to glide, reaching the trees on the north side of the valley, sweeping high, then low, then high again, and finding his peace in a cave. As soon as the darkness enveloped him, his human eyes sprang open and he looked around the townhouse. His human senses gradually returned to him. His head and body felt heavy, a stark contrast to his lighter woodpecker spirit, and he closed his eyes and let his head drop into his hands.

He looked up at a hand on his shoulder. It was Gvnagadoga.

"It's a difficult thing," the old man said. "Go now. Rest. Be patient."

Anagalisgi nodded tiredly, stood on stiff legs, and left the townhouse. The morning sunlight was far too bright in his opinion, and he wished only for the comfort of his bed. He'd been up since early this morning, long before the sun rose. Troubled by a dream, he sought the advice of Gvnagadoga and the adawehi. They told him that he was of an age now where he ought to try asking the spirits themselves for answers.

The spirits had answered all right, taking him through the future on great wings, examining his dream from within. He didn't like what he saw, and he was afraid to tell anyone. But if he was to become a dreaming man, adawehi of the people one day, he would have to learn to speak the good and the bad. Problem was, it seemed he spoke only the bad lately. Some people had taken to calling him a bad omen. He couldn't help what he dreamed.

He found himself wishing for a Christian pastor to speak to, if only for perspective, but there were none in Itsa'ti or Tanasi anymore, and no missionaries were visiting now. The chapel in Taliqua had been tolerated, but things were a little more tense in Itsa'ti and Tanasi. Love for Europeans was low, and both the British and the French were trying to sway the people into siding with them in what they now perceived to be an inevitable war. Some believed that in order to protect the people, they ought to withdraw and do their best to turn the Europeans against each other. Others favored one side or the other.

Gvnagadoga and his council were always very pleasant with the Europeans that Anagaliasgi saw, and only Gvnagadoga's patience and cool-headedness kept them from declaring a side in haste, though he was known to lean toward the French—thanks not in part to Ulisi and her women. The word now was that the French wanted to build one of their military forts near Itsa'ti, something that did not sit well with her residents.

And yet when Anagalisgi closed his eyes, he saw only bad news. Death, destruction, displacement. He couldn't conjure up a dream about a blessed marriage or the birth of a child if his life depended on it. Every night, the same thing, with only minor variances. At one point, he tried to see if he couldn't manipulate his dream and perhaps find a path to avoid the destruction he saw, but to no avail. He did not know if he was just unskilled in such manipulation, or if the things he saw were unavoidable.

When he arrived home, only Ulisi and Ulvsati were around. The men were all out hunting, and the one daughter who remained at home was in the fields. The children were also out and about, playing and pretending to be warriors and whatnot. Things had cleared out in the last couple years, and Anagalisgi looked forward to a quiet nap.

"I thought you might have taken up residence in the townhouse," Ulisi said, not looking up from the clothing she was busy sewing.

"Not yet," Anagalisgi told her, stifling a yawn.

"Have the spirits shown you anything, then?"

"Only the same thing they've been showing me for the last few years."

He saw Ulisi frown, but still she did not look at him. "Well, Kiyuga is out scouting right now. The French are surveying the spot where they want to build their fort."

"Have they been given permission?"

She shook her head. "Not as such, though I suspect it will be soon."

"Do you approve?" Anagalisgi just wanted to go to sleep.

Ulisi turned over the garment. "Not as such. But if worse comes to worse, they build it, we can kick them out and use it for ourselves."

"I thought you liked the French?"

"Coyotes and crows, you know that. I will take the lesser of two evils if I must, but my first duty is to the people. I don't believe any good will come from the Europeans. The time of novelty and curiosity has passed, and now they press their hand. I think you know this."

He didn't want to admit it, but he did. Anagalisgi nodded sullenly and turned as if to make for his blankets, but Ulisi kept talking.

"If Kiyuga gets back before the sun goes down, I think you ought to go out with him, do some hunting. Dreaming is a fine thing, but it puts no rabbit in the stew, and I would hate to see your premonitions of death turn out to be true, not because of war, but because of starvation. You understand?"

"Vv, Agilisi."

"Good boy. Go on now, get some sleep."

As relieved as he was to be released, and as much as he craved sleep at the moment, he only feared it now. He did not like sleep, did not like to dream. What was the point of having the same dream over and over again, every night for two years, if it imparted no new information, if he didn't understand it, and if there was nothing he could do to change it anyway?

He was more relieved when his nap proved to be one of the rare instances when he did not dream, or did not remember his dreams, and as he stood, he could hear Kiyuga and the others just outside the house.

His brother had grown into a handsome, impressive man, and an equally impressive hunter and warrior. His name circulated well among the people, and some had begun calling him Yvgidahi, Young Spear. He could probably have his pick of women, and it wasn't difficult to envision him as a future skiagvsta.

Even now, Anagalisgi could hear him laughing and carrying on, cracking jokes about the French and the fort they wanted to build.

"Anagalisgi, your brother's home," Ulisi said. Raising her voice, "Kiyuga! Get your young spear in here and wake up your brother!"

Sighing, Anagalisgi sat up, stretched, and got to his feet. "That's not necessary, Agilisi. I'm awake."

Even as he said it, Kiyuga walked in, still smiling. Anagalisgi barely had time to register this before Kiyuga was dragging him out of the house and into the sunshine. His head was still throbbing and the sunshine was still too bright.

"Come on, little brother," Kiyuga said, shoving a bow and quiver of arrows in his hands. "Communing with the spirits is noble, but you can't forget about speaking to the living as well. How are you supposed to woo a woman when you never go hunting?"

It felt like it was all happening so fast. Anagalisgi could not keep up, at least in his mind, and the next thing he knew, he and Kiyuga were well away from the villages. Only here was he able to collect his thoughts and bring himself back to, as Kiyuga put it, the living. The waking world. He looked around, saw everything as it ought to be, felt the bow in his hand, knew his brother was nearby.

"Ah, he lives!" Kiyuga cried. "You had me worried, little brother. I thought perhaps the spirits had already taken your soul and left your body."

"Believe me, sometimes I think that as well," Anagalisgi told him, rubbing his eyes and becoming more oriented to the world.

"Sometimes I think you'd like that." His brother's tone was difficult to judge. "I worry about you."

"And I worry about the people. Bad things are coming. I can't control my dreams."

"Maybe not, but you can't let them control you either. The people are here. What good is a messenger if he can't deliver his message because his mind is not with the living?" Kiyuga put his hands on Anagalisgi's shoulders. "I am glad for you, little brother, that you seem to have this great destiny and great favor with the spirits. But as long as there is work for you to do here, you cannot go with them just yet. What have I always said?"

Anagalisgi managed a small smile. "You will go first to clear the way."

"Exactly. And I will make good on my promise, little brother." He put up a hand before Anagalisgi could speak. "And don't say anything about your prophetic dooms coming for us all. Let me fulfill my promise to you in the way that it will happen, not because you told me of it beforehand. As the spirits will it, so things shall happen. All right?"

Anagalisgi sighed but agreed. He looked at the bow in his hand. It was real, tangible. Looking around, this world was very real. He could see it, feel it, smell it. Here he was anchored within his human body.

The more he thought about it, the better he felt. Kiyuga seemed to sense this because he grinned once more and clapped him on the back. "Come on. Let's see if we can't scare up something for supper, hm?"

Gripping his bow harder, Anagalisgi agreed, and the two of them headed deeper into the forest.

It was late spring and all the critters were out. With last winter finally shaken off, it was time to prepare for the next winter. Everything was out looking for food, or trying to avoid becoming food for something else. Anagalisgi managed to catch himself a few rabbits while Kiyuga pursued the coyote that had been hunting them.

It felt good to be out and about, Anagalisgi thought, standing with two rabbits in hand. For just a little while, it was him and the earth around him. He took a breath, then knelt to thank the spirits a second time for the provision. As he stood again, the bushes rustled and

Kiyuga appeared, the coyote across his shoulders.

"We'll just say you got the coyote," Kiyuga said, hardly fazed by the weight on his back.

"No one would believe it," Anagalisgi told him, mirroring his brother's smile. "Besides, if I got the coyote, that would mean that you were stuck with two measly rabbits. It wouldn't look good for you to stoop so low."

"Maybe you're right. Guess I'll just have to get two coyotes next time."

"Now, now," Anagalisgi said as they turned toward home, "you don't need to get greedy on my account. Besides, someone might think you were trying to woo me instead of one of the pretty girls you like."

"Which girls are those?" Kiyuga raised a brow.

"I don't know. Which one is it?"

"Ah, clever brother. You mean to say the spirits have not whispered my heart's desires to you? You've not seen my future wife and wedding in your dreams?"

"Sadly, no. You'll just have to tell me yourself."

For a long moment, Anagalisgi was sure his brother wouldn't answer. Finally Kiyuga said, "To be honest, there isn't anyone. Not really."

"No one? At all? Kiyuga, there are a number of girls trying to catch your eye."

"I know. I see them all the time. I just...I don't know."

"What's stopping you? Don't you want warrior sons of your own?"

"Of course I do. I just don't want to stop being a warrior myself to do it."

"I don't understand."

Kiyuga sighed. "I know it sounds selfish. But Wolf Clan is the clan of warriors."

"You think a wife—any one of the girls who is enamored with you because of your strength and warrior and hunting prowess—would forbid you from being a warrior?"

"No."

"Then what's the problem?"

Anagalisgi was becoming worried by his brother's reactions. Kiyuga hummed a bit before answering, "Our parents never had any daughters. There is no one to carry on the family line and inherit what they built, not if we both get married."

"If we don't get married, no one will be around to inherit after us," Anagalisgi reminded him.

"And that's the other problem. I think I have a solution, but it's rather unconventional."

"Marry outside the people."

"How did you know?"

"It's the only thing I could come up with to get around the rules. If you take an outsider, she becomes one of us, you stay in the clan, you can have warrior children, and they will stand to inherit our parents" line through you." At his brother's embarrassed look, Anagalisgi laughed. "The spirits didn't tell me that; I figured it out on my own. I know you better than you think."

"Oh really? And you think I don't notice how you stare at Andatsi from across the entire village?"

Now it was Anagalisgi's turn to be embarrassed, and he tried to cover it up by saying, "She's married already."

"That doesn't mean you're not hoping to be a future contender if something happens."

Anagalisgi was saved from having to admit to anything as they reached the town. He saw all the girls from the other clans looking their way, but he knew they were just looking at Kiyuga. His older brother glanced at all the girls and acknowledged them, but Anagalisgi noticed that he did not appear to be paying any of them special attention.

They were the last ones home.

"I know it takes a lot to teach a young boy to hunt, Kiyuga, but if you're going to be gone on long trips, you ought to tell the rest of us," Ulisi scolded, taking the rabbits from Anagalisgi first before directing Kiyuga to lay out the coyote.

"He did well, Agilisi," Kiyuga told her. "Caught the rabbits all on his own."

"And did you give thanks?"

"With Anagalisgi around, he would not have let me get away with not giving thanks." At her look, he sighed and said, "Yes, I did. And I'm sure he did as well."

"Good boys. Off you go, then, but don't wander far. Dinner will be ready soon enough."

Once more, Kiyuga took Anagalisgi's arm and dragged him out of the house, this time to wander about the village. Once a small plot of land given no second thoughts and barely even considered separate towns, Gvnagadoga had turned it into the capital city of the Overhill people, maybe the whole Aniyvwiya nation. He was certainly making strides in bringing the Middle and Lower Towns together under one unified rule.

As they meandered, Anagalisgi noted how almost all of the young women watched them. Well, they watched Kiyuga. He just happened to be tagging along. But they smiled and batted their eyelashes. A few tried to catch his eye and be shy about it. A few tried to "accidentally" stumble into him in some fashion.

Strictly speaking, Anagalisgi was rather jealous of the attention his brother was getting. What was he, his brother's prisoner? His animal? Did none of the girls look at him the same way, wondering if he would look their way for just a moment? Or was he seen by everyone as a walking bad omen? Did the girls fear for themselves and their future children if they showed interest in him, or wanted him to show interest in them? Did no one think to ask how he felt about the whole thing? Did they think he enjoyed being plagued by bad visions?

"Cheer up," Kiyuga said, jerking Anagalisgi from his brooding. "Someone will catch your eye someday."

"It's not about me seeing them," Anagalisgi told him grudgingly.

"Well, it might help if you didn't always look so broody and mournful." He continued hastily, "I know, I know, you have dreams and visions and so forth. But once again, you live in the waking world.

This is your home. This is where you need to be. If all you are going to do is live in your mind, then there ought to be no room for thoughts of girls. A bird may touch both sky and earth, but he can't have both at the same time."

"Make a decision."

"Exactly. I'm not saying today. You're still young, just becoming a man. But don't put it off too long, or one day you'll wake up an old man who never made a decision in his life."

Anagalisgi raised a brow. "And when did you become a sagely elder, O Wise One?"

"You must be rubbing off on me."

They paused in their walk and glanced around.

"So, just for pretend," Anagalisgi began awkwardly, "who do you think would be good for me?"

Kiyuga grinned. "Who do I think would be good for you? Hm..." He looked around dramatically. He nodded toward a girl. "Her."

"Unega Tsisdu?"

"Why not? She's of an age, youngest of three daughters. Wild Potato Clan, so you know she's good at healing. You'd be great."

"You think so?"

"Sure, why not? A clan of healers and adawehi would love to have you."

Anagalisgi shifted his stance. "I mean, I guess you have a point."

Kiyuga elbowed him in the ribs. "You can always go over and talk to her."

"What? No. What would I say?"

"You could start by introducing yourself."

"Everyone knows me, though. I'm the one with the bad dreams."

"Yes, but that's not all you are, is it? If you want any girl to look your way, you have to show her, convince her that there is more to you than just bad omens."

Anagalisgi made a frustrated sound. "But I don't know if I can."

His brother shrugged. "Then I guess we'll never know, will we?"

Still frustrated, but not wanting to let his brother walk away with that smirk on his face, Anagalisgi gathered what little courage he had and approached Unega Tsisdu. His resolve wavered with each step, and by the time she realized he was heading for her, his pace had slowed to a crawl. All the same, he was committed, and arrived at last.

"Hi," he began awkwardly.

"Siyo," she replied cordially, if a bit shy.

"I'm Anagalisgi."

"I know. You're the one who sits with Gvnagadoga and tells him of the evils of the Europeans."

"Um...I suppose. I've never heard it said that way before."

She managed a small smile and shrugged. "Well, my mother and grandmother and sisters all say that you have only bad visions of the future, but I try to be kind. And what use is a dreamer who sees only the good and never warns of bad things to come? If we cannot be prepared, then surely we will fall."

"So you don't think I'm frightening?"

"No one thinks you're frightening, Anagalisgi. You're not your brother. As for your dreams, what are they but glimpses of the future? Should we be afraid of the future, of that which we cannot see? Perhaps, but it allows us to be ready for whatever may come."

"Oh." Anagalisgi was stunned. Was this real? She didn't think of him as frightening? She didn't mind his bad dreams? Was she just telling him what he wanted to hear? Had Kiyuga set him up? He didn't know what to think. Worse, he didn't know what to say.

"I think your brother is trying to get your attention," she said after a few awkward moments.

He turned to see Kiyuga motioning for him.

"Um, right," he managed. "Maybe I'll talk to you later?"

"Maybe you will," was all she said before turning and walking away, giving him one last shy smile over her shoulder.

Anagalisgi startled as someone laid a hand on his shoulder, but it was only Kiyuga.

"Well, that went better than expected," his brother said, evidently as stunned as him.

"Then why did you interrupt?" Anagalisgi half-wailed.

"I didn't interrupt. I rescued you. Before it broke down. Now that the conversation ended on good terms, you're more likely to get a second conversation. Keep it up, and soon you might be presenting a deer to her."

"That would be very far in the future, I think."

"If you can keep her interest that long, it's well worth it."

Anagalisgi felt the blood rush to his face. Kiyuga laughed and steered him back toward home.

"Well there you are," Ulisi said when she spied them. "I was about to send a search party."

"Apologies, Igilisi," Kiyuga told her, grinning. "Anagalisgi was busy talking to a girl. Trying to woo her."

"Oh really? Which girl?" She looked at Anagalisgi.

"Unega Tsisdu."

She thought for a moment. "Unega Tsisdu of Wild Potato Clan? Youngest of three daughters, her mother is Wahuhu?"

"That's right."

To his dismay, Ulisi did not look overly thrilled by the prospect, and she wasted no time in explaining why.

"Unega Tsisdu is a nice enough girl, to be sure, but Wahuhu is not someone you want to be related to. It's a wonder she was ever married or had children."

"It can't be that bad, can it?" Kiyuga wondered, echoing Anagalisgi's thoughts.

Ulisi chuckled darkly and gave them a look. "Wadagv, her eldest, didn't divorce her husband on her own. She wasn't even home when Wahuhu set his things outside. It was a bit of a messy situation."

The one girl who showed interest in him, and it was her mother who would likely be his undoing. Anagalisgi sighed and let his head drop.

"Don't fret, my son," Ulisi told him gently. "At least you're looking in the right direction. Wild Potato Clan would certainly be happy to have you. Unega Tsisdu is a nice girl. If her mother weren't around, I would encourage you to pursue the matter further, if you so desired. I'm only trying to protect you from Wahuhu. And if you don't have bad premonitions about that, then I don't think we can put any faith in your other premonitions."

The thought was oddly intriguing, but he assented.

"Besides, there are plenty of other girls out there. Believe me, if everyone thought you were a bad omen by yourself, you would have been driven off long ago."

He wasn't sure how he was supposed to take that, so he said nothing and instead accepted some leftover food and sat to eat. Kiyuga was soon back to his jovial self, speaking with the other men and bragging of his hunting exploits for the day, both in the wild animal sense and the hunting for a wife for his brother sense. The guys got a kick out of that, but Anagalisgi said nothing.

Maybe his brother had just been trying to motivate him. If Unega Tsisdu was willing to put up with his bad dreams, then she couldn't be the only one. Certainly girls from her clan were more accepting of it. And another girl might have a better family. He couldn't take his first loss as his only chance. If he missed the first rabbit, go for the second.

Maybe there really was a way for him to touch both earth and sky, a way he could have both worlds at the same time. He was more than his bad dreams and evil premonitions. He had to live in the waking world when he was awake.

But when he lay down that night to sleep, when the waking world and the nightmare world blended together so that he was divided between them, when he was on the cusp of unconsciousness, it seemed to be that the nightmare world was more real and far more powerful.

DᏈᏞᎯᎢ ᎦᎪᎠᎩ

Ayadohlv'i Hisgi

Friendly Competition

nagalisgi continued to skirt Unega Tsisdu's peripheral vision, and while they had a pleasant conversation here and there, he could understand what Ulisi meant by Wahuhu being someone not worth being related to. The woman ran a tight home. Her husband and her daughters and their husbands respected her only out of obligation rather than any true fondness. Anagalisgi did not have any explicit dreams or premonitions about them, though intuition and straight observation said that darkness was crowding around Wahuhu, like little creatures that gnawed at her flesh and whispered in her ear.

He tried not to feel so dejected about it, told himself that there were plenty of other girls in the village, and still more families were coming to Itsa'ti every season. Then he would look at Kiyuga and how easily he talked to girls, and despair would creep upon him.

Kiyuga seemed to have abandoned the notion of marrying outside the people and was apparently more concerned with talking to girls and trying to impress them with his skills as both hunter and warrior, the latter of which would be sorely needed.

It didn't take a dreamer to know that something was going to happen. European delegates were almost a permanent fixture in Itsa'ti anymore. Sometimes it was the British, sometimes the French, each trying to persuade Gvnagadoga to declare for their side. Gvnagadoga, with his calm demeanor and legendary patience, the skiagvsta, the uku, and the Women's Council, managed to carry them along for quite a while.

Europeans were rather impatient, Anagalisgi thought, and they only grew more impatient as hostilities between them heated up. They wanted declarations. They wanted warriors.

What the British did not know, however, was that Gvnagadoga had already given the French permission to build their fort. Officially, it was to be a trading and diplomatic outpost, somewhere the French could rest in their preferred way when they traveled many days or months to reach Itsa'ti. It was a way to keep the Europeans out of the town as much as possible. But no one who knew about the fort was fooled; it could be turned into a war fortress at a moment's notice.

Anagalisgi had seen the fort once, when he and Kiyuga were out hunting. As few people were to know about it as possible in order to keep the secret until the right time. Kiyuga was one of those people, and he'd been more than happy to show his younger brother, saying it was only right for a dreamer to understand what was happening.

Looking upon the fort for the first time, Anagalisgi had a terrible sensation wash over him, as if this fortress not only marked a place of trading and war, but also set a stone marker in time itself, as though everything were leading here, to this moment, this place. It was as though the fortress were fulfilling a dream, a prophecy he could not remember. But this moment was always going to happen. It was a fixture of destiny.

He'd had such sensations in the past, but they'd always been fairly minute, and he'd often dismissed them as inconsequential, even as Gvnagadoga and the adawehi told him not to. This, though, could not be dismissed or ignored.

The immediate sensation had lasted only a few moments, but there was a lingering fog of dread that clouded his mind after that. It dogged him until he finally brought it up to Gvnagadoga many days later. The old uku seemed rather perturbed, though whether it was from the vision Anagalisgi described, or the fact that he'd waited so long to speak of it, was unclear.

"You know that we have not yet declared for either side," Gvnagadoga said slowly. "Loathe am I to take a side in such a war, which is why I have been stalling them as much as possible. Perhaps I erred in permitting the French to build their fort."

"No," Anagalisgi told him. "That is what I am saying. It must be this way. It was always going to be this way."

The old uku, called Old Hop by the British because of his limp, frowned and murmured, perhaps to himself, "Often the dreamers tell us what will be in order to guide our steps. What am I to make of a dreamer who tells us the present and the past? How shall we learn from this in order to go forward wisely?"

"Often we look too much to the future and so lose sight of where we are."

Gvnagadoga managed a small smile. "Words of wisdom from one so young. An elder in a child's form, speaking of the past rather than the future. All is opposite of what it seems." He dipped his head. "Thank you, Anagalisgi. I will think on this some more. Go see what trouble your brother's gotten himself into."

Anagalisgi didn't feel satisfied of an answer, but he ceded to the elder and left the townhouse.

Had he said something wrong? Had something he did or said evoked something in Gvnagadoga? Anagalisgi was occasionally allowed to be present at council meetings, as he explored his dreams and premonitions and Gvnagadoga groomed him to, perhaps, one day be an adawehi or even possibly an uku. Now he found himself wondering what the rest of them would make of this. Would they have answers, or only more questions? He didn't understand.

He turned back to look at the townhouse, but was distracted by a shape on the roof. Peering closer, he saw that it was a woodpecker. Not just any woodpecker, however, but a white pileated woodpecker. It looked at him with a certain human intelligence in its unusual silver eyes, then spread its wings and swooped off toward the nearest tree. It did not look back or pause as it glided from tree to tree, finally disappearing into the thicker forest.

Anagalisgi saw the white woodpecker from time to time, almost exclusively in his dreams, and never for very long. He could not recall that it had spoken to him at all since that one day when he was a child.

What did it mean for it to show up here, now? What plan was this, and why couldn't he figure it out?

He returned home where Ulisi and a group of women were busy fussing over an animal called a sheep, trying to shear its wool. Anagalisgi stared in amazement as the big, fluffy creature was trimmed down to size.

He had seen sheep before, on the rare occasion that traders brought them along, but only recently had the Aniyvwiya begun to keep them for themselves. Nanyehi had a part in that, he knew. She'd insisted on sparing the life of a particular prisoner once and taken that woman into her own home. She and that prisoner had become very close lately, more like sisters now, and the woman had introduced livestock to Itsa'ti.

It was a bizarre thing, Anagalisgi thought, watching the wool fall to the ground. Keeping animals went against everything he knew and had been taught. The hunters weren't sure what to make of it either, and they asked if they were expected to still hunt, or perhaps stalk the sheep around the wooden pens built to contain them. Perhaps they ought to let one loose into the forest so they could still experience the thrill of the chase, though sheep were hardly a thrilling animal to watch.

The last of the wool was snipped off, cutting the apparent size of the sheep in half. A couple women took the sheep away, back to its wooden pen, and Ulisi gathered up the wool into a sack. She spotted Anagalisgi.

"Ah, agituta. Come help me, will you?"

"How is it, with the sheep?" he asked, bending to help stuff the fluff into the sack and tie it off.

"It's not natural," Ulisi stated, straightening, "but it did provide meat through a tough winter when the deer herds fled because of the Europeans and their skirmishes." She shook her head.

"And...?" Anagalisgi goaded, grinning.

"And what?"

"I saw you holding the first two lambs of the season."

Ulisi blushed but she tried to maintain a firm facade. "I'm glad that Nanyehi's insane idea is working and we're getting young, that's all." At her grandson's look, she relented. "And they are pretty cute and fun to watch."

"It's a side of nature we don't often get to see."

"That is true." She sighed. "I still don't know what to make of it, though. One cannot contain nature so, without giving something back in some way. And even then, one cannot contain nature so. At the same time..." They looked where another sheep was curiously licking at a half-rotted ear of corn while another group of women prepared to shear its wool. "I don't know that this aspect of nature could survive without us. Perhaps domestication bred the intelligence out of it." She huffed. "All the same, they're here now, and we maintain responsibility for them."

Anagalisgi took up the bag of wool and followed Ulisi to Nanyehi's home, where she and her former slave, a woman by the name of Inga, were demonstrating how to wash and spin the wool.

"The sheep have no complaints in the winter," Inga was saying in her broken language, "except, perhaps, that they are too warm. When done correctly, the yarn you spin will do the same for you."

It was a long process that took many days, Anagalisgi knew. For the Europeans, it was normally done by the women. Here in Itsa'ti, there were a good number of men present as well. Some were curious as to the processing of the wool. Others wanted to know more about this animal that could quickly make hunting unnecessary, thereby reducing their ability to woo the women. Who wanted a deer—which had to be skillfully tracked and brought down—when there was a sheep just up the hill?

Once the wool was spun into yarn, then Inga had to demonstrate the concepts of knitting, crocheting, and other such techniques, teaching her growing crowd of students—most of them women, seeing how they had the slender fingers required for such intricate work—how to make blankets, shawls, and even whole dresses. It used up every yard of yarn they had, but wool quickly became the fashion around Itsa'ti, at least until it got too warm.

"How am I supposed to woo Wadagv now?" Kiyuga opined to Anagalisgi one afternoon when it was just too hot to do much of anything. They lay in the grass a short distance from the village. "She's learned so much from Nanyehi and Inga that her sheep are likely to be the healthiest and most numerous of the year and produce the most young in the spring. What use does she have for me, approaching her home with a deer?"

"She likes you, right?" Anagalisgi asked.

"Well, yes. I mean, I think she's hinting that she wants a deer, but I don't know."

"Do you know anything about sheep?"

"Not really."

Of course not, Anagalisgi thought. Kiyuga had been spending more time competing with the sheep, going out on hunts and raids, trying to show that he was still important. Many of the girls in Itsa'ti had turned their attention from him and his prestige to their new roles as shepherdesses.

"Maybe you could learn," the younger brother suggested. "At least it would be a conversation you could both have. If she thinks you care about her sheep, maybe she'll care about your deer." He went on before Kiyuga could speak. "It's about survival, Kiyuga. Prey is plentiful in the summer. Not so much in the winter. There isn't a lot to do with the sheep right now, since they've been sheared. Most of the males were already butchered over the winter, and the ones that remain have to breed again this fall. The females have to raise their young, and the lambs are still very small. She has many sheep, but no meat to speak of. You can provide the meat."

Kiyuga shifted position and appeared contemplative. Anagalisgi briefly wondered if their father had looked the same way, tall and as big as a bear.

"Maybe you're right," Kiyuga said finally. "My selfishness shouldn't get in the way of survival." He frowned. "But do you think it's a good match?"

Anagalisgi barked a laugh. "Don't ask me. I have only bad premonitions."

"True. I suppose I'll have to ask one of the adawehi."

That gave Anagalisgi pause. "You're serious about this?"

"Why wouldn't I be? If it's a favorable match..."

"Have you spoken to Igilisi about this?"

"Of course I have. And Digvnige. They think it's a good idea. I just need to ask an adawehi."

"What about your lament of not being a warrior?"

Kiyuga gave him a look. "I think that if something happens with the Europeans, we will need all the warriors we can get."

Well, that much was true, Anagalisgi figured grimly. Still, he got a certain sense of loss considering it, his brother leaving and living in another house. They'd always been together.

And, if he wanted to be honest, there was a certain sense of jealousy, too. Any woman would be lucky to have Kiyuga for a husband, and many had tried to catch his eye over the years. His own pick of women was sorely limited. Many were wary of his bad dreams and premonitions, others had families who strongly advised against marrying him. A couple, like Unega Tsisdu, had families he didn't want to be married to. He told himself to wait and be patient—he was only just becoming a man after all—but it was hard.

"Do you ever think about our mother and father?" Anagalisgi wondered.

The question appeared to catch Kiyuga off guard, but he answered, "Sometimes. Why, do you?"

"I do. Sometimes I think I see them in dreams, or maybe I'll hear a whisper on the wind that I know deep down is one or even both of them. But I never knew them. Not like you did."

"Little brother, I barely remember them, and my most vivid memories, which are already faint and blurry, are of their sickness and suffering."

"You still knew them. You know what they looked like, in the living world." Kiyuga did not say anything, and Anagalisgi continued thoughtfully, "But I think I know them in the spirit world."

"Can you talk to them?"

"Not as such, I think, but it's like we understand each other. They've never stopped watching over us."

"Maybe next time, then, you can ask their opinion and blessing on the marriage."

Anagalisgi gave his brother a look but said nothing. Kiyuga was too preoccupied with this marriage idea to be of use for anything else, it seemed. Who needed to focus on living in the waking world now?

Then Kiyuga sat up and finally stood. "Come on. Let's go jump in the river."

He took off before his brother could answer, but Anagalisgi quickly followed. They were not the only ones with such an idea, and the water was thick with people from Itsa'ti on one side and Tanasi on the other. Meals were being cooked on the banks, and a group of men was out looking for fish, turtles, frogs, anything they could catch and eat.

The brothers stripped off their clothes and waded into the river. Anagalisgi was momentarily stunned by the frigid water, but he was determined to not be left behind. His determination only lasted until Kiyuga gave him the slip, or he figured that was what happened. When he caught sight of his brother again, he was just leaving a group of peers and heading toward a rock on which Wadagv lay, stretched out in the sun like a cat.

Dejected and quite unable to feel his toes, Anagalisgi climbed out of the river and pulled his clothes back on. He found his own sunning rock to sit on and observe the merry goings-on of the people.

"Has he told you his plans?"

Anagalisgi looked up as Ulisi sat beside him. They watched Kiyuga talk to Wadagv. He said something, she smiled and laughed.

"He wants to marry her," Anagalisgi stated.

"That's right," Ulisi said.

"Do you think he should?"

"If the spirits declare it a suitable match, then who am I to stand in the way?"

"But you don't think it's a good idea."

"Any woman would be lucky to have him for a husband, but I fear he is relying too much on his celebrity. He is a strong warrior and a good hunter, but he has never been tested, not truly. A dispute, maybe a skirmish, but nothing more. I fear that a European war is inevitable, and we will get trapped in it somehow."

"But if that's true, he should have sons and daughters to carry on his line."

Ulisi shifted. "You're right in that, no question. But he is still young and untested."

"How better to test him, then? If he is married and has children, he will have something to fight for. Or fight to get away from."

That got her to snicker. "Ah, my little dreamer, always quick of wit." She mussed his hair and looked around. "So tell me, which girl do you have an eye on?"

Anagalisgi blushed. "Ah, no one."

"Now I know that's not true. Boys are always looking at girls, even if they say they aren't, even if they believe them untouchable. Who is it?"

"No one, Agilisi, I promise. I am no one to desire, and I've been too preoccupied with the same dreams that make the girls and their families turn away."

She frowned. "There doesn't seem to be much difference between the dreaming and waking worlds for you, is there?"

"No, and the veil gets thinner with every season. I fear your war is coming, but I fear more that it will be greater than anything we've faced so far."

For a long moment, Ulisi just studied him. Finally she said, "Child, I pray you're wrong."

But he wasn't wrong. Over the summer, they got their usual bands of European diplomats, and the French continued to build their fort, but there were also bands of warriors from the other towns and villages. Sometimes it was the First Warrior himself of a particular town, sometimes a man or group of men sent in his stead.

Anagalisgi sat in on all of the meetings now, and he suspected that his confession to Gvnagadoga had something to do with it. He did not speak except for a rare occasion when posed a question. His job was to listen and consult the spirits, see if anything triggered any more unusual sensations.

Many of the tribal delegations came to inquire after Gvnagadoga's intentions regarding the brewing European war. Some came to swear loyalty and accept Gvnagadoga's leadership for their towns, others would not until he gave a definitive answer. The old uku declared his intent to stay neutral for as long as possible and refused to say who he would side with, if in fact he was forced to choose.

"Coyotes and crows," Gvnagadoga mused one evening after a ridiculously long meeting in which a delegation had indeed tried to force him to declare for the British. "One will kill us, the other will curse us, and both will pick our bones clean."

"Why not declare?" Anagalisgi wondered. "The European war is coming. Other peoples have already declared. The Anisawanugi and Anakwanki for the French, the Aninvdawegi for the British. The French have always had good relations, and we are peaceful with their allies. The British are not always so kind, and it speaks for itself that the Aninvdawegi have joined them. We can't fight for one and against the other, and either one is liable to stab us in the back."

"Your words are true, but we have more at stake. The Anakwanki, the Anisawanugi, they survive through alliance. We remain free and independent, the largest and most powerful nation. Wherever we go, others look to us, to see what we will do. If we declare, others will surely follow. And if we lose, we cannot protect ourselves, nor others. Itsa'ti is a town of many nations, small peoples driven here rather than extinction. What use are we if we fail? Where will they go? Where will we go? Always we must think of the people first, how we will adapt and survive. Do you understand?"

Anagalisgi blinked. "I think so."

Gvnagadoga frowned. "Well, it is a lesson not easily learned without experience." He made a motion. "Go now. I'm tired, and I expect you are as well. Perhaps you can discuss such politics with your brother, take his mind off his grief."

Anagalisgi took his leave of the elder uku and departed the townhouse for home. He wouldn't mind discussing politics, he just didn't want to do it with his brother.

Kiyuga had proposed to Wadagv. He brought her one deer, which she summarily rejected, as was custom. No self-respecting woman accepted the first offering. The second was also rejected, which both confused Kiyuga and strengthened his resolve. The third offering was where the answer was final. If she rejected it, it was a solid refusal. He could try again the next year, but if he persisted, her whole family, men and women alike, would be within their rights to teach him a lesson about respecting her wishes.

The third deer was turned away. Kiyuga was absolutely crushed. When he begged for a reason, she would not give him one. He tried to talk to her, her mother, her grandmother. He tried to talk to Ulisi and get her to talk to Wadagv and her family, to no avail. Her decision was made.

Kiyuga hadn't been himself since, in spite of everyone's encouragement. He often went on long hunts, and he inquired frequently as to the state of the impending European war. He was desperate to prove himself a warrior in battle, more than just training or a few small skirmishes. He wanted something big, something to show off.

He was the last person Anagalisgi wanted to discuss politics with. So instead he crawled quietly into bed and went to sleep.

It was still dark when he jolted awake, sweating and terrified of a nightmare that continued to dance before his eyes, though he could not say just what it was he saw.

In the morning, he went to see Gvnagadoga.

"You look troubled, son," the old uku observed. "What have the spirits told you?"

"I had a dream," Anagalisgi stated. "Only I can't remember what it was."

"An unsettling thing, to be certain. Go, child, seek the spirits. The ancestors sent you a vision, and evil spirits have stolen it. Get it restored to you."

"How do I do that?"

"Search for yourself, and take flight."

Still uncertain, Anagalisgi headed into the forest. He had a favorite thinking spot where he was able to be alone, undisturbed, and able to focus. He sat down on the rock there, warmed by the sun, and closed his eyes.

He saw nothing. He stayed there all day, and still nothing came to him. He returned the next day with the same results. The third day, he built a fire and burned sage, asking for guidance as he again took his customary position and closed his eyes, breathing in the bitter smoke.

Now he saw, although it took a moment for his spirit eyes to clear. He broke through a curtain of leaves, riding an air current. To his human body, the feeling was frightening and freeing, and joy lifted his soul. And yet, to his winged spirit, it was only frightening. This was not about enjoying the day, but simply surviving it. Something was in pursuit. Anything he could do, it could do. It was much bigger, and his only chance was finding a hole where he could fit and his attacker could not. But where? Where could such a hole be?

His winged spirit swooped under some branches, glided over others, twisted and turned through tangles of branches and undergrowth. He could hear and feel his pursuer still close behind. In a moment where he twisted through a couple twisting branches, he was able to just make out glossy black feathers amid the greenery. The maneuver had bought him a little distance, but it wouldn't be enough.

Just ahead, he saw the edge of the forest. He couldn't go there; the openness would only aid his attacker. He swooped over a branch into the open air and turned, intending to dart into the trees once more. He was too late. As he turned around, he was suddenly confronted by something huge, something black. For a fraction of a second, it was a crow. Then it morphed into a...into a...

Anagalisgi's eyes flew open and he immediately began coughing as he inhaled a huge plume of smoke. Struggling to bring his body and spirit back together, he stumbled off the rock, dazed and still trying to make sense of his vision. As he came back to himself, he had vivid memories of not only his vision just now, but the dream he'd forgotten.

He rushed back to the townhouse where Gvnagadoga was just waking from an afternoon nap.

"I remember," Anagalisgi blurted as soon as he saw the old uku. "I remember my dream."

Only then did he remember his courtesies, but Gvnagadoga simply waved it off and bid him come closer.

"What is your dream, son?" Gvnagadoga asked calmly.

"I saw the land and the mountains, and something moved in them, over them, from the east. Rot followed it, and everything it touched turned to death. From the north came another force. It did not cause the rot, but it was also far weaker. The forces collided here, and I saw that they were two hands. The one from the east was a fist made of stone and covered in blood. The one from the north was an open hand made of eggshells that have been crushed to dust and molded back together in its shape. The stony fist crushed the hand in a single blow, shattering it entirely, and the wind carried the dust north again. From the place where it happened, there was death and rot in all directions. Then the fist made of stone began to crack, and eventually, it, too, broke apart. The blood flowed from the rock to the rotted ground, and new things began to grow."

Gvnagadoga's gaze turned as hard as Anagalisgi had ever seen it, like a man who has made a decision and could not be swayed from it. Considering how long the old uku had been putting it off, Anagalisgi was honestly afraid to know what was going to happen next. Yet when Gvnagadoga spoke, he knew exactly what he would say.

He called together the skiagvsta and the uku, and a ceremony was held to inquire after confirmation from the spirits, which they apparently gave.

The old uku would not speak of his thoughts right away, instead asked his wife to prepare the hand of war, a leather object with Gvnagadoga's mark on it and a way to summon all of the First Warriors from all of the villages. He even sent Kiyuga with the party delivering the Hand. As each warrior agreed to come, he would pin his mark upon the hand. Kiyuga and the others would then return, and Gvnagadoga would know who to expect.

Anagalisgi thought things would happen very quickly; they'd only been pestering the uku to make a decision all summer. And yet, the leaves were beginning to turn colors when Kiyuga and the party returned, and autumn was more than half over before all the First Warriors arrived with their various posses.

"It will be too difficult for them to travel home again," Anagalisgi told Ulisi.

"They won't be traveling home," she replied. "The Hand of War has been sent, and the First Warriors have responded. They will stay the whole winter to discuss and plan. If Gvnagadoga intends to declare, the parties will leave when the thaw begins to return and prepare their warriors."

So it was that the townhouse was packed full every evening. Gvnagadoga was there with the skiagvsta, the uku, the adawehi, as well as the Women's Council, of which Ulisi was head. First Warriors from dozens of towns and villages were also present, and some of them had brought their own advisers. Anagalisgi sat with the adawehi, feeling very much at fault for anything and everything that happened that night, and every night they met.

It was just as well that everyone was staying the winter, for very little was agreed upon for many days. Everyone had inquired as to Gvnagadoga's position and intent, but no matter what he might have said, someone would have taken issue with it.

"We side with the British," the uku declared soundly.

"They are treacherous snakes and have allied with the Aninvdawegi," someone said. "What could we gain by this?"

"The hope that they would spare us in the aftermath if we help to deliver to them a great victory. If we lose to them, there will be no hope of such a thing."

"Can we not stay out of the war?" another inquired.

"We are too big of a target. Too many towns and villages over too great an area in land that too many want, too many people, and our ties to both parties is too great. One would become frustrated that we are not helping, or suspicious that we are helping the other."

"Gvnagadoga, it has been many years since illness swept through our people, but not so many that we have the warriors we need to send to this European war and defend ourselves at the same time," a third person, one of the Beloved Women, pointed out. "Children who were born after that time are only just becoming men and women, hardly seasoned warriors. Shall we send our experienced warriors to war and leave ourselves open with only boys to defend us? Or shall we send our boys to die in a pointless war?"

"And what of the French fort?" a fourth warrior asked. "What if they should attack Itsa'ti and Tanasi to take our food and supplies there to steel themselves in their fortress?"

"We will only side with the British, but we will not become their slaves," Gvnagadoga said firmly. "They may use the fort if they want to fight for it. And we will defend ourselves as we always have."

It was not a satisfactory answer for some, and talks went on long into the night for many days at a time. Sometimes there would be a night off, so everyone could rest and think some more about it without the constant bickering. Anagalisgi began to cherish those nights when he could stay home, get something to eat, and go to bed at a reasonable time.

"What if it's my fault we're here?" Anagalisgi posed as Ulisi handed him a bowl of soup.

"What do you mean?" she wondered.

He stared into his soup. "I had a dream, and I told Gvnagadoga. After that, he sent out the Hand of War." Now he looked at her. "What if I was wrong? What if this is all a huge mistake?"

"There are no mistakes here, love. Gvnagadoga is very aware of the seriousness of the situation. He does not send out the Hand of War lightly. He has consulted the spirits on many a thing regarding this, and I know he did so after your dream. Maybe something about your dream confirmed something else he had been told. Who can know? But you are not at fault for this. If the spirits will it so, then so it will be, whether through you or someone else."

He knew she meant well. While it did make him feel a little better, the more selfish part of him knew that this declaration meant he could be called upon to be a warrior. He would not pretend to be Kiyuga; likely he would be a scout or some other minor accessory. His selfishness wailed that it wasn't fair. He was a dreamer, a woodpecker, a messenger from the spirits to the people. Why should he also have to be everything his brother was also? Why did his brother not dream? What good were his dreams if nothing changed anyway?

But it was his calling in this life. And if he wanted to preserve his life, he would either have to learn to be more like his brother, fully in the waking world and ready to take on the threats to his life in the waking world...or he would have to learn to fly.

An idea crossed his mind then. He set down his soup, half-finished, got up, and left the house, ignoring Ulisi's questions. He made his way to his thinking spot in the dim twilight, sat down on the rock, and closed his eyes.

DᏲᎾᎩT ᎦᏜᏢ

Ayadohlv'i Sudali

The Snowball Effect

The French struck first. Or that was the claim. Months of minor disagreements and skirmishes finally erupted into war. It happened in the lands near the Aninvdawegi, as the French attacked the British Fort Necessity. Young Lieutenant Colonel Washington and Captain McKay and their men were overwhelmed and forced to retreat.

It was hard to keep all the names straight sometimes, Kiyuga thought, mindlessly shooting arrows into small targets. Any day now, some British commander would show up to meet with Gvnagadoga and the skiagvsta, and Kiyuga knew that a fighting force of Aniyvwiya would leave with him.

If there was any relief, it was that they weren't going to train with the British soldiers. Gvnagadoga had been very clear that if the people were going to fight for the British, they would fight in their own way, their own style. If the British commanders wanted more British soldiers, they could bring them over from Britain. If they were asking for Aniyvwiya help, they were getting Aniyvwiya warriors who would fight in Aniyvwiya style.

When the British commander did finally show up, everyone turned out to hear what he had to say to Gvnagadoga, and Kiyuga was right there near the front.

He was a short man, half a head shorter than Kiyuga, dressed well, though not half so well as some of the commanders who'd come through in the past. He had his sword on one hip, a couple pistols on his belt, and a hard journey on his clothes. He was young, Kiyuga saw, a grown man but no veteran of battle.

"And who might you be?" Gvnagadoga inquired, once respects had been paid.

"Lieutenant William Kettle," the man replied swiftly, handing a folded piece of paper to the old uku. "Under orders and authority of Governor Dinwiddie, I'm here to collect a thousand of your men for the war."

Kiyuga understood English fairly well and was immediately stunned and outraged by the demand. Once the words were translated for the benefit of the crowd, indignation grew.

"We don't have a thousand men to give you," Gvnagadoga told the man calmly. "And I know we went over this before in our meetings."

The young lieutenant looked perplexed, clearly not expecting a refusal. "But, the orders—"

"Order the coyote not to kill the hare. Order the crow to leave the corn be." The old uku handed the orders back to him. "You will not get a thousand men."

"You pledged—"

"I pledged our support. And I did indeed pledge warriors. But I cannot make them appear where they are not, else I should be able to conjure up ten thousand warriors. Surely this you can appreciate."

Gvnagadoga was so calm and so well-spoken, he could mesmerize an angry bear and put it back into hibernation, Kiyuga thought. The British lieutenant seemed unable to gather his anger and indignation, though he appeared to want to.

"What I will do," the old uku continued, "is send one hundred warriors with you. The rest are needed here."

"But the governor—"

"Is too busy with other affairs to be concerned with a bunch of savage warriors except to know that they have come, as promised. And I'm sure they will be directed by someone who is directed by someone who is directed by someone who is directed by your Governor Dinwiddie, whose main goal is simply victory. The means are less important than simply getting it done. Do I have that about right?"

Kettle was sweating and unable to answer. He opened his mouth once, then closed it. The small group of men with him looked equally conflicted.

"These hundred warriors will go with you. They will fight in your battle, and they will return home. All as we have already agreed. You need not concern yourself with the minor details, far too cumbersome to reiterate now, and it would serve no purpose. I imagine you are expected to return quickly."

"That's right," Kettle replied, almost tripping over himself, as if trying to gain control over a situation that was not in need of it.

Gvnagadoga dipped his head. "I will speak to my hundred warriors now, and they will be ready quickly. Unless there were other matters you wished to discuss?"

"No, not at all. I will await your warriors."

As the lieutenant and his men left the townhouse, Kiyuga was reminded of a story of a man who was outwitted by a crow but did not realize it until much later, far too late to do anything about it. Kettle had that look, as if trying to figure out how he'd been tricked, but unable to come up with it at the moment.

No one really trusted the British, which was why Gvnagadoga sent mostly seasoned warriors to go with Kettle. They would be better able to hold their own against treachery. And if treachery should occur, he would not send boys to their deaths before tasting true victory in battle.

So it was that Kiyuga watched them all go and wondered if he shouldn't go with them anyway.

"I know you're disappointed."

Kiyuga turned to see Gvnagadoga walking up beside him.

"Everyone tells me I'm going to be a great warrior, yet I've never seen battle. Shall it always be merely a dream, an illusion I can never catch, yet am told I have already attained?"

The old uku chuckled. "You can be as philosophical as your brother sometimes."

Kiyuga felt his face turn hot. "He's rubbed off on me a bit, I suppose."

Gvnagadoga put a hand on his shoulder. "Don't worry, young warrior. Your time is coming, but your place is here."

"Have the spirits shown you something about my destiny?"

"Indeed they have, but do not concern yourself with it. You will know what to do when the time comes."

Kiyuga was uncertain, but he trusted the old uku who offered a small smile and limped away. After a moment, he struck out on his own, looking for Anagalisgi. He'd spotted him briefly at the meeting, then lost track once the larger group dispersed. Indeed, it ended up being Anagalisgi who found him.

"You were hoping to go," the dreamer stated.

"Everyone says I'm a great warrior, yet I have never truly seen battle. It makes me feel dishonest," Kiyuga confessed, looking around at small clusters of people who were whispering amongst themselves. "As a boy, just the thought and the dream was enchanting. But here I am as a man, and nothing to show for myself. All of the warriors who are leaving now, if they are not married, they soon will be when they return." He looked at Anagalisgi. "Why is Gvnagadoga doing this to me? Have you seen anything?"

"You're asking the one who sees only bad things?"

"I'm asking the one who sees and speaks more candidly than some."

Anagalisgi could not deny that part. After a long moment of silence and a few false starts, he answered, "I have not seen anything, no. But I know Gvnagadoga's reasoning."

"What is that?"

"Right now, he's testing the British, testing their loyalties and their motivations. Once he is assured of them, then he will send you to the battles you crave. Until then, you will stay here, defend the people. And he will call you to more meetings."

Kiyuga stared at his brother. Anagalisgi sighed in exasperation and clarified, "He is trying to build you up as a leader, to become a skiagvsta one day."

"But leadership and skiagvsta are proven in war," Kiyuga protested.

"Not only, not anymore. We can't be the way we once were. The Europeans are here. The French wish for trade, the British for control, but no matter what, they're not leaving. Gvnagadoga sees this and is trying to adapt in order to save us. We take their weapons in order to defend ourselves. We take their structure in order to communicate effectively. It's no longer just about battle, but politics."

"And he wants to teach me this? Why me?"

"Because you will be great. You will be needed. More than anyone, more than Gvnagadoga, the people will one day look to you. This I know."

Kiyuga frowned. "And what about you?"

Anagalisgi shrugged and gave a sort of lopsided smile. "I don't know. The only thing I don't see is me. And I think that's intentional, the spirits' way of keeping me humble."

"Or maybe it is that nothing bad will happen to you," Kiyuga told him cheekily. "I still have to keep my promise to you, don't I?"

His brother nodded. "That you do."

Kiyuga let out a breath and slapped his brother on the back. "Come on. I've got some free time it seems. Dreamer or not, you are still a man of Wolf Clan and will have to fight at some point. Grab your gun and your knife and let's go. If I am to lead one day, I will need followers. You will be my first follower."

Anagalisgi gave him a look. "I was always your first follower."

They went out a short distance from the town and spent the afternoon shooting targets with their guns, and practicing close combat with knives and fists. They limited their practice with their pistols, as the British were not keen on giving the Aniyvwiya much ammunition, for fear they would turn on them.

They did this for several days in a row. A month went by. And another. Half a month. Summer was at its zenith and just beginning to wane. Finally, the hundred warriors returned.

As predicted, Gvnagadoga called for Kiyuga to join the meeting where a dozen of the most senior warriors gave their accounts of the British and the war overall.

"When the British are prepared, they are nearly unstoppable," one reported. "But they are a match only for themselves, it seems. The French have many Indian allies and are adapting their fighting to us. Guerrilla, they call it. Ambush. This the British cannot seem to understand, overcome, or pull off for themselves. When they hole up in their forts, it is like a turtle retreating into its shell, nearly impenetrable. When on the road..." The warrior shook his head.

"Were you treated well?" Gvnagadoga asked.

"We have all returned, and all wounds were those sustained in battle. But the British have no love for anyone but themselves. They gave us orders. Strange orders. We tried to do our best, but they snap at us and their young warriors like dogs fighting over a carcass.

"Our task was to engage the nations allied with the French, meet them in their own fighting style, leaving the Europeans to fight in their own way. But the French have amassed a great number of peoples to their side, those who we thought would never fight together have set aside their differences for this common enemy. Gvnagadoga, we should rethink our position, our alliance."

The old uku frowned, and for the first time, Kiyuga saw real doubt on his face. Had he been wrong? Had he misinterpreted an omen? Had he been too hasty, or perhaps not quick enough?

"Gvnagadoga —"

"No. We cannot reform our alliances now. Word has come that British soldiers are to take over the French fort over the ridge, and they will be here in ten days' time."

"Then we should take the fort for ourselves and use it." The words were out of Kiyuga's mouth before he could stop himself. "No one is there now. If we take it, we have defenses."

"Not enough for the whole town," Gvnagadoga said calmly. "We take the fort, they burn Itsa'ti and Tanasi. It is the way of snakes. No. We will remain allied with the British for the time being, but we will not be their subservients. Tsiyu, you will be our leader and our voice in the fort."

Tsiyu was one of Gvnagadoga's many sons and a warrior whom many respected, including Kiyuga. Looking very much like his father, Tsiyu dipped his head and accepted.

"Yvgi, Galegi, Kiyuga, you will go with him. Galegi, I want you specifically to look after Kiyuga."

Galegi agreed wordlessly. He was a large man of mixed parentage, his father a warrior who had been captured in a raid on the Anikusi and eventually married his mother, Uhyesadi of the Bird Clan. Even so, while Bird Clan were known as messengers and skilled with snares, it had been agreed early on that Galegi was never meant to be anything but a warrior. Kiyuga was too young to know for sure, but there were rumors that the man had killed a bear with his bare hands and that was how he wooed his wife to marry him.

"We may not take over the fort," Gvnagadoga was saying, "but I want you to be there before the British arrive, let them know that they impress upon this land we consider our territory with their guns and their wars. If they want an alliance, an alliance they shall have. But we are not theirs to command like dogs."

That, at least, could be agreed upon by all.

"What should we tell them if they ask for more warriors?" Tsiyu inquired.

"We are not so far away," the old uku said with a certain touch of amusement. "This is their war, not ours. We have our own daily affairs to attend to."

"Shall we go now?" Yvgi wondered.

"Wait two days. I'm certain your wives are well-missed."

For the married among them, the prospect was a welcome one. For Kiyuga, well, at least it was a step in the right direction. He left the townhouse. Ulisi, who had also been present at the meeting but remained silent, caught up to him.

"So, you finally get to go out and do something," she said conversationally.

"It's a start," he agreed. "Do you think there will be battle?"

Ulisi frowned. "I don't know. The Europeans don't fight like we do. They rely on words, politics, and pieces of paper. A man may win a battle but lose a war simply because of wordplay."

"Maybe, but it does prove an advantage to us, I think."

"How so?"

"They advance their warriors because of wordplay and pieces of paper, so that their commanders don't know how to fight in battle. It makes war that much easier when your enemy does not know how to fight."

Ulisi grinned. "Well, that much is true. Though it does not help when your ally is equally as helpless."

"Which is why we're staying here and at the fort. We're looking after ourselves first."

She nodded. "I think you'll be just fine. Galegi will teach you much. You would do well to listen to him, as well as Tsiyu and the others."

"I understand, Agilisi."

"In the morning, approach them. Do it humbly and ask to learn. Be attentive and learn what they have to teach. This way, you will be prepared to leave home confidently."

"I'm ready to go now."

"I said with confidence, not arrogance," Ulisi said sternly. "Only a fool presumes to know what he has not learned. Did I raise a fool?"

Kiyuga felt the blood rush to his face. "No, Agilisi." He sighed. "But I am ready for this opportunity to finally prove myself."

Ulisi nodded calmly. "I understand, my son, believe me. I have wanted nothing less for you even since before we came to Itsa'ti. You will make Wolf Clan proud."

"Proud enough to leave." He grinned stupidly.

"Perhaps. And don't forget to say goodbye to your brother as well. I know he dreams many things, most of them bad, but he does see good in them as well. He knows you will be great, but he still fears losing you."

Her statement troubled Kiyuga more than he thought it should, and he made the excuse to go find Anagalisgi at that moment. It didn't take long to find his little brother, and Ulisi was barely five steps behind him when he got home and discovered Anagalisgi just settling in to sleep. Kiyuga got down on his own mat.

"You thought I was going to leave without saying goodbye?" he said, trying to sound light-hearted.

"You're not leaving for two days. I thought you might say goodbye tomorrow," Anagalisgi told him. Kiyuga could detect hesitation in his brother's voice.

"Well...I'm supposed to go out with Galegi and the others tomorrow, and I didn't want to be gone so long that you would be asleep before I returned and I would not get a chance."

He could not see his brother's face, but his tone was enough. "You're a terrible liar, Kiyuga, and dishonesty is terribly inappropriate."

Kiyuga sighed. "I know. I suppose you will have to intercede for me with the spirits."

Anagalisgi chuckled softly. "More likely, I will have to intercede for you with Igilisi. She told you to speak to me."

"She did," Kiyuga admitted.

"I can guess what she told you. Yes, I do love you, Kiyuga. You are my brother. And I do want you to be well. But I also want you to do well. In battle. In leadership. Now is the time when you will rise, a fledgling chick, late to spread it wings, but becoming the greatest of all birds in the end."

"And will I join my woodpecker brother? Or will he join me?"

Anagalisgi made a strained sound that Kiyuga didn't like and said finally, "Yes."

"But...?"

"I don't want to talk about it. I don't want to influence your decisions now. It's too critical."

"Not telling me will only distract me more."

In the growing dark, Kiyuga felt his brother's hand on his own.

"Brother, trust me in this," Anagalisgi said seriously. "Your path lies in the waking world. You will lead the waking world. When the spirits come calling, then call upon me. But not before. Until then, you must trust me and you must trust the spirits."

Kiyuga frowned and was silent for a long moment. Then, "All right."

Except it wasn't all right. Not really. Kiyuga lay awake for a long while that night, long after everyone else had fallen asleep. He and his brother had been borne of the same parents and they'd been together all their lives, so why did it sometimes feel as though they existed so far apart? The waking world and the spirit world often overlapped, yet they were so far removed. How could they, he and his brother, walk the same places but be in two different worlds?

He was still bothered by this when he got up the following morning, but his unease vanished when he found Galegi and the others. They were sitting around a cookfire eating some fish from the river.

"Ah, there's our Young Spear," Tsiyu greeted. "Are you ready to make something of yourself?"

"More than ready," Kiyuga told him, grabbing a fish off the cooking plate. "What are we doing? What is the plan?"

Galegi grinned. "Nothing especially glorious, we assure you. At least, not at first. Tomorrow morning, we will go to the fort. The French supplied but never occupied. We will take some things for ourselves, bring weapons and goods back to the people. Then we will camp at the fort and be there when the British arrive to remind them whose territory they occupy."

"What will we do then?"

"We don't know," Tsiyu said, sounding perturbed by it himself. "We will see what the British have to say."

"But you've been out. You must have an idea."

The uku's son sighed. "We are but slaves to them, Kiyuga, and we will never be accepted as part of them. Inga may be Nanyehi's sister now, but if their roles were reversed, the same would not be true. In their eyes, we are less of an alliance between comrades and more of a tool to be used, to get what they want. Their war is with the French, and we are only one more weapon in their arsenal."

Kiyuga blinked. "Do you not support your father's decision?"

Tsiyu was slow in answering. "I support my father, and I believe in the spirits' provision for us as long as we are in balance according to their ways and purpose. But their ways can be difficult to discern, even for experienced dreamers, or your brother." There was a glint of amusement in his eyes as he added that last bit. Then he grew serious once more. "I hope they have seen something, for I see only conflict, if not now, then later."

Kiyuga shifted uncomfortably. "Will there be Aninvdawegi at the fort?"

"Gvnagadoga and myself have made it clear that we do not wish for this, but it is difficult to know whether the British will honor our request. Once they squat themselves in the fort, they will not be moved easily."

"You expect betrayal, then?"

"Not now, while they are on the defense against the French, but if the tide shifts and they foresee their ultimate victory, they will not want to share the glory. They will betray us. And the Aninvdawegi as well, and any others who have agreed to ally with them."

Yvgi spoke up before Kiyuga could speak. "Our first duty is to our people. Not the British, not the French, not their wars or their allies. We are here to protect the people, protect Itsa'ti, Tanasi, the skiagvsta, the uku, the Women's Council, everyone here who is one of us. That is our duty."

Kiyuga nodded, but Galegi now spoke. "Do not seek to ally yourself with the coyote and expect him to share the spoils of his catch. He will devour you as well."

It was difficult for Kiyuga to grasp why they would ally themselves with the British at all, but he was not a skiagvsta. He'd barely seen battle. His first real assignment appeared to be entirely political. What was going on here? What great destiny was this?

They finished their breakfast and stood.

"Prepare yourselves for anything," Tsiyu told them. "We don't know what we will find when we get to the fort, and we don't know how the British will treat us. Every breath is an eternity when you are waiting for help to arrive. We will meet here tomorrow at daybreak."

On that cheerful note, they dispersed. Kiyuga went out on a short hunt just to make it look like he was preparing, but uncertainty dogged his steps. When he returned home and surrendered his catch to Ulisi, he looked around and considered everything he might need. His knife was sharp, his club freshly oiled, and he inspected his skala galogwehi, too. If they were going to a European fort, they had to have ammunition for it. But what else? His blowgun, he supposed, if he ever got a chance to use it, if he managed to make distance between himself and a foe.

"You'll want to take this."

He turned and instinctively stooped as Ulisi put a beaded necklace over his head. She stood back to admire it. "For luck, protection when you are unable to watch all sides at once."

He examined the necklace, bones and shells and glittering beads traded from far away peoples, punctuated with the claws and teeth of bears and cougars and, of course, wolves.

"Thank you, Agilisi."

"I don't want to hear bad reports about you, agituta," she told him, her voice threaded with humor. "You are a great warrior and you are going to protect the people. Act like it."

"I will, Agilisi."

"Fight bravely and stay alert. Don't consume any of that rancid alcohol the Europeans so love."

"I understand."

She smiled and put her hands on his shoulders. She was about half a head shorter than him. Kiyuga remembered being a small boy and thinking about how tall she was. Now he looked just over her head.

"Fight for the people. Please the spirits. Make your father and mother proud."

He nodded solemnly. "I will, Agilisi, for you are also my mother."

Her expression wavered a bit, but she took a breath and said,

"Well. Off you go. See about your brother. I'll pack your things."

He gave her a cheeky grin. "Will there be a wife waiting for me when I get back, then?"

"Do your duty, and there just might."

She shooed him away and he went, laughing.

"What's so funny?"

He looked around and spied Anagalisgi just approaching. It was one of those good days when his brother didn't seem to be dogged by his dreams in the waking world.

Kiyuga shook his head. "Nothing."

"Did you speak to Galegi and the others?" Anagalisgi stopped in front of him.

"Yes, this morning. Are they looking for me again?"

"Not that I am aware."

"Good. Let's go out, me and you. One last time before I leave."

So they did. They spent the better part of the day hunting, talking, discussing politics and war, and imagining vivid fantasies about their lives.

"You would think that we were speaking as though we would never see each other again," Kiyuga said as they returned to Itsa'ti.

"Perhaps," Anagalisgi mused.

Kiyuga gave him a look. "What do you mean, 'perhaps'?"

His little brother grinned. "Perhaps we are speaking that way. But don't worry. We will see each other again."

"You're having good premonitions now?"

Anagalisgi laughed. "Not exactly, but I am learning to examine the small details of my dreams and extract more information from them, which can yield some good news." He continued, "Gvnagadoga wants me close and he wants to know my dreams as though he dreamed them himself. He is helping me, as are the adawehi."

"It's an improvement, anyway. Who knows? You may become useful in the end."

Kiyuga danced away as his brother swatted at him, laughing still as he headed into town.

This was not Kiyuga's first outing by any means, and his honest chances of seeing battle this time compared to other times seemed only marginally greater, but this mission still seemed to be the most important one yet. Maybe it was because there was a real war going on and they were going to meet with foreign leaders. That certainly sounded more important than merely going out on a raid or a patrol looking for something to stir up a little skirmish.

He looked around at girls. He'd recovered from Wadagv's rejection and now searched out someone new, though he had no one specific in mind just yet. He figured he ought to get an idea, maybe try to catch an eye and see who met his gaze. If he was going to bring any glory to himself while he was away, he wanted to be able to brag to someone, impress a specific girl rather than merely spread his words like a fishing net and hope something came by at the right time. He needed focus. He needed a goal. He needed to find a girl.

Some looked his way, some caught his interest, a few were happy to exchange pleasantries and make small talk. When he told of his mission, going to take the fort and meet the British, well, he liked to think some of them were mildly interested. It was hard to know for sure; women could be confusing like that. At the very least, he felt like he'd made some progress in his endeavors by the time he returned home.

Ulisi had packed his bag and readied his gear, and they waited for him by the door. Ulisi herself was working with some furs, already preparing for cooler days. She did not appear to notice him, but as he turned to make his way to his sleeping mat, she spoke.

"You know, Meli is in town now."

He paused and looked back. "Who?"

"Meli. From Taliqua. The girl you used to like."

Kiyuga blinked. "Really?"

"Mm-hm." Ulisi nodded, not looking at him. "Her family just arrived a few days ago. Taliqua Eghawa is little more than a few shacks now, I'm told, held together only by stubbornness but little else, what with the Europeans demanding more room for themselves and their settlements."

Kiyuga elected to remain silent.

Ulisi continued, "From what I understand, she's not married. Moving to a new town can be very disorienting. She'll need something familiar to help her settle in."

He sighed. "You could have told me this a couple days ago, Agilisi. I'm leaving in the morning."

"Then pleasantries will be made early and briefly." She gave him a look. "For goodness' sake, Kiyuga, I didn't know until a little while ago."

Kiyuga made a frustrated noise, then huffed. "Maybe I'll wait until I get back. At least then I will have something to boast of, rather than admit that I, the future great warrior of Taliqua, have accomplished nothing for my time in Itsa'ti and Tanasi."

Ulisi shrugged. "That is your decision."

More frustration bubbled in his heart and he hurried to his sleeping mat where he sat in a heap. He didn't know how long he sat there debating whether he shouldn't seek out Meli before sleeping, but it was long enough for the light to completely vanish and render the point moot. He had to leave early. He needed sleep.

Anagalisgi was not home when Kiyuga finally found sleep, nor had he returned by dawn. But when Kiyuga dragged himself back to wakefulness and went to meet Tsiyu and the others, he discovered Anagalisgi among them, standing there with Gvnagadoga and some of the other warriors.

"Send back what you can," Gvnagadoga was saying. "When the British arrive, make it well known that we are allies by choice, and we can discontinue being allies by choice. We will not be subservient to them when we have no part in their war."

"I understand," Tsiyu told his father solemnly.

"And ensure that you mentor this one." He touched Kiyuga's shoulder. "Train him well. Let him taste battle if it comes to that." The old uku grinned. "He has a few girls he wants to impress, I've seen it."

There was a little ribbing, then farewells were made. Kiyuga said goodbye to Anagalisgi, feeling very much as though he were stepping through a door, and when he returned, things would not be the same.

Now you're starting to sound like him, Kiyuga told himself as they left Itsa'ti. *Maybe you need to get away from your brother and be in the company and tutelage of real warriors for a while.*

"Are you hoping for battle?" Galegi asked, slapping him on the back. "Want to impress a girl?"

"I'd like to have something to show for myself," Kiyuga answered. "Do you think we'll see battle? It seems to me that the whole point of these forts is to avoid such things. Waging war from behind great walls...it makes no sense."

"It may be alien, but that's not to say there is no sense," Tsiyu said thoughtfully. "It is a shelter for brief reprieve, so a warrior may tend to his wounds and get food and water. If he has enough supplies, he may survive long enough to outlast his pursuers. But just as it is a haven, it can also quickly become a prison."

It took them until sunset to reach the fort, a huge, slumbering beast made of wood and stone, black and silent against the darkening sky. The French had done a good job, Kiyuga thought, not that he was proficient in such things, but it looked impressive.

They got in easily enough, eager to see what the Europeans had left behind.

"Stupid fools," Tsiyu said, looking around. "They have enough armaments and ammunition to withstand attack for many seasons. But they have no food."

"Perhaps it was scavenged by animals," Yvgi suggested.

"Unlikely," Galegi mused, prying open a barrel only to find gunpowder inside. "There are no remnants. And there are no barrels of alcohol, nor would animals drink such bitter liquid." He straightened. "Europeans go nowhere without alcohol."

"What should we do, then?" Kiyuga inquired. "These cannons are too heavy to take back to Itsa'ti."

Tsiyu laughed. "So they are. But the rifles, gunpowder, and ammunition are not. Gather what you can carry, and we will take it to

Itsa'ti in the morning."

They gathered several dozen rifles, filled powderhorns, and ate as much of their own food as they could stand in order to make room for the little lead balls that somehow had the power to kill. Even once that was done, there was still more of the fort to explore. With Tsiyu busy starting a fire and Galegi inspecting the arms, Yvgi and Kiyuga went to explore some more.

"How many people did they expect to be here?" Kiyuga wondered, pushing open a door to yet another armory.

"Living here, hard to say," Yvgi said. "But apparently they expected the world to be attacking."

The next door Kiyuga went to revealed living quarters that reminded him of a townhouse. Beds stacked on top of each other for long rows. He found the same thing next door.

"Evidently, they were expecting a war," Yvgi mused, trying to find humor but having little success.

"Is this really how Europeans fight?" Kiyuga entered the room and went to one of the beds, one stacked on top of the other. The frame was cold metal, the mat thin cloth stuffed with straw. A family of mice had already moved in. A small table sat between each set of beds, the legs open except for a small drawer which was empty.

"This is a dangerous place," Galegi said, his hulking form taking up the entire doorway. "If it were up to me, I would say we burn it to the ground."

"But it's not up to you," Yvgi told him, a little farther down the room from Kiyuga. "Though I can't say I disagree."

Kiyuga looked up from the empty drawer he had opened. "They're not going to leave, are they?"

Galegi shook his massive head. "No. The French may have been content to settle for trade, but they are still here. The British, they are the aggressors. As easily as they will use this fort to repel the French, so they will inevitably attack Itsa'ti and Tanasi. All they need is an excuse."

"Perhaps we ought to occupy this place, then. There are many beds, many armaments. Move the people here. Then we will control the fort and we will not be forced to leave."

"Then we will die here as well," Yvgi sighed. "Remember what Tsiyu said about this place being a prison as well as a haven. The British would only lay siege, and they have the numbers to ensure they have continual supplies. In here, there is nothing to hunt and nowhere to flee. We would starve."

Kiyuga frowned. "They must be good for something, though, if the Europeans use them so well."

"A fort is a tool," Galegi said. "It is one tool of many in warfare. It is not to be relied upon as one's only hope. In the same way that we use many weapons for different uses, many tools for different uses. But a knife does not discriminate in whose flesh it cuts."

Kiyuga had heard these lessons many times before when he was training with his uncles, but to be out here now applying them, they took on whole new meanings. Somehow it made him feel very inadequate, left behind in his training. Had Gvnagadoga really been so wise to keep him back for so long? Was he really going to improve and become such a great warrior and leader as his brother seemed to think? Anagalisgi wasn't known for his good news, after all.

The French had completed their fort just in time for Gvnagadoga to ask them to leave as they declared for the British. Some had expected the French to get violent over the news and use the opportunity to test out its capabilities on nearby Itsa'ti and Tanasi. But such a thing had not happened. The French had left, and now the British were coming.

They found more armories and weapon stashes, more barracks for soldiers. They also found living areas furnished with only basic necessities, apparently awaiting personal decor from whoever deigned to live there. There was also one large room, its use only speculative. Yvgi suggested it was for church services or other merriment. Galegi thought it was to train horses as the stables were not far away. Kiyuga guessed that perhaps it was for a sheltered market, so trade could take place in any weather. They would have to wait and see what the British used it for.

Overall, once investigated, the fort seemed to have no singular purpose. It was designed to be sealed off if under attack, yet it also seemed to be a town or market unto itself for anyone to move freely about within its walls. Parts of it made sense, yet it remained very perplexing to Kiyuga.

They returned to their campsite in the open air. Tsiyu still tended the fire and kept an eye and ear out for mischief. He seemed relieved when the rest of the group joined him.

The three of them took turns reporting their findings, and Tsiyu and Galegi left for a time so the large warrior could show him more of what they saw. By the time the two returned, it was late into the night, and Kiyuga half-expected to see the sun after each tired blink.

"Rest now," Tsiyu told him. "We have a long trek back to Itsa'ti tomorrow, and then we must also return."

Kiyuga didn't need to be told twice. He lay down and didn't even remember closing his eyes.

He could not say that he slept well, as the ground was hard and unfamiliar, but he felt somewhat rested by the time Galegi shook him awake.

"We will take these supplies back to Itsa'ti," Tsiyu was saying. "We will give them to Gvnagadoga and the skiagvsta and let them decide how they ought to be distributed. Then we will renew our food stores if possible and return."

"It will be long dark by the time we return," Kiyuga stated.

"Yes, but we have no time to waste. The British said they would be here in ten days. Nine days now. But we cannot be sure that they will not show up sooner, and we must be here when they do. We also have to get these back to the people."

Kiyuga did not like feeling so rushed, but it was what had to be done. He wandered off to relieve himself before returning for a quick meal of berries and bear fat mashed and mixed together with molasses and honey. It was a sticky mess, and the cloth it was wrapped in was also sticky, but it was delicious.

Galegi and Tsiyu took most of the rifles on themselves, giving

Kiyuga and Yvgi only four apiece. Conversely, Kiyuga was laden with most of the ammunition while Yvgi was decorated with powderhorns. Looking around, Kiyuga could see that Tsiyu was already figuring out that their return trip to Itsa'ti might take longer than anticipated. Kiyuga and Anagalisgi, traveling light, could reach the fort in half a day. The four them with their supplies had taken almost a whole day. Carrying all of this now, they might not be able to make such a quick trip to Itsa'ti and back. But the look on Galegi's face said they were going to try.

"Is everyone ready?" Tsiyu asked, trying to sound optimistic.

They all nodded their agreement. Taking a breath, Tsiyu muttered something vaguely positive and started toward the large gates that could seal the fort off when under attack.

They'd barely crossed the threshold back onto the trail before they paused. Something in the woods moved. It was big, if the snapping twigs were any indication. Kiyuga fumbled for a knife, or any weapon at all, suddenly feeling very slow and cumbersome with all the weight he was carrying. And loud, too, as the rifles clacked against each other and the ammunition rolled around with a metallic sway.

Whatever it was, it wasn't trying to be quiet or hide itself. A bear, Kiyuga thought, or a cougar. Something that didn't have to worry about anything else hunting it.

Before anyone could ask what they should do, Kiyuga spotted a flash of red amid the thick greenery. Then he heard grunts and growls of effort. When he heard a snapped order, he knew their adversary was human. Given the red color and the location, he could hazard a guess as to who it might be.

The four of them still kept a grip on their weapons, even as the same realization was dawning on the others' faces. A minute later, a small garrison of British soldiers—Kiyuga might have guessed fifty or so—came into view on the trail. On either side, as if an escort or a guard, Kiyuga recognized the dark scowls and broad shoulders of the bad-tempered Aninvdawegi, about a dozen or so total.

When Aniyvwiya and Aninvdawegi saw each other, both stopped

and weapons were raised. The British kept right on marching, stopping only when their leader—whom Kiyuga recognized as the man Kettle—realized that their escorts had fallen behind. For a long moment, the Indians stared at each other, each wondering what the other was doing, each wondering what the other was going to do.

A few tense heartbeats passed. Finally, Kettle gave the Aninvdawegi a certain regard. "Come on, then. We're all allies now. Have to play nice together for a while. Once we've won this war, you can go back to killing each other."

The Aninvdawegi were slow to move, but they never took their hands off their weapons.

"Well now," Kettle said, turning his attention back to the Aniyvwiya, "this is certainly an unexpected surprise." He nodded toward the rifles and other goods they carried. "Where do you think you're going with all of that, hm?"

DᏦᎪᏆꞱ ꞱᏢꝞꝞᎩ

Ayadohlv'i Gahlgwogi
Personal Retribution

Y ou want armed warriors," Tsiyu said. "We're simply ensuring that they are armed."

"You can always bring your warriors here," Kettle told him. "That way we know for certain that you'll not betray us."

"We could have set fire to this place, and then there would be no fort for you. And our people are not so far away. If you require assistance and find yourselves trapped in this prison, then it would be an asset to have a nearby ally."

"It could be considered theft as this fort and everything in it is property of the Crown."

"It was property of the French. Is this not theft also?"

For a long moment, Tsiyu and Kettle squared off. Kettle, now that he was apparently the one in charge, was very different from how he had been when approaching Gvnagadoga. And it seemed to Kiyuga that he, or perhaps the British in general, didn't like it when they, the Aniyvwiya—and probably others, too—could speak English well. Well enough to talk generally, not so well to turn their words against them; that was how they seemed to like it. But Gvnagadoga had diligently learned English and French—and even a bit of Spanish, too, if Kiyuga heard right—and ensured that his children learned also, so that their people would not be tricked.

At last, Kettle sniffed and relaxed his stance. His men followed suit. "Well, we have the better armaments inside the fort anyway. And this garrison is only the beginning. More will be coming."

"We'll be sure to be here to greet them," Tsiyu informed him.

The Aniyvwiya waited patiently for all of the British and Aninvdawegi to enter the fort before daring to continue down the trail. Kiyuga looked back once and saw all twelve Aninvdawegi standing there, watching them leave. Kiyuga did not ask the question, for he knew it would do no good.

The trek back to Itsa'ti did indeed take longer than the trip out to the fort, and the last colors of the sky had disappeared when they set foot in the town. Immediately the council was assembled. Tsiyu and the rest of them handed over their meager spoils and prepared to give a report.

"Fifty British and a dozen Aninvdawegi," Tsiyu told them. "And supposedly it is only the beginning. They are capable of housing and arming hundreds, even thousands of men."

Disgruntled murmurs swept through those assembled, but Gvnagadoga was firm when he said, "This is not a surprise. This is war, not merely a skirmish or a raid."

"What if they send those thousands of men here to Itsa'ti?" one of the Middle Town skiagvsta asked.

"We will fight to the last!" It was unclear who spoke, but everyone agreed.

"This is the Europeans' war," Gvnagadoga reiterated. "We are merely allies. As Tsiyu and the others are going to remind them."

"Do they even understand our own war with the Aninvdawegi?" a Lower Town skiagvsta demanded.

"The Aninvdawegi are at war with themselves," one of Gvnagadoga's senior warriors said calmly. "Some in the Confederacy have joined the French. Others refuse to declare."

"That should slow them down some," Kiyuga offered, "if they are too busy worrying about their own empire to pay mind to us."

"It depends on their relationship with the British," Galegi said. "If they are just as suspicious, then yes. But if they have forged a true alliance, then a broken Aninvdawegi empire means nothing if they have the British empire backing them."

"Then we must hope that they have no true alliance."

"Hope that they do not, plan as if they do," Gvnagadoga mused. "Do not presume to turn your backs on them." He shifted position and looked at his son. "Return to the fort in the morning, and do as we have already discussed. Establish ourselves and our position, and see if you cannot determine the nature of the alliance between the British and Aninvdawegi."

Everyone assented, though Kiyuga could see not everyone agreed. There were plenty of people gathered whose words did not match their expressions. They would do as Gvnagadoga said because he was currently the one in charge, but even his calm demeanor could not quell the exasperation forever. They were hard-pressed to ally themselves with the British in the first place. Having to ally with the Aninvdawegi also was a bit much to stomach.

Nevertheless, he returned home to Ulisi and Anagalisgi for the night.

"Forever is a long time," Kiyuga said, pinching his brother who tried to dance away. "I would have expected to be gone for so long, I would come back and find you an old man."

"And you the leader of the people," Anagalisgi said, meeting him head on, getting in a few jabs of his own. He calmed and turned semi-serious. "That doesn't mean this isn't important."

Kiyuga just sighed and said, "No."

Ulisi got them some food and set to work resupplying Kiyuga for his return journey.

Again, they set off at dawn, moving hurriedly in hopes of reaching the fort before sunset. They would not beg the British to open the gates so they might take shelter. Neither did they wish to camp too close, for fear that the British might kill them in the night and claim they thought it was an attack.

Coyotes and crows, Kiyuga thought, sighing.

They reached the fort when the sun was just resting on the tops of the trees.

With Kettle and his fifty men plus a dozen Aninvdawegi, as well as a number of "camp followers" as Kiyuga had heard them called, suddenly the fort seemed much smaller, even cramped, he thought, looking around. How could it have looked to house hundreds or thousands of men, when these sixty men and a dozen or more followers looked very close together indeed?

Like an animal puffing its chest to intimidate a rival, he concluded. They made it appear as though an army lay behind these walls when it was only a small party.

The main guard patrol was entirely British, yet they were stopped by an Aninvdawegi.

"What are you doing here?" he growled in broken English.

"What are you?" Tsiyu countered. "We understood that the Aninvdawegi were neutral."

"Some are. Some not. What is your business?"

"Our business is with Kettle. Or are you his dog to command?"

The man grunted and made a move as if to draw a blade, but Tsiyu was quick as a snake and caught his wrist. Kiyuga and the others carefully formed a sort of outward circle as other Aninvdawegi started to close in, hands resting lightly on knives and pistols.

"Calm down, gentlemen, there will be no battles today." Kettle's voice cut through the tension, deflating it as the Aninvdawegi and Tsiyu took stiff steps back, away from each other. The Englishman stood between them. "Surely we can act like civilized men and not savages?" He looked at Tsiyu. "Why are you here? Did you forget to take enough gunpowder for those guns you stole?"

"Surely in war, all weapons may be shared among allies," Tsiyu said spitefully, still looking at the Aninvdawegi, aware of their circle around the Aniyvwiya and Kettle. "We are here to ensure our agreement."

"You say that as if you don't trust us." Kettle frowned. "Well, no matter. We can discuss it later, after supper. As we are allies, it is only right that we extend our hospitality, I suppose. Then we will figure out what it is you require of us."

The Englishman departed, leaving the Aniyvwiya and the Aninvdawegi to face off. After a moment, Kettle spoke again, far enough away that he had to raise his voice so all in the vicinity could hear him.

"Honestly, Jameson, leave them alone. If you want to scalp each other, at least do it outside the gates in the wilderness, where the wild belong."

Kettle did not stick around to see if they complied, but Kiyuga noted that Tsiyu was the first to back down.

"Did he call you Jameson?" Tsiyu asked of the Aninvdawegi.

The man called Jameson grunted, his front faltering. He took a step back. "They gave us English names to be called. Easier for them to shout in battle."

"So you are their dogs," Yvgi stated.

"Red Hand pledged his support."

"Red Hand?" Tsiyu questioned. "What branch of the Confederacy are you from? What is your name?"

"My name is Shkwanaame."

"And your people?"

Shkwanaame told them.

"I've not heard of them," Tsiyu confessed.

"They were defeated and all enslaved by the Half King a generation ago," Galegi stated. "Isn't that right?"

"That's right," Shkwanaame replied stiffly. "My parents were made part of the household of one of their great warriors."

"All of you, then?" Kiyuga wondered.

The Aninvdawegi murmured agreement.

"Half King abandoned the British, though," Tsiyu said. "He humiliated their leader."

"And was punished for it," Shkwanaame countered. "His agreement to ally with the British will stand." He huffed. "We are payment as proof." Before any Aniyvwiya could make a snide remark, he added, "Just as you are payment for Old Hop allying with the British."

Tsiyu smirked. "We are not payment. We are diplomats."

Shkwanaame did not flinch, just said lowly, "You will be." He nodded gravely. "You will be."

Kiyuga tried not to make it obvious that the man's words haunted him as they walked away, safely passing out of the circle of Aninvdawegi.

The British had built a number of small fires around the fort over which they roasted game as well as some of the animals that the followers had brought along: a goat, a few chickens, some rabbits. Some of the women were running about, delivering loaves of bread and other goods to the men, including plenty of alcohol.

Ulisi had strictly forbade Kiyuga from touching the Europeans' alcohol, but he couldn't say he wasn't curious, especially as Tsiyu, Galegi, and Yvgi chose a spot around a fire and helped themselves to all the hospitality available to them. The three British men who were already around the fire moved elsewhere, but they were quickly replaced by two more younger soldiers as well as a few of the Aninvdawegi. English was the preferred language around the fire as it was the only one they all had in common, but only when the different peoples were speaking to each other.

"So, your chief, Old Hop," one of the Englishmen said, leaning heavily on his knees, facing Tsiyu with red eyes, "what's his story, eh? Does he really hop around like a rabbit?"

"My father had an accident as a young man that twisted his leg," Tsiyu answered, not sounding quite like himself either.

"Your father?" the other Englishman said. "Old Hop's your da?" He leaned toward his comrade as if to whisper, but he did a poor job of it. "Makes this one a valuable hostage I should think."

"Hostage for what?" the first wondered. "We already got all the goods they need. What good are people? We just stop selling them guns."

"We don't need your guns," Yvgi sputtered, spilling his own drink but not noticing. "We got Galegi and Kiyuga and the finest warriors the Aniyvwiya and the Anihwaya can produce."

"Well, we have the finest soldiers from His Majesty the King."

"Some good they are, I think, considering the beating the French are giving you."

"That's why we need allies. And if you're as strong as you say you are, we should have no trouble. Assuming your people even show up. This is a pretty sorry lot right here methinks."

Galegi stood. "If you want a challenge, I'll give you a challenge."

Both British men stood, unsteady on their feet.

"Come at you, then," one said.

Before either party could move, two things happened. First, one of the challenging Englishmen passed out and hit the ground. Second, another soldier, this one of apparent higher rank, walked over.

"What's this, then?" he demanded. Alcohol was on his breath, but it hadn't yet affected his demeanor. "There will be no fighting here tonight." He glared at Galegi, then at Tsiyu and Shkwanaame. "And stop giving ale to the savages. We don't need them turning on us in the night." Pause. "If you haven't completely lost your senses, Lieutenant Kettle would like to have a word."

Tsiyu and Yvgi both needed Galegi's help to stand. Tsiyu got his bearings, but Yvgi collapsed in a heap, laughing like a coyote. Kiyuga tried to get him up, but he waved him off.

"Ah, you don't need me," Yvgi said, still smiling. "I would only get in the way." He sniffed hard. "Maybe I'll crawl there on my belly, like a snake."

"You stay here," Tsiyu told him. "Keep an eye on the rest of these — how do you say it, sir? Rabble rousers, that's it. Keep an eye on these rabble rousers."

Tsiyu followed the soldier of higher rank, though not in much of a straight line. Galegi's steps were more steady, but he was unusually cranky for having almost no provocation. Kiyuga felt like a stranger in his own land, among his own people even.

Kiyuga remembered exploring the fort just a day or two before, remembered how huge it felt, how big the rooms were, how empty and haunted the land felt. Now, everything was smaller, and the lieutenant's office was no exception. Before, it seemed that it could fit a hundred men. Now, even ten would have been too many. Maybe it was because of all the furniture that had been moved in: a desk with maps, more maps on the wall, chairs, and things Kiyuga had no name for. Kettle himself stood behind the desk, studying papers with writing on them, whose purpose Kiyuga did not understand.

"Thank you, sergeant, that will be all," the lieutenant said, not looking up.

The man who had approached them at the fire and brought them here dipped his head and left, closing the door behind him.

Kettle looked up and raised a brow. "I see you have made yourselves quite comfortable."

"Your hospitality is quite fine," Tsiyu told him.

"Yes, of course. I am glad that it pleases you. Would you like to know what would please me?"

"Does it involve a woman?"

The British lieutenant was not amused. He turned his attention away from Tsiyu and Galegi, his gaze finally resting on Kiyuga. "Are you drunk as well?"

"No, sir," Kiyuga answered, electing to use an answer he'd heard the soldiers use many times. "Agilisi warned against it."

Kettle grunted and nodded only slightly. "Well, I don't know who this Agilisi is, but whoever he is, he appears intelligent."

"She. Agilisi is my mother's mother."

No reaction. "Whatever the case, you can speak English well enough, you come from an apparently intelligent family, and if I remember right, you are the one they call Young Spear."

"Yvgidahi is my name, but yes, Young Spear."

"Tsiyu is my name, sir," Tsiyu said. "My da is Old Hop."

Kettle raised a brow and gave him no more than a cursory glance. "A shame he has you for a son, then." He turned his attention back to Kiyuga. "Were there not four of you? I see only three."

"Yvgi is...outside," Kiyuga answered diplomatically.

"He's too drunk to walk. Lovely." The lieutenant huffed a sigh. "And you all seemed so promising yesterday morning. I had hoped that even if we butted heads that we might be able to negotiate and fight alongside one another like proper allies. Instead, this is what I get."

Kiyuga shifted his stance. "If you don't like alcohol, why bring it? Seems a waste of energy and space when you could easily replace it with provisions, or unload it to move more quickly."

"Yes, that is true, but ale keeps better on long journeys when we don't have time to go searching for every spring and river. We must make haste when ordered."

Kettle spoke firmly, but Kiyuga suspected there was more to it. He took a breath. "If I showed you where the river flows, would you get rid of the alcohol?"

"Come on, Kiyuga," Tsiyu said in their language. "Don't be a spoilsport."

Seeming to remember their existence, Kettle turned to Tsiyu and Galegi. "You may leave now."

"But we haven't finished talking about...whatever it was that you wanted to talk about."

"And we never will. Get out."

For a moment, Galegi looked ready to fight the lieutenant. But Tsiyu grumbled and turned to leave, touching Galegi and getting him to follow after a moment of consideration. Only Kettle and Kiyuga remained in the room.

"I much prefer to negotiate without an audience," Kettle said. "As to your question, the washer women are using the stream just north of here, and such is where we get our water."

"A stream is hardly filling, and there are no fish to catch," Kiyuga pointed out.

"Quite true. All right, where is this river of yours?"

"You will find it east of here, flowing south. It flows into the main river through Itsa'ti."

"We came from the east," Kettle said, folding his arms. "We crossed no river."

"The road you came on goes directly over it, but at that point, it is underground until it emerges just north of Itsa'ti. Go to the northeast of here, and you will find the mouth of the tunnel. I will show you tomorrow."

The British man looked thoughtful and finally nodded. "Very well. I will hold you to your word. You can show me on my way to Echota."

"You intend to go there again?"

"Of course. The governor of Virginia has business with your people, and I've been sent to deliver the message."

Kiyuga eyed the man suspiciously. "What is this message?"

Kettle was silent for a long time, studying Kiyuga. He said, "Only because you are the only one of your people here who is not drunk am I disclosing this to you, and because you have agreed to help us find this fishing river of yours. Braddock's Expedition was a disaster. Hundreds of men dead and no progress in defending our settlements from the French. We are on the defense, a position that the king does not like to be in. Hundreds of new soldiers are on their way from Great Britain, but until then, we need help."

"From the Aniyvwiya and the Aninvdawegi."

"Yes, sure, whatever you call yourselves. We need your...warriors to counter the tactics of the French and their allies."

"Gvnagadoga has already pledged our support."

"And we need that support, but not just here. We need them in Virginia. We have to break the French line."

"To do so would leave us vulnerable."

Kettle tilted his head. "How old are you?"

Kiyuga thought a moment. "Twenty winters, I think."

"Well, a decade ago, while you were yet little, your people asked us to build a fort, a safe haven for them to run to. At the time, you were under siege by French-backed tribes. Well, the war ended before construction began, but the agreement still stands, and we're cashing in on that agreement. We will build that fort to keep your people safe as long as we get warriors to take to Virginia."

"What about this fort?"

"We'll take as much as we can to aid in the construction of the new fort. Certainly all the supplies will be moved over there." Kettle sniffed. "Honestly, I don't know what the French were thinking when they built this here. But, no matter, it saved us the hassle of setting up camp, and it solves some logistical issues we might have had otherwise."

Kiyuga frowned. "And what happens after the war is over? What will happen to the fort? What will happen to Itsa'ti?"

Funny thing, Kiyuga thought. He'd only ever heard of forts being built. He'd never actually heard of them being taken down once they were no longer needed, except, perhaps, for this one which was to be moved. Nor had he heard of them being used for anything other than war. Certainly they were useful, and perhaps their uses were limited, but he couldn't shake the suspicion that if the British were permitted this foothold in Itsa'ti, they would never leave, at least, not voluntarily.

"Well, I suppose that all depends on how this war turns out," Kettle told him. "If your warriors do well by us and help us to break the French line and save Virginia, I see no reason you can't remain in control of the fort. After all, good warriors needs good protection. How savage would we have to be to take away all armor from our warrior allies?"

"Of course," Kiyuga said, thinking it the only safe reply. Coyotes and crows, he thought, yet the British seem to be able to play both roles flawlessly.

"Excellent. I am pleased that we have come to an understanding. First thing in the morning, you will show me and my men to this river of yours. Then we shall press on to Itsa'ti to speak again with—what was it you called him?"

"Gvnagadoga."

"—speak with Old Hop, and arrange for this fort to be built."

Kiyuga returned to the campfire where Yvgi was asleep and Galegi was wrestling one of the British soldiers while Tsiyu, Shkwanaame, and a small crowd had gathered to cheer on their favorite. Galegi won easily, which sparked some controversy among the British which led to an argument that might have devolved into real fighting if not for the late hour and excessive alcohol making everyone as tired as they were bad-tempered.

Sleep did not come easily to Kiyuga, for he was troubled by the events of the evening, as well as the events to follow in the morning. Had he really done that? Should not Tsiyu have been the one to speak with Kettle? Would Gvnagadoga be upset? Should he have done more? Less? Uncertainty saw Kiyuga into a fitful sleep.

The following morning, Kiyuga showed Kettle, a dozen of his men, and another two dozen followers, to the river he'd spoken of. Near the mouth of the tunnel, the water rushed in frothing rapids, but just a little father upstream was water gentle enough for washing, bathing, and fishing. Kettle set his followers to the task while he and his dozen men prepared to return to Itsa'ti with the Aniyvwiya.

"So, you showed them the river," Tsiyu said, looking wretched in the morning light.

"They are our allies, are they not?" Kiyuga asked. "Should we not see to their well-being?"

"As they are so concerned with ours?"

"Then they ought not be our allies at all."

Kiyuga hadn't realized it until that moment, but he'd lost a great deal of respect for Tsiyu just based on the events of the previous evening. He was the son of Gvnagadoga and a leader in his own right. He should have done better to control himself so he might have been able to speak to Kettle. Instead it had been left to Kiyuga, and he greatly doubted himself and his inexperience. Had Kettle seen it, too? Was he exploiting Kiyuga's inexperience even now?

Uneasiness dogged Kiyuga the entire trek to Itsa'ti. Their swift pace had delivered them before sunset and the council was quickly convened.

"I see you have arrived safely at the fort," Gvnagadoga began pleasantly.

"Indeed. Young Spear was kind enough to show us good fishing grounds as well," Kettle replied coolly. "However, there is another matter which must be discussed."

"Did Tsiyu and the others not sweep out the spiders to your

liking?" one of the other skiagvsta snickered.

"The spiders are fine. Actually, we wish to discuss an agreement between our peoples made approximately ten years ago to build a fort here at Itsa'ti."

That caused grumbling throughout those gathered, and Kiyuga saw disapproving looks from the Women's Council as well.

Gvnagadoga nodded calmly. "I see. I remember this agreement. However, if it pleases you, see that I am an old man about ready to sleep. I will advise these discussions, but I will not act upon them as I have in the past. My nephew, Atagulkalu, he will serve as mediator in these and future war negotiations."

Tsiyu left the room.

Kettle turned his attention to Atagulkalu. "Of course. My respect to you, sir, taking your uncle's place."

A few impromptu gifts were exchanged. The only thing the soldiers had to give to honor the new skiagvsta were their guns, which they reluctantly relinquished.

Atagulkalu wasn't even a new skiagvsta, not really. He was the mediator appointed by Gvnagadoga, but he was already skiagvsta of Tama'li. Now that they had declared and allowed the British to set up camp, the uku had only minor say in matters. But, as far as the British were concerned, Atagulkalu was the one they were dealing with. Looking at Gvnagadoga, Kiyuga suddenly realized the old uku's age and wondered whether there would be peace again in his lifetime.

"Ten years ago," Kettle began again, now addressing the skiagvsta, "your people were under siege from neighboring tribes who had the backing of the French. You came to us to ask for help. We offered to build a fort here that might keep your people safe. The war finished before the fort could be constructed. In this new war, we would like to acknowledge this old agreement and build the fort. It would, of course, be open to use should other tribes attack. We wish to be proactive, not reactive."

"And what do you want in exchange?" Atagulkalu asked.

"We want every warrior you can spare to march to Virginia and break the French line at Fort Duquesne."

More murmuring.

Atagulkalu called a recess so he could speak to the adawehi and the Women's Council. Kettle had prepared for a short discussion, but Kiyuga knew better. It was the following evening before the council was called back.

"You have brought this request before us," the skiagvsta said finally. "Ten years too late to stop the raids, aided by the French or not. Therefore, you are ten years late in honoring this agreement at all. You will build this fort for us first. Then we will supply our warriors to your cause. But not one day sooner."

The British soldiers were greatly displeased, but Kettle remained calm as he said, "Very well. You drive a hard bargain, but I respect it. I will send word at once."

"And know this," Atagulkalu cut in before the British could leave. "This fort will remain under the control of Itsa'ti and the Aniyvwiya afterwards and ever after. Our allies are welcome here, but this fort is for our use."

Kettle nodded once. "Of course. I shall inform my superiors."

The British departed, but the Aniyvwiya remained.

"Shall we hand over the town to them, too?" one warrior demanded. "Shall we sweep out the townhouse and invite their Virginia governor to sit here and dictate his will to us?"

"No one will sit here but the Aniyvwiya leaders, as it has been and as it will be," Atagulkalu told them. "But this fort will do us good. As we have turned European weapons against them, so we shall do with their defenses."

"These forts are as much a prison as a haven," Kiyuga said. "Those on the outside have the advantage."

The skiagvsta nodded, his eyes glittering with amusement. "Yes. We will."

They were dismissed. Kiyuga met up with Anagalisgi and Ulisi as they headed home.

"How was it?" Anagalisgi wondered. "Walking through the door of leadership?"

"I don't know what you mean," Kiyuga said, and he knew it was a lie. He had been the leader, if only for a moment, and only in Tsiyu's absence. But he had been the leader.

"At least you kept your wits about you," Ulisi said sourly. "Tsiyu, Galegi, and Yvgi were all drinking that alcohol last night, weren't they?"

"Vv. Quite heavily."

"That's what I suspected. But you remembered what I told you."

"Vv, Agilisi. I didn't touch it."

"Good boy. Nothing good comes from surrendering one's wits." She huffed. "Are you leaving tomorrow to return to the fort again?"

"Atagulkalu did not say anything about it, and I do not believe so. We made ourselves known to the British, which is all we were sent to do."

He could see she was displeased, but he didn't know what to say or do about it. Was it him she was upset with, or the situation? Had Atagulkalu heeded her advice as Ghigau? Was it merely a case of choosing the lesser evil, the coyote versus the crow?

"And how did my hopeless younger brother fare while I was away?" Kiyuga asked, turning his attention to Anagalisgi. "Did my absence inspire you in some way?"

"Yes, it inspired me to get to sleep faster since I don't have to deal with your snoring," Anagalisgi told him cheekily.

"Ah, so now he wants to sleep. You have dreamt yourself a wife, then?"

"Hardly. But I know we are on the path we are meant to be on."

Ulisi snorted indignantly but said nothing. Well, when their intended path was approved by the one who only dreamed up bad things, Kiyuga couldn't say he was too excited to see what lay in store. He was fine with going to battle and claiming his spoils, but he didn't want to destroy the people to get there.

Dinner proved to be a turkey which Anagalisgi had caught that morning. Despite giving their accounts of the fort for the skiagvsta,

Kiyuga was again asked for his side of the story and how he saw things, especially when it came to Kettle, a man who most agreed was so shifty as to perhaps be a shapeshifter and trickster.

"I don't trust him," Ulisi stated. "I didn't like the idea of the fort even a day's walk away, and now they want to bring it here?"

"Atagulkalu has spoken," Kiyuga said lamely. "And I think he has a plan for it. We may never see British soldiers here at all."

"And the coyote will stop his tricks."

There was nothing he could say or do to dissuade her, but Ulisi was not inclined to action. She declared herself too old for such things.

Even with Kettle now gone, there remained discontent among the various village leaders, and conferences were held for many days, very nearly a whole moon. There may have been more tension, had Atagulkalu been more intent on his position. His uncle and the uku, Gvnagadoga, was rightfully skeptical of the British, but supported them as he promised to do, even acknowledging King George II. But the skiagvsta was not so certain. Sensing his hesitation, the rest of the Overhill leaders, as well as some of the Middle and Lower Town skiagvsta who had come, tried to persuade him to throw off the British alliance and attack instead. The French were greatly victorious in the north, and had always been good to the people. Why did he persist in this folly?

"The British will not return until next spring to begin their fort," Saloli, now the First Warrior of Taliqua Eghawa, said harshly. "But who needs it? Attack them instead. Take their supplies. They are ill-suited to these hills. They lumber about as drunken bears while we move swiftly and silently as panthers."

"We will do as the dreamers have dreamed and the spirits have insisted," Atagulkalu informed him. "We do not know the work of the spirits and how we may be rewarded in the long run. This is how we will proceed."

"And there has been no fighting here," Kiyuga pointed out. "Much of the war is far north. The Anisawanugi and the Anikwanki and the north peoples are dealing with most of it."

"Then what reason do we have to send our warriors?" another skiagvsta asked. "The Europeans march through Aninvdawegi lands on a regular basis, yet they remain officially neutral. For what reason have we declared?"

"And for the worse side," Saloli hissed.

"We have declared, for we must," Atagulkalu cut in, sounding rather annoyed. He looked around at those gathered, a few dozen skiagvsta, a few uku, the Women's Council and the Ghigau, and some invited guests like Kiyuga and Anagalisgi. "You have all heard the dreams."

"Coyotes and crows!" Saloli snapped, standing. His two warriors followed suit. "We have been promised so much from the British, yet all they do is lie and swindle and cheat and dishonor us and take ever more, thinking that meager gifts will smooth out ruffled feathers, even as we become more dependent on them for these things. At least the French wish to trade and have respect for us and our ways. They fight for us and with us. Or they would."

He stormed out of the townhouse with his warriors.

For several long moments, there was silence among those gathered. Kiyuga could see that things could devolve very quickly, if anyone had a mind to follow.

Thankfully, Atagulkalu saw this as well, and he elected to release them for the night.

There were several days of rest for the warriors, as the skiagvsta inquired after the wisdom of the Ghigau and the spirits, imploring the dreamers to dream and commune with the spirits, even with the Creator, to assure him that they were on the correct path. Kiyuga spent many days and nights alone at home, while Anagalisgi dreamed and Ulisi imparted her wisdom.

On the fifth morning, the warriors were summoned again. When Kiyuga arrived, he saw that a young messenger had arrived and was standing next to Atagulkalu who looked grave.

"Saloli and his warriors chose to depart Itsa'ti a few nights ago," he began steadily. "However, they have returned to Taliqua Eghawa and declared for the French, and they are amassing a great gathering of warriors there to go north and support them with the French. There are rumors that the town of Si'tiku is following their lead and they are rallying under Saloli."

"What are we going to do?" someone asked.

"If Saloli won't listen, we cannot force him," someone else said.

"Maybe he has the right idea," said a third.

"We can't afford division," Kiyuga threw in. "The British will only exploit it, just as we have been playing on their divisions for years."

"And if they see Saloli defecting and heading north to support the French, they may believe that we have betrayed them as well," Atagulkalu mused. "They will come for us."

"We have to head them off," one of the Middle skiagvsta stated.

"Cut them down!" someone shouted, much to the glee of his immediate company.

"Conquering them will not reunite the people," Kiyuga said loudly, trying to make himself heard. "It will only force their submission, as the British attacking us will only force ours." As the crowd quieted, he lowered his voice some. "It is not unity, it is subjugation. And Saloli does not take kindly to subjugation."

"Neither do we," a Lower skiagvsta, called Tawodi, stated simply.

"A common enemy," Atagulkalu said. All eyes turned on him. "We must have a common enemy that we can agree upon and defeat and take spoils of war as has always been our way. We must relearn what it means to be Aniyvwiya and to walk in the way." He shifted position and looked at the Lower skiagvsta. "I trust you know well where the Anikusi make their homes?"

Tawodi's eyes glittered. "Oh, the lower people know this well. We have been fighting them for this fifty years' war."

Atagulkalu stood, and all rose with him. "Our warriors will go to Taliqua Eghawa. We will gather Saloli and his warriors and we will meet with you in your village. We will raid the Anikusi and take their spoils and plunder as we have always done. And we will be one people again. Then maybe Saloli will remember where his loyalties ought to lie."

It was a plan that, miraculously, all could agree on. Even Kiyuga found the prospect exciting, and he hoped he would be chosen to go. This would be a battle away from the Europeans and their petty skirmishes. They would be free to fight as they had done for generations, to take spoils and plunder and captives.

The Middle and Lower skiagvsta were dismissed so they might travel and make preparations. Atagulkalu and the Overhill skiagvsta remained, hastily making their own plans. Saloli had the advantage of time, but he would still have to travel through Overhill territory to get to the French.

"Aganstata will lead the party," Atagulkalu declared, looking at the respected warrior. "With luck, Saloli will be at your side."

"Is that wise?" one of the warriors wondered.

"When a man wishes to lead, and he is good at it, give him a chance to do what he is meant to do, and do not hinder him. One may redirect a river without losing its power."

"Even beavers may build great dams."

"Yes, but beavers have more time and resources to devote to such a cause. We have neither." Atagulkalu let out a breath. "Where is my cousin? Where is Tsiyu?"

There was some searching for him, but only Yvgi could provide an answer.

"He left Itsa'ti to join Saloli," the warrior told him. "He...disagreed with you and Gvnagadoga in...some things over the last moon or so."

Atagulkalu sighed. "Very well. Tawodi will also lead."

He began listing off the warriors he wanted to go, and Kiyuga was delighted to hear his name called. True, it might not be more than a skirmish, such as he'd partaken in before, but at least it was something. At least he would be able to fulfill the honor code. Perhaps he would find good spoils to impress a girl.

"We will travel by night," Aganstata concluded. "Go now, prepare yourselves. We leave at dusk."

The warriors dispersed, and Kiyuga hurried home, eager to be going and doing something. This time, he did not have to worry about leadership and politics. He could do what he did best, what he was meant to do. He was supposed to be a great warrior, but how was this to be if he'd never been to war?

He was jerked from his thoughts as Ulisi delicately took his bag from his hands, saying, "Get some rest. You will need it for the night's travels."

"Agilisi, I only just woke up," he said. "How can I sleep now?"

"Then go out and run. Run and catch food before you go. It will tire you, especially in the hot sun. I will pack your things."

Still uncertain but brimming with energy, Kiyuga left the bag to her and headed outside. He did not see his brother anywhere, so he elected to follow Ulisi's advice, taking off into the woods. He felt as though he could run all the way to the fort and back with time to spare, but he knew better. After a few laps of the town, as well as a lucky break with a squirrel, he returned home, handed the squirrel off to Ulisi, and went to rest.

DꙶᎯᎢ ᏩᏁᎳ

Ayadohlv'i Tsanela

Premonition

Anagalisgi couldn't help but feel a bit responsible for how things were unfolding, and he questioned himself more than once. Had he really seen what he thought he saw? Had he misinterpreted it? Could Gvnagadoga have misinterpreted it? Perhaps, as a single man might be proven wrong, but multiple dreamers and adawehi? They couldn't all be fooled, and it was gravely bad luck to make up dreams or intentionally misinterpret. Still, was all of this happening solely because of him? He knew Gvnagadoga had been leaning toward the French, assuming he was unable to sustain Aniyvwiya neutrality.

He hadn't dreamed that day, which he figured was a good thing. Although it might not be, given why he'd been asked to accompany the raiding party.

Kiyuga was already waiting with a few others at the road, all of them eagerly boasting of exploits yet unrealized. He saw Anagalisgi and waved him over.

"Come to wish me luck?" he asked.

"Only if you want bad luck," one of the other young men snickered.

"No, I'm coming with you," Anagalisgi told him.

"What? Why? Wolf Clan you may be, but you're no warrior."

"Aganstata wants me to come along and continue to dream. He wants to know of misfortune before it happens so we might avoid it."

Kiyuga considered this and nodded. "All right. Did you see anything today, then? Should we abandon our mission entirely?"

"Yes, should we?" Aganstata inquired, walking up behind Anagalisgi with a couple dozen warriors.

Feeling very conspicuous, Anagalisgi answered, "I saw nothing. I did not dream today."

Despite the lack of bad news, Aganstata still seemed troubled as he mused, "Well, it's a start."

Some two hundred and fifty warriors were traveling with Aganstata from the Overhill villages, and would meet up with them on the road. From Itsa'ti alone were over a hundred. Anagalisgi could tell Kiyuga was excited. This was already far bigger than an ordinary raid, which might normally comprise between six and sixty warriors. They were going to secure Saloli's loyalty and end the Aniyvwiya war with the Anikusi.

"Are you ready for this, brother?" Kiyuga asked, slapping him on the back. "Your job now may be to dream, but you are still an Anihwaya warrior."

"A moment ago, you said that Anihwaya I may be, but a warrior I am not," Anagalisgi reminded him, coughing once. "So which is it?"

"You are a dreamer and a warrior," Aganstata answered before Kiyuga could speak. He put a hand on each of their shoulders. "And I am counting on you both."

It was high praise, and Anagalisgi would have been lying if he said he didn't revel in the warrior's attention just a little. Because of his lack of warrior prowess, Anagalisgi had become accustomed to being passed over by the skiagvsta in such matters. This alone was a new experience.

With the warriors gathering to leave, so the rest of the town had gathered to wish them well. Some women said goodbye to their husbands, while others had decided to join them. Anagalisgi saw Nanyehi standing beside her husband, both of them saying goodbye to Inga, telling her to mind things while they were gone. He saw his brother, and the other unmarried men, looking around at the unmarried girls, trying to catch an eye and silently promise to bring back something pretty for them.

"You think this is your big chance, huh?" Anagalisgi teased, following Kiyuga's gaze to a pretty Bird Clan girl.

"The first of many chances, perhaps," Kiyuga said, not looking away from the girl. "First we shall beat the Anikusi, and then we shall defeat the French. If I don't have a wife by the end of this, I think I shall be a very poor excuse for a warrior."

Anagalisgi sighed, rolled his eyes, shook his head, and pressed back into the crowd. The sun had already disappeared behind the high hills and trees, and the colors were quickly fading from the sky, leaving only the waxing moon and their intimate knowledge of the road and landscape to guide their way.

When Aganstata was satisfied that all of his warriors had gathered, he addressed them.

"My people, my brothers! We set out this night on a quest, seeking the guidance of the spirits and the reunification of our people. More importantly, we seek to remember what it means to be Aniyvwiya. We will bring home our wayward brother Saloli. And then, we shall raid the Anikusi!" Small cheers. "We shall raid!" More cheers. "We shall plunder!" Even more cheers. "We shall take spoils and trophies!" Continuous cheering. "We shall reclaim what is rightfully ours and we shall make our people known and feared once more! We will be Aniyvwiya!"

With whoops and hollers, the raiding party set off on the road at a brisk pace. Anagalisgi lost sight of his brother and quickly dropped to the rear of the group. Aganstata's enthusiasm was infectious, and even he enjoyed the thrill of the chase for a time. But as the run wore on, it became merely a task, a chore. The yells and whooping died down and the pace became a little slower and more synchronized.

As the moon began to sink and the first hints of dawn pressed on the air, the party had slowed to a walk and a small detachment had gone ahead to spy a good place to camp. Anagalisgi had remained near the back of the group, yet his pace had been fairly steady. Only lack of sleep slowed him now, though his body felt invigorated.

They arrived at the camp site, each man staking out a claim to a sleeping spot, with Aganstata arranging watches. If Saloli was already on the move, there was no telling what he might do if he came upon them asleep. With their direction and numbers, it wasn't difficult to piece together what they might be doing.

"I thought I'd lost you," Kiyuga said, coming up beside Anagalisgi as he lay down.

"How many miles were you going to wait before turning back to come look for me?" Anagalisgi wondered.

"Well, I knew you would come eventually."

"Anagalisgi." Aganstata approached them. Anagalisgi sat up. "You remember what we spoke of? I wish to know all danger that you see."

"I understand," Anagalisgi told him respectfully. "I will share all I dream."

The skiagvsta's top warrior nodded once and wandered off. Kiyuga looked at Anagalisgi. "What if you don't dream anything?"

He sighed. "Then I don't dream anything. It would be better than dreaming bad things, right?"

"You think you could dream up something good if you tried?"

"I've been trying for years." Anagalisgi lay down once more. "I don't know that I can try any harder. I've even tried not trying. But the spirits will tell me what they will. If I am to be a bearer of bad news, then so it shall be."

He could see his brother was displeased, but he was telling the truth. Nothing he did could make the bad dreams leave or the good dreams come. He was merely a vessel, and a pot did not get to choose what was put into it.

Even as he closed his eyes, he felt his soul leaving his body, his arms becoming long and thin, clothing shredding into feathers, face stretching long and pointed. When he opened his eyes, he found himself sweeping upwards into a tree overlooking their camp. He saw his body and his brother beside him, just now falling asleep. Soon the area was quiet save for the sounds of the forest.

His first instinct was to fly ahead, search for Saloli or other dangers, but something deeper told him to remain where he was. Just as he was thinking this, movement on the ground caught his eye. He looked and saw a wolf circling the camp. It was alone, and unlike any wolf he had ever seen. For one, it was white. For two, it was enormous, like a small horse. It did not appear hostile to the sleeping warriors, but protective, as a guardian.

The branch shuddered as something landed. He looked and saw that it was a pileated woodpecker, the white one from his youth.

"Are we on the right path, then?" Anagalisgi inquired, speaking from a place outside even his spirit body.

"Darkness comes on the horizon," the woodpecker said. "For even as every cloud has a silver lining, so every blue sky holds the threat of storm. And every victory must be hard fought, to be both earned and kept."

"Should I warn Aganstata to turn back?"

"Face the storm, Anagalisgi. And remember your place in it."

With that, the woodpecker spread its wings and took off, disappearing into the canopy. Startled and frustrated, Anagalisgi spread his wings, intending to follow. But as he dove off the branch and took flight on a wind current, he found he had lost control of his spirit body. He was gliding, yes, but the white wolf had spotted him and now watched. As he neared, the wolf moved to intercept, opening its huge jaws.

Just as his spirit body hit the wolf's mouth, Anagalisgi came awake, sitting up and gasping for breath. Daylight momentarily blinded him and he struggled to all fours, bumping Kiyuga who came awake grumpily. Sitting back and looking around, most of the warriors were still asleep. Those who were awake were eating or talking quietly.

Beside him, Kiyuga yawned. "Are we moving?"

"Not yet," Anagalisgi said, mirroring his yawn.

He took a strip of jerky from his pack and gnawed on it a bit, just enough to ease the tightness in his stomach. He couldn't eat too much, for he didn't want to get sick if they intended to run the whole day. Around the clearing, more were waking up. Some chewed on provisions, others wandered off to relieve themselves or do other things.

"Anagalisgi, you're awake."

He looked up and stood as Aganstata approached.

"Did you dream?" the warrior wondered.

"I did dream," Anagalisgi confirmed.

"What did you see?"

"I saw a white wolf, circling our people here as they slept, but it moved as a guardian and protector, not an adversary, and it watched over the sleeping warriors. Then I saw a white woodpecker in the trees. It said to me, 'Face the storm, and remember your place.' "

"And you are confident in this?"

"I am, Aganstata. We must face this storm, but we are protected. We must remember what it means to be Aniyvwiya."

The great warrior nodded. "Very good. You are young, but I thank you for your honesty and insight."

Anagalisgi dipped his head. "Thank you."

With that, Aganstata turned away from him and started barking at the warriors to get up and be ready. The few who were still sleeping jumped to their feet, initially confused. Others hurried to finish off food or water or dash into the woods for a moment, Anagalisgi and Kiyuga among them. By the time they returned, most of the warriors had assembled and Aganstata was about ready to move out.

Anagalisgi felt a bit dishonest in his recitation of his dream to Aganstata. He knew in his heart that his interpretation was true, but there was also a deeper meaning that he knew was meant for him. What if he was wrong? He uneasily made his way toward the group.

"Shouldn't you be at the front?" one of the other warriors asked him as he approached the back of the group where he would likely stay. "Then you can warn us of danger to come." His friends snickered.

"What need is there for that?" Anagalisgi countered cheekily. "I have already seen the whole day. We will be well."

That got them to shut up even as they murmured apologies and pleas for absolution for mocking a dreamer.

Before anyone could say more, Aganstata called to move out. Slowly the hundred warriors got going, jogging along the road. This time, they did not whoop or holler or call out songs or prayers, just set their mind to the task at hand, set their body in a steady rhythm, and jogged.

The terrain around Itsa'ti was very hilly; no one could argue this. Moving south and then west along the road, the hills got steeper and more rugged. There were parts where they had to almost crawl up the hill, and then they were set running out of control down the other side. Anagalisgi tried to picture the journey he and Kiyuga and Ulisi had made years before and could only conclude that they had taken a different branch of the road, else things really had changed that much.

The only time he saw his brother was from a distance, typically when he was looking downhill and trying to judge a path where he could run and not trip and fall. Kiyuga would already be heading for the next hill, running right up there with the leaders and showing no signs of slowing down.

Anagalisgi was happy for his brother. Finally Kiyuga would partake in his glorious battle, plunder his spoils, and win over a girl. He himself was not so sure. He was a dreamer, not a warrior. But if he wanted any hope of finding a wife of his own, he had to fulfill his duties as a Anihwaya warrior first. If he could not fulfill his current clan duties, why should he fulfill any other duties as husband, father, and uncle? Why should he do anything at all for a wife and family?

He scrambled over the crest of another hill, determined to not be the last runner. He would not claim to be as athletic as those in front, but he could not allow himself to be the last one either. He spotted his trail of descent and let himself go, sliding down the rocky slope and using the momentum to carry him along through a dark glade, along a stream, and around a corner.

Once around the corner, Aganstata allowed them to stop for a brief rest. Many went to the river to drink and refill their water skins; others sat under trees to relax. Anagalisgi filled his skin and sat under a tree, just within earshot of Aganstata.

"How far do you think?" one warrior asked their party leader.

"I expect we will intercept Saloli tomorrow, if not sooner, depending on how quickly he is moving," Aganstata answered thoughtfully. "We will travel a little while longer, then camp and dispatch a hunting party. A peace offering may make him more receptive to our pleas and proposal."

"Agreed. Should we send scouts ahead?"

After a moment, Aganstata nodded. "Yes. We are well within our own lands here. Saloli would be a fool to become aggressive with only a small scouting party." He looked around, and his gaze settled on Anagalisgi. "Anagalisgi, come here."

He stood and approached the skiagvsta who called over another young warrior, Tolatsi.

"Go ahead of us, no later than when the sun is a finger's width above the trees, and find a place for us to stop and camp."

"Why me?" Anagalisgi blurted out, hoping he didn't sound disrespectful.

"Saloli knows you for a dreamer; you are no threat. He would be foolish to provoke a fight, a raiding party against two young warriors."

There was no room for argument, and, after quickly refilling their water skins, Anagalisgi and Tolatsi started off. Anagalisgi did not see Kiyuga.

It only took one hill to obscure sight and sound of the party by the river. Then it was just the warrior and the dreamer. Hailing from Bird Clan, Tolatsi was called such on account of his long legs and extraordinary running and leaping abilities. Why he'd been paired with Anagalisgi was anyone's guess, except, maybe, because they were of an age.

The running became less strenuous. Although they still had to climb hills, the overall landscape trended downwards. Of course, that only meant that the trek back would be largely upwards, but by then, they hopefully wouldn't be so pressed for time. Was this journey really this difficult the last time? Had he somehow not noticed it before?

Tolatsi was polite enough to not completely outrun Anagalisgi, but he could see the long-legged warrior was hardly using his body to its full potential, and it annoyed him.

"You may as well go ahead and find a camping spot," Anagalisgi told him as he caught up to Tolatsi yet again. "I will follow, don't worry."

"Of course not," Tolatsi said, sounding rather offended. "It's safer to stick together. Saloli is not the only danger out here."

"Yes, but then you won't have to keep stopping for me."

"Maybe, but it is better to move slowly and carefully and arrive alive, than quickly and foolishly and not arrive at all."

Anagalisgi couldn't deny that, but he also couldn't say anything more as they started off again, making for the next hill.

They did eventually find a good camping spot, situated on a hillside with a small lake just down the slope. A hunting party would have good luck there, Anagalisgi knew. They gathered up some firewood. Anagalisgi sat to start a fire while Tolatsi did a more thorough sweep of the immediate area and down to the lake.

"Good animal tracks in the mud," the warrior replied when he returned. "And plenty of fish, too."

"Plenty of food to go around," Anagalisgi said, adding another stick to the fire. "Hopefully Saloli understands that all we want is peace."

Tolatsi grunted but said nothing more about it.

It wasn't much later that the rest of the party arrived. Anagalisgi expected them to come flying over the hilltop, then come screaming down the slope, trying to stop themselves before they ran over the camp.

And they did.

The first dozen or so runners evidently weren't expecting to come upon the camp so suddenly, and about half of them were forced into wild acrobatics to avoid falling into the fire Anagalisgi had built. Their whoops and cries were enough to alert the rest of the group which managed to slow down and walk down from the top of the hill.

"You might have warned us," was all Aganstata said about it, picking himself up from where he had slid out and moving off to direct the rest of the group.

A hunting party and a fishing party were sent to the lake, and the remainder of the group went to work gathering firewood, plants, and erecting quick shelters for the night. More fires popped up here and there, each one serving about fifteen to twenty people. The fishing party returned with a small catch. As night began to fall, the hunting party also returned, bearing a young elk.

The men skinned and divided the elk while the women, with their swift, deft fingers, had it cooking over the various fires just as soon as they could. Large portions of elk roasted over the fires while fish were stuck on spears and held over or placed on the rocks ringing the pit. Anagalisgi saw Kiyuga and sat beside him.

"Where is Aganstata?" Anagalisgi inquired casually.

"Scouting ahead and taking watch so we may all eat before taking watch ourselves or sleeping," his brother answered flawlessly, peeling the skin back on his fish just enough to drizzle a touch of honey that someone had carefully harvested before handing the comb off to the next person. He took a bite of the fish. "You think Saloli is going to come with us?"

"Hard to say. He was very upset with Atagulkalu and Gvnagadoga. But I've not seen anything about division."

"Well, you didn't exactly predict his betrayal either," Tolatsi said across the fire.

"It's not a betrayal," Anagalisgi stated. "He's not going against the people. He's doing what he thinks is best for the people. Whether or not he is misguided—or we are—we all have the same goal. He's frustrated. We all are. He's just a little quicker to react."

"Then why don't you go talk to him?" the long-legged warrior said sourly. "Or join him yourself?"

"There is no reason to be angry with Anagalisgi," Aganstata said, pausing in his walk and appearing as a ghost in the firelight. "Understanding one's adversary is the first step in either helping or hurting him. Not understanding will only hurt both your adversary and yourself."

"Is Saloli interested in understanding?"

"And you will notice where we are because of it."

"Are the British interested in understanding?" another warrior at the fire asked intentionally.

Aganstata sighed. "And you will notice where we are because of it." He continued before anyone could speak. "Enough. We have our task. Kiyuga, you will be on the next watch."

Anagalisgi saw his brother beam with pride as he accepted an otherwise mundane task. But this was less mundane; the senior warrior had asked him personally to do it. He was puffing up like a bullfrog, Anagalisgi thought, taking a bite of elk to hide his smile.

"Your brother is arrogant," Tolatsi commented distastefully, glaring at Kiyuga but speaking to Anagalisgi. "He might be older, but he's not seen battle, and see how he struts like a bird to show himself off."

"Have you seen battle?" Anagalisgi wondered.

"That's why I'm here."

"Look around. Aganstata has senior warriors with him, yes, but many here are young and untested, like you, like Kiyuga, like me. He's giving us a chance to see battle and blood our weapons before fighting the Europeans."

"Why would he do that?" one of the others inquired.

"It's a strategy to get Saloli to comply," Kiyuga told them. "The Anikusi have raided and burned almost all of the Lower Towns, for they are a ferocious, savage people. It's madness for Aganstata to take so many untested warriors into battle against them. Saloli knows this as well. If he's rallying many warriors to his side in the name of protecting and defending the people, he won't be able to leave us to our fates with the Anikusi. He will have to join us."

Tolatsi still looked annoyed, but the others seemed intrigued by the idea. Anagalisgi wasn't sure how true the analysis was, but it certainly sounded plausible.

"Well, I don't recall there being a village here before."

Everyone turned to look as the present watch party led Saloli and what appeared to be approximately one hundred warriors into their camp. They'd painted themselves and moved in the firelight and shadows like demons. Aganstata met them.

"Welcome, Saloli. Will you join us? We've plenty to share. And much to discuss."

Saloli gave him a look. "We left the discussion. There is nothing left to talk about. You have declared for the British. We declare for the French."

"I'm not speaking of the Europeans. I'm speaking of the Anikusi and the raids on the Lower Towns."

"Raids?" Saloli's warriors shifted behind him.

"Four villages burned, warriors, women, and children all stolen. We received word in Itsa'ti not long after your departure. All other negotiations and discussions have been suspended. The Lower skiagvsta have already gone ahead to see what remains, what we can salvage. Atagulkalu sent us to help. And to fight."

Saloli and his warriors glanced around at those gathered. The painted warrior raised a brow. "This is who Atagulkalu sends? The skiagvsta sends his best warrior and a bunch of boys? Against the Anikusi?"

Aganstata shrugged. "You took off with your warriors and rallied others to you. Itsa'ti must be defended as well. This is who Atagulkalu sends."

Anagalisgi could tell Saloli was greatly displeased, and his warriors appeared no less annoyed.

"We'll be on our way in the morning, then," Aganstata said pleasantly.

Saloli growled something Anagalisgi did not catch. Then, "I cannot abandon you to those savages. What did you want to discuss?"

The painted warriors dispersed, dividing themselves among the other campfires or building their own as they became crowded. Saloli, Aganstata, and a few of their senior warriors moved off to the edge of camp to deliberate.

"I recognize you," one of Saloli's warriors said, sitting down across from Anagalisgi. "You're the dreamer, Gvnagadoga's prophet."

"I don't know about that," Anagalisgi murmured self-consciously, "but I do dream."

"And that makes you Kiyuga," a second warrior said, looking at his brother. "Do you remember me? Totsuwa?"

It took some jogging of memories, but eventually Kiyuga did remember Totsuwa, a warrior from Taliqua who was only a few years older.

With the size of the camp now numbering nearly three hundred, the young elk suddenly didn't provide very much food, and another hunting and fishing party was dispatched. When they returned, it was a hurried endeavor to skin it and cook it, but before they could settle in to sleep, Aganstata called for quiet so he could speak.

"Saloli has agreed to join us," he began.

The gathered warriors erupted into whoops and cheers, which Aganstata allowed to continue and die out on its own before speaking again.

"In the morning, we will travel to Nagutsi' to meet with Tawodi and his warriors. There we will combine our strengths into the single strength of the Aniyvwiya!" More cheers. "And we will raid the Anikusi as the warriors we are!" Even more cheers. "We will avenge our burned cities, take back our women and children, and take our spoils and plunder as we please!"

Anagalisgi could see that Aganstata said more, but the whooping and hollering was so loud that he could not make out the words. He would not say that he was not excited by the prospect, and he cheered along with the rest of them, but he preferred quiet resolve over such flagrant displays.

Aganstata had disappeared into the crowd as someone brought out a drum and began to beat and wail. There was more whooping as some began to dance around their fires, trying to outdo each other and brag and show off and outdo one another, although many of Aganstata's warriors had few things to boast of. Anagalisgi looked up at a hand on his shoulder and found it was Aganstata. He made a motion and they stepped away to the edge of the camp so they could hear each other speak.

"Have you seen or heard anything that should give us cause to be wary?" the warrior wondered.

"Nothing, but I've not yet slept," Anagalisgi told him.

Aganstata frowned but nodded, half to himself. Then, "I realize you are yet young and still learning under Gvnagadoga and the adawehi, but I require absolution before we proceed."

"Absolution?" Anagalisgi wondered.

The warrior nodded again and knelt in proper position. "For my lies and deception against our people. I pray the spirits understand that I wish only to unite our people and avoid our destruction."

It was a simple enough ritual, one Anagalisgi knew well and performed now, using the proper elements and water from his skin. He would have to pray for absolution himself for not being more prepared. Aganstata stood.

"Thank you, Anagalisgi," the warrior told him sincerely. "You will one day be an excellent uku. And I suspect your brother will be an equally great skiagvsta."

He headed back to camp, leaving Anagalisgi alone just inside the line of trees, bewildered but also beaming with pride. Was this the real reason that Aganstata had wanted him to come along? Not just because he was a young, untested Anihwaya warrior, but because he was the only one able to perform these rituals? What other plans had Aganstata made?

It wasn't long after that that things started settling down and the warriors began to settle in. Anagalisgi prayed fervently for a sign in his dreams to either confirm or deny their next journey. Then he too lay down his head.

He remembered wondering whether a deception might be excused if it produced a greater outcome than straight honesty might have. As he considered this, he saw in the darkness of his dream an even darker flow of something liquid. The ambient darkness lightened into a red color, like fire that was yet invisible for the thick smoke in the air.

Anagalisgi suddenly found himself standing in the middle of a forest that was little more than a silhouette against a sky stained with smoke and fire. All the animals had fled, the birds gone, and the people missing as well. He was all alone. The air felt like a void and he was unable to breathe.

Confusion swirled around him as he tried to make sense of it all, wondering if this was what was in store for them if they continued on to the Lower Towns.

Then, in the darkness, he saw the smoke and shadows begin to take shape. They came as animals, but they were not healthy. They were rotted, diseased, and not all there as they shifted and reformed with smoke and shadow.

This was not his home, he realized. He'd stepped beyond the waking world, perhaps even beyond the dreaming world. What lay past the dreaming world but the spirit world? Was this what awaited them at the end of the setting sun? Were their souls destined to be devoured by these...beasts?

Another creature rose up now, appearing as smoke and shadow, yet Anagalisgi knew instinctively that this was a solid, physical being. He had no words to describe it with its long neck and long, narrow face. Its eyes were narrow and slitted like a lizard's, and it was covered in scales. Over the tops of the trees, he saw it had at least two legs ending in massive feet with enormous claws. Wings sprouted from its back. Its head had two main horns but many smaller ones, and spines ran down its neck.

It stared at him, studied him as hunter studies prey. Then the thing opened its mouth and let out an ear-piercing shriek. It came at him, mouth gaping wide, crushing the trees like twigs, wings blocking out what little light there was.

Anagalisgi was rooted to the ground in fear. At the last minute, he saw a flash of white light, and something big and heavy crashed into him from the side.

He gasped awake, but found himself still in the dream as he was still alone and in a place not the campsite. He was in a large meadow, the sun shining brilliantly and all appearing well. Directly in front of him was the burning black forest. The trees at the border seemed to be divided between normal trees and black trees. Looking up, he saw in one of the normal trees, a white pileated woodpecker.

"Is this the spirit world?" Anagalisgi asked. "Am I dead?"

"No," the woodpecker replied. "And you will not. Not here. You will live on, as will your people."

"You've come to me before. I've seen you, in the forest, in the village. Am I right to follow your direction? Are we right to be doing this thing?"

"If both paths lead to destruction, does it really matter how fast you get there?"

"Help me lead my people. There must be a way to save them."

The woodpecker hopped around the tree a bit, getting closer to the ground. Anagalisgi approached until it was just above his head. The woodpecker paused, then hopped down a little more so they could almost see eye to eye.

"Sometimes, there is no good answer," the woodpecker said. "There is only the least bad."

"You're saying we're doomed? If I tell this to Aganstata, he will have us return to Itsa'ti. Is that what we're supposed to do? Saloli will likely abandon us and continue his mission."

The woodpecker looked unusually determined. "Division now will cause destruction. Division later will save you."

With that, the spirit spread its wings and flew away, right in front of Anagalisgi. He put his arms up reflexively and turned. When he opened his eyes to follow its path, he found himself once more in the waking world.

It didn't take long for Aganstata to realize he was awake. The warrior motioned for him to approach.

"I saw you were dreaming," he stated. "What did you see?"

Anagalisgi's gaze flickered to Saloli once, then twice, before he answered, "I saw the land covered in darkness, lit only by distant fire. It was devoid of all people and all natural beasts. But there were spirits in the land, dark spirits formed of smoke and shadow. And above it all was a great dark spirit, a beast whose likeness I cannot name, nor well describe except that it was a flying lizard with large claws and horns.

It came after me, but I was rescued by a white animal; I do not know which.

"Then I found myself standing outside the dark forest in a natural meadow. When I looked up, I saw the woodpecker, and it said to me, 'Division now will cause destruction. Division later will save you.' "

"Is this all you saw?" Aganstata wondered.

"It is."

The warrior frowned, but it was Saloli who spoke. "What is the meaning of this dream?"

Anagalisgi faltered, partially because he truly didn't know, not fully, and partially because he did not want to speak aloud the part he thought he did know. Finally he answered, "The Aniyvwiya must stand strong, together, as one unified people. If we split apart now, we will only be fighting each other, and we will be destroyed. We must stay focused on our goal, on our people, and not lose sight of the true enemy."

He would admit to being a tiny bit vague so as not to appear accusatory to either side, but Saloli was not fooled. He fixed Anagalisgi in a hard gaze for a long moment before turning to Aganstata.

"Who did you say would be the skiagvsta from the Lower Towns that we are to meet and raid with?"

"Tawodi is expecting us," the warrior replied calmly.

"And how many warriors is he raising?"

"As many as he can in the time that he has. But the Lower Towns have been decimated. What warriors are left will not be difficult to find and rally."

Saloli still appeared skeptical, but agreed. Together the two warriors stalked through the camp, waking anyone who was not already awake, telling them to be ready.

"Are we still going to the Lower Towns?" Kiyuga wondered, arranging his effects.

"Yes, we are," Anagalisgi told him, suddenly longing for more sleep.

The notion cheered Aganstata's young warriors, reaffirming their excitement and determination to go to battle and raid the Anikusi. Saloli seemed mildly suspicious of the endeavor, but his warriors were just as eager to go on a good raid. Even before everyone was completely ready, they'd started out, now three hundred and more strong.

Once again, Anagalisgi quickly lost sight of his brother and was left to slowly lose ground in the shuffle. Saloli's older, strong, more experienced warriors quickly took the lead, but not without a few healthy young warriors running in their shadows if not in their midst. Even when those who had fallen behind in camp caught up, Anagalisgi was one of the last, keeping pace with other young warriors, some who were younger than him and going on their first raid or skirmish of any form.

He found himself wondering what would have happened if Saloli had refused to go along with this. Would they have had to fight Saloli and his warriors? It was true that most of Aganstata's force had been young men, and most of Saloli's force was seasoned, and Saloli's men outnumbered Aganstata's two to one. There was little doubt in Anagalisgi's mind who would win that fight. Would they have gone to Nagutsi' anyway? Perhaps they would have gathered Tawodi and his warriors before returning and trailing Saloli, trying to catch up to him. It was impossible to know, and Anagalisgi was only thankful that they didn't have to find out, at least, not now.

So they continued running up and down hills, always trending downwards until they got to a particular hilltop and Anagalisgi could actually make out vast stretches of flat ground as far as the eye could see. Where did the hills go? Where did this flat earth come from? Why was there such disparity, and where had the mountains and the flat earth come from?

He paused at the top of the hill, a large clearing, and turned around, suddenly stunned to find the mountains behind him. They rose high into the red sky, dark against the setting sun. His home. He'd left his home. Yes, he was still in Aniyvwiya territory, but it was as far from any home as he'd been since leaving Taliqua for Itsa'ti. It was surreal, like moving between the waking world and the spirit world.

Then he was moving down the slope, putting the high ground ever more behind him. The foothills still continued on, the road snaking this way and that, but he was in a whole new world now. Some distance ahead, he saw smoke, as from a large bonfire. The line of warriors streamed out ahead of him on the road, quickly but carefully making their way ever more downhill. Anagalisgi left the clearing behind, left the view of both worlds behind, and plunged back into the forest. The shadows were longer and darker on the sunrise side of the hill as the sun hid behind the mountains, and there was a certain chill in the air.

Anagalisgi slid out once, stepping on a rock that crumbled beneath his foot and sent him careening down the slope. He tucked himself the best he could, but he quickly found himself at the mercy of the rocky road, slicing open his body in multiple places before crashing through a bush and ultimately slamming into a tree. Stars exploded in his vision and he squeezed his eyes shut. His body went rigid but he forced himself to relax.

After a moment of quiet moaning and groaning, he picked himself apart and tried to move. He heard footsteps coming down the hill and silently prayed that they were at least in control and wouldn't crash into him. Hands came under his arms and he was dragged out of the bush and away from the tree. He limply crumbled to the ground, then got to his feet.

"Are you all right?" someone asked.

"I'm fine," Anagalisgi told them, waving the group away. "I'm fine."

Every movement informed him of a new scratch or scrape, and when he finally dared look at himself, he found that he was already halfway to battle paint. By the time he got himself wiped clean and dusted off, the others handing him items that had fallen off his person or out of his pack, most of the pain had subsided, concentrating in three main places: his left side where his ribs ached something fierce, his right shoulder, and the back of his head where he hit the tree. The good news was that nothing appeared to be broken, and the worst injury was to his pride.

"We'll stay with you," the group promised.

Anagalisgi didn't want them to stay with him. He wanted to stew in his embarrassment by himself. But he did not refuse their offer, and they started off down the road at a brisk walk.

They were hardly an imposing force when they walked into Nagutsi', and Anagalisgi was swarmed by both healers and warriors. He timidly explained his fall, assured everyone he was fine, and went to try and find his brother. He found Kiyuga speaking to one of the Nagutsi' families, presumably the one they would be staying with.

"Out fighting Anikusi already?" Kiyuga joked upon seeing his scuffed up little brother. "Well, be sure to leave some for the rest of us."

"Oh, there's plenty out there, I'm sure," Anagalisgi sighed.

"Come inside, brother," the man of the house laughed. "You will fight well tomorrow."

The man's name was Svkta, and his wife was Gigi of Anisahoni, heavily pregnant with their first natural child. Two more small ones clung to her legs, afraid of the sudden company. Anagalisgi and Kiyuga were not the only warriors staying with them; a dozen or so joined them, packing in until there was no more floor space to sleep on.

"I know the Anikusi well," Svkta said as they gathered around the cook fire. "They raided my village when I was a boy just becoming a man, and they took me. I lived among them for four cycles until Tawodi and his warriors freed me and brought me back. Ever since then, I have gone on every raid and taken every prize I can. Some I have given away. Others I cherish." He looked at the two toddlers still huddling around Gigi. He nodded solemnly and looked around at the group. "I, and every warrior here, will most certainly appreciate your help and support."

"Do you know their language?" one of Aganstata's senior warriors inquired.

Svkta nodded confidently. "I do know it. I have spoken to their warriors on the rare occasion that we speak, and I mediate for new captives until they learn our language. I will know if they call out to attack or retreat."

That boosted the confidence of the warriors, and conversation soon turned to all their daring exploits, bragging about past glory and imagining what the new day would hold.

Strictly speaking, it would be another two days until they left Nagutsi'. The Lower Towns were not like the Overhill. Where the Overhill Aniyvwiya had been consolidated into one power and one capital via Gvnagadoga, the Lower Towns were still primarily independent, and it would take more time to raise more warriors. More were said to be coming. Then, even once they departed, it would be another couple days until they reached their raiding destination. Anagalisgi had heard it mentioned briefly when the healers had been fussing over him when he entered Nagutsi' and Aganstata and Saloli had been speaking with Tawodi.

Taliwa was the name of the village. Anikusi were converging there as well as one of their allies, who called themselves Appalachiola. The only reason for this was to launch another raid. Nagutsi' was one of the last Lower Towns still standing; they couldn't allow themselves to be wiped out.

With almost all of the Lower Town warriors assembled in Nagutsi'' as well as the three hundred from the Overhill, Anagalisgi estimated their numbers to be about four hundred or so. As more warriors came from the farther Lower Towns, as well as the Middle Towns, that number grew to be almost five hundred. It seemed every Aniyvwiya had descended upon the tiny Lower Town of Nagutsi'. They had to get moving or there would soon be no more room, regardless of any raid.

Excitement was high, and it was contagious. Even Anagalisgi felt as though he could take on a whole legion of Anikusi, and he found himself bragging right alongside his brother. He came back to the waking world when Aganstata called him for counsel the day before they were supposed to leave.

"You've not spoken of your dreams these last couple days," the warrior stated. "I assume this means you've had no ill omens or warnings of our mission?"

"None, Aganstata," Anagalisgi told him. "I've seen no ill fortune for us."

"Nor has Nakatiha," Tawodi said, indicating the Nagutsi' adawehi, "and all signs point to a great victory for us, such that we may even end this war with the Anikusi, so we may focus on our other problems and misfortunes."

"That would be a welcome thing."

"Indeed it would," Aganstata agreed. "We are leaving in the morning, but you will stay behind."

"But I am Anihwaya; I am expected to be a warrior."

"Yet the spirits have called you to be a dreamer. Your brother is warrior enough for both of you. I want you to stay here with Nakatiha and the others. You will bless our journey this evening at the fire and in the morning when we leave. And you will prepare our dead when we have returned. This is your calling, not as a warrior, but a dreamer."

Anagalisgi dipped his head. "Vv, Aganstata."

He was dismissed. He felt relieved but also anxious. He had the important role of foreseeing good and ill fortune, yet he seemed only to see evil omens. On top of that, it seemed to be entirely unrelated to this impending conquest and instead focused on something far more sinister. Furthermore, he could do little about it. He could speak his dreams and give interpretations, but there was little he could do in the waking world once the information was imparted.

That night, the warriors danced around the fire to the many drums echoing in the darkness, the women and elders wailing their songs and prayers and memories of past glory. Nakatiha, Anagalisgi, and other attending uku and adawehi from various villages called out blessings and fortune and might and power and victory upon their warriors. Anagalisgi took care to ensure that he was the one who touched Kiyuga during the proclamation, praying aloud for his success, silently praying that this was not the time for the Promise to be fulfilled. Then he moved on to the next warrior. And the first lights of dawn peeked over the horizon.

DᏨᎯᎻᎢ ᎤᎶᏗᎳ

Taliwa

It was dawn before the end of the dancing and the fire, but there was no time for rest. Invigorated by the energy and the blessings and the promise of glory in battle, the warriors left Nagutsi', Kiyuga momentarily lost in the fray until he could push himself toward the front of the pack. They kept up for a good while during the morning, but slowed as the heat of the day and fatigue began to wear on them.

They stopped in the heat of the day to drink and rest. Kiyuga thought himself far too excited to sleep in spite of his exhaustion, but was asleep just as soon as his head hit the ground.

He found himself dreaming of his brother, though he couldn't say why. Nor could he understand the dream. He stood in the forest as the sun was going down. He was on a trail he did not know, and just down the trail was Anagalisgi. His brother was just close enough for Kiyuga to know it was him, but still a fair distance away. Kiyuga started walking toward his brother, but about halfway there, he could go no farther. Something invisible prevented him from moving closer to Anagalisgi. He saw nothing, felt nothing, heard nothing out of the ordinary.

On the other side of this invisible barrier, Anagalisgi looked on, unsurprised. In fact, he seemed quite aware of what was happening, resigned to it, even.

"I'm not going to let you go," Kiyuga told him. "I have to go first, remember? I have to clear the way."

But his brother said nothing, and suddenly he was gone, leaving Kiyuga alone in the darkening forest. He reached out and discovered the barrier was still there, even without Anagalisgi.

He woke slowly, almost uncertain whether he was truly awake. He sat up and looked around at all the sleeping warriors to reassure himself. What did his dream mean? Should he return to Nagutsi' to ask for clarification? Was it an ill omen of the battle to come? Could it be something in the future? He did not believe that Anagalisgi would hide any bad visions, especially if they involved his family, but what if?

Kiyuga had little time to mull it over before Aganstata was rousing everyone from their slumber and bidding them rise. This was only meant to be a short nap so they might continue on until dusk. Then they would camp for the night and proceed in the morning once more. With the flattening of the land, they moved far more swiftly. The Overhill warriors especially moved quite fast as they were more accustomed to scrambling up and down great slopes.

Again he found himself toward the front of the pack alongside Tolatsi, the long-legged warrior who was equally as excited for his first real battle. Skirmishes and raids were all well and good, but this would be the defining moment for them as they worked to defeat the Anikusi once and for all. They exchanged a glance as they kept pace.

The sun went down and they made camp. Aganstata, Saloli, and Tawodi sent out hunters and conversed quietly for a bit. Kiyuga watched them, trying to study their behavior and figure out what they were saying. He could not, though he did spot Tsiyu hovering around them, close to their fire.

"Tsiyu will have much to answer for to Gvnagadoga," Tolatsi murmured, following Kiyuga's gaze. "More than Saloli, Tsiyu betrayed his father as well as his people."

Kiyuga sat around the fire with a dozen warriors his own age, some with good battle experience, a few even married.

"They are only doing what they think is right," Kiyuga said quietly. "It may be wrong, but we can't fault them for it entirely."

"What if they won't come with us, even if we win?"

"I don't know. It would do us no good to fight. The Europeans are not our only enemies, and we cannot afford to turn against each other."

"Surely Saloli would listen to an adawehi, if he spoke to the spirits and discovered their disapproval," Uhnvtsati stated. "Your brother has spoken many times of ill fortune. It is why Gvnagadoga chose to side with the British."

"Atagulkalu is also a friend of the British," Kiyuga said. "He traveled far away to their land, before most of us here were born. It makes sense to honor one's friends and become allies. And if the spirits decree it the better alliance, then so be it."

He did not inspire the enthusiasm he was hoping for, but he made no further mention of it. Instead, conversation turned toward their plans for exploits and glory, which steered them to talking about the girls they hoped to impress. There was a bit of a tussle when three of them expressed interest in the same girl, and it was quickly broken up by Totsuwa, one of Saloli's warriors.

"Foolish boys," the warrior said, though his tone betrayed amusement. "There will be plenty of time for battle in the coming days, with much glory and spoils to be had. But for now, speak not of foolish things. Be patient, and wait for Aganstata and the others to speak."

Those who had been tussling looked appropriately chastised, though Kiyuga and the rest who had been watching also looked a bit sheepish and meekly returned to their fire and their food. There were some mischievous glances exchanged among those in the group and a few chuckles at unvoiced jokes, but no one did anything further to prove their worth against each other.

They received no instruction from Aganstata or the other senior warriors that night, and Kiyuga and the rest went to sleep, eagerly anticipating what the morning would bring.

The following day was more of the same as they hurried to cover ground, and soon it all began to blur together for Kiyuga. Everyone always loved to tell stories of battle and glory, but the stories and songs always seemed to neglect the mundane parts of just getting there. Make no mistake, Kiyuga was still eager to prove himself and bring home spoils, but the trekking bored him.

One morning, Kiyuga woke up on his own, with no prodding from Aganstata or Saloli or any of the senior warriors. Looking around, those who were also awake were also confused. There was some murmuring about some of the warriors being gone. Had they deserted in the night? No, that couldn't be it. All of those who had gone had experience. Some were from Saloli's warriors, others Tawodi's, and a few Aganstata's.

Kiyuga was just stirring the coals back into flame when the call went up for intruders. He jumped to his feet, reaching for his knife. He couldn't see well beyond the camp, but he did hear friendly voices, and he noticed how everyone began to stand down. Reluctantly, and not a little disappointed, Kiyuga put away his knife and returned to the fire.

The missing warriors from earlier had been roused at the crack of dawn to scout ahead, search out the Anikusi, learn, and report back. They had done just that, and now they spoke to the leaders and senior warriors.

"It would be great to see battle and become a seasoned warrior," Tolatsi said. "Then we might know what they're saying."

"We will in time," Kiyuga said sagely. "But first we must listen to what they say today so we can well prove ourselves in battle. That is the first step to becoming a seasoned and senior warrior."

It didn't take long for the leaders to come up with a plan. They relayed it to their senior warriors who took it to the rest of those waiting who were busying themselves with refreshing their paint. A warrior called Uhtalugi'a approached Kiyuga and the rest, bringing along another group of hopeful warriors who were even more green. He divided them, sending some to see other warriors in other groups, but Kiyuga remained with Uhtalugi'a.

"The village they call Taliwa," Uhtalugi'a began. "It is not more than a short run, and we will be there before the morning is over. There are perhaps a thousand warriors, both Anikusi and their ally, Appalachiola. There are many women and children as well. By orders of Aganstata, in accordance with the old adawehi who proclaimed this war before us, there are to be no survivors save those children still on the breast. They may be spared and taken. The rest is up to you.

"Utsugi will take warriors first to surround the village and kill their scouts and sentries. Aganstata will lead the main attack with Saloli and Tawodi. We will follow Adahi and cut off their escape to the south. We shall crush them as between two rocks, and we will show them the might of the Aniyvwiya!"

The group cheered, as did the other groups as they were told of the plan. Then they all came together to hear Aganstata speak. Kiyuga looked on with wild admiration for the senior warrior. He was a splendid man, his body scarred deeply because of smallpox he had endured when he was but a child, in addition to the numerous wounds he had taken in battle. He was an accomplished leader and almost mythical as he was said to have never lost a man in battle.

"Even now we are in the midst of battle," Aganstata said. "As we speak, Utsugi and his warriors are ensuring our approach will be smooth so we may descend upon them as a fierce pack of wolves, working together to bring down our prey. We will end this war!" Cheers. "And we will reclaim ourselves as Aniyvwiya!"

The warriors, Kiyuga included, erupted into cheers and Aganstata led the charge through the forest. The whooping continued only for a short distance before it reduced to the calm determination of the chase.

Kiyuga was dizzy with excitement as he pushed through the trees and undergrowth. This was real. This was happening. They were going to battle. His heart raced and he could hear the blood pounding in his ears. More than just a quick raid, more than a happenstance skirmish, this was his first real, true battle.

He anxiously felt all of his weapons, reassuring himself that they were all there and in good order. Knives, one on each leg, one on his hip, and another on his left upper arm. Skala galogwehi, securely on his hip. Rifle, on his back where it had been hitting him for the entire trip. Extra ammunition and powder were in their respective places on his belt. Club, it had been attached to his rifle but now he held it in hand. He was ready for anything; he wanted to experience everything.

He wanted to push ahead as he had been over the last several days, but he refrained and stayed with his group. Uhtalugi'a was to his left, Adahi farther ahead. As they ran, the groups began to segregate more and more. Aganstata, Saloli, and Tawodi pushed ahead with their warriors while Adahi slipped back to be with Uhtalugi'a and the rest of them. Gradually, they began to slow from a run to a jog, and then down to a walk. Aganstata then slowed them even more, almost to a creep. He said something to his senior warriors that Kiyuga did not catch, but the orders eventually rippled through the group.

They moved off the main road, slipping into the trees. Where before they had been all about speed and moving quickly to get to their destination, now it was about stealth and silence. They ducked low into the ferns and slunk along like snakes. Kiyuga made a point of memorizing his group, what they wore, how they were painted, and their positions. Creeping around, he could only go by glimpses through the greenery and the sounds of their movements.

Kiyuga sucked in a breath as he pushed aside a clump of bracken and discovered a body, one of the sentries that Utsugi and his warriors had killed. He spotted a beaded charm around the man's wrist; his body had already been claimed for spoils. While spoils were typically a free-for-all, some allowances could be made, such as stealth attacks where time could not be taken to strip the body right away, and claims were made with such charms.

They crested the slope overlooking the town of Taliwa. Indeed it was too small of a town for such a large force, much as Nagutsi' was far too small for the many warriors that had rested there. The forest ended and opened up to vast, rolling hills. Kiyuga could not see much more than that as he could only peek through the greenery. To the left, he could make out a break in the grass and trees where the main road came through. To his right, he spotted Uhtalugi'a briefly as the warrior began moving away, following after Adahi.

They moved back a bit into the trees to hide themselves as they skirted around the town, now moving just a bit faster so they could be ready when Aganstata and the rest of them arrived.

South of Taliwa were the village crop fields. Adahi went with a couple groups through them, but Uhtalugi'a and his warriors, which included Kiyuga, slipped around them. Kiyuga never heard any cries of alarm, never more than a grunt of effort or pain, but as he peeked through the rows of corn and beans, he saw more bodies, with Aniyvwiya warriors quickly moving from one row to the next.

He lost track of Adahi, but managed to keep sight of Uhtalugi'a and the others. He saw several of them stop and crouch down even lower in the undergrowth until they were on their bellies. Kiyuga did the same, heart thudding hard against his chest. Which weapon did he want to grab? Their job was to cut off the Anikusi escape and crush them between themselves and Aganstata's warriors. His rifle wouldn't do much good; in the chaos, he was just as likely to hit one of his own people. His club and a knife would do well, then.

He froze when he heard a twig snap near him and movement in the undergrowth. Calmly, slowly, he reached for a knife and listened for the stranger's position.

"Kiyuga." It was Uhtalugi'a. He crawled through the dirt and whispered. Kiyuga could just barely make him out through a pile of brush. "Adahi and his warriors have gone to the other side of the road. When Aganstata comes and begins his attack, we will close the road with Adahi and move to crush the Anikusi in their town."

"I understand," Kiyuga hissed in reply.

Uhtalugi'a moved off.

The forest was quiet, as if all the birds and animals knew what was about to happen and so retreated to safety. Kiyuga could hear the sounds of the town, men and women working, children playing, people talking and laughing. He did not know the Anikusi language, but he was able to pick up on at least two different languages being spoken. Anikusi and Appalachiola, he guessed. What were they planning? Had they expected to raid Nagutsi' and fully destroy the remaining Lower Towns? It was just as well that they came, Saloli or no!

A thousand thoughts went through Kiyuga's mind as he adjusted his grip on his club and reached for a knife. What good service he was doing to defend his people! What spoils he would bring back! If this ended the war with the Anikusi, there would be stories told of this battle and the warriors who were here! He had to ensure that his name would be mentioned. He had to do something to distinguish himself, set himself apart.

He put the knife away and slipped the rifle off his back. If they were to move as Aganstata came down the hill, there would be ample time and space to get off at least one shot, two if he could get his skala galogwehi out in time. Then he would switch to his club and knife.

How he wanted to look above the grass and brush and see what was happening! He wanted to look and choose his target. If he killed an important warrior or leader, surely his name would be known! If he took great spoils, he would be known. But he could not look to see and plan. He puzzled over this.

He wondered where Aganstata had gotten off to. Had they been delayed? Held up? Had there been an argument between Aganstata and Saloli? Had one of them been injured in some way? Had they been ambushed by the Anikusi? How would the rest of them know? How long were they supposed to wait? Did Adahi know what was going on? Was he worried?

A spider crawled across Kiyuga's hand. He brushed it away.

He shifted position in the dirt, looking for the others. He did not see anyone. In a way, that was good, as it meant that no one could see him, or so he hoped. But why were they taking so long? What was the delay?

Kiyuga adjusted his grip on his rifle, carefully turning to look and plan his next move. When the time came, he would have to move quickly to get to the road and get off a shot before too many Aniyvwiya made firing impossible. He picked out the spot where he would run to. It looked decent enough, he thought. Near enough to the road, but it seemed to afford an excellent path into the town when they started moving and pushing the Anikusi back.

Back into position. He had to stay focused. He couldn't let his mind slip or else he would be slow. If he was slow, he looked foolish. If he looked foolish, no one would speak his name except, perhaps, in mourning, if foolishness got him killed. He couldn't let that happen, not at his first battle. He was going to be a great warrior. He would be the skiagvsta one day, and Anagalisgi would be the uku. He would be known, and it would start today, with this battle. He again readied himself and waited for the signal to attack.

It felt like an eternity, and Kiyuga briefly wondered if perhaps the battle had already been fought and he somehow missed it.

He jumped when he heard the alarm go up from the town, scraping his head on the brush, loosening his grip on his club, and dropping his rifle. Cursing, he scrambled to get everything back together and jump into position just as he'd planned. In the distance, on the other side of the town, he heard Aganstata and his warriors whooping and hollering as they streamed down the hillside.

Kiyuga leapt into the spot he'd chosen, dropped his club, readied his rifle, and fired. Around him, his fellow warriors emerged from their hiding spots. Those who had guns used them as best they could while the rest stood back and waited. Kiyuga saw a number of Anikusi fall, or else stumble as they were hit, but it was impossible to say whose bullets killed whom. On the north side of the town, Kiyuga could see a number of Aganstata's warriors had branched off to surround the town and fire upon the Anikusi until the Aniyvwiya arrived.

The Anikusi, taken by surprise and confused, struggled to defend themselves for the first few chaotic moments. Women scrambled to find their children and herd them to safety. Some went into their homes, others decided to take their chances and try to break through the line of warriors surrounding the town. A group of three women and half a dozen children of varying ages ran down the road, straight toward Kiyuga and the others. Kiyuga took down one woman, Adahi another. The last woman and several children got past them, but the warriors with clubs and knives set upon them. Kiyuga did not turn to look, but he heard.

Finally the Anikusi warriors got themselves together. To the north, they ran with clubs, spears, and anything they could grab. At the south end, they grabbed guns and did their best to stave off attack from Adahi and the warriors, providing cover fire for women and children to escape. Kiyuga jumped back to take cover behind a tree, squeezing his eyes shut as a bullet ripped through the bark, sending splinters everywhere.

He reloaded his rifle, quickly looked around the tree, and fired. He saw the warrior go down, but it was unclear if he was dead. Without thinking, Kiyuga abandoned his rifle, instead grabbing his club and running forth toward the village.

His heart hammered in his chest and the blood thundered through his ears. He grabbed one fleeing woman and used her as a sort of shield while the warriors with the rifles tried to figure out what to do. Do they fire at him, possibly harming one of their own, or at the other warriors still blocking the road? In the time it took them to decide, Kiyuga had released the woman so he could strike down another Anikusi warrior with his club, and Adahi and the others were able to shoot several more before calling for their own charge.

The north and west side of the town were inundated with Aniyvwiya warriors, forming almost a wall around the town, forcing the Anikusi to fight or attempt to flee. Aganstata's and Saloli's warriors held that line and pressed ever more while Tawodi's people made their way around to the east. With Kiyuga leading the charge from the south, that route was quickly becoming less of an option.

Kiyuga rounded a corner and was suddenly dazed as something hit him in the face. He heard and felt his nose break and the blood begin to flow. Looking inside the house, he found a dozen women and a plethora of children huddled together. He dodged another blow—discovering that he'd been hit with a cast iron frying pan—but she could not dodge his as he struck her with his club. The children screamed, some began to cry. Then Kiyuga saw the glow of fire as someone on the other side of the wall set the house on fire.

There was more screaming, and Kiyuga figured he delivered a

merciful death to any who tried to escape and met his club or knife. He left the house, and just as he was turning, fire erupted in his chest. He stumbled back, hit the house, found that it was hot and full of smoke, turned and tried to crawl away, discovered his right arm was painful to move and it hurt to breathe. He managed to stand and only just turned to look for his attacker when his attacker was suddenly upon him.

Kiyuga caught the man's arm as he tried to stab him with a knife. He dropped his club and tried to reach for his own knife, but the blow to the face and the pain in his chest made it difficult. He fumbled for the knife on his arm. His attacker saw what he was going for; he pressed down harder with his own knife, trying to break Kiyuga's strength while he reached for the knife. Gritting his teeth against the pain in his chest and the heat from the fire behind him, Kiyuga struck a hard blow upwards, into the man's jaw. He heard the man's teeth clack together even as his assault lessened.

Kiyuga was able to get his knife, but his attacker leapt back a few steps to get out of the way. Breathing hard, Kiyuga prepared for an assault, but before the man could take two steps, he went down courtesy of a shot to the head. Silently saying a prayer of thanks, Kiyuga let out a breath and tried to calm down, figure out exactly how and where he'd been hurt.

"Are you all right?" It was Adahi coming up beside him and getting him away from the house that was now engulfed in flame.

"Fine," Kiyuga told him.

"You've been shot."

"I'm fine."

Reflexes kicked in before he could process what was going on as he spotted an attacker coming up behind Adahi. He grabbed Adahi's skala galogwehi, aimed, and fired without thinking. The whole thing only took about two heartbeats. Adahi startled as he turned to see what had happened. He looked back at Kiyuga.

"Thank you, my brother."

"The battle is not yet over," Kiyuga said, straightening. "We are not done here."

Kiyuga went back to grab his club but found that the fire was consuming it. Elsewhere, more and more houses were being set on fire. As the Anikusi and their allies fled, Aganstata, Saloli, and Tawodi sent some small groups to start fires and sent others through the narrow streets to cut off any who tried to escape.

Kiyuga and Adahi turned down one of these narrow streets, catching a glimpse of some fleeing people and giving chase. In a moment of clarity, Kiyuga saw that there were six of them, three warriors, one woman, and two children. They were heading for the cornfields.

"Keep them heading this way," Adahi said. "I'm going to go around and cut them off."

Kiyuga could only nod, tasting blood in his mouth from his bloody nose. Now that he'd had time to understand the pain in his chest, his broken nose made itself known, and now his whole face felt enormous. Groaning, he forced himself to focus on the task at hand, pursuing those who tried to escape.

Kiyuga pursued the escapees into a row of corn. When he was about a quarter of the way through, the escapees more than half, Adahi appeared at the other end. Not even hesitating, the Anikusi broke through the row of corn to the adjacent row. Kiyuga followed while Adahi stayed just outside of the rows.

Three rows in, one of the children fell. The woman, still running, could not stop in time before Kiyuga was on the child, a young boy, perhaps two years of age. He started squalling. The woman, two rows ahead, looked at Kiyuga, her gaze filled with terror. Before she could do anything, she went down, succumbing to Adahi's club. One of the warriors had stayed behind to defend her, the other two had taken the second child.

Kiyuga looked at the small boy at his feet, still screaming. He did not have his club, and his strength and will was quickly waning, buried under the aching and throbbing throughout his body. Adahi looked through the broken corn and stepped into his row, the other two warriors and one child forgotten.

"Well?" he wondered.

"What?" Kiyuga asked.

"Are you going to kill it or adopt it?"

"A child of two isn't on the breast, I think, but I don't have my club."

Raising a brow, Adahi struck the child with no more thought than striking a fly. It went abruptly silent.

"I think you are wounded," the seasoned warrior stated. "Your head is full of clouds."

"I am wounded," Kiyuga sighed. "And I am tired. But I will not give up."

Adahi grinned and put his hand on his shoulder. "Well said. Come now. There are others trying to escape."

They searched the cornfields, killing any who tried to hide in them. When they emerged, Kiyuga saw that the town had been decimated and most of it was burning. Aganstata and the others were giving chase in all directions, across the open fields, into the forest, wherever fleeing Anikusi could be found. But not all warriors were needed for this, and some remained in the town, already on the hunt for spoils.

"I see you looking," Adahi said, grinning. "Go, brother. You have proven yourself well this day. Take your spoils."

Kiyuga hadn't realized he'd been holding his breath, but getting permission from Adahi saw its release. He looked at the older warrior but could only briefly nod his thanks before heading back to the town, or what used to be the town.

The smell of burning flesh would never leave Kiyuga, but in the moment, he was unconcerned. Few buildings were not on fire, but they burned quickly, leaving blackened husks. A few clouds rolled over the sun, and a chill breeze promised rain.

He stopped at the first body he found and started rummaging. The Anikusi had trade relations with the French as well as the Spanish, and he found many trinkets and baubles that he knew he could not get anywhere else. Exotic and rare jewelry would make a fine gift for a pretty girl, and it would help to prove his own conquests. Elsewhere, the warriors were joking around, showing off feathery hats and glittering jewelry, pretending to be this or that person.

Kiyuga ducked into one of the few houses that had been spared fire. While clearly a home to a family, he could see that many visiting warriors had slept here as well and left plenty of things to pillage. He took a bayonet, a few shirts, a pair of boots. He even found a few of the red coats the British were so fond of. He took feathers and jewelry and adornments. He took a large bag, such as the Europeans used to carry large packs of letters. He took things for which he had no name and other things he just thought were interesting.

A few more warriors entered the house just as he was exiting, and he found that most of the warriors who had given chase had returned, some still whooping and hollering, some already dancing. Some had already taken spoils from those they'd killed, chasing them down through the forest and fields. Despite any injuries, most were in a jovial mood. Kiyuga felt that way, truly he did, but he was exhausted. As the excitement died down, he began shaking, and he searched another body to cover it up. He was not a trembling coward, he told himself. He'd done his part to bring victory to his people. But, oh, how his face hurt. He could barely breathe, and he was afraid to know what he looked like. His face was probably enormous; it certainly felt that way.

Aganstata, Saloli, and Tawodi were among the last to return, smiling and laughing among themselves, picking up spoils here and there. Tawodi broke off first, going to speak to a few of his senior warriors who were standing around, satisfied with their spoils, and directing them to some task.

Kiyuga rejoined those from his group, all of them showing off their spoils and talking about the battle, some already bragging about their exploits.

"Kiyuga, brother!" Tolatsi greeted. "How—oh, goodness. What happened to your face?"

Gingerly, Kiyuga dared touch his face. The blood from his nose had finally dried, but his whole face was swollen and tender, his nose like fiery hornets when he touched it. After a moment, he said, "There were at least a dozen of them. At least I won."

That got them laughing uproariously. He might have joined them, except it hurt to do much more than talk, let alone smile and laugh.

Aganstata and Saloli made their way over to them.

"Well done, young warriors," Aganstata praised warmly. "We have — what happened to your face?"

Again, all eyes turned to Kiyuga.

"He looks a bit like a bloated toad, I think," Saloli teased. "Is that what we should call you from now on? Shall that be your great warrior name?"

"Come now, Saloli," Aganstata said, though he was still smiling. "We've all had our fair share of embarrassing moments in battle. But he is the victor here! We all are!" Loud agreement from the group. Aganstata nodded and looked at Kiyuga. "Adahi told me how you led the southern charge, distracting the Anikusi warriors and breaking their defense." The cheering got louder, and Kiyuga thought that Aganstata looked a little prouder. "Soon enough, when we have returned to Nagutsi', I will make sure all hear of it. And when we return to Itsa'ti, I will speak of you to Atagulkalu. You have shown yourself to be true today, Yvgidahi."

Kiyuga hoped he conveyed the appropriate amount of enthusiasm and respect, but with his swollen face, it was difficult to tell.

"But now," the senior warrior went on, very serious now, "we have tasks to attend to. If you are finished collecting your trophies, collect now the dead and help the wounded. We will return to Nagutsi' quickly."

The young warriors agreed and moved off to do just that.

Of the five hundred or so warriors who descended upon Taliwa that day, they suffered only fifty dead, including Nanyehi's husband. She refused to let anyone take him from her, nor tend to her own wounds until after his burial. Kiyuga watched her politely from a distance, to see if she might eventually ask for help. She never did.

Most everyone had injuries of one form or another, many of them scratches and scrapes, bumps and bruises. A few suffered broken limbs, and there were a couple twisted ankles, a dislocated finger here and there. Broken ribs and dislocated shoulders were also on the list.

"We will meet up with Nakatiha and the others tonight," Saloli was saying. "Do what you can until we can reach them."

The thrill of battle had died down, and the spoils had been divvied up. It was all over. It was a surreal feeling, Kiyuga thought. In the heat of the moment, every heartbeat was an eternity. Now he could barely remember anything about it. He thought about the charge he'd supposedly led. He remembered fumbling his club and his rifle. He remembered jumping up to fight. Vaguely he remembered grabbing something as he charged forward. It had been a person. Had he been helping someone? He couldn't recall.

He definitely remembered being hit in the face, and then it was blurry for a minute or two. He remembered being shot. Had Adahi been trying to help him up? Why had he struggled?

And then there was the cornfield, chasing the people trying to escape. He remembered catching a child. The child had been screaming mightily. He killed it and put an end to that. No. No, Adahi had been the one to strike the child. Kiyuga had lost his club in the fire. That's right, he remembered now.

And then it was over. Almost as if it hadn't happened. But it had. As evidenced by the town burned down around him.

High regard was paid to the bodies as they were wrapped and litters hastily constructed to carry them. If they could meet with the priests tonight, they could hold proper ceremonies for them to ensure proper care for the souls. More litters were built to assist a few who were unable to make the journey up and down the hills they would be crossing. Everything was arranged just so, and Aganstata looked ready to order them to move out.

Saloli and Tawodi, along with half a dozen more senior warriors, started up the road first, if only to ensure their safety in the event that the Anikusi had other warriors hiding in the area. It was unlikely, but they couldn't allow themselves to be caught off guard.

Next was the procession of the dead, each litter carried by family of the deceased. Nanyehi carried her husband. Aganstata assisted her, for she was his niece. She appeared stoic, though tears still flowed freely down her cheeks.

On either side of this procession, and for a good distance afterwards, was another contingent of warriors, their primary mission to ensure the deceased made it to the priests to be honored and buried. After them came the severely wounded, surrounded by another contingent of warriors, moving more slowly than the rest.

Adahi, Uhtalugi'a, Kiyuga, and the others brought up the rear.

Despite the fatigue that was settling over the group at large, there was still much talking and laughter, each man and woman bragging of his exploits and daring deeds. Everyone hoped to be spoken of to Atagalkula, their fearless bravery and great courage against their foe. Kiyuga smiled inwardly, knowing that Aganstata had said it himself that he would speak of him to Atagalkula.

"How is it that we ran here over days and have taken the town, yet we will meet up with the priests this evening?" Tolatsi was asking Adahi. "We are moving terribly slow now."

Adahi grinned. "Aganstata asked that the priests remain behind for a day in Nagutsi', then travel the same road so they could meet us quickly, to honor our dead and sing their songs. Then we will return to Nagutsi' for a great feast with our brothers and sisters from the Lower Towns. Then we shall return home to Itsa'ti and the other Overhill villages."

"Maybe by then, Kiyuga will not look like such a toad," another warrior, Saliksgwo, said.

"Yes, then he will be able to look at the girls and they will not be repulsed by him," Tolatsi laughed. "All the adornments of your spoils will not make a toad not a toad."

"At least I have a goal to strive for to be handsome again," Kiyuga told them smartly. "The rest of you must suffer with your faces all the time."

That started a bit of a tussle, but Adahi barked at them to knock it off and they did. Kiyuga was glad for it. It wasn't so much that his face hurt, but his chest was throbbing and his arm was quickly going numb. He didn't think he'd broken any bones, but the lead ball was still buried in his chest, and it ached. It hurt to breathe, feeling his body move, the ball lodged deep in the muscle.

He tried not to let it bother him, tried not to let the pain show. He was a brave warrior, fearlessly charging the southern line, breaking the Anikusi defense and crushing them against Aganstata's forces. He couldn't let this little hornet sting bring him down now. He would wait until tonight when wounds could be more appropriately tended to by the priests and healers.

More clouds rolled in and it began to sprinkle. A few people breathed a sigh of relief as some wounds were cooled. Others gritted their teeth as other wounds were cleaned and made noticeable. Kiyuga, for his part, felt relieved, and he turned his throbbing face to the sky. He could feel the paint washing off his body, but he didn't care. He'd done his part, and he no longer needed to intimidate his enemies.

He managed to wipe the blood off his face. As his meticulous paint became smudged and smeared beyond recognition, he wiped that off as well, using leaves or just his hands. Around him, as conversation had faded with the rain, he saw others had similar ideas. Soon the ground was stained with paint, running down the hill in a multicolor river.

Still they trekked on, seeming to go ever slower throughout the day. Those carrying the deceased refused to give up their vigils, and those with lesser wounds soon looked no better than those with greater wounds. Kiyuga wanted to ask when and where they were supposed to meet the priests and healers, but he did not. He was a warrior, not a child.

Somewhere in the group, a baby began to cry. A dozen infants had been taken, only those still on the breast, as ordained. They would be taken back to Itsa'ti and raised with an Aniyvwiya family. Some might be told of their heritage, but they would remain Aniyvwiya. It was their way. Atagulkalu himself had been stolen from the Nipissing as a young child, only a couple years old, and now he was the skiagvsta. Hearing the infant cry, Kiyuga wondered if any of them might be a leader one day.

It was late when they spotted the distant glow of a fire, and they were quickly upon the priests and healers all come from Nagutsi'. The returning warriors were met with cheers, prayers of thanks, and a song beaten out on several drums. Kiyuga felt his strength renewed. By the time he and the others at the back of the group reached the camp, there was activity everywhere. The dead had been taken to be prepared, the wounded waited their turn to see a healer, and all waited to be cleansed from battle and death.

Kiyuga found a spot at a fire at just sat down, taking it all in and glad to be back among his own people in their own land after a great victory. A young girl, likely a healer in training, brought him some soup and inquired after him.

"My nose is broken and my face hurts," he told her, "and I've been shot in the chest. But I'm no worse for wear."

He knew it meant he would have to wait a while, but he was not suffering. The soup again renewed his strength, and he waited eagerly to see what happened next. There would be songs and dancing and mourning of the dead. There would be tales of heroes of ages past and bragging of those in the present who thought they were heroes. Kiyuga would be among them, he knew. He rather enjoyed the attention, the thought of Aganstata going to Atagulkalu and speaking of his brave deeds.

When he finished the soup, he stood and walked around a bit. He did not see Anagalisgi, though he suspected his brother was busy preparing the dead. He paused by the large fire, stepping back from the heat and rush of air as the flames licked the sky. He listened. Aganstata, Saloli, and Tawodi were speaking. Perhaps they were discussing which warriors they would speak of before Atagulkalu.

"The Lower Towns will return and rebuild on that spot," Tawodi was saying. "We will reclaim the towns and the land that was ours, and build over their bodies."

"We should have no trouble from the Anikusi now," Aganstata said calmly. "Or any of their allies."

"Indeed," Saloli said. "For we are Aniyvwiya! And we have a strong leader." He slapped Aganstata on the back, then sighed and grew serious. "We cannot afford division. I see that now. If we split up, the Europeans will surely attack us and we will have no one to call on. We must stick together for the sake of the people." He shook his head. "Fool was I, but I still don't like the thought of allying with the British."

"Gvnagadoga and Atagulkalu do not make the decision lightly. And it is not about supporting this European people or that European people. It is about our people, the Aniyvwiya. You were only just becoming a man when Atagulkalu was captured in battle and taken to the French. Before that, he treated with the British king across the sea. He, like Gvnagadoga, has seen both European peoples, he has listened to all sides, and he has made his decision. We must do our part not to undermine it and jeopardize our people."

Saloli looked greatly chastened, a younger warrior being scolded by a senior warrior. Not just a senior warrior, but *the* senior warrior. It would not be surprising for him to become skiagvsta if something happened to Atagulkalu, Kiyuga thought.

"And just as we must be united, so we must also prepare our warriors," Aganstata went on. "I saw Nanyehi's husband killed, and she picked up his rifle and continued to fight, charging into the fray. This I will speak of to Atagulkalu."

Tawodi nodded. "And I saw Nvyohi kill three men with a single swing of his hatchet. He will be honored."

"Yvgidahi charged the south line to break Anikusi defenses and crushed them against our warriors. This I will speak of as well."

They listed off more warriors and their deeds to be honored, but Kiyuga had stopped listening. He was going to be spoken of to Atagulkalu! Such an honor, and it was his first true battle! He'd helped to completely destroy the Anikusi, bring peace for his people, and he was going to be honored! He felt his pride swell, but only as much as his chest would allow. He winced, flinched again at the pain in his face, and tried to walk away with some dignity left.

He'd no sooner returned to his spot at the fire than he heard Anagalisgi.

"Kiyuga, there you are!" His brother sat down beside him. "I was wondering—oh. What—?"

"My nose is broken," Kiyuga cut in. "I know. It hurts. The rest of my face hurts, too."

"Oh."

"What were you going to say?"

Anagalisgi fumbled for his words. Finally, "I was just wondering where you'd gotten off to. I didn't see you around here, but I didn't see you with the healers, either. I know I didn't see you among the dead."

"No, but I will be among the honored," Kiyuga told him proudly. "Aganstata told me earlier—and I heard him speaking again just now—he is going to speak of my bravery to Atagulkalu."

"That's great! I am happy for you! My brother Kiyuga, honored Anihwaya warrior."

"It seems I am capable of living up to the reputation others seem to think I have, or will have."

"Of course you are. And this is only the beginning of the things you are meant to do."

Kiyuga did not ask what he was talking about. He couldn't if he had wanted to, for Nakatiha stood and called for quiet. He named all of the fallen warriors, named their clans and their great deeds. He burned incense for them and called on the spirits for safe passage to the next world. At some point, Anagalisgi had left Kiyuga's side and gone to join Nakatiha and the other priests. Somewhere on the other side of the great fire, someone began beating on a drum. More drums joined.

Songs were sung in honor and memory of the dead. Family of the deceased wailed their songs and prayers. Some began to dance, waving beaded ribbons that belonged to those now gone.

Kiyuga could not say that he knew any of the dead on any intimate level. He only recognized about three quarters of them, knew the names of maybe half. But for all that, they were his people, his brothers and sisters. They were united this night.

So he, too, danced for them, for their spirits. There was no right or wrong way to dance, as there was no right or wrong way to mourn. He ignored the pain in his face and chest as he joined the others. It was only right, after all. A warrior may have done brave deeds such as he had done, but he was worthless as a man if he did not take the time to properly mourn and honor the dead.

DꭹᎧᎥᎿᎢ ᏰᎠᎫᎾ

Ayadohlv'i Sgohi

Passageways

Upon their return to Itsa'ti and news of their victory, there was more song and dance and great tales of bravery. As promised, Aganstata spoke to Atagulkalu of Kiyuga and the others who had shown tremendous courage, and their stories were repeated around the fire and for many moons to come. Nanyehi was made Ghigau, the youngest there ever was.

As for Kiyuga, he finally had a battle to match his purported reputation. He was popular again among the girls, but he turned his eye to one in particular, Advtowa of Wild Potato Clan. In addition to the customary deer, he also offered her many of the shiny trinkets and adornments he'd taken from the Anikusi warriors. For a long time, or so it seemed to him, she did not say anything as she rejected his first offer, though he noticed that she did take the trinkets.

Hoping it was a good sign, he offered a second deer and more adornments. And he waited. A whole moon had passed since Taliwa.

"I thought I was supposed to be marrying into the healing clan," Anagalisgi teased him as they went fishing in the river together.

"No one says you can't," Kiyuga told him. "Have you approached any girls since we returned? You may not have spoils, but you were there, and you were excellent at tending to the dead and wounded. I'm surprised you're not trying to woo Advtowa."

"Who is to say I didn't want to? But between me and you, you are the great warrior and the superb hunter. Atagulkalu praised you at the feast for all to behold. I can't measure up to that, not if she had to pick between us. I'll just have to wait until you're no longer eligible."

A splashing in the river interrupted their conversation, and they grabbed their nets, hauling in a dozen fish. They took their catch home for dinner.

"Have you — ?" Kiyuga began as he walked in the door.

"No, I haven't heard anything," Ulisi cut him off. "Be patient."

It was hard to be patient, though he told himself that no news was good news. At least he hoped so. If she rejected his second offer, he had only one more chance before he would be made to wait for another season. What more did he have to prove? Atagulkalu himself had praised him. He had won a great victory and brought back great spoils. He had taken care to hunt down the best deer to offer.

He was hungry, but his anxiety ruined his appetite. He would take a bite, stand, pace a bit. Ulisi would say something to get him to return. He would sit, take a bite, stand, and pace some more.

Finally he went outside, weaving his way through town toward where Advtowa lived. It was nearly sunset, and if the deer remained there after the sun went down, it was a rejection. Heart hammering, he turned the corner.

The deer was gone. Stunned and terribly conflicted, Kiyuga stopped in his tracks. It was gone. More than that, a green wood fire was burning outside, tended by one of her younger brothers. One of her sisters exited the home and set up a smoking rack over the fire. Kiyuga took a step closer.

"Does this mean...?" he wondered, half to himself.

Three woman walked out of the house then; it was Advtowa with her mother and grandmother. They spotted him and paused.

"Yvgidahi," her mother said. "We were just coming to see you and invite you and your family to the feast of your engagement."

"Yes," Kiyuga said, hardly able to comprehend her words. "Yes, I'll go get them now."

"Slow down, child," her grandmother chuckled. "The smoking will take several days, as will the gathering of other feast foods. The adawehi must also be consulted as to the match itself and a fortuitous day for the wedding, which must be announced. Come back in three days. Then we shall be ready."

Suddenly feeling very foolish, Kiyuga tripped over himself and his words as he tried to thank them, say something to Advtowa, and get back home all at the same time. He couldn't escape fast enough, and his grand entry into the house was evidently enough to tell Ulisi all that had happened.

"The feast is in three days," Kiyuga announced.

"Very good," Ulisi said calmly, standing. "That will be more than enough time to prepare the food and consult the adawehi." She took his head in her hands. "I am very happy for you, my son. I know your mother and father would be as well."

"Wado, Agilisi."

She nodded and huffed, letting her arms fall to her sides. "Well, I suppose this means that there is much work to be done. We all have to prepare. I will have to help her and her mother and her grandmother with the feast preparations. Anagalisgi will be working with the adawehi, I am sure. And you should speak to Digvnige about preparing yourself."

And just like that, the three of them scattered, each with his task. Ulisi moved in with Advtowa's family temporarily to help with the feast. Anagalisgi took up residence in the townhouse with the adawehi in order to divine an appropriate wedding day. Kiyuga moved in with his uncle Digvnige to prepare for his role.

As far as the acceptance feast went, his role was basically to brag himself up and let everyone know that he was a good choice for a husband, to present himself as a strong warrior and good hunter before Advtowa's entire clan, to prove that he was worthy of them. Likewise, Advtowa and her family would be bragging about her, proving that she would be a loving, caring, devoted wife and a good mother. There would be much food and dancing, very reminisce of the ceremony that would be held later, once the adawehi approved of the match and divined a day.

There was a bit of anxiety over that, waiting for the adawehi. What if the spirits disapproved, said it was a bad match? Kiyuga knew that everyone would walk away unharmed and there would be no ill will between families, but what then? He couldn't just ask someone else.

Three days may as well have been forever. He found himself incredibly anxious every time he went out hunting. What if he had bad luck and returned with nothing? What if Advtowa or her family saw this? They would think him incompetent! He couldn't let that happen.

The day of the feast was overcast with a hint of rain on the wind. This, too, caused Kiyuga great concern. What if it was a bad omen? He wanted to ask Anagalisgi about it, but his brother remained with the adawehi and they had not arrived yet.

Everything was set up and both families present, along with more members of both clans. Corn, squash, berries, and fish accompanied the smoked venison. He would have to bring another deer to present to Advtowa at their wedding, assuming there was one. They would not be permitted to eat until the adawehi had come to render the verdict of the spirits. Kiyuga's stomach grumbled in hunger even as his heart pounded in his chest.

Finally, they arrived. Gvnagadoga came first, followed by half a dozen others. Anagalisgi brought up the rear. Respects were paid to the adawehi, and then there was a long moment of anxious silence.

Kiyuga felt the sweat run down the back of his neck as he waited, and his heart skipped a beat when Gvnagadoga shifted his stance and opened his mouth to speak.

"The spirits have declared this a most suitable match," he said.

There were grins and smiles and whoops all around, not the least of which came from Kiyuga himself as he met his betrothed's gaze. Advtowa's posture was relaxed and her face beamed with sunlight.

"The ceremony shall take place in nine days," the old uku continued, "on the night of the half moon."

No more needed to be said as the acceptance feast began in earnest. Congratulations were passed around on all sides, and Kiyuga was slapped on the back so many times he was amazed his spine didn't break. He finally made his way to the food where he managed to eat all of one strip of jerky before he was slapped on the back again and he nearly choked.

He noticed Advtowa was a bit shy of the whole thing, but she dutifully kept up appearances, thanking those who congratulated her and listening patiently to the advice and gossip of the women who surrounded her.

Kiyuga wanted to say something, but he didn't know what. She looked at him and he looked away, feeling the blood rush to his face. He could hear her giggle and it only made him more embarrassed.

Then he looked up and saw Anagalisgi standing politely toward the edge of the crowd. Their gazes met, and Kiyuga noticed that this brother looked like he wanted to say something, too. Knowing Anagalisgi, it wasn't going to be good. Kiyuga deliberately avoided his brother for the rest of the evening.

He never asked, and Anagalisgi never told.

Nine days later, Kiyuga was preparing for his wedding. Ulisi braided his hair and gave him adornments fit for a warrior to wear, furs and talismans, as well as his knives and a hatchet, all sharpened and oiled so they gleamed. She also gave him several flowers to weave into his belt, to show that while he was strong and mighty, he was yet gentle and would be good to his wife, that he would consult and submit to her in the required manner.

Both bride and groom entered the townhouse at the same time, yet when Kiyuga laid eyes upon Advtowa, he found himself rooted to the ground in awe. She was dressed in a lovely doeskin adorned heavily with shells as well as small glass beads traded from the Europeans. Her hair was woven with flowers, and a belt of dry corn husks rested on one shoulder. She had but one knife on her person, to show that she would stand by his side and support him when he defended their family and people, that she would consult and submit to him in the required manner.

Ulisi prodded him in the ribs and he took a jerking step forward, feeling rather embarrassed. She had a similar shy look on her face as they entered the townhouse.

The sacred fire burned hot, Gvnagadoga looking little more than a dark specter as he stood between it and the couple, several more adawehi on either side of him just as dark. Before him, on a low table, lay a leg of venison and a large ear of corn. Guests assembled on either side of the large room, the couple going to stand before the uku. Behind Kiyuga stood Ulisi. Behind Advtowa stood her mother as well as her brother Gatsvnula.

"Welcome all," the elder uku began, "to the binding of this great hunter and warrior of Wolf Clan, and this beautiful peacemaker and healer of Wild Potato Clan, before the spirits and the ancestors of all who have gone before."

He made a gesture. Kiyuga picked up the venison, Advtowa the corn.

"Yvgidahi, with this leg of venison, you promise to provide for your wife and future children, that they may live and thrive and bring honor to your family, your clan, and your people." He looked at Advtowa. "Advtowa, with this ear of corn, you promise to be a good wife and mother for your children, that they will live and thrive and bring honor to your family, your clan, and your people." Next he looked at Ulisi. "Diwedalohi, ulisi of Kiyuga and Ghigau of Itsa'ti, and Ulogilv, utsi of Advtowa, in witnessing this ceremony, you promise to teach their children the traditions, customs, and ancient stories of our people, passing on your wisdom." Finally, Gvnagadoga looked at Gatsvnula. "Gatsvnula, udo of Advtowa, in witnessing this ceremony, you promise to teach their sons the ways of our people, to hunt and fish and defend and live as honorable Aniyvwiya."

Somewhere, music began to play, and ancient songs were sung, invoking blessing and prosperity, not only on the bride and groom, but their families, their clans, and all those in attendance. Kiyuga could only stare at his bride.

With everyone understanding and accepting of their roles, Kiyuga and Advtowa exchanged their gifts, him giving her the leg of venison, and her giving him the ear of corn. Ulisi draped a blue blanket over his shoulders while Ulogilv draped a similar blanket over Advtowa's shoulders.

One of the adawehi then approached with the wedding vase, a cup with two spouts. Gvnagadoga took it from the adawehi and gave it to Kiyuga and Advtowa, bidding them drink, which they did.

There was cheering then, and someone started a drumbeat. Kiyuga smiled dumbly and stared at Advtowa for what seemed to be a ridiculously long time. Was this real? Was this happening? He was in the waking world, right? This wasn't a dream?

Advtowa smiled shyly and held out her hand for him to take. He did and they circled around the sacred fire to the other side of the townhouse where a great feast was spread out along one wall. On the opposite side, near the sacred fire, the drummers and musicians picked up a lively tune. With the rest of the townhouse open and clear, those who did not take to the feast elected to dance in celebration.

Kiyuga was obligated to eat the ear of corn, cleaning off every kernel, showing that he trusted Advtowa to be a good housewife and that he appreciated her. Similarly, she was obligated to not eat the entire the leg of venison, as if to say that he provided so well that there was great abundance in their house, and she passed it along to her mother and brother to finish.

With that ritual complete, more food was brought for them, and the two-spouted wedding vase refilled. It would be the only thing they drank from until the end of the festivities, and they could not drink alone. Not for any taboo, Gvnagadoga told them cheekily, but because the drink would inevitably spill out the other side.

The song changed, and Kiyuga and Advtowa went out to dance. He was so enamored by the way she stepped and twirled, that he tripped over his own clumsy feet more than once.

When the sun began to set, the festivities still going strong, Gvnagadoga called for quiet. It took a short while, but eventually, he got everyone's attention. Kiyuga and Advtowa were summoned forth again to the sacred fire. There the blue blankets were removed from their shoulders, and a single, large, white blanket was laid over them, binding them together as one. Gvnagadoga offered up a prayer for them, proclaiming that each would be the other's shelter from the rain, their warmth from the cold, their companion in loneliness, two bodies becoming one.

Another song was sung, this one seeing them out of the townhouse as the two, bound together in the white blanket, headed for the house they would share together. It was a part of her mother's home, and empty, as expected. Kiyuga removed the blanket and laid it down on the floor, over the rug in their little room. A sleeping mat had already been laid out, and Advtowa meandered her way there, stripping off her small adornments, all while maintaining eye contact with Kiyuga.

Kiyuga felt his bow grow taut and he moved toward his new wife.

Afterwards, they returned to the festivities, letting all know that the wedding and marriage ceremonies were complete. There was more singing and dancing and feasting, lasting well until dawn. Kiyuga and Advtowa left a bit early, returning to their new home and new lives together.

Laying down, Kiyuga found himself too excited to sleep, and also distracted by the presence of someone so close. Even Anagalisgi hadn't slept so close since they were boys.

Later in the morning, Kiyuga and Advtowa returned to the townhouse. The festivities had finally come to an end, though a dozen or so people slept where they lay. Gvnagadoga and the adawehi did their best not to disturb them as they went about their duties. Kiyuga found Anagalisgi among them, and they went outside to speak.

"How is it, then, being married?" the dreamer asked, grinning.

"We've only just begun," Kiyuga told him, mirroring his smile.

"Well, I know you will be happy together."

"This coming from the adawehi of bad omens?" Advtowa wondered jokingly.

"I have my moments," Anagalisgi defended himself. "Besides, what is a great leader without a great woman?"

Advtowa blushed.

Ulisi found them later on in the day and gave them more congratulations. Kiyuga found himself unusually self-conscious and unsure just how to conduct himself. He wanted to show off his wife, show off that they were married. He wanted to go out and hunt again and bring down another large buck, like the one he'd won her approval with. He didn't want to leave as if abandoning her. He wanted to go out and raid and bring back spoils, pretty adornments and gifts for her. He wanted to couple with her again. He wanted to make it known that he was Yvgidahi, a warrior of the Aniyvwiya and protector of his wife and clan.

There was still food leftover from the festivities, and they ate this for several days until he had to go out and hunt again. He brought in a turkey and a fox, which Advtowa prepared with practiced skill. Later on, they escaped together into the trees to explore one another.

Life quickly settled into a new normal, one that was both rewarding and exhausting. Kiyuga was accustomed to being the provider, bringing home game for Ulisi to prepare. And he was accustomed to her authority. He had to adjust his thinking to accept Advtowa's authority and exercise his particular authority, but pleasing her was not the same thing as pleasing Ulisi. He didn't always get it right. He didn't always understand what he'd done wrong, either.

It was a learning experience for him, he was told, by Ulisi, his uncles, and any married man in the village. And he also had to consider that he not only had to adjust to her, she had to adjust to him. The learning went both ways. As long as they were both open to correction, they would be able to learn anything.

As autumn unfurled its colors and winter closed in, Advtowa let it be known that they would have much more learning to do in the near future, and for many years to come. She was pregnant. Kiyuga didn't know he could be any happier, but he found it that day.

"And how much happier you will be when the child is born," Ulisi teased when he told her.

It was then that Kiyuga really regarded Ulisi. No longer living together, he began to really notice all the changes that had once seemed so gradual. Her hair had gone gray and her skin and eyes had wizened from hardship and many seasons now gone. Her back was bent, fingers arthritic, movements more careful. When had she begun using a walking staff?

In fact, with the beginning of construction on the fort—Fort Loudoun as the British called it—and Anagalisgi spending more and more time with the adawehi, both Anagalisgi and Ulisi had simply moved into the townhouse and now lived there, him with the adawehi, and her with the elders and Women's Council. There were few goings-on now that all the feasts had been celebrated. Atagulkalu had returned to his home in Tama'li to be with his wife and family through the winter and was reportedly host to the British engineers in charge of the fort.

So it was that Kiyuga also took up the duty of providing meat for the adawehi and the elders, and he always delivered his catch to Ulisi who suddenly seemed so small and frail.

"It is better for her," Anagalisgi said when Kiyuga spoke with him later on.

"What do you mean?" Kiyuga wondered. "What's happened?"

His younger brother gave him a sympathetic look. "She's old, Kiyuga. She got old. That's what happens to all of us eventually."

"But she is being taken care of?"

"Of course she is. She has never not been taken care of, and you make well sure that she never wants for food. The spirits are good to her, for she has always been loyal to the people, and they will welcome her when it is her time. You need not worry yourself of her. Focus more on your wife and future family."

Kiyuga nodded, but his thoughts were more taken by Ulisi. He saw her across the room, sitting around the fire with the elders. "Will you tell me? When her time comes? Before she goes, I want to make sure I speak to her."

Anagalisgi frowned. "You won't not know when her time comes. You will be there beside her, lying between Igilisi and Advtowa."

Kiyuga's blood turned to ice. "What are you talking about?"

"Death is coming. A plague upon the people, the very same that took our parents from us when we were but infants."

There was nothing but absolute, prophetic certainty coming from the young dreamer.

"Do the others know? The adawehi, the skiagvsta and uku?"

"Of course they do. I dreamed this months ago, shortly after your wedding. Why do you think Atagulkalu and Gvnagadoga are entertaining the British in Tama'li? It's not just because they are hospitable in their homes. They want to know of illness, and they want to secure medicine for it if need be."

Kiyuga swallowed and stole a glance toward the fire. "Does Igilisi know?"

His younger brother sighed and nodded. "I went to tell her of my dream, but she already knew. The spirits have called to her. She knows, and she is ready."

"Why would she not tell me?"

"Because it is her time, as appointed. She has lived a good and full life, as she wishes this for you as well. Do not be discouraged by her bodily passing, for she will remain in spirit."

"And Advtowa?"

Anagalisgi shrugged. "I do not know details of all who will live and all who will die. I know only that you and she will both fall ill."

If his brother were lying—which was a grave offense, especially for an adawehi—he was very good at hiding it.

"What are we going to do, then?" Kiyuga asked. "Who knows of this plague?"

"The elders, the uku, and the adawehi. We are calling on the spirits and attempting to divine an auspicious day for burning and ceremonies. My duty is only to dream and tell what I see."

"What shall the rest of us do?"

"Return to your wife, brother," Anagalisgi told him. "Return to your family. Provide for them. Cherish them. Speak not of this. Let us commune with the spirits first."

It was a difficult thing to do, and there were many times when Kiyuga was but a feather's breath away from telling Advtowa everything, as her pregnancy dragged on and her belly got bigger, especially when the baby started kicking and even Kiyuga could feel its movements.

They'd heard nothing from the adawehi about the plague, and Anagalisgi had said nothing more. Kiyuga would hope that his brother would tell him if the spirits had diverted this impending misfortune so as to ease his burden of worry. Else the baby would be born before the sickness came, and Anagalisgi had said nothing about the fate of the child.

The British finished the construction of Fort Loudoun and departed, and no news came from Atagulkalu or Gvnagadoga of sickness in Tama'li.

As the land shook off the chill of winter, Kiyuga wondered if perhaps the ancestors and the good spirits watching over them had chased away the evil spirits looking to ravage their bodies. Maybe the adawehi had to conduct prolonged ceremonies to ward off these demons and Anagalisgi didn't want to provoke the spirits to anger with premature celebration. Of course, knowing his brother and his dreams, there was never a premature celebration about anything.

But the promise of spring was enough to drive away most of his dark, brooding thoughts, and he turned his attention to happier things, like the imminent birth of his first child. He counted himself lucky to have survived Advtowa's pregnancy, never mind any plague in his brother's dreams.

There were many tales to tell whether a coming child would be a girl or a boy. Some had to do with the seasons or stars. Others had to do with the cravings of the mother and her sleeping positions. Some tales said that it was determined by the position used while coupling. And still others said it had to do with the standing of the father.

Kiyuga thought he was in fairly good standing, or at least he'd always been told so and he had no reason to think otherwise. If such was the case, then they ought to be expecting a boy.

That was his desire, to have his firstborn child be a son. He wished for a son so that he may teach him hunting and how to be a warrior. Of course, a daughter would inherit the home, possessions, and place in the clan, but Kiyuga really wanted a son.

As the birth drew near, Kiyuga did not want to leave Advtowa's side. She moved slowly, deliberately, and often complained that she was as big as the rams with their thick winter wool. Even so, she, her mother, her grandmother, and any other relatives who happened to be nearby, all told him to go out and busy himself. The child would be born in due time and it was not his place to be near.

It didn't make it any easier, he thought, as he went down to the river for late winter, early spring fishing. Downstream, toward the fort, there was a group of British soldiers, also out fishing. They were laughing, though they were too far away to distinguish any conversation.

Were they plagued? True, only a small contingent of soldiers manned the fort through the winter, but everyone knew that more would be coming. They always did. Everyone also always suspected that the Europeans had brought demons with them to inflict terrible sickness upon the people to get them to give up their lands. Was that what was going to happen? Had Gvnagadoga and Atagulkalu been wrong to allow the British to build their fort? Would the plague be punishment from the ancestors for giving up yet more land?

Kiyuga wanted to ask his brother if he'd seen anything, if the adawehi had been successful in their prayers, but also dared not. The spirits would do as they willed, and it was up to the adawehi to be the interpreters and messengers. If there was anything that the people needed to do, they would surely tell them.

Still he thought of Advtowa and their child. He had brought her venison to show that he could provide meat. He brought her trinkets and baubles from raids to show that he could defend the family and the people. How did he show her that he could protect them from this evil?

He pondered this for a while, at least a few days, before being told, upon his return from a hunt, that Advtowa had at last had their child.

"A bow or a sifter?" Kiyuga asked, hurrying home, Adahi close behind.

"It's a bow," Adahi informed him.

A son! His prayers had been answered and he had a son!

When he arrived home, Advtowa had just returned from bathing in the river and was sitting up against a wall, a small bundle in her arms. Their son lay quietly, hands curled up together in front of his face, like an otter.

They named him Ayohli Tsiyo, Little Otter, for his favorite sleeping position was like that of an otter in the water.

Kiyuga had been nervous about having children and being a father, but once Ayohli Tsiyo was born, he found himself primarily confused. Yes, he understood that babies could not immediately walk and talk and hunt and fight, but...what could they do? What did he do with this little otter who seemed only to want to sleep most of the day? As the last scraps of winter melted into spring, he felt as though life ought to change more than it did.

Well, that wasn't to say it didn't change at all. Advtowa's days became far more focused on the infant. She often despaired over it, wondering what kind of life he should have with the Europeans fighting one another and growing ever closer to the Aniyvwiya.

The best part of Kiyuga's day was waking up and seeing his wife and son there beside him, in the quiet time as the sky began to change colors and light filtered into their home. He enjoyed being close to them. He loved them. But Ayohli Tsiyo was yet a baby and Advtowa now focused on him almost exclusively. She looked at the child with the same eyes she'd once had for Kiyuga. He was glad that she was a good and attentive mother, but he wanted some of that attention, too.

He told himself to be patient, but it was hard. It didn't help that his brother only seemed amused by his plight.

"Ah, so the great Yvgidahi, the warrior who will charge into battle and hunt down cougars without a second thought, is perplexed and cowed by a squirming infant and his mother," the young adawehi laughed. It was a rare time when Anagalisgi was light-hearted and mirthful and Kiyuga was not.

"I'm serious, Anagalisgi," Kiyuga said. "I don't know what to do. I knew there would be changes, and I was prepared for them, but now it feels like everyone else is changing and I'm not. I can't."

"What has changed?" Anagalisgi asked. "You continue to hunt and provide for your family. You are more than able and willing to fight when the time comes. You continue to do your duties within your clan. The change is that now you must also provide for and defend your son. You take time for him, and you take time for Advtowa."

"But she does not take time for me. Ayohli Tsiyo cannot take time for me."

"And this is the nature of sacrifice. You agreed to it when you got married. This is what you wanted, a family and children."

Kiyuga sighed. "I don't know that there will be more children."

Anagalisgi frowned. "I don't recall hearing that there was anything terrible about the birth. Of course, being childbirth, I may not hear of such things as the women tend to squirrel that away. Though I might have expected you to make mention of it, and you showed no distress. Unless..." He grinned. "This is about the coupling, isn't it?" He laughed. "You're mad because you haven't gotten any for a while."

Kiyuga felt his whole body burn with embarrassment, and his serious retort devolved into a whine by the time it went from his head to his mouth. "It's been moons! I understood that it would be impossible while she was late in her pregnancy, but it's been at least three, if not four moons since then!"

"Kiyuga, your son is barely over a moon," Anagalisgi told him.

"You see? It's been so long I can't even remember the last time!"

His brother burst into laughter yet again. "Ah, Kiyuga, how did you ever survive before marriage? What ever did you see in Advtowa beforehand that attracted you to her? And here you are..."

Kiyuga scowled. "You're not helping."

"What would you like me to do, exactly?"

"I don't know..."

"Gvnagadoga and Atagulkalu both have a dozen children. Believe me, they were not all born at once, nor did they appear out of thin air. You will couple again, and you will have more children."

"Has my brother suddenly become a prophet of good news? What about this dire sickness that you spoke of last autumn?"

Anagalisgi's smile quickly faded and he said quietly, "Go home. See your wife and son."

Kiyuga sighed and wandered off down the river. Sometimes he wished he had his brother's gift of foresight, to know what was to come, or have a vague inkling. He wanted direction. But perhaps, daily life was indeed just as mundane as it seemed to be. Not every step was a great feat. For it to be so would be to diminish the importance of the great feats.

He went and stood on the riverbank, looking across the water. There were a few British soldiers hanging around, taking a break from their trek to fish and trade with the people, making ready for the rest of the garrison to come. Kiyuga had been to the fort once, to have the blacksmith fix some tools. More often, the British came to Itsa'ti or the other nearby towns. None of them showed signs of sickness.

Frustrated, he returned home and took his little otter in his arms, giving his wife a brief reprieve. True to form, the infant slept with his hands curled up like an otter. Kiyuga felt his chest swell with pride. This little one would be great one day. He just knew it.

"Hardly a moon and already you look at him as though he will take his place as skiagvsta tomorrow," Advtowa said quietly as she reentered the home.

"Only dreaming," he told her. "Besides, it may be that he turns out to be an uku or an adawehi, like Anagalisgi."

"Your brother? Please, Kiyuga, if he should be an adawehi, I would rather he not be like Anagalisgi."

"Because he sees only bad things?"

"Exactly why." Advtowa shifted her stance. "Although, if we did happen to have a daughter, I would not complain if she took after Diwedalohi."

"True," Kiyuga said. Carefully, so as not to disturb the sleeping otter, he lay the bundle in his cradle, then straightened and faced his wife, putting his hands on her. "Although, if we were to have a daughter...we would need to do something else first to make that happen."

"Something?" She raised a brow. "Like what kind of something?"

"Would you like me to show you something?"

"You might have to show me something."

Their sleeping little otter was never disturbed, at least until Advtowa picked him up again. Then the infant made it abundantly clear that he was hungry. Kiyuga was a bit hungry as well, though he knew he would have to wait his turn, and he took the time to relax and collect himself. The spirits had heard his complaints and answered his prayers. For the moment, it was enough.

Advtowa handed Ayohli Tsiyo, now well-fed and content, to Kiyuga and went about preparing food for them. Ayohli Tsiyo looked up at Kiyuga with large, dark eyes. For the first time, Kiyuga thought he finally saw his son. He was still young, true, but he was not just a baby. He was life, a life full of great potential and great possibilities. He would be a great warrior, a great leader. Kiyuga could see it in him, and he didn't even need his brother's foresight to know this.

"He's not going to be skiagvsta tomorrow," Advtowa said, evidently seeing his thoughts. "He is still a babe."

"Maybe so, but that doesn't mean that he will not be great. I don't need my brother to tell me such things," Kiyuga said, not looking at her. Ayohli Tsiyo had one tiny hand wrapped around one of his fingers, and it was the first grip Kiyuga had ever been unable to break.

"Your brother would not tell you such things," his wife went on. "He sees only evil and misfortune. Why should he say our son will be great?"

There was a certain venom in her words that caught Kiyuga off guard, and he looked up. "What do you mean? Are you speaking ill of a dreamer? Anagalisgi cannot help what the spirits show him."

"But why should he see only evil unless perhaps he is with them?"

Kiyuga shifted his position. "Now you are speaking ill of a dreamer, and my brother besides."

"I understand you love your brother," Advtowa said. "But I don't want him or his evil prophecies near our son."

Kiyuga stood, mindful of Tsiyo in one arm. "You will not speak such words. Anagalisgi is a seer, and he has done much good for the people because he foresees evil and misfortune. I will not have you slander my brother or speak against a dreamer." He went on before she could continue. "You ought to go apologize now before your poor words do indeed bring misfortune upon us."

Advtowa, chastened, sighed but nodded and agreed. She served Kiyuga his food and left to speak to the adawehi. He settled in again, food on one side, infant son on the other.

"Your uncle is a bit strange," Kiyuga told his son. "Always has been. He's a little more attuned to the spirits than most, I think. He has a hard time distinguishing between the spirit world and the waking world sometimes. He says that they are more intertwined than even the other adawehi understand, that they are layered, and invisible, yet fully intermixed." He sighed. "It's something only he can see, I fear, for his explanations have always eluded me, in the same way that the warrior path has always eluded him. He can fight well enough, but it is not his calling. In the same way, I may dream, but I am not a dreamer. Even Gvnagadoga is not so powerful a dreamer.

"It frightens me to think on his premonitions of sickness and plague, and yet, could it be that with enough warning, it has not and will not come to pass? I should like to think so. Plague is what killed our parents when we were but children, and decimated Taliqua Eghawa. And other towns I expect. I would not want such a thing to happen to you. You should have a vibrant life with the fullness of the people around you, a chance to make your name known.

"Anagalisgi has told me that we will have more children, that you will have brothers and sisters. I suppose, then, that even if there is a plague, we shall be safe from it." He looked down at the infant who stared at him. "You see? My brother does not see only evil; he is also learning to pick out the good things. Perhaps then your mother will see and understand."

As expected, the infant did not reply, and Kiyuga ate in silence. Advtowa returned some time later.

"Absolution has been made," she reported. "And I spoke to your brother about the grievance. Our family is absolved for my error." She let out a breath. "Your brother found it rather amusing, I think."

"For you to ask forgiveness for an offense?"

"For you to be so protective of him. He said he understands why some mistrust him, and it is not on you to defend him."

"Of course it is. He's my little brother."

She smiled. "Well, with any luck, Ayohli Tsiyo will have a little brother by next summer as well."

"With luck. But if that is to happen, then he ought to understand how to protect his little brother. Or sister."

"Well, when he begins to walk, then you may take him anywhere you wish to go and show him how to be a great warrior."

He had every plan of it.

Part of being a great warrior was understanding one's enemy, and even making use of them. Only a few days after Advtowa's apologies to Anagalisgi, Kiyuga made the short trek to the British fort, the one they called Loudoun. The one in charge of building the fort, a man called Demeré, was crowing about something in the main yard, perhaps taking pride in his accomplishment. He was speaking to the man Kiyuga assumed to be the one in charge, saying that the fort was basically complete and ready for use. Kiyuga ignored them and went instead to the blacksmith who repaired several knives and tools that had worn or broken over the winter.

The garrison at the fort was still small. Kiyuga had heard, through others, that more soldiers were expected to come over the summer in smaller groups. Even as Kiyuga looked around at a new batch of soldiers marching in through the main gate, he wondered whether they were truly friend or foe. Would they be fighting together against their enemies, or would they be fighting as enemies themselves? Would he be forced to kill this blacksmith with the very tools he was even now repairing? The thought was disquieting.

Several days later, as he was returning from a hunt, he noticed a certain air of urgency within Itsa'ti, especially around the townhouse.

He headed home, intending to give Advtowa his kill and find out what was going on, but she apparently already knew.

"Sickness," she said quietly. "Some of the new British soldiers in the fort were ill when they arrived, and they've since set their demons upon Itsa'ti."

"How many are sick?" Kiyuga wondered.

"A dozen? Two? More? I don't know. When I have prepared this rabbit, I will take the broth to the sick and fetch water for them."

There was little Kiyuga could say or do. The sickness had finally come. Whatever his brother or the other adawehi had been doing to keep this evil at bay had stopped working. Perhaps the British really were evil spirits, bringing demons with them wherever they went. Perhaps the Aniyvwiya had been wrong to allow them to build their fort. Perhaps Gvnagadoga had been mistaken in declaring for the British. The spirits had given them time to rectify their mistake, but their patience had run out as the fort was completed. Now it was time for the Aniyvwiya to suffer the consequences.

While many of the adawehi burned incense and smudge, a new fire was built. Those who were well enough beseeched the spirits—with and without the intervention of the adawehi—for mercy. Kiyuga had been hardly a child when the plague last visited them, and that had destroyed the Aniyvwiya, turned lively villages into little more than empty cemeteries, with none to properly mourn or bury the last of the dead. Was this to be their fate now?

Some called for an immediate attack on the British, burn the fort to the ground and kill everyone in its walls. But even if everyone had agreed on this course of action, they did not have enough warriors to carry it out with any effectiveness. Some were gravely ill, others simply weakened.

Kiyuga was sent to keep a watchful eye on the fort, make sure the British were not going to attack them in their time of weakness. But as he sat and waited patiently, surveying the fort from a distance and up close, he noticed that the British were in no better shape. Once, a small group of soldiers, no more than three dozen, did appear, fully armed, but they went south to Taliqua Eghawa where Saloli was having trouble defending against invaders. Itsa'ti had no warriors to spare for itself, never mind any other villages.

When he was home, Kiyuga worried for his wife and child. Advtowa's parents had fallen ill and been moved to the townhouse, now Ayohli Tsiyo had a fever. Advtowa was weak and exhausted, though whether this was from worrying over his family or because she, too, was afflicted, was uncertain.

"You should go to the townhouse with the others," Kiyuga told her. "Take Ayohli Tsiyo. The fire and the burnt offerings are great there, as are the songs of our people and the prayers to the ancestors and the spirits.."

"I'm afraid," Advtowa told him, sounding tired though it was barely morning.

"Don't be. You will be safe there, and I will continue to defend the people as long as I have strength. The demons have not touched me yet, and so I must carry on."

She still seemed uncertain, but eventually agreed. Kiyuga held Ayohli Tsiyo, extremely hot and fussy and covered in the claw marks of the demon the British called smallpox, for a long moment before relinquishing him to Advtowa. Then he held her for another moment before sending them away. They would be safer with the adawehi and the others in the townhouse. Anagalisgi would know what to do. He might see evil things, but that meant that he understood them and knew how to defend against them, just as Kiyuga knew how to defend against the threats of the waking world.

Yet, as Kiyuga sat down in the empty house, there was also a certain feeling of fear and hopelessness, that many moons of knowledge and preparation for this plague had yielded nothing. If Anagalisgi or anyone had tried to stop this misfortune, their efforts had been in vain. What, then, did that say for the rest of them?

What did that mean for him, then, as he sat there in the empty silence? Taking a breath, he could only try to stay calm, even as he felt his body grow warm.

DᏲᎪᎥᎢ ᏘᏚᎩ

Ayadohlv'i So'duhi

Apart But Never Alone

As the British fort was built up, Anagalisgi could see only a growing certainty of doom. He rarely went to see it, had never actually be inside, but each day, as the British made progress in their endeavor, it was slowly closing a door upon the Aniyvwiya. Anagalisgi could not describe how he envisioned these things, as different realms layered on top of one another, that perhaps even the waking world and the spirit world were more than singular places; he simply did not have the words needed to convey what the spirits showed him.

He traveled to Tama'li once to speak of this to Gvnagadoga. The old uku, having watched the construction of the fort for many moons, had listened with his boundless patience, but had little insight to offer.

"You have greater knowledge than I, Anagalisgi," Gvnagadoga told him. "Your wisdom extends beyond what we have ever seen or known, to a place that only the spirits themselves know. I'm afraid I cannot help you. Your guidance now comes from the spirits alone, and you must guide the rest of us."

It was an honor Anagalisgi had always envisioned, but one he found he no longer wanted.

"As the keeper of the Aniyvwiya, I must ask you," the old uku continued, "is it wise to continue allying with the British? Shall we attack their fort before it is completed and kill their warriors?"

Anagalisgi shifted uncomfortably. "Is it still wrong if it is only the path of the least evil? Why can I not see good things? Why have the spirits not shown me a way out of this?"

Gvnagadoga frowned. "Now, Anagalisgi, that is a childish question, not one I would expect to come from you. You know better."

"I see death, Gvnagadoga. Death is here. It comes like the lapping of waves on shore, the tide as it rises and falls. We do not see the danger we are in until the water takes us under. Yet I sense this is the only way, that this is the way things must be. Why is that? Why should the greatest path be so rife with death?"

"If this is the greatest path, then what does the least path hold, I wonder?"

Anagalisgi sighed and looked away. "The great fist from the east is here. It is bringing death with it, and it knows no limits."

"Yes. But remember, too, that new growth came behind it. We will rise again, Anagalisgi. You are a dark seer, a prophet of doom. You feel it is a curse, but you are the reason we will get through this time, for you are able to see and shoulder the burden. And I believe your brother has a part in this as well. And following you will be a time of peace and prosperity. Such is the way of things. You are young, but you will learn the cycles of life beyond what you can see. Sickness and health. Death and life. I believe you do see such things, but as you said, you have not the words to convey what the spirits show you."

He nodded but said nothing.

"Return to Itsa'ti," Gvnagadoga told him kindly. "They have need of you there."

Anagalisgi did as he was told, though with some reluctance. He paused once on the banks of the river directly across from the fort. There he stayed for a couple days, praying and asking the spirits for guidance. What did he do? What could he do? What hope did they have when this predator camped out within sight of their homes and families?

He received no vision or guidance. He thought he might have, when he heard the welcome tapping of a woodpecker, and he looked around, hoping to spy the white spirit that had come to him on occasion. Unfortunately, this was not one such occasion, nor did this common woodpecker speak to him in any way. Disheartened,

Anagalisgi tore himself away from the riverbanks and headed back to Itsa'ti.

He went to Ulisi and the Ghigau, telling them of his fears and what Gvnagadoga said. But for all the prayers and beseeching an answer, no matter who it was, no one received an answer. Nanyehi thought to attack the British and burn their fort, but another Ghigau cautioned against it, citing reports that more British soldiers were on their way now that winter was beginning to shake its chill.

And as time passed and the air grew warmer, Anagalisgi began to wonder if something hadn't been effective, if the spirits had indeed heard their cries. Sickness did not befall them in the chilly winter. Perhaps his fears were for naught. Yet when he visited the spirit world in his dreams, he knew it was not so. When he went back to the uku and the adawehi and the Ghigau, a few of them questioned him, wondered if he'd really seen such things or if perhaps he was merely looking for attention because his prophecy had not come to pass.

Again disheartened, Anagalisgi kept to himself and went about his duties as normal. He spoke no more of his vision of plague, deciding that they knew his words, and if the misfortune should come to pass and death followed, it would not be for lack of warning. There was only so much that he could do. He thought of Kiyuga and his family. He knew Advtowa disliked him, even mistrusted him. Did they also dismiss his warnings, now that seasons had come and gone with no misfortune?

How frightened should he be that one of his premonitions had not come to pass? Should he not feel grateful instead, that he was actually wrong for once? Or should he continue to spread the word, knowing that there would always be more sickness and death? Eventually he would be right.

The days passed, the sun grew hot, and the British declared their fort completed. Now, if anything happened, the Aniyvwiya would be protected. But what if the true enemy lay within?

It was that same day when word of illness reached Itsa'ti. One of the British soldiers had been afflicted with disease. It had spread rapidly among them, and it soon spread to the people as well.

Suddenly, Anagalisgi found himself very busy. He was not permitted to tend to the sick, for he was regarded as something of a bad omen. If he went to the sick, it may be that death would soon follow. His job was to perform the death rites, burying the bodies of the deceased and destroying all their possessions in life, those not buried with them at least. Once death had touched a thing, it was no longer clean. Meanwhile, another adawehi took the family to the river to cleanse them, assuming they were well enough to do so.

Opinions over him were divided. Many begged him to sit with them and protect them from the approach of the Raven Mocker, an evil witch spirit that tormented the dying and ate their heart when they finally passed, stealing their years and cursing their spirit in the afterlife. Others accused him of being a Raven Mocker.

If Anagalisgi had any time to think, it was only to consider that those who would have been about his present age during the last plague were largely unaffected. Aganstata visited Itsa'ti once to visit ill relatives. The great warrior, his body scarred from his fight with the plague when he was a young man, remained entirely unaffected by the sickness now. Anagalisgi found this heartening as those who looked upon the great warrior held out hope that they, too, may be as strong as him against the evil spirits. Many were not.

Ulisi and the Ghigau were diligent in their duties as well, bringing water for the sick and comforting children whose parents were not strong enough to do so. Almost all of the children were ill to some degree. It was not uncommon for Anagalisgi to find Ulisi asleep with a dozen small children around her, desperate for a loving touch.

One morning Anagalisgi made his usual rounds and discovered Ulisi in her pile of children. Spots had broken out upon her skin. He managed to shake her awake.

"Oh, my child," she sighed, touching his face. "I must have fallen asleep." She shifted position. "Well, since you've gone and woken them, I might as well fetch the water."

"You're ill, Agilisi," Anagalisgi told her softly.

"Yes, the evil spirits don't appreciate those of us trying to foil their evil ways. But if they're here, it means I must be doing something right. Help me up."

"Let me fetch the water, Agilisi. You stay here with the children."

Ulisi smiled and assented, letting her body relax as though she'd just done great amounts of work just in holding a conversation.

Anagalisgi grabbed a couple pitchers and went down to the river to fill them. He'd known that Ulisi would become ill; that much he had seen. He knew that Kiyuga would also fall ill eventually. But to be faced with the reality of such things was terrifying. They would all pass on eventually, but he was suddenly afraid of losing Ulisi. She had been his mother, his mentor, his guide in the waking world. What would he do without her?

On his way back, he passed one of the adawehi leading a family down to the river. No words were spoken.

When he arrived at the townhouse, Ulisi was on her feet, making her away among the children, gathering them to her so she could tell them stories and sing songs. None of the children looked in much of a mood for stories and songs, but it helped to distract them from the pain and fatigue, he supposed. Mindful of the other adawehi watching him, he simply gave Ulisi the pitchers of water, then went to tend his duties, determining who had died and where they'd lived.

It was exhausting work in the hot sun. To save himself time, if he knew that many members of a household were ill, sometimes he would dig more than one grave if he had the time, more than happy to fill in any that were unused and unnecessary. Of course, this action combined with his reputation only served to frighten many people, but he had to do something to help himself.

He climbed out of the hole and wiped his face. With all of his hard work, he didn't know how he would be able to tell whether he was feverish. Didn't matter, he supposed, carefully lowering the body into the hole, muttering some prayers, and going to work to refill the hole. The demon called smallpox always scored its claws over its victims. That should be his clue, if nothing else.

He placed stones over the grave to keep out wild animals as much as evil spirits. With the death circulating around Itsa'ti, the scavengers had begun to circle: crows, vultures, coyotes, even an odd cougar, attracted to the smell of weakness and death.

He said another prayer when he was finished, then went to work destroying the deceased man's belongings. He took the scattered pieces to the fire, the one meant to send away the death and uncleanliness. Inside the townhouse, the sacred fire burned as big and as hot as it had ever been, with the wails of the adawehi, the sick and dying, and those still well enough to dance and cry out to the spirits.

Anagalisgi turned away, gathering up his tools. He went down to the river. One of the adawehi, one that Anagalisgi knew had been complaining of fever only a day before, was cleansing a family. Another family waited on the riverbank.

He moved downstream, toward a calm lagoon where he would not be seen, and sat on the bank. He was supposed to cleanse himself between each burial, that the death and uncleanliness of the last death did not taint the next burial, that the deceased spirit might emerge untainted.

The problem was, every spirit was doomed to travel west, to the land of the setting sun, where they would exist in misery, being so far from their natural home, until such time as they simply ceased to be. Sometimes they might take up residence within an animal in order to prolong themselves and give them more of an anchor in the waking world, but all eventually ceased to exist.

Why, then, should it matter whether he cleansed himself between each burial?

Because he was an adawehi, and certain things were expected of him, regardless of the mistrust some had of him. And Raven Mockers would not cleanse themselves so. Besides, there were others who expressed beliefs in the Divine Beings, and those who prayed to them and did good things would go to them after death. Those who did evil things would be tormented by evil spirits without the relief of nonexistence.

It was a conundrum, Anagalisgi thought, wading into the water. But if nothing else, it helped to cool him off after digging so many graves.

Then he returned, digging more graves, burying more people, destroying more possessions, and cleansing multiple times in the river. He checked in on Ulisi often, noting that for as exhausted as she had appeared in the morning, she looked ten times worse by sunset. She had ceased storytelling some time in the afternoon and instead merely rested, not quite sleeping, not quite awake, but only communing with the spirits.

When Anagalisgi pressed water to her lips, she returned to the waking world, taking the water and a bit of broth.

"Advtowa and Ayohli Tsiyo came here," she said quietly, nodding vaguely in a direction amidst a sea of sickness. "The child is so warm. He was taken by spirits and began to shake. Another adawehi cleansed him of the spirit, but the heat and sickness remain. Advtowa cares for him, but she is very weak."

Anagalisgi made as if to stand a search for them, but Ulisi touched his hand. "No, child. She mistrusts you and would only question your presence and intent."

"Then I should fetch Kiyuga."

"He's the one who sent them here. He's taken it upon himself to hunt and provide food for those here, meat for the adawehi and broth for the sick, but I can see the illness in him as well. He will be among us soon."

"He will survive," Anagalisgi said. "He still has a great destiny."

Ulisi smiled. "Indeed he does. I am happy to have seen him this far. I am sure he will do great things."

"What are you saying?"

"Oh, child. My time is here, and I will walk on." She squeezed his hand. "Don't give me that look. You have known it. I am the one who told you. I tell you, my son, I will not live to see the full moon." She sighed. "Mourn for me, child, and do well."

Anagalisgi felt tears slide down his cheeks. The full moon was but days away. He nodded. "I will, Agilisi. I promise."

"Good boy. Now then, give this water to someone who has a chance to live."

He stood, his legs as weak as a new sapling in a storm. He finished out his daily duties and lay down to sleep for a bit. Just the opportunity for sleep had become rare. Sleep itself was nearly impossible. He wanted to sleep, to relieve himself of these troubles, yet he was afraid to dream as if he might learn that they were only beginning, or that they had no end.

In the morning, Anagalisgi was just returning from another burial when he spied his brother bringing in meat and broth. Kiyuga did not look well. As Anagalisgi got closer, he saw Kiyuga bore the marks of smallpox. Judging by the meat, he'd taken much small game, rather than a single large animal, and it appeared to have exhausted him as nothing else had up until now.

He followed his brother just outside the townhouse where Kiyuga sat and tried to catch his breath.

"You should be in there," Anagalisgi told him gently.

For a long moment, Kiyuga did not answer. Then, "I cannot lie down just yet. I have to do my duty to protect and provide." He sighed. "I don't know how to protect them, but I can still provide."

"They are grateful, but you need to rest and get well. The sacred fire will drive away the demons. Better to be closer to it rather than out alone, a wolf separated from his pack."

Another pause. "I heard that Atagulkalu has bartered for medicine from the British, that it saved a man on the brink of death, even as Raven Mockers waited to eat his heart. He is bringing the medicine to all the towns. If it is well to use it up to the point of passing, then I have no need for it yet. Better to give it to those who need it more. Like Advtowa and Ayohli Tsiyo." Kiyuga looked up at Anagalisgi. "Do you know about them? Have you seen their fates? Will they survive?"

"I have seen nothing since the first person became ill," Anagalisgi said. It was the truth, but it felt like a lie. He knew his brother's wife and child would not survive. He had known that since they got married, and it was what had to happen. It was a thing-that-must-be. But Kiyuga, too tired and sick to think straight, accepted the answer without question. Anagalisgi felt sick himself for it, and he added, "And I know little of what goes on here while I am out."

His brother just nodded, sighed, and struggled to his feet. "I should go out again." He continued before Anagalisgi could protest. "My wife and child are in there. Her parents are in there. Her grandparents have already walked on. Igilisi is in there. Most, if not everyone, in Itsa'ti is ill to some degree. Who is left? I have to go out."

Anagalisgi sighed but nodded and got out of his brother's way.

The sun was not quite at its zenith the following day when Kiyuga took his place in the townhouse, between Ulisi, who had fallen into a deep sleep in the night, and Advtowa who was too weak to do much more than hold Ayohli Tsiyo. If she didn't know her child had died, no one had the heart to tell her just yet. Or Kiyuga.

As the sun went down on that day, Anagalisgi did something he'd not done before: he traveled the road and crossed the river and made for Fort Loudoun. More soldiers had arrived, but with the sickness ravaging everyone in the Overhill, they were hardly a spectacle to behold. Indeed, he met no resistance when he asked to be let in after they'd closed the doors for the night, and the young guards unceremoniously gave him directions to the chaplain's quarters.

It had been years since Anagalisgi had spoken to a Christian minister, at least since he was a child. He remembered their water rituals. He remembered being confused by the bread and wine. Now that he was older, he figured he could better understand their ways. Maybe their God would have more readily-available answers as to why this was happening and how to drive the demons away.

William Moore had only just arrived at Fort Loudoun, initially as merely the missionary to Itsa'ti, then suddenly the chaplain who would administer last rites and services for the soldiers and others who perished from the disease they themselves had brought with them. He was a rather gruff man in his demeanor, someone who clearly expected results from his proselytizing and appeared selfishly frustrated by the plague inhibiting whatever plans he had expected to carry out while at the fort.

Upon hearing that an Aniyvwiya adawehi wished to speak with him, the man was apparently quite ready for a battle of wills when Anagalisgi walked into his quarters.

"We don't need your devilry and witchcraft here, heathen," Moore declared.

"If I may say so," Anagalisgi said quietly, "you are the ones who brought your demons of sickness to us."

The missionary was evidently not prepared for such a rebuke, or perhaps for Anagalisgi to understand and speak English so well. But he had been there for every meeting Gvnagadoga and Atagulkalu had with the Europeans who tried to sway them to one side or another, and he had picked up both French and English to near-fluency and had often acted as an interpreter.

"Please, I have not come to argue," Anagalisgi went on. "I come with honest questions."

Moore, still apparently caught off guard, shifted position uncomfortably and made a motion for him to continue.

"This plague has come upon both our peoples. What spirits send this plague? Why does your powerful and mighty God not stop them? What wrong have you done, and how may it be righted so that we end this attack?"

"Sickness comes from the Devil," Moore answered, finally finding himself. "But the Lord God Almighty may use it to discipline his children."

"Are the Aniyvwiya his children? Or has your curse extended to us because of your sins, that we are guilty by association?"

"Those who accept the Lord Jesus as Savior are his children."

"But many have not," Anagalisgi pointed out. "This means, then, that you are passing your sins and punishment onto us." He went on before Moore could speak. "There are some who see this and wish to attack the fort, to prove to the spirits we are still Aniyvwiya, that we are our own people and not subservient to invaders. Please, tell me, what is your sin that has brought this upon us, and how do we satisfy your God to remove this plague?"

The missionary sighed, his thoughts impossible to judge. Finally, "It is by grace through faith alone that we are saved. From there, we must follow His will and way, and we shall be assured victory."

"There are soldiers here who I am sure have such faith, and they obey their commanders' orders without question. What hope do they have?"

Moore straightened indignantly. "Well, at least they have the hope that their souls belong to the Lord. From what I can gather, your people are more concerned with alcohol."

Anagalisgi frowned. "There are many who consume this drink as a way to forget the sorrow that has beset our people. I wish to end both problems."

"Perhaps it is that your evil spirits have attacked us first with this illness, and now the Lord sends his armies against you to do the same. ' "Vengeance is mine," saith the Lord.' Our number of ill is but a small fraction compared to yours, and we can still fight. If your people will repent and turn from their heathen ways—" He regarded Anagalisgi's garb. "—then this plague shall be lifted."

Sighing, Anagalisgi shifted his stance and tried to appear nonthreatening. "Please, I wish no ill between us. The soldiers and the warriors are charged with safeguarding our physical bodies. We—you and I are concerned with greater things, elements of the world we cannot see. I want to understand. I want to protect my people just as you want to protect yours."

The British man regarded him for a long moment. Then, "I want to help my people, yes. I also want to save yours."

"Tell me how," Anagalisgi pleaded. "If we do nothing, there won't be any souls left to save."

"Repent," the missionary told him. "Repent and turn to the Lord. Renounce your devil-worshiping ways and step into the light. Then your people will be saved."

Seeing he would get nothing more from him, Anagalisgi thanked him mildly and turned to leave. The quarters were not large, but when he got to the door, he paused and looked back.

"When I was a child, I lived in Taliqua Eghawa. A missionary came and he stayed there for many years. He held Christian services on Sunday, did all the rituals, and lived among us as an elder of sorts. He was always very kind, even if I did not always understand what he was saying. I am certain that he is dead by now, for he was very old when I was young."

"Did he win many souls?" Moore asked.

"I don't know. I was young," Anagalisgi repeated. "But he must have done something right, for it was his kindness and willingness to teach as an elder that brought me here tonight, hoping you would be the same way. Instead you are merely an invader like the rest of them, only in the sense of the spirit world. Perhaps you are the Raven Mocker my people fear flies over them at night. But I will stand in your way, Raven Mocker, and I will protect my people. Whether the Christian God helps me or not, I will defend my people."

He left before the man could say anything further and made it out of the fort without incident. He was more confused and frustrated than ever. If Moore was an evil spirit or a witch or even a dreaded Raven Mocker, then he could be expected to tell only lies and half-truths to twist Anagalisgi's thoughts and perceptions of understanding and somehow get around him to get to the dying souls. But if not, then how was he supposed to react to the man's words? Was this a judgment? By whom? On whom? Who held the blame? How would repentance save the Aniyvwiya if it didn't appear to be helping the British?

The road was difficult to make out in the dark, clouds drifting over the moon. He stumbled more than once. Even though they were but minor incidents, his soul was so shaken by the events of the sickness and his recent conversation with Moore that any one of these minor stumbles may as well have been a near-killing blow. The fourth time, he just knelt where he was and tried to breathe.

How did he save his people? Why did he see such evils and misfortunes, but no way to stop them or ward them off? A dozen adawehi had prayed and burned incense and offerings for moons to please the spirits, and gradually ceased when his predictions failed to materialize in their suspected way. Had they been expected to do these things forever? Were the British simply too great an evil to counter?

Anagalisgi knew his dream had promised new growth after the great fist had passed over them, but he was struggling with the weight of the fist currently settled upon them. And yet, somewhere deep down, he knew that this was only the beginning.

He felt tears running down his cheeks. He was hurting, and he felt alone. He felt an outcast among his own, given a fantastic gift that brought only pain, powerless to stop or mitigate this crisis. Should he even bother returning to Itsa'ti? Would anyone notice if he did not come back? Or would they be glad to be rid of his plague? What if he was the problem?

A chill wind buffeted him, uncharacteristic for the season. He looked up as another wind blasted him from behind. In the dim light just breaking through the thin clouds, he saw great black wings stretched wide over the sky, melting into the inky blackness of the stars as smoke and shadow as it passed overhead in the direction of the town. A raven's cry echoed in the air.

"Raven Mocker," he whispered.

As he stood, a flash caught his attention and he saw the white woodpecker swooping low over his head, also making for Itsa'ti. It was unclear whether the Raven Mocker was aware of the woodpecker's presence, but Anagalisgi knew he could not stand idly by.

He took off at a dead sprint, keeping his eyes on the woodpecker at all times. He did not stumble. He did not fall. Itsa'ti came into view, but it was shadowed by the Raven Mocker as its wings came down, shrouding the town. The darkness receded as the Raven Mocker likely changed forms, rearranging its smoky, shadowy body into that of a grotesque man or woman.

Anagalisgi had no trouble getting through Itsa'ti in the middle of the night, yet he seemed to have lost track of the Raven Mocker as well as the white woodpecker. Still, he knew his destination to be the townhouse where the sick and dying lay.

He entered the townhouse and less than gracefully picked his way toward where he knew Ulisi to lie. Another adawehi knelt beside her and looked up at Anagalisgi as he approached. The adawehi shook his head.

"I'm sorry. She has passed in her sleep."

A great scream of frustration erupted from Anagalisgi before he could stop it. He whirled and looked at the sacred fire just as another adawehi added wood and incense to the flames. In the great plume of smoke that billowed from the flames, Anagalisgi saw the Raven Mocker leave the townhouse, assuming its form of smoke and shadow and escaping into the night, cackling in victory.

"Anagalisgi?" a weak voice wondered.

Anagalisgi came back to himself and looked down to see his cry had woken Kiyuga. He knelt. "I'm sorry I woke you. Go back to sleep."

Kiyuga looked confused, as though still half in a dream. He settled himself once more and had no trouble drifting back to sleep. The adawehi kneeling beside Ulisi spoke again. "Advtowa has also passed. All three will have to be buried tomorrow, and you will need to be cleansed."

"I have done nothing but cleanse myself for days," Anagalisgi said, his voice thick with sorrow. "It did not save them."

"If you want, I will bury them so you may properly mourn them."

"No." He wiped his face uselessly. "I will do it. It is my duty." He sniffed. "Gvnagadoga should be told as well."

No one argued, and Anagalisgi was left alone. Eventually, he fell asleep where he was.

He wanted to wake Kiyuga so he might participate in the meager ceremonies, but his brother remained too weak to move about. Indeed, when Anagalisgi finally forced himself to stand and move, Kiyuga was still well asleep. Guiltily, Anagalisgi prepared his tools and went to start digging graves.

He went to the home where Advtowa and Kiyuga had lived. It was part of her parents' home, and they as well as her grandparents were already buried, the fresh-turned earth and stone still noticeable. He put shovel to dirt and began hefting soil. When it was ready, he returned to the townhouse. Sighing, he managed to rouse Kiyuga.

"What is it?" his older brother mumbled.

Wishing that he might spontaneously die himself so as to escape the sickness in his stomach, Anagalisgi replied, "You are too weak to move, but you ought..." Breath. "You ought to take time now to mourn. Before I take Advtowa and Ayohli Tsiyo."

If Kiyuga had any clouds in his mind, they suddenly cleared and he sat straight up. He turned to look at his wife and infant son, cold and still beside him. He let out a cry reminisce of Anagalisgi's the previous night. Kiyuga took Advtowa and his son and cradled them, weeping and repeating their names. Still holding them, he looked at Anagalisgi. "When?"

"In the night," Anagalisgi told him, electing to say nothing of the Raven Mocker. He sighed. "Igilisi, too."

Suddenly his brother seemed torn over which way to turn and who to mourn first, but he remained with his wife and child. Anagalisgi suspected that the only reason he let them go was because he exhausted himself so that he could not fight back.

"Everything has been done," Anagalisgi assured him. "You will mourn here. When you are stronger, you will go to the river to be cleansed."

Kiyuga did not argue, and he was still weeping as Anagalisgi took Advtowa and Ayohli Tsiyo out of the townhouse to be buried.

Mother and child were buried together. It seemed to take forever, Anagalisgi thought, even if his hands were the ones moving slowly. He found himself wondering if he shouldn't have warned Kiyuga earlier about their fate. Was his brother's destiny and future really worth the lives of his wife and infant son? What greatness could possibly be worth this pain? Would the spirits ever tell?

What if Kiyuga suspected that he'd known? Would he blame him? He'd defended Anagalisgi often enough when Advtowa had expressed misgivings over him, but what if her fears had been entirely justified? What if she'd been right to fear and mistrust him? What if the others were, too? He knew he was no Raven Mocker, but he was, at the very least, a bad omen waiting to happen. Some days—more often than not during this time of sorrow—he feared and mistrusted himself. He wanted to run himself out of Itsa'ti on more than one occasion. What good was his gift of foresight if he could do nothing to stop these tragedies?

He placed the last of the stones on Advtowa's grave, then headed to the river for cleansing. He did not have the luxury of new garments to wear after each burial, so instead he wore the burial garb during the day which he stripped off before heading into the river. After his last burial of the day, he would change into his normal clothing, saving the unclean burial garments for the next day.

He waded out into the water a dipped himself under, seven times in each direction, murmuring prayers and rituals and incantations, now more of a habit than anything sincere.

When he emerged from the water on his final submersion, he wiped his eyes and saw the white woodpecker sitting on a branch in a nearby tree, looking at him.

"Was this really necessary?" Anagalisgi asked. "The pain, the sickness, all of it? Did Advtowa and her son have to die? Did Kiyuga have to marry her? What is this all for? How do we make it right? Why show me this in advance if there was no way to stop it?"

"When a storm is on the horizon, do you expect to stop it?" the woodpecker asked. "Do you expect that begging will alter the course of the storm? Or do you take shelter and prepare?"

"How were we supposed to prepare for this? Why did I or any of the adawehi receive no answers? They shunned me because they thought me a liar at worst, and crazy at best."

"Look around, Anagalisgi. What do you see?"

Anagalisgi sighed and gave a cursory glance of his surroundings. "I see trees."

The woodpecker chittered. "You see trees. I see the forest. Was this plague a storm, or merely a preparation for things to come?"

"What do you mean?"

"In the coming moons, traders will come from the west, from people known to Nayanali. Take what they have to offer and seek the spirits."

Sighing again, Anagalisgi nodded. "All right. But what do I do now? Is there any way to stem this plague?"

"What is happening now is what is happening now. Do not seek to control things bigger than yourself. Focus on your place in the storm, and do your duty."

He didn't like the sound of that, but he could not argue with a spirit.

"Did the Raven Mocker take them because I discerned who he was?" he asked.

"He would have done so anyway, but now that you are aware of him, he will seek to destroy you," the woodpecker answered honestly. "Know that this will not happen, though it will feel like it at times, and you will be tempted to give up."

"And my brother?"

"Your brother will do as he needs to do. You should not interfere."

"Does he hate me? For not telling him?"

"At this point, he is too ill to think about such things. As I said, you will be tempted to give up. But you will persevere, as will your brother."

Anagalisgi wanted to ask more, but he could think of nothing else that had not already been said or did not sound petty and childish. He thanked the spirit who then flew off into the sky until he disappeared into a cloud. Then Anagalisgi trudged out of the water, donned his burial garments, and returned to the waking world.

Because Diwedalohi was Ghigau, there was a special time of mourning for the skiagvsta, uku, adawehi, elders, other Ghigau, and the Women's Council. Songs were sung of her and stories told, her great deeds, her knowledge and wisdom, her leadership to the uku and skiagvsta in times of peace and war. Stories were also told of her family, her service to her clan, her dedication to raising Kiyuga and Anagalisgi. All this was done in the townhouse, and the sick who still had strength also told stories of her as best they could. Perhaps she had mediated a dispute. Perhaps she had spared the life of a war prisoner who became a beloved brother or sister. Perhaps she had cared for a sick relative. Whatever it was that she had done, it was abundantly clear that she had more than earned her place as Ghigau.

Despite offers from other adawehi, Anagalisgi insisted on burying Ulisi himself. Because of her status, she was buried there in the townhouse. Anagalisgi dug the hole. Kiyuga, in spite of his illness, forced himself to assist in carefully lowering her down. More songs were sung as dirt was shoveled back in, then mixed with rocks at the top. A rug was laid over the spot, and all were forbidden from stepping there for seven days.

Gvnagadoga arrived in Itsa'ti a few days later, where he, too, mourned and sang songs.

Atagulkalu came with him, along with a couple British medicine men. They balked when they saw the devastation that the smallpox had wrought upon Itsa'ti. Tama'li was not nearly so bad, they said. They did not have enough medicine for everyone in Itsa'ti, and it would take time to get more. Nevertheless, what they did have, they shared.

Kiyuga was beginning to recover on his own. His fever had finally broken, though he would be scarred like Aganstata. Even so, he remained absent, sometimes openly mourning all that he had lost, and sometimes quietly brooding, as distant as Anagalisgi sometimes felt when he walked in the spirit world. His body was in the waking world, but his mind was far away.

"You knew that they would die," Kiyuga said quietly one morning as Anagalisgi made his rounds, checking for the dead. Kiyuga looked up at him from where he sat against one of the walls. "That's what you always wanted to say, but never did." His gaze was not malicious, but the confusion and disappointment was far worse, Anagalisgi thought. "You knew from the beginning, when we got married. Why didn't you tell me? Wouldn't that be an omen from the spirits that it shouldn't have happened?"

Anagalisgi frowned, sighed, and sat down beside his brother. "I did know. I knew from the moment Advtowa accepted your courtship that you would lose her. I knew from the moment you told me of her pregnancy that the child would not survive either."

"Why didn't you say anything? Why allow me to suffer so?"

"It is what the spirits have decreed. It is what must happen, or what had to happen." He did not look at Kiyuga.

"For me to have a great destiny?" Kiyuga guessed. "Little brother, you of all people ought to understand that you may sacrifice yourself for the people, but you never ask others to sacrifice themselves in order to increase your own esteem. Even worse, you sacrificed my family for my own glory. What is a man's glory but his family? What is a wolf without his pack?" He snorted and shook his head. "Maybe Advtowa was right. Maybe you do talk to the wrong spirits."

"Kiyuga—"

"Just go."

It was a long moment before Anagalisgi was able to pull himself away and go about his duties. And he did his duties that day with a certain slow but determined fervor, returning to the townhouse as few times as he could manage and not finishing until the first of the spirits came out at night. Even then, he took his time in cleansing himself in the river in the dark, looking around, wondering if he would see the Raven Mocker again. A Raven Mocker, once identified, died within seven days. Yet Moore remained at Fort Loudoun; Anagalisgi had seen him roaming through Itsa'ti proclaiming his gospel only a few days ago. The missionary was therefore not the Raven Mocker, but the coincidence was too great not to think he knew who it was. Likely he'd even sent the Raven Mocker after him when he'd left the fort.

Ulisi and Advtowa and Ayohli Tsiyo were all dead because of him. True, the woodpecker may have said otherwise, but how could he believe it?

He kept on in his duties.

Anagalisgi and Kiyuga did not speak much after their exchange, and a few days later, Kiyuga left the townhouse. The worst of his wounds were still healing, but he was well enough not to need the care of the adawehi or medicine men. Without Advtowa or Ulisi, he moved in with Digvnige and Sotsena. Anagalisgi did not call on them.

The worst of the sickness passed. More people were leaving the townhouse—one way or another—than were coming in. The British medicine men brought medicine to Itsa'ti and also traveled to other towns to see how they were faring. News from the smaller Overhill towns was more promising. The Middle Towns had few, if any problems. The Lower Towns were actually thriving, thanks to the victory at Taliwa that meant the Aniyvwiya could go out and reclaim their old lands.

It appeared to be only Itsa'ti that had suffered so, and many blamed this misfortune on the British and their fort. As late summer turned into fall and the number of ill dwindled to only a handful, these grumblings grew. There was some outrage when the British sent a delegation to Itsa'ti asking for warriors.

"We built the fort as you asked," Paul Demeré, the brother of the man who had designed the fort, said simply. "That was the agreement. We honor the agreement as negotiated ten years ago, and you supply warriors."

"You brought demons to our town," Aganstata growled. "We have no warriors to give."

"Yes, we realize that you have suffered great sickness. We are not asking for warriors now. It is not prudent, with winter coming quickly. But in the spring, General Forbes is going to lead an attack on Fort Duquense, against the French and her allies. If we can break the French there, their hold on the Ohio Valley will crumble. We'll have them on the run. It will be an easy victory, and you will all be home in time for the harvest."

There was a long moment of silence as the two sides considered each other.

"Anagalisgi," Gvnagadoga said, looking at him. "Have you seen anything?"

Anagalisgi rubbed his eyes. "Of this, I have not."

The old uku grunted. "Then we will reserve judgment at this time. Aganstata, Yvgidahi, please see our guests out."

When the British were gone, Gvnagadoga turned to Anagalisgi as if to speak, but Anagalisgi beat him to it. "I understand. I will seek the spirits in this matter."

"Do so," Gvnagadoga told him, sounding tired. He sighed. "Ah, but I wish that Diwedalohi were still here to advise us."

Anagalisgi looked away. "I know. I do, too."

"But we all walk on in our own time. If we do our duties well, as she certainly did, then her knowledge and wisdom is carried on in those who remain." His gaze was kind.

"I don't feel wise, or that I know anything. Sometimes I feel as though I know too much, yet I am forbidden to speak."

"It can be a burden, yes. But you must remain strong and do all you can to warn and protect our people. The spirits have chosen you, Anagalisgi."

"What shall we do in the meantime?" Atagulkalu asked, interrupting their conversation. "We are bound by our word to supply warriors—warriors we do not have—and yet should we make deals with demon bringers?"

Gvnagadoga stood, wincing at a pain in his hip. "We shall wait, give it thought, and see what the spirits have to say. The man himself said they are not looking for warriors now, so we have some time." He took one limping step. "Who knows? With this much foreknowledge, perhaps this time you will listen to Anagalisgi's guidance."

All eyes immediately turned to Anagalisgi who felt the blood rush to his face, and he wished for nothing more than to simply melt into the ground as water. Then the moment passed and the various skiagvsta and warriors and adawehi dispersed. Reluctantly, Anagalisgi headed for his sleeping mat and prepared to dream.

DꭹᎯᏝT WWSᎯ

Ayadohlv'i Tahlduhi
Chosen Warrior

Kiyuga sat on the riverbank, shaving a stick, glaring at the fort across the river. The Europeans brought nothing but trouble, it seemed. Gifts, words, and treachery. As he had heard it put once, they would shake your hand with their right hand and stab you in the back with their left.

And he was supposed to fight alongside them.

There had been many weeks of negotiations. Gvnagadoga still upheld his alliance with the British, and Atagulkalu agreed. If Anagalisgi had dreamed anything, Kiyuga was never present when he spoke of it to the others. And if he had dreamed anything, it only pointed more toward helping the British.

He and Anagalisgi did not speak as much as they used to. Anagalisgi spent his time with the adawehi in the townhouse, as was expected of him. Kiyuga remained with his uncle Digvnige and his aunt Sotsena, hunting, scouting, doing everything he had always done. He felt hollow, though. He remembered when he had purpose, when he had a wife and child to provide for, to defend. It may have been confusing and frustrating, but it was his calling in life. Now he did these things merely from habit. Perhaps it was only Ulisi's words echoing in his mind that he not touch alcohol that he did not indulge like some who had lost family due to the plague.

The British had brought the plague, yet they, the Aniyvwiya, were expected to remain loyal to their alliance. A warrior's honor meant everything, but the British had no honor. They had words, pieces of paper. Their soldiers were made great because his father would send a piece of paper with words saying it was so. He did not have to prove this on his own. Warriors without honor were shunned, and they were expected to keep on with this alliance?

They did not have enough warriors to be picky, and Kiyuga was told that he would be one of the six hundred warriors going north to try and break the French at Fort Duquense. Atagulkalu, Aganstata, and Mankiller would be leading the parties. Dismayed by Atagulkalu's insistence at loyalty to the British and wary of Aganstata's insistence at neutrality, Kiyuga had fallen in with Mankiller.

His name was Ustanaqua, but he greatly preferred to use the name the English had given him, the translation of his warrior's title, Mankiller. He said that while on the trip, it would constantly remind the British of just who they were allied with, and what they would be dealing with if they had any thoughts of treachery. He was of an age with Aganstata, and with Atagulkalu he had buried a hatchet to seal the alliance between Tama'li and the British, but he still appeared to have some fight left in him, Kiyuga thought.

Life seemed to be very confusing. He had gone out on a few occasions just to see if perhaps the Little People could help him, give him some idea of what he should do. Normally a practice for children, it was all he had left it seemed. He could go to the adawehi, but he didn't want to face his brother.

He could not fathom what purpose his loss served. If Anagalisgi had known from the very beginning that Advtowa and Ayohli Tsiyo were doomed to death, why not speak up? Maybe Advtowa would still be alive, maybe not, but at least he might have been spared such dreadful heartbreak. Bad enough that Ulisi had walked on as well. That his brother had spoken of. What rules bound his brother's tongue about that which he could or could not speak?

He sneezed as a gust of wind brought another cloud of spring pollen to his nose. Sighing and wiping his eyes and nose, he stood and left the riverbank, returning to Itsa'ti.

The town was markedly devoid of people. Sickness aside, with so many warriors leaving, some families were choosing to pack up and move within the walls of Fort Loudoun, until such time as the warriors returned home, or so the thinking went. There was great apprehension among the Aniyvwiya, but the people trusted Atagulkalu, Gvnagadoga, and the others, and would follow their lead. Hence why Kiyuga was willing to go on this expedition in spite of his great distaste for the British.

Some warriors still had families to say goodbye to before they left for the raiding season. Adahi had his wife and four remaining children. Galegi had lost his wife to sickness and ended up marrying her widowed sister, thus bringing the children to a combined total of seven.

Kiyuga watched these warriors with envy. He should have been speaking such things to Advtowa. He should have been promising to bring her back the trinkets and baubles he stripped from the bodies of his enemies.

He looked around at some of the young women out and about, few though there were. He felt nothing for any of them. Well, he would not say he felt absolutely nothing, for he still desired coupling, but it felt hollow, dirty, as an evil spirit comes to defile women.

Perhaps this was what he needed, to leave for a raid, for battle, even. He recalled how excited he'd been to go to Taliwa. He remembered the thrill of battle, the excitement of picking his prizes and spoils, the elation of knowing that he would be spoken of to Atagulkalu. He tried to muster up some of those same feelings, but it felt tainted by the knowledge that they were going to help the British.

At long last, the warriors assembled. The fires and dancing and prayers had faded with the night, and now all that remained was determination on the part of the warriors. Atagulkalu, Aganstata, and Mankiller were the last to appear, and Kiyuga noted that they had been speaking to Gvnagadoga and Anagalisgi. Given that they were not telling everyone to leave, Kiyuga assumed his brother had seen no ill fortune for them. Or perhaps this was only the path of the least ill fortune.

They traveled first to Fort Prince George to meet with the British soldiers they were supposed to fight beside. General Forbes was presently quite ill, so he left most all tasks to Lieutenant Colonel Henry Bouquet and Colonel George Washington. Bouquet was a rather astute military officer, his greatest flaw only that he was British. Opinions over Washington were divided, though they ranged from whether the man was completely stupid or merely incompetent, as he was blamed for mishandling the inter-tribal politics that led to the start of the war.

Whatever the case, Atagulkalu, Aganstata, and Mankiller paid the officers their due respects, reaffirming their great alliance and confirming that there were indeed six hundred Aniyvwiya warriors ready to march to Fort Duquense.

Kiyuga was never sure what to make of the British soldiers, dressed in their flashy coats. Red was a common paint color, meant to terrify the enemy, but the red coats seemed to speak more of pompous finery. Of course, their puffery and self-righteousness proclaimed that they feared nothing and that their red coats were a warning to their enemies that they were coming. But Kiyuga just saw them as good targets. He said none of this out loud, however, and instead tried to tell himself that he was going off on a great raid to a great battle, for glory and spoils. Sickness had stopped him the summer before, but now he was back on track to really proving his warrior prowess.

His illusion did not last long, and he found himself drawn back to the British. Not all wore red coats, only those from their homeland of England. The British who had been born and raised in this land wore different coats, blue ones, to distinguish them. Less of a target, but still flashy.

The British seemed to be studying the Aniyvwiya just as much, at least the younger ones were. Kiyuga glanced over them. Did any of them have wives and children yet? He'd heard that the Europeans tended to wait on such things. For the Aniyvwiya, a boy only had to prove himself adept at hunting and fighting. A girl had only to have her first blood. Kiyuga had been later than some at getting married, true, but he'd wanted to have something to actually brag about first.

Taliwa had been his shining moment. Were these British boys hoping for the same thing at Fort Duquense?

Kiyuga had thought that they were meeting up at Fort Prince George and quickly moving north to Fort Duquense. If anyone else was expecting the same thing, they were all sorely disappointed. They ended up waiting two days before actually leaving, mostly on account of General Forbes' illness, as well as waiting on supplies that were late to arrive and late to load. Then there was a small storm overnight. By the time they actually set out on their mission, few were in a good mood, and there was marked division between the Aniyvwiya and the British. Had Anagalisgi seen this miserable delay? Well, if he had, he obviously hadn't said anything to the skiagvsta, or else the skiagvsta chose to ignore him.

Moods lifted as the sun came out, or they did for the Aniyvwiya. The British looked terrible in their heavy uniforms, and this was made worse by the way they had to make formations and march in a certain fashion, to say nothing of all the gear and armaments they had to transport. Much of this was hauled along by the followers while the bulk of the fighting force carried on ahead, but it was still slow going. Almost painfully so.

"If nature moved as the British do, then the tortoise shall one day rule the land," Adahi complained.

"Slow yet determined, and quite tough to take," Kiyuga agreed.

"Now you understand why we are here," Atagulkalu said, "and why we chose to ally with the British."

It had become quite obvious, at least since they left Itsa'ti but most certainly since arriving at Fort Prince George, that Atagulkalu was a far greater supporter of the British than he typically let on. He had many friends among the officers and was often seen speaking to and laughing with them while on the road and sometimes around the fire at night. They had many disagreements over the particulars of war, but they appeared to be good friends on a personal level.

"He tries to keep the peace," Galegi said, as if sensing Kiyuga's thoughts. "You may betray an ally, but it is much more difficult and far more sinister to betray a friend."

Kiyuga picked at his food. "Maybe so, but who wants a friend who wishes them harm and brings evil upon them?"

"The adawehi divined that this campaign would bring great glory and fortune to us," Yvwi commented.

"All the adawehi said this?" Kiyuga questioned.

There was a moment of hesitation. Then, "No."

It was unclear who had spoken, but it was Mankiller who continued. "Anagalisgi foresaw misfortune, as he always does. One bear upon the ground robbed of its teeth and claws and attempting to eat upon a carrion carcass in the middle of summer, four crows upon one tree in its leaves of gold, twenty-three crows upon a tree crusted with snow. Then fire."

"Did my brother happen to explain what this vision meant?"

"He feared that the bear should represent how helpless we have left the people in Itsa'ti, but the crows stood for the deaths we shall expect."

"Four and twenty-three?" Adahi wondered. "That's not bad, for the six hundred here."

Mankiller made a sound in his throat. "Aganstata suggested that it was the dark side of the other adawehi divinations of victory and glory. Hence why we are here."

Kiyuga was still uncertain, and he glanced at Atagulkalu sitting at a fire with Forbes and Washington and other officers. He did not doubt the adawehi, but he found himself doubting the skiagvsta. What if Atagulkalu had agreed to this mission, not to prove this alliance to the British, for they seemed to have little to worry about, but to prove it to the people? So far, the British had brought nothing but sorrow and misery; he had to justify this continued alliance somehow, and a great victory in battle would do it.

He said none of this out loud. He did not wish to disrespect the skiagvsta, nor give the appearance that there were divisions among them. If Atagulkalu was aware of any of the misgivings from some of the warriors, he gave no indication of it.

Whenever there was a call for scouts, Kiyuga readily volunteered. He hated marching along with the British. It was dull and boring. Atagulkalu put a stop to any pranks upon them, or fun and games. He always gave some excuse about working together. At least if Aganstata got after them, he said it was to uphold Aniyvwiya honor. But when Kiyuga got a chance to get away, he took every opportunity.

Sometimes they were scouting ahead for enemy encampments, or looking for campsites of their own. Sometimes they were helping surveyors and cartographers confirm their maps or make new ones. Sometimes they were reporting on the lay of the land as they trudged around with cannons and carts and other gear that did not do well on uneven ground. Sometimes they were out hunting or foraging.

Kiyuga became very popular one evening when he returned with a basket full of sweet honeycomb. He carefully made his way through the camp, not because it was crowded, but because he'd been stung a number of times. He could barely defend his haul when he finally sat down and the others, once they realized what he'd gotten, began reaching and grabbing at the sticky comb. He managed to save a little bit for himself, eating hastily before it was stolen right out of his hands.

"Well now, it seems Yvgidahi is the first of us to do battle on this journey," Galegi laughed. "His skin was pricked many times but he has prevailed and brought us great spoils!"

Someone offered him water which he took and used to cool the worst of the stings.

"At least he found honeybees and not wasps," Yvgi said jokingly.

"Then he would have required reinforcements," Adahi agreed. "No one walks into that battle alone."

"Maybe so, but wasps do not make honey, so I have no need to bother them," Kiyuga sighed, minding his wounds.

"Maybe not, but do you remember the time Gvsga stepped in the ground wasp nest?" Galegi said. "He had no need to bother them, but he certainly had a need to jump in a river to hide from them. Problem was, there was no river nearby."

"What did he do?"

"He tried to run," Adahi answered. "I believe I heard he was stung over a hundred times, many of them in the face and neck. It's amazing he lived."

"Then we shall eat in memory of Gvsga," Kiyuga declared.

"In memory of?" Yvgi wondered. "He's sitting right over there." He pointed.

"Then we shall eat in gratitude that we are not so unlucky."

They agreed and had the honeycomb finished off in a matter of moments.

Kiyuga did not sleep especially well that night. The following day, he declined the scouting missions and instead elected to plod along with the rest of them, with the British. One of the followers, a young woman, gave him a paste and indicated that it was for his stings. He tried a little on some spots on his arm. The worst of the burning went away, and he used more on the rest of his wounds.

Their pace remained excruciatingly slow. If there was even a little rain and the road was even a little muddy, the carts and cannons could not move. If the road was too narrow in a place, they had to stop and wait for the lowest soldiers and the laboring followers to widen the road. If Kiyuga was grateful for anything, it was that Atagulkalu and the others had made very clear that the Aniyvwiya were not their slaves to command to do this or that thing. They were here to help the British fight their war. They would fight, but they would not be ordered around.

It was during these times when the Aniyvwiya instead went out scouting. Kiyuga and Adahi were sent out with Washington. While a British officer, he was a surveyor by trade. His rank afforded him the ability to command his men to do the work and slip away himself to do what he was trained to do.

So Kiyuga spent the afternoon helping Washington make his maps and determine their best course of action. It was there that Kiyuga learned that there was some animosity between the British officers.

"I was with Braddock, you know," Washington said as he peered through his spyglass and scribbled notes in a small journal. "Finest general I've had the pleasure to serve under. Now I'm here with Forbes. Don't get me wrong, he's a good soldier, a good general, a truly brilliant mind. But the man is ill more often than not. What's more, he's the one pushing this road west through Pennsylvania. I wanted to follow Braddock's road north through Virginia. For one, the road is already clear. We could be at Fort Duquense in half the time, I think. And there is that bit about having a major road through Virginia, bolster our trade a bit, help our standing. But no, we go west." He slapped his journal closed. "And here we are, stopping every other day to cut down trees and forge a new road. Is this a military campaign?" He looked at Kiyuga. "I forget our purpose."

Evidently frustrated, he wandered off into the trees. Kiyuga and Adahi glanced at each other and followed him. They returned to the group at the road. As if he hadn't said anything disparaging about his fellows, Washington greeted them as old friends and happily relayed his findings. Kiyuga heard bits of conversation, something about taking the river for a few miles. His suggestion was rejected by another officer. The road had to be completed on land in order to form an effective supply line. Washington sighed, assented, and walked away.

Washington was not the only one to suggest traveling by river, and he was not the only one to be rejected. General Forbes was trying to avoid a repeat of Braddock's mistakes in being too hasty, too cocky, and too unprepared. Therefore, this campaign was not only about reaching and capturing Fort Duquense, but firmly securing their own hold on the territory. That meant a stable supply line. Every fifty miles, he declared, he wanted small depots, weapons caches, a safe place to retreat to in order to rest and resupply should the French manage to drive them back.

As if cutting the road wasn't bad enough, then, they had to also stop and wait for the British to build their small supply forts every fifty miles. They were fairly accomplished fort builders, but it still ate up a lot of time. Kiyuga had no one to get back to in Itsa'ti, but most of the other warriors did. At this rate, they would not be back in time for the harvest, as promised.

It had been spring when they'd departed Itsa'ti; Kiyuga remembered the pollen well.

Now they were well into summer, and it felt like they were making no progress whatsoever. Well, at least roads only had to be cut once, Kiyuga figured. Small comfort.

They woke one morning to find that sixty warriors had left in the night. Forbes was utterly irate. Whatever their friendship with the British, Atagulkalu, Aganstata, and Mankiller were quick to defend the people and chastise Forbes for his slow pace and constant delays. They were here to help the British fight the French and take Fort Duquense, not draw maps, chop down trees, and build forts.

But if they expected any haste on the part of the British, they were thoroughly disappointed. In fact, because the warriors had deserted, there were even more delays as the British tried to figure out what to do about it, how to compensate for the loss. Forbes wondered whether it would be prudent to send a group of soldiers after them, bring them back for discipline. Atagulkalu promised that if they did that—and good luck finding the warriors, never mind bringing them back—then the rest of them would leave and the British would receive no support from the Aniyvwiya on this expedition. There were more harsh words from both sides, but very little changed that Kiyuga saw.

Then they were on the move again.

Another thing that slowed them down was Forbes' constant illness. He was quick to lie down in the evening, leaving the other officers to squabble amongst themselves as to their actions for the following day. He was slow to rouse and be ready himself in the morning, and they lost much daylight because of it. It was difficult enough to get six thousand men, a thousand laborers and followers, and another thousand Indians to move anywhere with any sort of speed. Forbes' personal problems, which seemed to range from dysentery to cancer to merely "a wasting disease," were hardly helpful.

Summer began to wane. Another hundred Aniyvwiya left the expedition for home, this time openly after a dispute in which the officers not only refused to take a more sensible river course, but ordered them to help the laborers if they were so impatient.

Only about three hundred and forty remained.

They pressed on still. As the leaves began to turn color, more groups of Aniyvwiya began to leave, sometimes openly, sometimes stealing away in the night, until only about a hundred and fifty remained.

"At this rate, there shall be no Aniyvwiya left to affirm this alliance," Aganstata told Atagulkalu one evening over the fire. Kiyuga sat across from them. "Kvhe is threatening to leave as well and half with him."

"We have well seen that there is no way to rush this slow-moving tortoise," Atagulkalu said, his tone and expression understandably frustrated. "But if we can hold out a few more days, we will be at the place of the last supply fort. From there, we will be within striking distance of Fort Duquense. Our progress is slow, but the victory should be swift."

"How so?" Kiyuga wondered. "We've not sent scouts ahead to survey the fort. You speak of the hopes and wishes of the British."

"The adawehi divined victory and glory for us, and your brother himself saw only twenty-seven deaths."

"That was a fine thought when we were six hundred in number. Now we are one hundred and fifty. If Kvhe takes half, we will be seventy-five. Twenty-seven deaths suddenly becomes a lot more difficult to consider, don't you think?"

Others around the fire thought on this and grumbled an agreement.

"The British are six thousand," someone said. "What are we to them, anyway? They have the Aninvdawegi, and they are in their own lands. We are in enemy territory. Once they build their last fort and reach Fort Duquense, they have no further need of scouts or surveyors. They will discard us, as they have always discarded us."

More murmurs of agreement.

"Enough!" Atagulkalu barked. "We have come too far to give up without cause. I would be lying if I said that I was not also frustrated.

But such is the nature of war and alliances." He sighed. "In a few days, we shall arrive at the location of the last fort. From there, we shall see what Forbes and Washington and Bouquet intend to do."

"And what if they insist on further delays?" Kvhe walked up, along with several of his closest friends and supporters. "How long shall we wait? Look at the leaves, Atagulkalu. The harvest is here. We were promised to be home by now, and we have yet to see battle. We have yet to pick up hatchet or rifle. We have yet to even see the field of battle or what we are supposed to be fighting for. What shall our women and children eat this winter? Or shall cold and starvation take those who were spared the plague?"

"We will wait," Atagulkalu repeated, "until the British complete their next fort and we hear their plan."

"You assume they have one."

Nevertheless, Kvhe stayed. Two days later, they reached the spot where the British began clearing trees and constructing their last fort.

Kvhe was not the only one with misgivings about the time it was taking for them to see battle and realize this "easy victory." Kiyuga also heard discontent among the blue-coated soldiers, those under the command of Washington. Unlike the red-coated soldiers, who were apparently soldiers only and did nothing else, the blue-coated men were mostly farmers and tradesmen. They, too, wanted to get home for the harvest. Kiyuga saw Kvhe speaking to some of the more vocal blue coats, and he wondered if the seeds of mutiny were being planted. From what Kiyuga had seen, defiance and mutiny were punished harshly within the British army, even including death.

Multiple scouting parties were dispatched into the wilds around the fort, as well as hunting parties. Kiyuga availed himself every opportunity to be out doing something other than watch the British build their wooden castles. A few also took the opportunity to steal away and return home. By the time the fort was completed, just over a hundred Aniyvwiya remained. Surprisingly, Kvhe and his supporters were still around, though Kiyuga suspected that if he were going to leave, he would not slink away, but make a grand show of it.

Days passed with no word, just more scouting parties, hunting parties, and taking stock of everyone and everything who had made it the length of the expedition. The British did whatever it was they did, and the Aniyvwiya and Aninvdawegi did the same. Kiyuga recognized one of the Aninvdawegi who had been at the first fort near Itsa'ti, but his name eluded him.

"You're far from home now," the warrior said. "You walk our lands."

"Yes, but do they know that?" Kiyuga asked, indicating the British.

"Of course. We have an alliance, and we will honor it. Unlike you pathetic cowards."

Yvgi stood and reached for a knife, along with several others. "Say it again."

The Aninvdawegi also had friends close by, but Kiyuga spoke first. "This is different. The last time we spoke, you said we would be dogs to the British. Yet you will notice that we are free to come and go and leave as we choose. Can you say the same?"

The Aninvdawegi was halfway to a strike upon Yvgi, but a large beast came between them. Kiyuga recognized Aganstata and wondered where the great warrior had come from.

"Enough!" he hissed. "There will be no fighting here."

"Where then?" the Aninvdawegi challenged. "Name the place."

"Not here," Aganstata repeated. "We are allied to the British; we are here to help them. We'll do no one any good to fight each other." Carefully he got out of the way of Yvgi and the warrior. "Another day."

Out of the corner of his eye, Kiyuga saw Kvhe standing a short distance away.

The following morning, there came news, even a plan. Major James Grant would be leading a reconnaissance mission to Fort Duquense, to see what they would be up against when they finally launched their true attack. He would take eight hundred men with him, including twenty Aninvdawegi.

"Mankiller," Atagulkalu said, "take twenty of our best warriors and scouts and join them."

Mankiller agreed and started making his way among the one hundred Aniyvwiya who remained, each warrior hoping for a chance to prove himself and actually do what they were supposed to do on this expedition. Kvhe was chosen, Kiyuga suspected, to placate the restless warrior, and to perhaps keep an eye on him. What Kiyuga did not expect, however, was to be selected himself. Pride swelled within him and he eagerly joined the small group, waiting for the order to move out.

"Finally," Adahi said, grinning. "We might actually fight in this war."

"One can only hope," Kvhe growled, still bad-tempered despite this promising turn of events.

"Bouquet believes there to be five hundred French and three hundred Anisawanugi and Anakwanki," Mankiller told them.

Kvhe shifted his stance. "Then why not descend upon the fort?"

"Because there is no 'descending' anywhere," Atagulkalu informed him, walking up. "The fort sits on a cliff overlooking the river. Just getting there will be difficult enough, more than enough time for the French to organize a defense." He took a breath and tried to remain calm. "The Europeans don't fight like we do. And we don't fight like they do. We must learn to compliment one another, learn from one another."

"Learn an enemy's ways, and you can defeat him. What happens when the British consider us an enemy?"

Before anyone could speak further, Grant made the call to move out.

Kiyuga knew from the scouting reports that Fort Duquense was easily two days' trek from the fort. Based on Kvhe's grumbling, he was forced to wonder whether the warrior either hadn't heard these reports or if he just enjoyed complaining. He was not the most pleasant company to have around the campfire, and he and his three friends made for a dreadful thundercloud to have hanging around.

"Why did you choose them?" Kiyuga asked Mankiller the following day, making sure Kvhe was out of earshot.

"An animal must be free to be as he is if his full potential is to be realized," Mankiller told him. "Atagulkalu, Aganstata, and myself are all just as frustrated and upset with the British over this expedition. But we have the wisdom to keep our mouths shut. Kvhe is still learning. He has the strength and the will, but not the patience. But we cannot continue to restrain him and fool ourselves into thinking that we would be better for it. He must stretch his legs and be permitted to run."

"Is that how the British break their horses to ride?"

"Is a horse ever anything more or less than a horse? How shall it be trained? By force, using ropes and chains such that it fears the one who rides it more than anything out there that could kill it? Or by understanding the spirit within and working beside it so that it moves with its rider as one being and it becomes as concerned and dedicated to its rider as it is to itself?"

Kiyuga considered this as they moved along. Even eight hundred men moved more swiftly than the six or seven thousand of the previous season, and they arrived at their main campsite in just two days. Aninvdawegi were dispatched as scouts while the rest of them made camp.

The scouts returned and spoke to their leader who relayed their findings to Grant. Grant called a meeting of the leaders. Mankiller returned to speak to the Aniyvwiya.

"Grant believes there to be just two hundred soldiers and warriors in the fort," he said. "With luck and provision, we can take the fort tonight." The prospect was a welcome one, and the Aniyvwiya shifted eagerly. "Captain McDonald is going to take a dozen of his men to lure them out of the fort. Grant will take four hundred and lie in wait for an ambush. Major Lewis will wait behind with the rest to guard the supplies and surprise any enemy attackers who may slip around."

"What will we do?" Kvhe asked, his tone divided between annoyance and anticipation.

"I and nine warriors will stay with Grant and attack in the initial ambush. The rest of you will remain with Lewis. We don't know how many Anisawanugi and Anakwanki, or others, the French have with them."

Kvhe obviously expected to be named in the initial ambush. Instead, he was put in charge of the Aniyvwiya staying behind with Lewis. Kiyuga was named to go with Mankiller.

Now he remembered the feeling from Taliwa, he thought as he lay down to rest. He could not sleep, but it didn't matter, for both the Aniyvwiya and Aninvdawegi were awake before dawn, mixing paints and coloring their bodies. Even a few of the British soldiers who were up early asked to be decorated in such a way. The group called the Highlanders, from a place called Scotland and wearing a piece of clothing called a kilt, were especially fond of the practice. Apparently they had a similar ancient practice in their homeland.

With the Highlanders appropriately dressed and excited for battle, Captain McDonald led them away. Some had drums, some had the most godawful screeching instruments Kiyuga had ever heard. Something called "bagpipes." Well, it would certainly get the attention of the French.

Grant, Mankiller, and the main force were not far behind, carefully positioning themselves, ready for an ambush. The Aniyvwiya and Aninvdawegi were positioned around the British soldiers, tasked with keeping an eye out for any of the French allies sneaking up behind them.

First came the drums, then the screaming bagpipes, echoing through the trees. The Highlanders who had neither of these bellowed their war cries and challenged the French. A moment later, Kiyuga could hear faint cries from the fort as the French tried to figure out what was going on, where the attack was coming from.

If Grant was right, and there were but two hundred manning the fort, then they would have their swift victory and much glory. Kiyuga swallowed and tried to stay focused. The French would soon be coming. He could hear them. They'd assembled and now they were on their way. The Highlanders continued to beat their drums, strangle their bagpipes, and shout challenges.

Crouched in thick foliage, Kiyuga felt his heart racing. He could hear the French approaching. They'd reached a point where the Highlanders had ceased their baiting cries and would even now be leading them to the ambush.

Kiyuga sneezed and dropped his skala galogwehi. Just as he bent to pick it up, something thwacked into the tree where his head had been only a moment before. Cautiously, he looked up as he bent down and discovered an arrow embedded in the bark.

He snatched up the pistol and got off a single shot just as a painted warrior burst through the undergrowth, swinging at him with a hatchet. The warrior's head snapped back and he fell to the ground just in front of Kiyuga.

Suddenly there were warriors and soldiers everywhere. Grant's soldiers had barely even moved from their position, still waiting in ambush, and now fought three French for every one British. Kiyuga heard cracks in the trees as their allies tried to encircle them, but he could see few.

Instinctively, he dropped to the ground and began slithering his way through the undergrowth like a snake. He could not tell friend or foe from this vantage, but if he could get outside the fighting, then perhaps he could strike down some of their attackers.

Somewhere in the chaos came the call of retreat. The British struggled to get out of the thick of things and flee back to camp. Kiyuga did not spring up from where he still crawled on his belly, but he made sure to keep his head below sight line, under cover of brush and bracken. He'd lost sight of Mankiller and the others. If he could just get outside the circle...the camp itself was situated on the top of a hill. If they could reach that vantage...

Halfway there, they ran into Lewis' men. Hearing the cries of battle gone wrong and the call for retreat, they'd elected to leave their positions and come to help. With their momentum streaming down the hill, they managed to buy the rest of them time to get to safety and regroup.

Kiyuga crawled to relative safety behind the line and dared to stand. He saw Mankiller also fleeing up the hill but stop when he saw the Anisawanugi were already there. He saw Lewis take on a French soldier, but behind him, two Anakwanki attacked, binding his arms and taking him prisoner. The last Kiyuga saw of Major Lewis, the man was swallowed up in the maw of battle.

But the French were not here only for prisoners, and they were quickly surrounding the hill, the Anisawanugi at its peak. Kiyuga grabbed Mankiller and pointed this out.

"Go," Mankiller told him, pushing him toward a rapidly closing hole on the east side. "Warn the others."

Kiyuga was reluctant but agreed, running around the hill as fast as he could, lowering himself below line of sight just as soon as he hit flat land. He heard shots fired, flinched as the bark of a tree sprayed on his back. He heard pursuit and dove for the ground, scuffing himself in the dirt. Not looking back, he again slithered his way along to a pile of brush where he crawled in and waited quietly.

Someone ran past, then someone else. Both shouted in a language he did not understand. A moment later, they returned, still talking to one another. Anisawanugi, he guessed. He might have tried to kill them from a distance with his skala galogwehi, but if there were any more, or if he was unsuccessful, he couldn't get out of the brush pile fast enough and he would be killed for sure. They did not appear to be looking very hard for him, if at all. He watched them walk around a bit, then move off, back toward the fighting.

Within his relative safety, Kiyuga checked himself for injuries. A few scratches and scrapes, as he might have expected, but nothing more. No broken bones, no musket balls, and he hadn't been hit in the face with a frying pan this time. Nor had he succumbed to a stealth arrow shot. Who knew that a sneeze might one day save his life? He might have laughed at the absurdity of it all, but decided to reserve that for later when he was bragging about his exploits. But then, how honorable was it to hide in the bushes like a frightened mouse?

Just when he considered leaving his hiding spot, he heard the sounds of flight. British, Aniyvwiya, Aninvdawegi, all running, fleeing, the French and their allies in pursuit. There were more shots, but close combat had since ceased. Even the Anisawanugi and Anakwanki were chasing them in the open.

Kiyuga remained where he was, as still as he could make himself lie. The French did not pursue very far, as Mankiller had perhaps feared, for they returned not much later. While they were occupied with the remnants of the camp at the top of the hill, Kiyuga made his escape. There was one shout behind him, but nothing more.

He ran as fast and as far as he could, uncertain of his surroundings but hoping to run into the rest of the soldiers at some point. Instead he stopped first at a small stream where he drank and washed his minor wounds. With the sun going down, he decided it best to simply stay there and wait until morning to continue.

The following evening, he stumbled upon the British fort more than he intentionally discovered it, but that was no matter to him. He was back, and so were the others, though not for very long. There was still some chaos as the survivors were taken for treatment of wounds or given something to eat and drink, seeing how food and water had been in short supply once the French took control of the camp and its necessities.

Eventually a report was made, and it was given the following morning. Majors Grant and Lewis had both been captured. Bouquet expected a writ of ransom or some similar negotiations in the following days. Of the eight hundred and some men who had gone out, there was an estimated three hundred forty casualties. Some were still missing, including four Aniyvwiya. Those four happened to be Kvhe and three of his closest friends who had all been with Lewis.

"We will return tomorrow and search the dead," Atagulkalu told the rest of them. "We will find them."

"They'll not be among the dead," someone said. "I was with them under Lewis' command. They left before the fighting began. They must have deserted."

"Kvhe is bad-tempered, but he is no coward," the skiagvsta said. "He would not shy from battle. I expect more that he deserted Lewis' men to join Grant. Therefore, we will search the dead."

Dinner was a somber affair. Everyone settled in to sleep that night with brooding thoughts and silent dreams.

Kiyuga came flying awake as cries of attack echoed throughout the fort. He grabbed his weapons and jumped to his feet, ready for anything. Around him, others did the same. But as nebulous noise became clear, he realized that the sounds outside the fort were not cries of war and battle, but songs of victory. He recognized those songs. He knew them as surely as he knew his own tongue, for it was. He also knew the men the voices belonged to.

Kvhe and his three friends stood outside the fort, dancing and singing songs of battle and victory. They waved long poles decorated with many scalps.

The warriors quieted only when the crude gates of the fort opened up for them. Bouquet stormed out to meet them, Atagulkalu and Aganstata close behind. The rest of the Aniyvwiya also exited the fort with them, but stayed several steps behind.

"What is the meaning of this?!" Bouquet demanded.

"We are celebrating the easy victory," Kvhe told him. "We have brought proof of the death of our enemies and want the reward that was promised."

"Victory?! You call such a humiliating rout an easy victory?!"

"Your failure to plan is not our problem. You asked us to fight and win, and we have done this. We bring you scalps as proof. What more do you want?"

Bouquet grunted. "Where did you get these scalps? I heard reports that you left your post."

"We were told to stand back," Kvhe informed him. "We did not come all this way to sit idly by."

"And how is it that you are so late to return?"

"We had to be careful. We do not parade ourselves in front of the enemy as you do. We had to take care to blend in while we walked in the midst of our enemies."

This only angered Bouquet further. One of his men came up beside him.

"Sir, from the position at the hill, it is just as likely they visited any of the nearby settlements."

"Why should we stray from a glorious battle with a guarantee of an 'easy victory' to raid meager settlements and farmhouses?" Kvhe wondered loudly, laughing. His friends laughed with him. "Or is it that you accuse us of your own wrongdoing?"

"Enough of this!" Bouquet snapped. He turned to his own men. "McConnell, I want you to disarm and detain all of the Cherokees. We will launch our own investigation into this matter. If necessary, we shall destroy Fort Duquense without them. Seeing how they've done nothing but complain of our slow movements and inaction thus far, well, this shall be nothing new to them, I think."

There was great protest from all the Aniyvwiya, even Atagulkalu. Suddenly Kiyuga was beset by half a dozen British soldiers, stripping everything from him but the most basic of coverings, then binding his hands behind him. He and the rest of them were forced back into the fort. They were tied to various posts and a makeshift fence was built around them, overhead tarps providing the barest of protection from rain and wind.

"Good job, Kvhe," someone growled. "See what your arrogance has done?"

"Did I bind us here?" Kvhe shot back. "No, our great allies, the British, did this to us because we did as they asked."

"You abandoned Lewis," someone else said. "Where did you really go?"

"Does it matter?" a third warrior scoffed. "We may as well all abandon the British for as much good as their alliance has done for us. Disease, death, ridicule, and now this! At least none were shamed by dying in vain for this cause. I envy those who left before now."

Atagulkalu did not say a word. He, Aganstata, and Mankiller had been separated so they could not speak without shouting. Indeed the skiagvsta looked rather perplexed by the whole ordeal. Perplexed...and disappointed.

Water was brought to them, as well as any rations that happened to be leftover from meals. Otherwise they stayed where they were, little better than snared animals. They heard nothing of any attack upon Fort Duquense or any other course of action.

The Aninvdawegi, however, took the opportunity to hurl insults and a number of unpleasant objects at the Aniyvwiya while they were unable to defend themselves. Kiyuga found himself pelted with rotten food and animal dung, all the while an Aninvdawegi warrior insulted him, his family, his clan, his people. A few of the soldiers joined in on the game. It was great sport for the Aninvdawegi to try and make the Aniyvwiya warriors dance to avoid the projectiles. Kiyuga did not oblige, and their tormentors focused their attention on those who did.

"Did I not warn you?" the warrior from the fort—Shkwanaame was his name—sneered, lazily chucking rotten fruit at the bound Aniyvwiya. "You will be their dogs. And here you are, as dogs."

A few days later, General Forbes himself called on them. He brought a dozen men who came bearing buckets of water, food, and drink. The Aniyvwiya were suspicious, but still they washed, ate, and drank. More men appeared, redistributing the weapons and clothing taken from the warriors.

"I apologize for this monstrous treatment," the general said. "It was most improper, hardly due for little more than a suspicion of wrongdoing. You and your people have been robbed of your dignity, humiliated, and disrespected as warriors. As such, it reflects most poorly upon myself, the whole of the British army, and our alliance."

"Alliance," Atagulkalu echoed with a sigh. "An alliance is more than words on a piece of paper. An alliance is a bond that should not be easily broken. An alliance is meant to be stronger than mere strangers, stronger than only friendship. It is a promise. A promise for one to do right by the other. We have tried to do right by you. We leave our homes and our families based only on a hope of victory. We fight in a style greatly foreign to us with weapons that cut both ways. We fight in wars that mean little to us. Yet we allied to you and promised to do right. We endured demons and death and came with you on this voyage, all for a promise.

"You have broken that promise, General. The Aniyvwiya risked much in your battle, and only those brave enough to return to the aftermath were rewarded with any spoils. Thankfully, no one was killed. No one died in vain. And yet this is how we are repaid. With words and delays and rotten fruit. I will not subject my people to this humiliation any longer. Autumn wanes and winter comes swiftly. Our women and children hunger for our return."

"Please, we are almost ready to—"

"No. You cannot humiliate us in such a way and then ask us to fight for you. You have betrayed our trust and insulted my warriors. We are going home."

Forbes stuttered and fought for words. Finally, "May we still call upon you in the future?"

"For what?" Aganstata asked. "If Fort Duquense falls, you have said it yourself that victory in the war is assured. If you fall, well, it won't be for lack of forts or supplies."

The Aniyvwiya began moving out, Atagulkalu at the head. Forbes called after him. "I will send a letter to Governor Fauquier, to ensure that you are justly compensated for your efforts here! It will not be forgotten!"

Atagulkalu paused and looked back. "Is that a promise, General?"

And they departed, the last hundred Aniyvwiya warriors of the six hundred who'd started out. The British were unsure what to make of it. Some seemed troubled, others smugly satisfied, but most appeared confused or indifferent. The Aninvdawegi howled and ridiculed them all the way into the trees and for at least another half mile. None of the Aniyvwiya even gave them a second glance.

They traveled together that first day, meandering down the road so painstakingly cut and drawn over the summer. Kiyuga did not feel loss in the sense of having lost a battle, though he did feel that, too. Rather, he felt loss in the sense of a goal being unattained, and it was one he could not attain again, not here. He'd come hoping for victory and spoils. Instead, he'd gotten...this.

That night, they camped by the river, any one of them wishing for a canoe to get home faster.

"Any who wish to go ahead, I'll not stop you," Atagulkalu said. "I think at this point, we only want to get home to our families."

There were murmurs of assent. Daydreams of seeing family again, grumbling over a broken promise to be home for the harvest, a few scattered tales of bravery in battle from those who had been there, these things circulated around the fire. Even Kiyuga could not help telling his story of how a sneeze saved his life.

By dawn, probably half of the warriors had packed up and moved on. Kiyuga was in no hurry — he had no one to get back to — and he instead stayed with the slower crowd, led by Atagulkalu.

"I am sorry you have no spoils to show," Atagulkalu told him as they walked together.

"Doesn't matter," Kiyuga said. "I've no one to impress."

The skiagvsta gave him a sideways glance. "Still mourning your wife and child."

"Yes."

"I understand. But know that such grief will not last forever. You are here, aren't you?"

"I hoped that normal activities would help. Being assaulted by rotten fruit and harangued by savage Aninvdawegi has not helped much."

Atagulkalu laughed once and sighed. "No, I expect not. It has been a hard year. But at the very least, I hope to continue the supply of trade goods with the British. They are not much for battle and warfare, but they have goods we need. Such trade is helpful when we are away on these long campaigns and our families require goods."

"Maybe so, but then what need have they for us? What spoils shall I bring home that a woman cannot barter for? What honor have I? What use am I except to give her children?"

They continued together in their travels, even as their group dwindled to only five. It was only about half a moon or so after they'd left the fort when one of their warriors came back. His name was

Ahtsehd.

"Is there trouble ahead?" Atagulkalu asked, seeing the man's distressed state.

"Trouble...and death. We don't know who started it, but there was battle here. Four of our warriors are dead."

Indeed, about a mile up the road, they came upon the warriors, hung from trees, gold leaves sitting on their heads and shoulders. Each one had a crow upon him.

DꙨΛꙅT KꙅSꙆ

Ayadohlv'i Tsogaduhi

Soothsayer

It was not the crows they had to be worried about, Anagalisgi thought, but the bear. The bear with no teeth or claws, gnawing upon carrion in the middle of summer. The other adawehi had it half-right, that this bear was Itsa'ti as the warriors left to aid the British in their campaign. But there was a deeper element to it as well, that said the vision went beyond just this season.

They were quite surprised when some of the warriors who had left returned to Itsa'ti. Had there been troubles? Battle? Where was everyone else?

Apparently, things weren't as smooth and quick and perfect as the British had proclaimed. They were slow on the road but quick to make excuses. There would be no battle, no glory. The warriors had better things to do at home, protecting their families in the here and now. More and more warriors trickled back to Itsa'ti, all with the same story, all saying that Atagulkalu insisted on seeing it through to the end, whenever that might be.

It was a few days after one of these groups returned that visitors came to Itsa'ti. As the woodpecker had predicted, they were traders from the west, and they had goods from the peoples of the far west, the Great Desert peoples. As much as they had beautiful trinkets and exotic furs, they also had something that might interest the adawehi.

Anagalisgi went to them, inquiring after this item.

He did not speak their language, and they spoke very little of his, but it turned out that they had French in common, having been exposed to or allied with the French.

"Le fruit de la vision," the trader said. (The seeing fruit.)

"Le fruit de la vision de quoi?" Anagalisgi wondered, turning it over in his hands. (The seeing fruit of what?)

To Anagalisgi's eyes, it looked like an orange, or perhaps a peach with bumpier, even prickly skin. He took it in his hands. Nothing sinister about it, he supposed.

"Eat the flesh, or burn it upon the sacred fire," the trader went on. "Commune with the spirits and the ancestors."

"You trade with the far west," Anagalisgi stated. "Do the Great Desert peoples walk near the land of the ancestors, the place of the setting sun?"

"Naturally. With this fruit, they speak to the ancestors and the spirits."

Anagalisgi considered this, looked at the fruit in his hands. Maybe this was a way where he could really reach the spirits when he needed to instead of relying upon chance in his dreams. "What do you want for it?"

Mostly the traders were looking for guns and ammunition, something the Aniyvwiya were not handing over readily. Both sides drove hard bargains. Some deals were broken, but Anagalisgi wanted to commune with the spirits.

"I will use this fruit tonight," he declared when he and the trader came to a standstill. "If I can commune with the spirits, you may take the guns and ammunition with you. If I do not, you get nothing except the return of half a fruit."

The trader agreed, apparently more than certain his claims would be proven truthful. Anagalisgi wasn't sure which he feared more: that the trader would be wrong and Anagalisgi would just make a fool of himself; or that the trader would be right and Anagalisgi would have unfettered access to the spirits.

That evening, he sat before the sacred fire, burning incense and saying prayers, holding the fruit in his hands. He intended no offense to the spirits for partaking of the fruit, but he needed answers. Finally, he cut it in half, peeled the skin off one half, and ate the flesh.

It tasted like a peach and an orange mixed together, he thought.

A log in the fire collapsed, sending sparks into the air with a plume of smoke. Anagalisgi fell over in his seat as a beast of smoke and shadow rose with it, and he thought it might have been some kind of horse, galloping upwards along the plume, through the ceiling and into the darkening sky. When he finally righted himself, he found that the sparks had transformed into small white moths. They formed a loose cloud and fluttered around the townhouse once before leaving through one of the entrances.

Anagalisgi stood and followed, unsure of his steps as lights were too bright, shadows too dark, and his ability to perceive depth and distance was woefully impaired. But he managed to stumble outside where the cloud of moths floated into the air to become stars and his gaze was distracted by the sight of Itsa'ti at night.

White spirits were everywhere. A white deer walked down the street. A white hummingbird perched upon a doorframe. A whole pack of white wolves circled the town protectively. And just in front of him sat the white woodpecker.

"I'm here now," Anagalisgi said, his voice sounding distant to his ears. "What am I to do?"

"Take this message only for yourself," the woodpecker said. "You will walk among us in the flesh."

"Am I to die?"

"No. You shall stand guardian over the door between worlds."

"How will this be?"

"You will know it, when the time comes to cross over."

Anagalisgi frowned. "Very well. What of my brother?"

Suddenly Anagalisgi felt himself being lifted, as if his spirit rose out of his body. His arms stretched thin and his body shrank, and soon he was gliding over the trees with the woodpecker. They rose higher and higher. He looked out over the whole earth and saw everything. He saw the forest beneath him, gray and brittle, waiting for winter to close in. He looked north and saw where winter already had a hold, great sheets of snow and ice stretching as far as the eye could see. He looked west, to greater mountains than he knew, surrounded by lush grasses and also a vast, barren desert. He saw a great ocean, the land of the sinking sun. He looked east and saw another great ocean. He looked south and saw places never touched by snow, and still another great ocean, this one dotted with islands. Overhead, he saw the sun, moon, and stars all at once, each shining in its own glory.

He felt the air under his wings, and suddenly he was moving more swiftly than before. Suddenly the forest beneath was coming up very fast, and he and the white woodpecker dove into the trees. They looped around trees and through branches. Anagalisgi was uncertain whether he even had control over his body, but regardless, he landed safely beside the spirit in one particular tree.

He looked down and saw a fort. It was not so illustrious as Fort Loudoun or any of the other British forts, but it was definitively a fort, its occupants definitively British. Then he saw in one area people tied to posts and covered poorly by drab tarps. He recognized his people. He recognized Atagulkalu and Aganstata and Mankiller. He recognized his brother.

"What's happening here?" Anagalisgi gasped.

"Betrayal and the seeds of betrayal," the woodpecker answered. "Come with me."

The spirit turned and hopped off the branch, taking to the air once more. Anagalisgi followed, through his free will or not, he was unsure. They soared over the canopy again, over the new road cut through the trees, and south. The air grew thick with smoke. Anagalisgi looked down and saw fire. Flames leapt from homes and he saw men on horseback running down the occupants as they tried to flee. Then they were past, and they landed in another tree. Once situated, they glided back to the ground. Or Anagalisgi did, assuming his human form while the white woodpecker landed on a nearby house.

"You have seen what will be," the spirit told him. "It is a thing that will come to pass."

"Can anything be done to stop it?" Anagalisgi asked, feeling rather helpless. "Something to give the people hope?"

"Division. Invaders cannot conquer what is not there. The people must hide. Until such time as it is safe to return."

"How will we do this?"

"When you have despaired, help will arrive. Listen to them, and make others listen as well, for they are powerful and will teach you many wonderful things."

Anagalisgi was still uncertain, but he could hardly say no to a spirit. Instead he nodded. "Wado, Ge'gwogv."

The woodpecker dipped its head. "I await the day when we shall speak together, when I will mentor you and you may help others, when you take your place as guardian of the door between worlds."

Then it spread its wings and took flight. Anagalisgi watched it go, then looked around at the rest of the spirits still walking around in the night, ensuring Itsa'ti's safety in the spirit world. He concluded that the white animals were good spirits, while the beings of smoke and shadow were evil spirits. Perhaps his sudden drop into the spirit world had startled the horse-like spirit and banished it from the townhouse.

He had just turned when he found himself torn between two places, even two bodies, the one he wore in the spirit world, and the one in the waking world beside the fire. Had it been a dream, a trance? Or had he actually gone outside?

Whatever the case, he had a wretched headache. It was dawn now, somehow, but he felt too ill to move. He directed another adawehi to gather the things he promised to the trader from the west, then asked to speak to the trader.

"How shall I acquire more of this seeing fruit?" he asked.

"You may ask nicely," the trader replied, "and if you remain this generous in your trades, I may see what I can do, if you so wish."

"I do so wish."

"Very well. I will see what I can do."

"This fruit," Anagalisgi continued before the man could leave, "is a stone fruit, like a peach. If I plant the seed, will it grow and bear more seeing fruit?"

"The tenders of the seeing fruit are very secretive of its management," the trader told him. "But I have heard that in order to plant it so that it grows and bears the correct fruit that allows you to commune with the spirits, it must be planted within the body of one whose heart has been eaten by what your people call the Raven Mocker. Only then shall the fruit provide sight into the spirit world."

"Is the fruit evil, then?"

"By no means. But the one whose heart has been eaten has no spirit and is hollow. Therefore it seeks a spirit to fill its empty vessel and so enter the afterlife, thus providing a gateway for you to seek the spirits."

Anagalisgi sighed, thanked the trader, and sent him on his way.

Later on, when he was well enough to walk about, Anagalisgi managed to track down Gvnagadoga who was quietly fishing in the same lagoon Anagalisgi had used to cleanse himself during the plague. The old uku noticed him and bid him join.

"You have that look, Anagalisgi," Gvnagadoga said.

"What look?"

"The one that says you've communed with the spirits and have bad news. Others call it your perpetual expression of dismay." He gave Anagalisgi a cheeky grin. "What troubles you?"

"I've had a vision."

"Incited by this seeing fruit from the trader, I assume? What did you see?"

"I saw our people, the warriors who traveled with Atagulkalu, being mistreated, bound and beaten, by the British."

Gvnagadoga frowned. "That seems unlikely; they are our allies."

"I know what I saw. There was great mistrust and bitterness. Our warriors experience hunger and sickness."

"The warriors who have returned have reported nothing of the sort."

Anagalisgi shrugged. "I don't know what to say. It is what I have seen."

The old uku nodded, still frowning. "Of course. Have you seen anything else?"

"I saw British soldiers upon horseback, burning villages and riding down the villagers, killing them as they tried to escape." He paused. "The great fist from the east is here, and it will settle upon us, and it will crush us if we don't do something."

"Did the spirits happen to say what this something shall be?"

"Not specifically, not yet. The ge'gwogv showed me this, and it said that we must divide. Invaders cannot conquer what is not there. Our people must divide and hide themselves and wait until the storm passes."

Gvnagadoga nodded slowly. "I will have to think on this and seek the spirits myself. You must continue to dream."

Anagalisgi nodded. "I was able to freely speak to the spirits using this seeing fruit from the west."

"Did you consume all of it, or is there more?"

"The trader brought only one fruit. I consumed half, and I have the other half here."

"Did he say anything about how to cultivate more?"

Now Anagalisgi hesitated. "He said the stone must be planted in the body of one whose heart has been consumed by a Raven Mocker. The vessel is devoid of a spirit and will act as a conduit to the spirit world, giving the fruit its power."

Gvnagadoga seemed as troubled by this as Anagalisgi. Finally he said, "I am not one so gifted in such things; I know not who has been visited by the demon."

"I do."

"Who would that be?"

"Agilisi. Diwedalohi. The night she died, I went to Fort Loudoun and inquired after their Christian minister. We had an argument. On my return, a Raven Mocker followed and came to Itsa'ti. It took her soul just as I arrived."

The old uku took a breath, his expression contorting in pain. "Oh, my son, I am so sorry. I had no idea. Why did you not say anything?"

"The shame of it, that such a great Ghigau would be defiled. For my iniquities. I do not believe the minister was the Raven Mocker, but

I believe he knew who it was and he sent it upon me and my family."

"Maybe so, but it appears as though good will now come from it, and Diwedalohi may continue to serve the people even in death."

"You think I should simply take the trader at his word?"

Gvnagadoga shook his head and waved a hand. "Of course not. Seek the spirits once more. Dream. Ask after them. Inquire what you should do. If the spirits tell you to do this, then who are we to question it?"

"Of course."

"Something else troubles you?"

Anagalisgi shifted his stance. "A message from the spirits, intended for me only."

"Of course. I understand if you cannot speak, but if it is something I may help with, you have only to ask."

Anagalisgi thanked him, turned, and went on his way.

There was so much he didn't understand. Atagulkalu, Aganstata, Mankiller, even Gvnagadoga, they all seemed to operate on a basis of politics and negotiations. Yes, they sought the spirits for guidance and wanted the best for the people, but it all seemed so narrow compared to what Anagalisgi saw. They saw things from the perspective of the beasts, where he flew over the trees as a bird. But how did he explain the things he saw when he could not show them the same way? How could an eagle explain flight to a cougar? How could an owl explain flight to a snake? Or even walking, for that matter?

He wished he had more of the seeing fruit, but also knew that until the trader returned — assuming he even did, and had more of the fruit — Anagalisgi had only half a fruit left. Maybe he could cut it in half once more and get two visits to the spirit world, even if they were shorter. Regardless, he ought to save it and use it wisely.

Or perhaps he should use it now, so he could ask the spirits about planting the seed. Would they approve of using Ulisi's body as the soil in which to grow the tree? Would he feel so conflicted if it were someone he was not related to and loved?

He sought the spirits the traditional way first, praying, burning offerings, and sleeping as much as he could that he might dream. But he dreamed only a repeat of his flight with the woodpecker, seeing first his brother and the others bound and kept under watch by the British, and then the horsemen burning villages and killing people.

One night, instead of his brother, he saw a length of rope, many strands braided together. But the strands were fraying. In some spots, there had been complete severance. In other spots, only a few strands still held. Each end of the rope pulled taut, though he could not say by what force. Then there was a noise and the dream changed to the same familiar one of the horsemen. The dream itself had not changed, but there was a certain urgency behind it that said this time was coming very close.

Anagalisgi woke but did not move right away. He stared at the ceiling, wondering what to do. Other adawehi were blessed with both dreams and a course of action. He was given bad omens with no way to counter them. What use was he?

He stood and made his way outside to relieve himself. Autumn was here and the harvest was well under way. The warriors were supposed to be back by now, but if the stories from the deserters was true, such a thing was highly unlikely. If his brother and the others were indeed captives of the British, then their chances of returning for the harvest was even less. Anagalisgi told himself that it couldn't last forever; his brother still had a great destiny to fulfill. But it was hard when he thought about him sitting out in the rain and cold, bound where he was and getting little food or water. What kind of destiny was that? What greatness could possibly come of it?

Aganstata was the first to return, with a group of eight. The rest of the council and the Women's Council were convened, but before the warrior could say anything, Gvnagadoga spoke.

"With respect, Aganstata, I wish for Anagalisgi to speak first, regarding a vision from the spirits. Speak if he is not telling the truth."

All eyes turned to Anagalisgi who swallowed and said, "I saw you, Atagulkalu, and others, perhaps a hundred warriors. You were bound and tied within a British fort. You sat under tarps with little food and water, and were mistreated."

"Did this happen?" Gvnagadoga asked.

Aganstata nodded gravely. "It did." Murmurs from those gathered. "We traveled with the British for many moons, indulging their whims and their fancies. They would not permit us to travel the river but insisted on cutting their road. We did not even arrive until Guyequoni, when we were promised to be home. By then, there were only about a hundred of us left. I see the rest of them made it back safely." His gaze went to a few warriors in particular, loitering around the outside of the townhouse. He shifted in his seat. "When we arrived, some eight hundred men were sent to scout the area around the fort, to determine our attack. Mankiller led twenty of our people while Atagulkalu and I stayed behind with the rest.

"From reports, the man in charge, Grant, attempted a foolhardy attack, and four hundred of the eight hundred were killed or wounded. He himself was taken captive by the French.

"None of our people were killed or wounded, but Kvhe and three others were reported to have deserted. They returned later with scalps, claiming victory and spoils. That is when we were disarmed and detained. And they did everything as Anagalisgi saw. Their Aninvdawegi allies were arguably the worst offenders." His disgust was undisguised.

"Eventually, we were freed. Then General Forbes had the nerve to ask us to fight again and take the fort. Atagulkalu refused, and we have returned home. We have traveled in smaller groups. I came first to ensure a clear path, but I cannot imagine the rest are far behind us. As I said, no one was wounded or killed in this foolhardy endeavor."

There were troubled countenances all around.

"We cannot continue this charade," one of the younger skiagvsta stated. "The British have lied, cheated, stolen, and humiliated us at every turn. They mock our ways and take advantage of our generosity."

"As we take advantage of theirs," Gvnagadoga said. "We still maintain open trade with them."

"Shall they buy our loyalty, then?" another warrior challenged. "Shall we deal in words and slips of paper as they do?"

"We will do nothing until Atagulkalu and Mankiller have returned, along with the rest of the warriors. Once everyone is home, then we will discuss what we should do."

It did nothing to ease the tension among those gathered as they dispersed and went about their lives. Anagalisgi heard more than a few grumblings about attacking the British for insulting their honor and denying them spoils. Aganstata certainly looked like he was thinking such things, even if he did not say them aloud.

Anagalisgi kept his thoughts to himself. It was one thing to have premonitions of future things; it was quite another to watch them unfold. He had seen many things in his short life, not the least significant being the deaths of Advtowa and her son. Yet he had a feeling deep in his soul that the events to come would be the culmination of evil prophecies that he had seen as a child, though he had not understood them as such at the time. It was unnerving.

The gatekeeper between worlds. That was what the woodpecker had told him he would become. But it was not about the world of the Aniyvwiya and the world of the British. He was not a diplomat. He would be the guardian between life and death. Just that thought was enough to make him weak in the knees. Who was he that he should be given such a task? Did the spirits really believe him up to the challenge?

No more warriors appeared that day, but few were worried about it. Most were still too consumed with fury over Aganstata's report. How dare the British treat their allies so! The Aniyvwiya had allowed them to build their fort. They had endured devastating plague (on more than one occasion, some said). They had sent their warriors to fight in this war that was not even theirs. And this was how the British repaid them! By binding their leaders and greatest warriors and treating them like animals, even worse than animals! It was utterly outrageous!

Another small group of warriors came the next day. They, too, reported the poor treatment at the fort. They also reported that any British travelers on the road back had been little better, insulting them and making mockery of them. They might have been robbed and beaten if not for sheer numbers.

Two more days and another group arrived. This one claimed that they had been attacked on the road, shot at and beaten with clubs and pitchforks. Some certainly bore wounds true to the story.

"Did you attack them?" Gvnagadoga inquired as they finished their tale.

"We had no choice but to defend ourselves," one warrior, Golisdayv'i, said sternly. "Or shall we meekly run away like deer?"

"Why would they attack you?"

"They do not respect us. We are little better than pack animals to them, to drive here and there at their whim, fighting their wars and receiving no reward. Now that we do not do as they wish, they beat us, as if trying to break a wild horse."

"But the last time they would have seen you, it would have been going north with the army."

"And now we return without the army. They think us the incompetent ones when their own officers got half of his men killed. Even Atagulkalu believes it foolish. Why are you defending them? Are you so enamored by them and bought by their goods that you would sell out the people?"

There was silence in the townhouse. Debate was encouraged. Argument permissible. But to openly defy and challenge an uku or skiagvsta was not without consequence. To challenge an uku during a time of war was highly unusual.

Nevertheless, Gvnagadoga remained calm. "I seek peace. It is my duty. As such, I am required to see with a bit of empathy, to understand all sides of an argument."

"Peace can mean many things," Golisdayv'i growled. "If peace is only that we are not at war, then even their Anigvnage'i slaves are at peace with them. If peace is freedom for all peoples and goodwill between us, then we cannot allow ourselves to be trodden upon as little better than worms in the dirt!"

"And how shall attacking them produce peace?"

"How does a buck mate with the doe except that he fights for respect and his place in the herd?"

"Then you admit that you attacked the British settlers first."

Another span of silence stretched over the people. Gvnagadoga and Golisdayv'i stared at one another. The uku remained calm and in control while the warrior seemed caught off guard by the sudden, and apparently true, accusation. Finally, Golisdayv'i stood.

"We cannot continue to allow them to abuse us. When you work for peace, consider what it means to be at peace. Are the cougar and the hare at peace?"

With that, Golisdayv'i left the townhouse with his followers.

"We cannot allow the British to divide us," one of the Women's Council said. "They know we are loyal and peaceful. They also know that ill treatment will stir the young warriors to anger as they seek glory for themselves and their families."

"Yes," Gvnagadoga mused. "And perhaps there is merit to the thought that we have allowed ourselves to be bought by their trade goods."

"Loyalty and neutrality incite the young men to anger," Anagalisgi said. "But making them an enemy will surely devastate us."

The old uku frowned. "Not if we do as the spirits have shown you."

"And what is that?" another woman inquired.

"We must divide, hide ourselves. You cannot conquer an enemy that does not exist."

"And did the spirits say how this must be accomplished?"

"No," Anagalisgi admitted.

"Typical," another adawehi scoffed quietly.

"Then we shall reserve it as a final course of action, or until the spirits do give instruction," Gvnagadoga said, giving the adawehi a look. "Until then, there are still warriors on the road who have not returned, Atagulkalu and Mankiller among them. As we are at war, they are our guides. We will heed their instruction."

The old uku looked tired, Anagalisgi thought, and his limp was far more pronounced than it had ever been. He claimed it was the chill of winter wreaking havoc on his bones, but the way he carried himself said it was more than that.

But Anagalisgi said nothing. He simply went about his day, managing to escape for a bit to sit on his thinking rock and snare a rabbit that was out rummaging for moss and bark.

He missed Ulisi's cooking. He missed watching her deft hands and sure movements. He missed hearing her stories about her husband, and the stories he would tell about his hunting trips. He missed hearing her stories about the times when she would go out hunting with him, and how they would compete. He missed her stories of how some young men tried to court her after his death, and how she always turned them down. Her sons provided for her, she said, and for a long time, she had no desire to replace the man who had been her best friend and companion in life. Eventually, Kiyuga got to be of an age where he could provide.

Anagalisgi sighed as he returned to the townhouse where he skinned the rabbit and divided the meat to cook. With any luck, Kiyuga would be home soon. Even with this betrayal by the British, Anagalisgi hoped his brother had found some renewal of spirit while away. Perhaps he would consider courting a woman again.

It was four days before Atagulkalu returned, Mankiller and Kiyuga with him. While all the returning warriors had been bitter about their treatment by the British and Aninvdawegi, Atagulkalu seemed especially troubled, and he wasted no time in convening the council. He told about the warriors hung from the tree, and Gvnagadoga spoke of Golisdayv'i's vengeance. The warrior himself was present and not looking any happier for it.

"Golisdayv'i may have admitted to attacking the British village," Atagulkalu said, "but it was Ani and the others who paid for it."

"Ani was not yet a warrior," Aganstata growled. "He went to Fort Duquense hoping to prove himself in that supposed 'easy victory.' He died for nothing."

"He died showing us the true form of the British," Golisdayv'i said. "They have disguised themselves as a Raven Mocker does. They have come and they are ready to eat the heart of our people, who we are, and leave us a shallow husk!" He pointed. "Anagalisgi has been trying to warn us for years, and yet you sit here and defend them!"

"Hush, child!" Atagulkalu said harshly.

"I speak the truth! You know I do! Our enemy—"

"Is not much of an enemy seeing how they are still trading us guns and ammunition and even increasing the flow of goods."

"So that they may continue to buy us? Shall we die on the battlefield with honor and glory and a place among the spirits, or slowly penned in as animals for the slaughter? At least if I were to go out to the fields and beat the sheep, they would be smart enough to run away at least. A dog would fight back. A wolf would fight back!"

"And you can speak of this, can you, Anigilohi?" Gvnagadoga asked in a rare display of anything but calm tranquility.

"What is that supposed to mean?"

"You style your hair and dress yourself well in their trinkets and goods," Mankiller observed. "You know the traders by name. It seems as though you have the lowest price for their loyalty."

To attack an uku or skiagvsta was grounds for death, but that didn't mean Golisdayv'i wasn't considering a challenge of some form. Looking around, everyone was won over by British goods to some degree. Maybe it was clothing, jewelry, trinkets. Certainly they all enjoyed the ease and convenience of the guns, rifles and skala galogwehi. Aganstata had a pair of spectacles that he especially cherished. Atagulkalu had traveled to England many years ago to forge an early alliance. Anagalisgi himself inquired after their Christian religion.

Were they somehow losing their identity as Aniyvwiya and becoming as slaves or work animals? Would anyone have questioned themselves in this way if the British treated them well?

"We should attack them now," Golisdayv'i declared. "If they are as pathetic and slow moving as they were going to Fort Duquense, they will be even slower coming back when they are exhausted. Their backs are turned. We should attack."

"Attack whom exactly?" Atagulkalu wondered.

"All of them! Their armies, their settlements, everything. If nothing else, we must replace the warriors we have lost because of the demons they let loose to sicken us, and for the deaths of Ani and the others."

"We cannot risk a war with the British. They are powerful and they are still our allies. I have already secured greater trade for the time being. Believe me when I say that I know we have few warriors, which is why we cannot risk a new war. We already have one to fight. In the spring, I will take a war party and we will raid and destroy Fort Massiac. We will use their soldiers and allies as replacements for our warriors, and we will mend this frayed rope with the British."

But Golisdayv'i was already shaking his head. "At least the French treat their allies with respect and honor them as is appropriate."

"French allies are abandoning them in droves," Mankiller said.

"Because they are losing," Golisdayv'i hissed.

"You see the problem, then," Atagulkalu stated. "We cannot switch sides. We cannot abandon our alliance. All we can do now is protect ourselves. That is what I am trying to do."

"I am not interested in safety if it means surrendering everything I am! We are Aniyvwiya! Great people, great warriors! Shall we slink away into the night? Shall all the warriors return to their wives and mothers as mere boys because it is safer? Or do we not have an obligation to protect our people? Is it not mercy to put a suffering animal out of its misery? But I do not intend to suffer. Nor should anyone else! I suffered enough at the hands of the British up there at the fort."

With that, he stood and departed. Kvhe and a few others left with him.

"This is not going to go well," Gvnagadoga fretted. "The young men want to be the warriors we always told them to be."

"Perhaps the British are erasing our identity as a people,"

Atagulkalu said. "If our young men and women are unable to grow and learn as we did, as our ancestors did since the beginning."

"Was Taliwa not a battle as we have always fought?" Aganstata questioned. "Many boys became warriors that day."

"Yes, but then we were fighting others like ourselves," Mankiller said. "The Europeans are not like us. They do not respect us. The problem is that they have the power to ensure they never have to. Whether they conquer us in battle or buy us with their goods, their influence upon us is far greater than anything we have given them. We tell stories of a world that the young men don't see, and will probably never see. The world was already changing when we were boys."

"This is true," Atagulkalu agreed solemnly. "But I think I speak for all of us when I say that we don't need Anagalisgi to tell us that something bad is going to come from this. Golisdayv'i is angry, and his followers are angry. Anger is terribly contagious, and I fear that they will strike out against the British, burn their towns and kill their settlers, those they do not take captive."

"How shall we stop him?"

"We stop him," Gvnagadoga said, "by giving in." At their expressions, he clarified. "Only a little. We must buy time. In a few days, tell Golisdayv'i that you will approve of the raids, but not now. Tell him to wait until early spring, after planting, when parties may leave and raid at will through the summer. They cannot leave now, not again, not so soon. After all, they must ensure that their wives are fertile so they may have sons and daughters."

"And what shall we do in the meantime?" Aganstata wondered. "It buys us time, but it does not solve the problem."

"All we need right now is time," Atagulkalu said. "It will give me time to gather warriors for a war party against Fort Massiac and meet with the British to negotiate."

"What happens when Golisdayv'i doesn't listen?" Anagalisgi interrupted. "You know he won't. He and Kvhe and the others, they will go down and raid. Saloli in Taliqua Eghawa and Amadoya in

Si'tiku have already abandoned the people once; they will do it again. And they have greater access to the French for weapons and supplies."

"Then it appears that our length of time is much shorter than we would hope," the skiagvsta said, clearly uncomfortable. "And it seems that I must make a more hasty departure."

They sat in silence for a long moment, each lost in his own thoughts. How did they get here? How did they get out? It was Atagulkalu who broke the silence first.

"I think we all know our duties, then. Gvnagadoga, Anagalisgi, I trust that you will seek the spirits. Mankiller, I suggest you return to Tama'li. Aganstata, please keep an eye on Golisdayv'i and the others, ensure they do not leave to go raiding. I wish to consult the Women's Council."

The rest of them dispersed, weary and longing for sense to return. Or Anagalisgi was, anyway. Looking at Gvnagadoga, Aganstata, Mankiller, and the rest of them, they all looked as though they wished for the days of their childhood, when things were simple. Or maybe it only seemed that way. Certainly the children playing outside now did not bear this burden. Perhaps the safety Golisdayv'i had referenced was only an illusion. And they were the guardians of that illusion.

Anagalisgi headed out to his thinking rock, hoping for some sort of inspiration. Perhaps the woodpecker would come to him. Or maybe he should go to the woodpecker. He still had his half a seeing fruit. It did not rot as quickly as other fruits, though it was starting to show signs.

Figuring he had little to lose, except maybe a bit of indigestion, he ate the fruit. It did not taste as sweet as before, and it certainly had a tinge of beginning rot, but he forced himself to chew and swallow, holding the stone in his hand as if he might lose it.

The sunlight seemed to dim a bit and the trees took on a shadowy characteristic. But where sun hit water, it shone ten times as brilliantly and blinded him. He put his hand up and looked away, up into the trees.

"Ge'gwogv?" he asked cautiously.

For a while, there was no answer. Or it seemed like a long time, anyway. He waited there on his thinking rock, watching the high branches of the trees wind and loop themselves around each other, as if weaving a basket. His rock stretched out long all around him until he seemed to be but an ant upon it. Then it snapped back to rights as something rustled in the bushes.

A great white wolf emerged into the cleared. High on a branch, the woodpecker swooped in and perched.

"You heard me call," Anagalisgi said, relieved.

"We always do," the woodpecker told him kindly. Then, more seriously, "You have seen and sensed the danger approaching."

"Yes. I fear the time of warnings is past, but I still don't know what to do."

"You already have the answer, Anagalisgi. But you neither like nor fully understand its implications."

Anagalisgi hesitated. "I am Wolf Clan. The people must stick together as pack. We cannot allow ourselves to become divided."

"Yet divide you must. Wolf will show you the way."

"When?"

"When it is time."

"Is this the help you promised, when I have despaired?"

The woodpecker did a single, awkward, shake of its head. "No. You have not yet begun to despair. But you will. And when that time comes, you will learn."

"Learn what?"

"Everything."

With that, the woodpecker took off, and the wolf turned tail and bolted into the forest.

Frustrated, Anagalisgi let out a cry of frustration, lay back on the rock, and closed his eyes.

"Anagalisgi? Are you all right?"

He blinked open his eyes. The sun had moved, but not much. His head ached, and he found himself looking up at Gvnagadoga.

"I was on my way out here to see you, and I heard you scream," the old uku said. "Are you all right?"

Anagalisgi sat up and rubbed his head. "I think so. I was speaking to the spirits."

"They said something you didn't want to hear, I think." Gvnagadoga carefully sat down beside him on the rock.

He sighed. "Yes. And no."

"They didn't tell you everything you wanted to know, and what they did tell you was not what you wanted to hear as well as less than helpful."

Anagalisgi nodded. "That is exactly it."

Gvnagadoga laughed. "Yes, the spirits can be fickle like that."

"What do we do, then?"

"We do what they have already told us to do. The reason we have not is because it is something that we don't want to do, so we feign indecision and uncertainty."

"Division."

The old uku nodded.

"So, what, we just send messengers around to all the villages and tell them they have to leave? Where will we go? Where will we hide? The British have already displaced many peoples, why is this different?"

"I don't know," Gvnagadoga admitted. "And I don't believe it to be now. But I think we have to start preparing for it."

"How?"

Gvnagadoga sighed. "If we are to save the people, we must protect the women and children, for they are our life. And we must protect the elders, for they hold our culture and identity."

"We must also protect the warriors, for they are our protection," Anagalisgi said. "Everyone is important, Gvnagadoga. We can't just choose some to save and some to sacrifice. It's one thing if such a decision must be made in battle, but in preparation...it's cruel."

"I know, my son. I know. As for where we shall go, I don't know that answer. But I feel that you do, even if you don't know that you know."

"How shall I learn what I don't know that I know?"

Gvnagadoga got off the rock. "It will come to you, in the dark hours of the morning, when all seems hopeless and you begin to despair."

That word again. Despair.

"And what will you do?"

"I will see about making the difficult decision of who to save and how. If you would like to help me?"

"Of course I will help."

"Then see if you cannot discover which towns are going to be burned by the horsemen. As you have said, invaders can cannot conquer what isn't there."

Anagalisgi nodded. He understood now. He just didn't know when. And he still didn't know where they were supposed to go.

He had no more seeing fruit, so the best he could do was sleep much and try to dream. Fall slipped away and winter came quickly on its tail. Anagalisgi was almost surprised to leave the townhouse one morning and find snow.

"I take it the spirit world has no snow."

He whirled around to see Kiyuga walking up to him. "What do you mean?"

"You sleep in order to dream and speak to the spirits. Given how much sleeping you've been doing lately, I could only assume that there is no snow in the spirit world, which is why you prefer to be there."

Anagalisgi managed a light chuckle, his breath puffing out in front of him. "Ah. Um, no, there is still snow in the spirit world."

Kiyuga sighed dramatically. "Well, it was worth a try. Have you seen anything worth sharing?"

"When Gvnagadoga hears of it, then you will, too."

"My great destiny?"

"Yes."

"Was it necessary for Advtowa and Ayohli Tsiyo to die for it?"

Anagalisgi hesitated. Then, "Yes."

"Was it necessary for me to marry in the first place for it?"

He nodded. "Yes."

Kiyuga huffed a sigh. "I don't know whether I hate you or not."

Anagalisgi said nothing, just waited patiently.

His brother continued, "I want to. You knew about Advtowa and Ayohli Tsiyo, that they would die. At the same time, I've always known that you were different, that you have a different path to walk. Igilisi often made jokes that I would one day be the skiagvsta and you would be the uku.

"I guess it was my own pride that said that you would always be my little brother, that I would always know everything going on with you, that you would tell me everything. But now I realize that you're a man, and you walk a different path than I do. The only way for me to know everything about it would be to be you or walk it for you. I can't do that. And you answer to powers greater than anyone here. I cannot blame you for that.

"I don't know what the spirits show you. I don't understand it. I never expected you to defy Igilisi. I would not expect you to defy Gvnagadoga. How can I expect you to defy the spirits? I trust you, Anagalisgi, and I'm sorry."

Anagalisgi smiled and clasped wrists with him. "Thank you. Believe me when I say that if I could have warned you, I would have. If I could warn everyone of every bad thing, I would. Sometimes I can't. I don't understand it enough to say what's wrong, or I can't speak of what I have seen."

"I understand. I mean, I don't, but it's not my place to say. You don't tell me how to go about fighting in battle; I should not tell you how to commune with the spirits."

"Thank you." He shivered once. "I suppose I should go out and do something before returning to the spirit world. Perhaps I will see an early spring."

Kiyuga shook his head, grinning. "No, that would be good news."

Anagalisgi headed out for a brisk walk around Itsa'ti. People were out and about, visiting, talking, watching children play. The crop fields were gone, vanished beneath snow, though Anagalisgi knew that there were some potatoes and carrots lurking within the frozen ground. Sheep nosed around the fields, picking off what grasses they could find and stripping bark from trees, all perfectly content in their thick wool coats.

He returned to the townhouse and sat by the fire, warming his hands and nibbling on a bit of jerky. After a while, as he was considering drinking the sleeping brew and hoping to sleep and dream again, Gvnagadoga sat down beside him. He moved slowly, every move deliberate.

"I saw you talking to your brother," the old uku said quietly.

Anagalisgi nodded. "I wasn't expecting it...but I know it had to happen."

"It did."

He could feel the old uku looking at him, but Anagalisgi did not return the look, instead studying his hands and pretending to warm them, though he was already quite warm.

"Is it time to tell him? Them?" he asked finally.

"Do you believe he is ready?" Gvnagadoga wondered politely.

"I think so. Before the fires start and the horsemen come. He will need direction, as will the skiagvsta."

Anagalisgi let out a breath. Gvnagadoga put a hand on his shoulder. "I know this is hard. You love your brother. You want him to be great, but you don't want to lose him."

He nodded, though that wasn't the whole truth. Yes, he loved Kiyuga. He would be devastated if anything happened to him. But there was another element, the lurking fear that Kiyuga would be the one dealing with the loss. Anagalisgi knew that he would be the guardian between worlds. He just had a sneaking suspicion that he would not be posted in the waking world.

"I will gather the skiagvsta and senior warriors," Gvnagadoga said. "You go find your brother."

That was not hard to do. Kiyuga was in the middle of a meal with Digvnige and Sotsena.

"Anagalisgi, please, join us," Sotsena said pleasantly.

"Wado," Anagalisgi replied softly, "but I can't. I've been sent to fetch Kiyuga."

There were glances all around, but Kiyuga did not argue. He hastily finished his cornbread and stood to follow Anagalisgi.

"Is something wrong?" Kiyuga wondered.

"Not yet," Anagalisgi told him. "I told you that I would tell you as much as I could when I was permitted. Gvnagadoga saw us earlier, and he believes you are ready to be told. He is gathering the skiagvsta now."

This was a slow endeavor seeing how Gvnagadoga did not move swiftly, if at all if he could help it, and it was some time before they were all assembled.

"What have the spirits shown you?" Atagulkalu inquired politely, looking back and forth between Gvnagadoga and Anagalisgi.

"They have shown us terrible things," Anagalisgi said. "But also a way to avoid them."

Before anyone could say more, there was a commotion outside. A moment later, a boy only just a man entered the townhouse.

"My respects and apologies," he said breathlessly. "I have news."

"Speak," Aganstata commanded.

"Saloli of Taliqua Eghawa and Amadoya of Si'tiku have gone down to the European settlements and begun burning. They've declared war on the British."

ᎠᏙᏢᎢᎢ ᎤᏍᏏᎠ

Ayadohlv'i Nvgaduhi
Never Surrender

It all started with horses, or so Amadoya said. He'd been one of the six hundred warriors originally chosen to go to Fort Duquense. He'd also been one of those who deserted before reaching the final fort. Frustrated with the British as the rest of them had been, he'd decided to take a few horses as compensation for his trouble. On his return to Si'tiku, a group of Virginia militiamen confronted him and his men about the horses. There was a struggle. Amadoya and his men lost, and the British took the horses.

Since then, Amadoya had been plotting his revenge. He got Saloli involved right away. With news of the hostilities at the fort, it didn't take much to convince others to join the crusade. Saloli led raids from the Middle and Lower Towns, while Amadoya, Kvhe, Golisdayv'i, and their followers headed the raids and war parties from the Overhill towns.

It wasn't hard to find followers. The first five hundred were nearly a given. While Amadoya and his first followers had initially slunk down the river in their canoes in order to bypass the road through Itsa'ti, now they traveled freely. They came dancing through Itsa'ti, painted for battle and singing war songs. Amadoya's adawehi also came with him, burning incense and invoking the spirits for protection and victory and glory in battle against the white demons.

Despite initially burning several farms and other small buildings in various settlements, Saloli and Amadoya were still fairly practical in their style of warfare. They preferred to take captives and ransom them back for goods.

"If we have open trade with them, why the captives?" Atagulkalu asked. It was Unolvtan, the Cold Moon. He had finally managed to get Amadoya and Saloli to come to Itsa'ti and speak their piece.

"We wish to make a point," Amadoya said. "We cannot be bought. But they can. We are not animals to be driven here and there at a whim. We are warriors, and we are to be respected as such. We have our ways and traditions passed down from our ancestors, from digilisi and Ghigau, and we will observe these ways as they have always been."

"And what is the price for peace?" Gvnagadoga wondered. The old uku lay abed nearby, nearly unable to move for the pain in his body and stiffness in his joints. "How many captives will you ransom before it is enough? When will you cease your attacks?"

"When the British cease their advance into our lands. When they acknowledge us as warriors worthy of respect."

"You were on the road to Fort Duquense," Aganstata said. "The British cut the tress and built their own road. Their laborers did not complain. We were not forced to labor beside them. They sent us to scout and report; these things we are good at. They asked us to guide, and we did."

"And now you defend even that!" Amadoya stood abruptly. "Have you somehow forgotten being bound and held captive yourselves?! Mocked by the Aninvdawegi? Pelted with rotten fruit? Even we do not treat our captives so poorly. Many of the women are happy to be with us. How many young warriors now have white blood in them from those grateful and willing to accept our ways and become our daughters and sisters and mothers?"

"How many of these young warriors are now facing potentially divided loyalties, knowing that they may be harming their mother's family?" Gvnagadoga asked quietly. "For to harm the one who brings life is an offense to the Creator, and to offend a woman's family is to harm her. Are these the ways and traditions you seek to uphold?"

"They will gather strength from their mother's family," Amadoya told him, not backing down but meeting the old uku's gaze perfectly.

"Her family may not be able to teach the warriors in our way, but their spirits will provide their inherent strength to them."

"And what will you do if the British do not listen?" Kiyuga wondered. "When they send for more soldiers from England? When they bring their armies and horses to bear against us? When they burn our towns and take our women with no intention of demanding ransom? They are defeating the French. Already the Anisawanugi have sued for peace, and many others have been cowed. What shall we do then?"

"I don't know," Saloli said smartly. "What are we doing? Seems Anagalisgi foresaw this misfortune—" He looked at the young adawehi. "—so it only stands to reason that this was predestined." He shifted position and looked at Kiyuga. "We know you've been visiting the Middle and Lower Towns. Nagutsi'. Wayatsi. Kituwa. Kuwayi'hi. Taliqua. You've not come to fight, so what is it?"

"We are preparing for the inevitable outcome of your foolhardiness," Mankiller told him. "What good is respect if no one is left alive to appreciate it?"

"What good is peace if we are trapped?" Amadoya asked incredulously. "If we are broken? Why shall we make peace with the British but not the Aninvdawegi? They've no interest in peace with us either."

No answer given could satisfy the angry warriors, Kiyuga observed, nor would they say what would make them stop their campaign, short of death. Amadoya seemed to be the driving force this time, unlike Saloli the last time Taliqua Eghawa and Si'tiku allied themselves and went on the attack. Aganstata confronted them about this.

"After Taliwa, you recognized that we could not afford division among the people," the senior warrior said. "And that was when the French appeared to have the upper hand. Things have changed greatly since then. We are not in a good position for anything but peace."

"What division?" Saloli asked. "There is little division among the people now. The question is not whether to support this or that

European power, the Anigilisi or the Anigalvhtsi. The only question that remains is where to attack next."

"We were fools," Amadoya told him. "The Anisawanugi sided with the French and were respected. Although the British have won, they have still allowed for your peace. But at what cost to themselves?"

"Amadoya, Saloli, your arguments cease to make sense," Atagulkalu said, sighing. "Perhaps we are all tired and require rest."

"Yes, maybe Anagalisgi can conjure up a dream to guide us," Amadoya stated, though his words were less than friendly.

Kiyuga saw his brother's obvious embarrassment but said nothing.

They recessed, but Kiyuga would not be surprised if Amadoya and Saloli left in the night, or in the morning, and simply refused to return to the meeting.

Amadoya, Saloli, and their supporters left the townhouse quickly. The rest of them remained for a moment.

"Saloli is right," Aganstata said. "There is little division among the people now. The British have treated us poorly, and our honor demands retribution for it."

"Amadoya will try foolish things now," Gvnagadoga said softly. "As much as he wants to be respected by the British, he also desires respect from us. He wishes to honor the old ways. Simple captive and ransom is insufficient, now that he has been rebuked for it."

"We cannot forbid our warriors to fight."

"No, but we can give them a different target," Atagulkalu decided. "I will gather warriors to raid and attack Fort Massiac, as I said I would do."

"Who will you take?" Mankiller asked.

"I will take some who believe in peace and some who believe in attacking the British. We will fight together as one, just as we did in Taliwa. When we return, victorious and with greater spoils than mere captives to ransom, then perhaps some of the more easily swayed warriors will rethink things."

"Would victory not impassion them for further battle?" Kiyuga wondered.

"One cannot stop a flowing river," Atagulkalu told him. "But you may redirect its flow and lose none of its power."

While sound advice, Kiyuga wondered if it was wise to attempt the same thing twice. The first time, there had been no guarantee that Saloli would agree and join them at Taliwa. This time, as Aganstata said, things were much different, far less in their favor. Would Amadoya and Saloli truly come to join them over a few spoils at a small French fort that may not even be occupied anymore?

"When do you expect to leave?" Aganstata inquired.

"As soon as possible," the skiagvsta replied. He looked at Kiyuga. "Travel among the towns. Find any who are willing to go. I wish to take one hundred warriors. You may also include yourself."

While Kiyuga was excited at the prospect of raiding and spoils, he was less enthusiastic about traveling north during Unolvtan. The cold and snow would only get worse, and it was a terrible time to raid north. Any who knew where Fort Massiac was would know this as well. Did Atagulkalu really expect to find one hundred warriors up to the challenge? Or maybe that was just it; he only wanted hardy warriors. And he wanted them to fight over who was strong enough and hardy enough to take on such a feat.

His pondering was cut short as he left the townhouse and was immediately buffeted by a crisp, icy wind. His journey was not much better, and he had a hard time finding willing warriors, even among those who agreed with and supported Atagulkalu.

Unolvtan turned into Kagali, the Bony Moon, before Kiyuga returned with one hundred warriors for the skiagvsta. Kiyuga found himself wondering whether it was really smart to go north to Fort Massiac. The cold and snow would only get worse, and it wouldn't make the warriors feel any better about the endeavor. When Amadoya went raiding, he took his followers south, toward pleasant weather. The harsh weather of the Overhill and Middle Towns discouraged pursuit from the British. There were French strongholds in the south. New Orleans, for instance, or the area around it. Was it really necessary to go north?

Kiyuga was not alone in these thoughts, but Atagulkalu had made a plan and put his mind to it, and he would not be easily swayed. New Orleans was too great a stronghold for one thousand warriors, and it was certain death for one hundred. Fort Massiac was smaller, less fortified, and with fewer soldiers. Chances were good that the French were already retreating from there and they would meet little resistance.

Of course, the last time they had been promised an easy victory, it had been decidedly less so. And there was no shame in a challenging victory. What glory was there in an easy victory? If the French were packing up, or if they had already packed up and left, there wouldn't be many spoils to bring back.

Kiyuga supported Atagulkalu, and even he was leery of this mission. They left as soon as possible, Atagulkalu already losing support to Amadoya and desperate to make things right. With any luck, they would be back in time for planting season. With an easy victory, good spoils, the changing of the seasons, and the hard work of planting crops, Atagulkalu hoped that he could sway some of the warriors toward peace and not depart with Amadoya or Saloli during raiding season.

Weather and terrain made the northerly trek treacherous and slow. No one attacked in the cold of winter, Kiyuga mused. They did not, even the Europeans did not; on that much they seemed to able to agree. Winter was a time for planning and nursing grudges. Summer was the time to raid and take revenge. Amadoya got away with it because they raided south. And here they were, one hundred warriors, out of their territory, going to raid to the north. Were they insane?

But Atagulkalu was committed, and he would not show weakness by turning back. So they trudged on, out of the mountains to the north and east, enduring a snowstorm that halted them for several days. Kiyuga could see that not a few of the warriors wished to return home, but they'd already come so far. Might as well see it through to the end and try to get something out of it.

When they did finally come upon Fort Massiac, they found it

abandoned, likely since the previous fall. They scavenged through what was left, taking boots and coats, some personal affects left behind, but it was woefully sparse pickings compared to the spoils they'd been promised.

The journey home was a little easier. Kagali became Anvyi, the Windy Moon, and going south brought warmer, southern winds. It was cold comfort to the disappointed warriors as they returned to their respective villages, and Atagulkalu had to admit both defeat and foolishness in his mission, the same things he'd been chastising Amadoya and Saloli for.

"At least we lost no warriors to hunger, sickness, or ambush," he finished, trying to find something positive. He sighed. "What of Amadoya? He was not in Si'tiku when we passed through; I can only assume he has gone raiding again."

"Yes," Mankiller told him simply. "But if there is good news, his warriors are beginning to tire of the constant raiding. Planting season is nearly here, and his warriors wish to plant children in their wives as much as corn in the ground. It may be that his own warriors will cease the raids simply by refusing to go, rather than anything we say."

"We can only hope. But that is good news." Atagulkalu looked at Anagalisgi. "Unless it isn't?"

Kiyuga looked at his brother. Winter had not been kind to him. He looked gaunt, as though he had neither eaten nor slept the entire time Kiyuga had been gone to Fort Massiac. His brother rubbed his eyes and answered, "His raid must be stopped, or we shall surely see fire. This is our last opportunity to avoid that fate."

The skiagvsta and uku exchanged uncertain glances.

"Yvgidahi," Aganstata said, looking at him. "Do you think you can track Amadoya and stop him?"

"I can track him," Kiyuga answered. "As for stopping him, I can only say that I will try."

"Very good. Anagalisgi, do you know where he will go?"

The young adawehi shook his head. "Not specifically, only Watsini."

"Good enough. Go now, Yvgidahi."

Kiyuga stood and left without question, stopping only to refresh his supplies from the home of his aunt and uncle where he was staying. He told them what he was doing, and they wished him well. Then it was back out into the wilds once more. At least this time he was not heading so far north, or so he hoped. The territory that the British called Virginia was vast, and there were more than a few unfriendly peoples in the area.

He did manage to locate Amadoya where he was camped within striking distance of a small village. It was too generous even to call it a village, more of a cluster of people who happened to be in the same area at the same time.

"Come to join us, Yvgidahi?" Amadoya invited casually, offering him a place at the fire. "Forty warriors, forty settlers, men, women, and children. If there should be any easy victory, it is here. And they've plenty of livestock to take as well." He grinned and shifted position. "How were things at Fort Massiac?"

"Deserted," Kiyuga admitted stiffly.

"And cold, I bet."

"I'm not here to join you, Amadoya. I'm here to stop you."

The warrior seemed entirely unaffected. He shrugged and looked around at the gathered warriors. "So stop me. Here I am. Strike me down if you must."

"Come back to Itsa'ti. Anagalisgi has had a vision—"

"A bad one?" another warrior chuckled.

Amadoya leaned forward. "Yvgidahi, if we huddled in our burrows like frightened mice every time your brother blinked, then we would already be overrun and enslaved, just like the Anigvnage'i. We cannot live in fear."

"We also cannot live in defiance of the spirits," Kiyuga said firmly.

"Who is defying? The Si'tiku adawehi have shown me victory."

"And Anagalisgi has seen destruction because of that victory."

"Your brother would see death just as soon as a child was born," Golisdayv'i said. "Oh, wait. He did. Didn't he?"

Kiyuga stood and drew his knife. Golisdayv'i did not rise to the challenge, merely grinned.

"We are not defying the spirits, Yvgidahi," Amadoya repeated. "We are defying the Anigilisi, the British."

"I'm sorry, Amadoya. I know you are trying to do the right thing, but I trust my brother and believe what he says is true. You can't go through with this attack."

"And I cannot sit idly by while our honor is defamed."

He made a motion. Two warriors stood and seized Kiyuga, binding his arms behind him.

"You would dishonor me to save your own?" Kiyuga demanded.

"If anyone wishes to leave and not fight tomorrow, put him on a horse and lead it back to Itsa'ti. We'll catch up afterwards."

Only one volunteered, a young Deer Clan warrior named Uhyesadv. Golisdayv'i hefted Kiyuga on the back of a horse, got him upright, and Uhyesadv took its lead. The horse snorted, shook its head, but turned and followed obediently.

"My regards to Atagulkalu," Amadoya said to his back.

Once they were out of sight and then a little farther, Kiyuga started looking around, judging his chances of falling without hurting himself too badly.

"You could just ask," Uhyesadv told him, not looking at him, though apparently able to read his thoughts.

Without being told, the young warrior stopped the horse and went to help Kiyuga get down. Then he cut the bindings.

"It's no use," he said when Kiyuga turned and started going back. "He'll just tie you to a tree."

Kiyuga stopped and huffed. He looked back. "Why is he doing this? Why won't he listen? Why are you helping me this way?"

Uhyseadv frowned and looked uncertain. "I don't know who to listen to. Usga'hi promised victory. Anagalisgi has foretold doom. But it is more honorable to withdraw from an uncertain fight than to bring misfortune upon the people."

"If only Amadoya were so wise. Why are you here, then?"

"I follow him because I desire the honor that I have been told is mine if I serve the people. If my service results in the destruction of the people, what good is my honor?"

Kiyuga sighed and nodded. "What will it take to make Amadoya understand that?"

"He has chosen whom he will follow, and Usga'hi has chosen him as skiagvsta. Everyone knows Anagalisgi sees only misfortune. We have heard it often enough that perhaps we have become deaf to his warnings."

"Well, at least you haven't."

Uhyesadv swelled a bit with pride at the praise. Then, "So what do we do now?"

Kiyuga frowned and scuffed the dirt. "You and I cannot stop forty warriors, and there is even greater shame in warning the enemy."

"Then you believe the British are the enemy?" Uhyesadv questioned.

"I don't know. But it would be a betrayal of the people. I won't do that. All that is left, then, is to return to Itsa'ti."

So they did. They didn't make it two days' travel before Amadoya and his warriors caught up to them, whooping and dancing, telling stories and singing songs of victory. All had spoils of some form. Some were riding new horses, others driving sheep and goats ahead of them, a few carrying chickens. Many had captives, bound and staggering before them. Despite their slower pace, Kiyuga slowed even more so that they would go ahead of him. Uhyesadv chose to stick with him. Some of Amadoya's warriors taunted him about it and flaunted their plunder, but that was the worst of it.

They arrived back in Itsa'ti well after Amadoya and his warriors had dispersed, and Kiyuga could only meekly approach the council, Uhyesadv by his side.

"Well, it wasn't the one we wanted you to stop," Atagulkalu sighed, "but at least you stopped one of them."

The empty humor fell flat.

Uhyesadv told them a little about Amadoya's plans. The Si'tiku skiagvsta had run his warriors hard through the winter with the raiding, and he'd decided that this last raid would be the final one for the time being, so that his warriors could rest and, as Atagulkalu had put it, plant children in their wives and corn in the ground.

"I would not say that it is impossible for him to raid this summer," Uhyesadv said, "but it is unlikely."

"Maybe it will buy us time for peaceful negotiations," Aganstata suggested. "We should plan to travel to Kuwayi'hi and Fort Prince George."

"Agreed," Atagulkalu said. "Anagalisgi?"

"It will not stop the fire," Anagalisgi told them. "But it will open a door for our escape and survival."

"I think that's the best news I've heard from you," Aganstata said.

"We should gather as many skiagvsta as possible to go together," Mankiller suggested. "In this way, they will see that Amadoya acts outside of the people, but the majority of us have peaceful intentions."

"But is that true?" Kiyuga blurted. He shifted uncomfortably and went on, "A man may proclaim himself a leader, but if he has no followers, then he is just a man out for a walk. Amadoya and Saloli have been successful because they have followers. A great deal of them. We cannot presume to tell them what to do or how to conduct their affairs. They are following the ways and traditions that they have been taught. Shall we tell them that everything they have been taught is a lie?"

"Change is not a lie," Gvnagadoga said. He no longer appeared as death upon his bed, but he still rarely moved very far. "Amadoya is a mighty oak, strong, rigid, unyielding. If he takes his campaign much further, I fear he shall be uprooted or cut down. Better to be flexible as grass in the wind."

"A tree cannot turn back into a seed, nor into any other plant," Kiyuga told him. "A cougar cannot eat grass with the deer. Rather than try to fight, would it not be better to see this through to the end? We know fire is coming. Rather than waste efforts on trying to clean up the messes Amadoya makes across the countryside, why not use the time to prepare ourselves for flight, as we have been doing?"

"We cannot give up on peace," Atagulkalu stated soundly. "Peace and the free flow of goods is the only way to ensure our continued way of life."

"But if that is not what Amadoya, Saloli, and a majority of the warriors want, what good will it do?" Kiyuga shifted again. "Please, skiagvsta, I mean no disrespect, but I hear the talk among the warriors of my age, and the boys who wish to prove themselves. Ani was not only disrespected, but he was murdered. By rights, his blood was avenged, but this by force and with no blessing from those who rule and try to preserve our culture. How shall the other boys act to know that they can be similarly disrespected, even murdered, and the skiagvsta, the uku, and the adawehi shall say that it would be in vain with no hope of retribution? Shall we doom their spirits to even greater misery?"

He could see it was not what the older warriors wanted to hear, yet even they knew it to be true. All the same, after several more days, consulting the Women's Council and the spirits, not one of them changed his position.

"We will have to gather as many skiagvsta as possible," Aganstata said. "We wish to appeared unified, that Amadoya acts of his own discretion."

"I will stay in the Overhill," Mankiller announced. "I will visit Talasi and Tsilhowi; they were quiet supporters of Amadoya last fall, but perhaps they can still be brought back. Daqua'i will surely align with us."

"Taskigi will not join us, though they are part of Tama'li. The warriors there are too anxious."

Mankiller nodded gravely. "The more they look at Fort Loudoun, the more they hate it and wish to attack."

"I will go to the Middle Towns," Aganstata said. "They are caught between Amadoya and Saloli; they may be weary of their treks."

"I will go to the Lower Towns," Atagulkalu finished. "They are the most at risk for attack. With our plans to evacuate them, I cannot imagine they are fond of Saloli constantly provoking the British to fight."

Indeed they were not, and it was not difficult for Atagulkalu to find supporters and bring them back to Itsa'ti. Aganstata also had little trouble, though not all could return with him. As for Mankiller, Talasi and Tsilhowi were too divided among themselves to commit fully one way or the other and so elected to remain out of the fight. Mialoquo was like Taskigi, the more they looked at the fort, the more they hated it. Daqua'i joined them.

But while they made great progress in bringing the skiagvsta together in great support for peace, Kiyuga feared it may have come too late. Not two days after the skiagvsta gathered, British traders arrived, along with official messenger soldiers. Because of the raid that killed four British settlers, Governor Lyttelton was placing an embargo on all guns and ammunition to the Aniyvwiya. That was, unless the murderers were handed over.

It was immediately agreed that they could not simply hand over Amadoya, even if he had led the raid that resulted in the deaths. Another point, there had been forty warriors with him, and forty warriors did not kill four settlers.

Atagulkalu made his way among the towns, visiting Si'tiku several times, asking for the murderers to turn themselves in and settle the matter. Bring peace back to the Aniyvwiya. Bring trade back. He may have gotten some support, but Captain Demeré, the British man in charge of Fort Loudoun, often walked with him. They'd hoped to be seen as allies, that their goals of justice were aligned. But it did nothing to bolster anyone's opinion of the situation.

The murderers were never found.

"Amadoya wants to uphold the old ways," Kiyuga told his brother one night. They sat outside, looking up at the stars. "He may very well get his wish. If we cannot obtain ammunition for our guns, the autumn hunts may not yield much."

Anagalisgi nodded absently. "Amadoya will get his wish, but he will not realize it in the same way that we will."

"I don't think the situation is going to yield peace. I think it will only drive more warriors to support Amadoya and Saloli. They're already trading with the French. The French may be more willing to give us ammunition if we will attack the British."

Anagalisgi waved a hand. "The French have little say in this anymore. They are seeking an opportunity that will not materialize. Their hand has been shattered, and so they retreat."

Before either could say more, their attention was taken by movement within the town. Activity at night was unusual, but for there to be people leaving the town and going on the road in the dark was suspicious. Kiyuga looked at his brother.

"Evil things?" he asked.

Anagalisgi managed an odd smile. "Amusing things, I think."

Now curious, Kiyuga decided to follow the group. It was dangerous to go out at night, for a variety of reasons: cougars, witches, ghosts, evil spirits. Yet he kept on. He could tell that the people were young warriors, but also young women.

They crept around Daqua'i and Tama'li and finally paused in Taskigi. Kiyuga tried to keep out of sight as best he could and still watch them. Many in the group stayed where they were, but a few went around to certain homes, waking certain people and returning. Now what were they up to?

Kiyuga quickly found out as the group, now constituting perhaps fifty people, moved down the slope toward Fort Loudoun. They weren't armed that he could see, and while they tried to be quiet and undetected, they did not appear interested in the fort itself.

The group paused as the guard dogs made another round of the fort. Once they were gone, they continued on.

Kiyuga almost laughed aloud when he saw what they were trying to do. The British had a herd of cattle that they kept for milk and meat. The cows freely roamed the slopes around the fort, save for the areas used for crops. If the British were going to keep ammunition from the Aniyvwiya and so diminish their ability to hunt, well, the favor was about to be repaid.

He made no move to stop them, and he simply watched in fascination. The thing about the cows, though, was that they were slow, lumbering beasts. They did not move readily except in alarm, but the warriors and women trying to move them did not want to raise an alarm. It was comical to watch them attempt to herd the beasts anywhere, never mind wherever it was they wanted them to go.

The best he could gather, they were trying to drive the cows into the river, perhaps to drown them. A few of the cows went into the river, inasmuch as they got a drink of water and wanted to get back out. The group would not let them, and they were having trouble getting them to go deeper, or in the water at all in some cases. Some of the cows began to panic and bellow their displeasure. Soon the whole herd was bellowing.

There was movement in the fort. Kiyuga saw men moving around on its wall, waving torches and lanterns, looking here and there, pointing toward the river.

The warriors, realizing their plan had been foiled, quickly disappeared into the trees, slinking from shadow to shadow until they were back in Taskigi. The British, meanwhile, apparently realizing the intent, not only brought the cows out of the river, but they took them into the safety of the fort.

By the time it was all over, dawn was just breaking over the mountains. Still amused, Kiyuga left his hiding spot and got back on the road, making his way back to Itsa'ti.

He found Anagalisgi in the townhouse, still sleeping. His brother lay near Gvnagadoga, in the event the old uku needed anything, but he, too, was yet sleeping. Kiyuga shook his brother awake.

"What?" his brother asked, yawning. "Did something happen?"

"Would you not be the one to tell me?" Kiyuga teased.

Anagalisgi sat up, rubbing his eyes. "What is it? What do you want? Did you find out what those people were doing last night?"

So Kiyuga told his brother about following the group down the road, all the way to Taskigi. There they met up with some more warriors and women and tried to drive the cattle from Fort Loudoun into the river.

"But the cows started to protest and their noise alerted the soldiers," Kiyuga said. "They came out and drove the cattle into the fort to keep them safe."

"Was anyone caught?" Anagalisgi wondered.

"Not that I saw." Kiyuga laughed once. "You were right. It was not evil things; it was indeed amusing things. It was funny to watch."

"Cows are not so easily moved, nor willing to drown themselves without making a bit of noise."

They turned to see that Gvnagadoga was awake, and it was he who had spoken. He appeared mildly amused by the tale as well.

But if they were amused by the cows, they were less amused when Saloli led an attack on a small three-man convoy that departed Fort Loudoun and was heading for Fort Prince George. All three men were killed, and Saloli made a point of letting everyone know that he had traded their scalps for ammunition from the French, which he would share with any who needed to provide for his family for the winter, or who wished to kill the British.

It wasn't long before all trade was suspended, and Fort Loudoun began preparing for siege. Kiyuga went with Atagulkalu, Aganstata, and the other skiagvsta to Taskigi to watch as the walls were reinforced, cannons were set and readied, and a supply train brought provisions to the fort, everything from flour to ammunition.

The supply train did not last long, for Amadoya was quick to take his warriors and block the roads. Any supply wagons that did meander their way up the road were attacked, the goods taken and distributed to Aniyvwiya families instead. With hostile activity at Fort Loudoun, Amadoya's support grew, and there was no shortage of warriors and women willing to block the road for certain lengths of time. Even a few of the skiagvsta withdrew their support from the peace envoy Atagulkalu wished to assemble.

"Should we start moving people out of the Lower Towns?" Kiyuga wondered. "We may have the Overhill roads blocked, but the Lower Towns are in great danger."

"Not yet," Atagulkalu said. "Aganstata and Mankiller will take the peace envoy to Charleston, straight to Governor Lyttelton as he prepares to send his army against us. Perhaps we can stop this pot from boiling over. I will remain in Tama'li and Taskigi to keep an eye on Fort Loudoun, and send word if violence breaks out."

"I want you and Anagalisgi to go with me," Aganstata told Kiyuga. "I wish for you to observe the Lower Towns and listen for word of any treachery. Anagalisgi, I shouldn't have to tell you why I want you there."

Kiyuga looked at his brother who nodded solemnly. As much as Kiyuga did not like the way things were happening, how much worse was it for Anagalisgi, who had known about this beforehand, warned of it, and yet went unheeded? Suddenly he no longer envied his brother his gifts.

They departed the following morning. It was fall again, but winter would not be long in coming. At least this time they were going south instead of north, Kiyuga thought ruefully.

"Here to plead with me again?" Amadoya asked sarcastically as their party approached his barrier.

"No," Aganstata told him. "Actually, we wish for you to maintain it until such time as we return and announce peace has been achieved."

"Suddenly I am a hero, then."

"You are the one who started this war, if indeed it happens. We are trying to prevent it."

Amadoya did not back down. "And here we are."

Aganstata grunted. "Here we are."

The tension between them lasted until they were well past the barrier. Kiyuga could see stoic determination in all their faces. Even if peace was achieved, they would not give up. What, then, did that say about what would happen if peace was not achieved? Kiyuga glanced at his brother but said nothing.

When they reached the Middle Towns, Kituwa and Taliqua had joined forces. Kituwa was already charged with protecting the Middle

Towns from Aninvdawegi invaders. Saloli's enthusiasm for raiding British settlements had brought the two towns closer together, and neither one was overly excited about the prospect of peace. The Overhill were protected by distance, terrain, and weather. The Middle and Lower Towns had only minimal defense from the mountains, and they would be the first ones attacked. Some wished to evacuate immediately; others were determined to die on their ancestral soil if they had to.

"What happens when children actually listen to the stories they are told, and fully believe in the values they are taught?" Anagalisgi mused that night around the fire. "What happens when they are later told to ignore everything? When their heroes turn out to be, not legends, but men? When grand adventures are not filled with spirits and monsters, but boredom and mistreatment? When evil does not always receive justice?"

"This is why you don't get invited to parties," Kiyuga told him, chuckling.

Anagalisgi did not react.

"Have you seen anything?"

His brother did not say anything for a long moment. Finally he sighed. "I've seen too much, I think. There is little left to see. All has been told."

"You have seen fire, yes, and you have given us a plan. Surely something must come after that? Do the British stop their attacks? Do they continue?" Kiyuga did not voice his other fears that Anagalisgi was not seeing beyond these things because there was nothing to see, they would all be killed.

"I know only what the spirits have told me. This is what we must focus on, and not be distracted by other things."

Well, it was a course of action, at least, and a simple one. Focus only on the task at hand. Right now, they just had to make it to Charleston.

Charleston was at once city and fort. They were met with great suspicion by the common folk. There were plenty of glares, insults both understood and implied, and a few near-collisions with rotten fruit or animal dung.

"Are we sure we're doing the right thing?" one of the skiagvsta asked. "Their people are just as hateful of us as our people are of them."

"Hatred has yet to solve any problems," another told him calmly. "And we cannot rightly walk away without offering every opportunity to make things right."

"But what have we done wrong?" a third questioned.

"Amadoya tainted our honor," the first said.

"The British tainted it. Amadoya tried to save it."

"Are we here for peace or not?" Aganstata asked irritably. "If you are having second thoughts, then you are free to leave. You know where Amadoya has made camp."

Any further discussion fell silent, but Kiyuga could feel the uncertainty. How much longer could they pretend that simple meeting and trade goods would be enough to force peace and cooperation? The honor of both sides was at stake.

The governor made his residence within the fort. The envoy was stopped at the gates by a dozen soldiers.

"What's your business here?" one demanded.

"We are here to negotiate peace terms," Aganstata said calmly, trying to appear nonthreatening. "We wish to do so with your governor."

The soldiers sized them up for a moment, judging their demeanor, their weapons, and just the group overall. Aganstata was certainly a warrior, no doubt, but he was easily fifty winters. Many of the other skiagvsta were of an age. Anagalisgi was the youngest in the group at only twenty winters or so, followed by Kiyuga at twenty-five winters. The next oldest, he believed, was about forty winters. But it was all a guess, anyway.

Suffice to say, they were not a bunch of young warriors looking for blood and honor. The British soldiers seemed to come to the same conclusion. They bid the envoy stay put while the youngest of the soldiers was dispatched to inform the governor of their arrival.

Kiyuga looked at his brother, but Anagalisgi's attention was taken by something upon the wall at the far end. He almost looked like he wanted to speak. But when Kiyuga looked around, trying to follow his brother's eyes as exactly as he could, he saw nothing.

"What do you see, little brother?" Kiyuga asked quietly.

Anagalisgi blinked and looked at him, initially looking confused. Finally he blinked again and answered, "The way forward."

"We are where we are supposed to be, then?" Aganstata asked.

"Yes," Anagalisgi told him. "We're getting there."

It helped to ease the latent anxiety of the envoy. They were on the right path. This was the will of the spirits. Kiyuga found himself wondering if that was really a good thing, when the spirits had also apparently mentioned that fire and destruction was inevitable at this point. Weren't they trying to avoid that?

Still, he did not say this out loud, just waited patiently with the rest of them. A cloud passed over the sun, providing relief from the heat, although distant skies said that rain was on the way.

At long last, the messenger returned.

"Governor Lyttelton will receive them in his quarters," the boy reported, casting a few hasty glances toward the envoy.

The soldiers grunted but assented and got out of their way, all but two who proceeded to escort them through the fort. Kiyuga got a sickening feeling, that he was suddenly one of the cows the soldiers had brought into Fort Loudoun. The cows believed themselves safe from drowning, but Kiyuga also knew that the soldiers had then slaughtered all the cows and salted the meat as part of their efforts to prepare for a siege.

He also found himself memorizing the layout of the fort, counting the cannons and trying to estimate the number of soldiers, in the event that there would ever be battle here. He knew just from briefly looking around that the Aniyvwiya would be no match for the British here. They were too powerful, too numerous, and they also had their large ships in the harbor for more support. The would have to lure them into their own lands, into the mountains and forests. They had to go back to what had worked in the beginning, when the French had been defeating them at every turn.

But they were here for peace, he reminded himself. They were trying to resolve problems and come to a compromise that all could be happy with. But one look at his brother said that even if they came to some form of agreement here, it wouldn't last long.

"I will rely on you to understand their words," Aganstata said, speaking to both Kiyuga and Anagalisgi. "They enjoy word trickery. Do not let them lay any traps."

The brothers promised to do their best. The word trickery of the British was well-known, how they used word play on their pieces of paper—their contracts and treaties—to steal from all the nations. They'd gotten away with it for many years because few understood their language well enough to understand their traps. Now the people were learning, getting smarter. Kiyuga was forced to wonder if it was too little, too late. The British were here, along with their armies and their ships and their guns. The pieces of paper meant less and less when there was no consequence for not following through on their promises. He looked at his brother for some indication of what to do or say, but found nothing.

The fort was built as a grand display of the might of the British army with its guns and its walls and the ships at sea, and the governor's quarters were no different.

"Welcome, friends," the governor began, standing and spreading his arms in a friendly gesture. "It brings me great joy to know you have come to negotiate peace."

"We are here as a show of solidarity, that Amadoya acts of his own accord and not with the wishes of the Aniyvwiya," Aganstata said respectfully.

"Of course, of course. I've had to deal with my fair share of rogue colonels in my day. It's a tragic thing when a good soldier goes bad, hm?"

Something about the man's demeanor was off, Kiyuga thought.

They'd sent no word of their arrival, had rarely dealt with him directly, and yet he spoke and acted as though theirs was an intimate bond. If that were so, why the invasion preparations? Why the poor treatment from everyone else?

Or perhaps Lyttelton was dealing with dissent among his own people. Atagulkalu, Aganstata, Mankiller, and the rest of the skiagvsta were all vying for peace, a peace many warriors did not want. Perhaps Lyttelton was in the same situation with the British.

But then, why the invasion preparations?

"I would like nothing more than to be able to come to an agreement right here, right now," the governor was saying. "We both know the situation, so why don't we talk terms, hm?"

"Our people need ammunition for their guns for the winter hunts," Aganstata said.

"No doubt, but even if we had an arrangement, the roads are blocked."

"Our people are anxious, with you storing up supplies in your fort as though you plan to attack. The fort is within sight of Tama'li, and Taskigi has grown about its lands. Families live there."

"Even so, those families are able to flee as necessary. If the fort comes under siege from your people, my soldiers shall be slaughtered with nowhere to run."

"No one is slaughtering anyone."

"Oh? How about the raids upon innocent settlers?" He went to a map laid out on his desk. "Four settlers killed here just this spring. Eight more here. One here."

"Twenty Aniyvwiya killed when your people confronted Amadoya," Mankiller stated.

"He was stealing horses."

"He was taking what was promised to him."

Lyttelton hummed uncomfortably. "Yes, Fort Duquense really was an unfortunate thing, wasn't it? I don't know if you know this, but when we finally took the fort, there was nothing in it. The French had set it on fire and left in the night. So, quite frankly, we didn't get anything out of the deal either. At least all your warriors were able to go home."

"And we should like to stay there. Peacefully."

"The same as any of the common settlers, I should think." The governor frowned. "Do you not believe that they find joy and honor in building their own lives?"

"When it does not involve killing our warriors, certainly," Aganstata said.

Lyttelton looked over the group. "You know what I see here? A coalition of headmen, saying that they represent the interests of their people, pretending that their people agree with what they are doing. Do you know what else I see? Old warriors." He vaguely indicated Aganstata. "You're what, fifty?" He looked at another chief. "And you, forty-five?" He raised a brow toward a third. "You look at least sixty." He looked back at Mankiller. "But the wisdom of the elders is not always echoed in the actions of the youth. And the youth are the ones driving this campaign. You have this...Amadoya in the Overhill, blocking the roads and raiding in Virginia. And here in the south, there is another force that has now formed a unified army between your towns of Taliqua and Kituwa. What am I to make of this?

"Your leader Little Carpenter is our friend, no doubt. But I doubt his ability to lead and take charge of your warriors. If trade goods were the only objective here, then a full winter and a full summer of increased open trade ought to have been enough. But I don't think that it's the goods they're after, not when they are freely given." Lyttelton nodded. "I think your warriors want blood. I think they want blood and they want war and they want plunder. Because it is what you have taught them, what they believe they must do for their honor."

"Do you soldiers have no desire for glory and honor and spoils?" Wilinawa wondered. "Or are they merely forced laborers?"

"We have a right to be here. Everyone knows that. Our boys are glad to be soldiers. Even the unfortunate colonials have shaped up to be something of a useful fighting force."

"Are we here to negotiate for peace, or aren't we?" Aganstata cut in irritably.

The governor huffed. "Yes, of course. Bravado is a wonderful thing, but it does tend to wear on the prospect of peace. Perhaps we shall simply agree that we are both formidable foes in our own right. The question then becomes, how do we make it so that we never have to test this formidability?"

"Withdraw your soldiers from Fort Loudoun," Mankiller said. "Turn it over to us. We will reopen the road for free trade."

"Your people wanted the fort in the first place for protection."

"And we shall use it for that purpose. But without you."

"Well, as I said before, I am more than willing to bargain for free trade, but your people are still blocking the road."

"They won't, if you withdraw your soldiers and leave the Overhill."

"And the Middle and Lower Towns," another skiagvsta quipped.

"Would you have us withdraw all the way to the coast? All the way back to England?" He raised a brow. "Even if this were to happen, we may continue in the trade, but the embargo on guns and ammunition will remain."

"We need these things for the winter hunts," Aganstata said firmly.

"And just as easily kill us? I'm sorry, sir, but I can't take that chance. Perhaps you ought to do things as you did before we gave your people guns and ammunition."

It was a stinging blow, if only because suddenly everyone, even the oldest of the warriors, realized how dependent they had become on European goods. There had once been a time when their warriors were so skilled with an atlatl, they could launch three projectiles for every bullet a European fired and be far more accurate and deadly.

"It appears we have come to a stalemate," Lyttelton observed. "You need guns and ammunition to stay alive, and yet you are not willing to guarantee the safety of my soldiers and the innocent civilians in may care. Well, even if you were willing, I don't know that your younger warriors would be so quick to agree and follow the rules. It's a funny thing you have going for you, this idea that, even as a man is expected to contribute to the community, he is somehow also separate from it.

You cannot give him orders and expect him to follow. Of course, I could be misreading things. Rogue colonels and all.

"So I have a different idea. Rather than play this back and forth game, sending messages here and there, hoping they get through, hoping they are understood, and waiting for replies—giving either of our warriors or soldiers ample time to carry out most unseemly actions—I think it would be more prudent if we all go together. Gather this Amadoya and also the one in charge of the force in the south. I wish to see the faces of these revolutionaries. Perhaps when evil has a face, its mask shall come off."

Kiyuga could have sworn that the governor looked at Anagalisgi when he said that last part.

"When will we meet?" Mankiller asked. "In the spring?"

Lyttelton shook his head. "No. As soon as possible."

"We will do so," Aganstata promised.

He turned as if to leave, but a couple soldiers blocked their exit.

"No, no, no," the governor chuckled. "No. I'm not relying on words. When I said we are going to go together, I meant that we will be going together. I will send a messenger to the Overhill, to Little Carpenter, with the day, time, and location to meet. I want him to bring me this Amadoya, and the southern leader, and any other murderers whom you have allowed to run free and kill British settlers. And you are going to stay here, with me, under my lavish hospitality, as a guarantee that they will come and be turned over."

The governor made a motion. The warriors were made to, once again, surrender all their weapons save one knife for practical use. And if they thought to use it in any other way, well, there would be consequences. When all was finished, Kiyuga could see that if any of the skiagvsta had continued to hold out some hope of peace, it was now gone. From here on out, there was only war.

Lyttelton had poured himself a drink, which he downed in a single gulp and set the glass on his desk. He looked up as though surprised to see the envoy before him. He gave a lazy glance toward one of the soldiers. "Get them out of my quarters. They don't leave the fort."

DᏎᏫᏁᎢT ᎯᏬᎠᏍᏚᎯ

Ayadohlv'i Hisgaduhi

Magic and Sorcery

At least they got free run of the fort, Anagalisgi thought, sitting in the grass and peeling apart stalks of grass. Well, free run with exception of the armory, for obvious reasons. They were forced to sleep in an old bunkhouse unfit for the British soldiers. It was rotting, moldy, and infested, so unless it was raining—and even if it was—they usually chose to sleep outside. They were given food, the same as the soldiers, but they were not permitted to eat near the soldiers or the other fort laborers, but in their own area. That was fine; none of the warriors wanted to sit with the soldiers anyway.

When Lyttelton made the statement that he wanted to move and meet as soon as possible, they'd all kind of assumed that meant he wished to get moving within a few days. Then he let it be known that such was not the case and to not get their hopes up of leaving any time soon.

There were worse places to be, Anagalisgi figured, though it was hollow comfort. At least they were not bound and left exposed to the elements. And they still had their single knives. Nevertheless, a prison was still a prison. No matter how far the sheep roamed, they were still intended for slaughter.

So they waited. Luckily, Yachtino happened to have brought a bag of marbles with him. As soon as the rain cleared on their first day of captivity, they'd staked out an area for a digadayosdi tournament. At first, the soldiers thought them plotting escape, or, worse, some sort of revolt. And it was true, the game was used to improve ones aim and accuracy, it was also an agreeable pastime. Pretty soon, they even had the soldiers playing in their off time.

It was a simple enough concept. A field about one hundred feet long, with five holes dug at equal distances down the length of the course, though forming an L-shape. Each player was to toss his marble as close to the first hole as possible, knocking others out of the way, and advance to the next hole. The first person to complete the course won. There were variations of the game depending on the number of players and teams.

At the moment, Aganstata and Mankiller were playing against two British soldiers of roughly the same age. Mankiller was nearly completed with the third hole, arguably the toughest as it was the corner of the L-shape, and he could not afford to have his marble land in either the second or fourth hole. The rest of the players were having a difficult time of it, and one of the soldiers kept having to repeat the second hole.

Mankiller won easily, but he had the greatest coordination out of all of them; even Aganstata said so. The British soldiers were upset and did not bother to congratulate the winning team, even under false pretense, before stomping away and arguing, quietly insulting Mankiller and Aganstata and the rest of them.

"Who is next?" Mankiller wondered, looking around.

"I will," Kiyuga volunteered, standing. He looked up the slope. "Anagalisgi, join me."

"I don't think so," Anagalisgi said shyly.

"Come on, Anagalisgi, you've ripped up more grass than the sheep over there," Aganstata goaded. "Come. Be involved in the waking world."

Anagalisgi stood, stretched, and made his way down to the field. Aganstata gave him a marble to use as he joined his brother. They played against Wilinawa of Daqua'i and Chola of Si'tiku, the only skiagvsta to oppose Amadoya.

Kiyuga went first, tossing his marble toward the first hole. He nearly put his marble in the hole in one toss, but not quite. Anagalisgi stood to take his turn. He knew he could not hope to land in the hole in one try, but he could help his brother. He aimed, let out a breath, and tossed his marble. His marble struck Kiyuga's and tipped it into the hole.

Wilinawa and Chola both got close. They two as well as Anagalisgi landed in the first hole in two tries while Kiyuga took his second turn to make his first attempt at the second hole.

Kiyuga and Wilinawa played exceptionally well, while Anagalisgi and Chola tended to lag behind.

It wasn't enough to just navigate the course one hole at a time, but then, once you reached the end, you have to go back. Soon, Kiyuga and Wilinawa had completed the fifth hole and were working their way back, running into Anagalisgi and Chola who were still on the fourth hole their first time down. It was a bit of a mess as they bumped into each other, and then they were moving on.

Chola pulled away from Anagalisgi. Soon it was Kiyuga and Wilinawa racing toward the first hole, Chola one hole or one turn behind them, Anagalisgi following sadly.

Wilinawa was the first to complete the course, beating Kiyuga by a single shot. Then Chola bested Anagalisgi, not that it had been that difficult of a competition. Any bets that had been made were collected, and marbles were passed off to the next players.

"You might have warned me of this misfortune," Kiyuga said, slapping Anagalisgi on the back. "Eh, little brother?"

Anagalisgi grinned. "It is of no consequence; therefore, I do not see."

"Glad to know the fate of our people does not rest upon a game of digadayosdi," Aganstata commented, his attention still on the game at hand. "If it should rest on a sport, I would prefer it to be anejodi. At least we have you to say the blessing beforehand and toss the ball."

"We would need younger warriors for anejodi, I think," Yachtino chuckled. "And seven women for the dance."

They were suddenly distracted by an excited whoop from the players. Someone had gotten a hole in one, and on the fourth hole no less. There was some conspiratorial muttering as the losing team tried to figure out a new strategy.

They whiled away the afternoon in this manner, occasionally getting a few British spectators to join them, and this carried on until dinner. There was some commotion as a delivery to the fort arrived late and the soldiers at the gate gave the new arrivals a hard time about it. Words were exchanged, and then life carried on. Anagalisgi watched as the new arrivals offloaded the supplies then went to see what scraps they could scrounge up so they weren't too hungry when they went to sleep that night.

"What do you think it is that makes them so successful?" Anagalisgi asked of Kiyuga. "We have the advantage of ancestral lands and spirits. We have become proficient in their guns. We have warrior strength. We have allies among our own. How is it that they have conquered so much?"

"Numbers," Kiyuga said, very matter-of-fact. "They may lose one battle, but they can always send for more reinforcements. Here, we have no such luxury. We can call upon allies, but we are limited in number. I cannot say for certain, but the British seem to be infinite." He shifted position. "They are also very quick to make things. They have not only skill, but speed. They are able to make many guns, many musket balls, many cannons, in a very short amount of time. You saw how quickly they built Fort Loudoun. I have seen Atagulkalu build homes quickly, but even he was no match for their skill and efficiency."

"Do you think that perhaps their spirits, their God, is greater than us, than our spirits?"

Kiyuga looked at him. "I don't know. That would be a question that I would have for you. If their God is greater than our spirits, than our ancestors, then what good does it do us to fight?"

"Well, even the British and the French fought, and both proclaimed the Christian God. Or perhaps one part of it. From what I understand, they worship three gods. Perhaps they each serve one part of the God. Perhaps the Spanish to the south serve the third part. I do not know."

"Whatever the case, the British God certainly favored them."

Anagalisgi nodded absently, still puzzling over things. How had they gotten to this place? Where were they expected to go? How was this going to end, really? Why could he not see past fire and destruction? It troubled him greatly, and he badly hoped to dream that night. He had seen the woodpecker upon the fort wall when they arrived. It had not said anything to him, but he took its presence to mean that they were on the right path. This was what was to happen. This was what was expected of them.

But was this the path to destruction, or the path to avoiding it? Why would the spirits lead them to their destruction? Shouldn't they be leading them away from such a thing? Or had they dishonored themselves and the spirits too greatly that they were now being punished? And who had done the dishonoring? Amadoya or Atagulkalu?

The following day saw them again playing digadayosdi. Anagalisgi sat in a new spot, watching the game and still picking grass.

"Mind if I sit here?"

He looked up, putting a hand up to shield his eyes from sun, but gesturing to sit down.

The man did so. He was British, clearly, his age a little older than Kiyuga. He had thick brown hair and looked like a man who preferred life on the road, or else on the farm, versus having to be among the soldiers. His dress pegged him as one of the blue-coated provincials, rather than the dedicated, red-coated soldiers.

"Interesting game," he observed mildly.

"It passes the time," Anagalisgi said levelly.

"Has Lyttelton said when he expects to leave for Fort Prince George?"

"Not yet. Do you know?"

"Not specifically, but it will be soon." The man pointed. "That's Christopher Gadsden, Captain of the artillery force. Lyttelton is going to have him and a thousand men escort you to Fort Prince George for negotiations."

"How do you know this?" Anagalisgi wondered. "Are you an

officer?"

The man laughed. "Ha! Hardly. No provincial is considered so highly. Even Colonel Washington was rejected for a commission, and he served under two generals. What chance do I have?" He sighed and grinned. "Ah, but I forget my manners. Nathan Wilde."

"Anagalisgi. I believe in English, it would translate to lightning."

Nathan waved a hand dismissively. "Anagalisgi is a fine name. You're a fine man from a fine people. It's tragic what Lyttelton has done to you. What he's going to do."

Anagalisgi raised a brow suspiciously. "What do you mean?"

"Lyttelton is going to have Gadsden escort you to Fort Prince George where he expects to trade you for Amadoya and the other headmen of the raids. He is going to establish a treaty saying as such, but he will not honor it. He is going to leave Fort Prince George for the safety of home, and the army has orders to not only execute the headmen, but all of these chiefs here, and start destroying towns if land concessions are not made. Why else would he order heavy artillery brought along?"

"Why are you telling me this?"

"Because it's not right. It's not right what they've done, what they're doing, what they're going to do. It is not right, it is not honorable. It certainly is not Godly."

"Yes, but why are you telling me? Aganstata and Mankiller—"

"Are the leaders, yes, I know that. But you are the seer. You are the medicine man, the priest, the prophet, whatever you call yourself. The point is, you see things. You dream."

Anagalisgi shifted uncomfortably, moving just a smidge away from the man. "How do you know these things? What do you know of me or my dreams?"

"Nothing, only that you have them and it is you I must see."

"Why? Who sent you?"

"We call her the Author."

"Who is we?"

"My companion, Andrew. He is running errands presently. He

wished to speak to you also, but when I saw you, I could not pass up the opportunity."

Anagalisgi searched Nathan's gaze but found only sincerity. "Who is the Author? What things has she written?"

Nathan frowned. "We have only fragments here and there, but they tell stories that have never been told. True stories that would have been lost if not for our diligence in keeping them. We've yet to find any complete manuscripts, but the time is nearing. We know it. Stories will be written again."

"What does this Author want with you? Or me?"

"She has sent me to help you, to help your people. You are in grave danger. We cannot bear to see you suffer."

"You...and your companion, Andrew."

"That's right."

"Two helpers..." Anagalisgi murmured. "In a time of despair." He felt Nathan looking at him. "The woodpecker...Ge'gwogv told me of you. It said that you would teach me wonderful and powerful things."

Nathan grinned, and there was a certain air between them then, as though two long lost brothers had finally found each other according to the will of the spirits. He nodded. "That's right, or that is my intent. I wish to show you the power of the Author, though it may be more prudent to show you Time first, until you get the hang of it."

"Is it difficult to learn?"

"It can take some getting used to. It is not a physical weapon that you hold. It is a matter of will, purely spirit."

So it was no wonder that they had sought him out first, because he had a great connection to the spirits. In his soul, he felt as though this were the beginning of the culmination of every dream and vision he'd had since he was a child.

"You look excited," Nathan observed, eyes laughing. "Shall we begin now?"

"That would be very good," Anagalisgi told him.

"Excellent. Then perhaps I will begin with a few demonstrations." Nathan stood.

"Shall I call over Aganstata and the others?"

"Not yet. You are the one who must see and understand this first."

Anagalisgi nodded and watched him, eager to see and learn.

"This is what we call a Band," the British man began.

Suddenly, it was as though Anagalisgi were looking through glass stained red. But more than that, he watched everything around him completely stop. A bird hopping around in the grass was completely still. The spectators of the game only a short distance away were silent, gestures frozen. The players were as still as their stone marbles which hung in the air.

"What is this?" Anagalisgi wondered, fearful and yet awed.

"A Band, as I said," Nathan answered humbly. "It is the ability to manipulate Time. Specifically, this is a Fast Band. We are moving so fast that everything around us appears to have stopped. Similarly, a Slow Band..."

The red glass was replaced with blue glass, and everything began moving very quickly. Birds jumped around wildly, and an entire digadayosdi game was completed in but moments. The tint turned from blue back to red, and Nathan continued to speak.

"—will make everything appear to happen very quickly, because we are moving slower than everything around us. This is just regular Time, which means you can see these things as they are happening, as you are doing them. But when you use the power of the Author, the Bands..." The red tint vanished, but everything else remained the same, frozen in place. "—become basically invisible."

For a long moment, Anagalisgi had no words. What did he say to this, except, "Are you a spirit? A witch, perhaps?"

Nathan shook his head. As he did so, life resumed. Anagalisgi thought he saw everything become clear again in that moment, but it was difficult to tell. The British man sat beside him again.

"I am no spirit, nor a witch, nor any other magical being. I am simply a servant of the Author."

"An adawehi, then. A conjurer."

"Not as such, though I can see how you might make that

comparison. This power does involve an element of Faith. And you can do many things with it."

Anagalisgi watched as the man's eyes suddenly turned color, from brown to blue. Then his skin darkened. The changes lasted only a moment, but they had been stark and obvious.

"Matter is another aspect of it." He picked up a small stone, tossed it in the air, but before it hit the ground, it stopped and remained suspended. "Energy is the third portion. Time, Matter, and Energy, the three facets of the universe, all held together by the element of Faith."

"But this...this is sorcery."

Confusing thoughts swirled through Anagalisgi's mind. This was far more than anything he had ever seen or heard except in tales of evil and witchcraft. And yet, had not the woodpecker proclaimed this encounter good, that it would bring salvation to the people? Had he been tricked his whole life? He could not believe that, not when the Raven Mocker stole Ulisi's heart. There was a distinct difference between the shadow spirits and the white spirits. Whatever trickery evil played, a spirit in its true form could not be or pretend to be another spirit.

What, then, did that say about this power? What did that mean for the Aniyvwiya as they strove for peace with the British? How would this magic help their cause? How would they learn it? How would they use it?

Well, he had an idea how Amadoya and Saloli would use it. But at the same time, was that not the nature of war? To find and use every resource and every advantage in order to win? Regardless of what happened here or at Fort Prince George, there would be war. Anagalisgi knew that as surely as he knew the sun would rise in the east and set in the west.

"How long does this take to learn?" he wondered.

"Learning is not an issue," Nathan told him. "But mastery can take years."

Anagalisgi frowned. "The Aniyvwiya don't have years to spare."

"No, you don't. But Andrew and I will help you as much as we can.

As much as you will allow us."

"I would like to learn. I want to help my people."

Nathan nodded. "Well then, there's no time to waste, is there?"

He made a motion and Anagalisgi stood up.

"The most important element is Faith. Belief in the Author and belief that our stories, whatever they may be, will turn out exactly as they need to. It may not be what we hoped for, but it is always what is needed. Since the advent of 'One day,' our stories have been set in motion. And they will be as the Author wills. Do you understand this?"

"Is there no belief in free will, then, as the Europeans believe about their Christian God?" Anagalisgi questioned.

"There is," Nathan said calmly. "But how shall you and I know it? Do you, by following the woodpecker in a prescribed manner of events leading to our happenstance meeting, give up your free will? Do you not have the choice to ignore the woodpecker? Or is it simply more fortuitous to do as the spirits bid?"

Anagalisgi thought on this a moment. Then, "I understand it."

"Good. Then tell Time to stop."

"How shall I do that?"

"Close your eyes. Be aware of yourself. Know thyself and thy place. Observe all that is around you. Be part of it. Be apart from it. Single yourself out of everything. Apart from the group here. Apart from the fort. Apart even from the sky and earth, from the soil and stone. Feel everything about yourself, where hair touches wind, where moccasins touch earth. Feel yourself moving with the environment, all as one the same plane, moving in synchronization as one. Now step apart from it. Move yourself outside of everything else, faster so that everything else seems to slow."

Anagalisgi opened his eyes as sounds began to disappear. Even Nathan's speaking had slowed momentarily. He found that everything around him had come to a stop, that is, except for Nathan.

In his surprise, he lost his focus, stumbling backwards and falling on his seat as everything resumed normally. Nathan laughed and offered him a hand up.

"That was good!" he exclaimed. "That was very good!"

Embarrassed, Anagalisgi brushed the dirt and grass from his clothes. "Where did you learn this? Did Andrew teach you?"

Nathan, still smiling, shook his head. "No. No, my father taught me. Well, to be specific, he introduced me to a similar concept, but then we went our separate ways."

"There is more to learn?"

"He...he learned something called Harvesting." The British man sighed, suddenly very uncomfortable. "There is an industry out there, a secret industry, whose whole existence is based on the buying and selling of time, of the years that people have lived. It is a Harvester's job to collect these years from the sick and dying."

"Raven Mockers," Anagalisgi stated. "Witches that eat the heart of the dying and absorb their years, cursing their spirits in the western lands."

"Something like that, I suppose."

"A Raven Mocker took my grandmother."

"I'm sorry to hear that."

Anagalisgi shook his head. "No. It was a good thing, for she may even now serve the people she loved. A special tree may only bear special fruit when planted in the body of one taken by a Raven Mocker. That which was meant for evil has been turned to good."

Nathan's expression was uncertain. "Very well, then...good luck? I think?"

Anagalisgi waved a hand. "It is not your concern. But I can now see the threads weaving together."

"As long as it makes sense to you, I suppose. Why don't you try Banding again?"

He came to call it Iyuwahnilvhi Adahnesagi'a, Conjuring Time, although he sometimes jokingly called it Galvdasga, "cutting it into strips." He and Nathan spent much time together over the next few days, both of them uncertain exactly when Lyttelton intended to move them to Fort Prince George. His companion Andrew O'Dell also joined them and assisted in instruction.

"I was part of the Time industry, too," the man from Ireland explained. "I was a Merchant. I bought the Time collected by the Harvesters and sold it for a profit to anyone who would buy."

"How does that work?" Anagalisgi asked. "How shall time and years be bought and sold? I understand the Raven Mockers, or Harvesters as you call them, but the rest I cannot comprehend."

"If you are truly interested in knowing, we will show you once this debacle has ended. Right now, our focus is on teaching you so you may save your people."

The concept was not difficult, but the execution was. He was accustomed to having to dance, pray, burn incense, meditate, and use artifacts in order to conjure. A simple effort of will, basing everything on Faith alone, was a terribly foreign idea. He thought he was understanding, and then it would slip away and his conjuring would fall apart. Nathan and Andrew tried to be encouraging, but it was difficult when the timetable was uncertain. Even when one man or the other used his Bands to lengthen the days so they could train and practice more, Anagalisgi felt woefully unprepared to help his people.

He was dealing with the power of the spirits, conjuring as no adawehi had ever conjured before. He could tell the sun to stop, and it would stop. This was the power as told in the stories he'd heard as a child. Was it any wonder he was a bit fearful of it? But did that fear erode his Faith? Was it not right to be in awe of the spirits and thankful that they would see fit to choose him as a conduit for such power?

He managed to Iyuwahnilvhi Uhlisda Adahnesagi'a, that is Conjure Fast Time, or Fast Band as they said in English. Then he was able to Iyuwahnilvhi Asganola Adahnesagi'a, that is Conjure Slow Time, or Slow Band. Once he had done this, Nathan and Andrew decided he had done enough for the day and told him to return to his own people to eat.

Anagalisgi did so, getting food and sitting with Kiyuga.

"Why do you spend so much time with them?" his brother asked quietly. "You have passed along their warning of Lyttelton's intended treachery, do they have more to say?"

"More to teach," Anagalisgi said. "They have spirit ways and conjuring that I have never seen before."

"Conjuring?" Kiyuga echoed. "Witches, then?"

"No, not witches. Adawehi of a being they call the Author. I am learning their sorceries in hopes of saving the people. The woodpecker has led me to them."

"Why should they teach you sorceries? Why should you want to learn their sorceries? They are British."

"Why should we use skala galogwehi to hunt this winter? That, too, is British. It is a tool, a sorcery of Faith."

"From this Author spirit?"

"Yes."

"You no longer follow our spirits and ancestors, then?"

Anagalisgi paused and hesitated. Finally, "I am still trying to understand what it is they believe. But as I said, it is a tool. A powerful, wonderful tool. I intend to use it to free our people. Once we are clear and have returned home, then I may explore more into their doctrines."

Kiyuga frowned. "Please be careful, little brother. I know you wish to do right and help our people, but this would not be the first time someone has accused you of talking to the wrong spirits. Do not give them cause to doubt you, not when our lives depend on it."

"I understand. I do. But I feel I must still learn. If it cannot help us here, in this present danger, it will not matter later."

His brother sighed but finally nodded. "You are right. All the same, please be careful."

To make a point of it, that he had not abandoned his people, Anagalisgi did not meet with Nathan and Andrew the following day, instead spending the time with his brother and the skiagvsta. When it was sunny, they played digadayosdi. When it rained, they still played digadayosdi, providing it was not too bad of rain. Anything to stay out of the old bunkhouse. If they were forced to take refuge, they went to the stables. The straw was nicer than the moldy mattresses, and the horses and barn cats proved better company than the rats.

Kiyuga made a bit of a show of himself when he decided to ride one of the horses. He did not bother with bridle or saddle, just a light blanket and a rope. He mounted it in its stall, got comfortable, and nodded to Aganstata who opened the door. Kiyuga urged the mount forward and then took off through the stable doors. It was great fun watching him ride around the fort—no intention of attempting escape—the British soldiers and other camp laborers trying to catch him. The fun was made even greater when it was revealed that the horse he'd taken belonged to the captain of the fort.

They were barred from the stables after that.

The morning after that incident, there was a big to-do about a company of soldiers arriving. Anagalisgi and the others stood back from the line of soldiers welcoming them in, all in crisp red coats and recently polished bayonets. The arriving company looked like they were supposed to look the same way, but time and travel had made them slightly less than overly flashy. They marched in step and formation, but it was by habit only. Their expressions were exhausted, and, if Anagalisgi was any judge, their stomachs were probably empty.

A small company of blue-coated provincial soldiers came in behind them, but they received far less attention. They were dismissed with much less flair, and they seemed grateful for it. Nathan and Andrew greeted a few of them and departed, no one paying any mind to the camp laborers or the Aniyvwiya in their midst.

"We should have escaped while we had the chance," Wilinawa growled at the next meal. "One by one, simply slip out of the gates."

"And be shot by an entire company of soldiers," Aganstata stated. "At least if we make it to Fort Prince George, we will be back in our own lands and can escape more easily. And there will be more warriors in Kuwayi'hi to fight and help us."

"One thousand soldiers," Mankiller said. "And heavy artillery. How do you plan to escape that?"

"I don't know yet. Believe me, I am considering all options, both peaceful and forceful."

It was a discussion they'd had many times, Anagalisgi knew. They'd come hoping for peace, but now it seemed their only option was war. The problem was, they had delivered themselves — thirty-two skiagvsta, uku, and senior warriors, the most valuable hostages a person could have — right into the hands of their enemies. They had no way to fight when so outnumbered, and it would be up to the younger warriors and dissenting skiagvsta like Amadoya to decide what happened next.

It was a terrifying prospect, and Anagalisgi returned to Nathan and Andrew the following day to continue to practice and train and learn as much as he could in the short time they had together. There was no telling when Lyttelton would want to leave, so he had to do his best now.

"We're working on pulling some strings and calling in favors," Andrew told him. "We're trying to make it so we can come with you to Fort Prince George. It will give us more time to train together."

"And even if we can't, we will still try to come to you," Nathan promised. "We will train you as long as we can."

"How is that?" Anagalisgi questioned, feeling the sweat bead on his forehead as he struggled to Iyuwahnilvhi Uhlisda Adahnesagi'a.

"Like this."

Suddenly, it was as though a door opened in front of him, but in the air. Suddenly he was seeing a forest and hills. In his surprise, he lost his conjuring, but Andrew was quick to pick it back up.

"This is a portal," Nathan said, his face now quickly becoming slick with sweat. "It is a door to anywhere you want to go."

Anagalisgi approached it. He felt the change between the present fort and the forest before him. Then it was gone and Nathan went to a knee, offering up his breakfast.

"Apologies," he said, spitting once he was done and standing. "Portals are tragically difficult to open, harder to sustain, and near lethal to traverse, especially if you don't know what to expect."

"Why not help us escape this way?" Anagalisgi asked, perhaps more forcefully than intended.

"Did you not hear him say it is near lethal to traverse?" Andrew questioned. "Portals are an Energy conjuring, tearing apart the fabric of the universe between two points. It's not something we can teach you in this short time we have, nor would we expect your people to weather that kind of physical pain."

"Pain?"

"As I said, an Energy conjuring. Not something you need to worry about. We need to focus on the here and now, the things we can teach you in the time we have."

So they did, though Anagalisgi's thoughts kept circling back around to the portal. A door to go anywhere? Imagine the possibilities! Actually, he didn't have to imagine. He had seen. And he knew.

But for the moment, they still had to go places as they always had. And then came the day when they woke up and discovered it was moving day. The artillery force had been assembled in the early morning, and just as soon as everyone was fed, they started out, heading for Fort Prince George. It was Vsgiyi now, what the British called December. It would be cold at home, Anagalisgi knew, but for the moment, in the Lower Towns, it was still fairly warm.

Nathan and Andrew had managed to pull some strings and they were sent with the small provincial force accompanying the eleven hundred red coats. Their time to train Anagalisgi was woefully sporadic, though their slow progress because of the heavy artillery allowed for some recess where this could be accomplished.

Like Fort Duquense, the Aniyvwiya were not forced to help with soldiering matters. They did not have to help when a cannon got stuck in the mud, or when a cart tipped over. Anagalisgi questioned the motivation behind this, except to perhaps confuse the hostages, make them believe they were not really hostages, for they had not been pressed into service. Willful compliance, he thought ruefully.

He thought about demanding that Nathan and Andrew use portals to help them escape. His only hesitation was that he had seen how much strain it had put on Nathan. The portal had not been open long, and if it was terrible to traverse, then they might not all make it. And if any of them remained while some escaped, it was not unreasonable to think that those remaining would be killed.

He mulled over this during meals and at night when he lay awake. He had seen the woodpecker once, when they were leaving Charleston, so he knew the spirits were still watching him. He had learned a great deal from Nathan and Andrew, but if he couldn't come up with a way to use it and save his people, what good was it? What good was a tool when the job it was designed for did not present itself?

They arrived at Fort Prince George, but the Aniyvwiya were more fixated on Kuwayi'hi just across the river. It was a welcome notion, just to know that they were back in their lands and home was so close.

Fort Prince George was not a large fort by any means. It had not even been built as a fort, but rather a trading post that had been commandeered by the British army for their war against the French. It was not meant to house more than a couple dozen men for any great length of time. Once the heavy artillery was moved in and positioned, many of the soldiers, especially the provincials, were forced to pitch tents outside the walls.

This gave Anagalisgi hope that perhaps they would be able to escape. Even if they were forced under guard and made to remain in the camp, then he would be able to continue training with Nathan and Andrew.

He really should have known better. The Aniyvwiya were taken inside the fort. It was even more cramped now with the artillery and supplies crowding most of the available space. Clearly they were preparing for conflict, but what good was the fort anyway? If things did come to blows, there were more guns than soldiers, and no British soldier would want to be caught outside when the fighting began and the gates closed.

Governor Lyttelton had traveled with them, his posture saying that he had been a soldier himself once. Now he and Captain Gadsden, along with a handful of soldiers, escorted the Aniyvwiya through the fort to a small building that may have served as a bunkhouse. Indeed, when Lyttelton opened the door, they found six bunks, two on either side of the room stretching from one wall to the other, another set on the far wall, and virtually nothing else.

"All right, in you go," the governor ordered.

"Sir, we will not all fit," Aganstata said.

"I think you can. You're a resourceful lot. In you go."

With a little prodding from the bayonets, the thirty-two Aniyvwiya pressed into the tiny room. There were four to a bed, the rest huddled on the floor, knees drawn up to their chins.

"So," Wilinawa said spitefully. "Who still believes we have a chance for peace?"

"We have to wait and see what Atagulkalu does," Aganstata said, though his tone was difficult to judge. "We are at a disadvantage."

"We are sheep penned up for slaughter," another skiagvsta spat. "If we get out of here, I will personally ally myself and the warriors of my village with Amadoya and Saloli."

The arguing went on for some time. Anagalisgi, who sat by the door, tested the door handle. No surprise, it was locked. Judging by the sound, the door had been barricaded as well. The only window in the building was also locked and wood had been nailed over it both inside and outside so they could not break out. A single lantern hung overhead. When checked, the oil was low, and they elected to leave it be. Probably if they lit it, the building would catch on fire and they would be burned alive.

They were allowed out once a day to eat and relieve themselves and stretch their legs, always under heavy guard. When Aganstata inquired about a meeting with the governor, he was informed that Lyttelton was preparing to return to Charleston, and in fact, would be returning to England.

"Who is in charge here, then?" Aganstata asked, always polite.

His name was Lieutenant Richard Cotymore, and he did not wish to speak with Aganstata or any of the hostages. He had his orders and he intended to carry them out. Right now, his orders were to hold them as they were until Atagulkalu arrived.

They were herded back to the tiny bunkhouse. The air was hot and humid, and several developed rashes on their skin and wetness in their lungs. Anagalisgi could do nothing for them. He had no medicines, no herbs, no incense. The only thing he could do was pray. It was the only time they lit the lantern, hoping the spirits would understand their attempts at a sacred fire, but the smoke from the oil quickly put a stop to that idea.

Tisto, ironically enough, the skiagvsta of Kuwayi'hi just across the river, was seated on the lower bunk in front of the window. While they sat and waited there in the dark, he worked on loosening the nails from the boards over the window. He managed to pry off three of the boards, and he broke one of the glass panes on the window. Carefully, he handed the larger shards to the others for use as weapons if necessary. When it came about time to go outside to eat, he slipped the boards back in place and waited patiently, calmly, as though nothing had happened.

And still they waited. Anagalisgi was able to practice his conjuring on his own, but he was yet at a loss as to how to use it productively. Yes, he could manipulate Time around himself, but could he use it on others? Could he bring the others into the conjuring so they might all move quickly and escape? He saw Nathan and Andrew once, during meals, but they were across the fort and did not see him. When he tried to call out, he was struck in the head and told to be quiet.

So they waited.

Finally there came word one day that Atagulkalu had arrived, ready to negotiate for peace.

The Aniyvwiya hostages were let out of the tiny bunkhouse and given the chance to wash themselves, have a full meal, and walk around almost freely.

Unlike their earlier implication, Lyttelton may have been preparing to return to Charleston, but had not yet done so. He was the one to meet Atagulkalu and usher him into the fort, to the quarters he was using, which happened to be much finer than anything else in the fort. This was speaking comparatively as nothing in the fort was particularly comfortable. The hostages were also ushered in, making the room almost as cramped as the bunkhouse.

"Now that I have your attention, maybe we can come to some real terms," Lyttelton said. Cotymore stood behind him. "When I say that I want the murderers handed over, I mean I want them handed over."

"I have encouraged them to turn themselves in, but they will not," Atagulkalu told him. "I am uncertain even as to their identities."

"Well, I can make a few educated guesses. Your Chief Amadoya, for one. That much has been confirmed."

"Confirmed how?"

Lyttelton went on as though he hadn't spoken. "And whoever it is who is leading the raids here in the south. I have your chief of Kuwayi'hi, so I know it cannot be him. So who is it?"

"His name is Saloli."

"Excellent. So we have two murderers who must be brought to justice. Who else?"

"I don't know."

Cotymore raised a brow. "Sounds like you don't have much control over your people, Chief. Is it that you are unable or unwilling to stop your warriors?"

"We don't have much faith in you right now, honestly," Atagulkalu said. "We don't trust that you would honor your word that turning them over would end the hostilities and protect our lands."

"As much as we are holding your chiefs here, you are holding our soldiers hostage in Fort Loudoun."

"We have done no such thing. They are free to leave at any time. In fact, we wish they would do so as quickly as possible, though we understand winter is a difficult time to be traveling. But rather than attempt to leave, they have prepared for a long stay under siege. How is that holding them hostage?"

"Let us draw up a formal treaty, then," Lyttelton suggested, suddenly sounding very amiable. "If you turn over the murderers we seek—this Amadoya and Saloli and whomever else—then we, the British, will withdraw from Fort Loudoun and Fort Prince George.

You unblock the roads, and trade will resume."

"With guns and ammunition," Aganstata threw in.

"Limited guns and ammunition," Cotymore countered.

Atagulkalu nodded thoughtfully. "I want some of the warriors released. You are right that Amadoya and Saloli will not listen to me. But they will listen to others."

After a moment of thought and quiet conference with Cotymore, Lyttelton agreed. "You may have seven, as a show of good faith."

Aganstata, Mankiller, Wilinawa, Tisto, Chola, Yachtino, and another senior warrior were all chosen. Anagalisgi wondered if Atagulkalu had planned for this ahead of time, and what he intended to do now that he had them.

The treaty was drafted, perused by both Kiyuga and Anagalisgi, confirmed to be as straightforward as it sounded, and signed.

"Excellent," Lyttelton proclaimed. "I am just returning to Charleston where I will then depart for England. I will take this treaty to the king himself."

"Thank you," Atagulkalu said mildly. "We will do our best, though winter does make traveling difficult."

"I understand. I am sure Lieutenant Cotymore will do a fine job taking care of your people."

They left the small quarters. Anagalisgi went to Atagulkalu.

"Please, Atagulkalu, I am certain Aganstata will tell you everything he knows and has seen, but there is more. Can you take a message to Gvnagadoga?"

Atagulkalu gave him a sympathetic look. "You know I will take a message for you. But you should know that Gvnagadoga has taken ill. He does not leave his bed, and he is not always in the waking world. It is unlikely he will see the spring. I pray you will see him before he walks on. But yes, I will deliver a message."

Anagalisgi felt his throat close up at this news of the great elder. He took a breath and said, "Just...tell him that I am learning of a way to help the people. And I will do my best here."

Atagulkalu managed a small smile. "I know you will. You and

your brother both. Stay strong and be encouraged, for we shall endure this storm."

With that, Atagulkalu left with seven of the hostages. Even before they were past the gates, Aganstata was telling of their travels and treatment. Had they planned for this from the beginning? What plans were they making now? Should Anagalisgi have told Atagulkalu of the sorcery he was learning? No, best not. Not until he understood it better and was able to use it well, as Nathan and Andrew did.

He looked around but did not see the two men, nor any provincials inside the fort. How could he get a message to them? What would he say? They had to know what was going on, if they'd warned him about it back in Charleston. What plans were they making out there? Should he have told Atagulkalu about Nathan and Andrew, offered them as potential allies, spies inside the enemy? What good would it do? They knew they were outnumbered and lacking in the necessary firepower. Even when the extra soldiers outside the fort walls were dismissed back to Charleston after the treaty—Nathan and Andrew with them, Anagalisgi figured—there was still very little that could be done.

They were ushered back into the bunkhouse. There were twenty-five of them now, four to each bunk with one either squeezing in on a bunk or stretching out on the floor. They rotated who got the floor, finding enough room for two to fit comfortably.

With Tisto now gone, a warrior called Dodidoya now worked at the boards over the window. His name in English meant "Maybe a Beaver." He had gotten this name because any time he went out hunting or raiding or scouting or just for a walk, and he heard a strange noise, he always said that it was "maybe a beaver." It was unclear what his fascination was or had been—popular rumor said he was always just trying to be silly—but the name stuck, so he was called Dodidoya. Who is coming to help? Maybe a beaver.

But the beaver put his metaphorical teeth to good use on the boards over the window and managed to remove all of them from the inside. He broke the rest of the glass, handing out shards as Tisto had done, then going to work on the outer boards. It was a slow process, and it took longer to clean up and hide it when the soldiers came around to let them out once a day. But there was no telling how much longer they would be there. It could indeed be spring before Atagulkalu returned, and who knew what his plan was?

"Have the spirits said anything?" Kiyuga asked one night as they lay on the floor, staring up into darkness.

"No," Anagalisgi replied, sighing.

"Since Nathan and Andrew are gone, were you able to learn any useful sorceries from them?"

"If he had, don't you think he would have used them by now?" someone asked irritably. "Tricks from these white demons, all it is."

Anagalisgi ignored him. "I know only very little. I know it will help me, but I don't know how to use it to help anyone else, which is why we are still here. I still practice, when I am able, but it is slow and difficult to progress when I have only the barest teaching."

"Should our spirits not be instructing you as well?" the same person sneered.

"I don't know what is expected of me," Anagalisgi said firmly. "I know only the present moment."

"Well that's fortunate," someone else said dryly. "Whenever you see the future, it ends up being bad."

Kiyuga let out a grumbling sigh. "Don't listen to them, little brother. We're all anxious to be home, or anywhere but here. I am certain that Atagulkalu and Aganstata will come up with something. And when they do, and when they return, you will know what to do, by the spirits' guidance, with or without these British sorceries."

Anagalisgi wished he could take the encouragement to heart, but it was hard. More than that, he wished for some seeing fruit, that he might talk to the spirits and ask them what he should do. Had he been misled by the conjuring? If not, what was he supposed to do with it? It was great and wonderful power, but how awesome could it be when it could be so easily contained in such a small room?

DᏣᎤᏁᎢᎢ ᏛᏫᏚᎯ

Ayadohlv'i Daladuhi

Humiliating Defeat

They waited.

The British celebrated Christmas, and even the hostages got an orange each.

They celebrated New Year's and declared it the Year of Our Lord Seventeen Sixty.

Dodidoya managed to pry loose all of the boards over the inside of the window and most of them over the outside. But when he stuck his head out to survey the landscape, discovered that they were blocked in on all sides anyway. Directly ahead was the outer wall of the fort, and to either side were heavy artillery and other heavy supplies. Assuming it was even feasible, they would not be able to move them without attracting attention, which meant no silent escape.

The space was only big enough for three men to lie comfortably. Nevertheless, it provided another area for them to spread out, at least at night, and fresh air to breathe and cool them off.

And they waited.

"My youngest daughter is supposed to have her first child this winter," someone said one quiet evening. "I wonder if I shall see it before spring?"

No one said anything. Conversation had dwindled to virtually nothing inside the bunkhouse, and they were hard-pressed to speak when they were let out once a day. If there was any comfort, at least they weren't being pelted with rotten fruit and animal dung, and this small building was a bit cleaner than the bunkhouse in Charleston and did more to keep the rain off them.

A cat came by one evening, when Kiyuga was outside, quietly laying on the ground outside the window. It was brown and gray with stripes. Its eyes were bright yellow in the dim light, and it bore the marks of many battles. It watched him and the the others warily as it slunk around the edge of the wall.

He wondered if they could dig under the wall. It was a regular wooden palisade, the same as most other forts. He tried to recall the construction of Fort Loudoun. It had to have been similar; neither fort was very old nor elaborate, and they'd both been built in haste. If they were really that similar, then he would expect that these outer logs would be sunk probably to a man's height. He frowned to himself. That was a lot of digging, and with no tools, it would take far too much time. They would be discovered.

Others had probably considered this idea on their nights to lay under the stars. Probably they had reached the same conclusion. Right now, they were trapped, but they'd not necessarily been harmed. If they could hold out just a little longer, maybe Aganstata and Atagulkalu would return with a solution. They had to be patient.

It was hard, though. For so long, they'd chastised Amadoya for reckless behavior. Now Kiyuga was beginning to understand his frustration. Now that they were the ones directly threatened, he wanted to get out, be free, like an animal in a snare. The threat was real. It had always been real. Maybe Amadoya had been hasty, but he had not been the fool. The rest of them had been fools.

But perhaps each party, in his own foolishness, had done some good. Amadoya had shed light upon this dark spot in their relationship with the British, far too trusting. But the rest of them had been quietly preparing for the tragic outcome Anagalisgi had predicted would come from it. If Amadoya had been stopped, would they have been ensnared by their own false sense of security? If they had encouraged his raiding and joined in, would they be so prepared for the fiery outcome?

Kiyuga used this line of thinking to try to help his brother on the days when he was distressed and uncertain of himself, or more so than normal.

"Have the spirits shown you anything?" Kiyuga asked as they ate together, sitting outside in the sun for just a little bit.

Anagalisgi shook his head. "No. I will tell you when they do. Although I sense something very grave is about to happen."

"What do you mean?"

"I mean we may want to consider some means of escape."

"Anagalisgi, your head is full of feathers if you think we haven't already been considering such things. The problem is detection. We can't all of us leave without being found. The fort has its guards inside and outside, with dogs. The time it would take...we don't have enough time. We would be discovered too easily."

"And what I'm saying is, we may not have a choice. And being shot while trying to escape may be the preferred way to die."

Kiyuga studied him. "What about—?"

"I don't know. The spirits are frustratingly silent on the matter, and I can get no message to Nathan or Andrew to help, assuming they are even still here. Barring that, I would not know how to get a message to Kuwayi'hi, and they are just across the river."

"What about a ruse? Ask if you can contact the adawehi in Kuwayi'hi. Tell them you must perform a ceremony and you need them. Even if we cannot escape with them, surely we can get a message out with them, something to send to Atagulkalu and Aganstata and the others."

Anagalisgi mulled this over. The other warriors in the immediate vicinity gave him sideways glances, letting him know that they were listening without listening.

"I suppose it could work," Anagalisgi said finally, seeming to come to life a little. "It's worth a try. What would we say? What do we want to tell them?"

"First that we are alive and well," Kiyuga said. "For the most part."

"Duwisgali has a cough," his brother interrupted. "I will use that to ask for the adawehi of Kuwayi'hi, whether they come here or I and able to go there."

As if to make a point, the senior warrior began coughing. It was a wretched, barking cough that had kept him and most everyone else awake for the last four nights.

"What else shall we say?" Anagalisgi wondered quietly. "We are alive and well. What else?"

"If they are able to bring food, that would be a welcome thing," someone mumbled.

"Weapons," someone else muttered.

"Anything they can," Kiyuga summarized. "Go now, while we're here and have a chance."

Anagalisgi turned pale and stared at him for a long moment.

"You are an adawehi, not a warrior," Kiyuga encouraged him. "They treat their adawehi with some deference. Maybe they will extend that courtesy to you."

His brother let out a breath, quickly finished off his food, stood, and wandered off to find someone to ask, preferably Cotymore.

They were outside long after they finished their meals, after they would have normally been herded back to the tiny cabin. After a while, they were, but without Anagalisgi.

Locked again in the bunkhouse, no one made any move to remove the window boards and slip outside for fear of being found out. So they sat. And waited.

They were let out around midday for food, and it was late evening when Anagalisgi finally returned, with help.

"This is Tsgili," Anagalisgi said as someone lit the overhead lantern. "I was permitted to go with an escort to Kuwayi'hi for help. He is here for Duwisgali, but that doesn't mean that he didn't bring other supplies."

Tsgili opened his pack, handing a few things to Anagalisgi before distributing small bundles of food for the rest of them. It wasn't much, as he had gathered in haste during a few moments when the British had their backs turned, but the hostages were too grateful. Nuts, jerky, even a couple cups of sheep's milk which they all took turns drinking from greedily.

Kiyuga thought their mirth must have gone on half the night, but it lasted barely long enough for Anagalisgi and Tsgili to move Duwisgali to the floor in the middle of the room. He couldn't eat more than one bite before he was coughing, barking like the dogs that roamed the outside at night. Tsgili gave him a special drink while Anagalisgi prayed, sang, and invoked the spirits for healing and strength. They did not burn incense, but they crushed the dried herbs into the warrior's drink which he obediently consumed.

This went on for most of the night, when Diwusgali's cough finally subsided enough that he—and everyone else—could get some sleep. Kiyuga settled in right where he was and drifted off.

"I do not know how you have lived like this for the past two moons," Tsgili growled the following morning. He looked as though he hadn't slept at all. "You have greater strength and determination than I do."

"We do what we must," someone said.

"I have heard that Atagulkalu and Aganstata are on their way back here. I have heard that they intend to make peace."

"They are going to turn over Amadoya and Saloli?" someone said spitefully.

"I don't know what their plan is," Tsgili replied calmly. "It could be it is only pretext. I don't know. All I know for sure is that they are on their way, and they should not be long in coming."

"Welcome news, regardless."

"As is the news that you are alive and mostly well." The adawehi glanced at Diwusgali who was still sleeping. "I will have word sent to them, a messenger to meet them on the road. This will give them hope, whatever their plans are."

"Thank you for what you have done here," Kiyuga told him. "Your presence renews our strength."

"I am glad it is so. I wish you well, and may we meet again soon."

Tsgili was made to leave when the rest of them took their meal.

"I also had him send word to Nathan and Andrew," Anagalisgi

told Kiyuga. "I had him tell of our plight, and ask if there might not be a way to continue training, or have them use their superior powers to free us."

"Don't you think they would have done so already, if they did mean to help us?"

"They do not want to disrupt a delicate balance. The balance is tipping, and we need help. Besides, if you don't know a problem exists, how do you help? We have not been able to call for help until now. Maybe now they will be able to help us."

Kiyuga frowned. "I don't know. I think you place too much faith in this European sorcery. But I will reserve judgment of it until we are safely home. You might persuade me more if it were to be used in our escape."

"Believe me, I am trying."

And that was that. Things went back to normal. Anagalisgi gave Diwusgali more herbs to put in his food and drink to quiet his coughing, and he continued to pray and invoke the spirits, but success was limited. The warrior resumed his coughing by nightfall, though it did not sound quite so horrible.

"How did you get them to allow Tsgili to come?" Kiyuga wondered when the coughing warrior slept at last.

"I simply told Cotymore that if any of us died while here, no matter the cause, it may be seen as an act of war and it would violate the treaty we just signed." Anagalisgi managed a light chuckle. "The Europeans do love their pieces of paper and their words."

Kiyuga grinned invisibly in the darkness. "Indeed they do. Has Tsgili's visit and getting word to Atagulkalu and Aganstata—and your British friends, I suppose—changed anything about your premonitions or feelings?"

"A bit," his brother said, sitting beside him. "It certainly feels more likely that we will have success, but it's not...here. Nothing about this place or sequence of events has changed. But our odds overall are significantly better."

"Well, I guess it's the best we're going to do for right now. Keep dreaming, little brother. Our people are depending on you to get through this."

"I know," Anagalisgi sighed. "Believe me, I know this very well. I wish to dream and speak to the spirits, but they are elusive. I wish I had more seeing fruit so I might force them to talk to me. But even that may be a dangerous thing, to try and force a spirit to do something."

"They will speak to you when you are ready and need to hear something. It's not as if they cannot find you."

Although Kiyuga secretly wondered if the spirits really could not reach Anagalisgi, being held here in this place. But it was not something he knew how to change, so he could only wait.

Four days later, Kiyuga found his brother outside, alone, looking terribly distressed.

"The spirits told you something?" he guessed.

Anagalisgi nodded. "Yes. And it is deeply troublesome."

"What is it?"

"The spirits have told me that everyone here will die."

"Everyone? Including me and you?"

"I don't know. And I don't know that it is everyone. The exact words were, 'everyone who is and will be of this place.' Before you ask, I don't understand what that means, what the distinction is, or who it is referencing."

A call went up from the gates.

"I think we're about to find out," Kiyuga said.

He crawled back through the window, Anagalisgi close behind, grabbing the boards and sliding them back into place with all the deft efficiency of a practiced thief.

"Do you think that could be them?" someone asked.

"I think it is," Anagalisgi said, trying not to sound as tragic as he'd looked outside.

"Do you think they've brought Amadoya and the others?"

"I think so, but not for the reasons the British believe."

"The spirits have shown you something, then," someone else stated.

"Yes. And it's not good."

"It never is," a third muttered. "Of all the prophets to get stuck with, it had to be you."

"You'll be asking for forgiveness for that when we get out of here," Kiyuga told him.

"I'll gladly do it, too. I just want to get out of here."

There was the scraping of wood as the barricade in front of the door was removed. The door swung open and soldiers began swiftly ushering the hostages outside. Rather than remain in the yard, they were herded to a small flight of stairs that led to the ramparts. The wall was not especially tall, seeing how the fort had been built for trade rather than siege, but they were still nearly a height over the men inside. On the outside, they were about a height and half a height, or perhaps it only seemed that way.

They were made to line up along the rampart overlooking the road. They saw Atagulkalu and Aganstata, standing freely and dressed almost as if for war, though lacking paint.

"Here are your chiefs, then," Cotymore said. "All well, as promised."

"Release them!" Aganstata demanded.

"We have an agreement! Who wants to lay claim to murderers? Who wants to boast about giving them bread and board? But these are your chiefs and warriors! These men are the essence of your people and your culture and your heritage! Would you not rather have them returned to you than to continue to harbor a few men who insist on terrorizing the countryside and driving a wedge between our peoples and this chance at peace?"

"Bring the hostages outside, Lieutenant," Atagulkalu said firmly.

"I have not even seen proof that you have brought the murderers," Cotymore said.

The men glanced at each other, then looked behind them and nodded.

From up the road, Kiyuga watched as Mankiller and the other hostages who had been released led Amadoya, Saloli, and several others closer to the fort. Their wrists were bound and they wore only basic coverings to show they had no weapons.

"Release the hostages," Atagulkalu repeated.

"Bring the murderers inside," Cotymore ordered.

"I will not deliver more hostages into your fortress. Bring the hostages outside."

"I'm afraid I can't do that."

"Then neither can we."

"A shame. Well, since we cannot come to an agreement at this time, I see no reason to continue speaking. Therefore, your murderers will remain outside with you, and my hostages will remain inside with me. You have until sunset tomorrow to decide who you would rather have."

Kiyuga looked and tried to judge his chances of jumping and not dying. They weren't looking good. Crude pikes had been set up around the base. Even if he didn't impale himself on one of those, he would almost assuredly break both legs, maybe his back. At worst, he would die.

So they were prodded and herded back down into the fort and to the small bunkhouse.

They were not given food.

"I will try to sleep," Anagalisgi said. "And see what the spirits wish for us to do."

It was some time before he actually fell asleep, and Kiyuga was soon left to think and ponder by himself. He went over the exchange in his mind, over and over again, picking it apart, every action, every word. It had been clear that Atagulkalu and Aganstata had been unwilling to merely hand over Amadoya in good faith. They knew the British intended to hold as many hostages as they could, or simply kill as many as possible.

They'd been trying to get all Aniyvwiya outside of the fort. They'd gone to great lengths to show that they had Amadoya and the others and that they were unarmed and helpless. Amadoya had hardly resisted, and he was too great a warrior to be led around by a single rope around his wrists.

A trick, then? Even if it had been, Cotymore obviously hadn't given in. What would they do now? They no longer had the luxury of time. They had only until sunset tomorrow when, presumably, if Amadoya was not delivered, the rest of them would be executed.

Fort Prince George was not a large fort, but it was well-armed, and Kuwayi'hi was just across the river, easily within striking distance. But that strike went both ways, Kiyuga mused, a double-edged sword cuts both ways, as the English saying went. Maybe they'd brought a fighting force to take the fort by storm if Cotymore would not willingly give up the hostages. All that needed to be done was open the gates.

Kiyuga ran through a hundred possible scenarios in his mind as the day wore on, the sun slowly setting. With the boards off the windows, there was a brief period in the evening when the sun would almost shine into the little bunkhouse. It was the best part of the day, Kiyuga thought, even better than getting out and eating food while under heavy guard. In the evenings, the sun was theirs to enjoy freely.

Then the sun vanished, and shadows cloaked the bunkhouse once more. After a while, Kiyuga climbed out the window, trying not to disturb those who lay out under the stars.

"Coming to enjoy the stars?" one asked. "It may be our last night to do so. You know how these British bastards are."

"I do know." Kiyuga sighed. "I don't know. Perhaps I was hoping for a spark of inspiration, that the spirits might show us an escape we hadn't seen before. Has anyone tried climbing the bunkhouse wall to the roof?"

"And for what? We were all lined up on the large wall today, and you will notice that no one attempted to jump to freedom," a second said. "Maybe we should have. If we are destined to die, maybe we ought to fight back and take as many of these British bastards with us as we can."

"That's what I plan to do," the third man said. "I am tired of being penned up here as a sheep, herded here and there and paraded before others before the slaughter."

"Maybe we should have listened to Amadoya to begin with," the first man grumbled. "Perhaps we were too naive to think the British would ever be grateful to anyone but themselves and actually reward their allies."

But it was too late to do anything about it. They had made their choices. Now they were going to have to make some more choices. Such as, what did they do if the British did try to kill them? Where were they supposed to run? What were they supposed to do? They still had their shards of glass and knives, and it seemed as though they were all prepared to die, but was there really no way to escape this prison? In this bunkhouse, even with the window open, they were still cornered animals.

Maybe they should just make a break for it when the gates opened. Maybe they should take their chances with the wall and the pikes. If death was inevitable, was it not only right to meet it on their own terms, as true Aniyvwiya warriors?

He ducked back inside and managed to get a little bit of sleep, though he did not dream. It was still dark when he woke.

"How are you?" Anagalisgi asked, somewhere in the darkness.

"Hungry, honestly," Kiyuga murmured sleepily. "Thirsty, too." He stretched as best he could and yawned. "Were you able to sleep and speak to the spirits?"

"Yes, sort of."

"Did they tell you anything?"

"Nothing new, except..."

"Except...?" Kiyuga goaded.

"Your promise to me will not be fulfilled today," Anagalisgi told him.

"But that's a good thing, isn't it?"

"For us. But there was nothing else new to speak of."

So there would still be death in their midst. Given that Atagulkalu had until sunset to turn over Amadoya, those deaths would be today. And for some in the bunkhouse now, it truly was their last night to see the stars.

Kiyuga licked dry lips. "Do you think it's better to know when your death will be, or have it surprise you?"

It was a moment before Anagalisgi answered. "I suppose it depends on your view of death, if you are afraid of it, ready for it, willing for it, or any other feeling. Igilisi knew when her death would be, and she accepted it. And she did her best to ensure that she still helped the people for as long as she could, even as she herself was sick.

"Many of us don't know when our time will come. We see it as a possibility, but few truly consider its implications, I think. And I suppose a part of it has to do with one's views on the afterlife, whether the spirit wanders west in misery, if it takes an animal form and eventually disappears, or if it ascends to a Divine Being."

Kiyuga shifted position. "And what do you think? We have sat here for two moons now, each speculating that we might die, knowing that we could, knowing that we would. Now you say that my promise shall not be fulfilled this day. Does it change your view of the world any, and what might be going on out there?"

"Not especially, but I know more than I can say about the matter."

"Do you know when you will die?"

"I don't know when I will die, but I do know that soon my time will come to cross over into a new life. As will yours, though our paths will diverge."

"I don't understand."

"Nor do I. As Gvnagadoga once put it, I don't have all the words to describe how the spirits speak or what they show me. But it always unfolds exactly how it should."

Kiyuga was uncertain, but he tried to take comfort in the fact that his promise to his little brother would not be tested this day. But it was cold comfort considering that he knew for certain that he and his brother would live while others with him in this room would die. Perhaps it really was better to let death surprise you. If death was always an option, then one would fight all the harder to make his life worthwhile in every moment. Or so he told himself.

The darkness of night faded and a cool, foggy dawn broke over the horizon. For some, they would enter into the eternal sleep this day, while others would, with luck, be returning to their homes. Either way, Kiyuga would be glad to get out of this tiny bunkhouse.

Everyone was not even awake when the call went up outside, similar to the one from yesterday. The warriors outside were woken up and they hastily scrambled into the bunkhouse, fumbling with the boards but eventually sliding them back into place. They waited anxiously.

Then there was the scraping of the barricade. A moment later, the door swung open, but the hostages were not ushered out. Two guards remained at the door, ready for their next command. But the open door allowed Kiyuga and the rest of them to better hear what was going on.

Aganstata had returned, waving a horse's bridle for peace. Reportedly he wished to meet with Cotymore outside the fort to negotiate how to best go about the exchange of warriors.

Cotymore had been asleep when Aganstata arrived, and he was little pleased with being woken so unceremoniously. Kiyuga briefly saw him walk by, trying to get his uniform in order before going up on the ramparts.

Aganstata and Cotymore exchanged some words from their respective positions, but Kiyuga could not make them out. Then Cotymore descended the rampart stairs and made for the gates that opened with a distinct creaking. Judging by other noises, Kiyuga guessed that a small contingent of soldiers went with him. Still the hostages were not released from the bunkhouse.

Should they try? Only two guards here, easily overpowered. Could they make the run from here to the gates and beyond? He could see others had similar ideas.

Uki'la was the only one willing to act on this idea, though he did not get far. His sudden movement startled Kiyuga as he knocked him aside into a bunk. The senior warrior pushed past the two guards, but it was nothing for them to reach out and grab him. Uki'la had his knife out and swung at them, but their reach with their bayonets was greater still. They put both blades into his stomach and dropped him to the ground. Without a word or even a look at their charges, the soldiers removed their bayonets and kicked his body back toward the bunkhouse.

Anagalisgi and a couple others dragged Uki'la inside and hoisted him onto a bunk. The warrior was spitting blood and shaking violently. Kiyuga turned away and looked outside, over the shoulders of their guards.

"We all should have gone," Duwisgali growled, trying to cover a cough. "Cut their throats and made a run for it."

His last word was cut short as there suddenly came noises from outside. Whoops and hollers and yowls like fighting cats. It was a sound Kiyuga knew too well and was grateful to hear.

There had been a plan. An ambush, as warriors rose up against Cotymore and his soldiers. Kiyuga heard musket fire and confused yelling, conflicting orders. He heard Amadoya's distinct war cry. It had been a ruse from the beginning. Heartened, Kiyuga could only hope that their force was large enough to overrun the fort entirely and rescue the hostages. He felt for his knife, ready to attack just as soon as the warriors breached the gates.

The bunkhouse guards were suddenly uncertain whether to pay more attention to the warriors outside the fort or the ones right behind them.

"For Uki'la!" someone shouted.

Kiyuga was knocked to all fours as the warriors charged, cutting the throats of their guards and swarming into the yard. There was more yelling and confusion. He grabbed his knife and stood. Before he entered the fray, he looked back at Anagalisgi, the only one left with Uki'la.

"He's dead," was all his brother said.

Kiyuga turned and launched himself into the fray.

"Close the gates!" someone shouted. "Close the gates! The savages have escaped! They're going to overrun us from both sides! Close the gates!"

There was more creaking as soldiers struggled to close the gates in a timely manner. A line of soldiers stood on the inside of the fort, shooting any Aniyvwiya who tried to leave. Another line of soldiers stood outside, covering the retreat of Cotymore and his men. Outside, there was more whooping and hollering, the sign of a successful battle, if not a victory. Still more soldiers were rounding up the interior Aniyvwiya any way they could.

Kiyuga was taken from behind, a rope around his neck. He was herded to the center of the yard with the rest of them. Some were wounded, a few severely. Almost all had blood on them; whether it was their own or their enemy's was impossible to say. The rope around Kiyuga's neck was released and they were held in a group, soldiers encircling them, all with muskets raised.

An officer came by, not Cotymore, but Kiyuga did not recognize him.

"Any savage with blood on his knife, shoot him," the officer said.

Kiyuga did not have blood on his knife, but that did not make it any easier when he and nine others were forced to watch the rest of them, thirteen warriors in all, be summarily executed. Their bodies were taken away, and the officer returned.

"Lieutenant Cotymore was gravely wounded in that little ambush your 'peace envoy' staged out there. If he dies, then so will the rest of you." He looked at one of his men. "Return them to the bunkhouse."

So they were herded back to their pen. Uki'la's body was taken away with as much respect as the British had had for those they'd just murdered.

They were down to eleven. With six bunks, it meant that one of them was able to have a bed to himself. The thin mattress that Uki'la had bled upon was put outside, the best Anagalisgi could do for destroying his possessions. All of their knives and shards of glass had been taken away. They still had not been given food, and Anagalisgi had no water to cleanse the bunkhouse. But it was all they had, and it was where they were forced to stay.

And they waited.

"Did we do the right thing?" someone asked. It was unclear whom he was speaking to, of it he meant for his question to be answered.

"We tried," someone else answered. "We knew that death was a possibility just as well as any raid or battle. Or, in this case, without needing to do anything at all. But we tried."

A few looked at Anagalisgi, but no one wanted to speak to him. No one wanted to know. As it had already been stated, of all prophets to be stuck with, it had to be him. He would have only bad news. Perhaps it was better to find out on their own.

The fog lifted and the day turned out well. And still they waited. As the sun crept through the sky, Kiyuga may have dared to even hope that Cotymore had survived his injuries. But why should he wish for the survival of his enemies, except that their deaths would only bring pain and suffering to him? And why should he be adverse to pain when facing his enemies? Why should he run into battle if he was unwilling to accept the possibility of death?

He hated to think that the British were changing his thoughts so much, and without ever having to speak to him. All they had to do was lock him in a room.

He couldn't let them get to him. He had to remain strong. Even if Anagalisgi said it would not be fulfilled today, he still had to be willing to fulfill his promise. He would not let Anagalisgi go, not without going before him to clear the way.

But then, Anagalisgi had only said the promise would not be fulfilled today. He'd said nothing about tomorrow.

They still were not given food or water, and Kiyuga was feeling greatly fatigued, in addition to dizzy. If he continued to go without water, he would start to feel nauseous. Even if there were another opportunity for escape, he wasn't sure he would take it. Or if he did, he would surely not survive.

The day continued to crawl by at a snail's pace. The warriors were hungry, some weakened from injuries, all of them very thirsty. They'd heard no word on Cotymore, but they decided that no news was good news. They were still alive at least.

Was Aganstata or Atagulkalu still outside the fort? What had they done after Cotymore retreated? What had their intentions been? To overrun the fort? To force the British to release the hostages? To show their strength and will? Had any warriors tried to break into the fort to rescue them?

Kiyuga remembered hearing stories of Atagulkalu being captured by the Anishinaabe and held captive for a good ten years before being released as part of some agreement. Had he ever attempted escape? Had he ever hoped for rescue? Had he ever been in such danger as they were in now, sitting here in this bunkhouse? Would Kiyuga ever get the chance to ask Atagulkalu himself?

The sun began to shine through the window. Kiyuga watched it until it began to disappear.

The barricade scratched against the door as it was removed, and the boards over the inside of the window were replaced. No one bothered to stand and face the soldiers as they crowded around the door. After a moment, they parted, and the new officer walked into the center of the room.

"A sorrowful day, to be certain," he said. "An ambush and an uprising cost the British empire forty-seven invaluable soldiers, and this great fort has lost a great commander in Lieutenant Cotymore. I am hereby declaring the peace treaty officially terminated, and assume all authority from the Governor and the Crown to execute His Majesty's enemies without delay."

He gave them a sweeping bow and an unreadable look as he turned to his soldiers. "Kill them all."

The soldiers parted to let him through. A short line of them managed to get into position and leveled their muskets.

Kiyuga closed his eyes.

"No!"

His head exploded into waves of dizziness as he heard the sound of musketfire very close to himself. He stumbled as something fell into him, perhaps the body of his warrior brother falling in battle. His ears were ringing and he waited for the second shot that would surely take him as well.

It did not.

He slowly opened his eyes and gasped as he saw a musketball only a finger's length from his face. Something had grabbed onto him, and he looked to see Anagalisgi was pressed close behind him, holding him around the waist.

All around them, everything had frozen. Stopped. Completely. Musket balls hung in the air. Smoke wafted from the ends of the barrels. Some of the warriors had been hit, but their expressions said they hadn't realized it yet. Only two were falling, arms splayed out, crumpling into the bunks.

The soldiers remained in formation, their expressions dark and resolute as they carried out orders to kill their king's enemies.

"Walk," Anagalisgi said quietly in his ear.

Kiyuga was so enamored by the way everything had stopped, he jumped when his brother spoke.

"What's going on?" he asked hoarsely.

"British sorcery. But I don't know how long it will last. Walk."

"Can we not save the others?"

"I don't know how. I wasn't even sure this would work to save you, except I knew you would not die today. Please, brother, stop asking questions and walk."

Kiyuga did so, stiffly moving one foot in front of the other, Anagalisgi holding tight around his waist. It was an awkward dance, the two of them joined so closely while still trying to push past the throng of soldiers blockading the doorway.

"Why did you not do this sooner?" Kiyuga asked. "The gates were open earlier. We could have made it."

"I did not know how or if it would work. Please, Kiyuga, I am as weak as you without food and water. I truly do not know how long this will last. My will is slipping as we speak."

He could feel his brother's grip slackening. Once they were past the soldiers and into the yard, Kiyuga used both of his hands to keep Anagalisgi's from slipping. His brother scuffed and stumbled after him, his breathing becoming more labored with each step.

Everything in the yard was as still as the bunkhouse. Everyone was frozen in his actions, whether it was moving cannons, lifting heavy bags of gunpowder, handing off muskets, or just walking around. It was as though life had become art. Kiyuga swallowed nervously.

What kind of sorcery was this? How was it that the spirits had imparted it to Anagalisgi via the British? How could two common British soldiers come to have such power? Or perhaps it had been a test. Perhaps the spirits had disguised themselves as Nathan and Andrew, to test Anagalisgi. Was he willing to accept help no matter where it came from, or would he allow pride to get in the way? If not for this sorcery, they would be dead, too.

They reached the gates. By this point, Anagalisgi was merely conscious, hardly awake. Heart pounding, Kiyuga let go of his brother's hands, put his hands on one of the gates and pushed. It moved, though not much. Taking a breath, he pushed again. It didn't need to open a lot, just enough for them to get out.

"Come on, little brother," Kiyuga told him, pushing a third time on the gate and maneuvering them out of the fort. "If we can make it to the trees, we can make it to Kuwayi'hi."

Anagalisgi mumbled something, then went completely slack, slumping to the ground. Life and sound resumed, and suddenly they were caught on the outside of the fort with no explanation and with a lot of guns around.

Kiyuga bent and grabbed Anagalisgi under his arms. He'd only gone two steps when life again became suspended.

"You made it!"

He looked up to see Nathan and Andrew running toward them. A glance at the fort said that everything there was still stopped. What sorcery was this? What were its rules? Who were its adawehi?

Nathan knelt beside Anagalisgi and Andrew faced Kiyuga.

"Are there others?" he demanded.

"They're dead," Kiyuga told him.

Andrew frowned, then turned and ran inside the fort. Nathan stood.

"He's only sleeping," he reported. "Banding is terribly taxing for a beginner. But he got you both out, and that's all that matters."

Andrew returned, making sure to close the gate as if nothing had happened.

"They're dead," he confirmed. "I'm sorry."

"We got here as fast as we could," Nathan said. "We knew that there were supposed to be negotiations, and we'd hoped that it would buy us some time. It seems we should have just opened a portal and come directly. That is our mistake, and we are deeply sorry."

Kiyuga opened his mouth, closed it, opened it again, no words. Finally, "I don't understand what is happening. I don't know why you are apologizing. We are both terribly weak. Please, can you help me take him to Kuwayi'hi to get him some help?"

The blue-coated British soldiers agreed. Andrew took Anagalisgi's shoulders, and Nathan got his legs. Once they were well into the trees, life again continued. Birds trapped in mid-flight suddenly moved again. A deer startled and ran off, snorting an alarm.

"What are you doing? What magic is this that you use to make things stop and go? What are you teaching my brother? Are you witches?"

Both men grinned as they shuffled along.

"No, not witches," Andrew said. "Servants of the Author. She sent us to find you, help you. First we had to find and instruct the one gifted in the spirits."

"That could be any adawehi," Kiyuga mentioned.

Nathan shook his head. "Not like your brother. Only the Author knows, but your brother is far greater than any ordinary adawehi."

Kiyuga said nothing to that.

Too much had happened, and he'd eaten too little to make sense of it all. After a few minutes, seeing no pursuit from the fort, they stopped to rest. Anagalisgi was sleeping still, but Kiyuga felt ready to join him. He sat against the trunk of a tree and closed his eyes.

"Here."

He looked up to see Nathan handing him a water flask. Kiyuga took it and drank the whole thing. It helped to slake his thirst and made him a bit more alert, but he was still very tired and very hungry.

Anagalisgi began to stir. Finally he groaned, mumbled something, and sat up. He looked around, half in a daze.

"How did I get here?" he murmured, falling back on the ground. "Did we make it?"

"We came to help," Nathan told him. "Sorry to say, we could do nothing for your chiefs and warriors still in the fort. But we saw you and your brother and did what we could."

Anagalisgi looked at the man as if he couldn't understand a word he was saying. Maybe in his present state of mind, he couldn't.

"We're still too close to the fort," Andrew said. "We need to cross the river to your village there."

"Kuwayi'hi," Anagalisgi stated sleepily.

"That's right," Nathan said. "Can you walk?"

Kiyuga scooted over to help his brother sit up. Once he could do that, both he and Nathan got Anagalisgi to an upright position. Kiyuga put his brother's arm around his shoulders.

"This conjuring is especially painful," Anagalisgi said, looking at the British men.

"Yes, it can be, at first," Nathan replied, grinning. "You are working with forces far more powerful than anything you have dealt with so far. It can feel overwhelming."

"Is there a way to conjure Time around others?"

"There is, but we weren't able to teach you in the time we had. I'm sorry. We would like to continue to help and teach, if you are willing."

Anagalisgi nodded. "It helped me. I want it to help others as well."

"We help no one by standing here," Andrew growled.

They moved off. Kiyuga looked back once at the fort, to see that they were not being pursued. But he saw only the fort through the trees and down the hill, twenty-three crows circling overhead.

Nathan led the way, Kiyuga and his brother behind him, moving slowly, and Andrew in the rear. By the time they reached the river, Anagalisgi was better able to walk on his own.

They crossed the river into Kuwayi'hi and were immediately confronted. Rather, Nathan and Andrew were confronted, Kiyuga and Anagalisgi whisked away to safety.

"Do not harm them!" Kiyuga said. "They rescued us!"

"The others are with you, then?" Aganstata asked, shouldering his way through the crowd that had formed. "You escaped?"

Kiyuga hesitated, then said, "Only we two escaped. We could not save the others. Andrew and Nathan got us away from the fort."

The senior warrior studied them, then looked at the two white men. After a moment of consideration, he said, "Let the Beloved Women decide their fates."

The men were disarmed, their possessions distributed among those gathered. Then they were taken to the townhouse where a council had been convened. Atagulkalu, Aganstata, Mankiller, Amadoya, Saloli, Tisto, Wilinawa, Yachtino, Chola, and more had gathered, along with a Women's Council and Kuwayi'hi's Beloved Women. Kiyuga watched the white men turn even whiter as they faced this gathering.

No doubt Aganstata had told all about the mistreatment the British had doled out to them. Kiyuga and Anagalisgi were likewise sworn to speak only truth as they told of the incidents inside the fort, the massacre in the yard and again in the bunkhouse.

"How did these two Anigilisi come to rescue you, then?" someone asked.

Anagalisgi hesitated. Then, "Through their sorceries. They taught me many things, that it may help us. We did not have time to learn much, and the best I could do was save my brother."

"Sorceries?" one of the adawehi asked. "What are these men? They look like no adawehi I have seen."

"Witches, then," another man accused.

"Not witches," Nathan began. "We only wish to help—"

"Be quiet!" one of the women snapped.

"Please," Anagalisgi said. "Without their help, we would not have made it. They saw us to safety. When I was too weak to travel, they carried me. They gave us shelter and water until we could make our escape here."

Arguments were made throughout the afternoon. Kiyuga was weary, but he could see his brother was exhausted.

At one point, the British men were finally asked to demonstrate the sorceries they possessed. They changed the color of their eyes and skin. They caused objects to float in the air. They made things appear to speed up or slow down. They made the air feel very hot, and then very cold.

"They are witches!" someone cried.

"Or perhaps conjurers of the spirits," one of the adawehi countered. "We should not anger them."

"Please, we are neither," Nathan said. "Not truly. Not in the sense you are thinking. We are still but men. We bleed as men."

"Do you die as men?" Wilinawa asked casually.

"We can, yes. But we serve another being. We wish you no harm. We have been sent to help."

"We do not need your help!" one warrior snarled.

"The last time a European offered to help, we were driven off, beaten, bloodied, and dishonored!" another agreed.

"But we cannot ignore that they have brought Kiyuga and Anagalisgi to us safely," Atagulkalu said calmly. "They could have easily killed them and we would have been none the wiser with the actions at the fort."

"And what do they expect of us in return?" Saloli wondered coldly. "Everything the Europeans say and do comes at a price."

"We understand that you have been greatly mistreated—" Nathan began.

"On this, you are correct," Amadoya said curtly.

"We want to help," Andrew stated. "We ask nothing in return."

"An unlikely prospect," someone scoffed.

"You are not liars," one of the Beloved Women began, her voice silencing the rest of those gathered. "However, you are not as truthful as you would have us believe. There is something you are holding back."

A ripple of indignation made its way through the warriors and women.

"However, you did return a warrior and an adawehi to us," she went on. "If payment is what you want, then you will be paid with your lives. Leave Kuwayi'hi. Take nothing with you except what you have on you now. Go."

Her word was final. Nathan and Andrew tried to appeal, but the Beloved Woman was the highest authority in the waking world and would not be easily defied.

Kiyuga and Anagalisgi walked with them to the edge of the town.

"What will you do? Where will you go?" Kiyuga wondered. "The British do not tolerate disorder from their warriors."

"They don't," Andrew confirmed. "And they hold provincials in even lesser regard."

"Don't worry about us," Nathan said, waving a hand. "You are safe and back with your own people."

"Back with our own people, yes," Kiyuga said. "But far from safe."

"How shall we continue to train?" Anagalisgi inquired. "I am still willing to learn if you are willing to teach."

Nathan hesitated. "We would very much like to continue to teach. We also do not want to cause more trouble among your own people. We do not wish to cause trouble for you either."

"If I can learn to conjure Time for others, and I can help others, maybe they will see that it is not witchcraft, and they will be more willing to learn themselves."

Nathan and Andrew glanced at each other.

"It is an idea," Andrew stated.

Nathan nodded and looked at Anagalisgi. "We will give you some time to continue to practice your skills on your own and perhaps try to explain what you already know."

"We will be returning to Itsa'ti soon, I expect," Kiyuga said. "How will you travel there?"

"In the spring, we will come," Andrew said.

"But the army —" Anagalisgi began.

"Don't worry about them. Don't worry about us. As you have seen, we have little to fear from our superiors."

"Then why do you answer to them?" Kiyuga asked. "If you have greater power and believe their mission dishonorable, why continue to serve them?"

"We did so according to the will of the Author, because we were meant to come and help," Nathan answered. "We now see that it is unfolding in a way we had not considered. We answer to the Author, not the army. We hold love for our country and our people, yes, but we cannot stand idly by when our calling is elsewhere."

"Even if that means betrayal?"

"Is it betrayal to help the ones your people mean to kill? Is it betrayal to tell someone that what they are doing is wrong?"

Anagalisgi shook his head. "No."

"No. Helping one person is not the same as betraying another. The world is not so sharply defined as some would have us believe, and we choose not to be trapped in such a deceptive dichotomy."

"You are wise men. I expect to learn much from you."

"In the spring," Andrew repeated. "In the spring, we will come."

They all clasped wrists, and the Englishmen went on their way, disappearing into the forest across the river. Kiyuga and Anagalisgi watched the spot for a short moment.

"Do you truly believe in them?" Kiyuga asked finally. "That they will make things better?"

"I don't know that it is about them," Anagalisgi replied. "They serve a different calling."

"This...Digohwelisgi? This Author? Is it to be trusted?"

"Why should the Creator not be known by many names to many people?"

"But it goes against their own Christian doctrine."

"Or perhaps it is a way to explain it."

"What do you mean?"

"I'm not sure, but I think the spirits will tell me when—" Anagalisgi abruptly cut himself off.

"When what?" Kiyuga goaded.

His brother was silent for a long moment. Then, "I think the spirits will tell me when I am ready. When I have learned more from these conjurers."

Kiyuga frowned and studied his brother. He sometimes worried about losing his brother to the spirit world long before he walked on. It was honorable to commune with the spirits, but sometimes he wondered about the connection his brother had, if it was too great for his mortal mind to handle. Finally he said, "Well, no matter what, we have been many days without good food and water, and I greatly desire some furs to lie upon."

Anagalisgi nodded, seeming to return to the waking world. "Agreed. We will stay in the townhouse with the skiagvsta and adawehi. They have much to discuss yet, but I believe we will be returning to Itsa'ti soon."

So they turned and headed away from the river, into Kuwayi'hi, back toward the townhouse. As they walked, there was a rush of wind and a flurry of birds high overhead, crows cawing and calling to one another. They did not fly in formation but haphazardly, toward a darkening sky.

DᏯᎪᎢᎢ ᏍᏈᏍ

Ayadohlv'i Gahlgwadu

Consider All Resources

Anagalisgi arrived in Itsa'ti just in time to touch Gvnagadoga's brow before he walked on.

There was a time of great mourning in Itsa'ti for the old uku. He'd had many sons and daughters, and all came to mourn over him for a time. Half the town, it seemed, had to be taken for cleansing, including all of the adawehi who had spent much time with Gvnagadoga.

The ground was yet frozen, so his body and a few possessions were wrapped in white cloth and placed in the spot where he would be buried when the time came, right in the townhouse near the sacred fire.

Because of these ceremonies, talk of what happened at Fort Prince George had been postponed. Indeed, half a moon had passed before the council was convened to discuss matters. Most of those gathered had already heard and discussed much in Kuwayi'hi, but when the remaining Overhill warriors heard the tales, the rage was ignited anew.

"We cannot let this go unpunished!" one declared.

"They have taken advantage of us for far too long!" another agreed.

"We should attack Fort Loudoun!" someone suggested.

"We will lure them from the fort, as we did at Kuwayi'hi," Aganstata said calmly but suredly.

"You, Aganstata?" Atagulkalu wondered in disbelief.

"Certainly not you," Wilinawa scoffed. "You would trade us all for British goods if you thought you could."

"Your plans have only ever failed us and gotten our warriors and skiagvsta killed," Yachtino growled. "Twenty-three perfectly good warriors died that day. Aganstata, Mankiller, myself, we could have been next. Because you wanted to sue for peace when you knew no one was interested."

Atagulkalu's face had turned pale. He looked to Chola for help, the only skiagvsta of Si'tiku who had opposed Amadoya. The man frowned and sighed. "I wanted to believe in you, Atagulkalu, that we had a chance for peace. But no more. We go to war."

So it was that the great warrior and diplomat was unsurreptitiously ignored, almost barred from discussions on how to best go about attacking Fort Loudoun. Aganstata decided that because no news had come from Fort Prince George about the attack, they ought to use a similar tactic, luring the soldiers from the fort. It would be the fastest, easiest way to kill all of the soldiers, or as many as possible. They had only a limited store of meat and grain, and planting season would begin soon, which meant that now was the time when their stores were lowest. Any who survived would surely starve.

Anagalisgi would not say that he did not hold similar feelings, that the time for peace was past. And he performed well his duties as an adawehi to bless the upcoming war party. But he could not shake his dreams of fire and destruction.

He was not the one to accompany the war party. They didn't need a bad omen with them, or so the thinking went. He did not mind. He did not have the fortitude for war, and without the ability to conjure Time around others, he would be of little use in a fight.

Kiyuga went, though. Anagalisgi saw his brother off the same as the rest of them. He wanted revenge for Fort Prince George as much as Aganstata. Perhaps even more, seeing how he'd had to endure even greater mistreatment after the first seven hostages had been released. And he had to watch the other hostages die.

Anagalisgi naturally worried about his brother, though he had a quiet confidence in his spirit that told him everything would be all right. His brother was doing exactly as he was meant to do. It was as the spirits intended.

Unfortunately, the attack did not go as the warriors intended. This might not have been so bad, except...

"You warned them!" Wilinawa roared, pointing at Atagulkalu. "You warned the British of our intent. Worse, you betrayed your people!"

"We cannot afford war," Atagulkalu said, trying to remain calm.

"We have the advantage here," Aganstata told him sternly. "Just as we were stuck in British lands surrounded by their soldiers, vulnerable to their whims, so they are here now."

"Should we provoke them to send their soldiers here?"

"Should we let them wipe their boots upon our heads?" Amadoya countered.

"Should we meekly hand over our lands without even the courtesy of being robbed?" Yachtino demanded.

"We may disagree on many things and yet find common ground on which to act," Mankiller said, level but stern. "But on this, we cannot disagree. It is a terrible offense to betray the people. If any of our warriors had died today, their blood would have been on your hands, for your warning to the British to give them the advantage."

"I wish no harm upon anyone," Atagulkalu defended. "I tried to stop the fighting before it began."

"It has already begun," Amadoya said. "You blamed me well enough for it. It was your insistence on forcing the sun to rise in the west that saw our skiagvsta and uku taken hostage. It was your insistence on forcing water to flow uphill that most of those hostages were killed."

"Perhaps we should have listened to Amadoya from the beginning," Chola suggested. "Perhaps we should have listened to those who listen to and consult the spirits, rather than those who bargain with these white-skinned demons."

Atagulkalu glanced at the Women's Council as if seeking support. He found little.

"We entrust our safety to our warriors," one woman said. "We trust our skiagvsta and uku to consult the spirits, us, each other, and make a decision that is best for the people. Betrayal is never what is best for the people. We entrusted the safety of our children—our daughters, our sons—to you. You betrayed them."

"I was trying to protect our honor," Atagulkalu stated.

"There is honor in peace, yes. There is no honor in rolling over as dogs, for our sons to be beaten and our daughters carelessly mounted."

"Our daughters have husbands who are soldiers of that fort, and have children."

"And there will be no shame or retribution for them when they return. The daughters inherit all lands and possessions and the children are hers by rights. All remains as it should be. Some have already returned and have been more than welcomed back."

Atagulkalu could make all the arguments for peace he wanted, but no one was listening anymore, and no one dissented as all the skiagvsta, the uku, the adawehi, and the women voted to both expel Atagulkalu from the council and his position as skiagvsta as well as banish him from Itsa'ti. The old warrior took it in stride and left the townhouse without another word.

As the remaining skiagvsta and warriors planned their next attack, spearheaded by Wilinawa and Gvnagadoga's nephew of the same name, Anagalisgi slipped outside and caught up to Atagulkalu as he left Itsa'ti.

"Tell me, Anagalisgi," the old warrior said. "Did you see this? Did the spirits tell you of my apparent downfall?"

Anagalisgi let out a breath. "No. Truly, they did not."

"I believe you. I do not expect you to know the hills and valleys of every man's path."

"Where will you go?"

"I shall return to Tama'li, tell my wife and children what has happened. Then we will go into the woods and live alone."

"What about the Middle and Lower Towns?"

"Word will spread. Amadoya will make sure of that, through Saloli. I am known, and so my disgrace shall be also. Better to leave entirely."

"A wolf, even the lowliest nanny wolf, should not separate himself from the pack. It is not safe."

Atagulkalu smiled. "Ah, young one. What is safe? I know not the meaning of this word."

"Do you think perhaps you could still help with the relocation of the Middle and Lower Towns?"

"Perhaps. Those who are fleeing the fighting may be more apt to listen to a peaceful voice. But we shall see how things turn out."

"Well and not well," Anagalisgi told him.

The old warrior laughed. "That's the spirits for you." He sighed and his smile vanished. "It is clear that the others intend to go to war. I fear this brings the fire and destruction of your dreams. It may be prudent to seek out the white-skinned sorcerers to continue to teach you in your sorceries, and perhaps teach others. This is not a fair war that they are waging; the Aniyvwiya are at a terrible disadvantage. They ought to consider all resources available to them."

"They will never listen to Nathan and Andrew. They were lucky to escape with their lives last time."

"I think sorcerers are a bit more capable than that. But even so, either you will have to make them listen, or you will have to become a sorcerer yourself. They will listen to you."

"I don't think so, not when I see only ill fortune."

"You have so little faith in yourself. Consult the spirits, Anagalisgi. Gvnagadoga taught you well. Use that knowledge."

With that, Atagulkalu took his leave, stepping ahead on the road and making for Tama'li to gather his family into exile. Anagalisgi watched him go.

Atagulkalu was right. This war brought the Aniyvwiya ever closer to the fire and destruction he had foreseen. He could not stop the fire and destruction, but he could help the people escape and hide for a time. But he would need the help of the sorcerers to do it.

He returned to Itsa'ti and pondered what he should do. He prayed. He burned incense. He slept and tried to dream. The other adawehi consulted the spirits on war. The British had holed up in their fort like rabbits in a burrow, prepared for a siege. Anagalisgi sought the spirits for a plan of action for the rest of the people, when the rabbit suddenly turned into a very nasty cougar with its back to the wall.

He wondered what would happen to Nathan and Andrew if they tried to come into the Overhill during this time. Probably they would be shot and killed before they could explain themselves. As Atagulkalu had said, sorcerers could well take care of themselves, but Anagalisgi really needed to meet with them, without attracting too much attention.

He wished he could speak to Gvnagadoga, ask his advice. He'd been the only one to truly understand the dreams and visions that plagued him, his connection to the spirits. Anagalisgi wished he could consult Gvnagadoga in his dreams. He wished he had more seeing fruit.

When the ground softened, Gvnagadoga was buried. Anagalisgi also took the opportunity to unearth Ulisi. Decay had begun to set in, and he tried not to look at her face. He took the seed of the seeing fruit and pressed it up under her sternum, into her heart, or where her heart should have been. With luck, and provision from the spirits, the trader's words would prove true and a seedling would sprout, and the resulting tree would bear more seeing fruit.

The problem was, he thought as he replaced the earth back over her body, trees took many years to grow and bear fruit. The Aniyvwiya did not have years. He might hope that the trader returned with more fruit, but there was no guarantee. He might hope that the spirits would visit him in a dream and give him a straight answer. But hope was waning and patience was no longer a viable currency. He needed to act to save his people. He had to find the sorcerers.

He left the townhouse and momentarily paused when he saw the white woodpecker sitting upon a rooftop, facing him. It made deliberate eye contact with him, then spread its wings, and took off.

Anagalisgi chased Ge'gwogv through Itsa'ti to the road where he lost it. The white woodpecker vanished into a tree as surely as if it had never been there in the first place.

This left Anagalisgi standing there, staring down the road. He had to follow this road, for it led to his destiny. He was to be the guardian between worlds. Once he made the decision, there was no turning back.

He stepped out, down the road, feeling as though he were crossing a threshold only he and the spirits could see and feel. His heart lurched and his breath caught, but he knew deep down that this was right. This was what he was meant for. He had to find the sorcerers and learn from them, even if he could not convince anyone else to listen.

About halfway to Daqua'i, it occurred to him that he had no food, and he had no idea how long his journey might be. But he did not stop in Daqua'i, instead continuing on to Tama'li and then to the adjacent Taskigi.

The fort's cannons had been successful in keeping most of the attacking warriors at bay, and now they camped around the fort, just out of range of cannon and musket, waiting out the soldiers inside. No one was permitted in or out. The soldiers happened to have a few pigeons which they tried to send out with messages, but they had so far all been shot down.

Anagalisgi located his brother.

"Come to join the fun?" Kiyuga asked, his tone divided between amusement and annoyance.

"I'm going to find the sorcerers," Anagalisgi told him. "Unfortunately, I've not brought any food with me."

"Yes, that might prove to be a problem." Kiyuga handed him a small bag. "Take mine. It will tide you over until you can snare a rabbit or a turkey." He paused. "Do you know where you will find them?"

"On the road, I expect. It is springtime, and they said they would be here at this time."

"As long as Saloli and his warriors did not find them first."

Anagalisgi shook his head. "No. They are coming. Sorcerers can well take care of themselves."

Kiyuga's expression was uncertain. "And you are sure that this sorcery will save us? We no longer have the luxury of time or mistakes." He gestured toward the fort.

"I am sure. It saved us, didn't it?"

"And only us."

"It is a tool, Kiyuga. A tool I must learn to master. And tools take no sides."

His brother nodded. "You are correct. Go, little brother. I will be the physical barrier. You be the spiritual one."

They clasped wrists, then Anagalisgi stood and started out once more. The camp around the fort was more than just the warriors; their families were with them as well. Taskigi had grown up around Fort Loudoun, an odd extension of Tama'li, but this camp was far closer. It was as if the entire town had been picked up and moved.

Anagalisgi navigated new paths and shelters that had never been here before, trying to find his way back to the main road. Some called out greetings to him, which he politely returned. He could not afford further delays; he had to get going on his mission.

Then he was on the road, leaving Taskigi. Warriors patrolled the river in canoes, ensuring no soldiers could escape by that route. The whole fort was blockaded.

He continued on the road until the whole scene was gone from view and he was alone in the woods. He let out a breath and sat down against a tree. He felt terribly unprepared and so very alone. Could he really hope to do what he set out to do? Even if he did find Nathan and Andrew, could he really learn what they had to teach? Even if he learned their sorceries, could he really convince others to learn? Even if he could convince others to learn, could he really teach them?

As he was pondering this, movement caught his attention. He looked to his right, then to his left. A noise. Movement. Shadow. He reached for his skala galogwehi and discovered it missing. He went for his knife and found the same. He heard more noise, saw more movement, saw more shadow. Or rather...no, it was not a thing to cast a shadow. The shadow itself was moving.

"Evil spirit," he whispered.

He stood, reached for a weapon, a talisman, anything at all. He found nothing. He had nothing but his clothing. Even his food had been stolen.

As the shadow got closer, Anagalisgi had a hard time discerning a shape. It was at once coyote and cougar and bear and buck, as if it had no true form other than shadow and smoke. But he could certainly see a powerful body, long claws, and sharp teeth. It stalked him openly now, a shadow breaking free of its object.

The thing lunged at him. As Anagalisgi put his arm up defensively, there was a blur of white in his peripheral vision and a sharp yelp of pain and surprise.

Anagalisgi jolted and found himself suddenly back in the waking world. A dream, then. It had been a dream. But a very potent one. He rubbed his eyes and looked around. Everything looked as it should have. The road, the trees, the sun overhead and heading for the horizon.

But something else caught his attention. Marks in the dirt on the road. He stood and edged closer.

Animal tracks, one set unidentifiable, at once coyote and cougar and bear and buck, their direction pointing toward where he'd been sleeping. The second set was definitively wolf.

Had it really happened, then? Had it not been a dream? Or had the spirit world simply been closer to the waking world than normal?

Anagalisgi checked himself, relieved to find that he still had his skala galogwehi, his knife, and his food. He also had some talismans and charms, just in case. He glanced at the animal tracks in the road. How close had he come to the spirits really? How close had he come to death?

But if evil spirits were trying that hard to stop his mission, he figured that this was the road he was supposed to take.

Anagalisgi continued down the road, not realizing he was shaking until now; he walked briskly to try and calm himself down.

He did not find Nathan and Andrew that day as he retraced his steps through the Overhill to Itsa'ti and beyond. He did not find them the next day as he left Talasi and the Overhill. By the fourth morning, he was beginning to doubt himself as he rested beside a stream and filled his water. Could he have been mistaken? Did he really expect anything to be easy when it came to following the spirits and fulfilling destiny? If destiny was this easy to fulfill, everyone would do it.

"Anagalisgi!"

He whirled around to see Nathan and Andrew walking toward him from the road, sliding down the embankment to the river beside him.

Maybe it really was that easy.

"We were just coming to see you," Andrew said.

"Did you think we wouldn't come?" Nathan asked, stooping to refill his water also.

"I was more worried that something had happened to you," Anagalisgi confessed. "Either from your own people, or on your journey through the Middle and Lower Towns."

"We're grateful for the concern, but there is no need to worry."

"Aganstata and the others have launched an attack on Fort Loudoun."

That gave the white men pause.

Anagalisgi continued, "They have it surrounded, trying to starve out the soldiers. No one gets in or out of the fort. No British are permitted in the Overhill. I was expecting perhaps a blockade, but most of the warriors are occupied with the fort."

The men frowned. It was Andrew who spoke. "That does make this a little more difficult, then."

"If you can teach me, I can teach others. They'll listen to me more than you."

"Have you taught anyone so far? Your brother, for example?"

Anagalisgi hesitated, then shook his head. "No. This has all happened so fast, I feel like I'm on the outside looking in, and everything inside is...like I'm Iyuwahnilvhi Asganola Adahnesagi'a. Slow Banding. And everything else is spinning out of control."

"Then there is certainly no time to waste," Nathan told him

seriously. He looked at Andrew. "I think we ought to teach him the basics of many things."

"And have him kill himself for ignorance?" Andrew wondered.

"He is a clever young man; he can work out some things for himself. Give him a foundation to work from. The abilities that he will need, he will use more frequently, and we can refine as such, rather than our typical step-by-step method."

"We have those steps for a reason."

"He doesn't have the time, Andrew. They're at war. He needs to learn so they can learn. Our time is cut in half, and we didn't have much to begin with."

Andrew growled unintelligibly about the prospect. He seemed to be a very methodical person, Anagalisgi thought, and Nathan more passionate. After a minute of Andrew mentally wrestling with the arguments, he agreed. "Fine." He looked at Anagalisgi. "But that means you have to pay attention to everything. Every detail, every word. Do exactly as we tell you. And when you return home, we expect you to deliver the same instructions to your people, and don't give them any excuse to slack off. Understand?"

"I understand."

"Good. Show us what you know, everything you have been practicing, whether we showed it to you or not."

So Anagalisgi did. He conjured Time as they had shown him, around himself. On the way back from Kuwayi'hi to Itsa'ti, he'd also been experimenting with trying to conjure Time around others, without having to touch them. He thought he'd managed it once, but as soon as it happened, it slipped away.

"Not a bad start," Nathan said encouragingly.

"We'll give you the basics of External Banding, conjuring Time around others," Andrew said decisively. "You learn it, you practice it. Then we'll move on to something else."

It wasn't especially difficult, very similar to conjuring Time around himself, but it was a slippery thing. There were small differences in conjuring around himself, around himself and others, and around just others. These differences were similar to observing the sun in the morning, noon, and evening. Obvious once there, but it was like trying to pinpoint the exact moment when the sun passed from the morning arc into its zenith, and then past to its evening arc.

He managed to get it a couple times, conjuring around Nathan, then Andrew, then both of them, then all three of them. Anagalisgi felt terribly unprepared as Andrew declared it good enough for him to practice on his own time. Time to move on.

They moved on from Time, into a new aspect of their conjuring: Gravity.

"Gravity is the force that keeps us standing on the ground," Andrew began. "Imagine that the whole world is a marble, a round ball, and it is spinning so fast that we are naturally attracted to its surface."

At Anagalisgi's blank look, Nathan clarified, "Imagine a whirlpool. The force of the center of the whirlpool attracts water and objects—leaves, for instance—into itself."

"How do you know this?" Anagalisgi wondered.

"There are many things about the world and the universe that most men have not yet discovered," Andrew answered dismissively. "But it is known to conjurers." He picked up a stone. "I release this stone, and gravity causes it to fall, for it is naturally attracted to the earth." He let go and the stone fell. He picked it up again. "Like Time and other forces, Gravity may be manipulated. I can change the gravitational constant in one area or along a track."

"Honestly, Andrew, you're confusing him," Nathan interrupted. "He doesn't have the benefit of being able to go to the Archives to learn these things."

"Well, it's important to understand the nuances of manipulating Gravity, or else someone really could get killed," Andrew argued.

"Then keep it simple."

"Do you want to teach this part?"

"Maybe I should."

Andrew held out his hand, a gesture for Nathan to take over.

Anagalisgi just watched.

"Gravity is the force that keeps us on the ground," Nathan started. "Left alone, it always moves one direction. In this case, down."

"Are there other cases?" Anagalisgi wondered.

"Yes, elsewhere in the universe. But for our purposes, Gravity only moves down."

"Elsewhere in the universe? You mean in the stars? Or the spirit world?"

Nathan sighed. "Anagalisgi, please focus. We're trying to save your people. Once they're safe, we'll talk about some of your questions. All right?"

Anagalisgi nodded and motioned for him to continue.

"When manipulating Gravity, you are working against this force in a single spot or pocket or along a track." Nathan took Andrew's stone and grabbed another, bigger rock. "The maximum gravitational constant is nine-point-eight meters per second squared. That means that whether this rock falls, or you or I do, we will fall at the same speed." He dropped both rocks and Banded so Anagalisgi could see that they fell the same. Then he bent and picked them up. "To make the rocks stay in place, we need a counteracting force of negative nine-point-eight meters per second squared." He tossed one rock away from himself. About two feet away, it stopped falling and stayed in place. "The Gravity pocket that I have created only affects that stone in that spot." He tossed the other rock over it, and it soared into a bush. "If I want to move the rock as it is, I need to be continually changing gravitational and other physical forces." Even as he spoke, the rock floated through the air back into his hand. "It's not about the rock, but the forces around it."

"And you said I was getting too technical," Andrew said, rolling his eyes.

Anagalisgi could only stare. Half of what Nathan had said was completely lost on him, and he figured that the language barrier was not entirely to blame. These were concepts beyond what anyone had ever suggested to him, or anyone he knew. He'd always known about the spirit of the earth and the land, yes, and all the spirits within animals and creatures. But these kinds of forces, this breath of the earth that it should keep all men to itself, was astounding.

"He doesn't understand," Andrew was saying, again arguing with Nathan.

"No," Anagalisgi said quietly. "I do understand. In an odd sort of way, I understand it, I think, better than you do."

Neither man said nothing, though Nathan raised a brow.

"You describe these things in terms of math and science, things that you can write down and calculate, all very precisely, as if only precision makes beauty and peace with the spirits. But these things I have known and felt my whole life as Aniyvwiya, the movement of earth, sun, and moon, the clouds over us by day and the stars by night. It is not about mathematics, but listening to the breath of the earth."

Without even needing to touch the stone, Anagalisgi willed it out of Nathan's hand and into his own. He felt the changing of this gravity as surely as he would feel the change in a current of water should he try to redirect it. The two British men stared at him.

"Maybe we should have started with that," Andrew said, clearly unsure what else to say.

"Energy is one of the most difficult and dangerous things to learn," Nathan agreed. "But perhaps he knows something we don't." He nodded, as if confirming something to himself. "Let us try one more thing. Then you can return to your people and begin teaching them."

"What about you?" Anagalisgi wondered.

"We will follow behind and be not more than a day's travel away," Andrew promised.

The next thing they did, then, was Sound. All sound was just waves in the air, as from a pond, that gradually dispersed or became blocked by objects. Like Gravity, Sound and these sound waves could be manipulated, dispersed more widely so that noise was softer, or amplified and so louder.

"This will be of great use," Anagalisgi said excitedly as he practiced putting up a Sound barrier, a sort of bubble that would dissipate all sounds they made. People may see them speaking, but they would hear no words, nor any other sound: shuffling in the dirt and leaves, rustling of clothing, nothing. "Stealth is key in both attack and retreat."

"You have learned a lot today," Nathan praised. "More than some with months of formal study. I think your spirits were wise to choose you to save them."

"The Author has crafted excellent teachers," Anagalisgi told him cheekily. "I will return to my people. I will teach all who wish to learn."

Andrew raised a brow. "It may be more prudent to teach only a small handful to start with. Then, as you learn more, you can teach them. And as they become proficient, they can teach others."

"Perhaps you are right."

"Your enthusiasm is not misplaced," Nathan said. "But as we have said many times today already, time is limited. Return to your people. Teach them. Help them."

Anagalisgi nodded and thanked them even as he was walking away. Time was limited, yes, but only for those who did not yet understand how to conjure. But he did, and he did so now. He Iyuwahnilvhi Uhlisda Adahnesagv'i and walked along the road in eerie silence. The birds did not sing, the squirrels did not chitter, and the deer did not flee. All remained frozen, pristine, devoid of life. His was the only soul moving about, and yet he did not feel alone. Even here, in this void, he knew the spirits were with him. Both the white animals and the creatures of smoke and shadow.

After a bit, as his head began to hurt, he ceased conjuring. Birds took off in flight, squirrels jumped from tree to tree, and a deer looked up from where it was eating. He took a drink of water and continued on.

He practiced his conjuring as much as he could stand on the road. The Gravity he decided to call Galo'ohndiha ale Agi'a, making it fall and picking it up. Andrew and Nathan seemed to think it a difficult feat, yet he had no trouble with it. They relied on math and calculations to tell them what he instinctively understood about the movements of the earth.

Sound he called Uhnoyv'nohyvhlga, making a noise, or, perhaps more simply, Uhnoyvgi, noise. He was able to quiet some noises and make others louder. He could silence the squirrels and listen for the hare. He could mask his footsteps and get closer than he ever had in order to catch one. He could Iyuwahnilvhi Uhlisda Adahnesagi'a even to prevent the rabbit from escaping. It never even knew he was there.

He gave thanks for the hare before he cooked it, but he couldn't help but feel a little guilty. He felt as if he'd cheated. By using these abilities, he'd diminished his own prowess, cheated himself of an honest victory and the hare of a chance to escape. But was it truly wrong if the spirits had brought the British men to him to learn such abilities? No one seemed to have a problem with using guns over bows, or bows over clubs. Or clubs over snares.

In the end, he decided that the method was not the issue. As long as he continued to give thanks for the food that was provided, he could use these abilities. He could not get proud or greedy. As surely as the spirits could show him this magic, they could take it away. Barring that, they could cause him terrible misfortune and punish him for arrogance.

He would have to reiterate all of this to those he taught, he decided. This conjuring was a gift from the spirits, not something to be taken lightly. It was sent as a way to help them hide from their enemies, maybe even defeat them in battle. But they were not to use it for evil purposes.

He didn't know how the people would react to this, or if they would listen. When he showed the warriors on their return to Itsa'ti, they had been awed and terribly frightened by it. Some commented on his incredible connection to the spirits. Others questioned which spirits he was connected to. Whatever the case, nothing more had been said about it.

Well, he thought as he finished the rabbit and carried on up the road, they didn't have time to not make a decision. He had learned more, and he knew he could teach it. Either it would save them, or it would destroy them. But they had to choose whether or not they would use this tool.

He passed a group of warriors heading the way he came. No surprise, they were going to block the road to the Overhill. They did not have the numbers to resist a fighting force if it came through, but they were comprised of Deer Clan runners. They would be able to warn the Overhill of any incoming threat.

"How are things in Taskigi?" he wondered.

"The same," one of the runners replied, shrugging. "The soldiers proclaim they have ample provisions until they are rescued, but they can plant little within their walls, and they do not have enough to feed their horses."

"Have you heard anything about a rescue coming for them?"

"Not yet. How can they be rescued when their fellows do not know there is a problem?"

It was only a matter of time, Anagalisgi figured, after what happened at Fort Prince George. But they were safe for the time being anyway. Anagalisgi wished them well and continued on his way. It occurred to him later that perhaps he should have stopped and given them some instruction in conjuring Time. If the runners could slow down time around them or speed themselves up, it would give them a greater advantage if they had to run an urgent message to the Overhill. For a long moment, he considered going back and doing just that.

He decided against it, if only because he was not going to stay and camp with them to give them longer instruction and more oversight. He had to get back to Taskigi at least, if not Itsa'ti, and instruct the warriors there. Nathan and Andrew would be waiting for him to begin training his people.

So he carried on. There were several times when he considered going back. He could conjure Time and be back there in an instant, after all. But he never did. He just kept his eyes fixed on the road ahead.

Soon enough, Talasi came into view. Anagalisgi paused and

breathed a sigh of relief. He has home again. Well, closer to it. He continued on, through Tsilhowi, Si'tiku, traveling through Itsa'ti on his way to Taskigi and the fort. The Europeans seemed to enjoy making a grand show of their buildings. He remembered hearing Atagulkalu's stories of going to England. Buildings as tall as trees and richly adorned. Every common man seemed a king to his eyes, and the king himself lived as a god. Anagalisgi pictured the things he'd seen in Charleston and tried to imagine them even more lavish, considering some of the spoils warriors had stripped from wealthy victims or hostages. Were such things really so common for the Europeans? Looking at the modest homes of the Aniyvwiya clustered here and there, was it any real wonder the Europeans considered themselves superior? When a man had an ax to cut down a tree for building, he did not think twice about it, nor did he consider working as the beaver did to build his dam.

It brought little comfort as Anagalisgi drew ever nearer to the wooden monstrosity, the homes and shelters of the camped warriors dotting the landscape around it, the canoes patrolling up and down the river.

As the runners had said, nothing had changed. The warriors remained camped around the fort. The soldiers remained trapped inside the fort. Anagalisgi could see the soldiers still made routine patrols from the inside, but that was about it. The warriors were just out of reach of cannon and musket. This was not a battle of strength, but willpower.

Anagalisgi found his brother in the same spot he had been the other day. He was busy cooking up a spring stew, adding chunks of meat as Anagalisgi approached.

Kiyuga looked up as Anagalisgi sat down. He grinned. "Little brother, you've returned!" Then he frowned. "And so soon. Were you unable to find Nathan and Andrew?"

"I did," Anagalisgi said. "They taught me much. Now they send me back to teach others."

"Very good." Kiyuga stirred his stew, releasing the pungent scent of spring onions. "Have you found many students?"

"No, I've not asked anyone. And I would like for you to be my first student."

Kiyuga looked up. "Me?"

"What support should I gain if my own brother does not learn?" Anagalisgi postulated. "You would be excellent at it."

"I'm not a dreamer like you. I don't have the connection to the spirits that you do."

"No one does. But that's all right. You can still learn. We all know that the British have no connection to the spirits, and yet it is two of them who showed me this." Anagalisgi shifted position. "They rely on math and calculations and words on paper to tell them what they need to learn. I have learned in a few days what they say it takes moons or years to learn. Because of my connection to the spirits. You may not be the same as me, but you are more than them."

Kiyuga hesitated. "I don't know. Wouldn't it be better to approach Aganstata or Wilinawa or any of them first? They are the skiagvsta, the ones who are leading this rebellion."

"I will approach them. I am willing to teach anyone who wishes to learn. I am asking only that you be my first student."

His brother still squirmed, pretending to be more interested in his stew that was simmering nicely. He took a spoon and brought a chunk of meat to the top to check it.

In a moment of cheeky curiosity, Anagalisgi focused on the stew. He considered the pot and the contents and the fire it sat over. As he went to conjure time around it, he discovered that it was more difficult than he expected. As he tried to contain the fire in his conjuring, it flared and writhed like a beast. Kiyuga, surprised, fell back on his seat and scooted away.

Embarrassed and hoping to save face, Anagalisgi released the fire from conjuring and instead focused just on the pot and stew. It bubbled a bit, then died down. And in a matter of only a few breaths, the meat was fully cooked, the stew ready. Kiyuga stared at him.

"You did that," he said dumbly.

"Yes," Anagalisgi replied simply. "When I was on the road, I slowed a hare so that I might catch it with my bare hands."

"What else can you do?"

"Would you like to learn?"

For a long moment, the brothers stared at each other. Anagalisgi could not explain the boost in confidence he felt except that he had done something amazing and maybe now he could actually teach it to someone else. Many things about the spirits were reserved for those with innate talent. But this could be taught to anyone willing to learn. He hoped.

Finally Kiyuga nodded. "I will learn."

"Excellent." Anagalisgi stood. "I will find four more students. Then we will begin."

"Start with the skiagvsta and senior warriors. If they will listen and learn, so may some of the skeptics."

Anagalisgi nodded and headed out.

Wilinawa and the younger Gvnagadoga were too preoccupied with maintaining the blockade to want to take time and learn the sorceries, and their demeanor said that they were still immensely skeptical, to the point of hostility if they didn't already have a bigger threat at hand. Still, Anagalisgi remained polite toward them and decided to leave them until either other skiagvsta and warriors convinced them otherwise, or he had greater understanding and abilities to make them want to learn. But then, if they were not amazed by the conjuring of time, what would amaze them?

Amadoya was out raiding with Saloli, though Anagalisgi imagined he would be more interested and more willing to learn. He had seen enough battle to know how to put this new tool to use. But it was unclear when the Si'tiku skiagvsta intended to return.

But another Si'tiku skiagvsta, Chola, was present and interested in learning. If he could learn and was impressed, he said, he would help Anagalisgi convince Yachtino to learn and take it to the outer reaches of the Overhill, to Amohi and Ayuhwa'si, who were dealing with other problems not involving the British. As for Usga'hi, the Si'tiku adawehi was terribly skeptical and preferred to remain in the old ways until the spirits told him otherwise.

Mankiller, who was personally conflicted over whether he should stay and help with the blockade or go out and raid with Amadoya and Saloli, was also leery of the sorcery, though he did say that if Aganstata agreed to it, then he would at least consider it.

So Anagalisgi went to Aganstata who divided his time between the blockade at Fort Loudoun and his regular duties at Itsa'ti. He had taken Atagulkalu's place as skiagvsta and now worked to better coordinate the raids and attacks on British forts and settlements. They were of one mind again, he reasoned, and they should strike as a single fist, strong, united.

"Our warriors have also laid siege to Fort Ninety-Six," Aganstata said. "And also to many smaller outposts and settlements in the area of the Lower Towns. Only Fort Ninety-Six has the advantage to win against our warriors."

"Then let us take that advantage away from future raids and sieges," Anagalisgi said. "Learn to conjure Time. Convince others to learn. How shall it be for an enemy to see us here—" Anagalisgi conjured fast Time and moved behind Aganstata. He stopped conjuring. "—and then suddenly here—" Aganstata whirled around, but Anagalisgi was already conjuring and moving around. "—and then suddenly here?"

Aganstata almost went through the roof. Anagalisgi had tried to demonstrate similar things on the way back from Fort Prince George, but now he finally had it more under control, enough to spook the skiagvsta.

"My brother and Chola have already agreed to learn. I wish to find three more students to teach. As I teach them, they can teach others. You are a great skiagvsta, and I know that you are well-suited to this."

Aganstata was still staring with eyes as big as the moon. Eventually he remembered how to blink, though he seemed to have forgotten whatever it was he was going to say. They continued to look at each other for a few moments.

At long last, the skiagvsta nodded. "Very well. Yes, I will learn this conjuring. And when I have learned, if it proves useful, then I will take it to others as well."

"Mankiller said he would learn if you did," Anagalisgi mentioned.

"I will teach him myself if that is the case."

"Thank you, Aganstata."

The skiagvsta dipped his head. "We should be thanking you, I think. Too often we have ignored your dreams and prophecies and warnings. Now we are paying the price for it. And still you have the patience and foresight to investigate these new sorceries to help the people. As I said, I think we should be thanking you."

"When this is over, perhaps."

Aganstata nodded. "Indeed." As Anagalisgi turned to leave, he spoke again. "You need two more students, do you?"

Anagalisgi turned. "You know of some?"

"I have only one suggestion. Seek out Atagulkalu. He lives in the woods just a few days north of Tama'li."

"You think he would be interested, seeing how we intend to use this for war?"

The skiagvsta frowned and sighed. "Maybe when this is over, Atagulkalu will be invited back. He cannot be seen as less than he was. As for his interest and willingness, that is up to him. But I think he will accept."

Anagalisgi considered this. Then, "I think I have an idea."

Atagulkalu was not difficult to track. His wife still made trips to Tama'li and Taskigi to see her family, and their children visited often. The exiled skiagvsta was more than happy to receive Anagalisgi and offer him some cornbread.

"You intend to teach this sorcery to the people, then," Atagulkalu stated when Anagalisgi finished. "Use their own weapons against them, the same as the musket and rifle and skala galogwehi."

"This conjuring, it is not a weapon. It is a tool," Anagalisgi told him. "A knife may cut reeds as easily as render flesh. It is not the fault of the knife."

To prove his point, he pulled a similar trick on Atagulkalu's meat as he had done to Kiyuga's stew. Then he said, "There was no weaponry there, only a tool."

Atagulkalu cut the meat and ate it thoughtfully. "Indeed, so it is. And how is it that you expect me to learn this? In case you had not guessed, both from your attendance at the meeting and my new dwelling here in the middle of the woods, I am no longer skiagvsta. I am barely part of Tama'li or Taskigi except for my wife."

"You will return," Anagalisgi told him certainly. "You will be called back to the people. You will one day lead again."

"You know this, do you?"

"I do." Even as he said it, he knew it to be true.

Atagulkalu did not speak for a long moment. Then, "How do you expect to teach me with the rest of your students, if I am days away?"

"I have an idea," Anagalisgi said. "The British sorcerers, Nathan and Andrew, they are camped about a day from Talasi. No one knows they are there. They are here to teach me, as I am still learning myself. Perhaps they could come and stay with you. They can teach you and me, and the three of you may be able to learn more from each other and keep the hopes of peace alive."

The exiled skiagvsta looked thoughtful at the proposal. "You know my sons are not overly fond of the British. Tsiyu has gone to the Lower Towns to raid. He is becoming quite popular with some of the younger warriors, perhaps even more popular than Saloli."

"But Nayanali hopes for peace. She supports her father doing what is right to defend the people, but she looks to you as well to nurture the seed of peace. And your sons would be fools to defy her if she invited Nathan and Andrew into her home."

Atagulkalu laughed mightily. "Ah, such truth! A father and uncle may scold, but few may withstand the wrath of an angry mother." He wiped a tear from his eye. "Ah, you are right. Such wisdom from a young one I have never heard. My uncle was right to train you. I think he was wise to seize upon your potential." He nodded. "Very well. Send these two men to me that we may both learn. I am sure in that time Nayanali will be more than ready for their arrival."

"Thank you. I will not disappoint you."

The old skiagvsta waved a hand. "You have never disappointed me, Anagalisgi, and I don't expect you to start now."

Anagalisgi left Atagulkalu's home feeling hopeful for the first time in a long time. For once it actually felt like something was going according to plan. Finally, things were going as they should and people were listening to him. Maybe now they had a chance at survival.

DᏯᏞᎯᎢ ᏂᏪᏚᏋ

Ayadohlv'i Neladuhi
The Tides of War

Kiyuga stared at the fort. Two men walked along the inside of the wall on patrol. A short distance from him, Wilinawa peered through a spyglass for a closer look. Any attempt to storm the fort was met with cannon and musket fire. Occasionally they picked off the patrolmen; Gvnagadoga was a particularly excellent shot with a rifle. But mostly they sat. And waited.

So far, no soldiers had been able to escape the fort, and no armies had come to rescue them. The blockade on the road reported no unusual activity in the Overhill, although Saloli and Atagulkalu's son Tsiyu Gansini reported that there appeared to be some rallying on the part of the British in Charleston. Could be a gathering of forces, Tsiyu said. They would keep an eye on things.

Otherwise, the days passed uneventfully. Certain warriors left the camp on certain days to go hunting or fishing, and the women came and went for tending crops or gathering forage. The people had no shortage of food, even as Kiyuga knew the British had to be hurting. One day the dogs walked with the soldiers on patrol...and the next day they didn't. And they heard no more barking at night.

The most interesting activity from the fort came from the soldiers who had taken Aniyvwiya wives and fathered children with them. These soldiers begged to see their wives and children, promising anything in trade for just a few minutes. But children belonged to their mother, and the Aniyvwiya women had divorced their husbands and returned to their people with their children. One woman, who had been pregnant, even went so far as to go to the fort and call to her former husband. When he came to the rampart to see her, she gave birth there in the grass, her mother and grandmother attending. Then she took the babe and made a show of turning her back on the soldier, not even giving him the courtesy of knowing whether it was a boy or girl, or its name. Kiyuga happened to hear that it was a girl whom the mother named Galiyesusdagi'a, meaning roughly in English, I am taking off a ring.

Kiyuga also heard that the soldier tried to break out of the fort just a few days after the birth and was unceremoniously killed by the warriors on the east side of the blockade, opposite of Kiyuga's position. The body was taken to the woman, if she wanted to mourn. She stripped him of spoils and told the bearing warriors to sink him in the river. And it was so.

There were no more pleas by the divorced soldiers to see their wives or children after that. Kiyuga could easily imagine that morale inside the fort was terribly low.

Had the soldiers heard about Fort Prince George, what was done to the hostages? Had the soldiers known about the room they'd been kept in? Their fort was far grander still than such a wretched place. Stuffing thirty-two men into a room meant for six. These soldiers still had room to walk about and patrol and cook and carry on as normal, just without being able to leave.

"What are we hoping for?" Kiyuga heard someone ask of Aganstata one morning as the skiagvsta made his rounds. "Are we hoping to starve them to death, or do you think they will surrender?"

"I expect they will attempt to surrender," Aganstata mused with a certain air of confidence.

"We will not let them?"

"We will do to them as they have done to us. We will allow them to leave, and then we will attack. Kill them, ransom them, as we have always done these things."

"When will we do this?" Kiyuga asked.

"Whenever they ask," Aganstata answered simply, shrugging. "At this point, they only punish themselves. If they choose starvation, then it will be so. But they are cowards, I think, and they will want to attempt to leave and salvage what little honor they think they possess."

This exchange produced much gossip that spread throughout the camp. Some began making bets on which soldiers would rather starve. Some began claiming their prizes, declaring which ones they wished to kill and strip for spoils, pointing them out as the soldiers made their patrols. If the soldiers had any clue as to what Aganstata had declared, they gave no sign. This was just as well, for it meant there were no traitors among them.

Atagulkalu remained in exile, though his wife made regular trips to Tama'li and Taskigi. She spent most of the time with her family and her children's families, but she also paid a visit to Kiyuga as well.

"Your brother is well," she told him. "Ever enthusiastic about his studies."

Among those gathered around Fort Loudoun, it was never explicitly mentioned that two British soldiers resided with Atagulkalu, even if they considered themselves former soldiers, "and provincials at that." A few knew that Atagulkalu was learning the British sorceries, but they only knew that it came from Anagalisgi, who was also teaching Aganstata and others. Kiyuga's younger brother had decided that he would teach his pupils in Taskigi and elsewhere for half a moon, then make the trek to "teach" Atagulkalu. To hear Anagalisgi talk about it, Kiyuga suspected that Atagulkalu, spending more time with Nathan and Andrew, would likely end up teaching him.

"Has he learned anything that will either defeat the British soundly or else hide us well away until their wrath passes over us?" Kiyuga inquired.

"They discuss these things at length," Nayanali told him. "It seems there is an idea that they entertain, but Atagulkalu is unsure how it would be received by the people, regardless of who may give voice to this idea."

Kiyuga sighed and nodded. "We're well settled here, anyway. Have you heard your father's plan?"

"Yes, he told me. Starve them or kill them upon surrender." He could see she was uncertain of this plan of action. "Do you think it can be avoided?"

"Do you think it should?" he countered.

"I don't know. The things these sorcerers teach...there is no reason we could not defeat the British and send them scurrying like rats back across the ocean to their homeland. But then how shall we be any different from them?"

"Is stealing something of yours from the thief who took it from you still stealing, or merely reclamation?"

"And how many generations shall we reclaim from others? Or others from us? Shall we bargain for land with the Anikusi? The Aniseneka? How much time must pass before a past wrong simply becomes something that is? How long shall we carry hate in our hearts?"

"Certainly more than a few moons, for the sake of those murdered at Fort Prince George," Kiyuga said severely.

Nayanali sighed but could not refute him. "Yes, there is that, I suppose."

"It is for the people, Nayanali," he told her gently. "Whether the sorceries grant us a means of sound victory or escaping and hiding, I will do it for the people, those who are here now, and those who are yet to be born. If I thought the British intended an honest surrender with honest terms, I would do it for the people. But they have no honor, nor do they know honesty. It is a dangerous thing to bargain with a trickster."

"Coyotes and crows, as Diwedalohi used to say."

"That's right."

Nayanali stood. "It seems we are all simply waiting now. Waiting, watching, and learning."

"When does Anagalisgi expect to return?" Kiyuga asked before she could leave.

"When I left to come here, he was speaking of leaving in a few days. I would expect to see him on the path as I return home."

Kiyuga nodded, thanked her, wished her well, and watched her leave. She had been taken as a young girl in a raid on the Aninotsi and brought back to the Overhill, raised by Aganstata as his daughter. She was as much Aniyvwiya as Kiyuga or Anagalisgi or anyone here. Did true peace mean that she would have to return to the Aninotsi? When did past wrongs simply become the state of things in the present? When did British or French presence in this place or that place simply become the way things were? How many generations had to pass? When did they give up wishing that things would go back to the way they were before?

Well, it would not be this day, he decided. He was still alive. He had survived Fort Prince George. He owed it to those who died to avenge their deaths and bring peace to their spirits. He did not desire to sit around and simply wish and hope that there may be peace. The British could not be allowed to win, not today.

He settled back and watched the fort, watched the patrolling soldiers make their rounds. Eventually, they would starve. Eventually, they would wave their white flag and sue for peace.

As he waited, he practiced some of the things Anagalisgi had shown him. As he'd predicted, he wasn't very good at any of it. He just didn't have the same skill and connection to the spirits that his brother did. He could conjure Time a bit, make things appear to move a bit faster or a bit slower, but he couldn't make things stop completely, not like his brother did.

As for Galo'ohndiha ale Agi'a, what the British men called Gravity, he was a bit better at that. He could cause things to levitate in place, but he was unable to make them move about at will, not like his brother did. Perhaps he was thinking about it in the wrong way, the British way with math and calculations rather than the Aniyvwiya way, as simply the movement of the earth. When he stopped trying to see these things as British things, and instead saw them as things he already knew, he had a little more success. It was the same concept to both peoples; he had to remember that, and think of it as he knew it, rather than try to figure out how the British thought of it and copy them. He already knew what to do.

His success was limited.

But there were a few things he was good at. Uhnoyvgi, for one, making sounds louder or softer. This he had learned quickly when he went out to hunt. He could use Uhnoyvgi to hear the rustling of prey in the bushes while masking his own steps.

He was also very good at Udilegv'i ale Uhyvtsa. The British sorcerers called it Thermodynamics, which could be summarized as hot and cold, so that was what Anagalisgi decided to call it. It had taken a little explanation in order to understand how it worked, how heat moved through something. Anagalisgi had explained it as simply as putting his hand on a rock. The rock felt cool, and it quickly made his hand feel cool because it was stealing his heat. The same with the chill of the river or a crisp wind. Thermodynamics, or Udilegv'i ale Uhyvtsa, was simply willing oneself to give or take heat.

Kiyuga had experimented with this a bit when he started his cookfires, and he'd even discovered how to manipulate the wind with Udilegv'i ale Uhyvtsa. It wasn't anything grand, but it was a very similar concept to how the wind changed around a forest fire.

He was doing this a few days later when his brother arrived in camp, looking as lively as Kiyuga had ever seen him.

"You must have good things to teach," he observed mildly.

"I do, and it pleases me to see that you are practicing," Anagalisgi told him.

"You have brought us a useful tool."

"I'm glad you see it that way."

Anagalisgi sat down and helped himself to some of the food Kiyuga was preparing. "How are things here?"

Kiyuga shrugged. "The same. Ever watching, ever waiting."

"Nayanali met me on the path. She said Aganstata plans to either starve them out or kill them when they surrender."

"She speaks the truth. You will have to discuss it with Aganstata when you see him."

"I think I will." His brother nodded gravely, losing some of his enthusiastic shine for just a moment. Then he came back to life. "But I have new things to teach."

"More new things? Do wonders never cease?"

"This is only the beginning."

Kiyuga sat back with his own food. "We should be able to overthrow them now, I think, if more people understood and learned. Or if Aganstata would allow us to use it. But he wants us to understand it well before we attempt to use it in battle, this way we are not cut down with our own weapons."

"Fair enough," Anagalisgi mused. "It is a powerful tool, certainly, and he is wise to be cautious. Besides, it is not as though you are in desperate need of it here."

Kiyuga gestured to his cookfire. "Of course I do."

His brother gave him a look. "In battle."

They made mild small talk while they ate and for a short time after. Then they left the camp and headed into the woods to train privately, away from those who were more skeptical or hostile toward the sorceries.

"What new thing are you showing me today?" Kiyuga inquired.

"Atsvstdi," Anagalisgi answered. "Light."

This was another thing Kiyuga proved to be decently talented at, perhaps because Anagalisgi did not try to use British math and calculations to explain it. It was tricky to grasp at first, telling light to get brighter or dimmer simply on a whim, but it was very much like Uhnoyvgi. Like Uhnoyvgi, Atsvstdi did not simply be, it existed as an actual element, something that could be manipulated. The two were very close together, both of them waves in the air like ripples in a pond. He simply had to put up obstacles and barriers to direct it a certain way, and there was a part of this manipulation, this conjuring, that was sheer willpower. Faith, Anagalisgi said. Faith that it will be done for good, for the Author's purpose.

Kiyuga was still uncertain of the Author, but he could not deny what he saw, what he could do.

While Kiyuga's initial instruction only went over lightening and darkening, Anagalisgi demonstrated how he'd learned to actually bend light.

Kiyuga watched as his little brother went over to a sunbeam filtering through the trees. With barely a motion of his hand, Anagalisgi twisted the sunbeam so it bent over his head and wrapped around his body. The more he tried to do with it, the more he tried to move it, the less coordinated it became, but the fact remained that Anagalisgi was moving light.

"Can you make the sun rise in the west as well?" Kiyuga wondered incredulously.

"I cannot," Anagalisgi replied meekly, letting go of the sunbeam so that it slowly righted itself back to where it had been. "For the sun is its own element, a fixture in the sky, that no conjurer dares touch. It is the same with the moon and stars." He sat down on a rock, looking tired but still excited. "There is so much to learn. I am so overjoyed by it, and then I remember why I must learn it."

Kiyuga sat next to him. "Nayanali said that there is a possible plan to save the people."

"Yes, but we wish to examine it from all sides and figure out how it would work. On its face, it would not go over well with the people, no matter who introduced it. As some are already wary of the sorcery, the details would no doubt be off-putting for most."

"The way you are speaking tells me that you're not going to tell me either."

His brother shook his head. "No. I am sorry. We do not know enough at this time. Once it becomes a feasible plan, or perhaps our only option, then I will tell you."

"Is it that you believe the sorcery will defeat the British army and we will not need this plan? Or perhaps that it will not be enough?"

"I don't know. I wish I did."

Kiyuga could tell his brother was lying, a rare thing for an adawehi and even rarer for Anagalisgi. He knew something. They—him, Atagulkalu, Nathan, and Andrew—knew something, and they didn't want to speak of it. All the same, Kiyuga did not call him out on it. He had to extend a measure of trust to his little brother.

"Just be ready to move and carry out Gvnagadoga's plan when the time comes," Anagalisgi said, apparently ceding a tiny bit of information. "Fire and destruction come swiftly."

Kiyuga promised him he would be ready, and the two of them returned to camp.

"Have you seen any of the others?" Anagalisgi wondered, looking around.

"Aganstata was here a few days ago," Kiyuga answered. "He may have returned to Itsa'ti. Chola returned to Si'tiku after you left the last time."

His brother nodded. "He said that he would come to Taskigi at the full moon, which is tonight. I expect I will find him soon. And if I do not find Mankiller here, he will be in Tama'li."

"Do you know if they are teaching others? Or swaying them to be more accepting of the sorceries?"

"Mankiller is more accepting, and he seems to be trying to teach his sons. Chola wishes to get the approval of the adawehi so that everyone in Si'tiku will learn. Aganstata wishes to learn and think on it some more."

"And Atagulkalu?"

"Nayanali has proven to be an adept student also, and she teaches three of her daughters. I do not believe that their sons are so convinced. Their hatred for the British is great, but they struggle with seeing their father as a traitor to the people. But if we can convince Tsiyu to learn, he may convince Saloli and the rest of the Lower and Middle Towns."

"One step at a time, I suppose," Kiyuga mused.

Anagalisgi nodded. "And I must make many more steps if I am to find my own students and teach them."

They wished each other farewell, and Anagalisgi headed off.

Kiyuga practiced as much as he dared, trying to somehow use Udilegv'i ale Uhyvtsa as well as Atsvstdi to manipulate his fire. When he did small trials, he had few problems. Any time he wanted to really change something, the fire always got away from him, once burning his arm.

He saw Aganstata a few days later. He appeared as he usually did, determined, resolute, proud of the people and how well they were keeping up with the blockade. That comradery was foiled before midday when one of the Deer Clan runners from the road blockade approached him.

If Kiyuga hadn't been watching, he probably would have missed the whole encounter, and that was probably the point. If the warriors were unaware of mischief, then the soldiers in the fort would be also. As it was, Kiyuga and a couple dozen warriors were quietly called aside, traveling with Aganstata and the runner to Tama'li before finding out what was going on.

"The British have sent a force of soldiers maybe fifteen hundred in number," Aganstata said. "They are burning our crops and villages. Estato has fallen already. The warriors are fleeing to Kuwayi'hi, hoping to get there before the soldiers reach Fort Prince George so they may meet them on the road."

"Are we going to attack?" someone asked.

Aganstata nodded. "We will send who we can spare, but we mustn't let the soldiers find out that their army is on the move, nor can we let our guard down here." He looked over those who had gathered, about thirty. "Go to Kuwayi'hi and help them fight." His gaze rested on Kiyuga. "Yvgidahi, if things go poorly, get the women, children, elderly, and wounded out of the Lower Towns, as we have been discussing."

Kiyuga dipped his head. "I understand."

"Will you be coming with us?" another warrior inquired.

"I will not, no. Mankiller will be with you. Amadoya will meet up with you on the road with his warriors. Saloli and Tsiyu are currently rallying the Lower and Middle Towns. Go now; we haven't time to waste."

The Tama'li adawehi provided the warriors with prayers and charms for good luck before hastily sending them on their way. The only reason Kiyuga got to say goodbye to Anagalisgi was because of the conjuring. He still wasn't very good about bringing everything to a complete standstill, but his brother picked up the slack and helped him. Kiyuga explained what was happening.

"Be safe, brother," Anagalisgi told him. "Use the gifts you have been given."

"This is the fire and destruction you have seen," Kiyuga stated.

"It is."

"You know how this ends."

"And you know what you must do."

Kiyuga still hesitated, but finally nodded. "I know. Aganstata told me to evacuate the people if things go poorly."

"They will," Anagalisgi told him. "Please, do not waste time. Help the people."

"I always try."

They clasped wrists. Anagalisgi said a prayer for him and let him go. Kiyuga rejoined the departing warriors and ceased conjuring Time.

They passed by Fort Loudoun in the evening, when darkness and shadows obscured their movements so the soldiers would not see them leaving the area. Kiyuga used Uhnoyvgi to mask their footsteps and Atsvstdi to darken them even more. If anyone suspected what he was doing, they made no mention of it, and they slipped through the camp and by the fort undetected.

They traveled for part of the night, slept a bit in the early morning, then continued on. Kiyuga kept pace with Adahi, who spoke to him.

"This sorcery your brother is teaching you," he began. "You think you can use it here, when it comes to battle?"

"Some of it, yes," Kiyuga replied, unsure just how confident he wanted to be. "I do not have the same talent as Anagalisgi, but I can do some things."

"You will have to show us and the others when we reach Kuwayi'hi. I heard Mankiller is also learning these sorceries?"

"Yes, he is. He learns as much from Aganstata as anyone."

"Does it take long to learn? We may have to train others quickly."

Kiyuga paused. "I have had little instruction and also little trouble, though I think one man using the sorcery is different than many men using it as an army. It would require great coordination so we did not end up fighting each other."

Adahi did not reply for a long moment. Then, "Perhaps it is something Mankiller will be able to orchestrate."

"Maybe. First we must see what we have and what we are up against."

It was another two days before Amadoya and his warriors joined them on the road as promised. Around the fire that evening, Kiyuga heard Mankiller make mention of the sorcery and even demonstrate a bit, Atsvstdi and Uhnoyvgi. He may have demonstrated Iyuwahnilvhi Adahnesagi'a, but Kiyuga could not be certain.

He noted that Mankiller and Amadoya seemed deep in discussion throughout the following days. Were they discussing the sorceries? Was Mankiller teaching Amadoya? Were they discussing perhaps how to use these sorceries in battle? They looked at him from time to time, but never did they include him in their conversation.

They descended from the Overhill and made their way through the Middle Towns. Kiyuga noted that some of the women, children, and elders from the Lower Towns had already evacuated, as planned. While Amadoya and Mankiller interviewed them to confirm stories and try to figure out the British army's next move—all accounts said Fort Prince George was the most likely—Kiyuga inquired after them personally. How many had fled? Where had they all gone? Had anyone stayed in the Lower Towns? Was anyone unable to make it? A dozen or more had been taken captive by the British, but otherwise they had all escaped without incident.

Amadoya and Mankiller were visibly displeased by this and they hurried on down the road toward Kuwayi'hi.

When they reached Kuwayi'hi, they found a council had already convened and were very animated in their discussions. Saloli and Tsiyu Gansini seemed relieved when they saw the Overhill warriors and herded them into the townhouse which was already overcrowded.

"The British army is but a day away," Saloli reported. "They have red-coated soldiers, blue-coated soldiers, the ones who wear kilts, soldiers on horses, and several dozen Anitagwi. Fifteen hundred men, maybe even two thousand, plus Fort Prince George just here at the river."

"I say we take the fort," Tsiyu said. "We can use their cannons and arms against them. We already have them under siege; they are starving."

"The fort would be as much a prison to us as it is to them," Mankiller told him. "Who is to say they would not turn the siege against us and starve us?"

"We can't ignore them," someone said. "Nagutsi' is burned as well, all the cropland scorched. Tawodi was taken captive, Nakatiha slaughtered. If Kuwayi'hi falls, all the Lower Towns will go with it."

"The British are not here to negotiate," Tsiyu said hotly. "They have come to kill and to burn and to destroy."

"We are not here to negotiate either," Amadoya cut in. "Or have you not heard of your father? He was deposed as skiagvsta and sent into exile. Aganstata rules in his place, and he has sent us to help you fight while the Overhill lay siege upon Fort Loudoun. Once the British have surrendered there, more warriors will be available to help."

"That does us no good now," Saloli said. "They will be here tomorrow, maybe the day after at the latest. You can already see the smoke where they burn our hunting grounds. Tomorrow it will be the croplands and the village itself. What are we to do?"

"We fight," Mankiller stated. "When we were here last, the young adawehi Anagalisgi and the two British men who rescued him from Fort Prince George demonstrated sorceries to you." The mood in the room shifted. "Anagalisgi continues to learn and teach these sorceries to those willing to learn. His brother Yvgidahi has learned, as have I."

"You have taken up with these witches?" someone, maybe one of the Kuwayi'hi adawehi, asked skeptically.

"I have taken up the sorcery as it is taught by Anagalisgi. It is a tool, one we as Aniyvwiya are inherently talented to use. Just as we tame and ride horses with no need for the cruelty of the British, so we may also use this sorcery." Mankiller looked around. "We don't have time to instruct everyone, and I do not wish for people to be harmed out of ignorance. Kiyuga and I are the only ones here trained in this sorcery. We will use it tomorrow, and we will drive back the British army."

Kiyuga suddenly felt very unprepared.

Plans were made and discussed. Kiyuga remembered very little as he was more preoccupied with thinking over what he knew, what he'd learned, and how he was going to have to use it reflexively, with little time to think. Could he do that in the thick of battle?

Mankiller visited him afterwards, and they went to speak privately.

"I don't know that I can use this sorcery in battle," Kiyuga confessed. "I don't want to mess up and hurt our people."

"I know," Mankiller said. "But I have a different job for you." He hesitated for a moment. Then, "Honestly, I do not have faith that Kuwayi'hi or the Lower Towns will survive the attack. The British soldiers outnumber us terribly, even if we counted our women and children. Perhaps if everyone knew this sorcery, we would have a chance, but it is only you and I, and we do not yet have the skill we need for something like this."

"What are you asking of me?"

"I want you to gather the women, children, and elders. I want you to move them to the Middle Towns. Take them north to Kituwa, or west to Ayuhwa'si Eghawa where they will be safe."

"You think you will be able to hold out that long?"

Mankiller grinned but shook his head. "No. I do not expect this battle to last long at all. I expect we shall meet up with you on the road before you reach Itse'yi. But if all else fails, do as I have asked."

Kiyuga's heart was pounding in his chest as he nodded. "All right."

"Use the sorceries however you have to in order to get them out of here."

He looked at the sun, the long day lingering still. "Should I take them now and move under cover of darkness?"

The skiagvsta smiled as if he'd finally understood something. "Yes, I think that would be a good idea."

"Will anyone else be coming with me?"

"Some of the warriors from Nagutsi' and Estato are unfit for battle, but they can still put up a fight if necessary. The women will also be armed. Never underestimate what a mother bear will do for her cubs."

Kiyuga nodded. "Do they know of this plan?"

"Yes. They are ready to leave at any time. I will help you gather them and get them to the road."

So it was that Kiyuga, Mankiller, Saloli, Tsiyu, and others spent the better part of the evening assembling those who would flee to the Middle Towns. If the spirits willed it, the worst that would happen was they would simply have to turn around and come back. Judging by the expressions on the warriors' faces, they did not expect such an outcome. Kiyuga felt his heart drop into his stomach.

"Lead the way," Mankiller told him. "Use the sorceries. Use Atsvstdi to find your way."

Kiyuga nodded, ensured once more that everyone was ready, and started out up the road. On the one hand, he was a little frustrated that he would not avenge his captivity and the deaths of the others in Fort Prince George. On the other hand, he was perhaps the only one defending these vulnerable people if Mankiller and the rest of them failed to do just that and the British army came for them.

The road was dark, but the moon was still sufficiently lit that Kiyuga was able to use Atsvstdi to brighten their way, without the need for fire which would only draw attention. If anyone noticed how the quarter moon shone like the full moon through the canopy of leaves, they made no mention of it.

Kiyuga had learned quickly that pushing himself too hard on the sorceries, using abilities he was unaccustomed to or unpracticed in, could produce some wretched headaches. He had a good handle on Atsvsdi he thought, but it was still very new to him. Soon the light of the moon appeared as bright as the sun to his eyes, and his head pounded like a drum. Eventually he dropped the ability and called for a halt. His excuse was that he wanted to make sure everyone was keeping up well, a plausible excuse seeing how some of the elders moved slowly. But even when everyone was accounted for, he was loathe to keep going. His head hurt and his stomach felt sour. But he did not feel as though he'd put enough distance between them and the town.

He forced himself and the rest of them to keep going for just a little while longer, at least until they found a decent spot to hide and sleep for a bit.

Kiyuga was exhausted, yet he found himself lying awake, wondering if he was doing the right thing, wondering what the day would bring. Mankiller expected to meet up with them on the road before they even reached Itse'yi, where they would have to make a decision between Ayuhwa'si Eghawa or Kituwa. He wasn't sure whether to be comforted or discouraged by the thought.

He wondered what his brother was doing, if he was learning anything, if he was figuring out ways to use the sorceries in battle. Kiyuga felt as though he'd learned so much and yet so little. Would Mankiller's knowledge and talent be enough to save Kuwayi'hi? In theory, all he had to do was slow down time enough that he could cut down every British soldier and they wouldn't even know it. But conjuring like that was painful, and if he lapsed even a little, he would be dead.

Eventually, Kiyuga figured he must have slept. The next thing he knew, it was late morning.

Fearing the worst, that battle had already been had and lost, Kiyuga jumped from his spot and roused the group. Few were pleasant about being woken so roughly, especially the elders, but once they remembered where they were and why they were, it was less trouble to get them to move. Food and drink were had on the road, though Kiyuga allowed them a brief respite after they'd traveled a fair distance as the sun arced overhead.

Kiyuga stood watch, looking back over the road, toward where he knew Kuwayi'hi to be. They'd been right; it was possible to see the smoke where the British burned the hunting grounds. He wondered whether some of it was merely carrying over, floating through the air, or whether some of it that he was seeing might not be Kuwayi'hi itself as the British attacked and set fire to the town. Or, more optimistically, maybe it was the warriors setting fire to Fort Prince George.

He could hope.

If they were able to make any progress, it was only thanks to their horses and the litters they pulled behind them, carrying the frailest of the refugees. Children were put on the horses' backs to entertain them and keep them quiet while the women and few warriors watched for any sign of attack.

They traveled all day and most of the night. They did not look back. They did not turn back. They were not trailed by Mankiller, nor beset by the British. They were not surprised by Anitagwi warriors, or any others. They were simply alone in the mountains.

When they reached Itse'yi, they were met by their skiagvsta, uku, adawehi, and warriors. They were given food, water, and the children and elders were allowed to sleep in the townhouse, or with relatives if they had any. The wounded warriors were treated and Ganedisgi spoke to Kiyuga.

"Does this mean that Kuwayi'hi is fallen?" the skiagvsta asked him severely.

"We don't know," Kiyuga answered truthfully. "The goal was to save the vulnerable in case Kuwayi'hi was defeated, take them to Kituwa or Ayuhwa'si Eghawa. If Mankiller and the others are victorious, then these refugees may return home. If they are defeated, then they will likely retreat to the Middle Towns."

Ganedisgi frowned but nodded thoughtfully. "Many of the outer Lower Towns have been abandoned for Ayuhwa'si Eghawa. I expect more to come through here if the Lower Towns around Kuwayi'hi are burned."

"Agreed."

"But for now, you are welcome to rest here."

Kiyuga was grateful for the reprieve and a chance to lie down and eat something substantial without constantly looking over his shoulder.

He fell asleep where he was out in the open. No one disturbed him. The following day, he went out and snared a rabbit. Then he returned to Itse'yi to inquire after the refugees and see what they wanted to do, where they wanted to go.

Many had relatives in Ayuhwa'si Eghawa, and a group of young warriors offered to escort them there the next day, once the elders had rested well and supplies were restocked. Kiyuga helped to ready the horses and the litters. Elders sat or lay in the litters, children sat upon the horses' backs, and the women and warriors took up defensive positions around them. The road from Itse'yi to Ayuhwa'si Eghawa was treacherous because it went over a mountain, but when considering the British army, it was safer than the road to Kituwa which followed the river.

A few of the Lower Town refugees elected to stay in Itse'yi. One elder knew his time was nearly come and he had not the strength to continue. Another woman was pregnant and did not want to give birth in the woods. Still another woman and her three children chose to stay with relatives.

So there were perhaps a dozen or so refugees who were prepared to make the trek to Kituwa, though a few mentioned stopping in one of the smaller towns along the way.

As the refugees were about to leave, Kiyuga and a group of Itse'yi warriors escorting, a runner appeared in the town from the north. Curious, Kiyuga delayed their departure. The runner first went to Ganedisgi. Then Ganedisgi approached the refugee party, motioning for Kiyuga specifically.

"Aganstata is on his way south with more warriors to aid Mankiller. They should be here soon. The refugees should continue, but he wants you to stay and join, if you would," Ganedisgi reported.

Kiyuga agreed, but he still saw the refugee party off through Itse'yi to the road.

Aganstata and Mankiller arrived in Itse'yi on the same day, at almost the same time. Aganstata and his warriors looked well ready to go into battle. Mankiller and his warriors looked as though they'd just come out of whatever battle Aganstata had been envisioning on his trek down from the Overhill.

Council was convened and Mankiller gave his tale.

"They did not come to negotiate. They did not come to parley. They had no words for us. All that was on their minds was death and destruction. They surrounded the town and began burning. The woodlands, the croplands, trying to force us all inside a ring of fire. Their horses were unafraid of the flames and their mounted soldiers cut through our warriors as wheat. We had no choice but to flee. The soldiers in Fort Prince George fired upon us as we tried to escape on the river—or on land, for that matter. Dozens were captured, many killed.

"I heard their leader, a man they call Montgomerie, order certain groups to go to other towns—Duksa'i, Tomasi, Tsiya'hi, and others—and burn them as well. Some of their warriors and refugees joined us on the road.

"I also heard that in one town, perhaps the last to be burned, Montgomerie did offer a parley, but he offered it only on terms of surrender. Otherwise, he intends to pursue us even here and continue to burn our towns and lands."

A ripple of indignation grew to a great wave among those gathered. No one moved to quiet it as warriors young and old, just returning and just arriving, all shouted to be heard, each one with a plan of what to do when they caught one of the British soldiers. Scalping was only just the beginning.

"I was able...!" Mankiller said, raising his voice and waiting for the noise to die down some. "I was able to use Anagalisgi's sorceries, both in battle and in retreat. I was able to see the British soldiers and estimate their numbers. Because I have faith in our warriors to attack our enemies even in retreat, I would assume that they may be lower, if they are in pursuit. Higher, if they are not."

"Why do you not believe they would be in pursuit?" someone asked.

"Their wagons and supplies cannot well navigate the mountain trails," Ganedisgi answered. "They must rely on pack animals if they wish to move with any speed, and their large armaments, their cannons, are useless here."

"How many soldiers do they have?" Aganstata inquired.

"I estimate four hundred men in red and blue coats, one thousand of those soldiers in kilts, three hundred or more horse soldiers, and fifty Anitagwi warriors, less four," Mankiller replied with a certain smug smirk.

"Less four?" Kiyuga wondered.

"A scouting party was sent after us to see where we retreated. That message will not be received by those waiting for it."

"How many are you?" Aganstata asked. "How many warriors do you have able to fight still?"

"We've not been able to count precisely, as some still trickle in from the road as they retreat from the burning towns. But I might estimate four hundred or so. How many have you brought?"

"I was able to convince seventy to join."

"So our fighting force totals about five hundred," Amadoya stated. His tone was grouchy, but his demeanor said he was exhausted and not well akin to such tragic defeat.

"What else can you tell us?" Aganstata wondered.

"The British have retaken Fort Ninety-Six, but the siege was ineffective anyway. To my knowledge, there were no deaths in that encounter." Mankiller shifted uncomfortably. "I also recognized one of the officers with Montgomerie. James Grant."

"James Grant," Aganstata echoed. "He was captured at Fort Duquense, wasn't he?"

"Yes, and later released. He leads with Montgomerie in these raids."

"What does he know of us?" someone asked.

"Not much, I think."

"It is still very disquieting," Aganstata mused.

There was some talk among those gathered, fresh warriors wanting to know what happened from those who had just come from the Lower Towns. While individual accounts varied, the main thread seemed to be that there was very little actual fighting, very little by way of battle. The British were uninterested in this and instead charged in with fire and death. The sheer force and brutality of their attacks was perhaps one of the main reasons why they had been so effective. It was a new strategy, one they had been unprepared for.

The skiagvsta and senior warriors withdrew to speak amongst themselves for a time, giving the rest of the warriors a chance to boast of any heroic feats they may have accomplished. A few had managed to cut down British soldiers, and soon they were shouting their tales of bravery, showing off their spoils and trying to outdo one another. Kiyuga sat back and listened, wondering if he might be able to brag of such heroics in the coming days. He would very much like to have something to show for his efforts here, something to impress the people back home. Maybe he would even impress a girl.

Before he could go down that line of thinking, the skiagvsta and senior warriors returned. They called for quiet. It was Aganstata who spoke.

"We will assume that the British army pursues us. When they do, they will have to follow the road here. When they do, they will have to go through Itse'yi Pass. That is where we will meet them. We will leave here and camp in the pass that we may be ready for them whenever they arrive."

This was a rather agreeable course of action for the warriors. Revenge was a grand thing, and there was now the added responsibility of ensuring the British army could not breach the Middle Towns, and that meant protecting the road in and out.

Kiyuga found himself wondering what Anagalisgi would say about all of this. He had seen fire and destruction, yes. But what about afterwards? Fire and destruction had come to the Lower Towns. Would it also come to the Middle Towns, or would they defeat their foe? What came afterwards?

"Furthermore, all warriors will be instructed in this sorcery," Aganstata was saying. "Even if you do not use it, it may prove a useful tool. We will not have much time for teaching, I think, but you will know what to do."

He said it confidently, but Kiyuga was unsure. Had he learned something from Anagalisgi that would help? Other warriors appeared equally dubious, but there was no time to complain. The British were coming and they had to be ready. They had to be open to using any useful tool, no matter where it came from.

There was more talk and more planning that day, and the five hundred warriors stayed overnight in Itse'yi. Kiyuga lay awake, wondering what the day would bring. Would they even make it to the pass before the British came? Would they be kept waiting, kept in suspense, the British trying to wear down their resolve, play tricks on their minds? How was he expected to not only use the sorceries in battle, but teach others? He barely understood it himself.

Knowledge of hunting and warfare was passed down through many generations, fathers and uncles to their sons and nephews, each generation building and growing and perfecting the techniques of their ancestors. The Europeans had changed all that when they brought their foreign weapons and their foreign wars. And the Europeans moved so quickly. The Aniyvwiya did not have the time to pass down knowledge through many generations. Things had changed just in the lifetime of the senior warriors, Aganstata, Mankiller. As fast as the people learned something, there was something else to learn, with no time to perfect the old knowledge.

Now they had this new sorcery which was beyond anything anyone could have even conceived. Adawehi had always used crystals, beads, talismans and such to divine futures, invoke the spirits for good fortune in hunting and battle, even just to find lost items. This knowledge had been given by the spirits and perfected through the ages. Suddenly there was a new sorcery that allowed its wielders to change the world around them. And they barely had time to learn it before they suddenly had to use it. How would the spirits react to such hasty, even reckless use of this power?

Kiyuga slept. And dreamt. He found himself having a dream he knew he'd had before. He stood on the road. Anagalisgi stood before him, some paces off. He went to his brother and found an invisible wall which prevented him from getting close. He did everything he could think of to break through, but to no avail. Anagalisgi merely watched him with a certain expression, as though he knew that all acts were futile, that this wall separated them permanently.

"What can I do to help you?" Kiyuga begged, finally just putting his hands on the wall and leaning forward, almost pushing.

"I need no help," Anagalisgi told him, his voice a mixture of certainty, serenity, but also terrible longing. "But I will always be here to help you."

There was a flash of light and Kiyuga stumbled back several steps. Someone ran past him. At first, he was excited, for he thought it might be his brother. When he stood and turned, he could only see the back of the man running, and he knew it was not his brother. When he turned back around, Anagalisgi remained behind the invisible wall.

"Do not be angry with him," Anagalisgi said.

"Angry? Why would I be angry? Who is that?" Kiyuga looked around, but the fleeing warrior had gone.

Before his brother could answer, the landscape began to fade and sounds became muffled so that he could not hear his brother speak. Kiyuga let out a frustrated cry and found himself sitting up suddenly, still snarling. The one who had woken him stumbled back on his seat.

Kiyuga muttered a hasty apology and stood, feeling trapped and needing to escape but unsure why.

"You look like your brother when he has something to say," Aganstata observed, approaching. "But also when he does not know what he needs to say."

"That is certainly how I feel," Kiyuga sighed.

"Something we should know?"

"I don't think so. It was a message for me, and only me."

"Will you be coming with us today?"

Kiyuga nodded. "Yes, I will. It had nothing to do with this." *I think.*

"Very good. You think you can use the sorceries in battle?"

"I think so."

"Can you teach others?"

Now he hesitated. "I can only say that I will try."

Aganstata nodded in understanding. "I am new at this as well, but I will be there to help you. We cannot allow the British to advance so far and burn more towns. We must use every tool we have."

"I understand. Did Anagalisgi tell you anything before you came?"

The skiagvsta shook his head. "No, though the other adawehi promised us good fortune. If they promise good and your brother says nothing, I choose to take it as a victory."

Kiyuga said nothing except to mutter an agreement.

"Cheer up, Yvgidahi. Do not be so like your brother. Be a warrior, intent on the victory."

He clapped him on the shoulder and headed off to wake the few remaining sleeping warriors. Kiyuga let out a breath and looked around.

War was what every boy and young man dreamed of, to earn his name, gain standing, and build a reputation known throughout his people and his enemies. It was what separated Aganstata and Mankiller from the rest of the average warriors of similar age, what made them skiagvsta. Even Kiyuga could not deny his excitement, the thought of taking spoils and reinforcing his name of Yvgidahi. But there was something deep down inside him that said this war was wrong. Not morally necessarily, but something about it was just off. Something wasn't right about it. It wasn't like any other war they'd ever waged. Maybe because the British were unlike any enemy they'd ever faced, but it felt deeper than that. Something fundamental about their people would be gained or lost in this war. And if they lost it, they wouldn't get it back.

Maybe he did sound a bit like his brother, Kiyuga sighed. Maybe when this was over, he ought to move to a new town. Maybe one of these Middle Towns.

He looked around and spied a pretty girl a few paces off, bringing cornbread for the warriors to take with them. She caught him staring and blushed, but she couldn't stop smiling at him. She stumbled a step, looking more at him than where she was going, blushed harder. He moved forward a step as if to catch her, but she was too far and already upright.

The whole exchange lasted hardly two breaths, and yet Kiyuga saw it all unfold as though it took all day, every moment an eternity. Even after the girl moved off, he could recall everything about her. Her hair, her eyes, the beads and feather adornments she wore, almost as if she were hoping a young warrior would look her way and bring her spoils.

"Not possible," someone whispered in his ear. Kiyuga turned to see Adahi. The warrior went on, "She's Anihwaya."

Kiyuga couldn't stop a frustrated stomp in the dirt. Of course she would be from the same clan. On the other hand, it only bespoke of how great Anihwaya were. Hoping to hide his embarrassment, Kiyuga pushed himself into the crowd of warriors ready to move out. The Itse'yi adawehi were saying more prayers as they gave beads and talismans to the warriors. For luck and bravery and courage and true aim and victory. Kiyuga received a wolf charm, whether by chance or intent he did not know. But he tied it around the end of his rifle and sent up his own prayers.

Then they were moving, out of Itse'yi, south to the pass where they would confront their enemies.

ᎠᏯᏙᎸᎢ ᏐᎣᏁᎳᏚᎯ

Ayadohlv'i So'oneladuhi

Like Mastering a Bow

Runners were sent ahead to keep watch for the British army or any of their allies, especially the Anitagwi. They were not going far; their intent was to set up camp in the narrowest point of the pass to try and pinch the British army. That point was just north of Estato. There were two Lower Towns called Estato. The one that was far south had been burned. The one that stood at the southernmost point of the pass had been abandoned, its residents moved farther north.

The warriors made camp in the abandoned town of Estato, Aganstata sending out more runners to keep watch and report back. They all settled in at the abandoned townhouse, their possessions arranged such that they could move at a moment's notice. Aganstata raked and brushed clear a part of the ground where he sat and drew a map of the pass in the dirt.

"When the British come into the pass, I will lead an ambush at the head. There are some hills and thick trees here that will hide us. Meanwhile, Mankiller will lead as the Owl around here, down the left flank and attack. Saloli will lead as the Wolf and take the right. Amadoya will take the Fox position and circle around to cut off their escape.

"They cannot bring their wagons and supplies through here, which means they will have pack animals, horses and donkeys. Kill them or take them at your leisure. An army is nothing if it has no weapons and no food."

Aganstata looked around at those gathered. "If anyone here is faint of heart or newly married, leave now."

No one moved.

The skiagvsta nodded. "Very good." He sat back. "I will take one hundred warriors on the ambush. Mankiller and Saloli will each take one hundred fifty. Amadoya will take the rest. Any questions?"

There were none, except for who was going to be in which company.

Kiyuga was chosen to accompany Mankiller in the Owl position. Mankiller himself wore an elaborate mantle of owl feathers painted red and woven with hard cane to form armor. For Kiyuga and the rest of them, he was given a necklace of owl feathers to wear to designate his position.

He looked around at the others. Aganstata was taking the Raven's position in the front. He wore a similar armor to Mankiller, except his boasted black raven feathers, and his company wore raven feather necklaces. Saloli wore the wolf skin about his neck and his men had either wolf tails pinned to their garments or wolf teeth or claws draped as necklaces. Nearby, Amadoya's company of Fox warriors were similar, but with fox tails, teeth, and claws.

They also painted their bodies and faces such that they were unrecognizable even to each other. Only the animal skins told where they were supposed to be.

All that remained, then, was for the runners to return and report the movements of the British. And also for Kiyuga, Aganstata, and Mankiller, to try and teach all of the warriors everything they knew about the sorceries.

Aganstata seemed the most well versed in Iyuwahnilvhi Adahnesagi'a, though it was a difficult thing to teach and understand. Once understood, it was easy. But they didn't have the necessary time for all the warriors to have such a breakthrough.

Mankiller taught them Udilegv'i ale Uhyvtsa as well as Galo'ohndiha ale Agi'a, for he was good at these things.

This left Kiyuga to teach Uhnoyvgi and Atsvstdi. He had become rather adept at Uhnoyvgi, or he thought so anyway, but Atsvstdi he'd learned only just before being called to war. Still, he did his best.

Even as they taught these sorceries to the warriors, Kiyuga found himself wondering if it was really meant for such widespread use. What happened if two warriors tried to conjure at the same time? What if two warriors tried to manipulate the same beam of light? What if one warrior tried to amplify a sound and another hush it? What if someone tried to pick something up while another person tried to move it elsewhere? What rules were at play here? What decided that one warrior's will was greater than another? Was it based on sheer will of the spirit, or perhaps his purity?

He did not voice his fears, for he did not wish to appear cowardly. Aganstata and Mankiller had the same training he did, and they appeared confident in their work, so he ought to imitate them.

Most of the warriors took well to the sorcery, whether it was one aspect or all. A few struggled with it, most often out of fear or uncertainty as to the origins of the sorcery and having faith more in Aganstata than anything else. A few tried because they were asked to but quickly abandoned the idea, either because they did not do well or they were still terribly skeptical.

Tsiyu was one such skeptic. It was unclear whether his skepticism came from reverence for the adawehi and the spirits, or because he knew his father Atagulkalu was learning the sorceries. Kiyuga wondered if Tsiyu also knew his father was hosting Nathan and Andrew in his home in exile. Only his disrespect for his father kept Tsiyu from being a more honored warrior than Saloli; otherwise he would be leading the Fox position, Kiyuga knew.

The sun went down on that day. The runners returned briefly to mention that the British army had not been sighted and also that they were still alive. Aganstata thanked them and sent out replacements for them for the night.

Sleep was fitful for Kiyuga, and he woke up several times. He tried to dream again of meeting his brother on the road with the invisible wall between them, see if he might discern the identity of the running warrior or perhaps get clarity on the meaning of the dream as a whole. But he could not make the dream come again. Just as well, he figured, for he was not the dreamer and interpreter that his brother was.

Then it was morning. Aganstata permitted a few fires as long as they were kept small. They did not need to give away their position, nor burn down their own town; the British would do that well enough.

"How long will we wait for the British?" someone wondered.

"They will come," Mankiller promised. "They must. But they must also prepare for a new expedition."

"That could take forever," someone else with an eye roll. Kiyuga recognized him as someone who went on the Forbes Expedition.

"They are too intent on our destruction," Amadoya told him. "They offer parley in bad faith to try and lure us into the open. We will not oblige them, and so they must give chase."

The British did not come that day. Or the next. Still the warriors waited patiently, Aganstata rotating the watchers and even going out himself one day.

"Do you think maybe they gave up?" someone wondered around the fire. "If they know the road to Estato is treacherous and they cannot easily bring their wagons, they must know that the road to Itse'yi and beyond is no better."

"Maybe they are bringing their wagons," Kiyuga suggested. "They may be slower moving, but they will be well-supplied."

It was not a pleasant thought, but also not unrealistic. It was also unclear which was the smarter option. The British were powerful, but not the most intelligent. In this case, both options—with wagons or without wagons—seemed equally bad. Their best bet, then, would be to not come at all and leave the Aniyvwiya alone. Experience said that they wouldn't.

So they waited.

Aganstata returned that evening with nothing new to report except to mention that he sent runners out a little farther to see if the British were even in the area.

Still Kiyuga could not dream what he wished to dream. Then he wondered if such a thing was appropriate. Even if he did discern his dream, was it going to change how he acted in the waking world?

Such a thing could prove dangerous in battle, even fatal. He had to focus on the here and now, just as he'd told his brother to do often enough. Spend his time in the waking world. Focus. The British would be coming, and he would have to be ready. He had to uphold his name and honor.

The British did not come in the night. The runners returned and rotated positions. The warriors gathered a bit of firewood and stoked their fires, inspected their weapons, quietly told stories of past endeavors and heroic feats. Kiyuga told of his part in the battle at Taliwa, and how long ago it felt! He told of his part in the Forbes Expedition, going with Mankiller to ambush the French at Fort Duquense. He spoke of both himself and Anagalisgi and how they fought to escape Fort Prince George. That reminder renewed the fire of why the warriors sat in abandoned Estato, and Kiyuga was glad to see their spirits refreshed.

The sun was not quite at its zenith when the runners returned.

"The British are on the move," they reported. "They come this way. A thousand, two thousand, it was hard to tell. Soldiers in red and blue, more in kilts, many on horses. Anitagwi warriors as well, scouting ahead and looking for us."

Aganstata nodded. "Then we will leave some for them to find." He turned. "Amadoya. You and your warriors will stay here. Wait for the Anitagwi. Kill them as you can, but do not pursue when they flee to alert the British. Stay behind and prepare to follow and launch your attack in the pass as we have planned."

Amadoya dipped his head.

Without needing to be told, the warriors put out their fires and scattered the ashes. They brushed and raked the ground to obscure tracks. They gathered their supplies and weapons and prepared to move out, back into the pass. Kiyuga fell in with Mankiller and the rest of the Owl company.

Suddenly the prospect of battle was very near, and although the warriors were silent, their spirits were excited and they moved quickly. Now was the time for brave deeds and heroic acts that may be sung about for future generations. Kiyuga shivered with excitement despite the heat.

The flattening ground turned treacherous quickly as rolling hills gave way to mountains, and still they were only in the lower lands. Even so, one thing they always maintained was perfect single file of each company. Every warrior stepped directly in the steps of the warrior before him, making it appear as though only three men passed this way. They spoke no words, only animal calls now, to call out warnings or movements. And still they moved swiftly up the road, carefully making their way up the mountain.

They walked the rest of the day and all that night until they reached their destination.

The pass began to narrow. Up ahead, Kiyuga saw the spot where they would wait in ambush. The road curved upwards sharply, and then there was a gentler descent on the other side, but enough that it would conceal Aganstata and his Ravens. The west side of the pass was also a steep slope, a hump at the top and cluster of trees perfect for hiding Saloli's Wolf warriors.

The east side of the pass was different, as there was a narrow chasm between the road and the east slope. It would stop the British from attacking them directly, but they would have a difficult time trying to escape if such a thing became necessary.

They continued up the road in perfect single file until they were all well into the spot where Aganstata and his Ravens prepared their ambush. From there, Saloli and his Wolves broke off—still maintaining single file—to the west, sliding up the slope and slinking into the trees, using wolf barks and howls to speak to each other.

Meanwhile, Mankiller and the Owls carried on a short distance farther up the road until they came to a better access to the slope on the east side. It was narrow, and even those not out for battle would be forced to trek single file. Kiyuga tried not to look down as rocks slid out from under someone's foot and went tumbling down into the river below.

They reached better ground and ducked into some thick tree cover and brush, moving carefully and still single file until Mankiller bade them stop. They spread out as best they could, a few climbing to a higher shelf on the slope or even into the trees themselves, sitting upon branches. Rifles were inspected, loaded, ready for anything.

And they waited.

Groups of warriors at a time were permitted brief naps, to shake off the fatigue of climbing the mountain and refresh their spirits. A few nibbled on food remnants.

Kiyuga watched the road and waited. He knew that Aganstata had set up runners here and there to warn of the British advance. He could not see where they were. He looked across the narrow pass to where he knew Saloli to be but could not spot any of the Wolves. Aganstata's Ravens were also hidden, just awaiting the signal.

Had Amadoya and his Foxes encountered the Anitagwi warriors yet? Would they know it if they had? Would the Anitagwi flee to report to the British, or stay and fight? How much time would there be between Amadoya's battle and theirs? Would Amadoya be able to sit back and wait for the army to pass in order to completely encircle them?

All these thoughts and more passed through Kiyuga's mind as he lay in the brush, rifle at his side.

The sun began to sink and the sky darkened. Stars peeked out of the black cloth overhead, what little Kiyuga could see through the canopy. More groups at a time were allowed short naps, but they could not allow themselves to be caught off-guard. They had to be ready when Aganstata launched his ambush.

Then there was movement down on the road. A moment later, Kiyuga heard a sound as if a growl from a cougar. A runner, then, trying to keep quiet even as he did not wish to be assaulted by his own people. Kiyuga saw only the faintest of outlines on the road as the lanky warrior slipped from shadow to shadow up the road, heading for Aganstata and the Ravens.

There was silence in the pass for a short time, save for the rustling of leaves, the rumble of water from the river, and the whisper of wind.

What message did the runner have? What plans were being made? Were the British still traveling the road, or had they turned back? How had Amadoya fared against the Anitagwi? Would they be forced to retreat before they ever got to see battle? Kiyuga kept his gaze fixed on the road, but his mind was elsewhere, a dangerous thing for any warrior but something he could not help.

Then came Aganstata's raven call, eerily similar to the real thing, signifying all was well, stick to the plan, and sound off. Mankiller was the first to reply with his owl call. On the other side of the pass, Saloli gave a wolf's howl. In the distance, another wolf answered back.

Kiyuga wondered what the runner had said, and where they'd gone. He did not see anyone moving down the road, back toward abandoned Estato.

Perhaps the British were camped in the abandoned village. And why not? It provided shelter, fire pits, and some food if they had been smart enough to harvest what was ready before burning the cropland. If that was the case, then they should expect the army within a day or two, depending on how fast they could maneuver their way through the pass.

He slept, though not for very long. Only short naps here and there, only when it was his turn. He nibbled on a bit of food from his pack, checked and rechecked his rifle, his supply of ammunition, and continued to watch the road, waiting for the army to appear. That evening, Aganstata called out his raven call, and Mankiller and Saloli answered. He did the same in the morning, to ensure all were well and accounted for.

The following morning, as fog hung low in the pass, Kiyuga saw movement on the road. This time the call came as a pack of coyotes, yipping and screaming over a meal. Aganstata answered with a raven call. There were three runners this time, and they moved quickly through the pass, up the slope, straight into the waiting Ravens.

More words were likely exchanged, and Kiyuga wondered what they were. There was quiet in the pass for a bit, and Aganstata did not do another raven call. Had something changed? Were they—?

Then he heard it, on the wind. The stomping and snorting of horses, the jangling of metal, the general rustle of many people on the move in difficult terrain.

All else ceased to matter as Kiyuga focused on himself, his place in the trees, his line of sight, his rifle and his ammunition, and his enemies approaching their doom. As he did this, he found that he felt not only himself and all these things, but also his place in the universe, in time. He felt that he could conjure Time and all the other sorceries with no issue except to ask. The sorcery was a living thing among them, much as the earth was a living thing. It was not a tool as a knife was a tool, or a weapon as a rifle was a weapon. It was a being, like a horse. In order to wield it effectively, he had to learn it, understand it, respect it, and use it for its intended purpose.

It was as Anagalisgi often said, something that existed within the realm of the spirits, and they as mere men had not the words to convey what the spirits showed them.

He held onto this feeling even as his mind returned to the waking world. The first of the soldiers appeared, urging their horses forward up the treacherous road. To Kiyuga's limited vision, they seemed to never stop coming. Dozens of them, over a hundred on horseback, plus more foot soldiers around them.

The army advanced up the hill, faltering, stumbling, cursing, complaining. Kiyuga picked out his first target, a man a little older than him perhaps. He had some bauble on his jacket that caught Kiyuga's eye. Barring that, he had a nice horse, a sort of silvery blue. Kiyuga wasn't much for the heavy saddles the British used, but maybe he could barter it back to the French.

He kept his rifle trained on that man as the soldiers continued ever forward, entirely unaware of the ambush prepared for them. Kiyuga did not move a muscle. He hardly dared to breathe. He did not worry about the warriors to his left or right, wherever they may have been hiding. He did not worry about Mankiller or Saloli or Aganstata. He did not wonder about Amadoya. All that mattered was what happened in every moment, every breath, every heartbeat.

The fog still hung low, just obscuring the top of the hill where Aganstata and his Ravens waited, but it would burn off quickly once the sun rose.

A raven call went up. Then another. Then a third. The Ravens were about to launch their attack. A few of the soldiers looked around, maybe said something Kiyuga couldn't hear, but the convoy never stopped moving. He kept his eye trained on the soldier whose horse and baubles he desired. He remained on the outside of the company toward the east, the fourth row back, looking rather displeased about the whole thing.

The leading soldier was only a few laborious steps from the top of the hill when the Ravens sprang from their position and rushed the company. Startled horses reared and went backwards down the hill, crushing riders and sending men scattering for safety. Other soldiers simply went back on their seats or stumbled back out of control.

In that breath and heartbeat, Kiyuga found himself slowing Time and watching the scene unfold. He watched one brown horse rear in slow motion, a majestic beast, hooves pawing the air, tossing its head in wide-eyed terror as its own weight threw it backwards. Its rider was in the middle of a twist as he tried to jump off before being crushed, but one foot had become trapped in the stirrup.

He watched as the target he had chosen tried to rein his horse in and get it out of the way of the initial chaos. He was off balance in the saddle, hands tight on the reins as he jerked them back. The horse's chin touched its chest as it danced backwards, trying to figure out what the man wanted it to do, both of them oblivious to the sudden drop-off from the road.

Kiyuga took that moment to fire his rifle. Once the lead ball left the rifle's barrel, it, too, slowed, allowed Kiyuga to watch it fly through the air.

He'd hoped to kill the man, and it was impossible to say whether the injury was fatal regardless. Kiyuga ceased his conjuring so he could watch and hope to tell. The man was stunned as he was hit. With a jerking motion, he released the reins. The startled horse jumped forward, away from the cliff, knocking aside one soldier and colliding with another confused horse as it danced around with a dead rider still in the saddle.

The Ravens streamed down the road like a tide of demons, whooping, hollering, and making raven calls. Aganstata led a direct charge to break the soldiers down the middle while the rest circled to the west, trying to prevent the soldiers from escaping up the hill into the trees where the Wolves waited, trying to push them off the road and into the chasm.

A sudden, loud owl call made Kiyuga jump as he reloaded his rifle. He looked around for Mankiller but could not see him. Uhnoyvgi, of course. He was amplifying the call so all would hear him. A second call told them to be ready.

Kiyuga lifted his rifle and slowed Time again so he might pick another target. He watched as rocks slid out from beneath one horse and it went tumbling into the river below, its rider flailing in midair, desperate for some way to survive the fall. Another horse, riderless, went careening back down the road. The mounted soldiers were struggling to keep their mounts under control and the foot soldiers were more concerned with not being crushed by the enormous beasts than they were the enemies bearing down upon them.

He picked a target. When Mankiller gave his third owl call, all of the Owl warriors fired their rifles. Kiyuga knew this only by the smoke from the barrel, for the entire volley was quiet, their Uhnoyvgi muffled into silence.

Another horse fell into the chasm, its rider able to jump to safety at the last possible moment. A foot soldier slid down, clawing at dirt and roots to slow his fall, which it did and maybe even saved him.

At last, the mounted soldiers were able to find some semblance of order, but not before the Owl warriors fired on them again. The mounted soldiers tried to keep the Ravens at bay while the foot soldiers looked around for the ones firing at them. They formed up into their two-row formation, muskets aimed haphazardly at the hillside where Kiyuga and the Owls lay.

The Owls kept their heads low as the foot soldiers fired harmlessly into dirt and trees. They got off three volleys but no more as the Ravens continued to batter upon the mounted soldiers, killing or maiming their horses, breaking the line, and forcing the foot soldiers to scatter to safety once more.

A cry went upon among the mounted soldiers and they turned to retreat, sending their horses skittering out of control back down the road even as a wave of new soldiers struggled their way up.

This new wave split into two parts. The red- and blue-coated soldiers forced their way up the road, driving the Ravens back to the crest of the hill. The second part, made up of different soldiers—these dressed in dark green—left the road and started up the west slope, as if trying to encircle the Ravens.

Saloli and his Wolves launched their attack at that moment, springing from their position and firing at close range. This move stunned the green-clad soldiers long enough for the Wolves to reload. Truthfully, it would not have been enough time to reload, no matter how swift, but Kiyuga was beginning to identify the slight visual distortions where someone was Iyuwahnilvhi Adahnesagi'a.

Kiyuga lifted his rifle and picked a new target. The green-clad soldiers were being forced off the slope and back into the road which was already terribly congested. There was little room to fight. This was little problem for the Aniyvwiya as they danced here and there in the chaos, but the British were unable to perform their flashy formations and maneuvers, not when they were trapped between their enemy and certain death in the chasm.

The red- and blue-coated soldiers were quite useless in the fight. Kiyuga saw more than one run away, or attempt to, often with a Raven chasing him away. The green-clad soldiers were the only ones thus far able to make the battle a challenge. They were able to finally right themselves and make something like a formation in order to charge the Wolves again.

While the green-clad soldiers tried to force their way up the slope like a slow-moving but impenetrable turtle, the Owls again took aim.

With their adeptness at hiding and Mankiller silencing the sound of their fire from the rear, the Owls were able to slow the advance of the soldiers on the Wolves who continued to rain heavy fire upon them from the front.

Kiyuga was seeing less and less use of the sorceries, and he understood why. It was painful to use at first, like learning any new thing that required great deals of strength. But this was strength of spirit rather than body. Was it shameful that they were all so weak in spirit? He saw a few of the warriors waver, but whether this was from use of the sorcery or fatigue from battle was uncertain.

The fog began to lift as shafts of light streamed through the trees, the sun peeking its face from behind the clouds. This would give them an easier time of using Light, but who had the strength for it now? Well, things weren't going all bad for them, Kiyuga figured. When one tool had served its purpose, it was time to use the rest. They would do this as they always had.

The green-clad warriors pressed hard up the hill, and a new company of soldiers joined them. These were the kilt-wearing ones, the Highlanders. Kiyuga remembered them from Fort Duquense. Even if they were enemies, at least the Highlanders possessed a personal honor that the British regulars did not. The Highlanders faced danger, death, and defeat with a defiant cry.

Where the green-clad warriors had been slow but determined, the Highlanders rushed the Wolves with no fear. Some did not even have weapons that Kiyuga could see, but were prepared to battle with their bare hands if need be. While they distracted the Wolves, the green-clad warriors tried to sneak around them, get between the Wolves and the Ravens.

Kiyuga picked another target and slowed Time. He exhaled just as slowly as he fired his rifle. He watched the lead ball slow as it left the rifle barrel and jettison through the air.

Saloli, with his great wolf skin, was bringing his hatchet down with all his mighty strength, aiming for one Highlander's head, even as that Highlander tried to bring his bayonet up and thrust it into Saloli's stomach. Kiyuga's bullet found the Highlander's massive shoulder, stunting his bayonet attack and giving Saloli an opening to bury his hatchet in the man's neck. Blood spurted from the wound and covered the wolf skin as the man went down.

Then, as Saloli looked down for just a moment to wrench his hatchet out of the man's neck, another Highlander descended upon him in uproarious fury. Saloli looked up just as the Highlander came down, using a rock to stun him, drawing blood from a massive wound on his forehead, then grabbing him and knocking their heads together. Saloli went down and the Highlander was on him, using the same rock to beat him until his face was no better than ground meat. The Highlander grabbed a wolf tail from Saloli's body, stood, lifted the tail, and used it as a rallying cry for the rest of the Highlanders.

Kiyuga fumbled to reload his rifle, chastising himself for not slowing Time, reloading, and firing again in time to save Saloli. He had to do better than this. He couldn't think about his own comfort, not when he was defending the people. His headaches, his comfort meant nothing if he was to face death if captured.

Saloli's demise forced a retreat of the Wolves who found themselves trapped between Highlanders and green-clad soldiers. They managed to fight their way out and meet up with the Ravens on the road. They could not stay on the road and get caught; the Highlanders were trying to encircle them already. They had to get to higher ground.

Aganstata turned and headed up the road just a little ways, just enough to put some distance between the two sides. From there, they turned and charged up a hill into the trees. This was a far steeper slope than before, much harder to attack. There they turned and continued firing upon the British.

With their position suddenly rendered moot, Mankiller ordered the Owls back along the path they had come so they might trap the soldiers. Before they could get very far, there was more movement on the road and even more soldiers appeared. Kiyuga did not know which one was Montgomerie, but he remembered Grant.

The Owls were halted and instead took the opportunity to fire upon Montgomerie and his remaining men. There was some shouting, and it was loud enough that Kiyuga could hear it without the need to use Uhnoygvi. Montgomerie ordered a hard push up the road, to Itse'yi, while the Highlanders and Royal Scots had the Ravens and Wolves distracted.

"Move!" Mankiller ordered. "Get to the west slope where the Wolves were!"

Whether it was through some trick of Atsvstdi or Iyuwahnilvhi Adahnesagi'a or some other ability Kiyuga did not know, the Owls were able to move down the slope to the narrow trail, then across the road, and to the slope formerly used by the Wolves without being seen either by Montgomerie's men or the Highlanders and Royal Scots fighting the Ravens and Wolves. They slipped into the trees and turned to face the next part of the advancing army.

They began firing right away. Montgomerie began shouting orders, telling most of his men to continue up the road and not to stop for anything. He then ordered another company of men to start firing back, distract the Owls while the rest of the army moved on.

But it was difficult to engage an enemy that could not be seen or heard. The warriors were masters of disguise and deception. Thanks to Mankiller's diligence, they were able to fight as silently as shadows. From this, they could well ignore the British soldiers firing blindly into the trees, hoping to hit an enemy, and instead focus on the main army.

With this invisible, silent enemy assaulting them, the soldiers' progress was remarkably slow. Montgomerie continued to shout orders, but fear was beginning to win out over the common men. Kiyuga watched a few desert, running back down the road, heedless of the threats hurled at their backs.

Up ahead on the road, the Ravens and Wolves held their ground and even managed to push back the Highlanders and Royal Scots, almost to the point of the original ambush. The Owls continued their silent assault, varying their targets, from the main army to the Highlanders and Royal Scots, and back again. There was no pattern to it, and, using Iyuwahnilvhi Adahnesagi'a, there were enough shots fired to make the British believe that there were many hundreds, perhaps even a thousand or more Aniyvwiya warriors firing upon them from the trees. Maybe even the warriors outnumbered the British. And then what?

Kiyuga fired once more. As his fingers reached for another lead ball, he was suddenly acutely aware of how little ammunition he had left. He hoped the British decided to retreat soon, or else the silent, invisible warriors would have to disappear and they might have to fight in the open with knife and hatchet. Or maybe they could improvise.

He picked up a small stone. If it moved fast enough, a stone wasn't much different than this lead ball he used in his rifle. Was there a way he might use the sorceries to achieve what he needed? How did he go about it? He needed it to fly as fast as his ammunition balls in the direction he wanted it to go.

He threw the stone, hoping that he could simply make it happen. He wouldn't say it worked, as Grant remained alive with no hole in his head, but he wouldn't say it didn't work either, as he knew he did not have a strong enough arm to throw it as far as he did.

But it was not something he could sit around experimenting with in the middle of a battle. He lifted his rifle and fired off a reliable lead ball.

Montgomerie ordered another push on the road. The Highlanders and Royal Scots gave it everything they had, rallying together under a savage war cry and charging the Ravens and Wolves with all the force they could muster.

Even as the Ravens and Wolves retreated to their steep hillside and the Owls continued to fire from their positions, Kiyuga was suddenly made aware of the last company of warriors, one Montgomerie clearly wasn't expecting. The Foxes had come to play.

With Montgomerie's men all in one place, the pack animals were within sight, just a short distance from the rear of the main army. Amadoya came charging up the road, stabbing and slicing and killing horses and donkeys laden with goods. Many he did not kill but simply maimed, cutting leg tendons and breaking bones. By the time the panicked whinnying and braying reached Montgomerie's ears and he realized what was happening, more than thirty pack animals were dead or maimed and the Foxes took the rear of the army by surprise.

Suddenly the British found themselves surrounded on three sides with their backs to the river a death's leap from the road. Kiyuga heard one officer ask if they should order a retreat. Montgomerie, shocked by this turn of events, was unable to answer. He looked around helplessly. The Wolves and Ravens had again pushed back the Highlanders and Royal Scots. The Owls continued to fire upon them, as silent and invisible as ever. Now the Foxes had come for the rear, killing more pack animals than soldiers.

At last Montgomerie ordered that the rear be protected and to save the pack animals. They might win the battle, but if they had no supplies going forward, it was useless.

The regular foot soldiers were suddenly diverted from their task of pushing hard on the road to retreating and chasing away the Foxes who continued to assault the animals. The Highlanders and Royal Scots fell back to protect the bulk of the army.

While they were still occupied by the Wolves and Ravens, the Owls turned their attention to distracting the retreating foot soldiers and buying as much time for the Foxes as possible.

The army was at a loss, and they scrambled in the chaos. Were they supposed to be fighting the enemy? Pushing on the road? Defending the animals? No one seemed to really know, and every man was left to fend for himself. More deserted, running back down the road, away from the confusion. The Foxes let them go.

The Wolves and Ravens managed to push the Highlanders and Royal Scots back over the crest of the hill, immediately swinging momentum to their side, and they crashed down upon the army like a tidal wave. Mankiller ordered a charge from the slope, and the Owls swooped down, the invisible enemy no longer invisible.

More soldiers and horses went over the edge of the road into the chasm. Some tried to flee, but now the Foxes no longer let them go, and they began to squeeze even harder. Montgomerie looked fearfully behind him as his horse danced ever closer to the edge. Beside him, Grant on his mount looked just as terrified.

"Retreat!" the commander finally ordered. "Retreat!"

The soldiers needed no second order. At the south end of the road, the Foxes continued to harass the British, but no more killing blows were dealt. Amadoya whooped and hollered and trotted around on a large horse he'd commandeered, waving his rifle and showing off some trophies he'd taken. To the north, the Ravens pecked at the fleeing Royal Scots and the Wolves snapped at the heels of the Highlanders, the only soldiers who did not appear ready to retreat.

The Owls ran alongside the fleeing soldiers, Kiyuga whooping and hollering with the rest of them, ensuring that they did not try to escape into the woods.

As the last of the fog burned off and the sun came out, Kiyuga even pulled a second trick on them, using Atsvstdi and darkening the road so the soldiers could not see where they were going. Many tripped and stumbled and they began to pile up like firewood. The Foxes started to circle them, still hollering, a few mocking the soldiers with victory dance and song. The soldiers, their faces whiter than snow, were almost killing each other as they scrambled to get away.

The Royal Scots and Highlanders saved the foot soldiers, putting themselves between the frightened men and the warriors, providing a barrier for them to run away, though it was difficult in the mysteriously dim light with an already poor road and all the dead and dying pack animals blocking their way.

Still Montgomerie was shouting orders, as if his men weren't already screaming for their lives, desperate for a good meal and a good woman. He forced his horse among the men, Grant close behind. Both steeds were difficult to control, and it was hard to tell whether the officers were shouting at the men or their mounts.

The soldiers finally got clear of the pack animals as well as the worst drop into the chasm and took off as fast as they could. The Foxes ran with them on one side, the Owls on the other, and the Wolves and Ravens remained hard behind.

The warriors chased the soldiers for that day and well into the evening. With Kiyuga, Mankiller, and Aganstata alternating their use of Atsvstdi light their own way, they confused and exhausted the British soldiers who could no longer keep up the pace. Their panic remained very much in evidence, but they did not have the same strength and endurance of the Aniyvwiya. Some collapsed, others ran off into the woods.

They did not stop until they had chased the British out of abandoned Estato. To Kiyuga's eyes, their force seemed much smaller than it had been on their trek into the hills. Certainly they were weaker and more afraid; even the Royal Scots and Highlanders had lost their gruff, honorable determination, instead focusing on just making it out alive.

The bulk of the warriors stopped in Estato, letting out grand war cries to follow the soldiers all the way back to Fort Prince George, or whatever hole they decided to hide in. There were a few groups who continued the chase, though they returned quickly enough.

There was a grand victory celebration there in Estato as the warriors broke out into song, dance, and any number of grand tales of personal heroics. Their merriment may have been mistaken for a battle in its own right as they waved their weapons, slapped each other on the back, and carried on in loud catharsis. Kiyuga readily joined in, shouting his own tales of bravery, unsure if anyone was even listening. But he didn't care. The story needed to be told. The winds needed to hear his song.

They camped in Estato for a bit so everyone could rest, eat, and drink. Many slept where they lay, out in the open, uncaring of the light rain that came in the evening. Kiyuga knew he slept, but he could not say as he recalled any dreams, nor could he say that it felt as though he'd slept at all. His mind was too active, his body only slowly recovering from the excitement. It wasn't until the next morning that he truly felt fatigue in his limbs, but by then, they were already on the move back to Itse'yi.

Some of the Foxes would stay behind for another day or two, just to make sure the British did not try to return and launch a surprise attack, but the rest of them—Ravens, Wolves, Owls, and all—started back up the road. They no longer walked in perfect single file, though it was a day before they allowed themselves more than fleeting, whispered conversation. When they stopped to camp that night on the road, Kiyuga did not bother with food or shelter, simple lay down and slept, resting his weary body.

They returned to the pass and collected their dead, forty in all. Saloli was identified only by his wolfskin armor, for his face was gone, smashed in by the Highlander whom Kiyuga had shot. Litters were constructed, and the few horses that had survived uninjured and stuck around were made to drag the litters behind them.

Spoils were taken now, and nothing was prohibited. Soldiers were stripped of everything, even their underclothes if they were in decent shape. Weapons and ammunition were fought over. Dying pack animals were put out of their misery, and dead pack animals were quickly sliced up to be made into furs and jerky. Kiyuga claimed a horse for himself, the silvery blue stallion with lighter mottling and spots on its rump, and black mane and tail. The great beast had a bit of an attitude, but Kiyuga remained calm and patiently waited the horse out. When he was able, he removed the heavy saddle but kept the attached bags, for they were stocked well with ammunition and a bit of food. He also removed the bridle. Something the original rider had done had caused the bit to cut into the horse's gums which had bled. Once the bridle was removed, the horse became far more agreeable and even allowed Kiyuga to get up on its back.

As expected, his horse was given a litter to pull. As if sensing what was going on, the large beast stood still, in line with the road in the direction they were headed, and waited patiently for the command to move.

With spoils divided and litters prepared, Aganstata, also mounted, led the way up the road.

Kiyuga decided to name his horse Amayi Tsinagi'e'a, or Amayi for short. When he asked the horse what he thought about it, Amayi just snorted and shook his head, all without missing a step.

If the soldiers thought this part of the road was tough, they hadn't seen anything yet. The British would be foolish to attempt a second push through the pass to try and reach the Middle Towns. If they thought they were going to get anywhere near Fort Loudoun, they were sorely mistaken.

They reached Itse'yi to no fanfare. Aganstata had sent the runners before the battle to evacuate Itse'yi to Tawsi. Now he sent a couple more runners to retrieve them.

The warriors could only untie the litters and turn out the horses. They could not start the fires for the Itse'yi residents to come back to, nor clean out the townhouse. They could do nothing outside of themselves until the adawehi returned and could cleanse them. They also could not eat for four days, or as long as the adawehi said.

With all this in mind, once their chores were done, the warriors simply sat and waited patiently. It was the next day before the Itse'yi residents returned. As they did, the warriors stood, took their horses, circled the townhouse three times and began to speak of their heroic deeds in the battle in the pass. After this, the adawehi ritually cleansed every warrior and their horses, then sent them to continue their fasting.

In the middle of this, the Fox warriors who had stayed behind also appeared. They, too, were cleansed and made to fast for four days.

The songs of the dead warriors of Itse'yi could be heard all day and most of the night. All of the dead were from the Middle and Lower Towns, and Kiyuga was thankful he would not have to listen to the sorrow when they returned to the Overhill. There was some debate over what to do with the warriors from the Lower Towns, as well as Saloli who would have certainly merited an honorable burial.

Eventually it was decided that the warriors would be given a similar honorable burial right in Itse'yi. The Lower Town families were already present, already mourning, and it was unclear that they would ever be able to return to the Lower Towns. Besides, it was more important how one was buried than where.

When all of the living warriors had been appropriately cleansed and fasted for the required time, the skiagvsta and senior warriors convened in the townhouse. They spoke at length of the battle, of the movements of the British, their numbers, their fighting style, their soldiers. It was agreed that the common soldiers, those in red and blue coats, were cowards well enough, easily frightened and driven off when there was enough confusion. The Royal Scots and Highlanders were the real threat. They were fearless, determined, ready to fight with any weapon or even their bare hands if they had to. They were the only honorable enemy worth fighting in many warriors' opinions.

Several warriors were spoken of by Aganstata, Mankiller, and Amadoya. Tsiyu, in Saloli's place, also spoke well of several Wolves. Kiyuga was pleased to hear his name mentioned, and that segued into the next part of the discussion.

"The British sorceries were utilized in battle," Aganstata said slowly, deliberately. "Iyuwahnilvhi Adahnesagi'a was difficult in the tumult, but it was used to buy more time to react to the chaos. I know Mankiller used Uhnoyvgi to great success in hiding the Owls as they fired on the soldiers from a distance. And Yvgidahi used Atsvstdi well to confuse and frighten the soldiers in their retreat." The skiagvsta looked around. "We have seen what these sorceries can do. We have used them, those of us who have been learning from Anagalisgi and those who learned only days before the battle.

"I trust Anagalisgi to know and do what is best for the people, even when he sees only misfortune. I would never accuse him of cavorting with evil spirits. But as adawehi opinions are divided over this sorcery, so, too, is warriors' opinions. I think now that we have seen this sorcery in use in common life and in battle, we should give consideration as to whether we should continue learning and using it."

"Should it not be the decision of each man?" Ganehisdi inquired. "Many were skeptical of the skala galogwehi, yet here we are."

"What does a skala galogwehi do that a bow does not?" Mankiller retorted. "These are physical tools. These sorceries are far greater than that, and for one man to wield it and another not provides one with a terrible advantage."

"Are you saying that it should be forbidden?" Kiyuga wondered incredulously. "With respect, Aganstata, you have already said that Anagalisgi is looking out for the people. This sorcery is what won us the battle today. Should we insult the spirits by ignoring this gift they have given us? Or should we stand aside and allow the British to burn the Middle Towns as well?"

"We are but men," one of the Itse'yi adawehi said harshly. "We may use the gifts of the spirits, but we should not seek to be like them. Even as some do will their spirits into animals upon death, even they are eventually expelled into nothing, as all become in the end."

"The spirits do not have to give us any gifts at all, except that Anagalisgi has communed with them since he was a child and followed their guidance. Now they offer us a gift and you would turn it down?"

"Tell me," another adawehi said haughtily. "Did the spirits teach Anagalisgi this sorcery, or did the British?"

Kiyuga gave the adawehi a look. "Both."

The answer was clearly unsatisfactory, but before either side could say more, Aganstata spoke.

"Please, we do not wish for conflict here. It may be that each man must decide for himself according to the spirits whether he chooses to embrace this sorcery. It is still very new, and there is still much that must be taught and learned. This war is not over yet, I think. Perhaps when it is, then we may decide the future of these sorceries among the Aniyvwiya."

Kiyuga glanced at the adawehi who still watched him sternly. He looked away, suppressing a frustrated sound. He would not say he did not understand their hesitation. But how could one praise the character of someone, and then in the same breath accuse him of treachery?

There were more discussions, but Kiyuga did not pay much attention. He wanted to go home. He probably could have, except there was still safety in numbers. Even a frustrated wolf did not leave the pack on a selfish whim.

When the announcement came that the Overhill warriors were leaving, Kiyuga was too happy to grab his bags, sling them over Amayi who was looking happier and more contented every day, climb on the horse's back, and start out on the road.

"I know you are frustrated," Aganstata observed once they were well away from Itse'yi. "I know you believe that I disrespected your brother."

"You cannot praise him and then indict him in the same sentence," Kiyuga said, perhaps more harshly than intended.

"Yvgidahi, it is not your brother I am worried about. I worry about what may happen if we encounter similar sorcerers in the British army, more than just the two who are, thankfully, sympathetic to us."

"Who is to say that we haven't been fighting such sorcerers and didn't know it, and that is how the British have been so successful despite their stupidity?"

"Who indeed? And what do you think will happen if they discover that we now also possess these sorceries?"

Kiyuga let out a breath. "Nothing good."

"Exactly. I wish for our people to have a plan and know what we're doing before the innocent suffer needlessly."

"Is any suffering of the innocent beneficial?"

Annoyed, Kiyuga nudged Amayi forward and continued up the road.

DᏍᏏᎥᏒᏔ WᏢᏬᎣᎠᎫ

Ayadohlv'i Tahlsgohi

Under Cover

Anagalisgi was overjoyed to see his brother return. Judging by the horse and the bags of spoils, he figured it was safe to say the battle or battles had been a success.

The warriors returned with great flourish, riding or dancing around the fort just out of range of cannon and musket, the soldiers peering over the ramparts to see what was going on. The warriors proclaimed many stories and songs of their great victory and many personal heroic feats. Anagalisgi got most of the battle reports from this marvelous display. He learned of the ambush, of the maneuvers of both warrior and soldier. He learned of Montgomerie's push and then retreat. He learned of Aganstata's plan. He learned of Saloli's bravery and death. He learned of Mankiller's greatness to disguise their rifle sounds. He learned of Amadoya's surprise attack from the rear. He learned how the warriors chased the soldiers all the way back to Estato and even farther, just to ensure their victory and their message were delivered. The British were not welcome here.

This went on for some time, and by the time it was finished, the demoralization of the soldiers in the fort was most evident. Then the warriors dispersed.

Anagalisgi met his brother in the camp.

"I understand things went well," Anagalisgi said pleasantly.

"What part told you that?" Kiyuga wondered.

"The horse told me."

Kiyuga grinned as he removed the bags from his horse and turned it loose to graze. "Yes, I suppose he might."

"What do you call him?"

"Amayi Tsinagi'e'a."

Anagalisgi laughed "Yes, of course you would. Amayi for short?"

"Naturally."

They settled in and Kiyuga offered him a bit of jerky. Anagalisgi gnawed on it, staring at the fort. "Soldiers have been deserting for the last few days. Some try to run. Others try to surrender."

"What happens to them?" Kiyuga wondered.

Anagalisgi shrugged. "If they're lucky, they're stripped down to their skin and run off. What happens to them after they reach the road is anyone's guess." He ripped off another bite of jerky. "I imagine, with your display here today, there may be talk of surrender, or else mutiny."

Kiyuga nodded. "No one is coming to save them. We made sure of that."

"Will a council be convened in Itsa'ti? I apologize, I've only just returned from visiting Atagulkalu."

"A council was already convened."

"Without me?"

"It was only brief, to inform the people of our victory. Another council will be convened shortly, I am certain."

And it was so, only a few days later. Where the first meeting had been brief, this one was not. It was called in the morning, and the whole morning was spent retelling tales of heroics and bravery and spoils. Anagalisgi had heard little over the last few days except tales of courage and bravery in the battle, and yet to hear the warriors speak of it again that morning, one would have thought that they had only just returned and were relating their tales for the first time. This went on until the early afternoon, and only then because the women were getting a bit impatient and the younger boys restless, eager for their own battles.

"Will we attack Fort Loudoun now, since we have this victory?" one such young warrior asked eagerly.

To many groans and complaints, Aganstata shook his head. "No.

Not yet. We will let them punish themselves as much as they wish. When they tire of punishing themselves, then we will take over their punishment."

This heartened the young warriors some, and they eagerly awaited the skiagvsta's next plan of action.

"One thing we should consider," Mankiller began seriously, "is the role of the British sorceries in battle. And our lives."

"It sounds as though they helped quite a lot," another young warrior said.

"But is it disrespectful to the spirits?" one of the women inquired. "To have this power over the world is...it's unconscionable. Men were made to adhere to the spirits, not become them."

"It brought us victory," Aganstata said.

"At what cost?" one of the adawehi asked.

"We have already lost much of our identity to European goods and European ways. Shall we now lose more to their sorceries?" one of the older warriors wondered.

"If we use it to beat back the Europeans, then we should have no further need for it," a young warrior, Kanunu, said. "I would like to learn and take it into battle with me."

"Hush, pup," someone scolded. "You've not seen battle."

"Well I'm going to." Kanunu stood. "We know the British will come again. Or else these cowards in the fort will try to take us out on their way down. If we have a weapon to use against them, what better one to use than their own?"

"It is not a weapon, it is a tool," Anagalisgi said calmly. "How you use it makes it a weapon or not. And it is a living weapon, forged from the spirits for our use, but only when utilized properly."

"If defeating the British were not proper, I think the outcome at the pass would have been different."

"Hush, pup," another warrior said harshly.

Kanunu sat down, though he was hardly chastened.

"It should be left to each man to decide for himself whether to learn or not," Chola said. "Who are we to say whether this is good or evil?

The spirits will surely sort it out for themselves, and we shall see, though I fully believe Anagalisgi capable of discernment."

"Indeed, he had an excellent guide," Aganstata agreed warmly. "And I would be inclined to agree, except we have seen the hostility that even the mention of it has caused among some. We cannot afford division among ourselves."

Anagalisgi's stomach tightened and his heart dropped as he made himself known. "Respectfully, skiagvsta, that is where we must disagree." His unspoken question was met with an affirmative answer. He stood and faced those gathered. "You all know me. Many of you call me a walking bad omen. Those held captive in Fort Prince George often lamented that I was the adawehi they got stuck with. But you also know me for a dreamer. And I have dreamed."

He paused and took a breath. "Sometimes, the path forward is not always easy. It is not what we want. But it is what is best. And sometimes, when we do not want these things to occur, we feign uncertainty or indecision, make the choice more difficult than it is in order to avoid making a choice. We pretend that if we choose to make no choice that it will have to go away eventually.

"Some of you know that the elder Gvnagadoga and I were working on plans to save the people in times such as these. My brother Kiyuga...Yvgidahi, has helped orchestrate these. He helped to evacuate the people of the Lower Towns and bring them safely to the Middle Towns, a few to the Overhill. We have been preparing as such, that if we cannot fight, then we must hide. The British cannot conquer what is not there.

"The problem is that we approached it from the wrong perspective. The British can and will conquer what is not there, for they believe that they must fill every empty space, every void, with their presence. And they will conquer what is there, for they believe themselves superior in every way.

"Many seasons ago, I had a vision, a visit from the spirits, from Ge'gwogv. It told me that we must hide until it is safe to return. For many seasons, I believed this to mean that we must stay in the towns that the British cannot travel to, such as the difficulty it takes them to come over the hills. Except their poison is already here. It is already in the veins of this land."

He hesitated again. "Then the men Nathan and Andrew showed me their sorceries, this power of Digohwelisgi. And as they have shown me more of this power and this Digohwelisgi, I have come to realize that we are not merely meant to hide. We are meant to leave.

"We cannot merely leave this place, these towns, for there is nowhere the British will not follow, will not infect. I have seen the blood run from these rivers across great plains, flood even greater mountains than these, and touch the western lands where the sun sets and the ancestor spirits roam. And other conquerors will come, in time.

"Instead, we are called to leave this island entirely."

That snapped the patience and intrigue of everyone listening. Anagalisgi closed his eyes and tried to breathe even as dozens of warriors young and old, elders, women, skiagvsta, uku, adawehi, and even children started shouting at once. Most of it was utter surprise that he could even suggest such a thing. Everyone knew the Middle World was suspended between the Upper World and the Lower World, the sun and the moon. How did one leave the Middle World, the island, except upon death?

He did not attempt to quiet them, simply let the noise run its course. It was Aganstata who finally made himself known and spoke through the din of dying conversation.

"What are you saying, Anagalisgi? Shall we march to the western lands and save the British the trouble of sending us there?"

Anagalisgi shook his head. "I am not saying such a thing, not at all." He fought to find words, but the ways of the spirits often eluded the words of men. "There is more than one Middle World. There are many islands out there. Islands that the British cannot access."

"Except for the two who showed you this," one adawehi stated skeptically. "The two British men."

"They are not British men," a new voice said.

Everyone turned as Nayanali entered the townhouse and took her place among the Aniwodi. She glanced around at those gathered. "Some may know, some may not, but they have been staying with Atagulkalu and myself in exile. In that time, we have adopted them as kin, as brothers. They are not Anigilisi any longer. They are as Aniyvwiya as anyone here."

"You have done this to protect them, spare their lives?" one of the Aniwodi behind her spat.

Nayanali met the challenge head-on. "As they have spared our lives and helped us against the British, yes."

There was some grumbling among those gathered, but no one could speak against it. Even in exile, or perhaps especially, they had the right to do such a thing. Nathan and Andrew were Aniyvwiya now. Depending on who adopted them, they were either Anihwaya or Aniwodi and afforded full clan protections as such. It also meant that these were no longer European sorceries being taught.

"What do you expect us to do, then?" someone asked, turning back to Anagalisgi. "How shall we leave this island for another? The British have come conquering from their lands to ours. They will come for us eventually, no matter where we go."

"Which is why we cannot merely hide upon this new island. We must be alert, active, and continue to train in these sorceries," Anagalisgi said. "I was not there, but I would say that we got lucky in the pass. But if we have any hope of driving back this army, we must have more than a couple moons' worth of training, or even a couple days, as I have heard from some. We must become one with the spirits again, one with nature. We cannot do that here, not as we must."

"You suggest hiding a force to train in these sorceries, then," one of the women stated. "On this other island?"

"Yes. As well as provide protection for the women, children, and elders. If we are unsuccessful, and the British do come to the Middle Towns and the Overhill, we must still preserve the people always."

"Then who shall be left behind? If there is no one here to defend us, then we shall be overrun. If there is no one here to defend, then we lose the reason for fighting."

"I don't know. Perhaps it should be as Mankiller suggested. To each man his own decision. To those who wish to learn this sorcery or be protected by it, he should come with us to this island. To those who wish nothing to do with it, stay behind and defend the people as we have always done. We work toward the same goal, but division over this issue will surely see us fall. We cannot trip over each other in battle. If the old ways work, then we do not need to get in the way. If the old ways do not work, then it would be better for us to be well-trained and ready for combat."

"When would we have to go to this new island?" one of the elders inquired.

"Nathan and Andrew plan to show it to me when I return. I expect a few others may wish to go as well," Anagalisgi answered. "If we are satisfied that we may live there for a time, then we will make a plan."

Naturally, many wished to go and see this new island, but only so many would be allowed. It was a difficult journey, made more difficult for the sorcerers because they had to get everyone there safely. The more people, the harder it would be. Atagulkalu would be going. Aganstata and Mankiller also declared their interest, as did Yachtino. Nanyehi would go as a representative for the Women's Council. Others vied for the opportunity to go, but no further absolute decisions were made that day.

Other issues were addressed, speaking of the British, their leaders, their numbers, their soldiers. Peace was now entirely out of the realm of possibility. Even the most hopeful, the most staunch supporters of Atagulkalu and his campaign for peace, were now resigned to the necessity and inevitability of the war. The young warriors looked forward to their chance to prove themselves in battle. Even the elder, retired warriors regained a youthful spark as their wisdom was consulted.

Anagalisgi watched and listened to every word, every gesture. For the first time, he felt truly alive, living in the waking world. He no longer felt as though he walked in the daze of a dim, nebulous future. Now he was living that future that he had always seen. Finally, he was present. He was active. And he even had a plan of action.

He returned to Taskigi with Kiyuga when the council was dismissed.

"Atagulkalu remains in exile, and Aganstata, Mankiller, and I went to battle," Kiyuga observed. "What have you been doing while we were away? Have you taken on more students?"

"I continued to train Chola," Anagalisgi answered. "And he trains other in Si'tiku now. And I also made plans with Atagulkalu, Andrew, and Nathan."

"Yes, it sounds like you have. Where does this notion come from? Leaving the earth? Leaving the island? Can such a thing be done?"

"It is possible, according to Andrew and Nathan. They have been to the new island, a whole new world for us to live."

Kiyuga frowned. "My brother, I have never doubted you, even as you have played your part as a dark seer, even as you have been both reviled and shunned for the terrible things you see and some of your more outlandish ideas. But I am only one person, and Gvnagadoga is dead. How far do you expect people to follow you?"

Anagalisgi shook his head. "I am not a leader. I am a guide. You will be the leader. And I want you to come to the new island with us that you may see."

"Of course. I understand when you expect to leave, but how shall we get there? What supplies must be taken?"

"They use another sorcery element that I call Galohisdi. It is how we will get to the new island. As for supplies, expect to take the supplies you would normally take on an exploratory journey."

"Do they anticipate trouble?" his brother wondered.

"No. That is the point. We will have this new island to ourselves."

Kiyuga's expression was puzzled. "Are you sure?"

"Very sure."

Anagalisgi could see his brother was not convinced, but there was no convincing in words. They would have to see the new island for themselves.

"Do you want to practice more now or rest some?" Anagalisgi

wondered.

His brother sighed and broke into a yawn. "I think maybe we should both rest some."

"Tomorrow morning, then?"

"I expect to go out hunting tomorrow morning. Perhaps in the afternoon when I return. We can eat together and then practice."

Anagalisgi could agree to that, and so it was.

The last portion of training with Nathan and Andrew had introduced a new concept which they called Magnetism, though Anagalisgi had named it Gayalvnga. The idea was not so foreign as the men believed. It was known that some things were more attracted to other things. The British had simply revealed the math and calculations behind it. Anagalisgi had little trouble picking up on the more practical aspect of the sorcery, testing which things indeed had Galayvnga and which did not. If an object, usually a rock or a metal, had Galayvnga, then it could be manipulated, amplified or minified, much like Atsvstdi or Uhnoyvgi. If an object did not have Galayvnga, or if he had no other Galayvnga pieces to use with it, then he had to use Galo'ondiha ale Agi'a to move it willfully.

The white-skinned men, now officially adopted into Atagulkalu's family, promised that once they returned from the new island — or, if they wished, once they had reached the new island and settled in well — then they would break into a whole new aspect of the sorceries, which they simply called Matter, that was, everything that could be touched. Anagalisgi did not understand, but he was well set with Galayvnga, and too busy trying to prepare his speech to the people about the new island, to give much thought to their words.

Aganstata, for one, was simply enamored by Galayvnga and how certain metals could be manipulated with more ease using this sorcery versus Galo'ohndiha ale Agi'a. Steel, for instance, such as the primary product of casting cannons.

Anagalisgi knew where his thoughts were going the instant the skiagvsta made the connection.

"Please, skiagvsta," he began calmly. "Practice this sorcery first.

Learn it well. Cannons may have Galayvnga, true, but they are also very heavy for it, and we do not need to injure our own warriors for foolhardiness."

Aganstata made a gesture. "Of course, Anagalisgi, you are correct. And in practicing, I may learn more and be further inspired in how to use it effectively."

"Do you still intend to starve them out?"

"Their men desert under the cover of darkness. A bird was shot down yesterday carrying a message to their commanders. They subsist only on horse meat now and describe things as 'miserable beyond description.' Now that they have reached such a state, it may be in our interest to show them of our power, something that may also be taken back to their commanders, something to compare with Montgomerie's experience in the pass."

The man's mind was clearly working. Anagalisgi decided to end the lesson for that day and leave him to it. Mankiller and Amadoya had similar thoughts when Anagalisgi instructed them, and the three of them were soon conspiring, formulating a plan of attack to bring to the council and other skiagvsta. Chola, who'd stayed behind and already been instructed in Galayvnga, quickly joined them.

Anagalisgi prayed that night, looking for guidance as to what exactly he should do. He'd seen many of these things unfolding for months and even years beforehand, yet now that it was here, he felt lost. All he had was this insane plan to take part of the people to a new island. But that was where his visions stopped. Every time he tried to break through to the other side of this murky situation, Ge'gwogv would swoop down over him, blind his vision so that he could not see what lay ahead. Often, this was when he would wake.

It was about ten days later that a council was convened. Aganstata and the others had practiced with Galayvnga and come up with a plan to force the hand of the soldiers within the fort.

Anagalisgi listened to the plan, fearful that they were rushing things. While it was amazing that more warriors hadn't been hurt in the pass from misuse of sorcery, there was no telling how many had been injured because of it either. They really weren't ready. It took many months and years to master skala galogwehi; why should not sorcery be treated the same way? And here they were, not even a moon using Galayvnga, and they expected to use it in battle already. When had patience been replaced with such arrogance? It wasn't as though they were struggling to contain the soldiers in the fort; they could wait a bit while the Aniyvwiya trained some more.

He voiced these concerns, naturally, but as Aganstata explained his plan, it did not sound as an outright attack as Itse'yi had been. They would not storm the fort or engage in open combat. Rather, under cover of darkness and conjuring Time, they would destroy the fort's cannons, break the soldiers' ability to truly engage in defense of their fort. They would be forced to either starve, surrender, or engage in close combat which they were sorely unprepared for.

This Anagalisgi could not oppose. Stealth was of the utmost importance. If done correctly, they would have time to be cautious with their abilities and get it right. He hoped. He hadn't tried anything as ambitious as altering the Galayvnga to make it so forceful that something as large as a cannon would fold in on itself. But, he supposed that if Galayvnga didn't work, Galo'ondiha ale Agi'a might do the trick, just in a different way.

First they terrorized the fort a little, fasting and praying and dancing the same as they would before any battle, all within sight of the fort and the terrified soldiers who huddled about the ramparts, unsure how they should react and ultimately doing nothing.

The sun set and a sliver of a moon passed overhead, obscured by trees and mountain peaks. All fires were extinguished save for the sacred fire in the townhouse. Warriors gathered from all over the Overhill slipped through the Taskigi camp. Anagalisgi watched them go, using Atsvstsdi to cloak them in even greater shadow until they could not be seen even a couple paces off.

Kiyuga was among them, walking in the steps of Adahi and Amadoya.

The task was simple. They were to steal up to the fort and climb the walls to the ramparts. Those who knew the sorceries would climb, and those who did not know would help them up and down and keep watch. If they were all able to do this without being seen or heard, then they were to each choose a cannon or other heavy armament—even the armory itself if possible. Once all were in place, they would use Galayvnga to destroy the cannons. Depending on how this went, if they could do more than one apiece, then they would. Otherwise, they were to escape just as soon as an alarm was raised.

Anagalisgi could not see the warriors, so he could not say how things were going. Had they reached the fort yet? Were they able to climb the wall? Had they been found out and elected to retreat and try another day? Although, if there was no cry of alarm or shots fired in the night, he supposed that meant things were going well. He kept up the Atsvstdi just in case, fighting fatigue and a headache throbbing in the back of his mind.

At this rate, with how proficient Aganstata, Mankiller, and the others were becoming in this sorcery, maybe they wouldn't need to relocate to the new island.

On the other hand, if they would be truly left alone, why not move all of their peoples to the new island and forsake this place completely? Forget the Europeans, forget their wars. Go to this promised land and close the door. They could take their history and their traditions and no one could tell them otherwise. No one could interfere.

He rubbed his sore eyes and shook his head. He was tired, and the headache was not helping things, but he had to stay focused and keep up his part of the stealth operation for the warriors. For his brother's sake, he had to do this.

Crickets chirped and owls hooted. Something moved near the river.

Anagalisgi's eyes had trouble adjusting to his conjured darkness; they wanted to see, but there was nothing to see. He would not allow it. He wanted to see, to know what was going on, but he could not. He had to use the sorcery to help the warriors, and that meant blinding himself as well.

The moon disappeared overhead. Clouds drifted lazily by. A breeze stirred the leaves in the trees. It was hot and sticky, almost too unbearable even to sleep. Keeping his gaze focused on the fort and not allowing himself to waver in his resolve with the Atsvstdi, Anagalisgi carefully made his way down to the river. He blindly scooped some water in his hand and wiped his face. His skin was sticky with sweat, and the cool water was a welcome relief.

He returned to his former position and continued to wait. He could only conclude that the warriors were succeeding in some way, for no alarm had been raised, and there had been ample time for them to reach the fort, attempt to scale the wall, and make the decision whether to continue or turn back. Still he held his sorcery.

His head began to throb even more. How many cannons were they destroying? It was only a small fort, and Anagalisgi did not remember them bringing in very many, certainly not as many as Fort Prince George or Charleston. On the other hand, if they were successful with the cannons, they might go for the armory as well and destroy as many small arms as possible. If they were discovered and it turned into combat, the British would have nothing for weapons.

Or maybe they had been unsuccessful with the Gayalvnga and were resorting to other means of destroying the cannons and weaponry. That was equally as likely. Anagalisgi rubbed his face again, trying to stay awake and ignore his pounding brain. He silently willed the warriors to finish quickly and return.

Or maybe they were simply assassinating all the soldiers, just to get it over with and save everyone the trouble later. It would be as they had once done to the Anikusi. Except that had started a war. With luck, this would finish one. Between the events at Itse'yi and what was happening here, the British had to be getting the message.

But if they were, why were the Aniyvwiya being led to a new island?

Anagalisgi did a dangerous thing then. He sat down against a tree. His eyes hurt and he was tired; sitting was not a good idea. But he couldn't just keep standing there. He felt terrible about it. What kind of Anihwaya warrior was he if he could not help his brothers in so simple a task as this? Was he yet a boy? How shameful should he be to his brother who was a great warrior with a great destiny yet to be fulfilled?

Then, from the gloom he had caused to settle over the area, he saw figures. These figures materialized into men. As he began to recognize Aganstata and the others, he released his hold on the Atsvstdi. The great shadows eased back into the calm gloom of night. Aganstata approached him and put a hand on his shoulder.

"Thank you," the skiagvsta said with all sincerity.

"Are you accomplished, then?" Anagalisgi asked, hoping his stress and strain had not been in vain.

The skiagvsta merely nodded and said, "Yes. We will speak more of it in the morning. Get some sleep."

Anagalisgi breathed a sigh of relief. He found Kiyuga and they retired to bed without saying a word.

He found himself standing on a mountainside. Where he was, the trees had fallen away and the face was exposed to the wind. In the side of the mountain where he stood was a cave. It was small, big enough for a man but little else. A tree grew up from a crack in the rock beside the mouth of the cave. On one branch sat Ge'gwogv.

"Are you ready to go?" the woodpecker asked.

"Is this where we must go to reach the new island?" Anagalisgi wondered. He turned to look out over a broad valley. "I don't recognize this place. Where are we?"

"We are in the place where destinies are fulfilled. As you make them."

He looked back. "As I make them?"

"This is your gateway."

"The guardian between worlds."

Ge'gwogv dipped its head.

Anagalisgi frowned and again observed the valley. "This is the door I shall keep?"

"This is the door through which all destiny lies. Yours, your brother's, and many more."

He sighed. "I never asked for this."

"No, but it is why you were made."

"What if I don't want to?"

"Because you find yourself unwilling, or because you think yourself unable?"

"Either."

Ge'gwogv glided off the branch of the tree near the cave and rested on another only a few paces to Anagalisgi's left. "You are not unable. This the Author has written."

"This is the first time that you mention the Author. Nathan and Andrew were right, then?"

"You will learn much as the guardian. Which leads us to the question of your willingness. This is your story, Anagalisgi."

"Written by the Author. But the Aniyvwiya have no written language."

"Of course you do. It is written in the stars. And in the earth. And in the rock and the water. You have your language. You have your being, your connection to Elohi that you have always had. The Author simply articulates this, and in doing so, grants you this great power, this conjuring." The woodpecker climbed the tree trunk a bit and hopped onto a branch. "But you are not a puppet or a doll. If you choose, you can walk away. Your story will end here, and where the dice fall, they fall. All that will be known is that you walked away, the end. The Author will simply raise up another in time. Or you can choose to see this through to the ending you are meant to have."

Anagalisgi hesitated. "I'm afraid, Ge'gwogv. Is it right, what I'm doing? Am I helping my people or leading them astray? It is better to die with honor and purity than live with dishonor and a shameful spirit."

"What the Creator wills will be."

Wind swept through the valley and buffeted Anagalisgi. In the distance he saw dark clouds and they were approaching quickly.

Finally he nodded. "I'm willing."

"Excellent."

The wind died down for a moment, long enough for the woodpecker to glide down, turn around, then ride the next blast up the side of the mountain. Anagalisgi put his arms up instinctively.

When he lowered them, he found he was waking up. He sat up and found that all was as it was supposed to be.

There was great commotion in the fort that morning as the soldiers woke to find their cannons utterly destroyed, bent, crumpled, and folded like discarded clothing. Fear and panic overtook the soldiers, and it was some time before the chaos could be brought under any semblance of control.

Aganstata and the undercover warriors watched all of this with great satisfaction, standing at a distance from the fort, not saying a word but smiling smugly.

The sun had not even reached its highest point when the white flag was raised over the fort and Captain Demeré proclaimed that he was ready to negotiate terms of surrender. There was great cheering and merriment from the Aniyvwiya, and Aganstata was more than happy to receive them. They agreed to meet in Itsa'ti to speak, so all might hear and understand.

Two of the officers, John Stuart and James Adamson, were permitted out of the fort. Aganstata took the lead and a great troupe of warriors surrounded them the entire trip to Itsa'ti. Anagalisgi could see the soldiers were thin, hungry, and terrified to the point of exhaustion. Still they jumped like rabbits when one of the warriors even accidentally touched them, and they looked ready to bolt when intentionally provoked. Stuart ordered them not to react; they were going to negotiate quickly and get going back to civilization.

They arrived in Itsa'ti no worse for wear. All of the skiagvsta were present, their senior warriors, their advisers. A number of adawehi from all the Overhill towns were also present. And there were warriors from all of the Overhill villages, so many that they could not all fit into the townhouse. The seniormost warriors were allowed in first and on down to the youngest, though Kiyuga got in only because he had been part of the operation the previous night.

"We don't know what you did," Stuart sighed. "But it seems we have been bested. We wish to go home. Our own homes with our own people."

"We want you to go," Amadoya sneered. "And never return."

Aganstata leaned back in his seat. "We sneaked into your fort last night. We destroyed your cannons and other weapons of war. We could have easily killed you and your men while they slept, or as they drank and gambled. Always know this, and do not forget it. We spare you your lives. Take them back to your commanders for they mean nothing to us."

"We understand," Stuart said humbly, though his color had drained from his face when Aganstata told him what they had done, how close the soldiers had come to death.

"You will leave the fort," Mankiller told him firmly. "The cannons are destroyed. Your armaments are destroyed. You will leave them here. But you will take all the gunpowder with you. There will be no more destruction here."

"I ask kindly that my men be permitted to keep their personal affects. Their clothes, their baggage, things they will need for the trip back. The road is treacherous."

"Indeed it is," Aganstata said, smiling knowingly. The other warriors from the Battle of Itse'yi grinned likewise.

The terms were simple enough, and the British soldiers—having run out of food and being almost completely disarmed—were more than ready to comply.

"I would expect Atagulkalu to be leading surrender and peace negotiations," Stuart ventured cautiously. Anagalisgi knew that Stuart and Atagulkalu were very close friends, to the point of brothers as Nathan and Andrew were now brothers.

"Atagulkalu is no longer skiagvsta," Aganstata informed him levelly. "Nor is he uku. He is not here to negotiate, nor to save you. Now then, return to your fort and tell your soldiers what we have discussed here. When you reach your fort, you have one day to leave."

Stuart, looking crestfallen, nodded in resignation. "We understand. We will leave you in peace."

The officers left the townhouse and given another escort of warriors back to Taskigi, but the skiagvsta remained. Aganstata looked around.

"That's all?" someone asked. "We are going to let them walk away?"

"Of course not," Amadoya scoffed. "Do you think us fools? We shall take revenge upon them for Fort Prince George and pay the blood price for our warriors who were slaughtered that day."

"Twenty-three must die," an adawehi, Agodehi, declared, "in order to avenge our fallen. No more, no less."

"We will allow them to leave and travel upon the road," Aganstata said. "We will follow them and kill them where they camp. Anyone who wishes for revenge or seeks spoils or captives is welcome to come."

That stirred a great many warriors, from the very oldest ready to retire to become elders all the way down to the boys looking for their first blood. It seemed to Anagalisgi that there might be more warriors in this raid than there had been at Itse'yi as men began to speak amongst themselves of their plans for revenge. There were around one hundred or so men left in Fort Loudoun, the rest having died or deserted. If only twenty-three were permitted to be killed, that left a lot of room for captives. Once word got around that anyone seeking revenge was welcome, there would be more warriors than enemies. There would be disputes over captives, Anagalisgi was sure.

The skiagvsta made more plans for the attack, making sure to tell everyone to keep quiet about it until the disgraced soldiers had completely gone. Then they were dismissed. Still warriors continued to make their plans. Older warriors told tales of past glory, and a few declared this their last raid before retiring in the fall and assuming elder status. Younger warriors spoke excitedly of proving themselves as great warriors, the spoils they desired, and the girls they wanted to impress. The townhouse was slow to clear out, and the council was the last to leave.

Anagalisgi was just about to move when there was a hand on his shoulder. Turning, it was Amadoya. The hot-headed skiagvsta leaned in close.

"I want you to come with us," he hissed. "You don't have to fight, but I want you there."

"Do you want me to use the sorceries?" Anagalisgi inquired.

"No. I think they won't be necessary. No, I want you there because I don't trust you. We both know that John Stuart is Atagulkalu's friend. We don't need you running off to Atagulkalu to tell him of our plans and have him tell his good friend John Stuart." He fixed Anagalisgi in a serious gaze. "We don't need more problems than we already have. Do we?"

Stunned by the turn of events, he could only answer, "No."

"Just stay in Itsa'ti. Stay in the townhouse and go about your adawehi duties."

Anagalisgi blinked and came back to the waking world. He turned to face Amadoya face-to-face. "Mind yourself, Amadoya. A prophecy you don't like does not make it a prophecy you can ignore, and the same goes for its prophets. You would do well to remember who you are talking to. Age matters not for adawehi, and as Atagulkalu was expelled for his betrayal of the people on account of the British, so you may be expelled for betrayal of the people on account of disrespecting the adawehi and the spirits we serve."

Amadoya was a bit chastened from the exchange, but he still gave Anagalisgi a look and asked, "Do we? I know who I serve. Can you say the same?"

The skiagvsta left the townhouse. Anagalisgi watched him go, then sat down in a heap. Had that just happened?

Why would Amadoya think that he would betray the people? He wasn't going to run off to tell Atagulkalu of the attack so he could warn Stuart. Even if he did manage to Iyuwahnilvhi Adahnesagi'a part of the time, that was still a trip of many days. The garrison had only one day to get their things and leave, and Aganstata intended to attack their camp on the road that night. He would never make it. Perhaps it was that Amadoya did not understand the uses or limits of the sorceries. Perhaps he thought Anagalisgi had more power than he really did. Perhaps it was that Amadoya feared him, feared that he may be a Kutani, involved in deception, witchcraft, and the taking of women.

Nevertheless, Anagalisgi did not wish to provoke a fight, so he stayed in Itsa'ti. He did not stay in the townhouse at all times, but he made sure that Amadoya saw him frequently throughout the day. The skiagvsta said nothing to him, nor did he make any expression or gesture reminisce of their conversation.

The soldiers from Fort Loudoun came through Itsa'ti a couple days later. They were again escorted by many warriors and skiagvsta. Wilinawa and his warriors had come from Daqua'i, Mankiller from Tama'li. They shouted, whooped, hollered, and made a variety of animal noises, all of them to frighten and patronize the British who cowered like starved dogs, for such they appeared, as ungroomed and thin as they were.

The warriors were all painted and decorated and armed for battle, though none of them touched the soldiers just yet. Aganstata and his warriors followed them through Itsa'ti and down the road, still shouting, to Si'tiku. There they picked up Amadoya and Chola, the number of warriors growing into the hundreds. Yachtino and his warriors met them in Talasi. Once the soldiers were clear of Talasi and continuing down the road toward the Middle Towns—by now they were haggard, some even weeping—the warriors stopped their escort, though they continued to shout and insult them from afar, seeing them off into the forest.

Anagalisgi had come along as well, quietly following. What the soldiers hadn't seen was the following of women and boys, bearing the warriors' horses and needed supplies for warfare, everything from weapons to food. Anagalisgi took Amayi from a boy of twelve winters and led the horse to Kiyuga.

"Perhaps now we shall end this war," Kiyuga said. "Perhaps we shall make it known to the British the might of the Aniyvwiya!"

"They will know us," Anagalisgi said absently.

"What's wrong? Do you know something?"

"Nothing that will make a difference. The British will still come."

Kiyuga took the reins and mounted his horse. "Let them. We will be ready, and they will be short one hundred soldiers."

"At least twenty-three," Anagalisgi confirmed.

His brother grinned and nudged Amayi forward.

Aganstata sent out runners after the British to follow them and see where they camped, then report back. It was not long until sundown, so the soldiers would have to camp soon. It might be that they continued on for part of the night, wishing only to get as far away from the Overhill as possible, escape the ridicule.

At one point, Kiyuga returned to speak to Anagalisgi.

"Do you wish to ride as well?" he wondered. "At least until we reach the camp and go into battle?"

Anagalisgi had never actually ridden a horse before; he'd never needed to. Amayi looked at him as if asking the same question. Finally he shrugged and accepted a hand up, sitting behind his brother.

The view was certainly something to behold, but what was more stunning was the sudden surge of strength, power, and life force as he and animal became one. He felt the strong muscles, the enormous lungs of the beast, its desire to run and show off and display himself.

The runners returned and reported on the soldiers' position. Aganstata urged his mount forward, and the whole group of warriors— Anagalisgi estimated between two and four hundred—started out down the road. Aganstata assumed the Raven position. Amadoya was the Wolf this time, and Mankiller again the Owl. Wilinawa was the Fox. Kiyuga bore a wolf tail ornament on his armor, Anagalisgi saw.

They did not bother with single file stealth this time. In a rare show of pure vengeance, the Aniyvwiya warriors were going for a full, overwhelming, absolute frontal assault. There was nowhere the soldiers could run, not when they were in the heart of Aniyvwiya territory. They would be hunted down wherever they went.

The sun was well down before the runners slowed them and indicated the nearness of the British camp.

"Anagalisgi, are you here?" Aganstata wondered.

Kiyuga brought Amayi around.

"I'm here," Anagalisgi told him.

"Do not bother with Atsvstdi, and when we begin our attack, do nothing. But if you would, silence our approach."

Anagalisgi agreed. He ungracefully slid off Amayi's rump and stumbled a few steps before righting himself. He quietly followed the runner who pointed out the British camp right alongside a small river. Their appearance was as death in the firelight, and Anagalisgi briefly wondered if they would be fighting dead men. Was it even a fight worth having?

He picked out Captain Demeré, John Stuart, and others he recognized. They were trying to boost morale, telling the men that they were finally out of "that lousy hellhole" and on their way home. Few seemed satisfied with this observation and instead declared that they wouldn't be happy until they were home again "in right proper civilization where civilized men belong."

Anagalisgi looked at the runner and made a motion. Bring them in.

He remained hidden behind a tree, watching and waiting for the warriors. At the first rustling of leaves, he used Uhnoyvgi to silence the approach. None of the British suspected a thing and no alarm was raised.

Aganstata waited until the silence before urging the warriors into a full attack. It was an awesome thing to watch hundreds of horses bearing down upon him, all as silent as ghosts. Anagalisgi conjured Time and just watched, breathless, the slow, perfect movements of his people. They came with guns. They came with hatchets. They came with knives. They came with fire in their eyes and vengeance in their veins. With their painted skin and the growing darkness, with their singularity with their mounts, the warriors moved as effortlessly as a breath of wind, and for a moment, Anagalisgi was beholden to a dalliance of the spirits themselves.

Then the Raven warriors were past. Anagalisgi ceased all conjuring and the world erupted into shouts, whoops, hollers, the thunder of horse hooves, and the surprise of the soldiers as half a thousand Aniyvwiya warriors descended upon them in the darkness, swarming as wasps and just as precise in their stings. There was some gunfire and a lot of panicked shouting from the soldiers.

Still the warriors kept coming, overwhelming the soldiers as a flooded river overwhelmed its banks and filled the moats around the Aniyvwiya towns.

Anagalisgi looked around the tree once the last of the warriors had passed, and it seemed to him that the battle, if that was indeed what had happened, was over. Warriors circled their horses around the site, whooping in victory. The soldiers were herded into the center of the group. He could see some were dead already, though he could not say how many.

The warriors calmed down, staying their horses, some dismounting. Anagalisgi slipped through the crowd to see what was happening.

He watched as Amadoya grabbed Captain Demeré and threw him to the ground. The skiagvsta, in his Wolf attire, knelt, bound Demeré's hands behind his back and stuffed mud into his mouth. Then he hoisted the man to his feet and, with an improvised whip made from reeds, snapped them across the back of his legs and bade him dance.

Demeré, with his arms bound, did not comply at first, but another snap of the whip saw him do an awkward jig around the small campfire. The warriors laughed uproariously and picked several more soldiers to do the same.

After ten or eleven times around the fire, Demeré growing weaker and more uncoordinated with each loop, Amadoya simply took his skala galogwehi, pointed it at the man's head, and fired. The rest of the dancing soldiers met the same fate.

"Anagalisgi, come here," Mankiller ordered.

Anagalisgi approached.

"Ensure that there are twenty-three dead, as required."

The bodies were laid out and lined up. Anagalisgi counted seventeen bodies at first. When the site was searched again and no more bodies could be found, it was Amadoya's pleasure to pick six more to execute, all of them officers. When he looked around again afterwards, he spotted a man who Anagalisgi eventually recognized as John Stuart.

"You're lucky," Amadoya said. "We cannot kill more than twenty-three here tonight. But that isn't to say we cannot do more tomorrow."

"Claim your captives and your spoils," Aganstata said, addressing the group at large. He remained seated on his horse. "We will camp here until morning, then return to our homes."

The captives were bound and tied to trees while the warriors made camp. The warriors picked over the bodies and took spoils as they saw fit, with a few squabbles, as expected. Anagalisgi watched all of this, feeling rather distant from the whole thing, though he performed post-battle rites and rituals to purify the warriors and announce their warrior spirit for all to behold.

The next morning, the warriors rose early and prepared to leave. The captives were untied from the trees and instead tied to the horses of the warriors they belonged to now. Kiyuga had no captives, though he had taken some spoils. Anagalisgi climbed up behind him again, and they left the camp, heading for home.

ᎠᏃᎵᎢᏘ ᏭᏢᎣᎠ ᏖᏬ

Ayadohlv'i Tahlsgo Sogwu
Stone Wolf

When Atagulkalu heard of the massacre, he was deeply troubled.

When Atagulkalu heard that John Stuart had survived, he immediately left his home in exile and went to Itsa'ti to claim him.

When Nayanali learned that he traded everything he owned, all the way down to the clothes off his back, she was less than pleased and immediately set about making him some new clothes.

Indeed, all the man wore upon his return was a simple loincloth. Even his boots were gone, and his feet were scratched and bloodied from the return trek, a grateful John Stuart in tow.

"Is he to learn the sorceries now as well?" Aganstata hissed at Atagulkalu while Stuart spoke amiably with Nathan and Andrew. "Or has he had them all this time and said and done nothing?"

"He does not know the sorceries," Atagulkalu said, "and I've not said a word of it. He will stay here while we are away. I have said only that we are going on a hunt. Nayanali will look after him; she is a more than capable woman."

"And what of continued training? That was the reason you took in Nathan and Andrew, made them your brothers as much as your friend John Stuart."

"It was my understanding that training was the reason for going to this new island, so warriors may learn without interruption and our most vulnerable would be protected."

"Did you not intend to go to this new island as well? What shall we do with him?"

Atagulkalu shifted his stance. "Maybe I will not be going to this island." At Aganstata's sigh, he went on, "I believe we still have a chance for peace—"

"Peace! You still speak of peace? There will be no peace until these British demons are run out of our lands completely!"

The skiagvsta in exile was unmoved. He simply turned and gestured toward the three white-skinned men a short distance away. "My household proves otherwise."

Aganstata growled something but did not rebut. Instead he folded his arms and changed topic, asking, "When are we leaving on this 'hunt' of yours? We are already late, given that you had to take more time to rescue this captive."

"We may leave at any time. We may stay on this new island as long as we wish before returning."

Mankiller looked uneasy. "New lands, we should be cautious, take our time in exploration."

"And your wife still has to make you something to wear," Yachtino chuckled. "There is no telling what we may encounter, and you would do well to cover yourself."

The comment helped to ease the tension around the skiagvsta, and the group returned to the house. To Anagalisgi's eyes, Nathan and Andrew had become right at home, and John Stuart was quickly settling in. Nayanali regarded all of them well, he thought. They received the skiagvsta and sat to eat and talk of happier things, such as this fictional hunt they were supposed to be going on. Atagulkalu made mention of a very large buck he had seen, and conversation went from there.

At one point, Anagalisgi found himself able to speak privately with Nathan.

"What do you know of John Stuart?" he asked.

Nathan shrugged. "Not much. He's an officer, or he was. We never crossed paths, or if we did, it was merely in passing."

"Is there a way to know whether he knows of the sorceries?"

"There is, and I can tell you he does not. Believe me, when Andrew and I go to new places, we always check to see if there are others where we are going. He does not know."

"Do you think he should?"

"I think that would depend on your friend Atagulkalu there."

"The other skiagvsta don't trust him to act in the best interests of the people."

"So I've noticed. Unfortunately, I don't understand your people enough to make an opinion one way or the other. He has tried to explain it, but I think there will always be a cultural barrier that will block true, full understanding."

Anagalisgi nodded absently. "Even so, we still have to see this new island and make our decision whether to go there and train or stay here and take our chances."

"Agreed. One step at a time. Atagulkalu mentioned something about leaving in the early morning before the sun rises."

"That makes sense," Nathan said. He looked up at the sky. "Judging by the lack of sun now, perhaps we should get some sleep."

But it was another night where it was so hot and sticky, it was impossible to even get comfortable, never mind try to sleep. Anagalisgi would fall asleep, then wake up only a short time later because of how hot he was. He would wipe himself down, get a drink of water, try to use Udilegv'i ale Uhyvtsa to cool off some, lie down again, try to sleep. He would sleep a bit more, wake up again, and repeat.

He did this four or five times, and he saw others do it, too. Finally he and the rest of them decided to give up on trying to sleep and instead start their day. Andrew, who appeared to be the only one who'd managed to fall asleep and stay asleep the entire time, was shaken awake and told to get ready.

They all had their skala galogwehi—except for Atagulkalu who had traded his for Stuart, and Stuart himself who had been disarmed after being taken captive—and a bit of ammunition, something that was hard to come by these days, even from the French. Atagulkalu simply stated that he would have to do things the old-fashioned way and grabbed his grandfather's bow and some arrows. Few warriors had bows anymore, and Anagalisgi saw the look of awe and longing on Kiyuga's face.

Nayanali wished them well, giving her husband a new set of deerskin clothing that she'd worked on for most of the night. They were not as well done as they would have been, given more time, but they would do for a short expedition.

John Stuart also wished them good luck and good hunting, clasping wrists with Atagulkalu.

Then they set off. Nathan and Andrew had said several times that there was no special road they had to take. Whenever they wanted to go to the new island, they would take them there. The plan, then was to go out for half a day, as if on a hunt, in order to get deep into the woods, beyond where someone might accidentally stumble upon them and the sorceries. Anagalisgi noted an odd expression—something resembling exasperation—on Nathan and Andrew's face when the skiagvsta said this, but they did not correct them in any manner. But at least they agreed that they needed to get out of range of John Stuart.

So they traveled north and east, over rolling hills and through thick forests. Kiyuga once suggested hunting first that they might keep up their strength on the journey. Yachtino inquired whether it wouldn't have been better to fast first, to make themselves pure before traveling among the spirits. Aganstata rebutted this, mentioning how they'd eaten just the day before. Nathan and Andrew then assured them that fasting was not necessary, although having food in the stomach wasn't the best idea. Better to wait until they reached the new island.

They trekked on and the sky turned blue, the sun arcing overhead. It grew hot, even in the shade of the trees. They stopped once at a river to immerse themselves, cool off, and refill their water skins.

"This new island," Yachtino said, standing beside Nathan. "Is it as hot as it is here?"

"That depends on where you want to live," Nathan told him. "You are free to make your home anywhere. In the mountains. The open plains. The forest. We are merely your guides. Everything you do is by your choice."

"I like that idea very much," Aganstata said, slogging out of the river. "Let us get out of the open and travel to this new island, then, if indeed it can be reached from anywhere."

Anagalisgi, who had been reclining lazily on the riverbank, rolled and punched his brother in the arm to wake him up. Kiyuga startled, yawned, and got his stuff around.

"You didn't have to punch me," Kiyuga said as they started back into the trees.

"Of course I did," Anagalisgi told him. "I had to make sure you're ready for anything."

"How is waking me up and punching me the same as making sure I'm ready for anything?"

"You fell asleep in the open. Anything could have happened."

"Yes, but I know that you and the others would have warned me if things were amiss."

"You would have been the first target," Mankiller said from up ahead. He yawned. "Although I don't blame you for sleeping. I was not so comfortable last night myself."

The rest of them, less Andrew, murmured their agreement to that sentiment.

They came to a stop in the forest, the river just barely visible from their position. They stood in a circle.

"What we will do is create a doorway to this island," Andrew instructed them. "It is very taxing on us to do this. I understand that it will appear as magic. It will be startling. It is very new. We understand. But please, for our sake, when we tell you to go through the doorway, please do so in swift order. We promise, everything is well on the other side."

There were uncertain glances among the warriors, but Atagulkalu made a motion for them to proceed.

The warriors were directed to stand in a group. Nathan and Andrew stood a few paces in front of them and a few paces apart from each other.

For a moment, it did not appear that they did anything. Then Anagalisgi noticed the sweat dripping down their faces.

Suddenly, it was as though a door opened in front of them, though there was no physical thing there. The best way to describe, truly, was Galohisdi, an opening but no door. On the other side was an unfamiliar forest, draped in the shadow of a setting — or possibly rising — sun.

"Go!" Andrew spat, as if struggling to carry something very heavy.

Kiyuga was the first to lurch forward with about as much coordination as a child receiving his first blowgun. But with that awkward step, it got the others to remember themselves. Aganstata went through the doorway first, then Mankiller, Nanyehi, Atagulkalu, and Yachtino. Kiyuga glanced at Anagalisgi who was still staring himself. Then his brother grabbed his hand and they went through together.

It was like being punched in the face and the gut at the same time. Anagalisgi couldn't breathe and yet his head and his stomach begged him to throw up to relieve some ailment. He couldn't see, wasn't even sure he was conscious, and still he felt miserable. He may as well have fought a thousand battles, conjured a thousand sorceries, and suffered through a thousand sleepless nights.

The smell of earth greeted his nose, and he breathed in the sweet scent of dead leaves in the aftermath of a cool rain. He squeezed his hands and found soft earth sifting through his fingers.

When he finally opened his eyes, he was staring up at a sky quickly turning black. Perhaps the most unusual thing, though, was that he did not recognize any of the stars. He saw nothing he recognized. He could pick out no constellations or any directions, except perhaps that his head was facing west where the last of the colors were disappearing.

His stomach was still rather upset, so he decided to stay where he was for the time being. If it was dark, maybe he could take a quick nap.

He thought he must have done this, for when he opened his eyes again, the moon was overhead. When they'd left, there had been no moon. Now there was a nearly full moon. An almost full moon and new stars, had he been in hibernation? No, he still did not recognize any of the stars. No matter the season, he knew the stars. These were unfamiliar stars.

He sat up, mindful of some lingering nausea, and looked around.

Atsvstdi helped to shed a little light on his surroundings, though he was careful to keep it to a minimum, just enough to assure himself that all was well. He saw the others also on the ground, sleeping soundly. A short distance away, he thought he saw a fire. As his head came back to him, he saw that it was, indeed, a fire. Two people sat beside it. One pointed in his direction. The other looked and motioned him over.

Anagalisgi tried several times to stand before finally getting his feet under him. He stumbled on his way up a slope toward the fire. The light was terrible on him. He discovered that the two men around the fire were Nathan and Andrew, and he helped himself to a seat.

"We figured it best to let you rest as you were," Andrew said. "Portal travel is quite exhausting, even for seasoned sorcerers. We've not been awake long ourselves."

"Are we truly on the new island?" Anagalisgi wondered. "I see new stars, and we are not where we were, but this dark forest looks very much like any dark forest at home."

"It will look different in the morning," Nathan promised.

"Why didn't you build the fire closer, or bring us closer to it?"

"Vantage. This was a better spot to build a fire. And as Andrew said, we haven't been awake very long ourselves. The others will wake in time, so we'll not disturb them."

Anagalisgi nodded, took a drink.

Over the course of the night, as the sun began to rise, the warriors started to come around and make their way toward the fire. Kiyuga was first. Andrew suspected it was because he was young, like Anagalisgi. Then it was Aganstata, Yachtino, Nanyehi, Mankiller, and finally Atagulkalu. The older warriors did look pretty terrible,

Anagalisgi thought. Probably they would end up staying for a few days just to recover enough to return home.

They tentatively shared a bit of food. Yachtino promptly excused himself to utilize a bush a short distance away. When he returned, they lay down again to sleep some more.

When Anagalisgi woke once more, the sky was blue, white clouds billowing lazily overhead. His mind noted several things it did not immediately comprehend, and it wasn't until he sat up and poked the fire a bit that he was able to put it into words.

Just as he had not recognized the stars overhead, so he also did not recognize the leaves on the trees, or the patterns of the bark. He looked at the debris on the ground. He saw needles like pine, but nothing he'd seen before. There were nuts littering the ground, though he did not recognize them either.

He looked around at the forest. It looked very much like any other forest, where the tall trees loomed ominously, shafts of sunlight penetrated the thick canopy to shine on the saplings below. Ferns, bushes, brush, and other undergrowth filled in the lower layers. Yet he knew none of the trees. He did not see any maple, oak, none of it. He heard something scurry or slither under the leaves, but he saw nothing. The bushes were strange, the ferns more like feathers and string than leaves.

"Is this your home?" Anagalisgi found himself asking. "Is this where sorcerers come from?"

"No," Nathan said, grinning and poking at the fire. "No, this world is completely uninhabited."

"Truly? No man has set foot here before?"

Andrew spoke, cutting off his companion. "There is evidence of ancient ruins far to the south. Remains of towns, scattered bones, pottery and artifacts, but nothing is known. No sentient species calls this planet home now."

Anagalisgi frowned but said nothing about it. A land entirely devoid of people. A place to call their own. But for how long?

"You're certain the British cannot reach us here?" he wondered.

"Quite certain," Nathan told him confidently.

"How can you know this? If you have such sorceries, and you say that others have it, that there is a business for it, who is to say that other British men less noble than yourselves cannot use it for evil?"

"Because first they would have to find this place." Nathan shifted position. "Anagalisgi, there is much you don't know, so you will just have to trust us. But there are many, many planets, many islands, in the universe, all of them scattered among the stars. Thousands of islands. Thousands and thousands and ten thousand times ten thousand. We found this place only by the will of the Author. Ill-intentioned men would have no such blessing. You will be safe here."

"And when we have mastered the sorceries and are able to do battle and defeat the British...we will also be able to return to our ancestral lands?"

"If you master the sorceries, you can do whatever you want."

Anagalisgi thought on this while the others woke and composed themselves. They looked a bit better, less ill, but still weary from the journey. Now that it was daylight, many of them also looked around in wonder, finally seeing that they were indeed in a new forest on a new island, a new planet as Nathan had called it. New leaves, new trees, new plants of all forms. Now they saw creatures flying overhead, unlike any bird any of them had ever seen, all with new calls echoing overhead.

"Perhaps we should give you some time to look around and acclimate yourselves to this new environment," Andrew suggested.

If any of the warriors had heard him, they gave no indication of it. Indeed, they were already doing such things on their own as they stood and slowly made their way around the immediate vicinity, investigating everything.

"We truly are in a new place," Mankiller said breathlessly.

"Indeed so," Nathan agreed mildly.

They went nowhere that day, instead spending the time merely becoming acquainted with this new land. They had no names for anything, so they either tried to equate it with something similar or make up something new entirely. Mankiller found a small furry creature he named akatiha, for it frequently peeked over the rim of its burrow. Nanyehi named a tree agatena diga'galvnvhida, for its broad swath reminded them of the great diga'galvnvdiha, though the leaves appeared loosely twisted together as in agatena.

They attempted to catch one of Mankiller's akatiha for dinner that evening, but the creature proved terribly elusive, and not even the sorceries could wrest it from its burrow once it had gone. So instead, they made do with the rations they had packed.

"Tomorrow, we can start traveling," Nathan told them, looking as excited as the rest of them felt bewildered.

"Where?" Atagulkalu wondered.

"Anywhere you want," Andrew said. His demeanor had become less agreeable the more tired he appeared to become. "You're the ones looking for a temporary home. You already move your villages when it becomes necessary. This ought to be no different."

"We have only brought you here," Nathan cut in. "It's up to you to decide whether you like it and where it would most benefit you to settle down."

For a long moment, no one spoke. Then Atagulkalu stood.

"I thank you most kindly, Andrew and Nathan, for your willingness to help, to teach us these sorceries and to extend your knowledge and power for the benefit of our people."

"We wish you only the best," Nathan told him. "Truly we do."

"To that end, perhaps we should all get some sleep," Andrew suggested, growing more irritable. "We can start fresh at dawn."

No one argued.

Anagalisgi lay back on the ground, looking up at stars he had never seen before. He could not say which way was north except perhaps from the direction of the sunset. But what if that was also different here?

How did these stars get here? Why did the akatiha burrow so? What gave the birds their unique calls? All these things, he'd always had answers for. He knew all the stories. Here, though, he was in new lands with new skies. He did not know their spirits, did not know their stories and songs. These things, which normally brought him comfort, now eluded him, and he was afraid.

If they brought the people here, to this new land to learn new sorceries, they would wish for something familiar, some reason to come, some reason to stay. Would it really be as simple as a short absence in order to learn? Or should they plan for a longer stay? If the British really were unable to find them here, why should they want to return and fight? Why not stay and live as they always had? Why not learn the stories and songs of this new land and new sky?

He wished he could have spoken to Ge'gwogv, but the white woodpecker did not appear to him that night. Was it simply unwilling to visit, or was it barred from flying these skies? He prayed for an answer, a vision. If this was the land they were meant to be in, even for a short time, surely they must bring something of their own lands as a comfort and a guide. They could not abandon the spirits of their ancestors in their old lands. This was looking more and more like a very bad idea.

The sun rose, and Anagalisgi found himself grateful for it, for it had been the first night in his life he'd been truly afraid it might not. He got up and spent a good portion of time praying and burning incense, looking for guidance of some form.

"What do the spirits tell you?" Nanyehi asked, gently putting a hand on his shoulder as he knelt before his casting crystals.

"North and east," Anagalisgi reported. "To a land of stone wolves."

It felt good to have a direction to go. Aganstata took the lead, Anagalisgi following. Behind him came Yachtino, Nanyehi, Mankiller, Kiyuga, Atagulkalu, Nathan in the rear, and Andrew off to one side keeping watch. It was just as well, for the Aniyvwiya warriors were too distracted by the wonders of the new island to be fully on guard.

They did not stop for anything, else they would never get going again, they knew. They saw many new birds flying overhead, though it was impossible to say what kind of birds they were. Some appeared very colorful with majestic fans of feathers. Others appeared very smooth, sleek and fast. And they saw many small creatures running around in the trees. Some appeared as squirrels, others as raccoons, others as things they had no name for or words to describe.

Once they came across a large beast, surprising it in the trees. Anagalisgi was so stunned that he could only remember later that it was dappled gray in color, had four stocky legs, a thick neck, an unusually large muzzle, an enormous mouth, and a whip-like tail. It bared its teeth and hissed in a threatening manner but ultimately ran off, yipping and screaming.

"I suggest we move on," Andrew said, shouldering his rifle, "before it comes back with friends."

"Will it?" Kiyuga wondered.

"Do you want to find out?"

They pressed on, north and east. The land began to slope upwards, and a clearing revealed mountains in the distance, just a gray haze against a gray sky.

"At least the spirits still speak to you here," Aganstata said to Anagalisgi as they stopped to rest beside a stream. "I admit, I had feared they might not."

"The Upper World covers all islands," Anagalisgi told him, trying to sound confident and not let on that he'd been having the same fears. He still had them. What if his interpretation was wrong? What if there were no stone wolves? How would he even know these stone wolves?

"Yes, I suppose they do."

They continued on for a time until darkness and fatigue drove them to shelter for the night.

"Do sorcerers have children, Andrew and Nathan?" Nanyehi inquired as they sat around the fire.

"Some do," Nathan answered politely. "My father was a sorcerer, although he was of a less altruistic persuasion. Anagalisgi and Atagulkalu have educated me about what your people call Raven Mockers. I suppose that truly would be the best way to describe him. He preyed on the sick and dying, stealing their years."

"Why do you not follow in his footsteps? Such a prospect is a temptation to many, to lengthen one's years."

"The Author, Digohwelisgi, imparts the same gift to her followers, but with power to do good, with no need to thieve life from others."

"How old are you?" Mankiller asked.

"Older than we look," Andrew answered.

"Is that what will happen to us?" Kiyuga inquired. "Now that we are learning the sorceries, will we also gain extended years?"

"It takes a lot of time and practice for such things to occur," Nathan told him. "You must use it on a much more frequent basis for years before it will take hold. It requires a certain degree of commitment."

"If you have such extended years," Aganstata began, "what happens when you die? Or do you simply live forever?"

"Ah..." Nathan looked a bit embarrassed by the question. "Well, we do have many long years ahead of us. And if we continue to use the sorceries and follow the Author, we could very well live forever. In fact, I know of one particular sorcerer who's been alive for more than fifteen hundred years, since the time of Christ."

He let that sink in a moment. Anagalisgi could hardly wrap his head around it. The Europeans called it the Year of Our Lord Seventeen Sixty, and there was a sorcerer who had witnessed all one thousand seven hundred and sixty years?

"But we can die," Andrew went on. "We are very much mortal men, same as anyone here."

"What happens after you die?" Nanyehi wondered.

"All we know is that the Author says we will remain with her forever. And that's good enough for us. We don't know what it means specifically, but it's good enough for us."

Good enough for Nathan and Andrew maybe, but rather unsatisfying for the rest of them. Whether one believed that the spirits traveled west to the darkening lands, took on the form of an animal until oblivion, or went to Heaven or Hell as in the Christian faith, at least there was some kind of answer. Maybe being with the Author was some form of Heaven, but it still wasn't the most satisfying answer.

"Is this true for all sorcerers?" Nanyehi pressed. "Whether they do good as you do, or evil as your father did, do they all go to be with the Author?"

"Only followers of the Author get to be with the Author, and they are called Beloved. Evil sorcerers...we don't know except, perhaps, oblivion."

There were uncertain glances all around, and Anagalisgi would be lying if he said he didn't have doubts. The power was incredible, no one could deny, but what did it mean for them in the grand scheme of things? How did it help or hurt their purity of spirit, their bond with their surroundings and their brethren? If they were going to do something so drastic as split up their people, or even move them entirely, then they ought to know some of these things. Life was about more than mere food and water, mere physical survival; it was about purity of the soul.

Anagalisgi looked up at the stars, now only intermittently seen amid the clouds. What were the stories of this land? What did he tell them about this place and its spirits? Why had he not seen Ge'gwogv? He tried to tell himself the same thing he'd told Aganstata; the Upper World was above all islands. There was no reason the spirits should not speak to him here. Or so he hoped. So why weren't they speaking to him in this critical time?

He leaned forward and stared at the coals in the fire. Only a handful of adawehi in all of Aniyvwiya history had the talent to divine from the fire, and he was fairly certain he was not one of them. Clearly it had to be an inborn talent and could not be taught. Still, he could hope something would come to him.

"You are certain we must still travel north and east?" Aganstata asked of him.

Anagalisgi looked up. "Such is the last guidance I received. Unless the spirits tell me otherwise as I sleep and dream, that is the way we shall continue."

He desperately wanted to dream. For so long, he'd dreaded sleep on account of his terrible visions. And yet it had become familiar, so that now when he did not dream and was uncertain whether he could even speak to the spirits, he craved it. He would take the terrible visions, if only because it meant that he could still communicate with them.

When he lay down to sleep and discovered that he was indeed dreaming, he was so excited he almost woke himself up. But he stayed anchored in the dream and tried to focus.

He dreamed of a wooden table, and upon it sat a bowl. The bowl was broken in half, one half shattered into many small pieces. By some unknown force, he was directed to pick up the shattered pieces and begin to put them back together. As he did so, he knew instinctively that they were not going back together as the second half of the larger bowl, but as a new bowl, a cup really. When the pieces had been fashioned into the cup, he filled it from a pitcher of water and drank from it.

Then, still directed by the unknown force, he refilled the cup and placed it in the part of the large bowl that was still broken and useless.

"Not useless," he whispered, knowledge flowing into his soul. "Broken, yes, but useful in a new way."

His gaze shifted to the pitcher of water, and when he looked back at the bowl, he saw something beside it. A figurine had appeared, a stone carving of a wolf. He picked it up and turned it in his hands. He placed the wolf in the cup of water in the broken bowl.

The stone began to soften until it turned into clay, smooth and malleable, soaking up the water like moss. Details began to appear in the clay, and the clay turned to fur. The once-stone wolf then stood, jumped out of the cup, and shook out its fur. As it did so, it began to grow until it turned into a normal wolf pup. Normal, except it was solid white with silver eyes.

Anagalisgi looked up as a shadow appeared beside him. He saw more wolves join him around the table, all of them white, all of them with the wisdom of the spirits and the ancestors.

"One more pup," Anagalisgi said. "A new pup in the pack, alone for a time, but still protected." He studied the ball of fur. "And perhaps to become the mightiest of them all." He scratched the pup behind the ears. The pup smiled, its tongue lolling. "You will be called Yawi, for Waya, the Wolf, and Aniyvwiya, the People."

The wolves around the table lifted their voices in melodic approval, and even the pup gave its gratitude.

Then the pack turned and disappeared into the shadows, leaving only Anagalisgi and Yawi.

"I have a feeling that I will be seeing you soon," Anagalisgi said. The pup sneezed. "Until then, even as a pup spirit, I think you have greater power and ability than an entire pack of ordinary wolves and will be able to take care of yourself for a while."

The pup sneezed again but sat down beside the bowl and the cup as if on guard.

Anagalisgi nodded. "Well then, as you were. You seem to know your purpose."

He backed away from the table. When he turned to face the darkness, he found the dim light of dawn on his eyelids and he blinked sleepily awake.

Breakfast was swift and they were on their way soon enough. Anagalisgi felt more confident now in his directions, and he felt as though someone else walked in his shoes, showing him where to go.

They continued ever upward into the mountains until they came to a ridge. From there, they looked out across the range and the valley below.

"The stone wolves," Anagalisgi breathed and pointed.

Directly in front of them was, indeed, a stone wolf. Its back was curved ridgeline, its belly open to the south sun from a rockslide, lush and green. Its tail was a curved path from the ridge, down and around, protecting its belly. More formations and rock slides had carved out its head and paws, and with the wind cutting narrow gaps in the surface of the rock creating the appearance of fur, it appeared as though a great wolf had chosen this spot to rest.

Now with great enthusiasm, they hurried toward the stone wolf. It required moving down the ridge they stood upon and crossing a very wide expanse of forest. Then they were back upon stone. The trees turned into shrubs. A stone path led from the forest to the tail of the wolf where a narrow opening would allow them to go through. But they could not do so just yet.

Anagalisgi went forward and put his hand on the wolf's tail. It was easily ten times his height. Looking east toward the paws and head, he knew the story of this place.

"She has been waiting for us," he said, his soul swelling with such pride that he finally had something to give.

"She has?" Nathan blurted.

Anagalisgi nodded and ran his hand over the smooth stone. "Long ago she walked these lands. She made the valleys with her great paws, as safe havens for the people who were here before, whom she called her own. Other great ones did the same, beasts of the desert and the plains and even the birds of the sky.

"But the men of the beasts became jealous of the men of the birds. There was a time of great war and greater sorrow." Anagalisgi frowned. "All the men are gone now. And the wolf laid here to rest, to protect that which was hers, in hopes that she may do her duty once again, when men return."

He gave offering and thanks to the wolf before the group climbed through the path and into the broken bowl. There was a vast expanse of grasses waving in the wind and shrubs here and there, but no trees.

Indeed, there must have been men here at one time, for there were dwellings carved into the rock, homes devoid of all life. A few had bones that were nearly dust now; several had remnants of stone tools or pottery. But there was no life to be found.

"Do any spirits remain here?" Mankiller asked cautiously, looking at Anagalisgi.

"None, not a trace," Anagalisgi replied. "The bones are devoid of life and soul, and no spirits of the dead walk this land anymore. It has been a long time since anyone walked here, dead or alive."

"What do you suppose happened to them?" Andrew wondered.

"As our young adawehi said," Nanyehi told him. "Great war and greater sorrow. That's all we need to know."

Yachtino frowned. "Do you suppose this is what awaits us if we stay where we are?"

"It can't be," Kiyuga said. "Not when we have them on the run with the sorceries. If we use this place to train in the sorceries, then—"

"We will leave it up to each man to decide," Aganstata cut in. "But now we know that we have found this place, and it is worthy of our time. More importantly, we are worthy of its protection."

They spent three days in the old town, each of them fasting while Anagalisgi prayed and gave thanks to the stone wolf and the spirits for their guidance and protection. He also found himself thanking Digohwelisgi for bringing Nathan and Andrew to them to show them this new path and new island. He burned incense in the dwelling where they stayed and around the whole town, and Nanyehi sung songs that were perhaps the first to echo through the deserted town in many generations.

After three days, they went out and took greater stock of the town and surrounding area, each man to a task until they reconvened that evening.

"Fifty-two dwellings," Atagulkalu reported, "and one gathering place. And there is no reason to think more could not be carved out or built." He looked around. "This place is most ideal, smiled upon by the sun and protected from the north wind."

"Easy to defend as well," Aganstata said. "The only viable way in or out is through the broken tail. Warriors cannot scale the south stone where the paws and tail meet, and it is a treacherous thing to try and climb the ridge outright."

"Whom do we expect to attack?" Nanyehi wondered. "If this place truly is deserted and no men walk here save us, then such things are not necessary."

"We can never be too careful," Kiyuga told her. "There may not be men here, but we still don't know what that beast was, its nature and habits. We don't want it sneaking up on us in the middle of the night, be it one or a whole pack."

Mankiller grunted his agreement, then, "And was your task successful?"

She dipped her head. "The slope is grassy, good for grazing animals. The soil is stony, so it would require work to make crops grow, but it can be done. And the forest below is thick with vegetation. Unfortunately, I know not whether it is edible. But we will learn."

"We also have water within this bowl," Yachtino reported. "Kiyuga and I discovered a stream here to the east. It runs from the ridgeline along the inner edge of the bottom of the bowl until it goes into the wolf's mouth and disappears."

"As it sustains her, it will also sustain us," Anagalisgi murmured.

"And you, Mankiller?" Aganstata prompted.

"The forest is rich with game, of both birds and beasts. Not knowing their natures, I refrained from hunting them for the time being."

"Anagalisgi?"

The adawehi nodded slowly. "The townhouse will suffice. It will need to be properly blessed and purified, but it is appropriate."

Kiyuga added more sticks to the fire.

"And what do you see?" Aganstata asked of Nathan and Andrew. "Have you seen something that we have not that should give us pause to reconsider?"

The white-skinned man shook their heads.

"No," Nathan answered. "You know what you are looking for. You know what you need. In fact, this place seems as though it has been made just for you."

"We will not presume to tell you what to do," Andrew agreed.

"Maybe not," Mankiller said, "but you are Atagulkalu's brothers now."

"Atagulkalu is still in exile," Aganstata reminded him.

"Yes, but if that were a worry, I think he would not be here," Yachtino commented.

Atagulkalu said nothing.

"What shall we tell the people, then?" Nanyehi wondered. "How shall we show them what we have seen here? How do we convince them of this place?"

"We will bring back things from this island," Mankiller said. "The leaves of these news trees, bark from their trunks. We will capture an animal and—"

"You are bound and determined to catch one of those akatiha, aren't you?" Aganstata joked, jabbing him in the ribs.

Mankiller gave him a look even as the rest of them snickered. "We will bring back an animal such that they have never seen before. We will bring back grass and soil and the dust of these dwellings. And we will have our testimony of these things. Anagalisgi himself will testify to the stone wolf."

"The stone wolf and the stars and the spirits of this place," Anagalisgi confirmed.

"They speak to you now," Nanyehi stated, smiling.

"They do. They are glad to see people walk among them again, the caretakers of Creation."

"You must tell this to the people," Atagulkalu told him. "You must make them see and understand."

"I will."

Aganstata leaned back and folded his arms. "What are we attempting to persuade them of exactly? I am as happy as the rest of you that we have found this place and been accepted. But is this not meant to be a temporary place, where we can train in safety so we can fight to remain where we are at home, in our ancestral lands?"

"True training takes time," Andrew said. "Many years. Now, we have done our best to speed it up, and you are certainly more than capable of shortening that time, but it will not be an instant thing. Not a moon or a season, but many seasons. If the intent is also to protect the women, children, and elders, they will not likely be training. And someone must go out to hunt and fetch water and care for the elders. And I am certain that you will continue to observe your festivals and rituals."

The skiagvsta frowned deeply. "It seems to me that this will be far longer than just a few seasons. It seems to me that this may be an attempt to move us, as the Europeans have done to us, taking our lands and moving us out of our homes."

"We bring no contracts or treaties," Nathan said calmly before Andrew could argue. "We are not forcing you into anything. We present only an option. And as you have said, let each man decide for himself. It may be that no one wishes to leave. If that is so, then no harm has been done. If some wish to leave, then we will assist however we can."

The following day, Nathan and Andrew found themselves assisting Mankiller in the apprehension of the elusive akatiha. Anagalisgi and Nanyehi set about gathering plants to take back and show the people. Atagulkalu, Aganstata, Yachtino, and Kiyuga were in conference, probably arguing over Aganstata's misgivings.

Anagalisgi wouldn't say he didn't understand, because he did. They were a patient people. They could take the time to train and prepare and think about their wars. The Europeans had no such inclination. They were impatient, reckless, and they would not wait for the Aniyvwiya to be prepared. Could they really give up part of their fighting force in hopes that they could train fast enough to be ready and able to return and defeat the British?

When they were all done, they reconvened in the town. Mankiller finally had his akatiha in a bag. It no longer kicked and fought, but there was a distinct noise of chewing, as if it were trying to chew its way out, which it probably was.

"We will return to the place where we left," Andrew said. "Let me tell you something. Portals do not get easier over time. They are exhausting and dangerous. Just keep that in mind. Once again, when we tell you to move, please move quickly."

"What happens if this Galohisdi closes when someone is midway through?" Nanyehi inquired.

"No one knows, other than that person just vanishes forever," Nathan told her. "We'll do our best, but it takes only a moment to walk through. Quickly, please."

Anagalisgi clutched his bag full of plants and watched as the sorcerers again opened a doorway in midair. It looked so simple a task and yet such an effort as the men broke out into profuse sweating.

"Go!" Nathan gasped.

Mankiller jumped through first with his akatiha. Then Nanyehi, Aganstata, Yachtino, Atagulkalu, Kiyuga, and finally Anagalisgi.

Andrew was right. It didn't get easier. Anagalisgi felt as terrible on the return trip as he did going out. When he finally blinked back to wakefulness, his head felt heavy, his stomach sick, and he couldn't remember which way was up even though he stared at the sky.

But he recognized the stars. And the leaves on the trees and the patterns of the bark. He recognized home. He heaved a sigh of relief and managed to relieve some of the stress and nausea that had him rooted to the ground.

He sat up. All the others appeared to have made it, and they, too, were beginning to rouse.

By the time they made it back to Atagulkalu's home, Kiyuga had recovered enough to take down a deer, just as something to show for the "hunt" they supposedly went on. Nayanali immediately started preparing it for her husband.

"You're not coming with us?" Kiyuga wondered as Atagulkalu sat to rest.

"Best not," the disgraced skiagvsta said. "I have no voice with which to speak, and no influence to wield. Better to remove myself completely and let your testimony persuade them, with no taint from me."

Taint or not, it was a tragic thing when they called everyone together in the townhouse in Itsa'ti. Everyone marveled at the akatiha which Mankiller so proudly showed off. The women and adawehi set about studying the plants that Nanyehi showed them. And everyone sat in rapturous awe as Anagalisgi told them of the stories he'd learned of the island, the stone wolf and the other great ones, the men they once protected and how they perished.

Telling of their discoveries was no different than the time

Atagulkalu had gone to England and so relayed his tales of that place. But it was much harder to convince them to leave.

They had two grand victories against the British, stopped their advance in the pass with a mighty ambush, and showed their might against the soldiers of the fort. Even now, messages were being sent back and forth about ransom.

Winter was coming, and only fools trekked into the mountains during winter. They would have a whole season to learn the sorceries so that when spring arrived, they could chase the British all the way back to England.

Perhaps the worst part was that Aganstata and Mankiller, who were supposed to be swaying the people, were instead being swayed themselves.

"It will take more than a season to learn," Kiyuga said. "Over one season, this summer, I have learned only a tiny fraction of what is available."

"And we have two great victories for it," someone told him. "We have no need for a cannon when a rifle will do."

"We cannot presume to think that this is it. That somehow we've won. The British will return. And what if they do come over winter? What if they return and we haven't the numbers to beat them back? What if we are caught unprepared? Are you willing to sacrifice the people because we are untrained and unprepared?"

"Are you prepared to sacrifice the people by taking away warriors to this place when we need them the most here?" someone countered.

"If we take the most vulnerable among us, the women, children, and elders, away to safety, then the fighting force that remains will be more than enough and we will not be risking lives unnecessarily." He went on before anyone could say more. "Let each man decide for himself. Let each woman decide for herself and her children. This new island is not free from danger, for there are wild beasts, but there are no wars to fight. No armies coming to burn and pillage and destroy."

Unfortunately, there was little support for this among the younger warriors and untested young men and boys, who craved battle to make their names known. But among the elders and the women, there appeared to be great interest. Anagalisgi tried to judge the reactions from the rest of the skiagvsta, but it was hard to tell. Even the adawehi seemed rather divided, though that was probably them trying to figure out why the dark seer was suddenly speaking good things.

"Is winter about there?" one of the elders, Ugidahli, wondered.

"We would expect there to be snow, but it has not yet touched the ridge," Kiyuga answered. "It appears that way, though, for the stone is bleached white."

"If there is no snow there when winter comes here, then perhaps the vulnerable may go there to spend the season. We will decide whether it is a place worth living. We will clean the homes, plant the fields, and build fire in the townhouse. When spring returns and war with it, then we will know what we must do."

There was more discussion, but in the end, there was great support for Ugidahli's idea. Nothing was decided that day, for it appeared as though it would be a more personal discussion to be had among one's family and clan first.

The meeting was dismissed shortly after that. Anagalisgi and Kiyuga went down to the river to sit, watch the water go by, and speak together.

"What do you think of Ugidahli's idea?" Kiyuga asked. "Think it could work?"

"It's a sensible plan," Anagalisgi stated levelly. "My worry is how the elders will weather the crossing. Or how they will react to the Galohisdi at all."

"Each man makes his own choices. If he grows fearful and does not wish to go, he does not have to." Kiyuga sighed. "But I understand. It is a difficult journey."

"Some warriors will have to go as well, in order to provide meat while the women plant the crops. We don't know the foraging yet."

Kiyuga nodded. "I will go."

"You?" Anagalisgi had to admit he was surprised.

"I have made my name known. And how shall it look for you to go there and I not support you?"

I'm not going there, though. Anagalisgi almost said it, but stopped himself at the last moment. Finally he said, "I do not expect that I will go with them initially. As many have said, no one enjoys a bad omen hanging around. I will stay here for a time, until spring comes and we must make our decision."

"What about training?"

"Training will continue here. The vulnerable are going only to establish themselves and see if it is suitable. That takes a lot of work, and it cannot be disrupted by training. The most powerful warriors are but mewling pups if they have no food and water. Let them decide for themselves whether it is a worthy pursuit. Then we will go there to train."

Kiyuga mulled this over for a moment, then nodded. "All right. But this is all assuming that there is no snow there."

"True, but maybe we can convince them to go anyway and prepare the land. The British are burning our hunting lands and our croplands. It may be that we come to rely on this new island to sustain us."

"I pray you're wrong."

Anagalisgi sighed. "I have prayed that for many years about many things, and it has yet to be answered."

DᏇᏁᎥᎢ ᏪᏢᎧᎠᎠ ᏪᏢ

Ayadohlv'i Tahlsgo Tali
War Tortoise

There was indeed snow in the mountains, but the elders and women did find the sheltered town carved into the side of the mountain much more agreeable than the openness of the Overhill towns. They'd been terribly afraid when Nathan and Andrew opened a Galohisdi to the place, but, once situated, got right to work.

Kiyuga agreed to go with them for a time to assist, most often by hunting and bringing meat to the people while they figured out how to make the town their own. Some sheep had been brought, and they nosed around the snowy slope for anything to eat. About half the flock ended up being butchered.

But they made it. Winter was not so terrible when the wind was blocked and snow did not pile up around homes. The spring pond that formed at the base of the slope, where the grass touched the paws and tail of the great stone wolf, was excellent to draw in migrating waterfowl. And the women were soon hard at work tilling part of the slope for crops.

It was, by all accounts, a success. There was no rampant disease, and most people were too busy working about the town to pay much attention to the cold and snow. Indeed, the snow touched only the lowest homes, those that were not completely sheltered by the mountain. So the elders could move from their homes to the townhouse freely, and children could play summer games and still be protected.

Some from the new town even began to call for their counterparts in the Overhill to leave the towns entirely and come into the protection of the stone wolf. Leave the wars behind and come to this new place.

As spring came, some took them up on the offer, and they came from all over Aniyvwiya lands, the Overhill, the Middle Towns, and the displaced Lower peoples. The last time Kiyuga looked upon the town, that now called itself Aktiya Waya, it appeared as bright and bustling a town as any other. Some had even captured the animals of their homeland to take to the new island, to bring some familiarity to the people there.

The warriors, however, were less enthusiastic about leaving. Some had trained in the sorceries over the winter, but few stuck with it. When spring came, along with the news that the British were mounting a massive offense against the Aniyvwiya, there was little desire to flee, and few really considered what had truly ensured their victory at Itse'yi. It wasn't just skill and provision from the spirits, but the sorceries as well. The words fell on deaf ears, however. The young warriors were invincible and craving great glory; they wanted to show off their own prowess, not hide behind foreign sorceries.

The older warriors and elders who had remained—even those who were wary of the sorceries—chastised the younger warriors for not sitting down and paying attention to instruction. But the younger warriors only paid attention to who was proclaiming to lead the greatest raids when winter finally lost its grip on the land.

Some devised easy plans, to go against the British on the roads and in remote farmlands and settlements. It would be good practice for boys who'd not yet seen battle or blood. Kiyuga watched three such raiding parties depart even before the snow was well melted.

Many touted greater challenges and greater glory, attacking larger towns and settlements and killing the boy soldiers of the British army. If it must come to war, let them face worthy opponents. These were the most popular gatherings.

There were a few—who had "testicles bigger than their brains" as some of the elders grumbled—who proclaimed that they would march against Charleston or Jamestown itself and show the governor just what the Aniyvwiya could do. Unfortunately (or perhaps fortunately) these raids were never more than boastful dreams.

With Aktiya Waya well flourishing, Kiyuga returned to stay in Itsa'ti. He was not there long before he went out on the road. He, Adahi, Yvgi, and several others were to head to Itse'yi and then on to old Estato, to see what news and movements of the British.

Going through the Middle Towns, Kiyuga was reminded of the expedition the previous year, the journey to Charleston, being taken hostage, being freed only because of sorcery, fleeing to Kuwayi'hi and then to Itse'yi. Looking around at the mountains on either side of him, he recalled the battle in the pass. He remembered it in vivid detail, crouching and waiting for the enemy's advance. Watching them walk obliviously into their trap.

"Yvgidahi."

Kiyuga blinked. He realized he'd stopped and Amayi was pawing, eager to get going. Adahi and the others were farther down the road. They were indeed in the pass. He looked back, half-expecting to see Aganstata in his raven gear, ready for ambush.

"Something wrong?" Adahi asked, turning his horse and returning to him.

Kiyuga blinked again and shook his head, nudging Amayi forward to meet them. "No. No, though I heard something, but it's nothing. Just an animal."

Yvgi raised a brow. "An animal may refer to the beasts that the spirits have graced us with, or those red-coated sons of bitches. Which is it?"

"It was only a deer."

Another warrior, Nage'i barked a laugh. "If Yvgidahi shall be able to hear and warn us of deer, then he shall have no trouble warning us of a British assault."

And they continued on.

They reached old Estato with little problem. Some of the residents had returned, all of them young and able-bodied. They were less interested in truly living in Estato, but were instead tasked with fleeing to Itse'yi to warn the people of a British advance.

Kiyuga and the others took it one step further. They rested in Estato for the night, then rode out in the morning toward the south and east. Conflict was not their goal, though it was certainly a possibility. They just had to gather information about their enemy and where they might be.

The Lower Towns of Tsiya'hi and Tomasi remained abandoned. They were not far from Kuwayi'hi and Fort Prince George when they were able to get the information they needed, and they returned to Estato just as fast as they could.

"Are the Anigilisi coming?" one of the Estato warriors asked. A crowd quickly gathered.

"They will be," Adahi told them. "They are gathering supplies. Many supplies."

"The pass will slow them down, same as before," a young warrior, perhaps still a boy, declared.

"Even so, they will come," Yvgi warned severely. "Whether we win the battle or not matters little to you if you're dead. Remember that."

The younger warriors bobbed their heads expectantly.

And they were off again. They reported similarly to Itse'yi to forewarn them, then made haste for Itsa'ti.

Aganstata, Mankiller, and Yachtino had gone to Aktiya Waya only once, then returned, claiming that regardless if men stayed or went, if battle was to be fought and war was to be won, then the younger warriors would need guidance. It would be a gross insult for them to abandon those who chose to stay behind. They would continue to train, and they would hope that Digohwelisgi showed them favor in battle with the sorceries.

With some of the more haughty warriors still trying to convince others to come with them on this or that raid, the desire for battle was plainly evident, in the same way that one would get wet by walking through the river. Elder men spoke of their younger, more heroic days. Elder women spoke of their heroic fathers, uncles, brothers, and sons. Married women boasted of the battles their husbands had to fight in order to win their hearts. Younger women told the eligible warriors what they had to bring back in order to catch their attention.

Kiyuga and the rest rode purposefully through Itsa'ti, seeking out Aganstata. Amadoya, Yachtino, Chola, and others they picked up along the way. All they needed now was the skiagvsta of Itsa'ti.

He turned up eventually. Seeing the size of the search party and the expressions on their faces, he did not question them and instead headed to the townhouse surrounded by a number of warriors on foot and on horseback.

"Where have the Anigilisi attacked?" he demanded as they convened in the townhouse. "Speak what you have seen."

"They have not destroyed any towns yet," Adahi began. "We traveled to the Middle Towns and to Estato and beyond, to Kuwayi'hi and Fort Prince George. Then we retraced our steps. The warriors at Estato still kept watch when we left. The rest of the old Lower Towns remain abandoned or they are being occupied by Anigilisi forces. Kuwayi'hi has been completely overrun by the army at the fort, but that was to be expected."

"Judging by your hasty return, I would presume that there was some manner of activity at Fort Prince George?" Amadoya guessed, his tone half-sarcastic and half-annoyed. He leaned forward, as if he could will the information out of them.

"Much activity," Kiyuga told him, giving him a certain look. Addressing the skiagvsta in general, "We estimate between two and three thousand red- and blue-coated soldiers, many of their fierce Highlanders, plus another thousand upon horseback."

"They are going to raid and burn our villages again," someone said.

"They will try," another scoffed. "We stopped them at Itse'yi before, we can do it again."

Nage'i shook his head. "It will not be the same. They are preparing pack animals, wagons, heavy armaments, and many more supplies. They are not intending a short raid, but a prolonged siege upon our lands. They will move as a tortoise does, slowly but confidently, for few creatures can crack its shell. They will not be run off so easily.

They have learned. They must have, for James Grant leads them now."

Aganstata frowned at this.

"Word should be sent to all raiding parties and warriors," Chola said. "We can't lose them to chance encounters in the woods or in the fields, and we will need as much strength as we can muster."

"Agreed," Aganstata murmured.

"Many Anikawi live in Daqua'i," Wilinawa said. "I will send them as messengers."

"Good."

"Were the Anigilisi on the road when you saw them?" Yachtino asked of the returning warriors.

"Not then, but it is very likely they could be now," Kiyuga replied.

"We should send a party to the French, to trade for weapons and ammunition," Chola suggested. "We are terribly low on such things after the winter. We will be helpless without them."

"Agreed," Aganstata repeated, stretching out his legs. "We cannot afford a delay; our enemies move swiftly. Wilinawa, as your Anikawi messengers find the warriors and raiding parties, send them to Itse'yi if they will, to be ready if something happens. James Grant will not be distracted by the Lower Towns now; he will certainly move on the Middle Towns. Tolatsi, I want you to pick five warriors to escort a trading party to the French. Take whatever you believe they will trade for weapons and ammunition."

The long-legged warrior dipped his head.

"Shall we send all our warriors to Itse'yi then?" Mankiller wondered.

"That would be must unwise," one of the elders said.

"No, we cannot send them all," Aganstata said, reclining a bit. "It would leave us defenseless."

"We could make use of the fort," someone suggested.

"We could just as easily escape to Aktiya Waya," someone else pointed out.

"We cannot flee like prey," Amadoya spat. "We must be willing to defend what is ours. They have destroyed the Lower Towns! Shall we give up the Middle Towns without a fight? Shall we simply hand over the Overhill?" He went on before anyone could speak. "Aktiya Waya is protecting the vulnerable among us, our women, children, and elders. But what shall we be thought of if we run away at the first sign of trouble? We have our victory at the pass and here at the fort. We can't give that up!"

Without the most vulnerable present, them being squirreled away in Aktiya Waya, there was far less opposition than Kiyuga might have expected.

"Any who wish to flee to Aktiya Waya should do so now," Aganstata said slowly. "Our warriors and our boys who wish to be warriors will defend our ancestral lands as we have always done."

"How shall we get there?" one woman inquired.

"Yvgidahi will take you to Atagulkalu and the sorcerers in the morning. They will take you to Aktiya Waya."

"Is it wise to send so many away?" one man asked. "If there is no one to live in a village, the Anigilisi may mistake it for surrender, that we are fleeing. We cannot follow them around here to there to there and leave our back sides bare to the wind. They will surely have us surrounded."

"The Lower Towns are already abandoned," Aganstata mused. "How will the Anigilisi know if our towns are populated well or not, except that they see them? And if they see them, it will be because we have failed. We cannot give them prisoners to take, especially our vulnerable. They may see our towns, but they will find nothing. We cannot fail."

"We cannot send all our warriors to one spot either," Mankiller said. "If the Anigilisi take Itse'yi, then we must have fresh warriors in Tawsi and Nikwasi ready to relieve them. And all the way up the river to Tesenti."

"What happens if they reach Tesenti?" a woman asked.

"Then we have the Kituwa warriors," Amadoya said, seeming annoyed by the implication that the Anigilisi would get that far. "They have defended the people from greater savages than the Anigilisi."

Nods and grunts of agreement ran through those gathered.

The meeting lasted all day and most of the night. Kiyuga returned to the home of his aunt and uncle to eat and rest before his mission to take those who wished to leave to Aktiya Waya.

"Do you wish to leave?" Kiyuga asked his relatives.

Digvnige and Sotsena were not yet elders. Digvnige still had plenty of fight left in him, and he, too, was preparing to go to battle. Sotsena, however, was not so fortunate. Her health had begun leaving her as water leaks from a pot with a crack in the bottom.

"I'll not leave our ancestral lands," Digvnige said as they ate. "Do not mistake me, nephew. I do not despise those who have gone to Aktiya Waya, nor do I believe your brother to be misleading anyone. But my place is here. It always has been. I was born on this island, and this island is where I will die."

Kiyuga looked at his aunt who seemed conflicted. She sighed. "I cannot leave your uncle to fend for himself."

"You don't have to go away permanently," Kiyuga told her. "Prepare Digvnige to go to war, then go to Aktiya Waya until he returns."

Sotsena gave him a look. "And how shall I ensure that there will be food and clothing for him when he returns? How shall this be done if I am not here to do it? I cannot take food and supplies from Aktiya Waya, for I hear such things are yet scarce there; I could not deplete their resources further." She shook her head. "No. I will stay here. The Overhill is yet protected. If the Middle Towns should fall and the Anigilisi war tortoise make its way over the mountains, I expect we would hear about it in good time to make our escape to Aktiya Waya, if it indeed comes to that."

He could not deny her words, but he also did not want to test them.

"Don't worry about us, Kiyuga," she told him, as if hearing his thoughts. "Do what you can, what you are called to do, and protect those who are leaving. The journey to Atagulkalu's home is not very long. The Anigilisi will still be here when you return to go to battle yourself." She took his bowl and refilled it.

"I don't doubt that," he murmured, taking a bite of soup.

After a moment of silence, Sotsena spoke again. "While you are away, shall I brag of you to any of the girls who remain here?"

Kiyuga paused, mid-bite, feeling the blood rush to his face. Finally he said, "No, I don't think so."

"Really? None of them? Or perhaps she has already gone to Aktiya Waya?"

He shook his head. "No. There is no one."

Digvnige made a disapproving sound. "Kiyuga, it is not good for you to be alone this way. Advtowa is gone. Ayohli Tsiyo is also gone. It was a terrible loss. But it is time now for you to find a new wife and have children. This way you are not forgotten, and you will have someone to prepare you for battle when we are gone, to cook your food and mend your clothes. It is not good for a man to be alone for so long. I worry about Anagalisgi as well, but you are the one going to battle now."

"Please, uncle, I have not looked for a wife since Advtowa," Kiyuga sighed. "Even if I were, would it not be better for me to go to battle first, to claim spoils and return with them?"

"You already have plenty of spoils. You have a fine horse and many trinkets from the Anigilisi. The sorceries and Aktiya Waya consumed much of your time over the winter. This war will consume your summer. And then it will be winter again. Do not let time slip away from you so. Find a wife and have children. At least do so before your brother, and we both know he's not in a hurry."

It was a stunted attempt at humor, but Kiyuga couldn't help but grin. He couldn't speak as to why he was putting off remarriage. Yes, the sorceries and Aktiya Waya took up most of his time. Yes, the wound from Advtowa and Ayohli Tsiyo's deaths was healing. Yes, he'd forgiven his brother for withholding their deaths from him. What was it, then, that was holding him back from marriage now?

This war, for one, he figured, and he found himself with too little sleep behind his eyes as the sun rose. Digvnige woke him, and Sotsena both gave him a bit more food before sending them both off, Kiyuga to gather those who were leaving, Digvnige to the townhouse where he would fast and purify himself before battle, along with the rest of the warriors.

The group that was leaving was comprised mostly of elders and young children. Few women were in the group. Most were determined to assist their husbands as they went to war, whether through provisions and supplies or even going to war themselves. Some would stay behind the warriors, making camp here and there as needed. Others were prepared to take up arms, availing themselves as warriors against the Anigilisi. He was able, however, to convince a few of them to act as escort for the group. The Anigilisi were not yet arrived, but that didn't mean there were not other dangers in the mountains; he would need help.

Some of the horses dragged litters behind them, for the elders who could not well make the trip on their own power, or for those caring for especially young children who could not sit atop the beasts' backs. Kiyuga sat upon Amayi, circling the group a few times to ensure everyone was rounded up and well-prepared.

He'd sent two boys to run ahead to Atagulkalu and tell him and the sorcerers of their arrival. Perhaps they could meet on the trail so they did not have to make such a long journey, and then come up with some excuse for John Stuart who still knew nothing of the sorceries, or so Anagalisgi said.

There was no time left for tiptoeing around the issue. The Anigilisi were coming. They were a threat. Kiyuga had to get these elders and children to safety and then return swiftly to help his brothers in the fight. Part of him hated to be sent on this errand like a boy, and yet he could not deny the great responsibility placed upon him.

They started out later than he would have preferred, and they seemed to move excruciatingly slow. He tried to keep his mouth shut about it, told himself many times that it was only his perception. He could not allow himself to get so worked up, so anxious. The threat was real, but he had to face it with clarity, with certainty of mind. How would it be for him to jump and attack every shadow? How would it be for him to raise an alarm every time a snake moved in the brush? He was the leader here; he had to act like one.

All the same, any time they stopped to rest, he offered up any horses that had room on their backs. Many children could ride upon one, or a child and an elder, or perhaps two elders. A few took up the offer. Most were just as impatient as him to get to safety, but their bodies no longer responded to the wishes of their minds and spirits, and they were yet bound by a frail mortal shell.

Kiyuga wondered about that as well. It was a terrible endeavor for even one such as himself—young, strong, and strong-willed—to pass through the Galohisdi to Aktiya Waya. Traveling back and forth through the winter had been brutal. He'd watched elders go through before. While none had died, it had put a number of them in very precarious health, and some were not recovering well.

They did not make it very far the first day, in Kiyuga's opinion. He wanted to be there faster.

Wait. He could make that happen. What was he thinking? He could Iyuwahnilvhi Uhlisda Adahnesagi'a and make it so they arrived in half the time. Maybe they could even catch up to the runners he'd sent. Ha! And because they would be moving so swiftly, they would not have to worry about enemies in the trees. It would also give him a chance to show the sorcery to these people, who had been the most skeptical of it. He would show that it could be used for good, that it was not something to be feared, when used properly.

The following day, he did use the sorceries, conjuring Time as his brother had taught him. He did his best to explain it to the people beforehand, what he was going to do, and he knew that everyone had at least been exposed to the sorceries, that no one could claim ignorance. Nevertheless, it spooked several people when he did finally Iyuwhanilvhi Adahnesagi'a and brought everything around them to a standstill.

Conjuring was taxing work, though, especially for those who did not use it every day as Anagalisgi did. After a little while, with the sun still exactly where it had been in the early morning, Kiyuga began to get a headache that only worsened the more he thought about it. He was too grateful when the frightened elders asked him to stop conjuring for a while.

There was great debate on the road for a while after that. Elders traded their own theories on whether the magic was good or evil, where it had come from, and Anagalisgi's intentions. Kiyuga tried to defend his brother the best he could, but he was relieved when the children began asking for more stories and legends of ages past and the elders obliged.

Eventually, they stopped to rest a bit, let the children run around, give the elders a chance to slow down or stretch old bones, and give everyone a chance to refill their water skins.

"You really believe in this sorcery, don't you?" one of the elders asked, sitting next to him on the riverbank. "More than just indulging your brother or satisfying an idle curiosity, you truly believe in it."

"I believe it will save our people, yes," Kiyuga answered. "I believe it is a gift from the spirits to preserve our traditions and way of life."

The elder nodded. "If the spirits see fit to grant the stewards of the land the power to completely tear apart the fabric of that land, we are in very dire straits indeed."

"All will be well. You will be delivered to safety, and the warriors will defend the land."

He could see that few truly believed his words, but most were looking for any kind of reassurance, and they took it where they could get it.

Children and elders were rounded up, placed on horseback or in litters, and then they were off again. This time, Kiyuga did not conjure. His head throbbed, and he figured they'd made some decent progress from what conjuring he had done. He also told himself that he didn't need to spook anyone any more than he already had. He had demonstrated the sorceries, as he'd wanted. He also needed to demonstrate some restraint, that he was not dependent upon them. He was not addicted to them, as many of the Anigilisi goods were terribly addictive.

He wouldn't say he didn't want to use the sorceries, for he still felt very slow, but he couldn't.

And they plodded on.

The sun passed overhead, but the shade of the trees made the journey tolerable. Elders occupied the children with more stories. Warrior women kept an eye out for trouble.

They made camp that evening with no trouble. They lit a couple small fires, more for comfort than heat or cooking. Kiyuga volunteered for first watch as elders and children tucked in for the night.

He woke the following morning, grateful that his headache had subsided. He elected to refrain from conjuring until the evening, if it appeared that they would not reach Atagulkalu's cottage by the evening.

They had no such troubles. Atagulkalu and his household, including the two runners, met them on the road as the sun made its descending arc toward the horizon. Many were happy to speak to the skiagvsta in exile, but there were a few yet who disdained him, though they could not deny his help. It was their own choice, after all; they knew what they had agreed to.

"Thank you, Yvgidahi," Atagulkalu told him as they started toward his cottage. "You have done well to bring them here."

"I trust the runners told you of the plan?" Kiyuga questioned.

"Yes, they have told me everything. Nathan, Andrew, and I will see the children and elders to Aktiya Waya safely, so that you may return to Itsa'ti, or wherever the fighting may be." He grinned. "But until then, stay with us the night. You need to rest. I suspect that your return journey will not be so long as the trip up here."

Kiyuga felt his face burn hot. "I admit, I did conjure a bit to get us here faster."

"And you did well. Your brother is proud of you. So am I."

Atagulkalu put a hand on his shoulder briefly before moving to speak to someone else.

They arrived at Atagulkalu's home shortly before dark. A

comforting smell of herbs and meat wafted from it as Nayanali stood over a large fire. Nathan, Andrew, and John Stuart came to greet the party, taking their personal affects and horses and escorting the people closer to the fire. Many were leery of the white-skinned men, watching them as though they could turn on them at any moment. Kiyuga could not imagine that the men did not notice the subtle—and occasionally less subtle—animosity, but they said nothing about it. There were no confrontations, and they all took their places around the fire without incident.

Well, the adults took their places. The children, happy to be back in a home and able to freely run about, did just that. The darkness and the spirits beyond, as much as the temptation of food and a safe spot to sleep, kept them close to the cottage.

There were many questions about Aktiya Waya from the elders. How was it doing? How were the crops? The livestock? What foraging was there? How was the hunting? Kiyuga made a small gesture and managed to get Nathan's attention to speak privately.

"What does John Stuart know of Aktiya Waya?" Kiyuga asked quietly.

"He knows that it is an Aniyvwiya town, the last town, a secret town to hide the people from the British," Nathan answered.

"What do you tell him of it?"

"He's not been there, and he does not know even of the existence of the sorceries."

"That is not what I asked. What do you tell him of Aktiya Waya, and why you may go but he does not?"

"We tell him that Aktiya Waya is a secret town. We go only part of the way, as protection, for that is all we are permitted. We are allowed that much only by Atagulkalu's insistence. John Stuart is looked upon less favorably, despite being bought as Atagulkalu's brother, and it would be in his best interest to not press the matter."

Kiyuga frowned, but it was the best he was going to get. He'd wondered about it all winter but said nothing, trusting Atagulkalu to know how to handle it. But the Anigilisi were upon them now, and they couldn't mess up. They had been pushing so hard for people to go to Aktiya Waya for safety; they didn't need to bring an army to them now.

"I understand your fears," Nathan began. "Believe me when I say we share them. If the British army were to find us here and find out what we've been doing, that we've been helping you train to attack them, we could be hung as traitors."

For a long moment, they studied each other. Finally Kiyuga said, "Teach me Galohisdi."

"Portals?" Nathan wondered, eyebrows rising quite prominently on his face. "That's not something I would recommend. Even your brother is only just—"

"If things in battle go poorly, and if we must evacuate the towns swiftly to Aktiya Waya, we cannot wait for you or Andrew or my brother. Even the warriors with lesser abilities will be of little such assistance. Someone must know how to do this."

The sorcerer hummed and hawed and rocked on his heels a bit. He opened his mouth several times as if to say something, perhaps to protest, but nothing coherent was said for many moments. Finally he growled a bit to himself, rolled his neck and shoulders, made another long noise and said, "All right. All right, fine, you...you are correct. In a dire situation such as you describe, it might be advantageous to be able to open an emergency portal to Aktiya Waya. Yes, I will give you that argument."

"Then teach me."

"Yes, but not here in front of everyone."

"Where shall we go, then?"

"Now? Isn't it dangerous to go out in the dark?"

"What should a sorcerer of the spirits have to fear in the dark? Is his power inadequate? Is not Atsvstdi made for such an occasion?"

Nathan grunted. "You and your brother are more alike than you realize." He sighed. "Very well. I know a place."

He returned to the cottage just long enough to tell Andrew what they were doing. As expected, Andrew greatly disapproved, but it was happening. Then Nathan returned and he and Kiyuga headed off into the woods. After only a short trek, Nathan used Atsvstdi to light their way.

They came to a clearing and stopped. In the stillness of the evening, they could hear those gathered at the cottage. From a certain vantage, the faintest of light could be seen from the fire. Otherwise, they were secluded.

"Portals..." Nathan began awkwardly. "Portals appear as doors, but they are not like doors. A door may be opened a thousand times and it will always lead to the same place. Portals...Galohisdi, are a manipulation of the threshold that controls the destination."

"You speak foreign to me," Kiyuga cut in.

"You may open a door and discover where it leads. Galohisdi, you tell the door where it opens up to, wherever you are, and wherever you want to go."

"My only wish at this time would be to go to Aktiya Waya."

Nathan nodded once. "In order to do this, you must be aware of yourself, where you are, and you must also be aware of the place you wish to go. You must know it well, know it intimately. You must be a part of it."

Kiyuga frowned. "Is that why they are so difficult for you and Andrew? Because you are not part of this land or that land?"

The white-skinned man made another noise that tapered off into, "You and your brother are more alike than you realize." Then, normally, "Well, as I have told you many times and you have experienced for yourself, it never gets any easier. It is just as taxing when you are the one opening the portal.

"So, as I have said, you must be aware of yourself and the place you are in. You must know it well. You must know the earth, the air, the wind and rain. Likewise, you must know where you are going. You must be able to call it to mind as readily and as intimately as your own home. Do you understand what I am saying?"

Kiyuga shifted his stance. "I think I understand it well. I wonder whether you understand what you are saying."

Nathan winced at the comment but carried on. "Once you have become aware of yourself and where you are, as well as where you wish to go, you must then connect the two. It is not something easily explained, even in proper jargon, but to use terms you are familiar with, you must bridge the gap between islands."

Kiyuga considered this for a moment or two. "How does my brother do this? How does he see it?"

"Your brother has yet to open a stable portal, though he has begun to grasp the concept. How he does it, his method of bridging the gap, he has not disclosed to me."

"I would imagine it would be unique to him anyway." Kiyuga folded his arms.

"To be fair, the water between the islands that you must traverse is not a still pond. There is quite a current that you must fight."

"Does this current lead somewhere, or are you speaking only in metaphor?"

"It does lead somewhere," Nathan said surprisingly. "It leads to a maelstrom called the Wheel of Time."

"The business you have spoken of in the past."

"That's right. The Wheel holds the monopoly over interdimensional travel and similar portals, which sucks most of the energy away from transdimensional—I lost you, didn't I?" Nathan looked at Kiyuga guiltily.

Kiyuga just blinked.

Nathan shook his head and waved a hand. "No matter. Let's go back to the simple stuff. You need to get from one island to another, and you have to fight a great current into to build that bridge."

It was a simple enough explanation, but Kiyuga felt like he was missing something as he stood there, focused, concentrated, willed himself to do anything, and nothing happened. Once, he thought he may have felt a whisper of wind from the slopes outside of Aktiya Waya, but there was no Galohisdi to take him there.

After a while, still unsuccessful, and getting hungry and tired, Kiyuga finally gave up for the evening.

"Don't feel bad," Nathan told him as they returned to the cottage. "Galohisdi is one of the most difficult things to learn. It wouldn't be except for the current called the Wheel."

"I could feel it, I think," Kiyuga said. "It's as though something grabbed at me from dark waters and tried to pull me in."

Nathan nodded. "That would be it. That is the current you must fight in order to go from island to island."

"How are new islands discovered, then, if one is not aware of their existence, nor where or how far one must travel to reach them? How did you find Aktiya Waya?"

"It's an exploration, but always with the current trying to pull you under." Nathan shrugged. "As I said, it shouldn't be as difficult as it is except for the Wheel."

"Is there any way to make it easier?"

Nathan chuckled. "This is 'easier.' Most human Time Agents can't even travel to the Wheel by themselves because the current will drown them, the Galohisdi collapses. It takes a group of them to pull it off, or they have to seek out the Dominion Timekeeper who is probably the only one strong enough to open Galohisdi single-handedly."

"Why not teach everyone the sorceries, then, if it is in their best interest?"

By now they had reached the cottage. Nathan gave Kiyuga a look and said, "Because that's assuming that people want what's best for themselves and others."

They spoke no more of the training or the sorceries that night, and Kiyuga was awake before dawn the following morning, ready to go. Atagulkalu thanked him, assured him the elders and children would be well, and sent him on his way.

Once the sun was well up and he was a fair distance away from Atagulkalu, Kiyuga began conjuring. He felt as though he'd lost a whole moon since leaving Itsa'ti, though it had been only a few days. He had to hurry and make up for lost time. He had to catch up to the warriors heading to Itse'yi and help them.

He kept up the conjuring as long as he could, figuring he got about half a day of travel before he could stand it no longer. He hadn't done excessive conjuring necessarily—he hadn't made it so everything around him came to a complete standstill—instead electing to just move quickly. Nevertheless, his head throbbed, his eyes hurt, and even the gentle movement of Amayi under him was making him nauseous. He carried on for the rest of the day, grateful for the sinking sun and retreating light.

He managed to shave a little time off his return trip, though he was unsure if his illness was worth it. He knew it would eventually subside once he got a few days' rest, but illness could make an otherwise stoic warrior blanch at the thought of battle, and Kiyuga was no exception. He stayed at his aunt and uncle's home overnight in Itsa'ti before carrying on.

The rest of the war party had already gone, left for Itse'yi. Many elders, women, children, and a few others had fled for the safety of Aktiya Waya. As Kiyuga passed through the various towns on his way out of the Overhill, he was struck by how empty they all looked. It was more than just an empty home that someone intended to return to, for one would leave a fire burning, food cooking, clothes that needed mending, a basket that needed weaving, or any number of small projects to come back for. Rather, there was the feeling of total abandonment, that whoever had lived here had no intention of returning soon. Few items had been left in the empty houses. Even among those who had stayed behind, Kiyuga could see that they were half-packed, ready to move quickly if need be.

It made the hair on the back of his neck stand up, as though he were prey being hunted. The Anigilisi were coming. The war tortoise was moving. The Aniyvwiya had to turn them back at Itse'yi or there would be no hope. The pass was their best bet.

The thought put a fire under Kiyuga once more, and he started conjuring again, willing himself and Amayi to go faster. His head ached and he scaled it back a bit, hoping that less effort would carry him longer than a burst of strength quickly fizzled out. He was uncertain of his success in this line of thinking, and he became less certain of it the more his head throbbed.

Nevertheless, he caught up to the war party in good time as they traversed the road through the Middle Towns.

"Ah, Yvgidahi!" Adahi greeted cheerfully, slapping him on the back from his own mount. Kiyuga nearly fell off Amayi. "You made it!"

"I couldn't let you have all the fun," Kiyuga said, trying to stay upright and not be ill.

"I think there will be more than enough fun to go around," Yvgi told him. "If the war tortoise intends on suffering through battle to advance its cause, we may have to strike at it numerous times."

The traveling itself was a rather solemn affair. Kiyuga attempted to conjure Time around the entire war party, but it was a rather stressful endeavor, and illness and fatigue was not good for a traveler in the high hills and mountains. They were moving swiftly enough, he figured. They didn't need his help. The conjuring would be better saved for battle when lives were at stake.

Sitting around campfires at night, however, proved a much different atmosphere. Camping just north of Tesenti, solemnity was replaced with great boasting of deeds long past or conquests yet to be had. Not a few stories of the last battle at Itse'yi worked their way through the party, each man bragging of his daring exploits against the Anigilisi. This quickly turned into great songs of Saloli and his sacrifice, as well as the others who had died in the pass.

Kiyuga was honored as well, for his role in serving under Mankiller and using the sorceries to aid the warriors. Looking around, he saw that many appeared enthusiastic about the sorceries, giddy at the thought of using the British sorceries against the British themselves. And yet, Kiyuga knew that only a few handfuls of the warriors had any decent sort of skill. The rest, if they knew anything at all, only had paltry skills. What was it, then? Did they expect it to be as the adawehi, where many may show a bit of talent but only a few were chosen to master it? Perhaps. He supposed it made sense.

But he was no adawehi, and there were several warriors who couldn't interpret visions to save their lives but could conjure quite readily. How did this Author choose her servants? Clearly Anagalisgi was the best of them, but he was an adawehi. What about the rest of them?

A couple of runners came to them in the morning with a relayed message from the watchers at Estato.

"The war tortoise is moving," they reported. "Many thousands of soldiers and a great train of pack animals. They are coming up out of Fort Prince George. It looks as though they will attempt the same advance as before. They send scouts ahead to burn fields and forest."

"They will do the same to the villages," someone said with an echo of agreement among the party.

"We must hurry to reach Itse'yi," Amadoya stated, raising his voice some. "We cannot allow the Anigilisi to breach the pass or we will be overrun."

That set a fire under the war party and they redoubled their efforts to move quickly through the mountains. The only comfort Kiyuga could take in their travels was that if they were having this much trouble moving their war party through the mountains, how much more difficult would it be for the Anigilisi? The Anigilisi were very good at force and brute strength, but such things could only take a man or an army so far. With any luck, the mountains themselves would push them back and grant the Aniyvwiya victory.

They did not stop in Tesenti as originally planned, nor Kawise or Nikwasi except for small groups of warriors designated to stay in Nikwasi or Tawsi to act as relief warriors if things did not go as planned in Itse'yi. Kiyuga was not part of those small groups and he continued on with the rest of them.

When they reached Itse'yi, the village itself was mostly abandoned, the residents fled to nearby towns or into the forest. Only a few remained, including a couple of messengers from Estato.

"What news?" Mankiller demanded of them.

"The war tortoise comes, and it grows bigger with each day," one reported.

"How far out?" Aganstata asked.

"Some days," the second messenger said.

Mankiller frowned. "Either they weight themselves too heavily, or they are not concerned with speed."

"Whatever the case, they cannot claim to be attempting to conceal themselves," Amadoya scoffed. "They are arrogant fools."

"Maybe, but a fool can still inflict great damage if our backs are turned," Aganstata mused sagely. "We will stay here for tonight and move into the pass tomorrow." To the runners he said, "Return to Estato and report back when they are within two days of us."

The messengers nodded, turned, and ran off.

So it was that the war party stayed in Itse'yi that night. Kiyuga lay awake, staring at the sky, wondering if they would be so lucky this second time, or if this great war tortoise would indeed prevail and trick the hare.

DᏯᎧᏁᏍT ᏔᏢᏍᏗᎪ ᏦT

Ayadohlv'i Tahlsgo Tso'i

The Rules of the Enemy

There was a story told among the people of the tortoise and the hare. The hare challenged the tortoise to a race, and so they agreed on a time and place. The tortoise went home and spoke to his family of the race and how he might win. When the tortoise and the hare came together at the appointed time and place for this race, the hare gave the tortoise a head start, figuring that he himself was so fast that it wouldn't matter. And they started, the tortoise moving first in his head start.

When the tortoise reached the first of seven hills, the hare saw him go up and over the top, and he took off. When the hare reached the top of the first hill, he looked at the second hill and saw the tortoise going up and over the top. And the same for the third, fourth, fifth, and sixth hills. Each time, the hare moved faster and faster, and when he reached the seventh hill, he looked down and saw the tortoise crossing the finish line. The hare, too exhausted to see how all tortoises look the same, tried to sprint to the finish line but he collapsed before crossing.

The secret to the race was that the tortoise and his family had taken up a relay. The first tortoise went to the start line. The second tortoise went to the first hill that the rabbit might see him. The next tortoise went to the next hill and so on, all the way to the finish line.

So it was that the Aniyvwiya were also tricked. The war tortoise of the Anigilisi made a grand show of things around Estato, aggravating the warriors who were waiting for them but not moving especially fast. Five days into the wait, Mankiller himself went to Estato and sneaked up close to the Anigilisi camp.

"It's a ruse!" he cried as he rode back to the war party, still camped north of the pass. "We've been tricked! Hurry up! Ride! Ride!"

"What's going on?!" Amadoya demanded, throwing his few possessions over the back of his horse and quickly mounting.

"It has been all a trick of smoke and shadows," Mankiller said. "The war tortoise moves west. They will reach Gatogatsa'yi by sunset tomorrow. Hunters from Gatogatsa'yi told me this in Estato."

"How shall we get there so quickly?" someone wondered.

"It will take too long to go to Estato and around," Aganstata considered. "And their smoke and shadows are likely to engage in battle and keep us distracted while the tortoise moves toward Ayuhwa'si Eghawa."

"We'll have to cut across," Chola decided. "We can go back to Itse'yi and cut across to the west, come at Gatogatsa'yi from the north."

"Agreed," Aganstata said, nodding. He motioned Kiyuga closer. "Yvgidahi, can you conjure us there quicker?"

Kiyuga inwardly balked. "I can do my best, and I will, but we would have to get there in good enough time so I may rest before battle."

Amadoya snorted indignantly.

"Good enough," the skiagvsta figured. He turned his horse and started off, barking commands to any who were still slacking to hurry up.

Once everyone was rounded up, Kiyuga did his best to conjure Time for the whole party. He had a difficult time of it in the beginning for all the worry on his mind. They had been tricked, distracted by the smoke and shadows near Estato while the war tortoise marched happily unopposed to Gatogatsa'yi. They could not go by way of Estato, for they would surely be engaged by the distracting force. But while the soldiers near Estato may have been a distraction now, that did not mean they were distraction only. Once they learned that the war party had moved west to Gatogatsa'yi, they would still have the strength to attempt to move through the pass to Itse'yi.

When they reached Itse'yi, Kiyuga rode up beside Aganstata and voiced these fears. The skiagvsta appeared grave but unsurprised.

"Yes, Yvgidahi," he said calmly. "I have considered this. Some warriors will stay here to defend Itse'yi. But I still want you with us, to conjure Time to get us there before our enemies."

Kiyuga frowned. "I can only try, skiagvsta."

"That is all I can ask. I will help how I can, but I'm counting on you."

They did not stay in Itse'yi long, just long enough to separate out a small warrior force to stay in Itse'yi, water the horses, and quickly eat a bit of food before their hard press to Gatogatsa'yi.

Kiyuga's heart was racing as he conjured for all he was worth. He found himself thinking that they should have brought Anagalisgi. Even if he stayed on the sidelines to merely observe the battlefield, he was the one they needed for this kind of conjuring. Kiyuga was not the conjurer his brother was, even with Aganstata helping.

Worry aside, the ride itself was also very distracting for him. It was easy to ride cross-country around the Overhill or the Lower Towns, and perhaps the easy terrain with the conjuring would have delivered them faster. The Middle Town landscape was not so forgiving with steep slopes, sharp rocks, thick trees, and any number of threats about. There were several occasions when they had to slow to a crawl and make their way through a narrow pass only three abreast, navigating treacherous footing that made even the most stoic of horses nervous. Having to pay attention to such things waned Kiyuga's ability to conjure.

They kept on as long as Kiyuga assured Aganstata he could still manage. His head hurt and he felt sick to his stomach, but he felt just as bad about himself and his inability to conjure well like his brother. Only when he was in danger of falling off his horse did Aganstata call for them to rest.

When they'd left Itse'yi, it had been midmorning. It was late afternoon now of the same day, though they had been traveling for two days with few breaks.

"Rest, Yvgidahi," Aganstata told him. "You have done well."

The skiagvsta didn't look so excellent himself, Kiyuga thought. Aganstata looked a bit pale, a bit tight in the stomach as though he were about to have a fateful episode of either the stomach or bowels, and he moved with such deliberation that came about only when a drunk man is putting all his effort into appearing not drunk.

Kiyuga decided to wait to eat until after he'd rested. Sleep was not difficult to find and he happily lapsed into slumber.

He again dreamed of seeing his brother on the road but with an invisible wall between them. Again, Kiyuga saw the man running away, but when he turned, he saw only the man's back and could not identify who it was. Nor could he get his attention or ascertain exactly what was happening, how it would come to be, or what it meant. He looked at Anagalisgi for answers, but when his brother spoke, it was not in his voice. Nor were they words that made sense.

"Wake up," he said.

That was something Kiyuga might say to Anagalisgi. Wake up, little brother, and join us in the waking world.

"Wake up, Kiyuga," he said again, still not in his voice.

The waking world found Kiyuga as violently as a club to the head and he startled awake, momentarily confused why the running man looked like Adahi. Then he realized that it was Adahi who was trying to shake him awake.

"Is there trouble?" Kiyuga asked dumbly, looking around in the dim light as the sun sank below the horizon.

"No," Adahi answered. "We're moving again. Do you think you can conjure?"

Just the thought of conjuring was enough to make Kiyuga's head throb. Nevertheless, he sighed and nodded. Adahi gave him a hand up and the warrior brought Amayi to him.

"I figured I would get your horse and things ready so you could rest," Adahi told him. "I don't know if you notice much when you are conjuring, but many here can see the effort you put into it."

"Oh," Kiyuga said, unsure how to respond. "Thank you."

"Some may question the sorceries still, but I don't know of any warrior who questions you."

Kiyuga tried to take pride in the statement, but from the corner of his eye, he saw Amadoya on his horse, looking around. Amadoya had little love for the sorceries, everyone knew. How was he reacting to this, then?

Trying not to dwell on it, Kiyuga got on Amayi's back and turned the horse around to join the others. Aganstata nosed his horse up beside him.

"Did you sleep well?" he asked kindly.

"I would have slept better if I'd been allowed to rest for a few more moons," Kiyuga said, trying to find some humor.

Aganstata managed a polite smile. "Yes, I understand. Truly, I do. Can you continue to conjure us through another leg of our journey? I want to take advantage of what light remains."

"I understand," Kiyuga told him humbly.

When the rest of the warriors had been roused and readied, they started off again in the dusky twilight. Kiyuga forced himself not to balk as he conjured again, bringing everyone in as they rode.

He could well say that he did not conjure as long or as well as he had before. While he knew they rode well past what they normally would have been able to with the onset of darkness, it was not the same as what he'd hoped to accomplish, nor what they'd done earlier. When they finally stopped for the night, a few warriors gave him uncertain or sideways glances, but Aganstata merely thanked him and told him to sleep well.

"I'll take care of Amayi," Adahi said, taking the reins as Kiyuga stumbled along. "You should take care of yourself. We will need all the warriors we have to beat back the Anigilisi."

Kiyuga may have thanked him; he couldn't remember. He couldn't remember where he lay down or even when he fell asleep, it happened so quickly.

They were awake at the first light of dawn, when murky blackness turned to a just discernible gray. Kiyuga would say he felt pretty good, though it was still a chore to slog back to consciousness and be ready.

Blearily, he mounted Amayi and joined the group.

"I attempted to conjure Time for you," Aganstata said. "So that you might get more sleep. Did it help?"

"I believe it did," Kiyuga told him. "But it would take more than one rest to fully recover."

"Yes, the conjuring is as strenuous as Nathan and Andrew said, and even more besides."

"I will still conjure us as best I can."

"For the morning, yes. We must get as close as possible to Gatogatsa'yi. But in the afternoon, you will not. You will rest and recover well so that you may fight alongside us."

The relief that Kiyuga felt upon hearing this was probably what kept up his strength for the first ride that morning. They had navigated the worst part of the terrain, twisting and turning through the mountains, and were now moving largely downhill. By the time they stopped to rest, with the sun just hovering over the horizon, Kiyuga felt confident that they would reach their destination well ahead of the Anigilisi.

They got in two rides before the sun reached its high point and Aganstata told Kiyuga not to conjure anymore. Mankiller objected.

"We are not yet well near to Gatogatsa'yi," he said. "The Anigilisi will be there before sunset, if they are not there now. We must press on. We may suffer one less warrior to fight than have nothing to fight over when we arrive."

"The rest of us must rest also," Aganstata told him. "The conjuring is unusual and wreaks havoc upon any caught in its wake. We cannot let our own spirits and bodies betray us in our time of need."

Mankiller looked as though he had more to say. Amadoya, a few steps away but still within the conversation, looked displeased as well. But whatever the two warriors were thinking, they did not say aloud. Instead, after a moment of tense hesitation, they ceded to Aganstata.

"We are not so far from Gatogatsa'yi," the skiavsta went on, apparently attempting to lighten the mood and encourage them. "Over this hill and the next and it will be a swift descent upon our enemies."

If his words had any uplifting effect, it was muted at best, Kiyuga thought. He did not offer his opinion as he dismounted and went to find a good place to lie down.

He would not say he was not tired, but with the thought of battle so close, he found that fatigue alone was not enough to bring him to sleep. Eventually he fell asleep, but not before wondering how much time and sleep his nerves had cost him.

He again dreamed of his brother, although it was not the same dream of separation and the running man. This time, it appeared as a simple forest clearing, and Anagalisgi looked rather pleased about something.

"Ah ha, so it can be done!" his brother said, grinning.

"What can be done?" Kiyuga wondered, moving closer until they were within comfortable conversation range.

"Conversing through dreams."

"It's the middle of the day. Why should you be asleep?"

Anagalisgi gave him an odd look. "I don't sleep to rest, Kiyuga, or not only. I sleep to dream and to learn."

"How did you know I would be asleep, then?"

"I didn't. I got lucky, I suppose. Or the spirits guided me to you."

"Do you have a message for me?" Kiyuga intended to stop there and wait politely for an answer, but then the words started tumbling from his mouth. "We encountered the soldiers south of Estato. We retreated to Itse'yi to wait for them to come into the pass, but it was only a distraction. The war tortoise heads for Gatogatsa'yi. We've ridden hard over the mountains and I have worked hard to conjure our war party so we may reach them in time but I am not as skilled as you and I don't know if we'll make it."

He went to his knees in utter exhaustion. He didn't even know it was possible to be tired in a dream. Was that not the point of sleep?

Anagalisgi frowned and knelt in front of him. He put his hands on Kiyuga's shoulders.

"Be strong, brother," Anagalisgi said softly. "We have done all we can. Our time is coming."

"Our time to die?" Kiyuga questioned.

"Our time to fulfill our destinies, the ones spoken of us since we were children."

For a long moment, neither of them spoke. Then Kiyuga asked, "Who is the running man?"

His brother blinked. "The running man?" He looked around.

"I have a dream that comes to me from time to time. You and I stand apart on a road. I go to you, but there is an invisible wall between us and I never reach you. Lately, there has been more to the dream that when I reach the wall, someone comes out of it. I don't see his face beforehand, and when I turn, I see only his back. I call out, but he does not turn or slow down. Do you know who it is? Or the meaning of this dream?"

Anagalisgi frowned and huffed a sigh. "As I said, our time is coming when we will fulfill our destinies."

"But you know who the running man is?"

"I do not."

"You know the meaning of the dream?"

His brother hesitated. "Think not on it yet. I expect you will be waking soon and going to battle even sooner. Focus your energy on that. We will speak when you return."

Kiyuga didn't like the sound of that, didn't like where it was going, but he couldn't question an adawehi about his dreams. He wasn't even certain that this was real. On the other hand, if he returned to Itsa'ti and his brother brought it up, then it would only prove that his brother could communicate in dreams.

"Is there anything you wish for me to impart to those who remain here?" Anagalisgi wondered. "Anything I should tell them, or perhaps Atagulkalu?"

For a moment, Kiyuga couldn't remember anything. Finally he said, "The Anigilisi are heavily armed and well supplied. They will not be stopping at this town or that outpost to rest and resupply. This war tortoise intends to continue on until it has fulfilled its mission."

Anagalisgi frowned. "Well, I think we know what its mission is.

Thank you. I will let them know."

"How are things at home? How is Sotsena, that I may tell Digvnige?"

"She longs for him, naturally, but she is well. Otherwise, we wait only for you and the others."

Kiyuga was ready to say more, but the dream began to fade, twisting into light that became the sun. He squinted and put his hand up to shield his eyes until he could sit up and look around.

The sun hadn't moved much, and yet Kiyuga felt oddly refreshed. Around him, others were also waking, digging into food stores, grabbing water, and wandering off to find a tree or bush. While there was no shouting to hurry and wake up, there was a certain sense of urgency that told Kiyuga that they were going to ride into battle, and the skiagvsta wanted to be quiet about it.

Kiyuga freshened himself and went to find Amayi, grazing contentedly amid the throng of horses scattered through the forested hillside. The stallion snorted and pawed irritably as Kiyuga guided it away, back toward the camp.

"I think we're about to ride into something really terrible," Kiyuga murmured as he readied his mount. "We are one body, one soul. Your strength shall become my strength. If you bleed, I bleed."

The horse looked at him with dark eyes, then snorted again, tossed his head, and pawed the ground once as Kiyuga climbed on his back.

"I think he's ready to go to battle," Adahi said, riding up beside him on an equally anxious steed. "I think they all are. They know what must be done."

Kiyuga frowned and looked toward the hill they had to climb. "I hope so, because I don't."

"Trust his instincts, and let the spirits guide you."

Soon enough, Aganstata was rounding everyone up and they were moving out, riding down the short slope to the next hill. As they reached the top of the hill, Kiyuga could see faint smoke in the distance. He was not the only one, as the party picked up the pace. They neared the last rise and finally broke.

Gatogatsa'yi was little more than smoldering rubble, the grassy pastures and full croplands now charred ruins. To the north, the war party could see the war tortoise moving off, up river, to its next target.

Sudden rage overtaking them, Amadoya, Aganstata, and Mankiller led the charge. Amayi, seeing the wide open land and the spirits of his brothers, bolted down the hill with the rest of them, powerful muscles gliding with the wind, Kiyuga merely a minor inconvenience on his back.

They came upon the Anigilisi as a great wave. Their cover was limited, though the thunder of hooves and the whoops and hollers of the warriors gave them away well in advance regardless. Kiyuga, still just a thing on his horse's back, bounced along haphazardly in the confusion, occasionally swinging out with his knife or firing off a wild shot from his pistol. Then Amayi peeled off toward the right— whichever direction that happened to be—following a small group of warriors as they fled while the Anigilisi made their proper formations.

They snaked through the trees, heading back the way they came, circling around to the tail of the tortoise. Kiyuga cut down a couple of the pack animals before being run off. He circled again, following another group of warriors trying to break a group of riflemen who had formed up. They couldn't get close enough and eventually broke off the attack.

By now, more soldiers had come to reinforce their fellows. Somewhere in the confusion of battle, Kiyuga heard Aganstata call for a retreat. As swiftly as the attack had begun, it was over. Word got around quickly, and the war party retreated south, back to Gatogatsa'yi.

The ride was swift, but no longer a panicked rage, and Kiyuga and Amayi once again rode as one entity. Head still swirling from battle, they found themselves in the middle of the herd.

"One warrior for a town!" Amadoya was saying when Kiyuga arrived. Amadoya, Aganstata, Mankiller, and some of the other skiagvsta and senior warriors stood in a circle in what used to be the townhouse of Gatogatsa'yi.

"We did more than we would have, had we continued to wait in Itse'yi or tried any other route," Mankiller rebutted. "We are fortunate to have done what we did."

"And what did we do?" Amadoya hissed. "Kill a few donkeys and perhaps a few helping hands? The war tortoise barely felt a scratch."

"Maybe, but we are still well within striking distance now," Aganstata stated. "The tortoise follows the river. With or without conjuring sorceries, we can cut across the land straight to Aquohi and arrive well before them. We will have a good vantage there to defend Aquonatutse, Aquohi, and Ayuhwa'si Eghawa. The tortoise cannot take all three at once, and they will be tired from the journey. If we conjure Time and get there even faster, we will have more time to rest and gather our strength."

Amadoya did not seem overly enthused about the idea, but it placated him for the time being.

"We will rest and see to our wounded," Mankiller said calmly. "In the morning, we will head for Aquohi."

Kiyuga joined a group of warriors tasked with scouring the ruined village for bodies, survivors, or anything of use. The Anigilisi had done a thorough job in their attack, for little remained for them to salvage. If there was any good news, it was that there had been few people left in the village and they found no bodies.

Once they were certain that they'd scavenged everything they could and made sure the war tortoise wasn't coming back for a secondary attack, they got together around a fire to eat and brood.

"I suppose we shouldn't be surprised," one warrior grumbled. "The Anigilisi are master deceivers."

"They make the rabbit look almost angelic," another muttered in agreement.

"The armor of a tortoise, the claws of a cougar, and the cleverness of a coyote," a third, hardly more than a boy, said. "How are we supposed to defeat them?"

"The sorceries brought us this far," Kiyuga mentioned casually. "They will get us to Aquohi, and they can carry us in battle. They did at Itse'yi."

"Then why didn't they carry us in battle today?"

Kiyuga met the boy's gaze but could fashion no good answer. Because he was inexperienced. Because he was weak. Because he was exhausted. These were all the truth, but the truth was no comfort here. Finally he said, "We can only do what we can do. The sorcery is a tool, and a tool is not salvation. It is our faith, our trust, and our purity that will save us."

He knew the look the boy had. He knew what the boy was feeling. The boy was finally realizing the difference between the stories he had heard from the elders, both of war and of myth, and the reality of life. He wanted to believe that things were like the stories, and that war was always glorious. He was slowly learning that neither was true. Kiyuga knew this because he remembered feeling the same way once.

"Well, if nothing else, we always have Aktiya Waya," the first warrior mused. "I'm no coward for war, which is why I'm here, but I think I'd much rather leave this place and go there where the tortoise cannot crush us."

"And leave our ancestral lands and spirits?" someone challenged. "There is a fine line between caution and cowardice, but that to me sounds like cowardice."

"What good will the lands do if it is scorched and devastated? What good will the spirits do if there are no reverent living to guide?" a third wondered.

Kiyuga took a measured breath and did his best not to get involved. He struggled with these questions himself almost daily, assuming he could spare a thought to them when he wasn't conjuring. It hurt to consider the thought of leaving their lands and spirits. Moving from one village to another was one thing, for it was all Aniyvwiya land. But to abandon it completely? And the burial mounds and the bodies and spirits of their dead?

And yet, Anagalisgi had said that the wolf had been waiting for them. Was that a sign from the spirits that they must leave? Had they foreseen this tragedy and so given the living a way to avoid it? Were they foolish for trying to fight? Was this all a vain effort and they should flee while they had the chance?

He looked around the burned village at the warriors gathered around their various campfires. If they had to choose today whether to stay or flee, and if that decision were to be permanent, he knew a good majority of this group would follow Amadoya and stay. But if he had to make that choice, he would follow his brother and go to Aktiya Waya. Would he be considered a coward? Maybe. But what good was being alive when even the chance of going back to the old life was gone?

The same conversation was happening at many of the campfires, all just slightly varied. If things got tense and loud, usually someone would step in to quiet them. Even if the tortoise had moved on, they did not need to advertise their position to anything else that could be out there. They still didn't know what had happened to the distracting force at Estato.

Gradually, the warriors fell into slumber, less a small watch force. The voices quieted and the fires died down. Eventually, the warriors around Kiyuga's fire decided sleep to be their best option, and he wasn't going to argue with them.

He slept better than he thought he would, but he supposed that could be attributed to having to recover from all his conjuring. His mind was awake and struggling with many things, but his body demanded rest, and so rest it got. He knew he slept. He knew when he was sleeping. He did not remember any dreams from that night. When he woke, he felt rather refreshed. He did not feel fully perfect, but he certainly felt very good. When he caught Mankiller's eye across the clearing and made a quizzical gesture, the skiagvsta simply nodded once and carried on with whatever he had been doing.

It was simple enough to pack up, and with the threat of the war tortoise on the move, motivation to get going was high. Kiyuga was soon on Amayi's back, waiting for everyone to assemble and be underway.

He wasn't even sure that the skiagvsta ensured everyone's

preparedness before moving out. Perhaps by this point, they expected everyone to have an idea of what was required and to either keep up or drop out. Time was of the essence. They had missed their last chance by half a day; they could not afford to be late to their next battle.

Kiyuga did not conjure that day as they sprinted northwest toward Aquohi. Scouts were frequently sent out to report on the tortoise's progress, which they said was remarkably speedy. James Grant was no fool. He'd evidently spent the winter planning every detail of his attack, not only the maneuvers in battle, but all the boring stuff in between. It was both respectable and infuriating.

The second day, Kiyuga conjured. He was not asked, but he couldn't not do it. The last time he had rested, Gatogatsa'yi had burned. One man for a village was unacceptable. His brothers could fight well without him, but there would be no fighting at all if they were not there to stop this war tortoise from burning more villages.

It was frustrating enough to see the smoke rising above the trees, many miles from where they rode. The tortoise burned everything in front of and behind it. Kiyuga remembered the sorcerers Nathan and Andrew once saying that fire was difficult, if not impossible to control, and conjuring could actually make it worse. As Kiyuga looked at the smoke overhead, he wondered how true it was, and if he wasn't indeed making things worse by conjuring. But they would be near Aquohi soon enough, several days' travel in only half a day. Then he could stop conjuring, letting himself and the fire rest a bit.

They were able to gather a few more warriors in Aquohi before heading east to Aquonatutse, where the tortoise would arrive first.

Anyone who had even the most paltry conjuring abilities was made to rest so that they would be ready when the Anigilisi finally came. Warriors were posted on watch at all times of day, and scouts were sent out frequently. Finally, one returned with news, and it wasn't good.

"Grant has split his forces. The distraction force at Estato breached the pass and burned Itse'yi. They are making their way through the Middle Towns even now. The tortoise from Gatogatsa'yi has also split itself, some coming this way, another force seeking to cross over the hills to Konehete."

Kiyuga watched Aganstata's countenance become paler and more slack with each word.

"We don't have the warriors to split in such a way and fight all three," Mankiller hissed.

"We don't have the same numbers," Amadoya growled. "But we have the warriors." He knelt beside Aganstata. "Send me and a thousand warriors to chase the tortoise bound for Konehete. We will stop them there and travel north and east to meet the force in the valley and stop them before they reach Tesenti, or Kawise, or wherever they may be."

Aganstata hesitated. Finally, "Agreed. Take as many warriors as you feel is necessary. No doubt this is the distracting force now so that Grant may reach the Overhill. He is heading for Itsa'ti. Of this I am certain."

Grumbling rippled through the gathered warriors.

Aganstata looked at Amadoya. "Go, now, before the tortoise reaches Aquonatutse and the Anigilisi see you, think that we are abandoning the village."

Amadoya did not need to be told twice. In fact, he was already hollering for his chosen warriors who were already packed up and mounting their horses. Kiyuga was not among them.

"Have we done the right thing?" Mankiller wondered aloud.

"The spirits will guide us, as they have always done," Aganstata said. "If this is the distracting force coming upon us, then we should have no trouble defeating them. Amadoya took no skilled sorcerers. Once we have finished with the Anigilisi here, we will join him."

Mankiller frowned but did not argue.

If Aganstata had any advantage, it was that his force was comprised of mostly seasoned warriors or sensible young men. Amadoya had taken many of the anxious warriors, most of them younger and less experienced. Their youth and ambition would serve them better than bumbling sorcery, Kiyuga knew. He would not say he was not worried, but he did not fear as he might have otherwise.

"So what do we do?" he dared to ask aloud.

"We will stay here and wait for the tortoise to come to us," Aganstata stated. "Force the enemy to expend himself to get to us. In the meantime, we will plan."

"What about when the fires come?" Adahi wondered. "The Anigilisi burn everything in their path, and the fires will spread and reach us before the tortoise gets here. He tries to smoke us out, like animals fleeing before a fire. Then he meets no resistance in the towns which he then burns to ensure we cannot return."

"We will wait," Aganstata repeated firmly. He pointed east. "When the scouts return and report the tortoise is just over that rise, then we will disappear into the surrounding land. When they come upon Aquonatutse and set it on fire, we will surround them, force them to burn in their own flames!" He looked around at those gathered. "As they have left our towns and lands, so we will leave them!" He lowered his voice. "Nothing left."

There was much cheering and excited chatter after that, each man again boasting of his past victories or future endeavors. Kiyuga also partook, but eventually made his way to the townhouse to speak to Aganstata again.

"I can see the concern on your face," Aganstata began, taking a drink from his skin. "I don't need to be your brother or a dreamer to see such things. What troubles you?"

"The conjuring," Kiyuga answered. "Anagalisgi, Nathan, and Andrew have repeatedly warned of the dangers of attempting to conjure fire, or even near fire. I know my brother has attempted such, and has been successful, but never without injury to himself, even minor wounds around small cooking fires. If we are to ambush them in the flames, I will not be able to conjure us."

Aganstata nodded slowly. "I understand. They told me the same things, and I've no reason to doubt them. But I also have no reason to think that this will be a difficult fight. They use fire as a weapon, but I do not believe they understand it, and they are certainly not in control of it. Turn that weapon against them, and they will panic. They will try to escape. And we will not let them."

"Aquonatutse is a small village."

"Yes, but a distracting force is just that. A distraction. Smoke and shadows, as a small bird puffs out its chest to make itself appear bigger. They are meant to buy Grant time to split his forces, decimate the Middle Towns, and regroup before heading for Itsa'ti. But they underestimate our own capabilities, such as our scouts to tell us that he has done these things, and so anticipate them, and resist them, as Amadoya is doing even now."

"They don't fight like we do."

Aganstata laughed at that. "You are quite right. They certainly do not fight as we do. They are louder, more obvious, bumbling—"

"Stronger, faster, and with greater weapons," Kiyuga interrupted. "Aganstata, we make jest of them and laugh at their ways, but if their ways were not superior, I don't think we would be here. I don't think we would be relying on sorceries to give us a chance. I don't think we would be discussing how to turn their weapons against them if ours were superior in any way."

Now the skiagvsta looked rather displeased, but not without a shadow of understanding. He sighed. "I understand, Yvgidahi. We all do. The safety and stability of the people is all we care about. Sometimes, this is achieved through words. Sometimes, in battle. But a lost battle does not mean a lost war. And if words may achieve more than fighting, if it will preserve the people, then that is what we will do. In this moment, the Anigilisi believe that peace means that we will simply submit, as their slaves submit. That is not our definition of peace. Our peace may now only be achieved through battle."

"I want to understand, but I don't. This is an enemy unlike any in the stories."

Aganstata nodded. "I know." He sighed and murmured. "I know." He looked up at Kiyuga. "Go now and rest. When the time comes, conjure when you can, but know well when it is more beneficial to stop."

Kiyuga dipped his head and left the townhouse. He would not say he was afraid of battle, for that was a given, and so common that it may as well be ignored. He could not say that he was afraid of the Anigilisi, for that was largely untrue. He did not fear death, for it was the way of things.

If anything, he supposed he feared failure. He feared having to return to Itsa'ti—or perhaps whatever remained of it—and explain himself, his lack of skill in battle or conjuring, perhaps a lack of courage. He feared having to go to Aktiya Waya and tell the people that they would never return home, for there was no home to return to. Somehow, he feared it would be his fault.

His fear saw him into a fitful sleep. If there was any comfort, it was that he did not have the dream of his brother on the road. Somehow, he was afraid that would be his fault, too, whatever it meant.

It was another two days before the scouts reported the tortoise within striking distance. They were camping just over the hill where they could not be seen from Aquonatutse. When asked if they had been able to get close enough to hear anything of value, anything of the tortoise's strategic plans, the scouts said no.

"Distraction or not, they are very well-armed, well-prepared for whatever it is they intend to do," one of the scouts said.

"Naturally," Mankiller said, his voice level. "They were not planning on stopping at Aquonatutse, but to carry on to Ayuhwa'si Eghawa, then northeast to Konehete and beyond, meeting up with the rest of their forces from Gatogatsa'yi, carry on to Tesenti, and then to Itsa'ti."

"You don't think they would instead go north through Talula?"

"Doesn't matter," Aganstata said, shifting position. "What matters now is that they are here. No doubt they will come in the morning with fire. And we must be ready."

Kiyuga leaned forward. "What do you want us to do?"

"I will take the Raven position and lead a small force to the Anigilisi camp. Early, before they have had a chance to get ready. We will draw them out of their camp and back to the village. No doubt there will only be a small force that follows while some stay behind to assemble as they do. There will be some waiting just this side of the hill to fight those who follow and keep them busy. The faster we slaughter them, the faster the others must move, and the sloppier they will be about it.

"When the rest of the Anigilisi come to pursue us, we will retreat to the village. I have no doubt the Anigilisi will begin burning just as soon as they can. Mankiller will take the Owl position. Galegi will take Wolf. The fire will be the Fox position. Always keep it in front of you and behind the Anigilisi. Never allow the fire to surround you. If it comes to this, escape if you can, or take the Anigilisi with you."

Anticipatory grunts and murmurs rumbled through the warriors.

Kiyuga was assigned under Mankiller once more. At one time, he remembered thinking that he wanted to do all the positions, and that it would be terribly boring to do the same one over and over. Now he was beginning to understand. He was beginning to learn, to master the Owl. He was also learning how to work with Mankiller and those frequently assigned under him. He was part of them, a functional member of the pack, not a pup bouncing from here to there in deluded excitement.

So it was that he fell into place among the Owls like a piece of a chipped rock being put back in its place, and they became whole. He knew what Mankiller wanted and expected of it, and there was a certain respect between them for it.

"Yvgidahi, I want you to stay on your horse," Mankiller said as they prepared their positions that evening. "I want you to ride down any Anigilisi who try to flee past us, whether they are attacking or trying to escape. We take no prisoners here, only prizes."

Kiyuga dipped his head in acknowledgment.

The following morning, Aganstata and his distracting force were awake and moving even before Kiyuga was awake. Only when the Raven force was moving toward the Anigilisi camp were the rest of them woken and told to be ready. Blearily, Kiyuga hurried to relieve himself and ready Amayi. The horse snorted and pawed once, as if sensing the bloodshed that was about to ensue.

"Be silent as you can, and watch for Aganstata," Mankiller was telling the Owls. "Always keep the fire to your front. We attempt to use the fire, but it can be controlled by no man. It is as much an enemy as any of the Anigilisi. If it closes in or circles around you, flee. If you cannot flee, then take as many Anigilisi to the afterlife with you as you can."

Now was not the time for whoops of agreement, but there was a certain ripple of strength and surety that said the warriors were prepared to do everything necessary to defeat these white-skinned demons.

"Yvgidahi and others on horseback," Mankiller went on, "you must be our net and our wall. Strike down all who try to make it past us. It does not matter if they are attacking or attempting to flee. Show no mercy this day." Again addressing all the Owls. "We take no prisoner, we demand no ransom. When we have killed their soldiers, we will strip their bodies, take their weapons, their trinkets, their pieces of paper. We will make it easy for the scavengers to reach their flesh."

Now was not the time for whoops of agreement, but there was much shuffling of anticipation in the undergrowth among those hidden in the leaves, and the mounted warriors hiding in thickets.

Mankiller continued. "We take no prisoners, but we shall take enough scalps that we shall bind them together that we shall each create a new man. And we will gain such strength of these many soldiers that we will use it against those who still live, if indeed, any shall."

Now was not the time for whoops of agreement, but there was a serious tension among the warriors that bespoke of such yearning. Kiyuga shifting on Amayi's back, fingering the reins. The stallion, sensing the excitement, pawed and did a small dance, snorting indignantly and tossing his head once when Kiyuga tugged gently on the reins.

"I know," Kiyuga whispered, leaning on the horse's thick neck. "I know. We will have our chance, just as we always do."

Amayi snorted again but remained still, at least for a moment until he spotted a leaf he wanted. Kiyuga sighed but let him have it, figuring there was no harm in it. Aganstata and his Ravens were not back yet.

Even as he thought it, the wind carried distant sound to his ears. Looking down, Amayi's ears were also pricked, even as the horse still nosed for greens. The noise got louder and the horse lifted his head.

Looking between the stallion's ears, Kiyuga did not see anything at first. But then, the undergrowth was thick, and they were supposed to be hiding. The noise continued to grow and be carried to them by the wind. There was no mistaking the sounds of battle and the pops of gunfire. From this distance, it was as very sharp thunderclaps, often in rapid succession. He heard the hollers of his people, Aganstata and his Ravens.

The wind carried something else to him, then. The smell of smoke. Beneath him, Amayi grunted and shifted anxiously. Kiyuga tried to hold him still and keep him calm, but he knew the horse could feel his anxiety as well. Fire was not something any man truly controlled. They used fire in many ways, but this was a gamble if there ever was one, to use fire in battle in such a way. It did make him nervous, and that only fueled the nervousness of his mount.

Kiyuga took a calming breath and reminded himself to stay in the moment. He had a task. Focus on the task. The Ravens were distracting the Anigilisi, trying to draw them out before they were ready, use their unpreparedness to the advantage. The Owls and the Wolves flanked them on either side, using the fire as the Fox position. Kiyuga and the other mounted warriors were merely a way to ensure the fleeing soldiers could not escape.

As he focused his thoughts, he noticed Amayi calm down as well, though the horse was still distracted between the sounds of fighting and the increasing smell of smoke.

The noise of battle, which had stalled as the Ravens executed their plan, suddenly began to draw closer.

"Aganstata and the Ravens approach," the word came, rippling through the Owls. "The Fox is to the east, moving west, but slowly."

Kiyuga let out a breath as evenly as he could. The noise got louder until it became more than noise, but sight as well. Fleeing Ravens running on foot or horseback toward the village, now abandoned. When they reached the center of the village, they turned to engage the soldiers, now swarming from the camp over the hill like ants.

Shifting position and gripping his hatchet, Kiyuga turned Amayi and waited for the first soldier to foolishly attempt to flee.

ᎠᏯᏙᏁᎸᎢ ᏔᎵᏍᎪ ᏅᎩ

Ayadohlv'i Tahlsgo Nvki

A Brother's Words

It was some time after Kiyuga left that the traders returned, and with more of the seeing fruit. Anagalisgi took to acquiring everything he could command in order to trade for it.

"You have no idea what I had to go through to obtain this," the trader said, showing him the fruit. He had three small fruits in his bag. "The Great Desert peoples offered it as a sort of gift, a kindness, not a regular barter item."

"Surely they must have known that such an item would be highly sought after by those who understand it?" Anagalisgi wondered.

"I expect so. As I said, you don't know what I had to do in order to acquire this for you. I hope you were wise with your last one, and perhaps attempted to make use of the stone?"

Anagalisgi took him into the townhouse and showed him the small shoot that had sprung up from Ulisi's grave. "A tree grows. But it will be many years before it bears fruit."

"That is true enough. From the news I have heard, you may not have years left to tend it."

"Agreed. Which is why I must have the fruits you have brought in order to seek the spirits. What do you want for them? Last time you asked for guns and ammunition."

"And if you have more, that would certainly be a start."

Anagalisgi frowned and hesitated. The trader pressed harder. "From what I've heard, the British are well on their way here to Itsa'ti. You've won some, you've lost some, but the redcoats keep coming."

"We have a chance to choke them in the pass, before they reach

Talasi. We will need every gun and ball to hand."

"And will those guns and balls feed your families through the winter after the British have burned all the hunting grounds?" the trader countered. "Or will you trust the spirits again?"

Anagalisgi let out a breath and made a few paces. Finally he relented. "All right. But this is the last that I have."

"That works well, then, for I have every reason to believe that this will be the last of the seeing fruit I shall be able to acquire."

He hated giving up his last good means of protection, but when he finally held the seeing fruit in his hands, he knew it had been the right thing to do. He was not Kiyuga. He was not a warrior. He was an adawehi, and he had different obligations to his people. He would protect them in a different way.

While the traders were welcome guests, and certainly a welcome distraction, they were not as profitable as before. With many of the people gone fighting or escaped to Aktiya Waya, few people were left to trade. Those who remained were not as keen on giving up what they had, at least as far as weapons were concerned. There were many hard bargains and even more broken deals.

"Tell me honestly," the trader said to Anagalisgi before he and his brethren departed, several days after their arrival. "Do you think, if the British defeat your people, they will continue west?"

Anagalisgi sighed. "Yes. I know they will. For they are conquerors. It is all they know to do."

The trader said nothing to that, just nodded, wished him and all of the people well, and left Itsa'ti.

Anagalisgi had not partaken of any of the seeing fruit while the traders were present. He did not want them inquiring about any visions, nor did he want them present if he had a vision that required immediate attention or intervention. It was another day before he finally relented and cut into one of the fruits.

He did not remember falling asleep after eating the piece of fruit. He'd no sooner swallowed than he heard the tapping of the woodpecker on a tree outside the townhouse. He stood and went to it.

"I'm here," Anagalisgi said.

The woodpecker hopped up the side of the tree to a branch and looked down at him. "We know you are. Soon you will come to us and stay."

"When will this happen?"

"Soon. When you have been freed from your cage."

Anagalisgi looked around. "I see no cage. Are you saying that the Anigilisi will come to Itsa'ti? Will they kill and enslave us?"

"They will come to your village. And the next and the next. And they will not stop. But that is beyond your concern at this time, for it is written. You will be removed from this place so that you might prepare for the next day that you are needed."

"I don't understand."

"You will when the time comes. Soon. Very soon."

Then the woodpecker spread its wings and swooped away into the forest. Anagalisgi did not follow. He could not if he wanted to, for his head felt heavy and his eyes drooped. He dragged himself back to the townhouse and lay down in his spot.

When he woke, he felt very tired.

"Did you have a vision from the seeing fruit?" one of the other adawehi asked politely.

Anagalisgi nodded and yawned. "I did." He rubbed his eyes. "But it was a personal vision, the spirits speaking to me alone. I'm afraid I cannot share."

His answered was accepted with no malice, and everyone went about his day. Anagalisgi felt dreadfully slow and quite unalert for any goings-on. It was a terrible state to be in, and he wanted only to sleep more, but he somehow knew that if he did lie down, he would not yet be able to sleep.

He went about his chores in an almost trance-like state, caught between the spirit world and the waking world, and he found himself pondering whether there were truly a difference between the two, or if perhaps the spirit world was the waking world, and the world in which he now walked was something entirely different.

He wished Gvnagadoga were still alive, that he might speak to him. He wondered if he there were a way to commune with him if he again ate the seeing fruit. But then, considering how much energy it drained from him to enter the spirit world through that doorway, it would be a few days before he tried that. It had been difficult enough trying to get through to Kiyuga, even with Nathan's instruction.

He would wait a day or two, let his body recover. Maybe he would fast for seven days and then try again. Perhaps the spirits would be kinder to him if he better observed the rituals.

He did not dream about the warriors or any battles that may have been going on or yet to come. He saw almost nothing of the waking world and the things going on concerning his people. Everything he dreamed, if he dreamed, revolved around the woodpecker or his journey to the spirit world. Ge'gwogv often proclaimed that his journey would not be through death, but he would remain the guardian between worlds.

Anagalisgi did not understand what that meant, although he had a sneaking suspicion that he would not be waiting much longer to find out. Indeed, he found himself more and more certain, through a particular spiritual knowledge, that he would not see another winter. Part of him hoped he was wrong, that he was merely anxious over the state of things between the Aniyvwiya and the Anigilisi. Part of him knew better.

Spring shook off winter, and summer shook off spring. The days grew longer. Every so often, a young boy would return, sent by Aganstata or one of the skiagvsta with a message. Rarely was it good. Grant was a good soldier and an excellent commander, having learned much from the failed attack on Fort Duquense. The Middle Towns were burning, the villages and most of the surrounding cropland and hunting grounds.

Refugees from the Middle Towns made their way to the Overhill, all with the same message. The red coats were coming. They divided, regrouped, came together, like a serpent or flowing water. Smooth, fast, hard to pin down, difficult to catch. But their power was great, swift as a cougar, strong as a bear.

As for the warriors, they fought valiantly, and they killed many soldiers. But the war tortoise of the Anigilisi never ceased. It pressed on, unrelenting, unforgiving. Few prisoners were taken, some children, a young woman or two, almost no men. The Anigilisi were not here for diplomacy or reasoning. They did not bring their little pieces of paper with their serpent words. They brought only their guns and an iron will to kill the Aniyvwiya or destroy everything that makes him who he is.

Anagalisgi found himself searching for his brother each night as Nathan had instructed, walking in his dreams if only to reassure himself that Kiyuga was still alive. Sometimes he wondered whether this dreamwalking was real, or his own lively sleeping imagination bringing him false comfort.

He was able to relieve his doubts and fears one afternoon when Aganstata, Amadoya, Mankiller, and the others returned to Itsa'ti, Kiyuga with them. Despite the way they paraded their trophies around and sung of their heroics in battle, Anagalisgi perceived a certain heavy exhaustion, coupled with a rather intense amount of fear.

Once the warriors had cleansed themselves from battle and been given a chance to eat and revive themselves, Anagalisgi sought out his brother. He found Kiyuga with their aunt and uncle.

"The great warrior returns," Anagalisgi said lightly, grinning.

Kiyuga did not return the expression. Instead he frowned. "How great of a warrior can I be if I cannot help our people in our time of greatest need with these marvelous sorceries?"

Anagalisgi blinked. "I don't understand."

"If Nathan and Andrew know the secrets of using the sorceries to counter fire, they would by now be too late to disclose those secrets." He went on before Anagalisgi could speak. "The sorceries do not work well on fire. It can even make it worse, far worse. Had we been in open battle with the Anigilisi, the sorceries would have seen us to victory even before the first battle. But the fire, little brother. The fire made such things impossible, and we were overrun. Again and again.

"We tried these things in battle and failed. Those of us who knew the sorceries became too tired, so we rested while the others fought in the open, in hopes that we might regain our strength. When we were rested, we tried to attack the Anigilisi in secret, while they slept. But they are snakes, and they set many traps for us. Twice I was captured, but I managed to free myself, or someone helped me. The war tortoise is too great, little brother, even for the sorceries and the Author."

Kiyuga was as defeated as Anagalisgi had ever seen him, and it was heartbreaking to behold. Anagalisgi swallowed hard and said, "What are the skiagvsta going to do?"

"They will discuss this soon," Kiyuga sighed. "Grant is on his way to the Overhill. He means to take Itsa'ti."

Anagalisgi wondered whether the reason he was not having dreams beyond the war was because no one would be around to realize them.

Shortly after that, the council was convened. Few of the council or the warriors were not exhausted, and no one looked especially excited to be present.

Aganstata gave an account of things after they departed the Overhill. They went to wait at Itse'yi but were fooled by a distraction force of soldiers. Grant and his men made it to Gatogatsa'yi and burned it to the ground. When the warriors attempted to cut across to Aquonatutse to cut them off, the Anigilisi split up. Amadoya tried to head them off but could not. Meanwhile, Aganstata tried to turn back the force from Aquonatutse but failed. Then the distracting force from Itse'yi made its way through the pass and along the river. The warriors were left scrambling, unsure where their enemy was, where the greater force lay, and which way it would move next.

And through it all was fire. At least a dozen towns burned and all the crops and forest for three days' walk surrounding them. These raging fires also made conjuring the sorceries next to impossible, taking away the warriors' one great advantage.

It was more than disheartening, Anagalisgi thought; it was

absolutely soul crushing. The Aniyvwiya had suffered defeats in the past in their many conflicts with other nations. Some of those defeats had been quite brutal. But it was nothing compared to the anguish on the warriors' faces now, the haunted looks as they considered the devastated land and decimated villages and how the Anigilisi war tortoise continued to press on, their only comfort coming from the knowledge that most of the people were well safe in Akitya Waya. Still, it was bitter comfort, that they may have to join them as a pack of fleeing cowards.

"Are we going to surrender?" someone wondered, finally daring to say the word.

Murmurs rippled through those gathered. Aniyvwiya did not surrender; they just bided their time until revenge could be appropriately taken. But the Anigilisi did not believe in such things. They pushed on, pressed harder, and there seemed to be no way to stop them. The Aniyvwiya were the powerful nation and had no more allies to call upon. They were alone now, the last barrier between the Anigilisi and the lands west of the mountains.

"Not yet," Aganstata answered finally. "Not yet."

"We cannot give up the Overhill without a fight," Amadoya continued. "We cannot let them walk into Itsa'ti without paying the price in blood."

That did not lift the spirits of the warriors so much as keep a drowning man afloat in great rapids. Some looked uncertain, others simply exhausted. They would fight, but would it be as fierce as before? Probably not. The thought of defeat and surrender, especially given how likely it was, almost guaranteed such things.

"We will fast for seven days," Mankiller announced. "All of us. Every man, woman, and child left in the Overhill will fast for seven days. The adawehi will pray and prepare for a great feast and dance, that our continued dedication to our people will see us through the coming battle. We will fight. If necessary, we will die. For such is the way of things, as they have always been, from our grandfathers, to our fathers and uncles, to us, and to our sons and nephews, and their sons as well."

Again, it did little to lift spirits, though it got their heads above the water, Anagalisgi thought.

"What of Aktiya Waya?" someone asked. "Should we bring back some of the warriors to fight? Should we prepare to leave if things go badly?"

"Any who wish to return and fight may do so," Amadoya said, cutting off Aganstata. "But as Mankiller said, we will fight and die if necessary."

Some looked uneasy at his words. Every warrior knew death was likely when it came to battle, but there was no honor in worthless sacrifice. Sometimes the better path was giving in and waiting to fight another day. A man could not fight if he was not alive, and sometimes he had to choose his battles.

That did not make the idea any easier to bear. Somehow, it felt like a terrible, absolute surrender. Surrender on the Anigilisi's terms. The Anigilisi, who did not fight like any enemy they had faced before, and who, for all their deception, trickery, and witchcraft, still appeared to be far superior in warfare.

Anagalisgi came down hard on these thoughts as they entered his mind. He could not give in to despair. His people needed him, now more than ever. He had to fast. He had to pray. He had to prepare. Most importantly, he had to dream.

In that moment, the meeting started to annoy him and he wished them all gone so that he might...

Wait.

He couldn't use the seeing fruit, for that would interrupt the fast. Wouldn't it? He pondered this. Incense and offerings frequently accompanied praying and fasting as a way to invoke the spirits. They'd never had the seeing fruit before. But the seeing fruit was used to speak to the spirits. It seemed to him a bit of a contradiction. If he ate the fruit, it would break the fast, but it would let him speak to the spirits, as the fasting and praying was intended to do.

He found himself in a conundrum, one that distracted him while the rest of the warriors made their plans and told their stories.

"Anagalisgi?"

Anagalisgi blinked and looked around, searching for whoever had spoken. "Yes?"

"I said I want you with us when we go to fight the Anigilisi." It was Aganstata.

"Me?" Anagalisgi said dumbly.

"Anagalisgi, you have often been maligned as a persistent bad omen. But it may be that we have simply misjudged you, blinded by our own fear and unwillingness to accept the coming dangers. Please. Forgive us. We need you now. We need your dreams, we need your guidance."

Anagalisgi was as unprepared as he could be for such a vote of confidence, to say nothing of the request for forgiveness. He'd simply come to accept that he was an unwanted omen, tolerated rather than embraced. Now it seemed as though the people were finally considering that maybe he was right. Maybe there was more to this than what they could see. They'd wanted to believe that everything would be fine, but now they were faced with the possibility that it might not be.

But were they too late?

"Um, all right. I'll go." He nodded. "I will pray to the spirits and attempt to dream."

Aganstata chuckled. "Anagalisgi, for you to say that you will pray and dream is the same as if I said I would breathe and drink water. We know you will do nothing less."

And as swiftly as their attention had turned on him, now it turned back to other matters. Anagalisgi blinked and shook his head. Had that just happened?

He also resolved in that moment that he would eat the seeing fruit, but only the first day of the fasting. The spirits would quickly tell him if he was offending them, and it would be easier to begin the fasting again from the beginning, rather than wait until the end. Fasting was a means of purification, but warriors could be a cranky bunch if it stretched into starvation, especially for a fool's error.

The meeting stretched long into the night, and even when everyone left to sleep, it still wasn't resolved. Everyone would reconvene in the morning. Anagalisgi noticed his brother staying behind to speak to the skiagvsta, but he himself did not approach. He only had the hope of acceptance; he didn't need to push it, not until he had some message from the spirits to give in return.

He sat by the fire and stared. He wished he could be a fire seer, but such gifts were exceedingly rare, and for all his connections to the spirits, it seemed he was not so gifted. Perhaps it was just as well, for if he could master the fire, he could not master the sorceries.

On the other hand, what good had the sorceries done to help them win the war? It seemed that they were only good to help them flee, run like frightened animals. Mastering the fire might help them to save their own lands while turning it back on the Anigilisi. Somehow, it felt dishonorable. Had they truly been tricked? But if so, would not Ge'gwogv have told him? Anagalisgi sighed. Some days he didn't know what to believe.

He waited until everyone else had left the townhouse or fallen asleep before bringing out the seeing fruit and cutting a piece to eat. Suddenly unsure of himself, he ate quickly before he could doubt himself or change his mind. He lay back and waited.

A breeze swept through the townhouse. Anagalisgi shifted position, and as he did, something caught his attention. Before he could fully register his peripheral vision, a white deer went bounding through. Then another. And then a third.

Anagalisgi jumped up and faltered, unsure if he should follow. He was waiting for Ge'gwogv. But then, maybe the deer would lead him there.

Finally he decided to follow. It felt like a year between when the deer bounded through and when he finally turned to follow, but it really couldn't have been more than a few moments.

He left the townhouse and stopped suddenly. He looked around. White spirits were everywhere, of all forms. From the smallest mouse to the great bear and cougar, all were present in Itsa'ti. Some looked as though they were busy working, doing things as animals did, and others appeared to be roaming, as if checking for danger. High above, clear as day though it was surely nighttime, Anagalisgi saw an eagle and a hawk circling lazily, keen eyes intent on the activity below.

"At least I know eating the seeing fruit did not dismay the spirits," he found himself saying.

"You commune with us in your own way."

Anagalisgi looked up as Ge'gwogv swooped in and landed on a nearby roof.

"I have never seen so many spirits," Anagalisgi said. "What are they all doing?"

"Everything that is necessary," the woodpecker replied. "As are you."

"I don't feel like I'm doing anything. Nothing useful, anyway. I don't know what to say or do, and my dreams have abandoned me."

Ge'gwogv tilted its head curiously. "When a plan is put in motion, eventually it must be fulfilled. And when it comes to its conclusion, has the plan abandoned you, or has it simply been fulfilled and is no longer needed?"

Anagalisgi blinked. "You're saying that...my dreams...they were all plans leading to this place?"

"As it has been written, yes."

"And my time is coming, when I will be the guardian between worlds."

"The time for planning has almost passed, but it exists now only in the waking world. Your dreams, these plans, they are complete."

"Then you know how this will end."

Ge'gwogv made a noise Anagalisgi could not interpret. He tried to take an even breath and not sigh, but he couldn't help himself. "Ge'gwogv, surely you have seen the things of which the warriors speak, how the Anigilisi trick them and overpower them, and how the fire renders the sorceries useless. Is death the fate of our people?"

"The Aniyvwiya will live on. This is known. Take comfort in it."

Anagalisgi dipped his head. "That is good to know. And Kiyuga? What of my brother?"

The woodpecker shifted. "Why do you ask of things you already know?"

"Because I want to believe that things can change." The words were out of his mouth before he could think about them. "You may tell me that he lives, and I would be grateful and not wish for it to change. But you may also tell me that, in the same way, half of the warriors will die, in which case, I would wish for it to change. Is the future fixed, Ge'gwogv?"

"A man may decide at any point not to loose an arrow upon his prey. But once the arrow is loosed, he cannot call it back," Ge'gwogv answered severely. "A man's destiny is only as resolute as his actions to get there."

Anagalisgi frowned but dipped his head. "Thank you, Ge'gwogv. I understand now."

"I knew you would." The woodpecker shifted position again. "I also know you have more questions."

"Why does fire stop the sorceries? I thought the sorceries were supposed to save us?"

"Have they not delivered the people to Aktiya Waya?"

"Well, yes, but the idea was not permanent residence. It was to keep the vulnerable safe, until we could defeat the Anigilisi and then bring them home. Are you saying that we must move to Aktiya Waya?"

"Are your people not vulnerable now? You saw the faces of the warriors when they returned. You saw their reaction to the skiagvsta. And as you have known for many years, you are not their first choice for a good luck charm, yet now they call on you."

He looked away. "I know. I believe I know what must be done."

Ge'gwogv dipped its head. "I know you do. But until you make the decision, your resolve is no stronger than a leaf on its stem."

"I understand. Thank you, Ge'gwogv."

"We will see each other again soon. Guardian of the door between worlds."

Anagalisgi hesitated at that, but eventually turned and walked back to the townhouse. All around him, the white animals continued in their work. A rabbit was digging burrows with other like-minded creatures. A beaver built a second wall around the village. A cougar prowled through the shadows. An owl kept watch from a post while bats fluttered about. Even the spirits were preparing for battle, it seemed.

Anagalisgi recalled pieces of a conversation he'd once had with a Christian preacher. The preacher had spoken of angels and demons, the armies of God and Satan. When God was on a man's side, angelic armies would come to his aid and the gates of Hell would not prevail. But if God was against a man, no amount of force could make something happen, and often, punishment would instead come down upon his head.

At this point, it certainly seemed as though God was with Grant and his army. Did that mean that the Aniyvwiya were better off surrendering and hoping God would have mercy? What of the sorceries? Fire was often attributed to Hell, and fire rendered the sorceries useless. Did that mean that the sorceries were from God, a way for the Aniyvwiya to prevail? Was His method of deliverance escape rather than victory? Could God be for both sides of the fight at the same time? Is that how the outcomes could be known and written for both sides?

Or what if both sides were equally futile in their efforts? What if God was on neither side? What if He watched as a frustrated parent, annoyed by the fighting between His children? What if He provided Aktiya Waya as a way to save the weaker child without harming the stronger? Certainly no parent would wish to harm the stronger child and so cause him to despise the parent, any more than he would ignore the cries of the weaker child.

Anagalisgi didn't know what to think as he found his way back to where he'd been resting. Already the visions of the spirits were fading and his head felt muddy and tired. He needed to sleep for a while, he figured, let his mind sort everything out while his body rested. There were plenty of days left for fasting and praying. If the spirits wanted to impart more information to him, they knew where to find him.

He slept through most of the day, and even when he woke, he did not feel especially rested. He spent the day with the rest of the adawehi, praying, burning incense and offerings.

He tried to offer hope to the skiagvsta and the warriors, telling them of his visions of the spirits in Itsa'ti, preparing for battle alongside them. He told them of the message from Ge'gwogv, that the Aniyvwiya would live on. He omitted any mention of how they would live, in what conditions, and thankfully no one asked. It lifted the warriors' spirits some, enough to wipe away the exhaustion and sow the seeds of confidence once more, and Anagalisgi prayed he would have more hope to give them over the next several days.

Despite the great temptation, he did not eat of the seeing fruit every night during the fasting. It would be improper to barge in on them so, and so often. There was a time for it, but there was also a time to be calm, be humble, and approach them reverently, appropriately. Perhaps he would eat of the seeing fruit the night before the feast, that he might have something great and uplifting to say to the warriors before they departed.

And so he did as the other adawehi did, fasting, praying, burning incense, burning offerings, singing and chanting. He was relieved when he heard that other adawehi had dreams and visions of the spirits. One declared that the bear would give them strength. The cougar would protect them from the bayonets and musket balls of the Anigilisi. A pack of wolves surrounded them, warding off any witchcraft.

Never did any of the adawehi report that the spirits assured them of victory. Never did they definitively say that they would defeat their enemies. Not one of them spoke words saying that Itsa'ti would be spared. No one ever said that the people of Aktiya Waya would be coming home. The spirits would be present, Anagalisgi mused, but that seemed only to speak of their survival, not their victory. If anyone else realized this, they did not say it aloud.

It was the sixth day of the fast when Kiyuga approached Anagalisgi and asked to speak alone. Stretching tired legs, Anagalisgi followed his brother out of the townhouse.

"I've not heard more from the spirits since the first night, but I think I will tonight," Anagalisgi told him.

"That's not why I'm here," Kiyuga said. "Aganstata asked me to speak with you. I was going to wait until we were leaving, but he suggested it would be better to do so now, while you are praying."

"Does he not want me to go with you now?"

"No, he does. But he has a plan he wishes for us to carry out."

"Both of us?"

"Yes." Kiyuga hesitated and lowered his voice. "Aganstata prays for victory, as do we all. And he prepares for that end. But there is another avenue we must also prepare for."

"Defeat."

"Yes. If we should be unsuccessful in our attack, if we must retreat, he wants us to lead it."

Anagalisgi raised a brow. "Lead in what way?"

"We are to take the weak and wounded to Aktiya Waya, but we mustn't do so in the Overhill. Grant and his army march for Itsa'ti. Aganstata does not want to give them easy prey. We have to leave the Overhill before going to Aktiya Waya."

"But to leave the Overhill in such a way means going north into Aninvdawegi territory. We will be easy prey for them as well."

"A more honorable death, or so says Amadoya." Kiyuga snorted indignantly. "Aganstata believes we can do it. The Aninvdawegi have been abused by the Anigilisi just as much as we have, and their strength and numbers are not so great as they would have others believe. They suffer greatly also. Aganstata also believes that we will have many weak and wounded, and the Aninvdawegi would not bother such a large group, no matter our condition."

Anagalisgi frowned. "It is a chance and a risk, but no better or worse than dying in battle or being trapped in Itsa'ti."

Kiyuga nodded. "These were Mankiller's thoughts also."

"How are we to accomplish this in battle? Won't the Anigilisi notice when we take a large part of our warriors and flee?"

"I think Aganstata expects the sorceries to be used to cover our escape, and the Anigilisi will be too focused on pressing forward to Itsa'ti to notice."

"That would be reasonable." Anagalisgi shifted his stance. "Did the skiagvsta say anything else?"

"Only to do what we can and get as many weak and wounded to Aktiya Waya as possible. If things turn out well here, then it should be no trouble bringing them back. If things do not go well, then we have saved as many as we can."

"Agreed," Anagalisgi murmured. "We've reached the end of the plan, the end of the road."

"What was that?" Kiyuga wondered.

Anagalisgi shook his head. "Nothing. I will dream and consult the spirits."

Kiyuga managed a small smile. "And I will breathe and drink water."

Kiyuga left to tend to his affairs, and Anagalisgi returned to the townhouse. He lit more incense and said a prayer. The guardian of the door between worlds. He would be helping to lead the retreat for the weak and wounded. They would be his responsibility. By his actions or inaction, dozens or hundreds of warriors could live or die. Aktiya Waya could be exposed and their whole nation could be eradicated. They would have to flee far, deep into the mountains, well away from the Anigilisi before chancing the trek. It would take time to get the weak and wounded across; it was not something they could do in a day.

His destiny was only as resolute as the actions it would take to get him there. He would need strength and clarity of mind to accomplish this task as the guardian of the door between worlds.

He studied the seeing fruit. He had one whole fruit and a part of a fruit. He decided to eat the part now, on the sixth night of fasting, and save the whole fruit. He may need it at some point during or after the battle, when they were fleeing.

He closed his eyes as he ate the fruit, forcing his breath to remain even. When he opened his eyes, he couldn't help a small gasp.

The townhouse was packed with white animals. The larger ones ringed the outer wall while the smaller ones gathered close to the fire. Smaller birds perched on the walls, tiny claws finding purchase in the stone, while the larger birds perched in the rafters. They stared at the fire and smoke, all appearing almost completely still, like carved stone. Even when Anagalisgi dared to move, to stand and look around, they did not react.

"What are you doing here?" Anagalisgi wondered. "Have all your preparations been made? Is your work finished? Are we purified to go into battle now?"

"Now is the time of our rest." He heard Ge'gwogv but could not see it in the dim light and shadows of the townhouse. "When we, too, give thanks and ask for strength and courage."

"But you are spirits. Good spirits. What need have you to ask for these things?"

"What need indeed, except that we are not the finality of being?"

"Who do you pray to? Who does a spirit pray to?"

"The same thing that every creatures looks to for guidance. His father."

"You pray to God, then?" Anagalisgi wondered, still searching the walls and rafters for the woodpecker. "Did you not speak of the Author?"

"Do you think the Raven Mockers pray to God?" Ge'gwogv asked rhetorically. "Or someone else? Everyone prays to his father. But not everyone has the same father."

"I wish to know your Father, the One Who loves His children and does good, Who rescues those who ask." Anagalisgi paused. "That is the answer to the riddle, isn't it? We are all petty children, and a good father will not readily favor one child over another. But neither will he turn his back on one who suffers at the hand of another and asks for help rather than giving in to stubborn pride and selfishness. The Anigilisi will not be destroyed. But neither will we."

"Such words are the beginning of wisdom and understanding."

Finally Ge'gwogv appeared, gliding down from the rafters to perch on a tall stick jutting up from a log near the fire.

"You will learn much more when you take your place as the guardian," the white woodpecker told him.

"There is so much I do not know or understand," Anagalisgi sighed.

"There is only so much this world can teach you. Your time is coming quickly."

"What should I bring?"

"You will be provided with everything you need. All that is required is a willingness to trust and to learn. Can you do this?"

"I can try," he offered weakly.

"The first step is willingness," the woodpecker said. "You will understand."

Anagalisgi took a breath and let it out, trying to remain calm, trying to remind himself that his destiny was only as resolute as his actions. He had to be strong now, and not shy away from the future and what may come.

"I'm ready," he said.

"Yes," Ge'gwogv acknowledged. "You are."

Anagalisgi blinked then, but it seemed to take a long time, like falling asleep. When his eyes opened, he found himself where he had been before. The spirits were gone, including Ge'gwogv, and it was still dark.

He stood uncertainly and made his way to the door. Dawn was not far off. The sky had shifted from the pitch of darkness to the light and color that came even before the first grays of dawn. It did not last long, and soon the grays appeared. Bats began returning to their caves and hollowed-out trees. Skunks and possums began returning to their burrows, and raccoons to their trees. Small birds woke from their slumber and began priming their voices. As the gray became more noticeable, the first notes were sung in delight.

He looked around, remembering everything he had seen over the night, all the white animals working, preparing for their own battle. Now all appeared quiet, the calm before the storm.

As gray sky turned into true dawn, colors streaking across the horizon to announce the coming of the sun, life slowly returned to the village. There were no children under eight left, all of them migrating to Aktiya Waya. But the children eight and older were still up early, playing quiet games or doing chores until the adults woke.

There were few women left as well, and their absence was particularly noted. Every boy was taught how to field dress and cook his own meal, that he would never starve when in the wilds, but it was the women who did the real cooking. The women who did remain did their best to cook for all the men, not just their own, but it took much time and great care. This fasting now was a welcome excuse to explain why the warriors would not have the home-cooked meals they so craved after returning from war, but it would make for a very different feast come the evening.

The women also brought a sense of home and normalcy to the village, a place where a man could forget, at least for a time, the things he'd seen and the things he knew he had to do still. He could relax for a day, let someone else do the work, before he took up his knife and gun once more.

With few women around, the village looked and felt more like a large camp for a war party. In a way, he supposed it was. War had come to the Overhill. And it wasn't just raids and skirmishes with other nations, but the true threat of war and even possible extinction. Or at least it would be had they not found Aktiya Waya.

Anagalisgi sighed. The sorceries had proven well to be the power of creation, to command earth and sky. So why were they still losing so badly? Why had they been put in this position? What was it about fire that it brought this sorcery to its knees? Why go through all the trouble of learning it if it could be undone so easily? Was Grant even aware of what he was doing? Had he planned this? Or was it merely a happy accident for him?

As he had many times in the past, Anagalisgi wished Gvnagadoga were still alive. He would have words of wisdom, some sort of insight. But there was an Anigilisi saying, "If wishes were horses, beggars would ride."

It would do him no good to wish for Gvnagadoga. He could wish for Ulisi and be just as successful. Briefly he considered seeking out Atagulkalu. Conjuring Time would see him there and back faster than normal. But what would he say? What would he ask? What could Atagulkalu tell him that he did not already know? What insight could the exiled leader provide that even Ge'gwogv could not or would not?

The sun broached the horizon, and it seemed to Anagalisgi that it chased away a creature of smoke and shadow from the sky itself. Perhaps he was imagining things. Or perhaps he was seeing and understanding something for the first time.

He turned around and startled when he nearly ran into Usga'hi, from Si'tiku.

"Forgive me," Usga'hi said. "You looked deep in thought and I didn't want to disturb you."

"No, it's all right," Anagalisgi told him. "Have you seen something?"

"I was going to ask that of you."

"Why should you want to know what I have seen?"

Usga'hi sighed. "For many years, we have dismissed you as a walking bad omen. No one likes to hear bad news, and when it is so constant, no one wants to hear it at all. But our willingness to blind ourselves in this way has brought us here. But now we have removed the blindfold. Some are blinded by what they see, but others are willing to adjust and learn. We want to hear you, Anagalisgi. We want to know and heed your warnings."

Anagalisgi frowned and regarded him. "Our destiny is only as resolute as our actions. For my lifetime, the people acted quite resolutely when they ignored, scorned, and discarded my warnings and dreams, and so here we are." He went on before his fellow adawehi could speak. "We are out of time, Usga'hi. There is no more time for warnings or preparation. The fast ends today. The plan, our destiny, is unfolding even now, as it has been as we have directed it. We have already jumped off the cliff. All we can control now is how well we land."

With that, he brushed past Usga'hi into the townhouse.

DᏆᏗᎯᎢ ᏔᏢᏙᎠ ᏗᎣᏉᎩ

Ayadohlv'i Tahlsgo Hisgi

A Prayer For Victory

It was up to the adawehi to prepare the food for the feast. After seven days of not eating, it was the last test of resolve. Anagalisgi found himself thankful to be sent on the more mundane errands, such as gathering wood and building fires. Multiple fires had to be built and maintained a certain way, and the most important fire, the sacred fire, had to be kept in a certain manner also. This required much wood. Anagalisgi had to collect the wood because he was an adawehi, but there was no rule that said he could not borrow his brother's horse to help the cause.

Using Amayi to pull large logs or bundles of smaller logs proved quite useful in keeping the firewood sufficiently stocked for all the fires. Every time he returned to Itsa'ti, he smelled the game over the smaller fires. His urges were divided between ripping the carcass off its spit and tearing into it like a wild animal, and riding away on Amayi's back as fast as he could so he didn't have to smell it and be reminded of food.

He had once asked Gvnagadoga if his hunger on the seventh day and his conflicting desire for food and purity meant that he was yet impure and that the fast had been futile. The old uku had chuckled and said that it was not the physical hunger that made him pure or impure, but the spiritual hunger, the willingness to continue on and not give in. Hunger was only natural and not to be despised. It was his strength of will that determined whether the fast had been successful.

So Anagalisgi did not feel guilty about his torn nature as he headed back into the forest once more, gathering still more wood. He was hungry, yes, but he was also determined to do whatever it took, garner every last drip of favor from the spirits, in order to ensure the greatest chance of success for the impending battle.

He was not the only adawehi out gathering wood, but the task was typically left to the acolytes, boys who had either been accepted into training for the adawehi or were still being tested for it. They could not perform the ceremonies and rituals, but they could gather firewood at least. Anagalisgi directed them here and there as needed, occasionally correcting behavior when one or more of the younger boys got distracted or too rowdy. At least they listened to him, if only because it was expected of them, to show deference to an elder and an adawehi.

He paused in his work and looked around. Despite a certain knowledge that Grant's army was yet far away, and they would likely have ample warning from the other Overhill towns of his advance, Anagalisgi still kept his head circling, as if expecting the red coats to come bursting through the trees at any moment and catch them off guard, unprepared and weak from their days of fasting and preparation.

But no such attack came. Anagalisgi tied the last bundle of sticks to Amayi's pack and took the horse's rope in hand. The steed snorted, tossed his head once, pawed irritably a few times, then agreed to follow. The noble stallion was clearly more interested in going to war with Kiyuga, or else he was more interested in the mares in the field, some of which had been showing interest in him.

"Come on, Amayi," Anagalisgi sighed. "Maybe Kiyuga will win a great prize in the coming battle and will bring back a mare for you. Maybe he will let you choose your own mare, your own spoils for a job well done in battle. How would that be?"

The horse snorted again.

The sun was near the western horizon when Anagalisgi returned to Itsa'ti. The red flag of war had been raised, freshly painted. Soon the feast would begin, followed by dancing and stories and many blessings and prayers. The town itself was bustling with activity, everyone ready and eager for festivities and the excitement that followed. Anagalisgi had a difficult time making rounds to the various fires to drop off wood. At least this was his last trip. For the rest of the evening and through the night, if they needed more wood, the younger boys would be sent to fetch it. But, if the current stores were any indication, they could host a feast for many more days.

As Anagalisgi untied the last bundle of wood from Amayi's pack, he saw his brother approach. Kiyuga took Amayi's rope and patted the horse's neck.

"He hasn't got you seeing bad omens, has he?" Kiyuga asked. "You still want to go to war, don't you?"

"I think he wants to talk to the mares in the field more than me or you," Anagalisgi told him.

"I think he wants to do more than talk to them."

"As for your comment about me causing him to see bad omens, he's too stubborn for that. He's learned from you."

Kiyuga laughed. "Of course he has. Well, maybe I'll introduce him to some of those mares in the field and they can get to know each other."

Anagalisgi made his way back to the townhouse, joining the other adawehi.

"Our wood supplies look good," one commented. "And as everyone has been diligent in his fasting and prayers, I'm sure the spirits will be very pleased and well inclined to offer blessings."

The rest murmured their agreement.

Personally, Anagalisgi wasn't so sure, though he did not say this aloud. Somehow he had the sneaking suspicion that he was not going to assume his role as the guardian of the door between worlds if the warriors were victorious.

But this was a feast of victory and honor and glory. He could not be speaking of his bad omens now. He had a duty to fulfill.

With the rest of the adawehi distracted by their apparent assurance of good fortune, they did not notice the dismay which Anagalisgi was sure was spread across his face. He tried to muster up an expression of heroism and courage and stoic determination, but was uncertain as to his success. Well, with any luck, no one would notice. They would be too focused on the food and festivities to give him much thought. And if anyone did see, well, his dismay was nothing new. As Gvnagadoga had once said, he wore an expression of perpetual dismay.

Everything was exactly as it should be.

All that remained was the ritual water purification of the adawehi, the last to be purified as several of them had been purifying the warriors and the rest of the villagers throughout the day during preparation. Now the adawehi went down to the river and, under the eye of the setting sun, immersed themselves in the water, taking turns to purify each other and be purified themselves. They would do this again in the morning, themselves and all the warriors, before going to war.

Anagalisgi obediently went out and submerged himself seven times, facing the cardinal directions while another adawehi said prayers over him. As he came up the final time, his attention was caught, dragged away from the adawehi and toward something in the distance.

At first it was difficult to see because of the sun, both its disappearance as it sank below the horizon, but also the certain glare that came from the last fingers clawing over the hills and treetops, blinding him. He could not say for certain what he saw, only that it was some kind of bird. He would have liked to have believed it was Ge'gwogv, somehow trying to reassure him that all was well. He would have also been partial to an eagle, a good omen to pass along to the others, a good start to the feast.

He did not know for certain what he saw, and so he did not say anything. However, he was fairly certain, looking upon it, that everything was exactly as it should be. Everything had come to this point. It was the fulfillment of his many dreams and prophecies over the years, the many bad and the occasional good. It was a thing-that-must-be.

A man's destiny was only as resolute as the actions he took to get him there, and that seemed to be true of the people as a whole as well.

They were about to cross an invisible gateway into destiny.

Had he perhaps always been the guardian of the door between worlds, then? Had he always been leading his people this way, just by his mere existence? Had the resolve finally sealed itself and could no longer be moved or influenced? It was a disquieting thought as he stepped out of the river and followed the other adawehi back into town. He did not know what to make of it, but he had no more time to sleep and dream and pray. The time for planning and preparation was past. All that remained now was resolute action.

The return of the adawehi signaled the end of the fast, or near enough. More prayers were offered, blessings given, and finally, after seven long days, with the last of the sun gone from the sky, food was consumed. Finally, after seven days of denying himself anything but water, and a whole day of smelling sweet, roasting flesh and searing vegetables, Anagalisgi was able to satisfy the grumbling of his stomach. He could not get enough, yet he knew that if he ate too fast, he would make himself sick. He could see a few of the younger boys, eager to become warriors, were about to learn this lesson the hard way.

He ate slowly and observed his surroundings, having a distinct feeling that this would be the last time he would see such a sight. It should have frightened him, he thought, except it didn't. Somehow, he also knew that everything would be all right.

Maybe he was being fanciful. Maybe he was delusional from the fasting or complacent from the sudden influx of food. He didn't want to think about it. The time for planning was past, which meant he had to devote himself to the waking world, at least for a little while.

He could see the looks on the warriors' faces as they cast nervous glances at the adawehi. What else had they seen? What proclamations would be made? Would they have good fortune, and so ride off in eager anticipation of battle? Or would they have to listen to a noble speech about going forth with the spirits against evils that foretold their failure? Either way they were going into battle; all that remained to be seen was in what mood they rode forth.

While the adawehi had spoken of their dreams and visions during the days of fasting, on the last day, they could not speak of them until the appointed time. More serious or important dreams from the fasting may also have been withheld until this time, a final warning or encouragement for the warriors as they left.

Anagalisgi tried to catch his brother's eye, but Kiyuga was as elusive as Anagalisgi was sure he himself had been many times. To see it on his brother now was both unusual and unnerving. Had his brother seen something perhaps?

Some while ago, Nathan had instructed him in the art of communication across great distances, usually in the form of walking in another's dreams. He gave some long-winded explanation about manipulating lightning in the brain, none of which made sense to Anagalisgi. He figured it was better explained as the joining of spirits. Given that Kiyuga was his brother, they were similar in spirit, which ought to be enough.

Anagalisgi had made contact, and it was then that he learned of Kiyuga's dream, the two of them on the same road and yet separated. And then there was the mysterious running man whom Kiyuga could not identify.

Perhaps Kiyuga had learned the man's identity during the fasting time. Perhaps he'd had another dream. Kiyuga was not an adawehi, in the same way that Anagalisgi was not a warrior, but that did not mean that Anagalisgi could not fight, or that Kiyuga could not dream.

His attention was on Kiyuga for only a few moments before they both became distracted by other goings-on.

"Anagalisgi, are you ready to go into battle?" someone asked. "It will be your first time as the battle adawehi, won't it?"

"Yes. Sort of." Anagalisgi replied, feeling the blood rush to his face. "I went with Aganstata years ago, when Saloli attempted to ally himself with the French. But I was only a boy still, an adawehi in training. And I was there when John Stuart and the others were killed or captured after leaving the fort."

"True battle is much different," Usga'hi told him severely. "When you are faced with the real possibility of death, that is when you begin to understand and appreciate the magnitude and importance of our prayers and blessings, and the spirits' provision, of course."

"I understand."

The man grinned and shook his head. "No. Not yet. Such a thing may only be understood once it is experienced."

Anagalisgi elected to say nothing and instead wordlessly agree. He understood well that he had not seen true battle, not as his brother had seen it. He understood well that his entire worldview would change once he did. But he also knew that he had seen beyond this battle. He walked a longer path than the present day. He could not hope to make them understand, nor did he want to. It was his path, and his alone.

Adawehi did not always fight as much as the warriors, depending on the battle and the circumstances, but they had their own stories to tell, those from the outside perspective of things, which could be just as interesting and entertaining.

Anagalisgi reached for some more venison and a bit of cornbread, acutely aware that the main festivities would begin soon. Already he could see the drummers hurrying to finish their food so they could get into position. The warriors shifted excitedly, each one silently taking inventory of himself, to ensure he had all he needed. With one hand, Kiyuga ate of a piece of fruit. With the other, he touched his weapons and belts. Someone made a comment to him to which he laughed and said something in reply.

As if instinctively copying the motions, Anagalisgi also felt around on his person, looking for his rocks and crystals, his charms and talismans, the herbs he would offer into the fire. He glanced at one of the deer being feasted upon. Its tongue would be cut and used for divining later also, to foretell the warriors' victory or defeat.

A thrill of nervous excitement shivered through him. In spite of his apparent perpetual dismay, he enjoyed the ceremonies and the feasts. He enjoyed being one of those who communed with the spirits to divine the future endeavors of his people. Not that he was conceited in that regard, but it was one of the things in life that brought him true joy and pleasure.

"Eat up," someone said, slapping him on the back. "The drummers and warriors are impatient."

"Give me a break," Anagalisgi coughed. "I've been fasting the same as you. I need food as well."

"We will be eating all night," another man told him. "There is plenty here for all."

"You don't have the same duties that we do," one of the adawehi said, only half-joking. "We must eat when we can."

Anagalisgi was grateful for the defense, but still he tried to eat more swiftly. His stomach protested such a move and twisted unhappily. He paused briefly. He could not pass off the food to any of the warriors, for he was an adawehi and they could not eat of his food once he'd touched it. At the same time, he was the only adawehi still eating, and the rest looked quite finished. He could not waste it. He really did not want to eat it. But he had no choice.

He slowed his eating a bit, and it only got slower as the discomfort in his stomach got worse. He looked around, quietly wondering if there was anyone else in the same predicament. Some of the younger warriors had already offered up their food, but as for the more experienced, few were still eating. It seemed as though everyone was now waiting on him. He felt his face turn hot, and he reluctantly forced himself to take another bite.

Finally he made a last push, stripping the last of the venison off its bone and drinking the last of the hominy broth.

"Do you need to give your dinner as the first offering of the night?" someone teased.

"Just give me a moment," Anagalisgi sighed.

He dragged himself to his feet and went rummaging for a small skin of hickory milk. Normally a delicious seasoning for most meats, it also had mild healing properties, to calm a disgruntled stomach.

"So, our great prophet is a man after all," one warrior teased when he returned. He wouldn't say his stomach felt fully healed, but he no longer questioned whether he would be vomiting in the middle of the ceremony.

"Maybe so, but he is still a speaker of the spirits," another adawehi rebuked him. "And you would do well to show him such respect, even when he is in such a state."

The warrior, chastened, said nothing, and instead retreated back to his spot.

Everyone had well gathered where they needed to be. The warriors had divided up, and the drummers sat around their drums, drumsticks ready. All eyes were on the adawehi, waiting for their word to begin.

Anagalisgi knew a moment of sadness then. Whatever it meant to become the guardian of the door between worlds, he would never be the head adawehi. He would never be the uku. He would never lead a ceremony like this.

He told himself not to be selfish, that he should be honored to be chosen as the guardian. Whatever it meant, whatever he was to do, it meant more than simply being the head adawehi and reciting words. All the same, it would be a dream forever unrealized.

The first offering was given to the fire, a possum. It was not a regarded animal, though its fur was used to crown the uku. A blessing was said, the spirits invoked. They asked for the blessing of the spirits, that they would look down and see that the people had fasted well over the last seven days, that they had prepared themselves properly. Now they were about to engage in greater ceremony that would preface what they wished to be a great victory.

"The white-skinned men are coming," the adawehi prayerfully murmured, still loud enough to be heard all around the fire. "Hear our prayers and protect our warriors, for they do great deeds of honor and sacrifice."

Oration was a cornerstone of Aniyvwiya culture. Anagalisgi had heard many Europeans—British, French, and others—marvel at the grand speeches given by the people, and the greatest of them coming from the leaders. When Mankiller had traveled to England, he had given a farewell speech that lasted half the night, or so it was said. Prayers and invocations were no exception to this, and Anagalisgi found himself growing more patient as he listened. War had a way of stirring a man's blood and worrying his mind, but the great words of a gifted speaker could remind a man of himself and his place in the world. He was but one small creature here. Nature did not hurry, yet it accomplished everything it needed to. So must a man also be.

Anagalisgi took an even breath and allowed himself to be calm. He knew the prayers and the rituals, and he had given a speech a time or two, but he knew he would never be as great as Mankiller or Gvnagadoga or any of them. He knew only riddles and vaguery. That was all right, though. The spirits would help him interpret, once he'd assumed his place.

He forced himself out of that line of thought and back to the present moment, back to the speech and the ceremonies. It was a scene he'd witnessed a dozen times as warriors prepared for battle, yet each time he found himself in awe. These were his people. This was his family. This community and these lands were their home. It was their heritage. They did not own it as the Europeans claimed to own it, yet it was theirs, a gift from the spirits, one they were obligated to protect. And their families were waiting. They waited in Aktiya Waya. Waited for the day they could come home. It was their duty to secure these lands once more, to bring peace and make them safe. To let the Anigilisi know that they were not welcome here.

The prayer came to a close, and as it did, the first beats of the drum were tapped out. As soon as the adawehi finished, one of the drummers gave a loud whoop. The others joined in and the drums beat out in full force. So began the first incantation, which would swing upwards with the smoke from the fire and carry to their enemies to drive them mad.

Your Pathways are Black; you have become wood, not a human being!
Dog excrement will cling nastily to you.
You will be living intermittently,
"Woof!" You will be saying along toward the Nightland.
Your Black Viscera will be lying all about. You will be all alone.
You will be like the Brown Dog in heat.

You are changed; you have just become old.
This is your clan: Anigilisi.
In the very middle of the Prairie, changed, you will be carrying dog stools.
"Woof!" you will be saying.
Your Pathway lies towards the Nightland!

This incantation was repeated many times, each time the voices growing louder, more forceful, as if the people could will it to become even more strongly applied to their enemies. The warriors whooped along with the singers and joined in themselves, often singing, but also shouting the things they would do to the Anigilisi in battle. With the recitation of this incantation, the Anigilisi were now little better than wooden figures, wooden dogs, to be captured and burned, having no souls worth saving, if they had souls at all.

Anagalisgi almost did not hear when the incantation of madness ended. He knew it better when the groups of warriors began to move. Each town formed a company of men, and each company had their own war song to be sung and played now. With this song, each company moved around the fire, each man demonstrating his skill and boasting of his past deeds as well as what he intended to do in battle.

One man bragged of his skill with the rifle and how his eyesight was as keen as the falcon's. He would pick off his enemies before they had a chance to react. Another man boasted of his strength and how he would use this strength with his war club to crush his enemies in a single blow. Still a third man demonstrated many clever knife tricks with a couple of steel daggers, twirling them about and making motions as though slashing at his foes to disembowel them or sneaking up behind them to cut their throats.

The first company did not so much end their song as other companies ended it for them, the second company eager to get their chance to boast of their own exploits. There was a bit of pushing and shoving, some friendly banter as the first company was ushered out of the circle to make way for the next company. The song changed, but the bragging and boasting did not.

Anagalisgi watched with awe, fascination, and a great sense of pride. Several of the adawehi were still praying, and the boys and acolytes tended the fires well. Even with most of the women and all of the children gone away, the festival was as lively as it had ever been. Perhaps because this was a war unlike any other their people had known.

The second company finished their dance and was quickly replaced by the third. Here, a warrior carried a bayonet in one hand and a broken stock in the other. He bragged about how he'd taken the broken gun from one of the Anigilisi. He bragged about how he could yet use these broken pieces as greater weapons than anything whole the Anigilisi had to offer. He showed how he could use the bayonet still as a dagger or spear, and the broken stock as a club. He claimed to wash his teeth with their useless gunpowder and so gain the strength of this fire weapon, to spit fire on his enemies.

In his peripheral vision, Anagalisgi saw one of the other adawehi frown at this man. Fire was a useful tool, yes, but it was also a dark sorcery. This much was obvious, given that the Anigilisi were using it as they were. Fire had been a dark sorcery since the beginning of the world. Perhaps it was the only thing that kept Anagalisgi in good standing still, even for the sorceries he wielded, that they were not fire-based. Still, nothing was said aloud, and the man continued on in his boasting. There was much eccentric bragging here tonight, and not everything could be taken literally.

At least, that was what Anagalisgi told himself. He did not recognize the man as one of the sorcery students, though he was torn whether this was a good or bad thing.

The dances lasted a long time. Anagalisgi remembered a particular missionary who had once visited Itsa'ti and observed the dances. He'd commented that the dances lasted an average of fifteen minutes. When someone asked the missionary if that was a long time, the missionary had remarked that many European dances lasted only a fraction of that time, perhaps three or four minutes. But then, the European dances were purely social affairs, for fun and delight and entertainment; they were not endeavors of strength and endurance, meant to mimic the hardships of war and battle and hunting game.

Anagalisgi could not imagine a dance lasting only a few minutes, if what the missionary had said was true. Social or not, how was one supposed to really get into the rhythm, into the meaning of the song and dance, in such a short time? By the time he found himself and began to express his soul, it would be over. And by the time the next song got going and he was able to find his soul again, it would again be finished. No, the songs had to last as long as they did, for it was the only way to truly express oneself and ensure he said and did everything he needed to do in order to please the spirits and refresh his soul.

The next company came through, each man bragging of his deeds and desires for battle. Next up would be the company from Itsa'ti, in which Kiyuga would dance. Anagalisgi searched for his brother in the crowd but did not see him immediately. Likely he was speaking to one of his warrior brothers, perhaps already dancing a bit on his toes, eager to put himself on display.

The companies who had already gone through and danced their songs were crowded well around the circle, now mingling freely. Some still bragged of themselves, others joined in with the singers, and still others let out whoops and hollers, encouraging whoever was currently dancing. Many still stomped in time with the drums, doing small dances on the side.

When all companies had gone through individually, the whole force gathered again for the final war song. It was nearly dawn by now, the black sky just giving way to gray and the first hint of colors on the horizon. If anyone had noticed the night passing by, they gave no indication of it, for spirits had remained well high and excited by the festivities. Even Anagalisgi found himself only mildly tinged with fatigue. If anyone appeared tired, it was the boys and acolytes still tending to the fires, heaping them high with wood to illuminate everyone in Itsa'ti.

With everyone assembled, the drummers began beating out a

rapturous tune, jolting the heart and energizing the spirit. Aganstata led his army into the circle, and all the warriors cried out in song.

> *Where'er the earth's enlighten'd by the sun,*
> *Moon shines by night, grass grows, or waters run,*
> *Be't known that we are going, like men, afar,*
> *In hostile fields to wage destructive war;*
> *Like men we go, to meet our country's foes,*
> *Who, woman-like, shall fly our dreaded blows;*
> *Yes, as a woman, who beholds a snake,*
> *In gaudy horror, glisten thro' the brake,*
> *Starts trembling back, and stares with wild surprize,*
> *Or pale thro' fear, unconscious, panting, flies.*
> *Just so these foes, more tim'rous than the hind,*
> *Shall leave their arms and only cloaths behind;*
> *Pinch'd by each blast, by ev'ry thicket torn,*
> *Run back to their own nation, now its scorn:*
> *Or in the winter, when the barren wood*
> *Denies their gnawing entrails nature's food,*
> *Let them sit down, from friends and country far,*
> *And wish, with tears, they ne'er had come to war.*

> *We'll leave our clubs, dew'd with their country show'rs,*
> *And, if they dare to bring them back to our's,*
> *Their painted scalps shall be a step to fame,*
> *And grace our own and glorious country's name.*
> *Or if we warriors spare the yielding foe,*
> *Torments at home the wretch must undergo.*
> *But when we go, who knows which shall return,*
> *When growing dangers rise with each new morn?*
> *Farewel, ye little ones, ye tender wives,*
> *For you alone we would conserve our lives!*
> *But cease to mourn, 'tis unavailing pain,*
> *If not fore-doom'd, we soon shall meet again.*

But, O ye friends! in case your comrades fall,
Think that on you our deaths for vengeance call;
With uprais'd tommahawkes pursue our blood,
And stain, with hostile streams, the conscious wood,
That pointing enemies may never tell
The boasted place where we, their victims, fell.

The song was repeated more times than Anagalisgi could count, and yet he did not grow weary of it. He found himself mesmerized by the display. He watched the older, seasoned warriors dance with the grace of water and the ferocity of fire, so sure of themselves and the skills which had kept them alive and made them heroes for many generations. He watched the younger warriors, brimming with energy and determination, their strength certain to inflict terror on any enemies not fortunate enough to merely die.

When the last rendition hit its second verse, Anagalisgi followed the rest of the adawehi to the river. There they waited and watched as the final song ended, yet the dance continued, Aganstata leading the warriors down to the water. It took a moment to get everyone calmed down, enough to get everyone sorted out again.

One at a time, each company waded out into the water to the adawehi. Anagalisgi called out prayers and blessings on the warriors as they plunged into the current seven times, then waded out and returned to Itsa'ti.

Kiyuga's company waded into the water, and Kiyuga himself went to Anagalisgi.

"Be blessed, my brother," Anagalisgi told him. "You will be great."

He knew it to be true, and he hoped his brother knew this as well as he went under the first time, then the second, and again and again until he'd gone under seven times. They made eye contact as Kiyuga came up, then turned and headed for the shore.

The next company pushed into the current.

Color made its way into the sky. With all of the warriors now purified, the adawehi returned to Itsa'ti. Anagalisgi was not the designated war adawehi, but he was going with them and would be performing adawehi duties. For that, he now participated in the next matter of the ceremony, the first of many divinations of success or failure.

He put great bundles of fresh wood into the sacred fire and coaxed the flames to life such as the sun had come and now rested in Itsa'ti. Then, the designated adawehi cut the tongue from the feast deer and cast it into the fire. Aganstata, Mankiller, and the others gathered around as the adawehi watched the flames most intently. For a long moment, no one spoke, and no one dared to breathe. And it seemed as though the fire burned brightly. If it consumed the deer tongue, victory was certain. If it was consumed and popped to the east, they would slaughter their enemies such that they would never again return to this land and all would be well. They watched the tongue in the flames as a cougar watched a rabbit in the grass.

But after several agonizing moments where the tongue was not consumed, the designated adawehi let out a hesitant breath.

"I am afraid," he sighed, "victory is not certain."

As if to emphasize the point, the tongue sizzled and popped toward the west.

"Defeat," Amadoya hissed. "Why do the spirits abandon us so? Did they not witness our fasting and prayers? Did someone break the fast in secret and so defile us?"

"Peace, Amadoya," Mankiller said. "This is but one sign. There are others yet to be sought."

As the sun made its way over the horizon, the adawehi then went outside with the sacred beads. Anagalisgi watched from behind as he took up a bead in each hand. He prayed to the first heaven, calling for guidance, mercy, and blessing. He gave honor to the spirits and prayed for victory. He raised his hands a bit higher and began a prayer to the second heaven. Again he gave honor to the spirits, asking for guidance, mercy, and blessing, praying for victory. He prayed for the consideration of their women and children who would be alone and defenseless should their endeavor fail.

He raised his hands a bit higher and prayed to the third heaven. He gave honor to the spirits, asking for guidance, mercy, a blessing, asking for victory. He prayed for the consideration of the boys seeking to be warriors, asking for strength and honor for them that they might be great warriors one day.

He raised his hands a bit higher and prayed to the fourth heaven. He gave honor to the spirits, asking for guidance, mercy, blessing, and asking for victory. He prayed for the consideration of the young warriors seeking to woo women and so carry on the Aniyvwiya traditions, how tragic a thing for them to die out with no children to learn.

He raised his hands a bit higher and prayed to the fifth heaven. He gave honor to the spirits, asking for guidance, mercy, blessing, and asking for victory. He prayed for the consideration of the older warriors, those who had fought faithfully, served the people well, and honored the spirits all their lives. Their faithfulness ought to be rewarded well, and their wisdom was essential for the survival of future generations.

He raised his hands a bit higher and prayed to the sixth heaven. He gave honor to the spirits, asking for guidance, mercy, blessing, and asking for victory. He prayed for the consideration of the warriors already gone, those recently and those whose existence had been forgotten by the living. They had fought for their people, their survival and way of life, to ensure the continuance of the people. Their sacrifices should not be in vain; there must be a future of the Aniyvwiya.

Finally, the adawehi extended his hands up as high as they would go, the beads still in hand. Again he gave great honor to the spirits. He prayed now to the seventh heaven, pleading for mercy and guidance, asking for blessing and victory. He prayed for consideration for the uku, the skiagvsta, and the adawehi, those whom the spirits had chosen to lead the people. They had been chosen for the strength, their loyalty, and their great faith. Truly, they were pure of spirit, for such was why they had been chosen. Lead them now to victory for the people.

As he held his hands up and the sunlight caught the beads, it seemed to Anagalisgi that the one in his left hand was glittered far more brilliantly and seemed more alive. The one in his right hand was little more than a pretty rock.

The others apparently saw this as well, for Amadoya snorted in disgust.

"Defeat again. Surely someone must have broken the fast!"

Neither Mankiller nor Aganstata rebuked him this time. Instead, both skiagvsta looked thoughtful.

Behind them, Anagalisgi swallowed. Ge'gwogv had told him that his partaking of the seeing fruit had not impacted the fast in any way, and may have even been beneficial. That did not make him less nervous, though it did make him curious as to who may have broken the fast. Under normal circumstances, for a village-wide fast, it was not uncommon to have to constantly remind children of their obligations, and it was not a fun or easy task. But the elders, women, and children were gone. The only ones here for this fast were those who were directly impacted by it, who would live or die by their adherence to it, and whose failure could also get their friends and brothers killed. Who would be so foolish?

"We must find out who did this," Amadoya said sternly. "We cannot go into battle with such an impure fool among us. He will surely be the death of us all."

"Agreed," Aganstata said. "Adawehi?"

The adawehi nodded. "As the warriors pass by the divining stone, we will discern who it is who has done this to us."

"Will we tell them what we are doing?" Anagalisgi inquired.

"No. We cannot allow an evil spirit to know what we are doing, how we attempt to root it out. We must catch it by surprise." To the skiagvsta. "Go now, and prepare the warriors."

Again the warriors were gathered. This time, however, they were not arranged according to company, but by experience. The youngest and most inexperienced went first. Aganstata and the skiagvsta would be the last warriors to march, and the adawehi would finish the ritual in similar fashion, with the boys and acolytes going first, all the way up to the designated war adawehi.

One of the acolytes set up a post in the central area and Anagalisgi situated a divination crystal atop it. He looked up at the sky, judging the wind and weather. There could be no clouds to interrupt them and cast doubt on the signs. Looking around at the sky, there did not appear to be any danger of this. The clouds from the night were well to the horizon, and any new clouds were well away from the sun.

When the adawehi judged the crystal and conditions suitable, he gave the signal to Aganstata who oversaw the line of warriors, sending the youngest and most inexperienced first. If the crystal sparkled a certain way when the warrior passed by, he was likely to live. If it did not sparkle at all, he was likely to die. If the premonition was that he should die, he was given the chance to withdraw and stay home.

The first young boy to walk by did not sparkle, a bad omen in itself. But when asked if he should prefer to stay behind, he made the simple statement that if he wished for such a thing, he would have fled to Aktiya Waya with the women.

There were many such statements given for the younger boys and warriors. While the skiagvsta praised their courage and determination, Anagalisgi silently worried about how few warriors caused the crystal to sparkle. Were this a cloudy day where they had to frequently pause the march so the sun could show its face, he might have understood. But the sky was nearly clear. There was no reason for the crystal not to sparkle except that it meant that over half their inexperienced warriors would die.

A skiagvsta, or even just a warrior who led raids, who lost more than two men in a skirmish could be stripped of all war titles and reduced to little more than a boy in rank. War may have been seen differently and afforded more leeway, especially in situations like this, but if even a portion of these bad omens came to pass, Aganstata could be executed for such poor leadership.

But then, would the Anigilisi not do the same to them anyway? Was there truly no way to win?

"Stop!" the war adawehi barked suddenly, causing Anagalisgi to jump.

He walked up to the young man currently passing by the crystal. It did not sparkle, but the purpose of this pause was clearly not to ask if he wished to stay behind.

"You were the one who broke the fast," the adawehi said severely. He held up a bead in his hand. "I asked that this bead be warmed when the traitor passed by the crystal. It has shown me you to be the one."

The young man swallowed nervously. "Please, I—"

"Did you break the fast? Are you the one who has incurred the wrath of the spirits such that divination has produced nothing but predicted defeat? Are you the one condemning your little brothers to death?!" He gestured to the younger boys who had been foretold their deaths.

The young man gasped for breath. "It was just a bit of tea, I promise. I had a pain in my mouth. I thought that if I made a tea of the leaf instead of eating it—"

"You have done this!" the adawehi roared. "You have broken the fast and the faith of every warrior going into battle now! Their blood is on you!"

The adawehi made a motion and two more adawehi took the young man away. Likely he would be scratched, a razor-sharp comb drawn all over his body so that he bled. It would drain out any evil spirits that had possessed him to break the fast. Then he would be taken to the river for more purification. He would not be permitted to join them in battle. He would have to wait until their return, then be taken to Aktiya Waya in shame.

With the impure warrior rooted out, the warriors were made to start all over again in marching by the crystal. The results were now far more promising.

"Would it be correct to assume that the other signs would be favorable now as well?" Amadoya inquired.

"It would be," the adawehi replied. "We have exposed and shed this evil. We may proceed without hesitation."

Spirits had been well lifted after the impure fool had been discarded, and they lifted even higher when all of the skiagvsta passed by the crystal and it sparkled brilliantly. Suddenly the war did not look so hopeless. There was an excellent chance that they would see victory over the Anigilisi yet. Anagalisgi already knew it to be true, but he breathed a sigh of relief when the crystal sparkled when Kiyuga walked by.

With the warriors gone through, it was the adawehi's turn to walk by the crystal. Only those who were going to war walked by. Three young attendants were the first to go through. Two were predicted to live, one to die. He elected to stay behind and was replaced by another young acolyte who was predicted to live. Next was Anagalisgi. Heart racing, he walked forward.

The crystal sparkled.

For a moment, he was perplexed. He was not going to shrug off the gift of life, but somehow he'd always expected that taking the place of the guardian of the door between worlds meant he would have to first pass through death. Perhaps not. He'd never actually asked what it entailed, merely accepted the role and speculated on his own, so part of this confusion was his own fault.

And anyway, the crystal was only a likely prediction. That did not mean that someone who sparkled could not die, nor that someone who did not sparkle could not live. There were many variables in war, and life was certainly one of them.

All but one adawehi were predicted to live, and he decided to go anyway. He was an older adawehi and declared that he would rather die in service of his people than live in a land he did not recognize with people who were not his own.

With everyone now aware of his likely fate, and having been given the chance to stay behind if fate was likely to be unkind to him, all that remained was the guiding fire.

The war adawehi retrieved the ark from the townhouse. It was a clay box about as long as Anagalisgi's forearm or perhaps a little longer, plain, with a lid. The adawehi set basswood and goldenrod in the bottom, then took another small stick of goldenrod and held it to the sacred fire. When it caught, he took the fire to the ark and lit the contents within. The wood and goldenrod caught easily, and fragrant smoke lifted eagerly to the sky, another good omen. This greatly excited the warriors, some of whom let out shrieking war whoops, eager to get moving.

When the fire was going well, the adawehi placed the lid over the box and looked at Aganstata.

"Our success is assured. Gather the warriors. We may leave at any time."

His command to gather the warriors was wholly unnecessary, and no one needed to be told twice. No one needed to be gathered. They had all been waiting for such a command all night and all day.

Aganstata donned his raven skin and went first to the road. Mankiller, Amadoya, and Chola joined him, all in their respective skins. Behind them was the skatiloski, the speaker. Beside him stood the katate kanehi, red war banner in hand. Around them were the adawehi, Anagalisgi included.

It was the skatiloski's duty to orate and inspire the warriors. This was not difficult to do, and the reversal of the bad omens by the expulsion of the impure fool only excited them more.

The seven war counselors led the warriors, all formed into their companies and led by their greatest warriors. Anagalisgi spotted his brother in the crowd, already prepared for war with his owl skin.

Aganstata and the other skiagvsta went forward first as scouts. With the Anigilisi so close to the Overhill, they could not be too careful. While they were gone, the skatiloski continued speaking, asking the adawehi for prayers on several occasions. Then, when the animal calls came back from the skiagvsta, letting them know the road was clear, the warriors started off.

The proper formations and companies quickly fell away as everyone found their preferred friends, though Anagalisgi made certain to stay close to the other adawehi. It did not take long for

Kiyuga to catch up with him.

"The omens are sound, then, brother?" Kiyuga asked seriously. No joking or trivial conversation was permitted on the war road.

"So they seem to be," Anagalisgi replied evasively.

"You are not as enthusiastic as the other adawehi or the skatiloski. What's wrong?"

"Personal omens only, from the spirits, as I fasted."

"The crystal sparkled when you walked by. That should offer some measure of confidence."

"Confusion, not confidence."

"You expect to die?"

"I don't know," Anagalisgi answered honestly. "I do not expect to live, but neither do I expect to die."

"Does another option exist?" Kiyuga managed an uncertain grin.

"The guardian of the door between worlds. That is what Ge'gwogv has told me."

"But what does that mean?"

"I don't know. Not exactly. But I have the feeling that I am going to find out, one way or another."

DᏨᎯᎮᎢ ᏔᏢᏬᎠ ᎨᏞᏢ

Ayadohlv'i Tahlsgo Sudali
A Duel With Demons

The exhilaration of the fasting and the war dance and all that followed quickly turned into stony resolve for the warriors as they continued on down the road. They moved swiftly, with great purpose. They were not going off to distant lands of other nations to raid for a few slaves. This time, they were protecting their own homeland, their way of life, maybe even their very existence. It was frightening and thrilling at the same time.

If they succeeded, their songs would be sung and names known for generations. They would tell their sons and nephews and grandsons and grandnephews of this time. They would always know the day that the invaders came and were repelled by the might and the power and the enduring faith and honor of the Aniyvwiya. And the Anigilisi would know it as well.

But if they failed, the only ones who would sing their songs would be the frightened survivors, still waiting for them in Aktiya Waya. Those lonely peaks would echo with the wails of the women as their husbands and sons and brothers and fathers and uncles did not return to fetch them. There would be only a few elders to pass on stories of their ways and traditions to the young boys, and a terrible risk of the knowledge being lost forever.

Worse than that, Kiyuga thought, there would be no one to carry on his line. He had no sisters, nor a wife, nor any nieces or nephews. The proud line of his father and mother would end with him and Anagalisgi. Kiyuga could not let that happen.

The skatiloski was in charge of all details on the march, where they went, how fast, where they should camp once the scouts deemed it safe, and when, where, and how much to hunt or forage. While there were already understood rules of these marches, the skatiloski, with the aid of the adawehi, would also dictate any additional rules for this particular march.

It was already forbidden to speak of trivial matters while on the march. In light of current events, as well as some lingering doubt as to the nature of the omens, it was decreed that there should be no talking whatsoever, except to warn of attack, make official reports or plans, or, for the adawehi, to pray and invoke the spirits. The enemy was already in their territory; stealth was of the utmost importance.

Si'tiku, Tsilhowi, and Talasi were nearly deserted as they passed through. In a way, this was a comfort, for it meant that the Anigilisi were not yet into the Overhill. Or they were not this far. The last report had them coming down the river, north of Tesenti. It would not take long for them to traverse the river, but they would be forced to stop before the waterfall southeast of Talasi. On the other hand, if the Aniyvwiya could intercept them while they were still on the river, that would prove a great advantage also. They would not need to kill them individually, just put a few holes in their canoes. Few Anigilisi could swim, and it would render their cannons useless.

All of these things Kiyuga considered as they made their way up the road. It was not yet high summer, but the heat and humidity was already unforgiving. The shade made the trip bearable, but it was still terribly warm.

With everyone vowed to silence, they moved like a cougar through the trees, invisible and swift, sounding only like the wind as it rustled the leaves, or the river as the current rumbled against rocks.

Kiyuga always tried to keep his brother within sight. Anagalisgi was always a bit elusive with his dreams, premonitions, and omens, but now he had the look of a man who was seeing everything for the last time and desperate to remember every detail.

The guardian of the door between worlds. That was what he had said. That was what Ge'gwogv had told him. But who or what was that? What did it mean? He did not expect to live, he'd said, but he also did not expect to die. What were the spirits telling him? Kiyuga had always understood that the spirits spoke a language that men could not know, and yet, they seemed to be communicating ideas that no one had ever heard of.

Did the sorceries have something to do with it? Had Anagalisgi truly begun to grasp the power of Creation? Was he going to somehow be the bridge between the mortal and the immortal? Was he going to become some sort of spirit himself? What did that mean for the rest of the Aniyvwiya going forward? If the spirits were going to use Anagalisgi to channel their ancient wisdom and knowledge and power to save the people, they appeared to be cutting it a little close.

They made camp for the night. Before they could even think about rest or food, they had to go down to the river and immerse themselves seven times, to purify themselves in case battle came upon them in the night. The adawehi also said prayers and invoked the spirits for guidance, courage, and protection.

Once they were finished with ablutions, some set about to gather firewood, but Aganstata stopped them. No fires were permitted this night. A survey from a high hill indicated that the Anigilisi were not far away, likely making fires of their own on a distant hill. If the Aniyvwiya could see their smoke, if indeed that was what it was, then the Anigilisi would surely see theirs. They could not risk being seen. Younger, smaller, faster boys were sent to scout ahead a bit, to report on the Anigilisi, their location, and when they got in their canoes again.

So the best Kiyuga could do was draw up some water in a gourd in order to soften the hard bread and cornmeal he'd brought with him. A few warriors had strips of smoked jerky. A couple of them shared.

Kiyuga sat beside his brother, who also ate of hard bread and cornmeal, as well as a few berries he'd found on the riverbank. Neither of them said a word. Kiyuga was unsure whether he wanted to speak at all. Anagalisgi's expression was both puzzled and depressed. Had he dreamed more? If he had, it wasn't related to the impending battle, or else it wasn't enough to turn them back.

A long time ago, Kiyuga had made a promise to his younger brother, that he would go before him in all things, even death. As he became a warrior and Anagalisgi an adawehi, it seemed that promise was a simple one and certain to be fulfilled. Now was the first time Kiyuga had ever doubted himself in that regard. The crystal telling was only a likelihood, not a guarantee. What if Anagalisgi truly did not survive?

Kiyuga chastised himself for such thoughts. He could not bury his brother before he was dead. The battle had not even begun, and even so, they were tasked with a different mission, one that was more likely to save their lives. Anagalisgi himself was uniquely qualified for the task. If the spirits had chosen him, surely he would not meet his end so casually.

It was unclear just how far Anagalisgi's power with the sorceries extended. Conjuring Time and manipulating the Forces of the world was unnerving enough, but he seemed also to have broken into the power of dreams and the mind, the very soul. Kiyuga clearly remembered his brother coming to him in a dream. Seeing his expression now, as they quietly nibbled on bread and cornmeal, Kiyuga was forced to wonder if Anagalisgi was also able now to read a man's thoughts. Such powers were traditionally reserved for witches, except Anagalisgi was anything but a witch.

With his brother's penetrating stare hooked into him like a fish on a line, Kiyuga went back to his meal. His brother had his own unique relationship with the spirits, one that Kiyuga could not understand, nor pretend to. His job was to be a warrior. With their combined talents, their task would be to rescue as many wounded warriors as possible and get them to safety. That was their mission, laid out by Aganstata himself, and that was what they would do when the time came.

Kiyuga's thoughts went one way, but his confidence went another. Chancing another look at his brother, Kiyuga could see that Anagalisgi was not fooled. In fact, he was probably having similar thoughts.

Would they meet the Anigilisi in battle tomorrow? Would the attack be glorious and victorious? Would anyone be alive to sing the songs of their bravery? Or would they all be huddled up, frightened and defeated, like rabbits, in Aktiya Waya?

Not wishing to think about such things anymore, Kiyuga finished his meal and lay down to sleep, straight on the ground, for no beds were to be made while on the march toward war.

Dawn had not quite come when the scouts returned. They spoke to the skiagvsta who then roused the whole camp and told them to be ready. Then the four skiagvsta left to scout for themselves while the warriors woke, gathered themselves, and went down to the river for more ablutions. By the time they were moving on down the trail, the first colors of dawn graced the horizon.

They did not move as swiftly as before, as they did not want to haphazardly stumble upon their enemy. Now they moved more slowly, even more quietly than before, waiting for the calls of one or more of the skiagvsta that they had found the enemy. Once they had done that, the skiagvsta would return to make final plans and give directions.

The adawehi stayed to the front of the group while the warriors slowly reformed themselves according to their companies. Kiyuga lost sight of his brother, but he did not worry about that now. Aganstata and the others would return with the final plans. He would direct them accordingly.

Kiyuga could feel his heart pounding in his chest. This was it. War was coming. War was here; battle was coming. This was his chance for glory unlike anything any of them had ever known, greater than their ancestors could have dreamed. Everything was at stake.

Then came the raven call. Aganstata had found the enemy. The other skiagvsta answered with their own calls. The raven call came again. The warriors slowed and finally stopped. They would wait for the skiagvsta to return. Kiyuga spotted Anagalisgi momentarily, and then he was gone.

They did not make camp this time, but neither did they stand around like a flock of turkeys waiting for an arrow. Instead they got off the road and melted into the trees, almost as if they might ambush the skiagvsta when they returned. Each man took care to be aware of himself and others around him, patiently waiting, hardly moving, barely breathing.

When the skiagvsta returned, the warriors did not all rush to meet them. Rather, the skatiloski and one of the adawehi stepped forward to meet them and verify that they were who they said they were. They did not need to be fooled at the last moment by witchcraft, an Anigilisi spy posing as the skiagvsta in order to lure out the warriors for the slaughter.

Once the skiagvsta were properly verified, the warriors slowly came out of hiding and waited for orders. The adawehi declared the vow of silence over, so any man might speak and ask questions of the skiagvsta and their plans.

"The Anigilisi travel by river, as expected," Aganstata reported. "They are in the process of bringing their supplies down the slopes to the bottom of the waterfall. Now is the best time to strike, when they have all of their supplies packed up."

"What about firing on them on the river?" someone wondered. "They will be unable to easily reach us; they will be vulnerable for longer."

"That is what we are doing," Amadoya said irritably. "But they are a formidable force moving very slowly. If we wait for all of them to be on the river before we strike, they will already be set upon Itsa'ti."

"Any boy or green warrior who has a gun but does not have a horse will stay here and fan out along the banks," Mankiller said. "Hide in the trees and the bushes, and be invisible. When the Anigilisi come by, fire upon them. You do not have to kill all of them in the canoe. Aim for the canoe itself. Few Anigilisi can swim.

"Meanwhile, the rest of us will take our places on the south slope, facing the waterfall. First we will fire upon them as they have their backs to the cliffs. They will have to climb to escape, hardly an easy feat. If they retreat, they will be forced to abandon those on the river. If the soldiers on the river retreat, they will have to contend with our gunfire and a difficult escape."

"We will not give chase if they escape up the cliffs," Aganstata went on. He continued before anyone could protest. "The escape is difficult for them, and we would be just as vulnerable if an ambush were staged for our pursuit. If they choose to retreat, then we will wait for nightfall before pursuing them."

"And if they do not retreat?" someone behind Kiyuga asked.

"Then I will lead the Ravens on the offensive. The Owls will run along the flank and prevent soldiers from attempting to escape up the valley or encircle us. The Wolves will reinforce us along the riverbank, but their primary objective will be taking whatever supplies they can from the canoes and destroying the rest. The Foxes who have guns will reinforce those firing on the Anigilisi on the river, and the rest will focus on reinforcing the Ravens and Owls. Any questions?"

"And my brother and I?" Kiyuga inquired casually.

Aganstata picked Kiyuga out of the crowd and nodded once. "Of course. Come here. I will speak with you privately."

The rest of the warriors were dismissed. Kiyuga and Anagalisgi were taken aside by Aganstata.

"You understand what you are to do?" Aganstata asked.

"You want us to tend to the wounded with the doctors," Anagalisgi began, "and also to get them to safety."

The skiagvsta nodded. "Yes. This is the best location we will get for a chance at victory. The terrain is in our favor, as is the movement of the Anigilisi. But we cannot take chances. If we are unsuccessful, we are the last to stand between the Anigilisi and Itsa'ti. The Anigilisi will take many prisoners. They will make slaves of some and examples of the rest. They will seek to crush us.

"A remnant must be preserved, more than just the women and children, more than the elders. We must yet have a fighting force. A wounded warrior is a burden on the battlefield, but he may yet fight another day. Your job is to ensure that he sees that day."

"What do you want us to do?" Kiyuga asked.

"Take the wounded warriors up the valley; the Owls and Foxes will ensure your escape. Get well away from the fighting before attempting to cross to Aktiya Waya. I have seen it on the faces of Nathan and Andrew that it is a difficult task, and I cannot imagine it will be any easier for you, as talented as you may be, Anagalisgi. If you must travel for some days before you are able to cross, then so be it. Get the wounded to safety, but do not neglect yourselves. If any Anigilisi give chase, do what you must, whether it is to try and outrun them or engage in battle yourselves."

"What should we do when we have seen the warriors to safety? Shall we return to Itsa'ti?"

Aganstata shook his head. "No. If we are defeated, it would be too great a risk. Return to the place from where you leave, if you can, or go to Atagulkalu's home. He will welcome you, I am certain. And he will have news to tell."

The brothers agreed and were dismissed.

"How shall we do it, then?" Kiyuga wondered. "How shall we gather the wounded to escape?"

"Sorcery," Anagalisgi decided. "I will conjure Time that we can step into the battlefield. I will assess the warriors for their injuries. You will help me get them to a safe place behind the Owls and Foxes."

"How long will we wait before leaving? We cannot hope to open a door to Aktiya Waya for each warrior individually. That is far too taxing. As Aganstata said, it is difficult for Nathan and Andrew; it will not be any easier for you, in spite of your talent."

"We will wait as long as we can. If defeat appears likely, or certain, then we will leave. We will need a greater head start to get out of range. Inevitably, we will leave some behind."

Kiyuga frowned, but he knew it was true. "Maybe we can come back later and rescue any who are taken prisoner. Whether the Anigilisi move on to Itsa'ti or retreat to their own lands, they will take time to get there."

"Agreed." Anagalisgi looked at Amayi. "He can take some terribly wounded on his back. Do you have a litter for any more that he is unable to carry?"

Kiyuga unfastened the litter from the side of the horse's saddle. "It will only hold one or two, maybe three if they are boys."

"Then that will be one or two or maybe three more that we will be able to save."

He wished he had his brother's confidence. Even if it was a mask for terrible anxiety, Anagalisgi had a certain air of surety, as if he knew exactly how this was all going to turn out. For as often as he'd proclaimed it a curse, to have such foreknowledge, Kiyuga wished he could have but a drop in his brother's well of information.

The warriors sorted themselves quickly, Kiyuga and Anagalisgi among them. Now was the time for action. Once more, the warriors blended into the trees, moving into position as Aganstata directed them. The Ravens were sent to various places on the hillside facing the waterfall while the Owls and Wolves slipped down the slope, the Owls to cover the valley, and Wolves to attack the canoes. The Foxes spread out behind them as reinforcements.

They were not to attack until they heard the first gunshots from up the river. Those were Aganstata's orders. Because of the noise of the waterfall, they may not hear it, which would work to their advantage to take them by greater surprise. So, just in case, a runner would be coming as well to tell them that the first shots had been fired. Judging by what they knew of Anigilisi tactics, they would have several dozen canoes on the river by the time those on the bank attacked. Not many soldiers to kill, when one considered the force that had overtaken the Middle Towns, but anything was better than nothing.

The messenger reached the warriors only moments before a panicked canoe could be heard shouting to the Anigilisi. By the time the soldiers on the bank still loading canoes looked up to see their comrades, Aganstata was calling out a war whoop that was undoubtedly heard back in Itsa'ti. The hidden Aniyvwiya warriors opened with a great volley of gunfire that struck down many Anigilisi soldiers before they had a chance to react.

Confusion reigned among the soldiers. Some were crying out that they were under attack. Some wailed about their injuries. A few of the officers were trying to take charge, barking orders like a mad dog and trying to rally their men to some semblance of order.

The warriors fired again. By now, the soldiers were attempting to flee back up the cliffs to safety. The warriors got off a third and fourth shot before Aganstata's raven call bade them cease.

The warriors did not run after the soldiers. They did not change their position. They did not flee or regroup or even move from their present personal location. Every man remained exactly where he was, waiting quietly, listening intently. Kiyuga wished he could hear what the Anigilisi were saying, what they were planning to do. But even as the rush of the waterfall disguised their movements to the Anigilisi, it also did the same in reverse.

All the same, he knew they would be coming. It might not be right away, but they would be coming.

He blinked as a gun went off not far from him. He saw a soldier on the opposite hill, perhaps trying to sneak into a clump of bushes with his musket, fall and roll down the cliff, landing near one of the canoes. Several more were taken out in this manner. Kiyuga knew it was only to buy the soldiers time to get ready, but this had all been anticipated. No matter what, the soldiers were still going to have to climb back down the cliff, which would leave them especially vulnerable again. How many men would they sacrifice just to have a chance at reaching their attackers?

Movement at the top of the hill caught Kiyuga's attention. But what he expected and what he saw were two very different things.

He did not initially see soldiers, but warriors. His first thought was that these were Aninvdawegi and other Anigilisi allies. Then he realized that he knew some of those warriors. Then he became confused why those warriors should be over there and fighting with the Anigilisi.

Slowly he came to realize that they were not fighting with the soldiers. They had been captured in battle and taken prisoner. Now the Anigilisi were using them as shields. They'd bound the warriors as best they could to keep them from running away or fighting back, but the treacherous terrain proved difficult to that end.

All the same, the warriors on the hillside were momentarily frozen, unsure what to do. Any one of them would gladly die in battle, but could they really fire on the soldiers now and risk killing their own warriors? Would it be a mercy killing, or would it bring wrath upon their own heads from the spirits for killing a brother?

Any soldiers who did not have a warrior as a shield were fired upon, but those who did have the shields were able to safely navigate to the bottom of the cliffs. Some went to the canoes, others prepared for battle.

Once on more even ground, however, the game changed. Aganstata let out a great war whoop and led the charge, his Ravens flying out alongside him. Some Foxes on the hillside provided cover fire against the soldiers who stood upon the cliffs and tried to pick them off. The warriors being used as shields saw Aganstata coming and immediately set about trying to free themselves, wrenching against their bonds, using bites and kicks against their captors. One managed to get a knife and cut his ropes and then set about freeing his fellows.

As the Ravens engaged the soldiers, using the driving momentum of the run down the hill to break their line with ease, the Wolves moved in toward the canoes. The newly-freed warriors were already pawing through the supplies, looking for guns, knives, anything they could get their hands on.

A line of Anigilisi soldiers marched to the edge of the cliff at the top of the waterfall and began firing down at the warriors. The Foxes responded by trying to pick them off, little more than a variation of a boy trying to plink squirrel tails from a distance. The soldiers on the cliff, unable to see the Foxes, because of both the thick foliage as well as their camouflage body paint, could do little to protect themselves, though they did not retreat to safety. One soldier was shot and fell off the cliff. If the shot hadn't killed him, then his strike upon the ground surely would have, to say nothing of how he crashed through the bottom of a canoe as well.

Kiyuga jumped at a hand on his shoulder, but it was only Anagalisgi. His brother silently motioned for him to follow.

They slid along the top of the slope, still protected by foliage, circling the back of the Raven position, behind the Foxes still firing on the Anigilisi on the cliffs. A few Wolves slunk up the hill, delivering small packages of ammunition and gunpowder.

The Owls had silently fanned out down the slope and as far up the cliffs as they dared, blocking access to the valley. So far, the Anigilisi had not yet tried to escape this way, and the line was silent. Kiyuga and Anagalisgi circled behind them, a hill on either side, and watched and waited.

The Anigilisi had finally gotten some semblance of order to their ranks. Now, rather than sending the sacrificial lambs down the cliff to assess the situation and draw out the warriors, the soldiers came down, ready for a fight. The Foxes still tried to pick them off as they slid down the cliff, but sheer numbers threatened to overwhelm the warriors. A contingent of Owls waited patiently in the trees. They now began to fire upon the soldiers. Still it seemed a futile effort as the soldiers just kept coming, like swarms of bees that never ended.

Anagalisgi looked at Kiyuga. "Are you ready?"

Kiyuga frowned as he observed the scene before him. Finally, "I'm ready."

His brother began conjuring, then, and Kiyuga watched the scene before him slow and finally come to a stop. Multiple lead balls hung in the air like a scattering of insects. One warrior was bringing his hatchet down in a mighty swing, only a hand's width from a soldier's neck. Elsewhere, a soldier had grabbed a warrior by the shoulder and was in the process of driving a knife into his gut, the tip of the blade only just touching skin.

"We should help them," Kiyuga stated, looking around and carefully maneuvering a suddenly skittish Amayi through the carnage.

"Do what you can," Anagalisgi told him, sweat beading on his forehead from the effort on conjuring. "But remember that our first mission is to get the wounded to safety."

"If we help them now, there may be fewer wounded to worry about."

Nevertheless, they went their separate ways on the battlefield. Kiyuga took a number of lead balls out of the air, those he could reach, either putting them in the ground or redirecting them to be on a path toward a soldier and not a warrior. He rescued the warrior about to be gored, prying the soldier's hand off his shoulder and moving the warrior out of the way. The warrior had only a small scratch on his belly, but he was otherwise unharmed.

He saved several more warriors in this way before Anagalisgi called to him for help.

The warrior had been shot and then stabbed several times with a bayonet, but was somehow still alive. Anagalisgi had performed some sorcery to stabilize him, but the warrior was still unable to rescue himself.

Kiyuga hefted the man and laid him across Amayi's back. Anagalisgi kept the man outside of the conjuring, so he would be unaware of these events. Other wounded he had brought into the conjuring, and they were able to slowly limp along with them, back to the line of Owls where they slipped through safely.

"We could kill them, you know," Kiyuga stated before Anagalisgi could stop his conjuring. He looked back at the battlefield. "We could kill them all. They are at our mercy right now, entirely defenseless."

"Such a thing would be terribly dishonorable," Anagalisgi said, as if shocked he would suggest such a thing. He went on before Kiyuga could object. "The Anigilisi have no honor; this is known. Because of this, and the fact that they have not done the same to us, I am inclined to believe that they are unaware of the sorceries, as Nathan and Andrew have said. If we were to do this, we would have no more honor than they.

"Why have the spirits allowed us the use of this sorcery? We did not have it until our time of need. The gift of the sorceries is not to become conquerors as they are conquerors. It is meant for our protection and survival. We will not use them in wrath and dishonor. You will not speak of such things again."

Kiyuga, chastened, fell silent. His brother stopped conjuring and the battle resumed. From the noise, there was a brief moment of confusion, but it quickly faded back into the organized chaos that was battle.

He knew his brother's words and understood them, but he could not say he was not frustrated by them. Was survival all they were meant for? He did not need to conquer others, but he wanted to do more than exist. The warriors who had been captured still existed, but they were miserable. Would they not want to die in battle rather than exist?

The Anigilisi were not going to give up. The war was too long and hard-fought on both sides for one side to simply give up. One side had to defeat the other. The Anigilisi had great supplies and resources and many men. The only way they would be defeated was if they were defeated so soundly that all of their greatness meant nothing. What was the purpose of the sorceries except, perhaps, to do just that? Not merely allow for survival, but a sound defeat of their enemies that they might all live in peace?

But regardless of his personal feelings, his brother had spoken. Anagalisgi rarely gave orders, but if he ordered Kiyuga not to speak of such a thing again, then he would not speak of such a thing again.

A few of the doctors joined Anagalisgi as he tended the wounded. They had been able to bring fourteen out, including the one on Amayi, but Kiyuga knew there were more out there still. Many had been shot, others wounded in close combat. A few had the courage and willpower, once their heads had cleared, to pick up a weapon and return to the fight.

Kiyuga longed to be with them in the thick of battle, but he had a mission to complete. If they had to flee with the wounded, and if they were pursued, he would be their best chance of defending themselves. That meant more than offering just another body here.

The battle had reached a sort of stalemate. There was only so much room to fight in the narrow valley. More soldiers could not come down, and even if they did manage to push back the warriors a little, they would not blindly pursue them into the forest for fear of there being more hidden warriors just waiting for them, the same reason Aganstata would not pursue the soldiers until dark. Now it seemed to be a game of one side trying to outlast the other and kill as many enemies as possible before being forced to retreat.

The Anigilisi made another push, this time going after the Wolves, trying to drive them back, away from the canoes. Kiyuga heard an officer shouting at the soldiers, telling them to launch the canoes, launch the canoes, launch the bloody canoes. Get in the canoes and try to get around the damn savages.

By sheer numbers, the Anigilisi were able to force their way down the cliffs and effectively create a human wall in order to protect a contingent of soldiers as they prepared to launch some of the canoes.

Kiyuga glanced up the slope. He could not see the Foxes, but he hoped they could see what was going on. If the Anigilisi surrounded them, it would be a slaughter. Already some soldiers were testing the Owl line. They had no reason to try and escape this way, so Kiyuga could only conclude that it was a diversion. Get the warriors away from the river and give the high ground to the soldiers. Could no one else see this?

Fear gripped him as he saw one of the canoes get underway, twenty soldiers inside. A couple of shots were fired upon it, but the leading soldier barked at the men to keep going and put their backs into it.

Sensing his distress, Amayi was fidgety as well. The horse snorted and pawed a few times, turned toward the battle and then away from it, uncertain what it wanted to do, uncertain what Kiyuga wanted to do. Kiyuga knew what he wanted to do, but his mission was here, to protect his brother and those under his care.

At the same time, he was trained in the sorceries as well. He was not as skilled as Anagalisgi, but he was not helpless.

"I have to help them," Kiyuga said, more to himself than anyone.

He knew Anagalisgi looked at him, but if he said anything, it was lost to the wind as Kiyuga turned Amayi and kicked the horse into motion. The horse bounded up the slope, behind the Owls and Foxes, climbing up to the road where the Ravens had lain in wait. Kiyuga could hear the soldiers on the river, could see that most of the boys and green warriors had gone to the main battle after turning back the canoes. To his relief, some of the Foxes had seen what was going on and had returned, but it was terribly difficult to stop the Anigilisi from surrounding them.

Chola seemed to recognize this as well, but he appeared to have something of a plan. Kiyuga saw a couple of the warriors carrying one of the large two-man saws that the Anigilisi used to swiftly cut down trees.

"Yvgidahi!" Chola hissed, waving him down. Kiyuga went to him. "You are trained in the sorceries, yes?"

"Yes," Kiyuga said. "I have an idea."

"So do we. Do you know Udilegv'i ale Uhyvtsa?"

"Yes. That was my idea, to freeze the river to prevent them from—"

"Good. If you can do that, it will buy us time to cut down these trees. We will either crush them or dam the river like a beaver so they cannot move. It may also flood the valley and stop the battle, separate us for a time."

"Understood."

Kiyuga was already dismounting and slinking through the brush toward the river. The Anigilisi could move swiftly in their canoes when they wanted to, but he was faster still, conjuring Time so he could get ahead of them even more. He knew it could take time to use Udilegv'i ale Uhyvtsa, and he was fighting dreadful summer heat to turn water into ice. He didn't need to freeze the entire river, just this small expanse, enough to buy time for the others to fell trees upon the soldiers.

He slid down the bank and lay down under some bushes to hopefully hide himself. He would be defenseless while he did this. With any luck, if they did see him, they would think him dead from the earlier skirmish. Taking a breath, he slowly reached out one hand and touched the water with just a finger.

It was already cool and beautiful. He just needed to make it a little cooler. And a little cooler. And a little cooler.

Nathan and Andrew had called this particular sorcery Thermodynamics. They also explained that Thermodynamics was a principle of balance. When left alone, they would equal each other and become lukewarm. But there could be no vacuum between the two. If cold was taken away, heat had to take its place. Similarly, if heat were removed from something, cold must take its place. It was merely a shuffling of something that existed constantly.

So it was not that Kiyuga cooled the river so much as he took its heat. He could see ice crystals beginning to form on the water's surface, yet he was sweating terribly. No ice formed around his finger. The ice crystals began to stick together and form chunks. He could hear shouting from the soldiers, confused questions about what in bloody hell was wrong with the river. Kiyuga pushed himself harder. He was dizzy was heat fatigue and could barely breathe, but he had to do more. They could push aside ice chunks, but they would not pass through solid ice.

The ice flow solidified into a chunky mass. Orders were shouted to bring the canoes about, reverse course, and not crash into the damn thing, whatever it was and however it got there.

Kiyuga sighed and opened his eyes. Apparently he'd passed out. He didn't know for how long, though he decided it could not have been too long. There was still a large solid ice flow on the river, but the canoes had largely gone; several of them looked to have been smashed by large trees which Chola and the Foxes had cut down. So they had been successful. Why, then, did the sounds of battle seem so close?

Carefully, he picked his way out of the bushes. Farther down, he could see half a dozen canoes had landed on the shore. Panicking, Kiyuga made his way back to the road.

The Anigilisi had managed to land a small force behind the warriors. The Foxes and Wolves were driving them back easily, but with their attention diverted, the Ravens and Owls had to be overwhelmed, Kiyuga thought.

Taking hatchet in one hand and club in the other, Kiyuga approached the minor battle. In his peripheral vision, he saw Amayi galloping toward him. Without losing or holstering his weapons, Kiyuga threw himself over the horse's back as it came beside him and managed to right himself just in time to swing his hatchet down and split open the skull of a soldier who was very near to a Wolf warrior.

Kiyuga was still very warm from what he'd done to the river, and he was still fatigued from the heat he had taken into himself. Perhaps it was this fatigue that clouded his judgment so that he considered his brother's words for only a moment before grouchily disregarding them. Let the spirits punish him; at least there would still be warriors alive to care and fight another day.

So he conjured Time. It was clumsy and uncoordinated, hardly as rigid and perfect as Anagalisgi's conjuring had been. The soldiers and the scene of battle did not come to a complete stop, but it was close enough. Kiyuga rode among them, striking them down with hatchet and club until the small encircling force was all dead.

When he released his conjuring and Time was back to normal, he could hardly see for the dizziness, headache, and fatigue. It was amazing he remained upright on Amayi's back. Exhausted, he put his weapons away and looked for any wounded. Several warriors were dead, but of the injured, they could all walk. A few refused to hide behind the Owl line and instead returned to whatever they had been doing before the distraction. But there were other warriors who, despite their inner pride, would be unable to return to battle just yet. Reluctantly, they agreed to follow Kiyuga down the slope to be treated.

With the distraction of the Foxes and Wolves, the Anigilisi had made another push and all lines had fallen back. Kiyuga could see all of the warriors were exhausted, but the Anigilisi still had men to spare. Their biggest problem was how to relieve and treat the exhausted soldiers without having to make them climb back up the cliffs.

The Owls had managed to hold their position, but the wounded had been moved a short distance up the valley, out of sight of the battle. Kiyuga delivered the wounded to the doctors and nearly fell off Amayi himself.

"Kiyuga!" Anagalisgi exclaimed. "Are you wounded?"

Kiyuga sighed and shook his head as he sat down. "No, I don't think so."

"Why did you run off? Where did you go?"

"The Anigilisi were trying to get around us on the river. I had to stop them. I used Udilegv'i ale Uhyvtsa to freeze the river, but soldiers still came around from behind."

"Yes, the Foxes and Wolves dropped back to take care of them, but then the Anigilisi made another push."

"So I saw."

"Kiyuga, we have to be ready to flee. It's only a matter of time. We have sixty wounded —"

"Sixty?"

"Yes, and these are only the ones we've been able to save. There are more out there, and I want to get as many as possible before we finally retreat. Do you think you can walk?"

Kiyuga sighed again and got to his feet. "It seems I have no choice. When, do you think?"

Anagalisgi looked uncertain. "Soon. Sit and rest a moment. Have some water. Be ready."

It had now come to a point where some of their patients came to them. It wasn't just the injuries they'd sustained, but the exhaustion from fighting so hard for so long. This was not their way. The Aniyvwiya way was to surprise an enemy, scare him, take a few scalps, and melt back into the forest undetected. This open combat that the Europeans did was still very foreign and still very difficult. A few warriors returned to battle, but many were ready to return home. This was not their way, and this was not their day for victory.

Kiyuga tried not to let such despairing thoughts consume him, but he would be lying if he did not admit to wanting to go home, or at least to Aktiya Waya. He took a drink of water and waited. He listened to the sounds of battle only steps away. If he just stood and walked ten paces to the south, he would see it.

But he did not. He stayed where he was and waited.

Finally he heard the sound, the only sound that was even remotely similar to the great war whoops of the Aniyvwiya. The Highlanders had joined the battle.

The Highlanders were perhaps the only soldiers that were respected, even as adversaries. They wore the clothing of their homeland and ancestors, and they did not need "supplies" to go to battle. If he had a gun, he would use a gun. If he had a knife, he would use a knife. If he had no weapon at all, he would use his bare hands with just as much ferocity. A few of the greater Highlander warriors even carried great, heavy swords that could cleave a man in two in a single swing.

The Highlanders were not here to reinforce failing military tactics. They were here to put a stop to the warriors' attack, and to end this war.

Kiyuga stood and went to Anagalisgi. He put a hand on his brother's shoulder. "It's time to go."

Anagalisgi looked ready to protest. Then he, too, heard the bellow of the Highlanders descending upon the battlefield. Reluctantly, he nodded. "Agreed. We'll make one last rescue attempt, and then we'll leave."

They headed toward the battlefield. The roars of the Highlanders grew louder, and Kiyuga saw that even the common soldiers got out of their way, that they would not be struck down by haphazard fury. There was still cover fire from the cliffs for a time, but eventually that ceased as the Highlanders engaged the warriors. Most did not even have weapons, only brute strength. Kiyuga spotted one man with one of the heavy swords, a double hand guard distinguishing it from other similar swords.

The battlefield froze suddenly as Anagalisgi conjured Time. All sound died away and the brothers were left alone, as if the last two warriors alive. Judging by the new wave of kilted soldiers swarming down the cliffs, that could very well be the case if they did not escape soon.

At this point, there were very few wounded to gather. Some had died, others Anagalisgi judged unable to be saved. Any warriors who remained in battle were less wounded and more fatigued.

"We should bring them with us as well," Kiyuga said. "At the very least, they will provide greater defense as we escape. I cannot do it alone."

Anagalisgi frowned but agreed. They chose warriors who were in the path of the rampaging Highlanders or perhaps already engaged. One man was attempting to wrestle a Highlander barehanded, but it was like trying to wrestle a bear. The warrior was initially confused as he was pulled out of the battle, but was no less grateful for the rescue from certain death.

"They are animals," the man said, puffing with exhaustion. "Savages. Absolute savages." He sighed. "But they are a worthy opponent."

"A worthy opponent will kill you as readily as an unworthy one," Kiyuga told him. "Come now. The wounded need help to reach Aktiya Waya."

The man nodded. "How many horses will we need? I will gather some."

Because of the terrain, once the initial attack was over and battle shrank into close combat, many of the horses were turned loose. The man went to gather some of them now while Kiyuga stayed with his brother to help the wounded and take a few more able-bodied warriors. Only one protested and demanded to be sent back to battle. He would not flee like a woman; if he must die, he would die as a warrior. No amount of reasoning or pleading would dissuade him, so Anagalisgi sent him back.

They did as much as they could, but Anagalisgi was exhausted from conjuring and could not continue for as long as he had earlier. Kiyuga understood how he felt; he was still quite weary from his own sorcery use. All the same, it did little to comfort as Anagalisgi finally admitted his own defeat and turned to leave the battlefield. There were still more wounded to be saved. Now they would either die or be captured by the Anigilisi. There were still able-bodied warriors who could help them escape. But they could not take everyone away, and some would inevitably be wounded or killed.

"We can't save everyone in the present," Kiyuga found himself saying. "But what we can do is our best to save our future."

Anagalisgi nodded, not looking at him. "I know. It doesn't make it any easier, though. How many of these warriors were foretold that they would live, and they will not? How many were told that they would die, and they will not? What purpose does it serve?" He looked back longingly at the battlefield before it disappeared around the corner and he ceased his conjuring.

Thirteen horses were brought, including Amayi. All took wounded upon their backs, and a few would pull litters behind them as well. It reminded Kiyuga of his trek to take the women, children, and elders to Aktiya Waya. Except here, danger was far closer.

"We'll have to travel for several days before we can leave," Anagalisgi was saying. "We are too close to the battle to conjure and save you, and too weak to try except as a last resort. We must get far away and rest. Then we will go to Aktiya Waya."

The able-bodied warriors agreed wordlessly. Some of the wounded looked uncertain, as if assessing themselves to determine how useful they might be in a battle to escape.

There were about eighty of them, Kiyuga judged, all of them good warriors, experience ranging from still a boy to well seasoned. He did not see any of the skiagvsta or senior warriors, had not seen them on the battlefield, knew nothing of what had become of them. There was no one to give them orders now, nothing except for Anagalisgi and his dreams. At this point, they had only each other and a hope.

DꙄΛᎥT ᏢᏢᏬᎠA ᏚᏢᏘᏯ

Ayadohlv'i Tahlsgo Gahlgwogi
Divide and Conquer

They used the final wave of battle as cover for their escape, but it was not long before they suspected pursuit. A couple of the able-bodied warriors took the Fox position, to report on their pursuers. A couple more took the Wolf and Owl positions to their flanks, and Kiyuga went ahead as the Raven.

They would not be leaving for Aktiya Waya today; that much he knew. They were all too tired to make the crossing, let alone try to open Galohisdi. Some were injured badly and needed care if they were going to survive until nightfall. Pursuit was evident, but danger was not imminent as long as they kept moving.

They had to go north. North and east, farther into the mountains. The Anigilisi were not so keen about climbing the mountains, and pursuers would not want to stray so far from the main army. At least, that was the hope. The French had not fared well against the British in the war and were on the run themselves, meaning the red coats now swarmed all over the fields and mountains.

They could expect no help.

They were on their own until they could cross to Aktiya Waya.

Kiyuga did not want to stray too far from the group himself in case they were attacked. They did not have the luxury of numbers or strength. He needed to be with them. He needed to be out front to help them. There was just no good or easy way to do this. Even escorting the women and children now seemed a far easier task.

He spent much of his scouting time simply listening and waiting. He would go out ahead of the group a fair distance, then pause and wait. He might hide behind a bush or climb a tree, and just listen. The Anigilisi knew nothing of stealth when out in the wilds, which proved to be a distinct advantage for the Aniyvwiya.

He would stay in his hiding spot until he heard or caught a glimpse of his party come upon him. Once he was satisfied that all was well, he would move ahead of them again.

He dropped back to them only once that first day to ask how things were.

"I don't expect Ulodskv to see the morning," Anagalisgi said quietly. "He has lost a great deal of blood and has fallen asleep, not to be roused. He breathes still, but he is very weak."

"Would it help to stop for a bit?" Kiyuga wondered. "There is a river not far ahead. Have you heard from the Fox?"

"Not long before you returned, he also reported it clear a fair distance, though he still suspects pursuit." His brother frowned. "It would not hurt to stop for a moment, as long as we do not fall asleep."

That was the challenge, wasn't it? There were several times where Kiyuga was sure he'd nodded off while hiding. Maybe, then, he wasn't hiding and waiting for any potential attackers, but simply looking for a place to sleep.

Nevertheless, he went ahead once more to ensure a clear road for the party to the river. Once there, he searched the area, upstream, downstream, the road beyond. All was quiet, as if great tragedy had not happened only earlier in the day. But then, to a tree that may outlive ten men, what was one day? What was conflict to a tree?

Kiyuga went to the river and drank. Not much later, the party arrived, as well as the other scouts.

"Anything?" Kiyuga inquired of the scouts while the party drank water and Anagalisgi tended to the wounded once more.

"A trapper cabin to the east, but that's it," the Wolf reported.

"Nothing," the Owl said.

"And behind us?" Kiyuga asked of the Fox.

"We have pursuers, though not enthusiastic ones," the Fox reported. "They complain much and often stray from the road, easily distracted by anything that will cause them to be slow without stopping. If we can stay ahead of them for a day or two, they may lose interest and return."

"Better than having to stay ahead of attentive hunters," Kiyuga mused. "Take a rest here, and we will travel a bit more this evening."

The days were long, but the mountains still hid the sun easily past the noontime. They could travel a bit more. He was hoping that their lazy pursuers might give up early and afford them greater distance.

Kiyuga went to his brother. "How is everyone?"

"Exhausted," Anagalisgi replied, yawning even as he said it.

"How is Ulodskv?"

"He will be dead before morning. I don't need to divine this; it is certain."

"Should we wait here, then, so he may be buried and you can purify yourself before continuing?"

Anagalisgi hesitated. "It would be a respectful thing to do, but it will do no good if our pursuers catch up to us. The dead cannot bury the dead."

"Fox says our pursuers are lazy and sluggish. Surely one night will not do us harm? If we collapse from exhaustion, we run a similar risk."

After another moment, his brother nodded. "Your assessment is fair and accurate. If we rest now and do well, we may be able to cross to Aktiya Waya in the morning and have no fear of pursuit."

Kiyuga frowned. "You don't think you could open Galohisdi now and send at least Ulodskv to Aktiya Waya?"

"Kiyuga, I can barely open my eyes, never mind Galohisdi. Even so, I don't believe there is anything that can be done for him now."

Nevertheless, Anagalisgi got water for himself to drink as well as more to wipe down the dying man's face. He had several terrible wounds that had since bled him dry, or so it seemed. It was likely his blood that had kept their pursuers interested. Maybe if the blood trail ended here, their pursuers would give up and go home, leaving the rest of them free to travel at their own pace and make the crossing when they were ready.

It was a hope.

Kiyuga nibbled on a bit of cornmeal, suddenly aware of how hungry he was. Only a stone's throw upstream, a couple of the lesser wounded warriors were rigging together a quick fish net which they lowered into the water.

"Do we want to risk a fire?" someone asked as the warriors started tossing fish onto the bank.

On the one hand, they needed to stay as invisible as possible to hide from their pursuers. On the other hand, they needed food to keep going. Or perhaps they ought to fast again? Would it bring them any favor from the spirits to help their escape? Had it done them any good to fast and keep faith before the battle?

Kiyuga was torn, and he hated himself for it. He felt disloyal in a way, faithless. But he was hungry and exhausted, both physically and spiritually. Finally he nodded. "Only one. Keep it small. Dead wood only, so there is no smoke."

It was an odd sensation, being the one in charge. He was not necessarily the most senior warrior here, but Aganstata had chosen him for this mission and others were respecting him for it. They were looking to him to get them through this. Well, he would certainly try.

They ate fish that evening, as the sun went down. Even with the darkness, Kiyuga did not allow the fire to get very big. Just enough to see each other across the fire, just enough to cook what they ate and cure the rest, which they would take with them in the morning.

Once his own hunger was satisfied, Kiyuga realized his brother was nowhere to be seen, though he was located quickly enough.

"He's dead," Anagalisgi said before he could ask the question.

"He will be remembered," was all he could offer.

"He will." His brother stood. "I will bury him tonight and purify myself as I must. We will continue in the morning."

"When will you sleep? We are relying on you to make the crossing. You are asleep on your feet as it is. We will not be able to cross if you are too weak or injured or anything."

"Kiyuga, this must be done; you know that. I will sleep when I am done burying Ulodskv and have been purified. Besides, there are still other weak and wounded among us. We may have to wait another day or two."

Kiyuga sighed. "I suppose, as long as we are not in immediate danger."

"Trust me, brother."

"I do."

With that, they separated. Anagalisgi went off to fulfill his duties, and Kiyuga returned to the fire where he informed the others of Ulodskv's passing. There were a few murmurs, but little more.

"We must be awake with the sun, in order to stay ahead of our pursuers," Kiyuga said. "Another day, maybe two, and then we will make the crossing to Aktiya Waya, to safety."

More murmurs. No objections, no excitement. Only fatigue.

Kiyuga knew exactly how they felt, and soon enough, his eyes had closed and he was drifting off.

He did not remember his dreams, and even if he had, he was given no time to consider them, for he was startled awake by shouts of alarm. As he scrambled to his feet, he saw that it was well past dawn. Around him, the party was hastily gathering themselves and making ready to leave. Horses snorted and pawed, and Anagalisgi was trying to juggle the wounded, getting people on horses or in litters and ready to go.

"What's going on?" Kiyuga demanded.

"We slept late and the Anigilisi are close," someone told him.

No more needed to be said.

Having come from battle, where they already packed only what they needed, there was very little they had to gather. The thing that slowed them down was trying to accommodate the wounded, get them situated on horses or in litters.

Kiyuga sent out a Fox scout even before they were ready to move, and just as soon as he felt comfortable in leaving them to move on their own, he also darted ahead as the Raven. There was no use running from one enemy right into the hands of another.

All the same, a full night's rest was very refreshing, and he actually felt up to his task. He wanted to scout far ahead, but he didn't want to get so far from the party that he would not hear any cries for help. Although, the Anigilisi had their guns, and gunfire echo would carry much farther than he was likely to travel. But still, he did not want to be unable to return in good time if the need arose.

He did not scout as he had the previous day, slinking from bush to bush, or branch to branch. While he remained cautious, quiet, and alert, he also moved much faster and covered a broader range. In addition to seeking out enemies, he also looked for secret, private areas where they might rest a bit, gather their strength, and cross over to Aktiya Waya without being spotted.

Several times he wanted to return and check on the party, but he refrained. He could not worry over them as a mother; he had to lead them as a worthy warrior. Their confidence would directly mirror his strength; he couldn't let them down.

He came across a small cluster of homes once, a few French trappers outside fleshing some furs. He paused and considered whether he should approach. Perhaps they would have knowledge of any Anigilisi in the area. Perhaps they would have something for trade like ammunition, something the Aniyvwiya sorely lacked. Or perhaps they would aid their pursuers.

That last part was unlikely. Even if they had lost the European war, that did not make the two peoples allies. These Frenchmen were unlikely to give them away, not anymore than they were already given away. Taking a breath and saying a prayer, Kiyuga made himself known.

"Bonjour! Je suis un ami!" he said as the Frenchmen startled and reached for their guns. *"Un ami! Ami!"*

He put his hands up as he'd seen others do. One of the trappers put his gun down.

"Comment vous appelez-vous?" he asked.

"Yvgidahi. Je suis Ayvwiya. Tsalagi. Cherokee. Un ami."

He could see the trappers were still wary, but they at least lowered their weapons.

"Going to war, I see," the first trapper commented.

"Escaping from it."

"Oh?"

"We are being pursued from the south. Do you know of any British in the area ahead, to the north?"

For a long moment, Kiyuga was afraid the man would not reply. Then, "You're going to want to cut east. British are coming back from Pennsylvania, Canada, all those places. They're coming back from the Ohio, too, but they'll cut north, follow the shoreline rather than risk the mountains. If you're looking to hide, go east first, higher into the hills."

"There are no British there?"

"What am I, a fortune teller? I can only tell you what I know and make a guess. Your guess is as good as mine. You might run into some Moravians, but they're no threat."

"Moravians?"

"Missionaries. They're moving west. As I said, no threat to you."

Kiyuga nodded. "*Merci, monsieur.* Do you have anything for trade? Ammunition, perhaps?"

The man barked a laugh. "I wish. All of the ammunition went to the soldiers. Problem was, ammunition is only good if you have weapons and soldiers to wield them. We had neither. So I have none for you. If you come across some, let me know."

Kiyuga took his leave of the man and vanished back into the forest.

So, north was likely to find Anigilisi as they cleaned up and returned from their war with the French. East was their better bet, climbing higher into the mountains. With any luck, their pursuers would grow weary or bored and break off the chase.

He made his way back to the party. The sun was just beginning to fall to the west.

"We were beginning to think something had happened to you," Anagalisgi said.

The party moved with some speed, although their urgency was nowhere to be found.

"I came across some Frenchmen. I asked if they knew of any Anigilisi in the area."

"Did they?"

"To the north, yes, as they return from war. But they are likely to stay north. Our best path takes us east, higher into the hills."

Anagalisgi frowned, his expression turning to that of some sort of spiritual consideration. Then, "Yes, I suppose it does."

"Do you know something?"

"For myself only."

"And the others?"

"We have not encountered the Anigilisi following us, nor have we heard them, though the Fox has not returned. Owl and Wolf returned once to say that all appeared clear so far. Then they went out again."

Kiyuga nodded. "I will also go out again. We must turn our path east."

"We must pray to outrun the Anigilisi in good time, then. The hills will slow them down, but it will also slow us down a great deal, with the wounded."

"None have recovered enough to walk well and keep up?"

His brother gave him a look. "The pack is only as strong as its weakest member. We can only move as fast as our slowest member."

Just because it was true didn't mean Kiyuga had to like it. He looked around at the party, tried to gauge the slowest and weakest members, tried to figure out if there was any way to speed them up and put greater distance between them and the Anigilisi.

"We are doing the best we can," Angalisgi told him. "And I know that you will readily return and fight if there is trouble. But until then, you must be our leader. Go, be the Raven."

After a second of hesitation, Kiyuga nodded. "Of course. Be well, little brother."

Anagalisgi's expression turned unreadable. Kiyuga did not stop to dwell on it as he moved ahead of the group, the Raven once more.

He went ahead north on the trail, looking for a good spot to turn east. He had to be mindful that they were a large party moving through the hills. They had wounded who would not be able to climb well, and some of the horses had litters behind them which, if they weren't careful, could dump the wounded on the ground.

When he found such a spot, he made a mark on a tree and laid out a bundle of raven feathers pointing in the new direction. There was no trail as such, but it was not difficult to grasp that he wanted them to go up a certain slope which appeared much gentler than some of the surrounding hills. When the party came this way, Anagalisgi or someone would pick up the bundle of feathers so the Anigilisi did not see them and also follow. The mark on the tree could be anything, and he made it to look as though a bear had clawed the bark to mark territory.

They could only hope.

He set out east and north from that spot, following the slope and trying to judge ease of escape. If they could just make it to a safe spot where they could hide for a bit, allow his brother to rest and gather his strength, they might have a chance. There were plenty of caves in the mountains; he just needed to find a suitable one without having to travel inward too far. They were only trying to outrun or outwit the Anigilisi. They didn't need to anger any evil spirits in the caves. Even with Anagalisgi as an attending adawehi, angry spirits were a little harder to outrun than mere soldiers.

The slope was fairly gentle and eventually led to a pass down into another valley. The problem was that there appeared to be some kind of small settlement in the valley. It was impossible to tell from this distance who it was, but he decided to err on the side of caution and assume they were enemies until he had reason to believe otherwise.

And anyway, the narrowest part of the pass proved to be a good spot to camp for the night. It was surrounded by large trees and thick vegetation, steep slopes on either side narrowed the area considerably, making it far easier for a smaller force to hold off a larger force if the need arose.

He retraced his steps back down the mountain until he found the party, a short distance up from his directional marker. Anagalisgi gave him a knowing look as he returned the bundle of feathers.

"You've found a good road for us, then?" he wondered.

Kiyuga nodded. "We'll camp in a narrow pass tonight. It is covered and easily defended. As long as we do not have a large fire, we should not be spotted by those in the valley settlement."

"Is it an Anigilisi settlement?"

"I don't know, I couldn't tell. But it's the best spot to camp for the night; we can avoid the settlement easily enough tomorrow."

Some still looked uneasy, but they trusted him and did not say anything about it.

"How are you doing, brother?" Kiyuga asked.

"Still very weary, but better," Anagalisgi replied.

"Do you think you could open Galohisdi? At least for the most terribly wounded, that they might receive help? As you have said, we are only as fast as our slowest member. If we can get them to Aktiya Waya for help, they can receive care and we can move more quickly, assuming we cannot all make the crossing."

His brother chuckled nervously. "We would not all be able to make the crossing. Honestly, the thought of more conjuring makes me ill at this time. But your point is well understood. I will attempt Galohisdi in the morning, to send the worst injured among us to Aktiya Waya. Then we must hurry and get away."

It was all Kiyuga could ask, and more than he'd hoped for. But he was also uncertain about how he felt about being so dependent on the sorceries. What would they be doing if they had no sorceries? For one, they probably never would have left the battle. In that case, they would probably be dead or captured. He was grateful for a chance to fight another day, but were they perhaps becoming too dependent on the sorceries? Or, as Anagalisgi had suggested, was their need so great that the only help the spirits could give them was literally the power to manipulate the very fabric of Creation?

He considered this as they traveled. He went ahead of them, but not as far as he had, instead guiding them toward the narrow spot in the pass where they could make camp. Once the first few of the party trickled in, he scouted out the surrounding area to ensure their safety and privacy.

They made a quick camp with a small fire. The Wolf Scout returned, but Fox and Owl never showed up.

"We can only conclude that they have been captured," someone said. "We must be on the move earlier and faster tomorrow than we were today."

"Agreed," Kiyuga said. "But in the morning, Anagalisgi will conjure Galohisdi and send the worst injured to Aktiya Waya for care. Once they are gone, we can move that much faster."

"Why can't we all go?" someone else inquired.

"The stress of the conjuring is too great," Anagalisgi replied. "I am yet weary from conjuring yesterday. Performing Galohisdi will sap my strength, and I may require a litter myself if I cannot stand. To hold Galohisdi for so long would not go well, and if someone is caught in the middle and I am unable to hold it, Galohisdi will close and that person will perish." He let that sink in. It was not actually known what happened to a man if he were caught in the middle of the doorway when it closed, but he did vanish, never to return. "Better to be cautious and ensure that all make the crossing, while we are still able to be cautious."

No one could argue with his logic, nor did anyone want to. Instead, they prepared to settle in for another night, many of them uneasy about it. Would they be found in the night? Would they sleep too long? Where had the two scouts gone? Had they been captured? Gotten lost? Would they see them again?

Kiyuga lay awake for a while, staring at the branches overhead, barely visible against a dark sky except for the faintest light from the dying fire. He felt as though he should be doing more for his people. He'd barely fought in battle, had barely helped with the wounded. He was trying to scout them a safe path to he knew not where, trying to find a place for them to rest so Anagalisgi could send them to Aktiya Waya, and two other scouts had disappeared without a trace. So here they were, camping in fear and unsure of the dawn. He should be doing more, but when he thought about it, he didn't know what more he could do. He was only one man.

The following morning, they were awake and ready early, though they still had to wait for Anagalisgi as he prayed and prepared himself to conjure Galohisdi. The eight weakest in the group had been chosen to send over. If he was able to hold the doorway open for longer, then more could go through, but he was uncertain of his ability to even get the eight through.

Finally Anagalisgi stood and took a large breath, readying himself. Even in the cool dawn air, he began sweating. He seemed to stumble, and nothing had happened yet. The other warriors looked at each other uncertainly. Would even one of the injured make it to Aktiya Waya?

There was a flash of light and a doorway began to open. It sputtered at first, like sparks from fire, but then it opened all the way. Through it they could see Aktiya Waya and several startled expressions from women and elders on the other side.

"Move!" Anagalisgi sputtered.

Several warriors began helping the eight wounded through to Aktiya Waya, explaining to the spectators that this was only a brief visit and it was not safe to return. Some protested, others had more questions, but Anagalisgi did not have the strength to hold Galohisdi forever. He went to a knee. Kiyuga went to his brother's side and barked at the warriors to hurry up.

Seven of the eight wounded and three warriors made it to the other side before Anagalisgi passed out and the doorway abruptly closed.

"Is he all right?" someone asked.

Kiyuga felt his brother's neck, slick with sweat so that he was like a fish. He breathed a sigh of relief. "He's alive. I think he'll be all right. Put him in a litter and let's get moving."

The eighth wounded man who did not make it across did not complain, just continued as he had been, and Anagalisgi was laid in Amayi's litter.

Kiyuga faced his remaining party.

"We need scouts," he stated.

The Owl and the Fox still hadn't returned from the previous day, and this fact was not lost on the rest of them. Nevertheless, he got volunteers for the Owl, Fox, and Wolf positions. He himself remained as the Raven.

With everything taken care of, they started out, Kiyuga tracing a path along the high ridge of the valley, avoiding the settlement as much as possible.

Having handed off the weakest members, the party was able to travel much faster, and Kiyuga did not feel so anxious about scouting ahead as far as he did. If they could keep up this pace, if he could find a good spot to stop and settle down...

So many ifs and uncertainties. He didn't like it. But if there was anything he knew for sure, it was that they couldn't stick around this valley with its settlements. If they could get to the next valley, they might have more luck.

They made it to the next valley by nightfall with no one really any worse for wear. Anagalisgi had woken up at some point in the day but was still very weak from his ordeal, barely strong enough to feed himself.

"In the morning, I will try again to send some through," he whispered.

Kiyuga shook his head. "You are too weak. You yourself said the risk is too great. We must wait until we are certain we can make it through."

"I will pray for strength. If it is as the Author intends, then it is what will happen."

"And if it is not?"

Anagalisgi frowned and did not answer for a long moment. Then, "The soldiers are coming. We must move quickly. To do so, we must shed the weight of the weakest slowing us down."

"Right now, you are the weakest one here," Kiyuga informed him. "The others are recovering well enough that most can walk. Those who can't are riding."

"Four have wounds that are terribly infected. Eleven more will become infected if they don't get help."

"And what help will they get if something happens to you? Then they will not be able to go to Aktiya Waya, and you will not be able to help them out here."

"I am not the only one here with knowledge of medicine."

Kiyuga sighed.

"Kiyuga. Brother. We must," Anagalisgi insisted.

Still he hesitated. Then, "All right. Is there any way I can help you conjure Galohisdi?"

"It would make you as weak as it has made me, and we need you to lead us. Don't worry. I'll be fine."

He was still unsure, but he knew it was pointless to argue. Anagalisgi was on his path, and nothing would sway him from it.

The following morning, Anagalisgi conjured Galohisdi, but only three were able to make it through. This time, when he collapsed, Kiyuga was almost certain he was dead except for slow, shallow breathing. He frowned and addressed the rest of them who were ready to leave.

"You will be with him when he wakes, I imagine. When he does, inform him that there will be no more conjuring until we find a safe place to rest and recover our strength."

The best he got was reluctant agreement. No one told an adawehi what to do or not do, especially one as powerful as Anagalisgi. Still, Kiyuga knew his brother was humble enough to agree, at least until they could speak again in the evening.

"Keep an eye on him," he said quietly to one warrior.

The man nodded, and Kiyuga headed into the forest as the Raven. He needed to find a safe place to hide soon. Anagalisgi was weak, but he knew well the infections he'd spoken of. The doctors gave what care they could, but without being able to rest, to bathe and purify themselves, and allow the medicines to work, the infection would only spread. Soon they would have many more wounded slowing them down.

He kept them going through the valley, hoping that the spirits might guide him as readily as they guided his brother. Ge'gwogv spoke to Anagalisgi often and showed him where to go, what must be done. Perhaps he ought to be the one in the Raven position, Kiyuga thought. Then they might get somewhere.

He scaled the hillside a bit, looking for a better vantage point. As he did so, a happenstance glance to the east showed him what he had been looking for, and he knew it was where they must go.

It was a depression in the landscape, like a bowl, a narrow river running through it. Three great peaks rose up around it in near-perfect triangle formation. One side was a rocky ledge not easily traversed. The second side appeared similar, though it was impossible to say what lay on the other side. The third side was a narrow pass, the only way in and out, though shrouded well by trees.

Excited, he returned to the party to inform them of his find and guide them there. Some questioned whether it was wise to corner themselves so. When Kiyuga pointed out the area to them, he noted that it was invisible in the larger scheme of things. The trees made it seem as though the slope were solid and absolute, with no sign of the depression. There was still a bit of hesitation, but the party followed his lead.

The depression was at once comforting and foreboding, Kiyuga thought as they made camp. Comforting, because it felt as though this was where they were supposed to be and they could settle down for a few days. Foreboding, because they were, truly, trapped here. Well, not completely trapped, but not everyone was strong enough to be able to scale the rocky slopes in the event they had to escape through some means other than the gentle slope they'd taken.

And with any luck, the soldiers, if indeed they came this far, would think the same thing and avoid it. If it was a foolish place to go, why go there to check on what seemed like a bad idea? Or so Kiyuga hoped.

He allowed for a small fire. Anagalisgi was awake, but only just barely, and Kiyuga had to tip water in his mouth which he promptly coughed up.

"Where are we?" Anagalisgi asked, coughing once from the water.

"In a safe spot. I hope," Kiyuga told him. "We can stay here for a few days so you can get some rest. When you're feeling up to it—which will not be tomorrow morning—then we can cross to Aktiya Waya."

"Have the scouts reported anything?"

"No, and they all returned. Maybe we finally got rid of our pursuers."

"For a time, anyway."

"Hopefully enough time." Kiyuga lifted the water skin. "Here."

Anagalisgi drank properly this time, then slipped back into sleep. Kiyuga returned to the fire with the rest of the warriors.

"Has he had any dreams or premonitions?" someone asked. "Are we safe here?"

"For now," Kiyuga answered. "But we must take no chances. We will continue to send out scouts to the north, the south, the east and west. We must be vigilant, ready for anything. Only the scouts may leave the bowl, no one else, and that includes the horses. If the doctors need to forage for medicines, another warrior must go with them. We cannot risk losing our healers. As soon as my brother is strong enough, we will continue sending people to Aktiya Waya."

Finally there seemed to be some relief and certainty among the warriors. Now they were no longer merely hunted prey. They were warriors again, with a task and a mission, ground and honor to defend.

They were also yet wounded. Some were healing well, but many only had a short time before infection became severe. A few had infections that were already severe and getting worse. The doctors would have to go out searching for herbs and plants in the morning. Else if the soldiers did somehow find them, they would only find corpses.

They rested well that night, or so Kiyuga thought. He slept better than he had the last few nights. He knew he had a dream, and he had a sneaking suspicion that it was the same recurring dream about him and his brother on the road, but if it offered any new insight as to why they were on the road or the identity of the running man, he did not recall.

Nevertheless, he woke feeling rather refreshed and ready for the day. They didn't need to camp here long, only a few days, just long enough for Anagalisgi to gather his strength and conjure Galohisdi once more. Considering the size of their group, it might take a while for all of them to cross over. Perhaps ten or twelve the first time, another dozen a few days later. Each time, the strength of the group would grow as they shed their weakest members. They would not only be better prepared to fight, but they could move more swiftly in the event they had to abandon their camp. Or if they decided to return to Itsa'ti, to see what had become of their brethren.

Kiyuga sent out the scouts that day, while he chose to accompany one of the doctors on a foraging mission. Success proved to be limited, if only because they were trying to be extra cautious. Even so, it was better than returning with nothing, and what had been gathered was quickly put to use.

Kiyuga spotted his brother sitting by the fire with his knees drawn up, looking as though he had fallen asleep, his head resting on his knees, breathing slowly, not moving. Kiyuga sat beside him.

"Did you sleep well?" he asked.

For a long moment, his brother did not answer. Then he mumbled something into his knees.

"I don't understand you, brother," Kiyuga said teasingly.

Anagalisgi lifted his head. "I know I must have slept, but the rest of me hasn't caught up to it yet."

"Did you walk over here by yourself?"

"It was all I could do. I was happy enough just to be able to stand and find a spot to relieve myself so I did not soil myself like an infant."

"You must be patient. Gather your strength. We are well hidden here. The doctors have found some healing medicines, so—"

"What have they found?" Anagalisgi interrupted, moving as if to get up. Kiyuga expended virtually no effort keeping him where he was.

"If they need help, they know who to ask," he said gently. "You're not going anywhere."

"I'm supposed to be helping them."

"You have already helped a dozen warriors to Aktiya Waya. Rest, gather your strength, and help a dozen more."

"I have to help," his brother repeated, though he was clearly exhausted and did not make any more move to stand. "I have to help...before I can't...There isn't much time..."

Anagalisgi sighed, laid his head back on his knees, and said no more.

Kiyuga watched his brother for a moment or two more before quietly standing and moving away.

The scouts reported nothing unusual that day. The doctors went out again to look for more medicines. That evening around the fire was spent in healing more wounds and fighting infection. Anagalisgi offered up prayers and a bit of incense he'd brought with him from home. He asked for guidance, strength, and mercy.

"And may our stories have a happy ending," he murmured at the end. Kiyuga was unsure if anyone had been meant to hear that part, and he said nothing of it.

The next day, Kiyuga again sent out scouts. It wasn't that he did not want to scout, for he did, but he wanted to keep an eye on his brother and make sure he didn't try to conjure when he was not yet strong enough. Instead, Kiyuga accompanied Anagalisgi into the forest to forage for herbs and medicines.

Anagalisgi winded easily, and soon they stopped on the riverbank to rest.

"Kiyuga, do you remember the promise you made me, when we were children?" he asked suddenly. "That you would go on before me in all things?"

Kiyuga managed a lop-sided smile. "I made that promise when you were still an infant."

"We would repeat it to each other all the time when we were young. It meant everything to us, but we still had no idea what it meant, not really."

"I think our spirits knew. My spirit understood the grief of the loss of our parents. Your spirit...you have always been more deeply rooted with the spirits."

His brother nodded. "I think we both understood on some level, in our spirits, in the quiet places of our hearts. I also think we are coming to a conscious understanding of what it will mean, when the spirit world connects with the waking world."

"Does this have to do with being the guardian of the door between worlds?"

"Yes. The time is coming soon." Anagalisgi looked at him. "You must not be afraid, Kiyuga."

Kiyuga studied him. "What is going to happen to you?"

"I will walk as the living among the spirits."

"Some would argue that you walk as a spirit among the living already."

His brother smiled. "Maybe. But there is so much more out there that I must know and learn."

Kiyuga frowned. "Will you be alone? I don't understand."

"The spirits will guide me. No." Anagalisgi looked thoughtful. "Digohwelisgi will guide me. The spirits will teach me."

"And the rest of us?"

"You will carry on. As you have promised, you will go before me."

When he sighed, his brother added, "I do not know how this will come to be, but I feel that it is soon. I am ready, but you must also be. When I tell you to do something, you must do it without hesitation. Do you understand?"

Kiyuga nodded reluctantly.

Anagalisgi attempted to search more for herbs, but he was still very weary. They returned to camp with only a handful of herbs which disappeared quickly.

The scouts reported nothing unusual that day. Perhaps they really had managed to shake off their pursuers. They could not truly rest until they reached Aktiya Waya, but it was a relief to not have to constantly watch every leaf and shadow, wondering if an enemy might be nearby. If there was any good news, it was that the soldiers—indeed, Europeans in general—were not very good at stealth.

The next day was very much the same. The scouts went out, as did a few hunters. Kiyuga accompanied Anagalisgi who was stronger and again went out looking for herbs. When they returned, they tended to the wounded. With the herbs that they had found, many mild infections were cleared, and more severe infections were curbed. Weak and wounded warriors became stronger. Kiyuga even managed to conjure Time for a few of them and heal their wounds before their very eyes.

Night came, as it always did. The scouts returned and reported nothing unusual. The Wolf had found a vantage to spy upon the settlement in the next valley. He did not see anything strange going on there; no red coat army was coming through. They appeared to be in the clear.

So it was that the following morning, the fourth morning since camping in the bowl, Anagalisgi announced that he would attempt to conjure Galohisdi. As always, the weakest among them would cross over first. There was no set number, simply as many as could go through as long as he could hold the doorway open.

Kiyuga was sure to keep an eye on his brother even as he gathered up the weakest in the group. Of course, their weakest now was a great deal stronger than their weakest when they had first started out from the battle. They no longer needed to carry anyone through, which would be a great help.

Anagalisgi looked as calm and as sure as Kiyuga had ever seen him as he focused himself on his task, whatever concentration or silent prayers or incantations were required to open the doorway to Aktiya Waya. His skin gleamed with sweat and the doorway opened. This time it appeared to be just a little outside the village proper, looking up the slope to the stone homes.

Immediately, warriors began crossing over, far less hesitant now than they had been only a few days ago. Kiyuga watched his brother as he sweated and shook, trying to keep the doorway open for as long as possible.

"Stop!" Kiyuga barked suddenly, leaping forward toward his brother.

One last wounded warrior went through the doorway, but the one behind him came to a sudden stop only a heartbeat before the doorway snapped shut. Anagalisgi collapsed, but Kiyuga was right there to catch him and lower him gently to the ground.

Kiyuga got his brother, sweaty but sleeping soundly, situated near the fire, then stood to take stock of who was left.

There were maybe twenty of them remaining, and few of them had injuries worth speaking of. If they wanted to, they could return to the Overhill. They were strong enough, and their small group could move much faster than before. All except Anagalisgi, anyway.

Kiyuga sent out the scouts and other tasks which had become routine the last few days, then went to his brother.

Anagalisgi slept most of the day, rousing a little before sunset.

"How many left?" he asked weakly.

"Eighteen," Kiyuga answered. "Rest a few more days and we may all be able to cross the next time."

Anagalisgi shook his head. "No. The time has come."

"What time?"

"You know the time. The time for you to go ahead of me. And for me to take my place."

"As the guardian of the door between worlds."

His brother nodded but drifted off to sleep before he could elaborate.

Worried, Kiyuga went out scouting himself the following day, taking the Wolf position so he could look upon the settlement and see if he could spot anything unusual. He could not, and the other scouts also reported nothing strange.

Even more worrisome was how Anagalisgi suddenly became silent. Even as he regained strength and moved about, he would not speak to anyone about anything. He would not answer questions. It was as though his spirit had already left his body for the spirit world, and all that remained was a shell. When Kiyuga finally looked him in the eye, he saw something remarkable. It was a depth of understanding he could not comprehend, eyes that saw two worlds—no, three worlds—simultaneously. His brother saw the world around them, but also saw the Upper and Lower Worlds. He saw the spirits, walked among them.

"Have you gone?" Kiyuga asked him that night at the fire. "Have you taken your place as the guardian?"

But his brother just looked at him, his expression something Kiyuga did not want to interpret, for the only answer he saw was, "No. Not yet."

He remained that way all day, and none disturbed him from his spiritual trance.

The scouts reported nothing unusual as they returned for the evening. Kiyuga glanced at Anagalisgi who did not react to the news, for good or for ill. What did he see? What did the spirits tell him?

Hold on, brother, Kiyuga thought. *Just another day or two and we will all be in Aktiya Waya.*

He'd never willed for something more forcefully than he did that night. He lay there by the light of the low fire, staring up into darkness, wondering what was going to happen. He could not remember feeling so uncertain and so afraid, not since his parents died and he made his promise to his brother.

A thought entered his mind then. Could his promise have started this whole thing? Had he somehow invoked a spiritual power so great that he had literally formed and shaped their destinies and the destinies of all of their people? Could Anagalisgi have been given such great spiritual power, as well as the sorceries, in order to try and counteract his deed?

It sounded foolish, but his mind was far too active to consider anything rational.

Eventually, he managed to sleep. He found himself on the road, Anagalisgi only a few paces away. His brother said nothing, just looked at him with that terrible expression of deep spiritual knowing and certain resignation. As in the past, Kiyuga walked toward him. He found the invisible wall and the flash of light. Then there was the man running away from him.

In a change from the norm, Anagalisgi said something then, but for some reason, Kiyuga could not hear him clearly. Still, the unknown man stopped running. He was probably ten or more paces away. He turned.

In the dream, Kiyuga recognized the man, but his head was cloudy. He knew it was someone still in their party. He knew it was someone he trusted a great deal. They had fought together before. Then, just as the man's identity broke through the clouds in Kiyuga's mind, just as he was about to speak the warrior's name, everything vanished.

Kiyuga quickly forgot his dream as the alarm was raised and he was shaken awake. He scrambled to his feet and looked around.

It was dawn, the sun just peeking over the hills. Around him, the warriors were making ready to fight even as Anagalisgi prayed silently by the fire now dead.

"What is it?" Kiyuga demanded.

"A hunting party," someone told him. "A group of soldiers and some fierce-looking men from the settlement in the valley."

"Do we know they are hunting for us?"

A shout down the slope quickly answered his question.

"Anagalisgi!" Kiyuga snapped. "We need Galohisdi!"

"We don't have time here," his brother said calmly as he stood, rising almost as a god from the earth. "Follow me."

They had little choice but to obey. Anything they did not immediately have on hand was left behind; there would be more for them in Aktiya Waya.

Anagalisgi took them up one of the steeper slopes on the southern side of the bowl, following the ridge and staying well within the trees. The soldiers and hunters could be heard coming up to the narrow pass, the only kind passage into and out of the bowl. They would be distracted for a while as they rummaged through the abandoned camp. Hopefully it would buy them enough time to escape.

Just ahead, the hill fell away to a steep cliff, but the ancient rockslide had revealed a cave, barely big enough for a man to stand up. Anagalisgi stood at the mouth of the cave and motioned for the rest of them to move in.

"I will conjure Galohisdi," he said, still remarkably calm for the situation. "Go through, all of you."

"What about you?" Kiyuga asked.

"My time is nearly here. Please, do not be afraid. And do as I say."

Before either could say more, there were the sounds of the hunting party getting closer.

Kiyuga looked into his brother's eyes one last time. They clasped wrists. Anagalisgi nodded once, then broke the gaze as he concentrated on his conjuring.

He had not regained as much strength as he had previously, and even so, the frequency of this difficult conjuring was taking its toll. Kiyuga could see that he struggled, but there was little he could do.

"There they are!" someone shouted just down the slope.

At the same time, the doorway opened in the cave.

"Move!" Kiyuga ordered.

The warriors began ducking into the cave and all but leaping through the doorway to Aktiya Waya.

Down the slope, the Anigilisi had broken through the tree line and now came at them unhindered. A few took haphazard shots with rifles or muskets.

Most of the warriors were through, but as the Anigilisi drew nearer, a few hesitated, wondering whether it wouldn't be better to fight. They wanted to escape, yet they could not allow the Anigilisi to get to Aktiya Waya.

Someone burst past Kiyuga on his right, charging the hunting party. Kiyuga felt a moment of disorientation as his dream came back to him in a rush.

"Adahi!"

But the warrior did not listen. When he reached the party, it was nothing for the Anigilisi to subdue him, hitting him over the head so that he stumbled but did not go down.

"Kiyuga," Anagalisgi groaned.

Snarling a bit in frustration, Kiyuga raced down the hill, determined to simply grab Adahi and go. Somewhere in his panic, he conjured Time just enough to get a hold of the dazed warrior and drag him away from the enemy's grasp. He turned the warrior around, got him pointed toward the cave, and told him to go.

Adahi was slow, but the two of them got back to the cave. Still the Anigilisi closed in, clearly believing they had the warriors cornered in the cave.

As Kiyuga ducked into the cave, he turned just in time to see his brother go to a knee and then be seized by the Anigilisi.

"Anagalisgi!" Kiyuga cried, lurching toward the mouth of the cave.

Adahi, following his lead, stumbled outside, only to be seized himself once more. Kiyuga took his hatchet and swung wildly, hearing a blood-curdling howl as blade met flesh. Adahi was released, but Anagalisgi was nowhere to be seen.

Then Kiyuga spotted him being dragged down the hill. He fell once and got himself turned around. The brothers locked gazes one last time.

Suddenly, it was as if Time slowed down, and all sounds melted away until Kiyuga could hear only his own terrified heart thudding in his chest. Knowing Anagalisgi, that was probably exactly what happened. Indeed, his brother did not appeared concerned at all about his predicament. Then, in the dimness of sound that blanketed them, his brother's voice carried on the wind.

"Go, Kiyuga. Save the pack." He paused. "I love you, brother."

The next moment stretched on for a lifetime.

Then, suddenly, life resumed. Kiyuga did not have time to think as he grabbed Adahi and started back into the cave, to the doorway that was starting to sputter.

Kiyuga leapt through, and it felt like diving into icy water. His whole body froze, contracted, and he hit the ground with no tact or grace. It took a second before he could suck in a breath, and the first thing he did was sit up and turn toward the spot where the doorway had been. It was not there any longer, and Adahi was nowhere to be seen.

His brother was gone.

DᏯᎧᏞᎥᎢ ᏔᏢᎧᏗᎠᏗᎠ ᏣᎫᎳ

Ayadohlv'i Tahlsgo Tsanela
Prison

Somehow, Anagalisgi knew that his brother had made it through the doorway before it closed.

The Anigilisi had grabbed him and forced him roughly away from the cave. He did not remember much about it; on top of his exhaustion from the conjuring, things started to get really blurry when the soldiers began beating him and tying him up. He knew his wrists were bound with rope and then manacled with cold iron shackles. A bag was placed over his head and he was made to stumble along down the slope.

He could not say for sure, at least at first, whether others had been captured. He did not believe so. He was fairly certain they had all made it through to Aktiya Waya.

Then he was made to sit, thumping to the ground on his seat but grateful for the brief rest. The bag was not removed, nor were his wrists unbound, but he could sit still and listen well enough to make up for his lack of sight.

"We can't send our men in there," one soldier was saying. "The damn savages will ambush them and we may never know. No, we'll wait them out. Post guards at the entrance and keep a few close at hand. We'll have to wait them out."

"For how long?" a second man wondered. "They know these caves better than we do. What if there is another exit? That's probably why they ran up there. We can post guards all we want, but if they escape out the back door, the front door doesn't matter."

Anagalisgi did not have to think hard on what the first man's expression must have been.

"We'll give them five days. Unless there's water in the cave, or a back door as you say, they'll have to come out at some point for water."

"And this one?" a third man inquired lazily, his accent making Anagalisgi believe him to be a Highlander.

Someone shoved Anagalisgi in the back with a staff of some form, or more likely the butt of a musket. He went forward but did not fall.

"He can stay here a day or two," the first man decided. "Maybe they'll try a rescue mission for him."

"Doesn't look like much of a warrior," a fourth man commented. "And I seen some of them bastards in battle. They're big and strong. He can't be much more than a boy."

Anagalisgi startled as someone grabbed his belt and his satchel and forced it back over his head, rubbing the burlap bag against his face. There was the sound of rummaging as the Anigilisi pawed through his herbs and medicines, his crystals and stones. The burglar made some unintelligible noises, and a fifth man spoke up.

"Witchcraft," he said. "I'd say he's one of their priests."

"Well, keep everything together there. We'll give it to the Reverend to be properly destroyed and any evil spirits driven away."

Murmurs of agreement all around, and Anagalisgi imagined them making the sign of the cross upon their breasts.

"What do we do with him until then?" someone, maybe the fourth man, asked.

"Should at least take the bag off his head," the Highlander suggested. "Not as though he doesn't know where we are or who we are."

A moment later, the bag was ripped off his head, and Anagalisgi blinked against the sudden light. He instinctively drew back as someone knelt close in front of him.

"Well, well. Look at him, would you?" He raised his voice in the way that Anagalisgi had learned they did when they thought it might somehow bridge a language gap. "Your people made a big mistake turning against us. Do you understand me? Big—mistake. We—" He gestured to the group. "—do not—" He made an X with his fingers. "—like you." He pointed at Anagalisgi. "You—" Another point. "—attacked —"

"I speak English, thank you," Anagalisgi interrupted. "The yelling and the charades are not necessary."

That gave the first man pause even as a couple of his men snickered and badly tried to hide it. Anagalisgi did not react as the first man slapped him with the back of his hand.

"I will not be made a fool of, especially in front of my own men. Do you understand me?" he sneered. Anagalisgi did not speak, just nodded once. "Good. Now you're just going to stay right here for a while. In a few days, we'll take you back to town to decide your fate."

My fate has already been decided, Anagalisgi thought, though he was wise enough not to say this aloud.

"But if you want to take your life in your own hands, you can always try to escape," the man went on. "In which case, you will be pursued. If you're recaptured, well, you'll just be summarily executed at that point. British army is in a pretty bad mood after this war, and I'm no exception. We're not suffering too many prisoners, especially those who come from the peoples who betrayed us."

There were a number of things Anagalisgi could have said to that, but it would accomplish nothing. And besides that, he was still very tired from the conjuring. If the man could stop talking, he might be able to get some sleep.

Two men were posted as guards, and the head man in charge went off to do something or other. No one bothered him, though the guards got a bit anxious when he started to wiggle around. They relaxed as he got himself situated to lie down and quickly go to sleep.

When he opened his eyes in the spirit world, he did not know where he was initially, though it looked familiar. It took a moment for him to realize that he was on the road in his brother's recurring dream. Hope flared within him and he looked around for his brother, hoping to tell him that he was alive and well for the time being. He did not want his brother to worry about him, though he knew it was inevitable given the separation they would soon face. Still, if there was any way that he could assuage his brother's fears, he would do it, or he would try.

He spotted someone on the road and started toward him. As he got closer, he saw that it was not Kiyuga. Disappointed and yet curious now, Anagalisgi continued his approach.

Whoever it was, he was certainly afraid. He paced, looked around nervously. His hands frequently touched his weapons and his belt, unsure what he should grab or if anything would even help.

As Anagalisgi drew nearer, he finally discerned the worried man's identity.

"Adahi," he stated.

The man jumped and whirled around. When he spotted Anagalisgi, he visibly relaxed and started walking toward him, then running.

Both Adahi and Anagalisgi startled when Adahi suddenly hit something and fell backwards onto his back in the road. Anagalisgi skidded to a halt. As Adahi picked himself up, Anagalisgi reached out with a tentative hand. He felt the invisible wall. Adahi also reached out and touched it. Their hands were very nearly touching, except for a wall that was impossibly thin separating them.

"The guardian of the door between worlds," Anagalisgi murmured, feeling more along the wall. "You are where I must be."

Adahi began speaking. Anagalisgi knew this only because his mouth was open, lips moving. Yet he could hear no words.

"I am sorry, Adahi. I cannot hear you."

The warrior blinked, said a few more words, then backed away from the invisible wall, clearly distressed.

"But I know where you are," Anagalisgi went on. "And I am coming for you. I promise."

Adahi did not look all that comforted as he approached the wall again, put his hands upon it, and continued speaking. Anagalisgi studied the movements of his lips and determined his words to be, "Where am I?"

"You are in the spirit world, Adahi, though I do not believe you to be dead. You are in a Land in Between. You are where I must be, and I believe your entrapment paves the way for my own destiny. So you can be assured that I will come for you."

Adahi searched him. Then, silently, "How?"

"I don't know," Anagalisgi admitted. "Not yet. The spirits will guide me, but you must stay close to me."

The trapped warrior nodded.

"We are not without hope or a solution. We simply have not discovered their form yet."

Again Adahi did not appear especially comforted, though he did calm down a bit, enough that he agreed to stay near Anagalisgi. As the two of them stepped away from their respective sides of the invisible wall, the spirit world began to fade, and Anagalisgi found himself again in the waking world. It was later in the day, or perhaps the next day.

He got himself to a stiff sitting position, muscles cramping from the uncomfortable position of his slumber. He looked around. While nothing had physically changed around the Anigilisi camp, he was almost certain that he felt Adahi nearby.

He did not dream of Adahi again that day or during the night. He was taken out of the camp several times to relieve himself and given meager rations once a day for the four days they remained in the bowl.

"They're not coming," the Highlander, McDowell, said to the leader, Baker. "At least they're not coming for him."

"There's been no activity in or around the cave either," another soldier, Johnson, sighed. "They're not coming out, sir."

Baker was clearly displeased with this assessment, though his only other option was to lead an offensive into the cave, something he had already made very clear he would not risk.

"Very well," he growled. "We'll leave first thing in the morning."

As the men dispersed, Baker came and knelt before Anagalisgi.

"How do you like that?" he jeered. "Your friends aren't coming for you. And you're their damn priest! Thought your people were supposed to be a pious folk? And yet they abandoned you here to us."

"I always understood the British to be a pious folk as well," Anagalisgi said. "And yet here you are, destroying your neighbors, dishonoring God's creation, and doing treachery to the least of these."

He fully expected and was fully prepared for the punch in the face the commander gave him, and he did not resist, simply went with the force of the impact and went backwards. As he got back into a sitting position, he could taste blood on his lips.

"Now you listen to me, redskin. I will not be insulted, nor will I stand for an attack on my king or my faith. I would tell you to get behind me, Satan, but I will be more than happy to send you up to the gallows first."

"Does that mean you intend to swing beside me, condemned as a murderer for being angry at your brother?"

Baker stood suddenly, kicked Anagalisgi in the jaw, and stalked off, barking orders to his men.

No one came to help him sit up. No one offered to wipe the blood away. No one offered him any water. No one asked if he might need some of the herbs in his pack, squirreled away by the commander. He merely stayed where he was, alone, silent, and with a few new bruises blossoming on his face.

He did not dream of Adahi that night either, nor did he expect to, and the following morning, he was roughly shaken awake and hauled to his feet. The camp was very nearly packed and ready to leave, but Baker apparently had a few more choice words for him.

"Maybe you don't understand this yet, but we are superior. We British are chosen by God to expand and conquer, and by the grace of God and the wisdom of our king, we will do just that. You and all your people have been conquered. You may as well learn to live with it, at least for as long as you are alive."

With that, they were ordered to move out.

Several men went forward, then one of Anagalisgi's guards, then Anagalisgi himself, then McDowell, then a few more men, Baker, and a couple more bringing up the rear.

A few miles in the walk, the man in front of Anagalisgi, hardly more than a boy, slowed a step to walk beside him.

"Come on," he said eagerly. "Aren't you the least bit curious how we found you?"

"Does it matter?" Anagalisgi wondered.

The boy frowned. "Well, no, I suppose not. But aren't you curious? Even a little?"

"Dormer," someone said lazily. "Stop talking to the prisoner."

The boy, Dormer, did not listen. "We actually gave up, initially. Tracked you savages from the battle across the river, over hill and dale. Followed the blood as long as we could, but you know these hills better than we do. So we gave up and went to town. Told Captain Baker there what happened. He knew you'd be on the lookout for soldiers, so he sent out a bunch of hunting parties. Average men and boys, you know? One of them's the ones that found you. Came back to us to report and we came out and what do you know? Here you were. Some invisible ghosts you are if you can't even—"

"Dormer, shut your trap," McDowell growled. "Or I'll shut it for you."

The boy heeded that threat, though his expression said he had a lot more he wanted to say.

Anagalisgi did his best not to react to the boy's words, telling himself that all was as it should be. The spirits had brought him here, and the Author was going to deliver him into something great. The guardian of the door between worlds. He breathed in a contended sigh and gave only brief glances to either side of him, half-expecting to find Adahi right there.

Instead, he saw something much more promising. There, flitting from tree to tree, was Ge'gwogv. He did not stare at the spirit for long, lest he draw unwanted attention to it, but its mere presence was a comfort, an assurance that he was on the right path.

This did not mean that he was unafraid, for he most certainly was afraid. As much as he trusted the spirits to guide him through, the transition itself scared him. Giving up his life and everything he had ever known. Leaving his brother. For as much as things had changed just over the course of his life, he'd always had the comfort and familiarity of family and friends. He'd always had his brother's promise. Now that promise was going to be fulfilled, and he didn't understand what was supposed to happen afterwards. More than that, he would not have his brother there to help him through it.

He also feared for his brother. He'd dedicated his life to being a good brother as much as a good warrior. He seemed confused as to why their paths would diverge so. Anagalisgi understood this confusion, for he shared it. Many brothers would hope to go into battle together, share their lives as warriors, even as their daily lives went their separate ways with family obligations. And even with their dynamic, one brother being a warrior, the other being an adawehi, they still had the hope and opportunity to share their lives. And a warrior's life was always dangerous; there was never a guarantee of returning from a raid, or even some of the more dangerous hunts.

But this would not be like that, not truly. Anagalisgi knew for a fact that they would both live through this experience, the transition as he became the guardian of the door between worlds, but it would feel like a death. It would be a separation they could not overcome, the invisible wall upon the road.

They camped that night in sight of the town. The trek down the slopes combined with the gathering darkness cut their journey short, much to Baker's annoyance. He took it out on his men, snapping at them, less like a dog, and more like a snake. Beware any who was unlucky enough to be struck by his venomous fangs.

Anagalisgi was not immune to this, and he took his fair share of kicks and shoves. He did his best to not react, telling himself to be as lively as a statue. Eventually the man would tire of beating something that did not fight back, and in fact inflicted pain of its own without the need to move. All the same, his upper lip still had crusted blood on it and his jaw was yet tender.

Sleep was a welcome relief. Anagalisgi did not see Adahi in his dreams, though he knew the trapped warrior was present. He was sticking with Anagalisgi, as he had asked. He still wasn't entirely certain what the plan was, how to free Adahi and take his place, but he trusted the spirits to guide him and the Author to deliver them both where they needed to be.

The following morning, Baker wasted no time in rousing his men and getting them on the road. If they hadn't been so lackadaisical the previous day, he said, they might have made it to town in time for a drink and maybe a woman, too. Instead, they'd had to sleep out, so they were setting out early. If they made good time, he might just consider letting them off with only a few lashes for sloth. The man looked at Dormer as he said it. The boy's face and ears turned red, and he made himself scarce.

Anagalisgi was again guarded by Dormer and McDowell as they headed down the trail. It was steep and rocky, and Anagalisgi had to navigate while having only limited use of his bound hands. He fell more than once, and the big Highlander was always too happy to roughly pick him back up and set him on his feet, shoving him in the back just as soon as he was upright and barking at him to move.

They arrived in town while it was still morning. Baker gave orders to some of his men, things to be done, while he and McDowell took Anagalisgi to another building. Inside, they found another officer and an attendant of some form; Anagalisgi did not fully understand the ranks of the slaves the Anigilisi held.

"One prisoner?" the new officer asked, raising a brow. "Are the rest dead, then?"

"Yes, sir," Baker lied expertly. "We chased them into a cave. There was no escape for them."

"Good. And what do you intend to do with this one?"

"Execute him, sir. He's one of their pagan priests. I have his bag of witchcraft items; I figured the good Reverend could properly dispose of them."

"Indeed." The officer waved a hand. "Very good. Away with him, then. Have an execution order drawn up."

And again they were moving, Anagalisgi being herded along like a cow or a sheep. He was taken from the building with the officer to another building that was poorly lit and smelled wretched. They descended a flight of stairs and came to a long corridor filled with rooms. These rooms were made of stone for three walls and had iron bars facing the corridor.

Baker grabbed a ring of keys and went to one of the cells. He unlocked a door. McDowell dragged Anagalisgi to the cell and pushed him in, following him menacingly. But the Highlander merely untied his bindings, unlocked the shackles, and left without so much as a word or even a glare.

"The Reverend will be by soon enough," Baker said as he locked the door. "I suggest you take the opportunity to speak to him and get right with our Lord, Whom you have blasphemed with your witchcraft. But He is forgiving in His perfection."

"Only greater proof that you are imperfect people," Anagalisgi said, a little more confident in his quips seeing that there was iron between them now.

Baker smirked. "No more than you."

Then he and the Highlander departed. Anagalisgi watched them walk up the stairs and disappear.

He was not alone in the corridor of many cells, but his state of mind did not allow for interruption by petty whining and pathetic pleas for mercy. He could not allow himself to give in to fear and panic. He had to remain focused on the moment and the task at hand. He had to come up with a way out.

Before his thoughts could progress very far, the door at the top of the stairs opened with a groan. A moment later, a man descended. He was perhaps forty years of age with thinning brown hair, a clean face, small spectacles, and the clothes of a Catholic priest. Anagalisgi concluded that this was the Reverend.

Upon realizing who it was who had joined them in their misery, the other prisoners began shouting and wailing for him, begging for mercy and intercession. The man did not flinch or balk at the conditions, either of the place or its occupants, but dutifully went to each cell in turn, speaking with each prisoner for a moment before continuing on.

Anagalisgi was the last one he visited.

"So, you're the Aniyvwiya priest," the Reverend stated calmly.

"My name is Anagalisgi."

"Ah. Lightning, if I remember correctly."

Anagalisgi gave the man a look. "You know the tongue of my people?"

"Yes, and several others. I spent many years as a missionary to the various tribes. Unfortunately, I suffered a hip injury and cannot traverse the wilds as I once did."

"Then you know that I am not a witch."

The Reverend frowned, stood, and went to grab Anagalisgi's pack which hung near the stairs. He opened it and rummaged through it as he returned.

"Stones and crystals for divination. Herbs for potionry..."

"Even your priests called down fire from heaven in times past," Anagalisgi pointed out. "And Gideon divined his future by use of a sheep's fleece."

The Reverend's expression turned contemplative. He nodded slowly and set the pack aside. "Yes, I suppose so. Perhaps, then, it is not the method in question, but the intended recipient."

"I pray to God the Creator the same as you. We simply see the spirit world differently."

"On that much, we can agree. And what of your salvation? Have you trusted your soul to Jesus Christ?"

Now Anagalisgi frowned. "This I have not understood. My people have always believed that the soul travels west to the Darkening Lands, eventually to vanish into the wind. How does one of the Middle World join the spirits of the Upper World?"

"Such is the power of our Lord. If He made our souls, why would He not have the power to take them back to Himself?"

He could not argue with that, but still he was troubled. How did he go about explaining the sorceries and everything he had learned from Nathan and Andrew? Would the Reverend understand, or call it heresy and witchcraft? Furthermore, how did he explain the destiny he now faced? How did he explain his becoming the guardian of the door between worlds?

"I have not the power to save you," the Reverend went on. "I cannot rescue you from the gallows, nor the maw of Hell."

"You believe my execution just, then?" Anagalisgi inquired. "Do I deserve it? I've not killed anyone. I have done my duties as healer for my people."

"It is the order of the colonel."

"Is it automatically correct?"

"It is not my place to question those whom God has appointed over me."

"But all men are imperfect, are they not? What if the one whom God has appointed gives an egregious order that you cannot agree with?"

"Naturally my first duty is to the Lord."

"So again I ask. Is my execution just? What offense have I given?"

The Reverend hesitated. "The execution order defines your crime as assisting in the escape of war criminals."

Anagalisgi shifted his stance. "You say you spent many years as a missionary among the peoples. You have no doubt seen and lived with our warriors. Look at me. What do you think I could accomplish that a warrior could not? Except, perhaps, healing. And healing the sick and wounded is no crime."

For a long moment, they regarded one another. The Reverend looked as though he had a lot that he wanted to say, but was unsure if he wanted to speak aloud. Other prisoners still begged for mercy, but a few were now pleading for mercy that their sentences were not just. Anagalisgi simply watched him with calm dignity.

"We will speak again when you are taken for your sentence to be carried out," the Reverend said at last. "I encourage you to consider the fate of your soul. Seeing how you seem to know some Scripture, I expect you also at least understand how to pray for salvation. But if you need help, as I said, we will speak again later."

Anagalisgi frowned. "When is my execution scheduled?"

"Two days from now."

"Do you know if any others of my people have been captured and are being brought here?"

"I've not heard anything." He continued before Anagalisgi could speak. "Until then, Anagalisgi. Please, consider my words carefully, and your soul even more so."

Then he turned and left, walking stiffly on one side. The other prisoners cried out after him, but the Reverend simply ascended the stairs once more, dragged the door open, and disappeared. Anagalisgi stared after him a moment longer before making a lap of his small cell.

When he circled back to the door, he looked down and realized that the Reverend had left his bag right outside the door. Anagalisgi knelt and slipped a hand through the bars, easily grasping the satchel. He dragged it to the bars and carefully wiggled it into his cell where he opened it.

Near as he could tell, nothing was missing. The soldiers had been too worried about the evil of its contents that they dared not touch anything if they didn't have to. That included the seeing fruit.

Anagalisgi breathed a sigh of relief. He looked around his little cell for someplace to hide his bag, but there was only straw and stone. Eventually he settled for hiding it under some old straw. With any luck, the Reverend would have forgotten about it completely, and the soldiers would just assume the Reverend had discarded it as he saw fit. And with exception of the seeing fruit, everything in the bag was replaceable, seeing how he wouldn't be able to take it with him to the gallows, he was sure.

For a while, he sat and meditated, considering his options, his plan for escape. He would have to eat at least part of the seeing fruit in the next day so he might speak to the spirits, and perhaps Adahi as well. He had only one chance to escape before his strength would be sapped beyond his ability to fight back if need be.

The prison was not well lit to begin with, and it only got darker as the day went on. As fatigue crept up on Anagalisgi, he dug his bag out of the straw, grabbed his seeing fruit, and ate about a quarter of it. He would save the rest for his actual escape, when he would need greater guidance from the spirits.

He turned and saw Adahi standing at the door of the cell, looking nervous.

"I don't like this place, Anagalisgi," he said anxiously. "Why don't you escape? Surely you've recovered well by now?"

"Because in this escape, I must take my place as the guardian," Anagalisgi said. "And I must also rescue you. To do so now would bring you here, and I will not condemn you to this cell. We must get out and leave this place, to give you a chance to escape and be free."

The warrior could not argue that.

"If this is the case, then you have a plan?" he asked instead.

"I'm working on it," Anagalisgi sighed. "I don't know the layout of this town to plan an escape."

"Maybe not," Adahi mused, "but I can move freely. I will go and learn this town."

"The seeing fruit will likely lose its effects by the time you return, and I don't want to take any more until I am being taken from here."

"Then I will visit you in your dreams. The spirits will show me how."

Anagalisgi smiled. "Yes, I'm sure they will. Go, then. Learn an escape route and bring it to me. And know that you will have to help me on the day that I am taken."

"I'll not leave your side."

With that, Adahi turned and left, running up the stairs though his footfalls made no sound. Anagalisgi stared after him for a moment, then went and found as comfortable a place to sit as he could. The other prisoners yelled at him, laughed at him, called him insane. A few asked to go with him when he made his escape. He ignored all of them and instead tried to focus on the task at hand. Two days from now, he would be taken out for execution. He had to have something planned before then.

He lay down to sleep, and he prayed silently for the spirits to visit him, for Ge'gwogv to guide him, and for Adahi to be able to enter his dreams and speak to him. He whispered this prayer several times before sleep finally claimed him.

He did not have any especially enlightening dreams. His only dream was that he stood at the mouth of the cave, and a voice came from it, saying, "Come...come...come..."

It was the only guidance he got that night. He saw no spirits. Ge'gwogv was silent. Adahi did not appear. He would not say he was not disappointed, but he tried to tell himself that the time for plans was past; he had to live in the moment.

All the same, there was still the very real threat of hanging looming over his head.

When he woke, nothing had changed. There was still the dim light, the tragic smell, and the audible misery of the other prisoners. No food was brought, and Anagalisgi's stomach grumbled. He sighed, but decided to treat this as a fasting situation. He did not have seven days to give for his purification, but the mindset helped to quell his hunger and take the edge off his fears.

So he sat and meditated and prayed. He thought about bringing out his stones and crystals, then decided against it. In the event a soldier or guard did come down, he did not want to be caught with them. It wasn't the stones he was worried about losing, but the seeing fruit. He was also committed to not using any sorceries until his escape, and that included minor instances of conjuring Time so as to retrieve or hide his things. He would need everything he had in order to pull this off.

He meditated. He prayed. He sang several songs, ignoring the shouts and whines of his fellow prisoners. Some called him a dirty savage, pagan heretic and blasphemer. Others just wanted him to shut up so his singing didn't drown out their pitiful cries for mercy, as if any mortal man could hear them.

The day passed on. No one brought any food, though a guard did come down to make a brief inspection, make sure no one had died or was attempting escape.

Anagalisgi was still singing, but he startled and cut off at a banging on the iron.

"You just shut that up, you understand?" the guard growled. "We don't need you bringing any devils down here."

Several prisoners called out rough agreement, but if they thought it would win them any favors, they were sorely disappointed as the guard snapped at them to keep quiet.

"Your pagan gods can't help you now," the guard told him, looking back at Anagalisgi.

"Maybe not," Anagalisgi said. "But what if your God did?"

The man thought this immensely hilarious, and he left the prison bellowing with laughter.

And that was all the prisoners saw of their captors that day. No food was brought, and Anagalisgi remained meditative. He continued to sing, continued to pray, asking for guidance and mercy. Surely he could not have been brought all this way just for his life to end upon a rope? The spirits had promised him great things. Hanging at the end of a rope was not a great thing.

He could not say he felt no trepidation as he finally lay down to sleep that night. He wanted, no, needed guidance from Ge'gwogv and the spirits. He needed to speak to Adahi about what he'd seen, if he'd found a path to escape. He would still attempt his escape no matter what; the end would be the same as hanging if he were recaptured, though he imagined that it would not be so swift and merciful as the rope. He had heard many tales of some of the tortures the Anigilisi would inflict upon their prisoners.

He fell into an uneasy sleep and was relieved when he found himself upon the road, Adahi a few paces away behind the invisible wall.

"I am sorry," Adahi said. "I was not able to enter your dreams last night. I did not know how, and even this night, I was unable but for Ge'gwogv's help."

Anagalisgi looked around and spotted the white woodpecker upon a branch, watching them curiously.

"Thank you, Ge'gwogv," Anagalisgi said humbly.

"Fear not, Anagalisgi," Ge'gwogv told him. "You will be with us soon."

Then the woodpecker spread its wings and glided away, across the road and into the forest.

"I still don't understand what's going on," Adahi said, still looking a bit fearful. "I don't understand where I am, how I got here, or how to get out. Ge'gwogv has tried to explain it, but the only thing I understand is that I must stay by you, and you will see that everything is put to rights."

"Well, I can only try my best," Anagalisgi told him.

Adahi nodded. "Yes. I know. As I can only do my best to help you. And know that if something goes wrong, I hold no ill will toward you for it. As I'm sure your brother will understand also. If he ever hears what happens."

"He will know," Anagalisgi said with all certainty. "You will tell him, and I will show him."

The warrior shifted his stance, nodded, and knelt upon the road. He brushed away some leaves and picked some tufts of grass to reveal bare dirt beneath. He grabbed a stick. "Well, I will leave the final rescue plan up to you. Your connection to the spirits has endowed you with great knowledge that I cannot begin to comprehend, and I trust you to know what to do. But in order to get there, first you must get out of the town."

"You have learned the town well, then?"

"Yes. Better than expected. When I could not enter your dreams, I returned to the town to learn it even better so that I could be of more use when I was finally able to speak with you. I have learned all the streets, all the alleys, and many of the buildings as well, in the event you should need to hide."

Anagalisgi nodded. "You are a good warrior, Adahi."

Adahi did not respond to that, merely readied his stick and began drawing in the dirt.

"I do not know the history of this town well, but from other Anigilisi towns that I have seen, I can say that there were several minor skirmishes here during the war. Their wall is damaged, undergoing repairs, but these repairs are only just beginning. Naturally, they are starting in the most heavily damaged sections, but I believe that some of the areas of lighter damage may prove enough to get you out.

"There are several holes here, here, and here." Adahi marked the spots in his drawing. "They look like places where cannonballs struck the wood. Animals, or perhaps courageous soldiers, have since been digging at them. This one and this one would be big enough for a man to get through. This one looks big enough for a child, but you are small and slender; you may be able to fit."

"How do I get there?" Anagalisgi asked.

"This is the prison where you are now being held." Adahi took a small pebble and placed it appropriately. He grabbed another pebble. "This is their law building, and the gallows here. There are five streets going here, here, here, here, and here. More streets run this way and this way. Their streets are laid out as bees lay out honeycomb, though the Europeans seem to prefer more square shapes."

They spent a good portion of time just going over the map of the town, considering all possible routes: major routes, diversions, doubling back, and more. And yet, Anagalisgi knew that plans, especially navigational plans, could be much different once flat drawings were brought to life in a big world.

"I will go ahead and direct you to better ways, if necessary," Adahi told him. "And I will show you where to hide."

"That is a good thing, while the seeing fruit lasts," Anagalisgi said. "If it does not last, if it wears off before I have escaped the town, I may need to know some good hiding places."

"There are several small sheds here, here, and here that may be of interest. I noticed several children playing a game of hide-and-seek, and they seemed to favor this area where there are many barrels and crate of provisions. Otherwise, I would think it will depend on the movement of the people."

"Agreed."

Anagalisgi sat back on his heels. "I would be lying if I said I was not anxious about this."

Adahi nodded. "I think my own fears are quite noticeable."

"But we must have faith, trust in the paths the spirits have laid out for us. Sometimes our paths are dangerous and uncertain, but we will always end up exactly where we need to be."

Adahi looked uncertain. "Do you think...?"

"Yes?"

"This...Author...that Nathan and Andrew spoke of. Do you think she's real? Do you think she cares?"

"Great power has certainly been demonstrated and credited to her," Anagalisgi said. "Based on that, I've no reason to think she is not real. Who she is and whether she cares, I think, will be discovered shortly."

"Depending on whether or not she delivers you from the gallows?"

"No. Depending on whether something is learned from either my delivery or my execution."

"Isn't that a bit presumptuous?"

"It's called faith, that even in misfortune, something far more valuable may be gained."

Adahi scuffed the dirt, looking a bit like a child who has been shamed for wrongdoing. "You have far greater faith than I. I think many have given up hope, and yet you never have."

"Having faith does not mean that you ignore the waking world," Anagalisgi told him. "It simply means that your heart is fixed on the spiritual one."

"You are younger than me, and yet you have the wisdom of Gvnagadoga."

Anagalisgi laughed and put up a hand. "Oh, I don't deserve that honor. No, I don't deserve that for many more years, and it may be that I never achieve his great wisdom and gentle disposition."

"I think you will. If I have faith in anything, I have faith in you."

"Thank you. And if you would, I have something to ask of you."

"Anything."

"You will be freed to the waking world, and I have every intention of seeing you safely to Aktiya Waya. But I will not be going with you. I have my own destiny to fulfill. When you see my brother—"

"I will tell him," Adahi promised. "I will tell him of your bravery and your wisdom and your courage and your loyalty and your never-ending faith. I will make sure that everyone knows this and your name and your deeds—not just here, but all your life, even those many deeds and warnings that we ignored—will not be forgotten."

Anagalisgi smiled. "Thank you. But make sure you tell Kiyuga...tell him that he has fulfilled his promise. Even if he does not yet realize it, even though he will not understand it, let him know that his promise has been fulfilled. He will know what it means."

"I will do that." Pause. "Will we ever see you again?"

"I expect so. I expect that I will never truly leave you, though it may be that you must seek me out. I expect that such things will be revealed in time."

"You speak of things that will happen after you escape, but you speak them as a man who expects to die."

"I don't know what to expect, honestly," Anagalisgi admitted, "except that it will all be revealed rather quickly in the near future, and we will not have much of a choice in how we learn how things will be."

The two of them stood, still on the road, still separated by an invisible wall.

"Know that regardless of the seeing fruit, I will stay by your side until the end," Adahi said. "It is only right."

Anagalisgi dipped his head. "I thank you, my brother. You are a true friend and a great warrior. Kiyuga will be lucky to have you back."

Adahi was the one who turned and walked away from the invisible wall, and Anagalisgi watched him go. He felt the pull of the place beyond the invisible wall, the spirit world. So close and yet unable to touch it. But soon. Soon he would walk where Adahi now tread.

Instead of leaving, Anagalisgi sat down to meditate and pray. It might be his last chance before morning, when the guards would come and take him away to be hanged.

DᏯᎾᏞᎥT WᏢꬲᎠA ᏪᏙᏁW

Ayadohlv'i Tahlsgo So'onela

Escape and Sacrifice

Anagalisgi woke. It was the day of his execution. The light in the prison was barely enough to make out the bars of his cell. Still early dawn, then. From what he understood, the Anigilisi preferred to execute their prisoners around midday. This way they could witness a spectacle before settling in for their midday meal; it would provide much gossip fodder for the women, and political speculation for the men. Well, with any luck, Anagalisgi would give them much to talk about.

Feeling around in the dark, he located his bag under the straw. He would not be able to take it with him, but that was all right. Everything inside was replaceable, and all he really needed was the seeing fruit. He intended to eat it just before they took him away. It was not a whole seeing fruit, obviously, but there was enough there that it should sustain him for the entirety of his escape, or a good portion of it, anyway. He only needed it to last until he was a good distance from the town.

Anagalisgi got himself situated on the cell floor. Grasping the seeing fruit firmly in one hand, he began to pray. In the cool dimness of the prison, he whispered his prayers. He prayed for peace; his spirit was anxious and troubled by the coming events. He prayed for faith; he wanted to believe that his life did not end this day, and yet fear still gnawed at him. He prayed for understanding; this was for his brother and the others who would miss him, who would not fully grasp just what he was doing. He was not entirely certain himself, so how could he expect it of others? He knew only that this was what he must do. He could accept it. They would have to understand it.

The light gradually increased, and the other prisoners began whimpering their customary pleas, their frantic wails and prayers that hardly resembled anything of a true faith-based invocation. With life returning to the prison, Anagalisgi ceased his whispers and instead prayed aloud. This gave way to singing and chanting, much of which was ridiculed by the others.

At one point, several soldiers appeared. Some prisoners fell silent, others increased their wailing. Anagalisgi did not react. The soldiers did a cursory inspection of the place, yelled at them to be quiet. They stopped in front of Anagalisgi's cell.

"Sounds to me like he has no interest in repentance," one said.

"Well, he's still alive, and the Reverend has to see him," a second grumbled.

"We see him just fine," a third complained.

"We'll send the Reverend down. What are you whining about? It'll be over quick enough."

The trio departed, going up the stairs and opening the door. A moment later, a single set of footsteps could be heard, and the Reverend appeared. Cries went up from the others, begging for him to do something, anything, everything from saving their souls, to getting them a bit of food, to getting them out of their cells. The Reverend ignored them and went to Anagalisgi who ceased his chanting.

"Have you considered what I spoke of, salvation for your soul?" the Reverend inquired.

"I have given it a great deal of thought," Anagalisgi told him.

"And?"

"With all due respect, I feel that something is missing, that there is something greater here to behold."

The Reverend shifted his stance. "What do you mean?"

"I mean that you are attempting to create a true image on a flat surface, and you attempt to use words to do so."

"I'm afraid I don't follow."

Anagalisgi sighed. "Often I have been told that I attempt to describe things that have no equal in our limited tongues, but even that, I think, is an adequate metaphor. You write words on paper to record accounts of your days, yes?"

"Yes."

"And while the words may be accurate in their own degree, they can never truly encompass the magnitude of any event or person, because the words themselves have no life. Even spoken word is insufficient, for they come at the interpretation of the orator. So I feel it is here, that you and I, standing here and speaking of greater spiritual things, are no better than these flat words upon paper, and even our spoken words are marred by our own biases upon imperfect lips."

The Reverend looked thoughtful. "I can see you are a young man of great wisdom and thoughtfulness. But consider that even if flat words are insufficient, if they are all we have, then we must be prepared to deal with that."

"Indeed this is true, and there is much that can be taught and learned. But if experience is impossible, then words have little meaning. How would you explain a sunrise to a blind man? Or thunder to a deaf man? Or the joy of laughter to a mute?"

"There are many things we cannot know as mere mortals. But going before our Lord is not the time to begin this study."

"You are correct, that death is not the proper time to discover life, but it is not merely souls that I am speaking of. I feel that there is more to be known here, something greater and far more powerful to be obtained. Again, as I said, I have not the words for this feeling or these experiences."

"I think I might." The Reverend shifted his stance again. "Witchcraft. You have been deceived by evil spirits and are embarking upon the path of Satan himself, believing that you may become like God and attempt to overthrow him. But God will not be mocked, nor is minor mortal rebellion of any danger to him."

Anagalisgi blinked. "That is not what I am talking about at all. I do not seek to overthrow God, nor do I believe that I shall ever possess such vast knowledge and power, for I am yet a mortal man. But that does not mean that there is not more that can be known and understood. While our peoples fight in endless wars and seek only destruction, what greater knowledge have we lost? What more could we have discovered if our souls were yet pure and unblemished?"

"Your heresy may be your downfall," the Reverend went on, his tone suggesting his mind had closed to all other conversation. "And yet, I will pray for your soul. Perhaps your intentions are yet pure enough that you will be shown mercy for actions as yet unrealized. And praise the Lord for it, for we do not need another Satan upon this world."

Anagalisgi sighed and said nothing as the preacher lifted his hands and wailed multiple fervent prayers, asking for forgiveness for his own sins, that God would cleanse the prison and the whole town of the evil spirits brought by the heretic. He prayed for mercy for an innocent soul led astray, the Devil tempting his spiritual curiosity and twisting it for sin and evil. He prayed for righteousness and peace, and he prayed for the salvation of all the Aniyvwiya left alive after the war, have mercy on them for allowing themselves to be led astray.

He said more, but Anagalisgi no longer paid any attention. He wished he had the words to convey what he meant. He wished he could explain the sorceries, but knew that would have no good effect. Even just using them in his escape would only further solidify the idea that he was a pagan witch who ought to be burned. How could he ever hope to make others understand? What good was having great knowledge and insight if no one listened because they were unable to understand him?

It was quite a conundrum, and it occupied his mind enough that he hardly noticed when the Reverend finished praying and departed.

Anagalisgi sighed, sat down in the straw, and thought. He did not resume his prayers or singing, merely considered his situation. The conversation had bothered him, even as he told himself that he had to be ready; the soldiers would be back for him at any moment. Still, it was hard to focus his thoughts.

If he escaped, his only option was to take his place as the guardian of the door between worlds. Ge'gwogv had told him so, and Adahi was counting on him. He still didn't know what it entailed, but it was as important a job as anything he had ever done so far as an adawehi for his people. But to what end? If this task was only going to give him greater knowledge and further separate him from his people, make him entirely incomprehensible to their ears and minds, then what was the point?

He hated himself for his doubt, but he could not deny it, either. On the other hand, even less knowledgeable men were sometimes ignored, if only because their audience was too stubborn or too stupid to understand. It was not always the fault of the teacher. A good teacher always tried to speak his student's tongue, but if a man did not want to listen, no words would persuade him otherwise.

Perhaps, then, it was the fault of the Reverend. If such was the case, Anagalisgi found it disheartening, for he'd hoped that a spiritual man such as the Reverend might have a better understanding of that which he'd spoken and tried, unsuccessfully, to convey. Again he found himself wishing to speak to Gvnagadoga.

It was not long before the soldiers came for him. There were six men: a judge, the Reverend, three soldiers, and another man whose purpose he did not know. As they descended the steps into the prison, Anagalisgi conjured Time, bringing everything around him to a standstill. In that moment, he ate the rest of the seeing fruit.

Adahi appeared beside him, looking anxious, but also resolute that this was what must happen. Ahead of him, perched on a wooden peg near the stairs, Ge'gwogv rested. There was also a white spirit on either side of the cell door, as though guarding him.

Once he saw these things, Anagalisgi ceased his conjuring. The men on the stairs approached. They all regarded Anagalisgi in silence for a long moment. Their expressions conveyed revulsion, as though he were a lowly creature to be summarily dismissed as unimportant and unclean.

"Bring him," the judge ordered.

One soldier opened the cell while the other two entered and seized him. They bound his wrists and put a bag over his head. It smelled like sweet earth, but also rot, blood, and death. His first instinct was to gag and recoil, but he could do nothing of the sort.

And yet, even with his head covered by stinking burlap, he could still see. He would not call it physical sight, for he could not make out the things around him, but he would call it spiritual sight. He could move by instinct, intuitively knowing where to set his feet, when to step over a pile of horse manure that the soldiers seemed to intentionally steer him towards. And he could feel the presence of the spirits. He knew Ge'gwogv flew ahead of him. An eagle flew high above. A deer walked on his right and a cougar on his left. A fox guarded his rear. And all around, a pack of white wolves scouted the area. His true escort was far more powerful than the soldiers who held him.

He also tried to visualize Adahi's map. He could remember where the prison was, where the gallows was, but it was difficult to bring them together now that he was walking in the real world. He could not quite tell where he was, how far he had to go, and which way was the best route for escape. He wanted to speak to Adahi, who he knew was close by, but he did not wish to alert his guards.

As if sensing his thoughts, the warrior spoke.

"I am right here, Anagalisgi," Adahi said. "We are very near to the gallows. Actually, as we turn this corner, we are within sight, and very close."

Even as he said it, Anagalisgi could feel the presence of many people gathered. When they saw him, walking forward with the bag over his head, being led to the gallows, there was an outbreak of whispers and murmurs, and a few raised voices. There were many names and insults thrown his way, ranging from common name-calling to rather atrocious analogies of himself, his people, and his parents. He did not react, and he told himself to ignore these things, but he would not say they did not wound his soul.

"Be strong, Anagalisgi," Adahi whispered in his ear. "Their words are but the croaks of frogs."

Yes. The croaks of frogs. Insignificant, dull, droning, and meaning nothing to men. He took a calm breath, resisted the urge to gag upon the stench of death in the bag, and carried on. As if he had a choice.

His foot touched a wooden step, and he started upwards, to the gallows platform.

Among his own people, when it was decided that a prisoner should be executed, he was given a chance to recite his greatest deeds and mightiest battles. He was also permitted to embellish these tales as much as he wished, no matter how grandiose to himself, or belittling to the audience. From what Anagalisgi understood, the Anigilisi offered no such rights to their condemned prisoners. A man was permitted to say some final words, ask for prayer from the preacher, and that was all. No one would know who he was, his daring deeds or bravery in battle. A condemned man was but a scoundrel, an insect to be quashed.

Anagalisgi would not have known what to speak of, anyway. He would not say that he had ever been particularly daring, and he had never fought in battle. He had blessed the warriors, offered guidance, tended wounds, but he had never actually fought. And to speak of his grand visions, insightful dreams, prophetic omens, and spiritual connections would likely only enrage his captors, perhaps encouraging them to execute him more swiftly, thereby making his escape that much more difficult.

His best option, then, would be to say nothing. He had to stay focused. He had to get this bag off his head, the bindings off his wrists, and flee.

He reached the top of the platform and was roughly maneuvered to a certain spot. He could feel a rough spot in the wood where a splinter stuck itself in his toe.

The bag was ripped off from his head, and he squinted against bright sunlight.

As his eyes adjusted, he saw two things. He saw the things before him, in the waking world. And he saw spiritual things. Things only he could see.

In the waking world, he stood over the heads of about a hundred spectators, maybe more. Most were men, perhaps soldiers at home. But there were also women and children among them. The women did not look afraid, but nearly as angry as the men, if not more. The children were wide-eyed and curious, pointing and pestering their parents with questions. On the platform, the three soldiers stood directly behind him. The judge stood in the rear corner on his left. The Reverend stood in the rear corner on his right. The executioner waited at the handle to the trap door. The man whose purpose was unknown stood in the front corner on his right.

In the spiritual world, the area was filled with many white spirits, all looking, watching, waiting to see what he would do. Ge'gwogv perched on a tree near the platform. The eagle sat atop a building. The pack of wolves roamed through the crowd. But overall, none of them made a move. They had immense power, but all that remained to be done hinged upon his will to do it. He had to take the initiative. He had to try and escape.

Adahi stood beside him.

"I am ready when you are," the warrior said quietly.

Anagalisgi did not react except for a nearly imperceptible nod. He knew what would happen. He knew what he had to do. He greatly desired to conjure Time and collect himself, but he had to save as much energy as possible in order to not only escape the town, but open a doorway and complete the rest of his journey.

He let out a breath as the executioner put the noose around his neck. As the thick hemp touched his neck, his throat closed and his heart began to race. The man with the unknown purpose brought out a scroll and began reading.

The man named a great many crimes of which he was accused. Some of them were war crimes or political in nature, citing broken treaties, hostilities against an ally, hostilities against soldiers of the Crown, hostilities against Crown holdings and properties, and others he did not understand. Actually, many of their laws he did not understand. Other crimes included heresy and witchcraft, invoking demonic powers against the Crown, her allies, her soldiers, and her citizens, and others.

What was interesting was that witchcraft was not a crime unique to the Europeans. The Aniyvwiya also had laws regarding witchcraft and the punishment of witches and those who consorted with them. If all of them were witches, then they must be of Satan, as the priest said. But if Satan could not be divided against himself, what did that say about the Aniyvwiya adawehi who condemned witchcraft on their own? What did God say about such things?

"And you shall be hanged by the neck until dead," the man said, rolling up his scroll. "May God have mercy upon your soul." He turned to face Anagalisgi. "Do you wish to make a final statement?"

Anagalisgi hesitated and looked out over the crowd. Even if he had wanted to say something, whether a simple statement or a recitation of his deeds, his tongue suddenly went dry and he could barely speak to reply, "No."

"Do you wish a final prayer from the Reverend?"

He shook his head. "No."

The man frowned and Anagalisgi could feel the disappointment from those gathered, both on the platform and in the crowd. Before anyone could do anything, he found his tongue again and said, "Actually. I do wish to make a statement."

Behind him, someone snorted indignantly.

The man with the scroll looked displeased still, but motioned for him to continue.

"My name is Anagalisgi," he said. "I am not a witch. I am an adawehi. I serve the Creator." He sighed. "Unfortunately, I cannot do so if I am dead. It seems that—"

He cut himself off as he reached above him, grabbed the noose above the knot, and, with mighty strength and a tiny bit of Galo'ohndiha ale Agi'a, heaved himself up onto the beam.

"Open fire!" someone shouted, perhaps the judge.

As the soldiers readied their muskets, Anagalisgi took the noose off from around his neck, then used it to swing back down from the beam, landing safely on the platform. He conjured Time, long enough to use the bayonets to cut the ropes from his wrists and get off the platform. There he ceased conjuring and called to Adahi.

"Where shall I go?" he puffed.

Adahi came beside him. Anagalisgi first ran south, just to get away from the crowd and the open square, but he knew he needed to get east and north.

"This way," the invisible warrior said, turning down another street.

Behind him, Anagalisgi could hear shouts of anger and confusion, calls for more soldiers and for every man to grab his gun and hunt down the escaped prisoner.

He followed Adahi partway down the street, then slid into a narrow opening between buildings, ducking behind some barrels. Adahi crouched beside him, partway inside the barrels and one of the buildings, as if they didn't even exist, or as if he didn't.

"From here, you have to go out this way, turn right, and run straight until you reach the end of the street," the warrior told him, keeping his voice low though no one else could hear him. "Turn right again; you'll be heading north. There's an alley there that I will show you."

Anagalisgi nodded, breathing heavily. The element of surprise was gone. All he had now was speed and cunning, as well as help from the spirits which no one else could see. He was in enemy territory, and he had no tricks to play here. He had to get out.

Taking a breath, Anagalisgi slid among the barrels like a snake, pausing and listening. There were still frustrated shouts from men, but they did not seem to be close by. He saw a group of armed men go by a short distance away, on an adjacent street, but in his immediate vicinity, he saw nothing.

"Go now!" Adahi hissed.

The warrior took off himself, and Anagalisgi followed, hard on his heels. A cougar guarded one side of him, perhaps blinding some men that they would not see him as he ran by. On the other wise, the pack of wolves distracted another group of men, clearing his passage.

Overhead, several birds kept a keen eye on the situation. And Ge'gwogv himself glided alongside Anagalisgi, flitting from building to building, landing on walls and rooftops to watch him go by.

The town was small, when seen from a distance, but there was no larger country in the world than enemy territory, and the street seemed to stretch on forever. He knew he was heading west. Perhaps he had died and was already making for the Darkening Lands in the west, toward the setting sun? A cut on his foot from a sharp stone quickly ended that thought.

He stumbled a bit, his feet slapping on hard ground. Up ahead, the street ended at a building of some form, and Adahi turned right, to the north, just as he'd said. A moment before Anagalisgi followed, he heard a shout behind him.

"They're coming," Anagalisgi told Adahi, hoping the warrior heard him.

"This way," Adahi said, veering off the main road and into another alley. The invisible warrior had no trouble with common obstacles, but Anagalisgi had to slow down and try to navigate barrels, crates, and assorted common goods of the people. He did not need to leave a trail for his pursuers to follow. Adahi motioned for him to hide under a small structure, which, when hastily investigated, proved to be a bird coop. The chickens, ducks, and geese were unsure what to make of his sudden presence, but similar white spirit animals seemed to convince them to stay quiet.

"From here, we only need to get over to the wall there." Adahi pointed to the timber palisade that surrounded the town. "It is not far to one of the holes. It is a child-sized hole, so even if they spot you, they should not be able to follow easily."

Anagalisgi nodded, breathing hard. The coop smelled obscene and he gagged.

"Shall I wait, then?" he whispered, unable to see much from his vantage.

Adahi looked at the sky. "Wait until the sun hides behind this building. The shadows should provide good cover for you. It will not be long."

Anagalisgi did not argue, although he wished for something, anything to smell besides the bird coop. By the same token, however, it kept his mind off his racing heart, sweaty palms, and anxious thoughts. It gave him a way to consolidate himself, refocus his energy. Trying not to gag and vomit, he took an even breath and waited for the sun to move around.

Elsewhere in the town, he heard calls to search every inch of every building and every street. Look up in the trees and under the rocks. Close the gates and have someone keep an eye on the wall. Women and children should also be guarded, and every man who could hold a gun ought to have one and help in some fashion. And make sure the other prisoners remained well-guarded, in the event one of them decided to attempt an escape of his own.

It amused him, in a way, the fuss they were making over him. It made him feel a little special, a little important. That feeling only last a short time before the sun finally disappeared behind the building Adahi had indicated. The warrior spoke.

"Come out, Anagalisgi," he said. "Follow me."

Anagalisgi was more than happy to wiggle out from under the bird coop, pulling himself across the ground and upright, trying to move swiftly and yet silently. Adahi was already moving, and Anagalisgi readily followed.

Just a short distance to the child-sized hole, he'd said. Even if he was spotted, as long as he could get through the hole, the others would not be able to follow. One of the advantages to being a more slender adawehi, rather than a large warrior like his brother.

They followed the wall, footsteps quiet in the grass. Up ahead, Anagalisgi could see the hole Adahi had spoken of. It was near the bottom of the wall, and it looked as though someone or something had tried to make it bigger with claws and teeth. Nevertheless, it was indeed small. Child-sized. But perhaps...too small. Fit for a toddler, not one such as himself who, despite being small, was not quite...that small.

"We can continue ahead," Adahi said. "There is another hole—"

Commotion farther along the wall made Anagalisgi shake his head. "No. There's no time." He knelt and began digging at the hole, prying away loose wood splinters, the soft earth below coming up easily. He looked around and saw a few white animals go on ahead to meet and perhaps distract the nearby hunting party.

"I will look ahead and see what to expect on the other said," Adahi told him, standing and moving through the wall to the outside.

Anagalisgi kept digging, throwing clods of dirt everywhere like a dog. Eventually, hearing the hunters nearing his position, he had no choice but to force himself through.

"Adahi!" he hissed, positioning himself to slide through the hole.

"You're clear on this side," the warrior said.

Anagalisgi slipped through the hole feet first, wiggling and forcing his way through, digging hard into the earth and sticking himself with a number of splinters. He bit his lip and wiggled more. He could hear the hunters only steps away. Once they rounded the corner, they would see him, and he would have nowhere to run.

"There he is!"

Too late.

Panicking, he conjured Time, stopping the hunters in their tracks and giving him time to get his shoulders through the hole, grabbing anything he could for leverage and force. Once his shoulders were through, his head followed easily.

Then he was out. He was mildly disoriented as he tried to stand, and he was on the ground again.

"Anagalisgi!" Adahi cried.

Anagalisgi put up a hand as he clambered to his feet. "I'm fine. Come on!"

He ceased his conjuring, hearing the shouts of the hunters behind him, but did not look back as he ran into the forest.

He was dirty, stinking of bird poop, and stuck with innumerable splinters. His foot ached from the cut he'd gotten, and he limped every fifth step. But he was free. He was away from that place. Now he just had to find a spot where he could safely conjure a doorway to Aktiya Waya and rescue Adahi. He decided to return to the cave they had used before. He was uncertain if it would make a difference, but it would put more distance between himself and his pursuers anyway.

Around him, the white animals had gathered. Ge'gwogv led the way, flying in front of him, while an eagle soared overhead, wolves ran on one side, a cougar slunk by on the other, and a fox kept watch behind him. Adahi also kept pace with him, changing positions in front of or behind him, from side to side.

Anagalisgi wanted to stop and rest when he came across the first stream, but he didn't dare. He knew the hunters would not give up so easily, not when they had been so close to victory, not when they had been outsmarted so brashly. They would continue to pursue. He could not stop.

He did, however, use the stream to his advantage, stepping in the chill water and running upstream, always following Ge'gwogv. The cool water numbed his aching foot and relieved the sting of some of the splinters. It would also confound the hounds for a time, as would the smell of the bird poop he'd lain in.

He did not stop. He did not slow down. He did not look back to see if the hunters were on his tail. He kept his gaze firmly fixed on Ge'gwogv's white tail feathers, deviating only inasmuch as he needed to navigate certain rocks and obstacles in the stream.

As the sun moved around the sky and the air grew warm and his feet grew numb, Anagalisgi did slow down, and Ge'gwogv took him to a sheltered spot to rest. He climbed up the bank as gently as he could and made his way to a large flat rock bathed in sunlight. It was wonderfully warm, and he lay down upon it. Or he tried to. Multiple splinters made themselves known, and he quickly sat up again, twitching in discomfort.

"Shall I attempt to conjure Galohisdi here?" he wondered, looking at Ge'gwogv, settled on the side of a tree. He started picking out his splinters.

As the white woodpecker hopped along the tree and looked at

him, Anagalisgi thought he seemed less...solid than before, like a reflection in a pool of water that was not quite still.

"Ge'gwogv? What is happening?" he asked. He looked at Adahi who appeared the same way, a rippled reflection.

It was a foolish question. The seeing fruit was wearing off, and his connection to the spirit world was slowly fading. Even now, aside from the poor reflections, he could not hear their voices clearly, could not hear Ge'gwogv's answer to his previous question. And then, the reflections became even poorer, more ripples in the water, until they all finally vanished, and he was alone once more.

"I don't know what your answer was, Ge'gwogv," Anagalisgi sighed. "I do not know if you told me to conjure here, or continue to the cave. I suppose the Author shall have to direct my path now, and as I previously said that I would conjure in the cave, that I will so do, unless I am directed otherwise."

All the same, he remained where he was for a short time, picking splinters out of his body, tending to the cut on his foot, and picking some mushrooms to eat and regain his strength.

He did not hear the hunters when he set off again, but he knew instinctively that they were still following him. He had stayed too long, lost too much ground; he had to make it up again, and then some.

Having warmed himself upon the sunlit rock, he was able to return to the stream and run through the water. He hoped that this was the way to the cave, or that he would find some marker to tell him which way to go. He remembered what the depression looked like, and he recalled the way. But there was no telling exactly where he was in relation to that.

He would have to trust the Author, that she would deliver him. He would have to trust the small, instinctive voice telling him where he needed to go.

Later in the day, as the sun began to sink behind the mountains, he got out of the stream. He could barely feel his feet, and he was fairly certain that he had a decent head start on the hunters. Besides, he was getting winded, and the mushrooms had long since worn off. His ability to convince his body that he was fasting was now severely depleted, and his body had discerned his lie.

Anagalisgi climbed out of the stream and looked around for a decent place to...eat? Sleep? He wasn't exactly sure. Did he keep going? Did he stop for the night? He was unaccustomed to being on his own like this. Whether he was giving orders to others or taking orders from someone else, he was accustomed to traveling with others, in groups large and small, where the needs of the pack determined their movements, their comings and goings. Now he was a pack of one. He had to make his own decisions based on his own needs. It was a strange sensation.

Unsure what else to do, he continued along the bank at a walk. His goal was less about making distance, but finding good forage. He picked some more mushrooms and ate them, and foraged from a clump of raspberries. It took the edge off his hunger, anyway.

Eventually he came to a small pond where cattails grew in great abundance. Sighing with relief, he dug up several and portioned them out by stems, leaves, and roots. He debated the wisdom of a fire, then decided against it. Better to remain as silent and as dark as the night, rather than give his pursuers hope of the chase. And the snare. Instead, he ate the pieces raw, wrapping the leaves around root and stem bundles and eating them together. He went out and managed to find another large cluster of raspberry bushes which he added to his meal.

It was not the same as cooking in the village. It was only vaguely similar to foraging while on the road, in that, in planned and prepared travels, he at least had some tools on him, such as a knife. He had only his hands now. A piece of river cane served as a crude knife, and a smooth stone mashed up the berries, stems, and roots, but he was not prepared for battle if the hunters came upon him.

He elected to try and rest under a large bush with fragrant flowers and broken lower limbs. With any luck, his scent would be masked and his body would be hidden should anything come upon him in the night. All the same, it was terribly difficult to get to sleep. He hoped and silently prayed that he would see Ge'gwogv and receive guidance.

Such did not happen. He did not see Ge'gwogv or any of the spirits. He did not see Adahi. He had no spiritual revelations or encounters of any kind. He could not recall that he had any dreams whatsoever.

When he crawled back to consciousness, he would admit to feeling a bit lonely and disappointed. Surely the spirits knew of his confusion and anxiety. Why would they not come to comfort and guide him? If he were on the wrong path, he would expect them to say so. He could not imagine that they would help deliver him from execution only to ignore him over a cliff.

All the same, he was back in the waking world. He wiggled out from under his bush and stood. When he looked up, he saw what he was looking for. He could not say how he knew that the place where he was looking was where he needed to go, only that it was. Maybe it was some familiar feature of the stone, or maybe it was subtle, spiritual intuition. Whatever the case, he suddenly felt deeply ashamed of his doubt. He had no seeing fruit, could not see the spirits, and had not dreamed of them, but that did not mean that they had abandoned him.

He still took a moment to gather a few things to eat and consider his surroundings, listen for any hunters on his trail. It was dawn now, and light enough to see by. If he was awake and ready to be moving, chances were good that any pursuers were thinking and doing the same thing. He still did not know if he had pursuers, or how long and how far they would pursue him, but he would take no chances.

So he fixed his eyes on the mountaintop, and in that direction he traveled, the same as when he'd followed Ge'gwogv. As he did so, as the mountain drew nearer, he began to pick out familiar features. A rock formation here. A cluster of trees and a broken log there. The land sloped in a way that he remembered as being strange, thinking that there must have been another river running through here many years ago.

He stumbled upon the depression more than he actively found it. It was as simple as looking around and somehow knowing that there was a good source of herbs just beyond a cluster of bushes there. He had come this way with Kiyuga, tending the wounded so they could escape to Aktiya Waya. Yes, he knew this place.

Suddenly excited, he took off down the slope, farther into the depression. He came across the camp they had made, and the soldiers after them, all exactly where it had been. A hat and a spoon had been left behind, but that was the only evidence aside from the fire pit left behind. And there to the east was the trail leading to the cave.

Anagalisgi couldn't help but grin. He let out a breath and knelt to give thanks to the spirits. He was nearly there. He was so close to completing his mission. All the same, he had to give thanks one last time. He had a feeling that pretty soon, he would be able to thank them in person.

He stood and, not wishing to waste any more time, started up the trail to the cave.

Despite his flight from the town, having to run in cold water and eating very little, he still felt vigorous and strong, ready to do whatever the spirits asked of him, whatever he needed to do to save Adahi and take his place as the guardian of the door between worlds. He was beginning to understand it now, what that meant. It was not a door between life and death, or between here and Aktiya Waya. It was the door between the waking world and the spirit world. He would learn the tongue of the spirits, that he would be able to communicate with more people in the future, that future adawehi would not have the same trouble he did, trying to verbalize ideas that, as of now, had no words.

His heart was racing with anticipation as he climbed the hill toward the cave. Up ahead, he could see where the tree line ended, where the rocks fell away and revealed the mouth of the earth.

He was just about to break through the tree line when he stopped. He heard dogs, baying in the distance. His fear lasted only a moment. He was already here, at the cave. He knew what he had to do. By the time the hunters arrived, there would be nothing left to find. Adahi would be in Aktiya Waya, and he would long gone, taking his place as the guardian.

He walked a few steps into the cave.

"Adahi," he said. "I am certain you are near. I will conjure Galohisdi for you to Aktiya Waya. You will walk through, and I will take your place."

There was no answer, not that he expected one. Taking a breath, he readied himself.

He felt the earth beneath his feet, felt the air and the cave around him. He felt his place upon the island, in the Middle World, between the Upper and Lower Worlds. He felt the current that ran between the islands. He reached out to navigate the rivers and touch the island of Aktiya Waya. He felt it, knew its island, knew its place. Taking a breath, he forced his will upon the river, bade it cease so that he may cross.

The chill air of the cave froze his sweaty skin, but when he looked up, he had conjured Galohisdi. On the other side, he saw Aktiya Waya. He stood and put a hand up as something flashed within the doorway. For a moment, he saw a blinding form that he realized was Adahi.

"Adahi?" he wondered. "Did you make it?"

He approached the doorway, but did not see the warrior on the other side. Confused but still determined, Anagalisgi placed himself at the threshold between islands. Outside, he could hear the baying of the hounds, but he worked to put it out of his mind.

He startled as something touched him, and he again saw a flash of light and the form of Adahi. This time, however, he was of a presence of mind to reach out and touch the warrior. They grasped wrists and Adahi appeared as a ghost, having form in all worlds and yet not present in any of them.

"Anagalisgi," Adahi gasped, sounding very much in pain. "Anagalisgi, I can't hold on."

"I know," Anagalisgi told him calmly, feeling the sensation of lightning creep up his arm. "Don't fight it. Let me come to you."

The feeling of crossing into the spirit world was unlike the feeling of crossing between islands. Traveling between islands was difficult, exhausting, and even a little painful. Moving into the spirit world was a bit like wrapping oneself in a thick fur blanket, warm and comforting, and then being removed from the world, as if free-floating, attached to nothing, floating through a tunnel.

The way into the spirit world was easier than one might have expected, Anagalisgi thought, like a trap for fish. But it could only be exited through one sacrificing himself for another. Adahi could never have hoped to escape on his own, but as Anagalisgi entered the spirit world through the warm tunnel, it was his only chance of getting out.

"Go, Adahi," Anagalisgi said, his voice sounding distant, even to himself. "Go to my brother. Tell him...I am all right. Tell him that his promise has been fulfilled."

Adahi's expression was a grave mixture of confusion, relief, and still pain. He let go of Anagaligi's wrist. At that moment, Anagalisgi gave him a hard shove, pushing him out of the spirit world and through the doorway to Aktiya Waya.

Only when the doorway closed did Anagalisgi feel pain, as though a porcupine quill had been ripped out of him. He dropped to his knees with an involuntary cry.

Outside, he heard the dogs getting closer. As he stood and exited the cave, he saw the dogs running up the hill, the hunters still down the slope. The dogs put their noses to the ground as they entered the cave, but the scent abruptly disappeared. None of them were aware of his presence. A short time later, the hunters caught up to them.

"Back into the cave, then," one man growled.

"The others got away, which means there must be an exit somewhere in there," a second said. "We'll have to go in after him."

The party groaned. One man said, "Is it worth it? For one escaped whelp?"

"We have to make an example of him, or the savages will walk all over us."

"The savages are defeated. They can't do anything more."

"Well we can't give them any reason to think otherwise."

As they debated and argued, Anagalisgi entered the cave. He went to the point where the light was so dim, it may as well have not existed. And yet, the light existed for him. He saw not only Light, but Time. And he began taking these threads of Time, like a single tapestry, and pulling on them, one by one. He took the tapestry and re-wove it, re-formed the pattern. The hunters would come in, and they would think little of it. But when they emerged, months or years would have passed. And they would be displaced, just as his people had been displaced.

When he emerged from the cave after finishing his new Time tapestry, passing the hunters on their way in, he found Ge'gwogv. If a woodpecker could look disapproving, disapproving it looked.

"You should not have done that," Ge'gwogv told him.

"They will not hurt my people again," Anagalisgi replied levelly.

He started off back down the slope.

DᏫᎥᏞᎢ ᎧᏙᏫᎠᏮ

Ayadohlv'i Tso'osgohi

A Lost Hope

Kiyuga paced angrily. Then he paced sadly. Then he paced angrily again. Then he paced with confusion in his mind. Then he was sad again. Then confused. Then angry. Then sad.

He could no longer tell where one emotion ended and another began as he continued to pace, worrying the rug until his feet hurt and his head was dizzy.

He shouldn't have left his brother behind. He should have grabbed him and pulled him through. He should have stayed and fought. He should have done any number of things. But he hadn't. And now, not only was Anagalisgi captured, but Adahi was also missing. And it was all his fault. He thought he'd had time. He thought they'd been able to hide and get away. He thought that they were safe enough to camp instead of moving after every Galohisdi to shed their weaker party members.

He had been the leader. He had been responsible. Aganstata himself had assigned the task to him because he trusted him. And now he had failed them.

When he had first stumbled through the doorway, he had been too weak to do much more than stumble alongside someone and be taken to the home of a cousin to recover. Once he was recovered, he demanded to know of the others, and most importantly, his brother.

Anagalisgi hadn't come through with him, and Adahi had vanished, he was told. Neither had been seen since.

He had gotten angry then, and been confined to his cousin's house until he could calm down.

He still was not calm. He was still angry, sad, confused, and other emotions he had no name for.

Finally he sat.

The home overall was about as big as the ones in the Overhill, but it was divided into more rooms. This particular one that his cousin lived in had three rooms. The stone walls were strange, and even stranger was the dim light outside. The sky could not be seen well from here, only the walls and ceiling of the cave the village was situated in. Furniture was still in the process of being made, so the only items to liven up the otherwise gray room were the rug on the floor, a pot in the corner, two hastily-built chairs, and a flat stone that had already been in the room that served as a table. There was one window behind him that pointed toward the outside of the cave, and at a certain angle, one could see a sliver of sky. Another window was near the door, facing inward, a piece of bad leather covering most of the opening.

He should be out there. He should go back. He had to rescue his brother.

Kiyuga stood and began pacing again, unsure what to do. He knew what his heart told him to do, and yet he could not forget how calm and assured Anagalisgi had seemed. His brother had always known things beyond the waking world. He had seen many things, things which could not be put into words. Was his capture somehow part of the Creator's greater plan? If so, who was he to interfere?

But what if it was not part of the plan? What if his brother had been mistaken? What if he truly needed rescue?

He turned as the door opened and his cousin, Ganulahsa'a, walked in, his demeanor that of approaching an agitated animal. Carefully he closed the door, always watching Kiyuga.

"Has there been news?" Kiyuga demanded. "A sign, perhaps?"

"Nothing," Ganulahsa'a answered quietly. "The adawehi are seeking the spirits as we speak. Anagalisgi always had one foot in the spirit world; if there is any place to look for him, it is there."

His words gave Kiyuga some hope, though he could not say

especially why. "May I join them, or shall I be locked in here forever until he returns to us?"

Ganulahsa'a hesitated. "I am not your father or mother, Kiyuga, nor are we of the same clan. I cannot tell you what to do. I ask only that you consider well your actions before you do something you will regret."

"I do not regret caring for my brother. I regret leaving him behind."

His cousin said nothing as he pushed past and left the house. He paused almost immediately, momentarily disoriented. For some reason, he had fully expected to walk out and see Itsa'ti, active and lively. Instead, he found the cave and its dim, twisting maze of homes and buildings.

He roamed the streets for a short while, jogging where possible in hopes of outrunning his rage and confusion. He wanted—needed to do something. He wanted to go back and save his brother. He wanted to go back and slaughter all of the Anigilisi. And what had happened to Adahi? Had he been captured as well?

When he finally exhausted himself, he returned to his cousin's home. Ganulahsa'a had been one of the few warriors chosen to come to Aktiya Waya when the migration was made. In addition to defending the women, children, and elders, and the heavy labor needed to see the village succeed, if worse came to worse, young, strong men would be needed to carry on the next generation. The elders could not, and they would not be able to wait for the young boys to come of age.

Case and point, when Kiyuga reached for the door to the home, he paused and listened before entering. He heard nothing unusual and let himself in.

"You have returned," Ganulahsa'a observed. "You look tired. Did you speak to the adawehi?"

Kiyuga shook his head. "I could not. I ran. And I continued running until I exhausted myself."

Ganvgi, Ganulahsa'a's wife, brought dinner for him.

"Is there a home here that is yours?" she wondered. "There are still many empty buildings; I am sure you may lay claim to any of them, if you haven't already."

Kiyuga sighed and shook his head. He had stayed with his cousin over the winter and had not given it much thought. "I have not had a chance to look. Do you know if my aunt and uncle have crossed?"

"Digvnige?" Ganulahsa'a asked. "I've not seen him, no. Or Sotsena."

Kiyuga frowned but said nothing.

He slept in the middle room that night, Ganulahsa'a and Ganvgi taking one of the side rooms. His comforts amounted only to a couple of deer furs, but it kept the chill of the stone at bay when the fire burned low.

He did not dream of his brother, or of any spirits. Truthfully, he did not recall his dreams except to know that they were meaningless in such regard. Even before his cousin was awake, Kiyuga was again running through the pre-dawn town. This time, he made his way to the townhouse where the elders and adawehi were. Many were asleep, but some were awake and tending to the fire.

"Ah, Yvgidahi," one said, motioning him over. "Come here, come here."

Kiyuga obeyed and went to join them at the fire.

"Have you news of my brother?"

"Only enough to say that he is well, and Adahi is with him."

Kiyuga thought he might melt into the stone with his relief. "Were you able to speak to him?"

"No." The adawehi shook their heads. "No, this was only a small message from the spirits. To you. To tell you not to worry."

"Thank you. Was there anything more?"

"No, but you best not get greedy. The spirits have shown you this in order to calm your restlessness. Seek not more than that."

A flash of irritation struck Kiyuga, but he said nothing of it. He merely thanked the elders, stood, and left the townhouse.

His brother was well, and Adahi was with him. Such tremendous news! Perhaps they managed to get away from the Anigilisi and were now hiding. It took time for his brother to recover from his conjuring, and he would be too weak to make another attempt so soon. If he and

Adahi could stay hidden for a few days, then there should be no problems for them to come to Aktiya Waya.

He could hope. He had to hope.

It settled his restless spirit, anyway, and he was better able to go about his day. He checked on some of the warriors who had been injured in battle and had to escape on the road, at every chance Anagalisgi had to conjure. He checked on other relatives he knew were there in Aktiya Waya. He checked on the women, children, and elders he had helped to bring to the town. He checked on the crops in the fields and asked after the hunters as they returned.

All seemed to be going well, exactly as they had hoped and planned, returning to the ways of their ancestors, without the Europeans and their words and their wars, and even without the Aninvdawegi and other enemy nations. Finally, the Aniyvwiya seemed to be at peace.

All he needed now was his brother.

Kiyuga spent his day productively, even going out on his own for a bit to hunt and forage. This was his home now, too, for a time; he ought to be a part of it. He also went on a walk through the town, inspecting some of the buildings yet empty. Aktiya Waya had come to life once more after many eons of only ghosts and spirits—and even they had abandoned it eventually—but even so, there were still many unoccupied homes. He ought to find one for himself, build his life and reputation, and maybe...maybe find a woman again, take a wife once more. Have a family again.

None of the houses especially spoke to him, but it was not an urgent matter, he figured. Ganulahsa'a was gracious, and Ganvgi was a good cook. Besides, there may be a chance of returning to the Overhill one day. Or so he hoped.

He returned to his cousin's home that evening.

"If you could return to the other island, to the other towns, would you?" Kiyuga asked of his cousin and his cousin's wife. "If you were told that you could go back first thing in the morning?"

Ganulahsa'a glanced at his wife as they ate. "Is that what is to happen?"

"No," Kiyuga sighed. "I've heard nothing. But if it were an option, an opportunity, would you take it?"

"Of course," Ganulahsa'a said. "Many of my brothers stayed behind to fight, as did Ganvgi's brothers."

But his wife seemed less certain. "Would there be peace?"

"What do you mean?" Kiyuga wondered.

"Would there be peace?" Ganvgi repeated. "Or would we yet fear for our lives from imminent threats from the Europeans? Would our history and our culture continue to be degraded by their forceful presence? Would our children continue to be slaughtered and taken captive by enemies against whom we have no defense? Of those children that survive, would we have anything left to teach them of our ways?"

"The sorceries—"

"Provided a means for escape. Perhaps, then, it was the intent of the spirits that we leave. Why should we return when our salvation was made so clear?"

Kiyuga frowned. "How, then, should boys and men be tested if we have no enemies? How should a boy prove himself a man? How should a man prove himself to a woman, a husband to his wife? Would that element of our culture and history not be abandoned if we stayed here?"

"Then send the boys on raids back to the other island," Ganvgi said. "We are safe here. And we yet have our way of life. We are learning the turn of the world, the moons and seasons, and so we plant crops. We are learning the movements of new animals, and some of the hunters have brought the animals we knew, so we continue to bring meat. We are learning the plants and trees, and some have brought familiar plants to cultivate, and so our healers continue to heal.

"Without enemies, our children are free to explore, to learn this world in which we reside. Our elders look to the stars and learn the tales and spirits of this place, as surely as the other island has its stories and spirits. We are not merely living here; we are alive again. We are the people our ancestors were, before the Europeans.

"The other day, I saw a young man return from a hunting trip. He had brought in a galogedi'a, a grazing animal that can be found south of the forest. He did this with a bow he had made himself from the knowledge of the oldest elders. Do you know how to make a bow, Yvgidahi? Can you use one?"

"I learned as a child, but was never so proficient," Kiyuga admitted.

"And our ancestors would weep for it. But now that knowledge will be preserved with greater strength and skill than the tales of elders."

Kiyuga glanced at his cousin. "And what do you think?"

Ganulahsa'a hesitated and hastily took a bite of food. Finally, "I would very much like for things to return to the way they were. I suppose, if I were told that we could return tomorrow, I would. But Ganvgi has a point. What would we return to, and how long would it last? Would we leave here tomorrow, after a terrible war, only to return in another ten years when we find that we can no longer fight and win?" He paused. "What would you do, cousin, if given the choice?"

That gave Kiyuga pause, and he did not answer for a long moment.

"I don't know," he sighed. "I don't know what battles may be won, as you said. I don't know what the Anigilisi or the other Europeans will do to us, now or in the future, but I cannot imagine it will be friendly."

"I have never been to war," Ganvgi said, "but Ganulahsa'a has told me that if a party cannot achieve the element of surprise, they will abandon the entire raid. A warrior must never fling himself into a foolhardy battle, for he will die as a fool. At what point does staying make us fools?"

"Shall we leave, then, every time there is danger?" Kiyuga argued. "Did we give up against any of our enemies in the past? Why the Europeans? Why can we not defeat them also, if we just have the patience?"

"The Europeans do not have our patience," Ganulahsa'a said. "They do not have our patience, our weapons, our tactics, or our honor. They take what they want and they will use any means necessary to destroy any opposition. They also have far greater numbers, large ships that bring them across the sea in endless tides. We have no such luxuries. We have no such advantages. That is why the spirits gave you and your brother the sorceries, that we could escape to this place before we became ghosts, as the peoples of Aktiya Waya—whoever they were— did long ago."

Kiyuga folded his arms. "You sound as though you have talked yourself out of returning."

His cousin shrugged. "Maybe I have."

It was an interesting argument to be had, one that no clearly defined sides. Kiyuga lay awake that night, wrestling with the question in his mind. Was it better to return and fight as they always had, even if it meant their destruction? Or remain in Aktiya Waya and salvage what they could, rebuild the lives of their ancestors so that they might have a future? Was it a wise thing to do, as retreating from a raid that has been discovered? Or cowardly, as running away from an honorable battle?

Was fighting the Europeans honorable? Was it worthwhile? How many of the warriors from that battle would have spoils to show off? How many would be able to brag of heroic deeds? How many would find a girl to impress? Or would they simply be grateful for their lives and move on?

Eventually he found sleep. He did not know if he wished for guidance from the spirits, or hoped to see his brother, but if he did, he did not receive it. He told himself to be patient. The elders said his brother was well and Adahi was with him. It took his brother a few days to recover from his conjuring, so there was time to wait.

Another day passed. And another. And another.

Five days after escaping to Aktiya Waya, Kiyuga returned to the elders and inquired if any of them had seen or heard more of his brother and Adahi. No one had.

Five days, his brother ought to be recovered enough to conjure Galohisdi. He was not attempting to send an entire party, only himself and Adahi. Worry gnawed at him, but he forced himself to think of other things. Perhaps the strain of so much conjuring meant Anagalisgi needed a little more time to recover. But again, it was only for two people. And once they were here, his brother would be able to rest as much as he wished, as long as he needed.

Of course, his brother was rather stubborn. He would insist on being up and about and helping just as soon as he was awake. All the same, though, he would be safe. Why was he not conjuring?

Or perhaps he had conjured Galohisdi, but he had done so at a distance and they would have to trek to the village. That was also a possibility. Being weakened, they would not go very far very fast.

Kiyuga hung onto this hope, as foolish as it felt, but something in his spirit said that something was wrong. He could not identify it exactly, but he knew that something was wrong.

Another day passed. No one had seen or heard from them, either physically or spiritually. The hunters and gatherers who went out promised to keep an eye out for him, but even he could see the confusion and uncertainty in their eyes. They did not believe it. He did not believe it, honestly.

The seventh day came and went. Kiyuga began to lose hope.

He did not know which day it was, perhaps eight, perhaps ten, but it was a day about midmorning, there came a commotion from the fields. Galohisdi had opened in the corn field, near the river. Someone had come through.

Kiyuga sprinted to the fields, intercepting a group who appeared to be assisting someone. He knew immediately it was not his brother.

"Adahi!" Kiyuga barked. "Adahi, look at me! Look at me!"

He put his hand under the man's chin and lifted it. Adahi looked tired and confused, hardly aware of his surroundings. Kiyuga sighed and let his head drop. He looked at those helping.

"Where is my brother? Where is Anagalisgi?"

"We didn't see anything," one man said. "We were told only to get him to his mother-in-law's home. But one of the women there might know something."

He nodded toward the corn field where a bunch of women remained gathered. Kiyuga ran to them.

"My brother," he stated. "Where is my brother?"

"We saw him," one woman stated incredulously. "By the spirits, we saw him. And then he was gone."

"What do you mean, gone?"

But the women had no answer.

Kiyuga spent the day scouring the fields and surrounding lower rocks. Maybe his brother had landed somewhere in the vicinity. Maybe he was wounded or unconscious and unable to move or call for help.

His search yielded nothing. He did not find his brother or anything of his person, not his satchel, not his crystals, not even a feather or a lock of hair. Absolutely nothing.

Frustrated, he returned to the village and made his way to the home of Adahi's mother-in-law. It was his wife who met Kiyuga at the door.

"I must speak to Adahi," he told her.

"He is still sleeping," she said. "He was very confused and disoriented."

"Can you wake him? Please, I must ask him—"

"I will not. I know what you are looking for. When he wakes, I will ask him."

Kiyuga shook his head. "I would like to ask him myself."

"If that is so, then you may wait here until he wakes. But I will not disturb him."

So he did. He sat and waited outside the door, drawing his knees up and willing Adahi to wake quickly. He would know what happened to his brother. He had to.

Adahi did not wake as soon as Kiyuga had hoped. Every time he knocked, he was told that the warrior still slept. When he asked, he was told that Adahi did not appear to have any injuries to his head, or anywhere else for that matter. He was simply exhausted from the crossing over, as many often were.

Still Kiyuga waited.

It was past dark when the door opened and Adahi's wife looked out.

"You're still here," she observed.

"Is he awake?" he asked.

She frowned but nodded. "Yes." He stood and she put up a hand. "He is still very tired and thinking very slowly. Do not be cross with him."

Kiyuga agreed and she let him inside.

Adahi was relaxing in a chair covered in furs, his posture making Kiyuga wonder if he hadn't again fallen asleep. A cup of tea sat on a table beside him. As Kiyuga approached, sitting in another chair opposite him, the warrior roused a bit and looked at him. His gaze was one of a man who had indulged in too much of the Europeans' alcohol. He did not seem to recognize Kiyuga at first, and even when he did, it was not an urgent recognition.

"Adahi," Kiyuga said, trying to keep his voice soft. "Adahi, do you know me?"

The warrior stared at him for a moment, then said, "You're Yvgidahi."

"That's right."

"Yvgidahi. Kiyuga. Anagalisgi's brother."

"Yes. Do you know where he is? Where is my brother? Where is Anagalisgi? What happened?"

Adahi's wife conspicuously cleared her throat. Kiyuga shifted in his seat. Perhaps his questions had come too quickly, for Adahi's gaze had become distant once more. He seemed to be thinking, but not quickly, as his wife had mentioned.

Then he began to speak.

"Anagalisgi was caught. By the Anigilisi. They took him back to their camp. They were going to stay there a while. They thought..." His brows furrowed as he tried to remember. "They thought that you...and the others...were hiding in the caves. They were going to try and wait you out. Use your brother as bait, trying to bring you out...like fish. But after four days...the soldiers were tired, restless. Said there must be an exit elsewhere and you had escaped. Said there was no use waiting around. They had captured your brother, and they were going to take him to town to be executed."

"Where were you?" Kiyuga asked.

"I was...also caught. But not by the Anigilisi. I...fell into the spirit world. The spirits rescued me from death as the doorway between worlds closed on me. I still walked among the lands we knew, but I was invisible, and I...walked alongside the spirits. I could see and hear everything, but they could not see or hear me."

"Except Anagalisgi."

Adahi nodded dumbly. "Except Anagalisgi, and only then when he was dreaming or he ate of the seeing fruit." Again he seemed to be trying to remember something important. "He said...he said that his time had come, and he needed to be where I was. His destiny was going to be fulfilled. But first he had to escape execution and figure out a way to save me so I did not take his place."

"What did he do?"

"He...was taken to the prison in the Anigilisi town. He spoke to their priest. The priest was supposed to take his satchel, but he forgot, and Anagalisgi was able to eat of the seeing fruit. We made a plan. I learned the roads of the town and found a way for him to escape. I would guide him out.

"He was taken to be executed, but he ate of the seeing fruit. He escaped the soldiers, and I guided him through the streets, out of the town through a hole in the wall. And we ran."

"Did the Anigilisi pursue you?" Kiyuga asked.

"They did," Adahi sighed. "And Anagalisgi had many small wounds, many splinters from crawling through the wall. But he ran in the river. At some point, the seeing fruit wore off and he could no longer see me or the spirits. But we had made a plan to return to the cave. He did not know if it would make a difference, but it was a safe enough distance from the town for me, if I came out on the wrong side of the doorway.

"We made it to the cave. And there..."

"There what?" Kiyuga demanded. "What happened at the cave?"

"Anagalisgi conjured Galohisdi. He opened a doorway to Aktiya Waya. But when I tried to go through, it was as though I had been struck by lightning, and I could not go through. The first time, I was surprised and did not understand what had happened. The second time... The second time he grabbed me, grabbed my wrist. And as he was anchored in the waking world, it opened a tunnel for me to escape."

"What about him? Why didn't he come with you?"

"I cannot describe it exactly, but it was as though he created a way for me to escape, and yet he was fixed in place, that he could only move one way."

"What do you mean?"

The warrior was silent, but his expression was thoughtful, as though waking from a dream and trying to put all the pieces together again.

"He said..."

"What? What did he say?"

Adahi's wife again cleared her throat, but Kiyuga paid her no mind. Adahi himself seemed to struggle, and Kiyuga could see both the struggle and the frustration.

"He said...to tell you...that he is all right. He said to tell you...that your promise has been fulfilled."

At those words, Adahi's gaze and posture righted itself, and he appeared to be back to normal. Kiyuga, meanwhile, stood suddenly from his seat, unsure what to say or do or feel.

"He said it was his destiny," Adahi said quietly. "He spoke of being the guardian of the door between worlds."

Kiyuga nodded. "He said something similar to me. He said he did not know what that meant, what it entailed exactly, only that it was tied to the spirits in neither life nor death. He told me...he told me some of his thoughts and intuition about it, before the battle, after the battle. He said that it would be soon. He told me not to worry." He paused and huffed. "Well, I suppose now he's figured it out."

He stormed out of Adahi's home, heedless of the words they spoke to his back. He did not know where he was going, only that he needed to get out of there.

He left the village, crossed the fields, and left the protection of the wolf, heading for the forest. He still did not know where he was going, or what he expected to do. Was he going to yell at his brother? Rescue him? Plead with him to return? How was he going to do any of those things?

Where had his brother gone that he walked among the spirits and yet did not die? Was he to be isolated forever? Was there no way to speak to him now?

By the time Kiyuga's head came back to him, he was well south and west from Aktiya Waya, deep in the forest, and the sun was midway to the horizon.

He didn't know what to do.

He had so hoped to have his brother by his side here.

It might have been easier if Anagalisgi had died, if Kiyuga had a body to mourn or a grave to visit. Then he would know that his brother's soul had well moved on into the spirit world that way. But to think that he had voluntarily left the waking world to pursue this... It may have been the aspiration of any adawehi to commune with the spirits so closely, and Kiyuga did not begrudge him that.

Perhaps the offense came, then, from the fact that he hadn't said goodbye to him. Adahi had been the last one to see him, the last one to speak to him. Kiyuga had run like a coward. He should have stayed. He should have been the one to help. He should have gone before his brother into the spirit world, to ensure his place was secure. Adahi told him that Anagalisgi said the promise was fulfilled. Kiyuga was not so sure.

He stayed where he was, in a calm glade, all night. He made a fire and burned a small offering, praying for guidance. Did the spirits back in the Overhill hear him in this place? Were they offended that he was not there? Did the spirits of this island hear him? Would they be able to help with a problem on another island? Could the Overhill spirits help him here?

Such questions puzzled the elders and adawehi in Aktiya Waya, though Kiyuga was fairly certain that his brother would have been able to tell them. Perhaps he already had, at another time. He did not know. His mind was still very confused, and his spirit was wounded.

He stayed up all night, praying, burning offerings, and considering what he should do. Perhaps the other adawehi could shed some light on this.

He returned to Aktiya Waya. No one seemed to have missed him, or maybe he just wasn't paying attention as he made his way to the townhouse.

"Welcome, Yvgidahi," Nage'i greeted. "What can we do for you?"

"My brother has gone to the spirit world, and I wish to speak with him," Kiyuga blurted.

The adawehi blinked. Then, "I am sorry, we had not heard that your brother died."

"He's not dead," Kiyuga insisted. "He went there voluntarily. He proclaimed himself to be the guardian of the door between worlds. Ask Adahi; he saved him."

There was a bit of deliberation among the adawehi who all seemed uncertain of what to make of his claim. Walking among the spirits as a living soul was a great aspiration, something few had achieved. Finally, one acolyte was sent to fetch Adahi.

When Adahi was at least retrieved, he again told the story of their flight to Aktiya Waya, becoming trapped and invisible, helping Anagalisgi escape, and then switching places in the spirit world. Now that he was more lucid, he was able to speak with more authority and better detail. The adawehi listened patiently, questioned him only occasionally, and said nothing for a long while after he was finished.

"We will seek the spirits on this matter," Nage'i decided at last. "We will verify the truth of your words and see what may be done to commune with your brother." He looked at Kiyuga.

It was the best he was going to get at the moment, and Kiyuga thanked them. He left the townhouse without a word to Adahi.

Several days passed, and the adawehi decided it best to fast for seven days, praying and burning offerings in order to elicit an answer. The elders also joined in, as did Kiyuga. He could not ask them to undertake this endeavor that was so important to him and not partake himself. His selfishness would reflect badly upon him, and he might not get the answers he sought.

On the eighth morning, one of the adawehi claimed a vision.

"I see..." he began curiously. "I see a light. It is a light of wisdom. And of love. It has...the form of a woman. And her name is Diwedalohi."

"Agilisi," Kiyuga said.

"Yes. The light fades. It remains only a kernel and...oh! A raven has snatched it away! All that remains is a shadow, and yet...there is a ray of light still. It is growing. Now it has the form of a tree. Fruit is growing on it."

The adawehi blinked, shook his head, and looked at Kiyuga. "This fruit. This is what you seek."

"Agilisi was no tree tender," Kiyuga said, confused. "She had no orchards."

"Perhaps it is not a literal fruit," another adawehi suggested.

Kiyuga shifted his stance. "Anagalisgi spoke with a trader from the west. He carried a seeing fruit that allowed adawehi visions of the spirits."

"Yes, he traded everything he had just to get it," Nage'i said. "But that fruit comes from the west, from a land and peoples known to us only by trade and very rare, very distant raids."

"What if he took one of the fruits and planted it? What if he was trying to cultivate it, so he did not have to trade everything he commanded in order to get it?"

"Even if this were true, what does it have to do with Diwedalohi? She died before the trader brought the first seeing fruit."

Kiyuga sighed. "I don't know. But I don't think these questions can be answered here. I have to return to the Overhill."

"How is that? Are you skilled in Galohisdi?"

He sighed. "Not well."

"Then unless you wish to end up in the same predicament as Adahi, or perhaps your brother, then I suggest you wait until one of the skilled conjurers arrives."

Only because of the current "predicament" did Kiyuga not attempt to conjure anyway. He did not wish to be in the same position as his brother, but separated across islands. From the sounds of it, if a man were accidentally trapped, the only way out was through willing sacrifice and replacement, and he did not wish for anyone to have to sacrifice themselves to save him, not when it might be prevented. So his only choice, then, would be to wait for Nathan, Andrew, or another skilled Galohisdi conjurer.

Five days passed.

Then ten.

And another ten.

The moon's cycle upon this island was forty days instead of twenty-eight, and a full cycle went by with no news or sighting of the conjurers.

Rumors began to circulate. What if they had been captured or killed? What if something else terrible had happened? What if there was nothing to return to? What if they were sealed off upon this island? What if they truly were stuck here in Aktiya Waya? Were they really prepared for such a task? Should someone attempt a conjuring, just to see what had happened?

Another cycle went by.

Two and a half cycles after the adawehi's vision, there was another commotion in the fields. Nathan and Atagulkalu had arrived.

There was much fanfare as people swarmed the two of them, asking questions about the battle, the war, the state of things in the towns, asking after this person or that person. The two men, at first happy to take questions from a few people, suddenly found themselves overwhelmed, and they fell silent until they reached the townhouse.

"It has been nearly three wolf moons since the last battle," Nage'i said. "What news of things? Were you victorious? Have the Anigilisi been defeated?"

Atagulkalu sighed and shifted uncomfortably.

"The battle was lost," he said. "I think you all knew that; you just wanted me to tell you otherwise in order to soothe your ears and hearts." He paused to let the whispering and murmuring take its course. "The battle was lost, and so was the war. The people were overrun, villages burned, homes and crops destroyed. We would not have had enough to continue waging war and feed ourselves through the winter, so a decision was regrettably made. We were forced to sue for peace."

Louder murmuring, a few loud noises of frustration.

"I was asked to return to the people," Atagulkalu continued. "The Anigilisi have named me king, and they will deal only with me from now on in political negotiations."

"And what have you negotiated?" someone sneered.

"Negotiate is perhaps too weak of a word," Atagulkalu said. "With no way to continue war...they laid out terms and I was forced to accept, or else they would destroy everything we had left and kill everyone they found.

"The Lower Towns are lost. The Anigilisi have claimed the land entirely, and they have also taken some of the more southern Middle Towns. All firearms and ammunition trade has been cut off for the time being. We managed to ransom back many of the captives, but not all, and they are still being kept as slaves."

"What are we going to do?" someone wondered.

"At this time, Aktiya Waya has the stronger position. I believe it is best if you remain here. You are yet the lifeblood of our people and must be protected. I, Aganstata, Amadoya, Mankiller, and the others will remain in the Overhill. We will deal with the politics and treachery of the Anigilisi. But we will not sacrifice you."

There was more talk after this, and Atagulkalu nor the adawehi made any move to quell it. It went on for some time. Some expressed disbelief at this turn of events. Others wept over being separated from their home for an even longer time. Others seemed to accept it with a certain resolve, closing one door and opening another. Only a handful seemed angry about it and asking to return so they might kill more of the Anigilisi.

Atagulkalu and Nathan stayed in the townhouse that night, speaking to the elders and adawehi. It was late when Kiyuga approached them.

"Ah, Yvgidahi," Atagulkalu said, sounding tired and not a little sad. "I thought I saw you earlier. I am glad. Aganstata will also be glad to know that your mission was an apparent success."

"Not entirely," Kiyuga told him. "My brother is missing."

"What do you mean, missing?"

Again Kiyuga repeated the story Adahi had told him. Atagulkalu, the new uku of Itsa'ti, listened patiently, not interrupting. Nathan, for the most part, seemed contemplative, if not a little confused. When Kiyuga was finished, the uku was silent for a long moment.

"It seems as though your brother has fulfilled a marvelous destiny, one any other adawehi might kill for," he said finally. "Why would you seek to take that away from him?"

"That's not what I want," Kiyuga said. "I only wish to speak with him. I've not spoken to him in my dreams, and I know he has the power to do so, to walk in the dreams of others. I want to know why. I want to know what has become of my little brother."

The uku nodded. "I understand. And you believe this seeing fruit will allow you to do this?"

"When Adahi was trapped, it is how Anagalisgi was able to communicate with him. I see no reason that should not still be the case. I would have returned to the Overhill, but my conjuring skills are poor in this matter, and I did not wish to end up in the same predicament, but a whole island away."

"A wise decision," Nathan murmured.

Atagulkalu agreed. "Indeed. Very well. Do you know what it is you seek?"

Kiyuga told them about the vision of the tree, as well as the seeing fruit from the trader.

"Anagalisgi did mention the seeing fruit once to me, and he attempted to cultivate such a tree in the townhouse, though it takes many years for a tree to bear fruit. I am uncertain as to when the trader will return, if at all, or whether he would have the seeing fruit you seek."

"I must try."

Surprisingly, Atagulkalu shook his head. "You are needed here."

"But—"

"There are no traders now; it is autumn and will be dangerous to travel and be so far from home. There is no other such seeing fruit in the Overhill or our ancestors would have found it long ago."

"You don't know that," Kiyuga cut in hotly. "It took but one generation to forget how to make and use a bow. Why shouldn't we have lost our knowledge and connection to the earth as well?"

He could see his words cut Atagulkalu, and he bumbled an apology.

"Do not worry yourself; you were only speaking your mind. And in this case, it is also the truth. But within that truth is the best course of action. You should stay here and keep our people and traditions alive. Protect the people and our heritage, and see that it is passed on. Train as a warrior and practice the sorceries as well. We may get a chance to return one day, and we will still need our warriors.

"As for the seeing fruit, we will keep an eye out for it, for the trader. Or perhaps a tree will be discovered which bears this fruit. Whatever the case, when it is found, we will let you know. I will come get you myself if I must. You will not be forgotten. Your brother will not be forgotten. But do not rush headlong into this, only to be disappointed. Do you understand?"

Reluctantly, Kiyuga nodded. He did not know how to adequately describe how he felt at that moment. Anger, hurt, frustration, disappointment, helplessness. Merely concepts, the sides of a structure but unable to portray the substance within. He swallowed hard.

"But what will my brother think if I do not at least try?" he asked, his voice small.

Atagulkalu sighed and smiled gently. "I think your brother knew this was coming for a long time. And just as he has accepted his role in this, I think he has also accepted yours. Because regardless if you speak to him today, tomorrow, or two moons from now, you and he will still be separated. He has his path to walk, and so do you. You must both carry on as you are meant to do. Do you understand?"

Kiyuga nodded, feeling tears start to flow. He sniffed and wiped his eyes. "I understand."

"I know it is not easy. But it is right."

Kiyuga merely thanked them and left the townhouse, returning to the home he had claimed as his own.

He did not speak to Atagulkalu in Aktiya Waya after that, nor did he go to see him and Nathan off, back to the Overhill. Instead, he went out hunting, wishing only to be alone. Wishing only to find his brother.

Anagalisgi did not know how far to believe the trader's words when he spoke of planting the seed of the seeing fruit in the body of one stolen by a Raven Mocker, but he was not surprised when a tree did indeed sprout from the place where Ulisi was buried. He watched over it very attentively, though he had no more say in its survival than anything else.

But he did see where the power of the spirits had intertwined with the tree. It was as though a sunbeam had enveloped the small sapling, imbuing it with great spiritual power and magic.

This magic did not cause the tree to grow any faster, however. He watched as it went from a small tuft of leaves to a single stem of a sapling. Then branches sprouted, and the tiny tree began to really grow.

It was several years before the first flower budded and the first fruit began to grow.

Anagalisgi did not know the details of what had happened in Aktiya Waya, but he had heard from conversations between Atagulkalu and Nathan that they were keeping an eye out for either the trader from the west or a tree that bore like fruit. The trader had never returned, but the tree was now finally bearing fruit. With that now accomplished, Atagulkalu went to Aktiya Waya to retrieve Kiyuga.

Anagalisgi had missed his brother dearly while they were separated. Often he wished to visit him, but as he walked in the spirit world, he appeared to be limited only to this island. He had managed, with some difficulty considering the great separation between islands, to go to his brother several times in dreams, but Kiyuga treated them only as that, dreams. Often it was only the spirits or the spirits of the dead who spoke in dreams, and he refused to believe his brother was dead. He wanted to eat of the seeing fruit, see his brother for real.

So he had waited years for this moment. When Kiyuga walked into Itsa'ti that hot summer day, Anagalisgi cried out for joy. His brother looked as though he wanted to rip a fruit from the tree's branches and devour it immediately, but he restrained himself.

Instead, he spent the day fasting and praying. Anagalisgi watched him intently, almost willing him to simply stand, take a fruit, and bite into it.

Kiyuga kept up his fasting and prayers all night. As dawn broke and colors streaked through the sky, he stood, went to the tree, and took one of the seeing fruits. He hesitated only a moment. No doubt he had been waiting just as long, just as anxiously. He had envisioned this many times; Anagalisgi certainly had. And now was the moment of truth, for both of them. Anagalisgi could see the magic within the tree, but still he was nervous. What if the fruit did not work at all? What if the fruit wasn't ripe and so did not work? What if it wasn't ready because it was only the first year of fruit for the tree?

So many questions, but only one way to find out the answer.

Kiyuga took a bite.

ᏔᏂᏔᎣᎠᏗ ᏗᎪᏍᎯᏇᎣᎩ

Igvne'isdi Digohwelisgi

I've always wanted to write a sidekick story, where the main character, while a hero in his own right, is not the main hero that we would come to expect, sort of like writing Batman from Robin's point of view. I find these kinds of stories interesting because I find that it gives more unique insight to stories that may otherwise be dull and predictable because we already instinctively know the story arc. In the case of historical fiction, we may already know the outcome, and so something new is needed to keep our interest.

Many of the primary and secondary characters in this book were real people that you may have read about in history, though their names are slightly different. Atagulkalu is Attakullakulla. Aganstata is Oganatoga. Ustanaqua is Ostenaco.

Due to the nature of transliteration, any of these men had dozens of different English spellings for their names. Someone probably picked one out of a hat to use for common, official usage such as in history textbooks. However, I wanted to get away from that, take you away from any perceptions that you have about these events, and take you inside their lives in a new way. It's also why I changed the town names back to something a little more true to form versus the common English transliteration.

Research of this magnitude is difficult, and I know that someone out there is already penning a nastygram telling me how I got something wrong or that I'm a racist. However, I do wish to thank the editors of *When Cherokees Were Cherokee*, Oukah and Lee Ross MacDonald, for compiling an extensive amount of information that is free to use for education and research. I would not have gotten this far without it because I would have buried myself in mountains of information with no way to get out.

While not technically the earliest chronological point in *The Timekeeper Chronicles* overall (*In the Hands of the Enemy* has it beat by about twenty years or so), *Wolf Pack* is the earliest point in the Akari timeline. Going forward, the *Lone Wolf* series, I think, will be one of the more serious entries in the Chronicles, as it tackles not only Native politics and other historical events, but also the nature of the Akari. It is no accident that Anagalisgi was chosen, and his relationship to other characters in the larger universe will become clearer. In a way, I hope he also begins to bond with you, Reader, and help you understand what I am trying to convey.

There is also another fun aspect to this that I wish to mention, and that is that, because I have no life and no friends, I made a game based on this book. It's not a card game or a board game, but a video game. It doesn't follow the story perfectly, but many major elements are involved. If you need something to pass the time and want to explore the world of Kiyuga and Anagalisgi, check it out.

www.ingramcontent.com/pod-product-compliance
Lightning Source LLC
Chambersburg PA
CBHW061335190726
48288CB00005B/1458